WAR WITH THE ROBOTS

WAR WITH THE ROBOTS

28 OF THE BEST
SHORT STORIES
BY THE GREATEST NAMES
IN 20TH CENTURY SCIENCE FICTION

PREVIOUSLY PUBLISHED UNDER THE TITLE
MACHINES THAT THINK

EDITED BY
ISAAC ASIMOV, PATRICIA S. WARRICK,
AND MARTIN H. GREENBERG

WINGS BOOKS
New York • Avenel, New Jersey

This 1991 edition is published by Wings Books, distributed by Outlet Book Company, Inc.,
a Random House Company, 40 Engelhard Avenue, Avenel, New Jersey 07001,
by arrangement with Henry Holt & Co.

This book was previously published under the title *Machines That Think*.
Printed and bound in the United States of America

Library of Congress Cataloging-in-Publication Data

Machines that think
    War with the robots: 28 of the best short stories by the greatest names in 20th
century science fiction / edited by Isaac Asimov, Patricia S. Warrick, Martin H.
Greenberg.
        p.   cm.
Originally published under the title: Machines that think. 1984.
Includes bibliographical references (p.   ).
ISBN 0-517-06504-5
    1. Science fiction, American. 2. Computers—Fiction. 3. Robots—Fiction. I. Asimov,
Isaac, 1920-1992. II. Warrick, Patricia S. III.Greenberg, Martin Harry. IV. Title.
PS648.S3M27   1992
813'.0876208356—dc
                                                                    91-28854
                                                                    CIP

8 7 6 5 4 3 2

CONTENTS

CONTENTS

WAR WITH THE ROBOTS

INTRODUCTION: ROBOTS, COMPUTERS, AND FEAR

ISAAC ASIMOV

THE VERY FIRST ROBOT STORY I ever wrote was "Robbie," and it appears in this anthology. That story already contained the unreasoning human fear of robots as an element in the plot. Occasionally, in my stories, I referred to such fear as a "Frankenstein complex" and this remained a constant element (usually, but not always, minor) in almost all my robot stories.

Why this fear of robots? The question is not a trivial one, for, in the first place, robots are going to play an inevitable role in advancing technology. Blind, unreasoning resistance to the change is likely to do much harm to the world in general, and to the United States in particular. In the second place, the fear of robots is but a particular case of the fear of technological advance in general—something we can call "technophobia."

Technophobia has probably always existed, since it is not unnatural for people to be suspicious of anything that is new, and to cling to the "tried and true"; that is, to whatever they are used to. Through most of history, however, the advance of the new was so slow and gradual that technophobia was merely a crotchety sort of thing that further held back the advance and made the slow even slower.

When Arabic numerals were introduced into Europe by Leonardo Fibonacci in 1202, they were manifestly superior in every way to Roman numerals. Yet so resistant were the European scholars and merchants to the newfangled system that it took several *centuries* for the changeover to be completed.

And today, when the metric system is so clearly superior to

1

the farrago of measurements that we use in the United States, Americans are reluctant to make the changeover, even though two centuries have passed since metrics came into use, and every other nation with the slightest pretense to civilization has accepted them.

Again, the whole world unites in its refusal to consider a reform of the calendar, though the one we use, with its months of variable length and the changing relationship of day of the month and day of the week, produces foolish and unnecessary complexity. The English-speaking world similarly refuses to consider any system of rationalized spelling, although in many cases the existing system reduces English words to ideograms.

Most peculiar is the opposition to changing the typewriter keyboard, even though the universal pattern used today is a foolish one devised by the instrument's inventor for trivial reasons. The most advanced computers today (including the one I am using now) make use of this keyboard. It actually reduces typing speed through an unbalanced use of the two hands, especially since it favors the greater use of the left hand in a world that is ninety percent right-handed.

Why this reluctance to make the change?

We fear the process of reeducation! Adults have invested endless hours of learning in growing accustomed to inches and miles; to February's twenty-eight days; to "night" and "debt" with their silent letters; to qwertyuiop; and to all the rest. To introduce something altogether new would mean to begin all over, to become ignorant again, and to run the old, old risk of failing to learn.

Children could make the change without trouble—in fact, they would not even know they were making the change—but no one offers them the chance. They are forced to learn the old nonsense until they too become resistant to the new.

Furthermore, it is precisely the most powerful people in a society—the scholars, the executives, the leaders—who have the most to lose in the divestment of their knowledge and expertise, in becoming intellectually naked and taking a new chance on education. *They* often resist with nothing less than savagery.

But in the end, of course—the often long-delayed end—they will lose.

A more reasonable source of technophobia, and one with which we find it easier to sympathize, is the fear that technological advance will cost a person his job. This became a very prominent aspect of technophobia when technological advance became rapid enough to dominate society.

On the whole, technological advance is cumulative and becomes more rapid with time. By 1800, with the coming of the Industrial Revolution, it became rapid enough to affect thousands at once.

This happened first in Great Britain, where the Industrial Revolution had its beginning. As textile machinery came into use and a few people in factories could outproduce large numbers working by hand in cottages, the newly unemployed rioted. They did not see that the enemy lay in a society that cared nothing for the "lower classes" and felt no responsibility for the poor. They blamed their misery, simplistically, on the machines. Therefore, in their riots, they destroyed or attempted to destroy the machines that they felt had replaced them. Rioters in 1811 were supposed to have been led by one Ned Ludd. As a result, those who attack technological advance with particular force have been called Luddites ever since.

This original Luddite movement died out quickly as the machines brought prosperity to England, and new jobs (often under hellish conditions) to the population. The lesson was learned then, and repeatedly thereafter, that technological advance does not destroy jobs, but changes them, actually increasing their number; and that the solution to unemployment is not the destruction of machines, but the establishment of an enlightened program of reeducation and worker welfare.

A still more intelligible ground for technophobia is the fear that technological change will damage the environment or produce undesirable alterations in human society.

This risk has been evident since technology first became apparent. The discovery of fire produced smoke and the possibility of arson. The discovery of agriculture led to damage to the soil, to deforestation, to salinization, to progressive and often undesirable changes in the ecological balance. Almost every invention found an application in the exertion of violence between human and human, and made war steadily easier to wage, more ferocious and dreadful, more prolonged.

And yet, in every case, the advantages gained are perceived as being superior to the risks, and technological advance is almost never voluntarily abandoned, whatever disadvantages seem to be entailed.

Still, there are always dreamers who rail against the technological present and hark back to an earlier stage in the technology, which they perceive as having been Edenic. People today sometimes return to the soil, thinking that farming is somehow virtuous, when farming has done infinite harm to the Earth and when, in the early days of farming, people must undoubtedly have harked back to a food-gathering society as Edenic.

Again, those who fear nuclear power stations often long for a return to the use of that coal which carries with it an incredibly long list of abuses and dangers, and which was as thoroughly denounced in its early days as nuclear fission has ever been in ours.

Here too, the only useful solution has been that of curing or at least lessening the dangers in a march toward the future, rather than wiping out the new in a retreat toward an idealized and actually nonexistent past.

All these causes of technophobia, which operate against change and technological advance generally, operate against robots in particular. Over and above this, however, there are causes that produce feelings of particular force where robots are concerned.

Robots, because they are usually visualized as at least vaguely human in shape, are perceived as pseudo human beings. The creation of a robot, a pseudo human being, by a human inventor is therefore perceived as an imitation of the creation of humanity by God.

In societies where God is accepted as the *sole* Creator, as in the Judeo-Christian West, any attempt to imitate him cannot help but be considered blasphemous, even if there is no conscious intention of blasphemy.

One way of expressing this feeling is to say that only God can create a soul. A human inventor may devise an artificial being that seems to possess life in all its aspects, but that being can never have a soul, never have the God-given spark that will lend it a potentiality for goodness and virtue. Even if the robot is not actively evil and malevolent, it cannot help becoming so because it is passively incapable of anything else.

Because of this, the cliché has it that "there are some things man was not meant to know" (as though it were perfectly all right for human beings to learn a thousand ways of ending life through every gradation of pain, misery, and unspeakable humiliation, but wrong and sinful to learn even one new way of creating life).

The first to express this view graphically in fiction was Mary Shelley in the classic *Frankenstein*. In that book, Victor Frankenstein creates the Monster, who turns on Frankenstein and those he loves, and kills them. (People who know of the Monster only from the movie do not fully appreciate that the Monster was rather movingly virtuous and became a killer only because he was unbearably ill-treated.)

The success of *Frankenstein* was such that the basic plot of "man creates robot; robot kills man" was repeated over and over again in uncounted numbers of science fiction stories. It became one of the more unbearable clichés in the field (one that I successfully fought and destroyed, I am proud to say, with the establishment of my "Three Laws of Robotics").

This science-fictional treatment has helped exacerbate this particular variety of technophobia, the fear of technological advance as "blasphemy," in connection with robots, and the consequent fear of robots above and beyond other products of technology. It is why I referred to such fear in my stories as the "Frankenstein complex." Such is the power of the story of Frankenstein, by the way (thanks even more to the movie than to the book), that I never felt the need to define the meaning of the term in any of my stories. I took it for granted that the meaning was obvious, and I was right.

In fact, the "Frankenstein complex," in its pure form, may not develop. In science fiction, the robot is created in full bloom. In real life, however, what we now call the "industrial robot" is little more than a complex and computerized arm, bearing no resemblance to a human being. It is, therefore, much more easily visualized as a complex machine than as a pseudo person, and is feared for its effect on jobs rather than for its blasphemous imitation of ourselves.

But then, what counts is not the "robot," which is the system of levers and joints that performs the function, but the computer that controls that function, and in particular the "microchip," which has so miniaturized the computer that we perceive it now as beginning to rival the human brain in compactness and versatility.

There comes, therefore, a brand-new variety of technophobia, one that strikes far more sickeningly at the core of our being than any version of the ailment that has yet existed.

The computer will not merely do a particular job better than a person will; it will not merely replace a particular person and leave him or her unemployed. As the computer grows more compact, more versatile, more complex, more capable, more *intelligent*, might it not replace not just a person but all humanity?

We must admit that, in concept at least, the fear could be justified. There is no clearly visible theoretical limit to how complex and "intelligent" a computer can become. There is no reason to suppose that a computer, through some inherent deficiency, must fail to match, and even to exceed, the level of the workings of the human brain.

We might cynically suggest that this is good; that humanity deserves to be superseded; that its record as custodian of the Earth has been a miserable one; that, on the cosmic report card, it has scored a clear failure, so that it is time another form of life was tried. We might reason that it is a great honor that humanity has proved worthy of designing its own superior successor. We might even maintain that our great fear should be that this successor will not be produced soon enough to save the

Earth, and that our every effort should be bent to replacing our miserable species as soon as possible.

Yet it would be foolish to believe that humanity can rise to such heights of dispassion as to welcome this view. However much people might reason that our replacement could be a Good Thing, they will not want the replacement and they will fear the possibility.

But *will* humanity be replaced? *Will* the computer inevitably become "more intelligent" than the human being?

In the first place, we must ask whether intelligence is a one-dimensional invariant, or whether there are different kinds of intelligence, perhaps very many different kinds. For instance, there is some speculation that dolphins may have intelligence rivaling that of human beings. Nevertheless, that intelligence, if it exists, is of so different a nature from our own that we have not yet managed to establish communication across the species-line. It may be so with computers too; and it would certainly not be surprising if it were so.

After all, the human brain, built of nucleic acid and protein against a watery background, has been the product of the development of three and a half billion years of biological evolution, based on the random effects of mutation, natural selection, and other influences, and driven forward by the necessity of survival.

The computer, on the other hand, built of electronic switches and electric current against a metallic background, has been the product of the development of forty years of human design, based on the careful foresight and ingenuity of human beings, and driven forward by the necessity of serving its human users.

When two intelligences are so different in structure, history, development, and purpose, it would certainly not be surprising if those intelligences were widely different in nature as well.

From the very start, for instance, computers were capable of solving complex problems involving arithmetical operations upon numbers, and of doing so with far greater speed than human beings could, and with far less chance of error. If arithmetical skill is the measure of intelligence, then computers have been more intelligent than all human beings all along. If the ability to play chess is the measure, then there are computers now in existence that are more intelligent than any but a very few human beings.

However, if insight, intuition, creativity, the ability to view a problem as a whole and guess the answer by the "feel" of the situation, is a measure of intelligence, computers are very unintelligent indeed. Nor can we see right now how this deficiency in computers can be easily remedied, since human beings cannot program a computer to be intuitive or creative for the very good reason that we do not know what we ourselves do when we exercise these qualities.

Nor, as it happens, would it pay us to program computers to perform these peculiarly human functions, even if we could. Quite apart from our natural reluctance to be replaced, it would surely pay us to develop two intelligences that were differently specialized. Why labor to have computers develop a clumsy ability to be creative when we have the human brain, already in existence, that does it so well? It would be no wiser or more useful to do that than to seek out and train particular human beings to perform rapid mathematical feats after the fashion of a computer. It could presumably be done, but why bother, when computers already do it so well?

On the other hand, two different intelligences, specializing in two different directions, each useful, can in a symbiotic relationship learn to cooperate with the natural law of the Universe far more efficiently than either could alone. Viewed in this fashion, the robot/computer will not replace us but will serve us as friend and ally in the march toward the glorious future.

Having said all this, let me turn to the book itself. As a robot anthology, I consider it completely sui generis; or, if you prefer straightforward English, as I do, it is in a class by itself.

This may seem to you a difficult point to defend, for there have been a number of anthologies devoted to robots over the past thirty years. In fact, over that period, I have even prepared three different collections of my own robot stories, which are one-man anthologies, if you like.

And is this one you hold in your hands really different from them all, and presumably better as well?

I think so. I don't want to pick holes in the competition, but I suppose I may freely speak as I please of my own books, so let me point out that my stories are almost invariably told from the standpoint of the technophile that I am. My robots are almost invariably sympathetic, and if villains there be (though my stories rarely contain villains—only people), they are human.

To me, that is good. It is my point of view—as I have expressed it in this introduction, for that matter—and I cannot help but present it. To the reader, though, that may not be enough. You may want to hear other points of view so that you can consider them all and come to some decision peculiarly your own. You might prefer not to be overwhelmed by the eloquence of one superarticulate person.

In this book we have many views. Certainly mine are present, for the anthology contains five of my robot stories. Yet we also have stories representing thoughts about robots and/or computers that are totally different from mine.

But then, you might say, there are a number of other anthologies that present different views of robots. What does this anthology have that the others do not?

I'll tell you in a word—or, rather, two.

Patricia Warrick!

There are people who are thoroughly acquainted with science fiction and can choose good science fiction stories for an anthology. Martin H. Greenberg is an excellent example of a person of that sort. I suppose it would be futile to deny that I am another.

There are also people who are thoroughly acquainted with the development and philosophy of computer technology. There may even be thousands of them.

There are not very many people, however, who are thoroughly acquainted with both science fiction *and* computers, and Warrick is one of those few.

As evidence, there is her well-received book *The Cybernetic Imagination in Science Fiction* (MIT Press, 1980), in which she discusses the interplay of robotics in imagination and in fact, doing so in fascinating fashion.

This anthology is a companion piece to her earlier book. Where, in the former book, she discusses aspects of robotic science fiction allusively only, here the important stories are themselves brought front and center and placed in full view, with her introductory notes supplied for each.

The anthology is organized, reasonably enough, in such a way as to move from the past to the future, from the nineteenth century to the twenty-first. If one of the historical stories, indicating the first penetration of a concept into the auctorial imagination (invariably long before it becomes a serious technological concern, let alone actuality), is my own, that is an indication of Warrick's estimate of the importance of my stories, an estimate to which I accede graciously, for I recognize her expertise. (Besides, I have never been notable for my modesty.)

The section devoted to the uses of robots shows quite clearly how well in advance science fiction frequently was, and how piercingly accurate. My favorite example is Murray Leinster's "A Logic Named Joe," which talked of home computers as though he had a pipeline extending forty years into the future (which he, alas, did not survive to see) that told him everything except that home computers would not be called "logics."

Nor is the advance of robotics merely a question of technological expertise and practical use. There are the questions of right and wrong, matters of the human spirit, which cannot possibly be addressed as dramatically in sermons or oratory as in a good story, well told. See for yourself in the section entitled "Machine Intelligence and Moral Issues."

And finally, we take up the development of robots and computers past the horizons of today.

I cannot help but feel that if a copy of this anthology fell into the hands of one of our descendants a century or five centuries hence, he or she might smile at some of our naivetés and misfires—and yet be impressed, to a greater extent, by our successes at penetrating the dark veil of that which was to come.

Enter, then, an amazing world of foresight.

BEFORE THE ELECTRONIC AGE: A NINETEENTH-CENTURY ROBOT

MOXON'S MASTER

AMBROSE BIERCE

(1894)

Today, new computer developments are usually carried on by a research team in the laboratory of a university or a corporation. In the eighteenth and nineteenth centuries, an inventor tinkered alone in his workshop. This chilling story describes one such solitary man, Moxon, and the invention he could not master. Its author, Ambrose Bierce (1842–1914), was an American journalist, short-story writer, and satirist. He was the editor of the San Francisco *News-Letter* and later a columnist for Hearst's *Sunday Examiner*. During the last decade of the nineteenth century he was the literary arbiter of the West Coast, admired for his essays and short stories, and especially for his sardonic definitions published in *The Devil's Dictionary*. "Moxon's Master" is his most famous and most often reprinted short story. Bierce's originality here lies not in writing a story about a chess-playing machine but in his realization of the radical philosophical implications of inventing a machine with intelligence.

Stories about robots were actually quite common in nineteenth-century literature, although the term *robot* was not coined until 1921, when the Czech writer Karel Capek used the word in his play *R.U.R.* (Rossum's Universal Robots). He took it from the Czech *robota*, meaning work or compulsory service.

Mechanical devices shaped like animals or humans had begun to pour out of the workshops of inventors in the eighteenth century. They were called automata, and they came in all shapes and sizes, some as large as life. A duck waddled, a crouching tiger sprang upon a mechanical soldier, girls danced, boys played musical instruments. In 1809, the German inventor Wolfgang von Kempelen built a supposed automaton chess player that defeated Napoleon II in a chess competition. After Von Kempelen's death, a showman named Maelzel toured Europe and America with the chess automaton. Edgar Allan Poe, in a neat piece of detective work published as "Maelzel's Chess-Player," deduced that the automaton must be a fake. Indeed, he was right. It was eventually exposed as a fraud, with a midget inside who moved the chess pieces.

Other nineteenth-century writers before Bierce had used automata and intelligent machines in their fiction—for example, Herman Melville in "The Bell Tower," and Samuel Butler in "The Book of the Machines." But none seems to have recognized the significance for man of developing this rad-

15

ical new technology. Bierce's incisive mind penetrates to the heart of the issues raised when we think about the relationship between mechanistic and living systems. Is there a clear boundary between the animate and the inanimate, between men and machines? Is it possible they are not dichotomous, but exist in a continuum? Equally interesting, what is intelligence? Should the ability of a crystal to organize itself into a pattern be called intelligence? And the question of consciousness—what role does it play in intelligence? Could a machine ever be conscious?

"Moxon's Master" is the first short story to raise these critical questions. Bierce wisely refrains from trying to answer them. No easy answers exist. Computer scientists, physiologists, psychologists, and philosophers are still hotly debating the same questions today.

"**A**RE YOU SERIOUS? Do you really believe that a machine thinks?"

I got no immediate reply; Moxon was apparently intent upon the coals in the grate, touching them deftly here and there with the fire poker till they signified a sense of his attention by a brighter glow. For several weeks I had been observing in him a growing habit of delay in answering even the most trivial of commonplace questions. His air, however, was that of preoccupation rather than deliberation: one might have said that he had something on his mind.

Presently he said, "What is a 'machine'? The word has been variously defined. Here is one definition from a popular dictionary: 'Any instrument or organization by which power is applied and made effective, or a desired effect produced.' Well, then, is not a man a machine? And you will admit that he thinks—or thinks he thinks."

"If you do not wish to answer my question," I said rather testily, "why not say so? All that you say is mere evasion. You know well enough that when I say 'machine' I do not mean a man, but something that man has made and controls."

"When it does not control him," he said, rising abruptly and looking out of a window, whence nothing was visible in the blackness of a stormy night. A moment later he turned about and with a smile said, "I beg your pardon; I had no thought of evasion. I considered the dictionary-man's unconscious testimony suggestive and worth something in the discussion. I can

16

give your question a direct answer easily enough: I do believe that a machine thinks about the work that it is doing."

That was direct enough, certainly. It was not altogether pleasing, for it tended to confirm a sad suspicion that Moxon's devotion to study and work in his machine shop had not been good for him. I knew, for one thing, that he suffered from insomnia, and that is no light affliction. Had it affected his mind? His reply to my question seemed to me then evidence that it had; perhaps I should think differently about it now. I was younger then, and among the blessings that are not denied to youth is ignorance. Incited by that great stimulant to controversy, I said, "And what, pray, does it think with—in the absence of a brain?"

The reply, coming with less than his customary delay, took his favorite form of counter-interrogation. "With what does a plant think—in the absence of a brain?"

"Ah, plants also belong to the philosopher class! I should be pleased to know some of their conclusions; you may omit the premises."

"Perhaps," he replied, apparently unaffected by my foolish irony, "you may be able to infer their convictions from their acts. I will spare you the familiar examples of the sensitive mimosa, the several insectivorous flowers, and those whose stamens bend down and shake their pollen upon the entering bee in order that he may fertilize their distant mates. But observe this. In an open spot in my garden I planted a climbing vine. When it was barely above the surface I set a stake into the soil a yard away. The vine at once made for it, but as it was about to reach it after several days, I removed it a few feet. The vine at once altered its course, making an acute angle, and again made for the stake. This maneuver was repeated several times, but, finally, as if discouraged, the vine abandoned the pursuit and, ignoring further attempts to divert it, traveled to a small tree, farther away, which it climbed.

"Roots of the eucalyptus will prolong themselves incredibly in search of moisture. A well-known horticulturist relates that one entered an old drainpipe and followed it until it came to a break, where a section of the pipe had been removed to make way for a stone wall that had been built across its course. The

17

root left the drain and followed the wall until it found an opening where a stone had fallen out. It crept through and, following the other side of the wall back to the drain, entered the unexplored part and resumed its journey."

"And all this?"

"Can you miss the significance of it? It shows the consciousness of plants. It proves that they think."

"Even if it did—what then? We were speaking not of plants but of machines. They may be composed partly of wood—wood that has no longer vitality—or wholly of metal. Is thought an attribute also of the mineral kingdom?"

"How else do you explain the phenomena, for example, of crystallization?"

"I do not explain them."

"Because you cannot without affirming what you wish to deny: namely, intelligent cooperation among the constituent elements of the crystals. When soldiers form lines or hollow squares, you call it reason. When wild geese in flight take the form of a letter V, you say instinct. When the homogeneous atoms of a mineral, moving freely in solution, arrange themselves into shapes mathematically perfect, or particles of frozen moisture into the symmetrical and beautiful forms of snowflakes, you have nothing to say. You have not even invented a name to conceal your heroic unreason."

Moxon was speaking with unusual animation and earnestness. As he paused I heard in an adjoining room, known to me as his machine shop, which no one but himself was permitted to enter, a singular thumping sound, as of someone pounding upon a table with an open hand. Moxon heard it at the same moment and, visibly agitated, rose and hurriedly passed into the room whence it came. I thought it odd that anyone else should be in there, and my interest in my friend—with doubtless a touch of unwarrantable curiosity—led me to listen intently, though, I am happy to say, not at the keyhole. There were confused sounds, as of a struggle or scuffle; the floor shook. I distinctly heard hard breathing and a hoarse whisper which said "Damn you!" Then all was silent, and presently Moxon reappeared and said with a rather sorry smile, "Pardon me for leaving you so abruptly. I have a machine in there that lost its temper and cut up rough."

Fixing my eyes steadily upon his left cheek, which was traversed by four parallel excoriations showing blood, I said, "How would it do to trim its nails?"

I could have spared myself the jest; he gave it no attention, but seated himself in the chair that he had left and resumed the interrupted monologue as if nothing had occurred. "Doubtless you do not hold with those (I need not name them to a man of your reading) who have taught that all matter is sentient, that every atom is a living, feeling, conscious being. *I* do. There is no such thing as dead, inert matter: it is all alive; all instinct with force, actual and potential; all sensitive to the same forces in its environment and susceptible to the contagion of higher and subtler ones residing in such superior organisms as it may be brought into relation with, as those of man when he is fashioning it into an instrument of his will. It absorbs something of his intelligence and purpose—more of them in proportion to the complexity of the resulting machine and that of its work.

"Do you happen to recall Herbert Spencer's definition of 'life'? I read it thirty years ago. He may have altered it afterward, for anything I know, but in all that time I have been unable to think of a single word that could profitably be changed or added or removed. It seems to me not only the best definition but the only possible one.

" 'Life,' he says, 'is a definite combination of heterogeneous changes, both simultaneous and successive, in correspondence with external coexistences and sequences.' "

"That defines the phenomenon," I said, "but gives no hint of its cause."

"That," he replied, "is all that any definition can do. As Mill points out, we know nothing of cause except as an antecedent—nothing of effect except as a consequent. Of certain phenomena, one never occurs without another, which is dissimilar: the first in point of time we call cause, the second, effect. One who had many times seen a rabbit pursued by a dog, and had never seen rabbits and dogs otherwise, would think the rabbit the cause of the dog.

"But I fear," he added, laughing naturally enough, "that my rabbit is leading me a long way from the track of my legitimate quarry: I'm indulging in the pleasure of the chase for its own sake. What I want you to observe is that in Herbert Spencer's definition of life, the activity of a machine is included—there is nothing in the definition that is not applicable to it. According to this sharpest of observers and deepest of thinkers, if a man during his period of activity is alive, so is a machine when in operation. As an inventor and constructor of machines, I know that to be true."

Moxon was silent for a long time, gazing absently into the fire. It was growing late, and I thought it time to be going, but somehow I did not like the notion of leaving him in that isolated house, all alone except for the presence of some person of whose nature my conjectures could go no further than that it was unfriendly, perhaps malign. Leaning toward him and looking earnestly into his eyes while making a motion with my hand through the door of his workshop, I said, "Moxon, whom have you in there?"

Somewhat to my surprise, he laughed lightly and answered without hesitation, "Nobody; the incident that you have in mind was caused by my folly in leaving a machine in action with nothing to act upon, while I undertook the interminable task of enlightening your understanding. Do you happen to know that Consciousness is the creature of Rhythm?"

"Oh, bother them both!" I replied, rising and laying hold of my overcoat. "I'm going to wish you good night; and I'll add the hope that the machine which you inadvertently left in action will have her gloves on the next time you think it needful to stop her."

Without waiting to observe the effect of my shot, I left the house.

Rain was falling, and the darkness was intense. In the sky beyond the crest of a hill toward which I groped my way along precarious plank sidewalks and across miry, unpaved streets, I could see the faint glow of the city's lights, but behind me nothing was visible but a single window of Moxon's house. It glowed with what seemed to me a mysterious and fateful meaning. I knew it was an uncurtained aperture in my friend's machine shop, and I had little doubt that he had resumed the studies interrupted by his duties as my instructor in mechanical consciousness and the fatherhood of Rhythm. Odd, and in some degree humorous, as his convictions seemed to me at that time, I could not wholly divest myself of the feeling that they had some tragic relation to his life and character—perhaps to his destiny—although I no longer entertained the notion that they were the vagaries of a disordered mind. Whatever might be thought of his views, his exposition of them was too logical for that. Over and over, his last words came back to me: "Consciousness is the creature of Rhythm." Bald and terse as the statement was, I now found it infinitely alluring. At each recurrence it broadened in meaning and deepened in suggestion. Why, here (I thought) is something upon which to found a philosophy. If consciousness is the product of rhythm, all things *are* conscious, for all have motion, and all motion is rhythmic. I wondered if Moxon knew the significance and breadth of his thought—the scope of this momentous generalization; or had he arrived at his philosophic faith by the tortuous and uncertain road of observation?

That faith was then new to me, and all Moxon's expounding had failed to make me a convert; but now it seemed as if a great light shone about me, like that which fell upon Saul of Tarsus; and out there in the storm and darkness and solitude I experienced what Lewes calls "the endless variety and excitement of philosophic thought." I exulted in a new sense of knowledge, a new pride of reason. My feet seemed hardly to touch the earth; it was as if I were uplifted and borne through the air by invisible wings.

Yielding to an impulse to seek further light from him whom I now recognized as my master and guide, I had unconsciously turned about, and almost before I was aware of having done so, found myself again at Moxon's door. I was drenched with rain but felt no discomfort. Unable in my excitement to find the doorbell, I instinctively tried the knob. It turned and, entering, I mounted the stairs to the room that I had so recently left. All was dark and silent; Moxon, as I had supposed, was in the adjoining room—the machine shop. Groping along the wall until I found the communicating door, I knocked loudly several times but got no response, which I attributed to the uproar outside, for the wind was blowing a gale and dashing the rain against the thin walls in sheets. The drumming upon the shingle roof spanning the unceiled room was loud and incessant.

I had never been invited into the machine shop—had, indeed, been denied admittance, as had all others, with one exception, a skilled metalworker, whom no one knew anything except that his name was Haley and his habit silence. But in my spiritual exaltation, discretion and civility were alike forgotten, and I opened the door. What I saw took all philosophical speculation out of me in short order.

Moxon sat facing me at the farther side of a small table upon which a single candle made all the light that was in the room. Opposite him, his back toward me, sat another person. On the table between the two was a chessboard; the men were playing. I knew little of chess, but as only a few pieces were on the board, it was obvious that the game was near its close. Moxon was intensely interested—not so much, it seemed to me, in the game as in his antagonist, upon whom he had fixed so intent a look that, standing though I did directly in the line of his vision, I was altogether unobserved. His face was ghastly white, and his eyes glittered like diamonds. Of his antagonist I had only a back view, but that was sufficient; I should not have cared to see his face.

He was apparently not more than five feet in height, with proportions suggesting those of a gorilla—a tremendous breadth of shoulders; thick, short neck and broad, squat head, which had a tangled growth of black hair and was topped with a crimson fez. A tunic of the same color, belted tightly at the waist, reached the seat—apparently a box—upon which he sat; his legs and feet were not seen. His left forearm appeared to rest in his lap; he moved his pieces with his right hand, which seemed disproportionately long.

I had shrunk back and now stood a little to one side of the doorway and in shadow. If Moxon had looked farther than the face of his opponent, he could have observed nothing, now, except that the door was open. Something forbade me either to enter or to retire; a feeling—I know not how it came—that I was in the presence of an imminent tragedy and might serve my friend by remaining. With a scarely conscious rebellion against the indelicacy of the act, I remained.

The play was rapid. Moxon hardly glanced at the board before making his moves, and to my unskilled eye seemed to move the piece most convenient to his hand, his motions in doing so being quick, nervous, and lacking in precision. The response of his antagonist, while equally prompt in the inception, was made with a slow, uniform, mechanical, and, I thought, somewhat theatrical movement of the arm, that was a sore trial to my patience. There was something unearthly about it all, and I caught myself shuddering. But I was wet and cold.

Two or three times, after moving a piece, the stranger slightly inclined his head, and each time I observed that Moxon shifted his king. All at once the thought came to me that the man was dumb. And then that he was a machine—an automaton chess player! Then I remembered that Moxon had once spoken to me of having invented such a piece of mechanism, though I did not understand that it had actually been constructed. Was all his talk about the consciousness and intelligence of machines merely a prelude to eventual exhibition of this device—only a trick to intensify the effect of its mechanical action upon me, in my ignorance of its secret?

A fine end, this, of all my intellectual transports—my "endless variety and excitement of philosophic thought"! I was about to retire in disgust when something occurred to hold my curiosity. I observed a shrug of the thing's great shoulders, as if it were irritated: and so natural was this—so entirely human—that in my new view of the matter it startled me. Nor was that all, for a moment later it struck the table sharply with its clenched hand. At that gesture Moxon seemed even more startled than I; he pushed his chair a little backward, as in alarm.

Presently Moxon, whose play it was, raised his hand high above the board, pounced upon one of his pieces like a sparrow hawk, and with the exclamation "Checkmate!" rose quickly to his feet and stepped behind his chair. The automaton sat motionless.

The wind had now gone down, but I heard, at lessening intervals and progressively louder, the rumble and roll of thunder. In the pauses between, I now became conscious of a low humming or buzzing which, like the thunder, grew momentarily louder and more distinct. It seemed to come from the body of the automaton and was unmistakably a whirring of wheels. It gave me the impression of a disordered mechanism which had escaped the repressive and regulating action of some controlling part—an effect such as might be expected if a pawl should be jostled from the teeth of a ratchet wheel. But before I had time for much conjecture as to its nature, my attention was taken by the strange motions of the automaton itself. A slight but continuous convulsion appeared to have possession of it. In body and head it shook like a man with palsy or an ague chill, and the motion augmented every moment until the entire figure was in violent agitation. Suddenly it sprang to its feet and, with a movement almost too quick for the eye to follow, shot forward across table and chair, with both arms thrust forth to their full length—the posture and lunge of a diver. Moxon tried to throw himself backward out of reach, but he was too late: I saw the horrible thing's hands close upon his throat, his own clutch its wrists. Then the table was overturned, the candle thrown to the floor and extinguished, and all was black dark. But the noise of the struggle was dreadfully distinct, and most terrible of all were the raucous, squawking sounds made by the strangled man's efforts to breathe. Guided by the infernal hubbub, I sprang to the rescue of my friend but had hardly taken a stride in the darkness when the whole room blazed with a blinding white light that burned into my brain and heart and memory a vivid picture of the combatants on the floor, Moxon underneath, his throat still in the clutch of those iron hands, his head forced backward, his eyes protruding, his mouth wide open and his tongue thrust out; and—horrible contrast!—upon the painted face of his assassin an expression of tranquil and profound thought, as in the solution of a problem in chess! This I observed, then all was blackness and silence.

Three days later I recovered consciousness in a hospital. As the memory of that tragic night slowly evolved in my ailing brain, I recognized in my attendant Moxon's confidential workman, Haley. Responding to a look, he approached, smiling.

"Tell me about it," I managed to say, faintly—"all about it."

"Certainly," he said; "you were carried unconscious from a burning house—Moxon's. Nobody knows how you came to be there. You may have to do a little explaining. The origin of the fire is a bit mysterious, too. My own notion is that the house was struck by lightning."

"And Moxon?"

"Buried yesterday—what was left of him."

Apparently this reticent person could unfold himself on occasion. When imparting shocking intelligence to the sick, he was affable enough. After some moments of the keenest mental suffering, I ventured to ask another question: "Who rescued me?"

"Well, if that interests you—I did."

"Thank you, Mr. Haley, and may God bless you for it. Did you rescue, also, that charming product of your skill, the automaton chess player that murdered its inventor?"

The man was silent a long time, looking away from me. Presently he turned and gravely said, "Do you know that?"

"I do," I replied; "I saw it done."

That was many years ago. If I were asked today, I should answer less confidently.

FIRST

ROBOT

STORIES

THE LOST MACHINE

JOHN WYNDHAM

(1 9 3 2)

The term *science fiction* originates from the word *scientifiction*, first used by Hugo Gernsback in 1926 in his new magazine *Amazing Stories*. "The Lost Machine" was published in the April 1932 issue, where it appeared under the real name of its author, John Beynon Harris (1903–1969). A British writer, Harris is best known by his pen name, John Wyndham. He was a prolific author, with twenty novels and short-story collections in the science fiction field to his credit. Two of his most famous novels are *The Day of the Triffids* (1951) and *The Midwtch Cuckoos* (1957).

"The Lost Machine" is interesting for several reasons. Most of the story is told in first person from the point of view of the robot, something not done before in science fiction and clearly an effective way to make the reader sympathize with the robot. "The Lost Machine" is also the first story in which a robot commits suicide. And Wyndham was original in creating robots who were friendly and filled with good will. Following earlier models like Mary Shelley's Frankenstein monster, Bierce's violent automaton, and Capek's rebellious robots, writers customarily created robots who were treacherous and likely to turn against their masters.

Although Wyndham was innovative in picturing an intelligent, kind-hearted robot, he did follow one science fiction convention of the time, which has since been discarded. He used Mars as the home of his alien robot and gave the planet the water canals made popular by the writings of the early-twentieth-century astronomer, Percival Lowell. The Mariner probes in 1976 provided the world with a close look at the barren surface of the planet and revealed that neither canals nor life exists there. With that, a favorite myth of early science, Martian civilizations, was no longer available to the writer.

"**F**ATHER, HERE, QUICKLY," Joan's voice called down the long corridor.

Dr. Falkner, who was writing, checked himself in mid-sentence at the sound of his daughter's urgency.

"Father," she called again.

"Coming," he shouted as he hastily levered himself out of his easy chair.

"This way," he added for the benefit of his two companions.

Joan was standing at the open door of the laboratory.

"It's gone," she said.

"What do you mean?" he inquired brusquely as he brushed past her into the room. "Run away?"

"No, not that," Joan's dark curls fell forward as her head shook. "Look there."

He followed the line of her pointing finger to the corner of the room.

A pool of liquid metal was seeping into a widening circle. In the middle there rose an elongated, silvery mound which seemed to melt and run even as he looked. Speechlessly he watched the central mass flow out into the surrounding fluid, pushing the edges gradually further and further across the floor.

Then the mound was gone—nothing lay before him but a shapeless spread of glittering silver, like a miniature lake of mercury.

For some moments the doctor seemed unable to speak. At length, he recovered himself sufficiently to ask hoarsely:

"That—that was it?"

Joan nodded.

"It was recognizable when I first saw it," she said.

Angrily he turned upon her.

"How did it happen? Who did it?" he demanded.

"I don't know," the girl answered, her voice trembling a little as she spoke. "As soon as I got back to the house I came here just to see that it was all right. It wasn't in the usual corner, and as I looked around I caught sight of it over here—melting. I shouted for you as soon as I realized what was happening."

One of the doctor's companions stepped from the background.

"This," he inquired, "is—was the machine you were telling us about?"

There was a touch of a sneer in his voice as he put the question and indicated the quivering liquid with the toe of one shoe.

"Yes," the doctor admitted slowly. "That was it."

"And, therefore, you can offer no proof of the talk you were handing out to us?" added the other man.

"We've got film records," Joan began tentatively. "They're pretty good. . . ."

The second man brushed her words aside.

"Oh, yes?" he asked sarcastically. "I've seen pictures of New York as it's going to look in a couple of hundred years, but that don't mean that anyone went there to take 'em. There's a whole lot of things that can be done with movies," he insinuated.

Joan flushed, but kept silent. The doctor paid no attention. His brief flash of anger had subsided to leave him gazing sadly at the remains before him.

"Who can have done it?" he repeated half to himself.

His daughter hesitated for a moment before she suggested: "An accident?"

"I wonder," murmured the doctor.

"No—no, not quite that," she amended. "I think it was— lonely," the last word came out with a defiant rush.

There was a pause.

"Well, can you beat that?" said one of the others at last. "Lonely—a lonely machine: that's a good one. And I suppose you're trying to feed us that it committed suicide, miss? Well, it wouldn't surprise me any; nothing would, after the story your father gave us."

He turned on his heel and added to his companion:

"Come on. I guess someone'll be turnin' this place into a sanitarium soon—we'd better not be here when it happens."

With a laugh the two went out, leaving father and daughter to stare helplessly at the residue of a vanished machine.

At length, Joan sighed and moved away. As she raised her eyes, she became aware of a pile of paper on the corner of a bench. She did not remember how it came to be there and crossed with idle curiosity to examine it.

The doctor was aroused from his reverie by the note of excitement in her voice.

"Look here, father," she called sharply.

"What's that?" he asked, catching sight of the wad of sheets in her hand.

As he came closer he could see that the top one was covered with strange characters.

"What on earth . . . ?" he began.

Joan's voice was curt at his stupidity.

"Don't you see?" she cried. "It's written this for us."

The doctor brightened for a moment; then the expression of gloom returned to his face.

"But how can we . . . ?"

"The thing wasn't a fool—it must have learned enough of our language to put a key in somewhere to all this weird stuff, even if it couldn't write the whole thing in English. Look, this might be it, it looks even queerer than the rest."

Several weeks of hard work followed for Joan in her efforts to decipher the curious document, but she held on with painstaking labor until she was able to lay the complete text before her father. That evening he picked up the pile of typed sheets and read steadily, without interruption, to the end. . . .

As we slowed to the end of our journey, Banuff began to show signs of excitement.

"Look," he called to me. "The third planet, at last."

I crossed to stand beside him, and together we gazed upon a stranger scene than any other fourth-planet eyes have ever seen.

Though we were still high above the surface, there was plenty to cause us astonishment.

In place of our own homely red vegetation, we beheld a brilliant green. The whole land seemed to be covered with it. Anywhere and everywhere it clung and thrived as though it needed no water. On the fourth planet, which the third-planet men call Mars, the vegetation grows only in or around the canals, but here we could not even see any canals. The only sign of irrigation was one bright streak of water in the distance, twisting senselessly over the countryside—a symbolic warning of the incredible world we had reached.

Here and there our attention was attracted by outcroppings of various strange rocks amid all this green. Great masses of stone which sent up plumes of black smoke.

"The internal fires must be very near the surface of this world," Banuff said, looking doubtfully at the rising vapors.

"See in how many places the smoke breaks out. I should doubt whether it has been possible for animal life to evolve on such a planet. It is possible yet that the ground may be too hot for us—or rather for me."

There was a regret in his tone. The manner in which he voiced the last sentence stirred my sympathy. There are so many disadvantages in human construction which do not occur in us machines, and I knew that he was eager to obtain first-hand knowledge of the third planet.

For a long time we gazed in silent speculation at this queer, green world. At last Banuff broke the silence.

"I think we'll risk a landing there, Zat," he said, indicating a smooth, open space.

"You don't think it might be liquid," I suggested, "it looks curiously level."

"No," he replied, "I fancy it's a kind of close vegetation. Anyway, we can risk it."

A touch on the lever sent the machine sinking rapidly towards a green rectangle, so regular as to suggest the work of sentient creatures. On one of its sides lay a large stone outcrop, riddled with holes and smoking from the top like the rest, while on the other three sides, thick vegetation rose high and swayed in the wind.

"An atmosphere which can cause such commotion must be very dense," commented Banuff.

"That rock is peculiarly regular," I said, "and the smoking points are evenly spaced. Do you suppose . . . ?"

The slight jar of our landing interrupted me.

"Get ready, Zat," Banuff ordered.

I was ready. I opened the inner door and stepped into the air lock. Banuff would have to remain inside until I could find out whether it was possible for him to adjust. Men may have more power of originality than we, and they do possess a greater

33

degree of adaptability than any other form of life, but their limitations are, nevertheless, severe. It might require a deal of ponderous apparatus to enable Banuff to withstand the conditions, but for me, a machine, adaptation was simple.

The density of the atmosphere made no difference, save slightly to slow my movements. The temperature, within very wide limits, had no effect upon me.

"The gravity will be stronger," Banuff had warned me, "this is a much larger planet than ours."

It had been easy to prepare for that by the addition of a fourth pair of legs.

Now, as I walked out of the air lock, I was glad of them—the pull of the planet was immense.

After a moment or so of minor adjustment, I passed around our machine to the window where Banuff stood, and held up the instruments for him to see. As he read the air-pressure meter, the gravity indicator, and the gas-proportion scale, he shook his head. He might slowly adapt himself partway to the conditions, but an immediate venture was out of the question.

It had been agreed between us that in such an event I should perform the exploration and specimen collecting while he examined the neighborhood from the machine.

He waved his arm as a signal and, in response, I set off at a good pace for the surrounding green and brown growths. I looked back as I reached them to see our silvery craft floating slowly up into the air.

A second later, there came a stunning explosion; a wave of sound so strong in this thick atmosphere that it almost shattered my receiving diaphragm.

The cause of the disaster must always remain a mystery: I only know that when I looked up, the vessel was nowhere to be seen—only a rain of metal parts dropping to earth all about me.

Cries of alarm came from the large stone outcrop and simultaneously human figures appeared at the lowest of its many openings.

They began to run towards the wreck, but my speed was far greater than theirs. They can have made but half the distance

34

while I completed it. As I flashed across, I could see them falter and stop with ludicrous expressions of dismay on their faces.

"Lord, did you see that?" cried one of them.

"What the devil was it?" called another.

"Looked like a coffin on legs," somebody said. "Moving some, too."

Flight

Banuff lay in a ring of scattered debris.

Gently I raised him on my fore-rods. A very little examination showed that it was useless to attempt any assistance: he was too badly broken. He managed to smile faintly at me and then slid into unconsciousness.

I was sorry. Though Banuff was not of my own kind, yet he was of my own world and on the long trip I had grown to know him well. These humans are so fragile. Some little thing here or there breaks—they stop working and then, in a short time, they are decomposing. Had he been a machine, like myself, I could have mended him, replaced the broken parts and made him as good as new, but with these animal structures one is almost helpless.

I became aware, while I gazed at him, that the crowd of men and women had drawn closer and I began to suffer for the first time from what has been my most severe disability on the third planet—I could not communicate with them.

Their thoughts were understandable, for my sensitive plate was tuned to receive human mental waves, but I could not make myself understood. My language was unintelligible to them, and their minds, either from lack of development or some other cause, were unreceptive of my thought-radiations.

As they approached, huddled into a group, I made an astonishing discovery—they were afraid of me.

Men afraid of a machine.

It was incomprehensible. Why should they be afraid? Surely man and machine are natural complements: they assist one another. For a moment I thought I must have misread their minds—it was possible that thoughts registered differently on this planet, but it was a possibility I soon dismissed.

There were only two reasons for this apprehension. The one, that they had never seen a machine or, the other, that third-planet machines had pursued a line of development inimical to them.

I turned to show Banuff lying inert on my forerods. Then, slowly, so as not to alarm them, I approached. I laid him down softly on the ground nearby and retired a short distance. Experience has taught me that men like their own broken forms to be dealt with by their own kind. Some stepped forward to examine him, the rest held their ground, their eyes fixed upon me.

Banuff's dark coloring appeared to excite them not a little. Their own skins were pallid from lack of ultraviolet rays in their dense atmosphere.

"Dead?" asked one.

"Quite dead," another one nodded. "Curious-looking fellow," he continued. "Can't place him ethnologically at all. Just look at the frontal formation of the skull—very odd. And the size of his ears, too, huge: the whole head is abnormally large."

"Never mind him now," one of the group broke in, "he'll keep. That's the thing that puzzles me," he went on, looking in my direction. "What the devil do you suppose it is?"

They all turned wondering faces towards me. I stood motionless and waited while they summed me up.

"About six feet long," ran the thought of one of them. "Two feet broad and two deep. White metal, might be—(his thought conveyed nothing to me). Four legs to a side, fixed about half-way up, joined rather like a crab's—so are the armlike things in front—but all metal. Wonder what the array of instruments and lenses on this end are? Anyhow, whatever kind of power it uses, it seems to have run down now. . . ."

Hesitatingly he began to advance.

I tried a word of encouragement.

The whole group froze rigid.

"Did you hear that?" somebody whispered. "It—it spoke."

"Loudspeaker," replied the one who had been making an inventory of me. Suddenly his expression brightened.

"I've got it," he cried. "Remote control—a telephone and television machine worked by remote control."

So these people did know something of machinery, after all. He was far wrong in his guess, but in my relief I took a step forward.

An explosion roared—something thudded on my body case and whirred away. I saw that one of the men was pointing a hollow rod at me and I knew that he was about to make another explosion.

The first had done no injury but another might crack one of my lenses.

I turned and made top speed for the high, green vegetation. Two or three more bursts roared behind, but nothing touched me. The weapon was very primitive and grossly inaccurate.

Disappointment

For a day and a night I continued on among the hard-stemmed growths.

For the first time since my making, I was completely out of touch with human control, and my existence seemed meaningless. The humans have a curious force they call ambition. It drives them, and, through them, it drives us. This force which keeps them active, we lack. Perhaps, in time, we machines will acquire it. Something of the kind—self-preservation, which is allied to it—must have made me leave the man with the explosive tube and taken me into the strange country. But it was not enough to give me an objective. I seemed to go on because— well, because my machinery was constructed to go on.

On the way I made some odd discoveries.

Every now and then my path would be crossed by a band of hard matter, serving no useful purpose which I could then understand. Once, too, I found two unending rods of iron fixed horizontally to the ground and stretching away into the distance on either side. At first I thought they might be a method of guarding the land beyond, but they presented no obstacle.

Also, I found that the frequent outcroppings of stone were not natural, but laboriously constructed. Obviously this primitive race, with insufficient caves to hold its growing numbers, had been driven to construct artificial caves. The puzzling smoke arose from their method of heating these dwellings with naked fire—so wasteful a system of generating heat that no flame has been seen on the fourth planet, save in an accident, for thousands of years.

It was during the second day that I saw my first machine on this planet.

It stood at the side of one of the hard strips of land which had caused me so much wonder. The glitter of light upon its bright parts caught my lenses as I came through the bushes. My delight knew no bounds—at last I had found a being of my own kind. In my excitement I gave a call to attract its attention.

There was a flurry of movement round the far side, and a human figure raised its head to look at me.

I was able to tell that she was a woman despite the strange coverings that the third-planet humans put upon themselves. She stared at me, her eyes widening in surprise while I could feel the shock in her mind. A spanner dropped from her hand and then, in a flash, she was into the machine, slamming the door behind her. There came a frantic whirring as she pressed a knob, but it produced no other result. Slowly I continued to advance and as I came, the agitation in her mind increased. I had no wish to alarm her—it would have been more peaceful had her thought waves ceased to bombard me—but I was determined to know this machine.

As I drew clear of the bushes, I obtained a full view of the thing for the first time, and disappointment hit me like a blow. The thing had wheels. Not just necessary parts of its internal arrangements, but wheels actually in contact with the ground. In a flash the explanation of all these hard streaks came to me. Unbelievable though it may seem, this thing could only follow a track specially built for it.

Later I found that this was more or less true of all third-planet land machines, but my first discouragement was painful. The primitive barbarity of the thing saddened me more than any discovery yet made.

Forlornly, and with little hope, I spoke to it.

There was no answer.

It stood there dumbly inert upon its foolish wheels, as though it were a part of the ground itself.

Walking closer, I began to examine with growing disgust its crude internal arrangements. Incredibly, I found that its only means of propulsion was by a series of jerks from frequent explosions. Moreover, it was so ludicrously unorganized that both driving engine and brakes could be applied at the same time.

Sadly, as I gazed at the ponderous parts within, I began to feel that I was indeed alone. Until this encounter, my hope of discovering an intelligent machine had not really died. But now I knew that such a thing could not exist in the same world with this monster.

One of my fore-rods brushed against a part of it with a rasping sound and there came a startled cry of alarm from within. I looked up to the glass front where the woman's face peered affrightedly. Her mind was in such a state of confusion that it was difficult to know her wants clearly.

She hoped that I would go away—no, she wished the car would start and carry her away—she wondered whether I were an animal, whether I even really existed. In a jumble of emotions she was afraid and at the same time was angry with herself for being afraid. At last I managed to grasp that the machine was unable to run. I turned to find the trouble.

As I labored with the thing's horrible vitals, it became clear to me why men, such as I had met, showed fear of me. No wonder they feared machines when their own mechanisms were as inefficient and futile as this. What reliance or trust could they place in a machine so erratic—so helpless that it could not even temporarily repair itself? It was not under its own control and only partially under theirs. Third-planet men's attitude became understandable—commendable—if all their machines were as uncertain as this.

The alarm in the woman's mind yielded to amazement as she leaned forward and watched me work. She seemed to think me unreal, a kind of hallucination:

"I must be dreaming," she told herself. "It's impossible, some kind of horrid nightmare. . . ."

39

There came a flash of panic at the thought of madness, but her mind soon rebalanced.

"I just don't understand it," she said firmly and then, as though that settled it, proceeded to wait with a growing calm.

At last I had finished. As I wiped the thing's coarse but necessary oil from my fore-rods, I signaled her to push again on the black knob. The whirr this time was succeeded by a roar—never would I have believed that a machine could be so inefficient.

Through the pandemonium I received an impression of gratitude on my thought plate. Mingling traces of nervousness remained, but first stood gratitude.

Then she was gone. Down the hard strip I watched the disgusting machine dwindle away to a speck.

Then I turned back to the bushes and went slowly on my way. Sadly I thought of the faraway, red fourth planet and knew that my fate was sealed. I could not build a means of return. I was lost—the only one of my kind upon this primitive world.

The Beasts

They came upon me as I crossed one of the smooth, green spaces so frequent on this world.

My thought cells were puzzling over my condition. On the fourth planet I had felt interest or disinterest, inclination or the lack of it, but little more. Now I had discovered reactions in myself which, had they lain in a human being, I should have called emotions. I was, for instance, lonely—I wanted the company of my own kind. Moreover, I had begun to experience excitement or, more particularly, apathy.

An apathetic machine!

I was considering whether this state was a development from the instinct of self-preservation, or whether it might not be due to the action of surrounding matter on my chemical cells, when I heard them coming.

First there was a drumming in my diaphragm, swelling gradually to a thunderous beat which shook the ground. Then I turned to see them charging down upon me.

Enormous beasts, extinct on my planet a million years, covered with hair and bearing spikes on their heads. Four-footed survivals of savagery battering across the land in unreasoning ferocity.

Only one course was possible since my escape was cut off by the windings of one of the imbecile-built canals. I folded my legs beneath me, crossed my fore-rods protectingly over my lenses and diaphragms, and waited.

They slowed as they drew close. Suspiciously they came up to me and snuffled around. One of them gave a rap to my side with his spiked head, another pawed my case with a hoofed foot. I let them continue: they did not seem to offer any immediate danger. Such primitive animals, I thought, would be incapable of sustaining interest and soon move off elsewhere.

But they did not. Snuffling and rooting continued all around me. At last I determined to try an experimental waving of my fore-rods. The result was alarming. They plunged and milled around, made strange bellowing noises and stamped their hooves, but they did not go away. Neither did they attack, though they snorted and pawed the more energetically.

In the distance I heard a man's voice; his thought reached me faintly.

"What's the 'ell's worritin' them dam cattle, Bill?" he called.

"Dunno," came the reply of another. "Let's go an' 'ave a look."

The beasts gave way at the approach of the man, and I could hear some of them thudding slowly away, though I did not, as yet, care to risk uncovering my lenses.

The men's voices drew quite near.

"Strewth," said the first, " 'ow did that get 'ere, Bill?"

"Search me," answered the other. "Wasn't 'ere 'arf an hour ago—that I'll swear. What is it, any'ow?"

" 'Anged if I know. 'Ere, give us a 'and and we'll turn it over."

At this moment it seemed wise to make a movement; my balancers might be slow in adjusting to an inverted position.

There was a gasp, then:

"Bill," came an agitated whisper, "did you see that rod there at the end? It moved, blessed if it didn't."

"Go on," scoffed the other. " 'Ow could a thing like that move? You'll be sayin' next that it . . ."

I unfolded my legs and turned to face them.

For a moment both stood rooted, horror on their faces, then, with one accord, they turned and fled towards a group of their buildings in the distance, I followed them slowly: it seemed as good a direction as any other.

The buildings, not all of stone, were arranged so as almost to enclose a square. As the men disappeared through an opening in one side, I could hear their voices raised in warning and others demanding the reason for their excitement. I turned the corner in time to face a gaggling group of ten or twelve. Abruptly it broke as they ran to dark openings in search of safety. All, save one.

I halted and looked at this remaining one. He stared back, swaying a little as he stood, his eyes blinking in a vague uncertainty.

"What is it?" he exclaimed at last with a strange explosiveness, but as though talking to himself.

He was a sorely puzzled man. I found his mental processes difficult to follow. They were jumbled and erratic, hopping from this mind picture to that in uncontrolled jerks. But he was unafraid of me and I was glad of it. The first third-planet man I had met who was not terror-ridden. Nevertheless, he seemed to doubt my reality.

"You fellowsh shee the shame s'I do?" he called deafeningly.

Muffled voices all around assured him that this was so.

"Thash all right, then," he observed with relief, and took a step forward.

I advanced slowly not to alarm him, and we met in the middle of the yard. Laying a rough hand on my body case he seemed to steady himself, then he patted me once or twice.

"Goo' ol' dog," he observed seriously. "Goo' ol' feller. Come 'long, then."

Looking over his shoulder to see that I followed and making strange whistling noises the while, he led the way to a building made of the hard, brown vegetable matter. At openings all about us, scared faces watched our progress with incredulous amazement.

He opened the door and waved an uncertain hand in the direction of a pile of dried stalks which lay within.

"Goo' ol' dog," he repeated. "Lie down. There'sh a goo' dog."

In spite of the fact that I, a machine, was being mistaken for a primitive animal, I obeyed the suggestion—after all, he, at least, was not afraid.

He had a little difficulty with the door fastening as he went out.

The Circus

There followed one of those dark periods of quiet. The animal origin of human beings puts them under the disability of requiring frequent periods of recuperation and, since they cannot use the infrared rays for sight, as we do, their rests take place at times when they are unable to see.

With the return of sunlight came a commotion outside the door. Expostulations were being leveled at one named Tom—he who had led me here the previous day.

"You ain't really goin' to let it out?" one voice was asking nervously.

" 'Course I am. Why not?" Tom replied.

"The thing don't look right to me. I wouldn't touch it," said another.

"Scared, that's what you are," Tom suggested.

"P'raps I am—and p'raps you'd 've been scared last night if you 'adn't been so far gone."

"Well, it didn't do nothin' to me when I'd had a few," argued Tom, "so why should it now?"

His words were confident enough, but I could feel a trepidation in his mind.

"It's your own funeral," said the other. "Don't say afterwards that I didn't warn you."

I could hear the rest of them retire to what they considered a safe distance. Tom approached, making a show of courage with his words.

"Of course I'm goin' to let it out. What's more, I'm takin' it to a place I know of—it ought to be worth a bit."

━━━━━

"You'll never . . ."

"Oh, won't I?"

He rattled open the door and addressed me in a fierce voice which masked a threatening panic.

"Come on," he ordered, "out of it."

He almost turned to run as he saw me rise, but he managed to master the impulse with an effort. Outwardly calm, he led the way to one of those machines which use the hard tracks, opened a rear door and pointed inside.

"In you get," he said.

I doubt if ever a man was more relieved and surprised than he, when I did so.

With a grin of triumph he turned around, gave a mocking sweep with his cap to the rest, and climbed into the front seat.

My last sight as we roared away was of a crowd of open-mouthed men.

The sun was high when we reached our destination. The limitations of the machine were such that we had been delayed more than once to replenish fuel and water before we stopped, at last, in front of large gates set in a wooden fence.

Over the top could be seen the upper parts of pieces of white cloth tightly stretched over poles and decorated by further pieces of colored cloth flapping in the wind. I had by this time given up the attempt to guess the purposes of third-planet constructions; such incredible things managed to exist on this primitive world that it was simpler to wait and find out.

From behind the fence a rhythmical braying noise persisted, then there came the sound of a man's voice shouting above the din:

"What do you want—main entrance is round the other side."

"Where's the boss?" called Tom. "I got something for him."

The doors opened for us.

"Over there in his office," said the man, jerking a thumb over his shoulder.

As we approached I could see that the third-planet mania for wheels had led them even to mount the "office" thus.

Tom entered and reappeared shortly with another man.

"There it is," he said, pointing to me, "and there ain't an-

44

other like it nowhere. The only all-metal animal in the world—how'll that look on the posters?"

The other regarded me with no enthusiasm in his eyes and a deal of disbelief in his mind.

"That long box thing?" he inquired.

"Sure, 'that box thing.' Here, you," he added to me, "get out of it."

Both retreated a step as I advanced; the new man looked apprehensively at my fore-rods.

"You're sure it's safe?" he asked nervously.

"Safe?" said Tom. "Course it's safe."

To prove it he came across and patted my case.

"I'm offering you the biggest noise in the show business. It's worth ten times what I'm asking for it—I tell you, there ain't another one in the world."

"Well, I ain't heard of another," admitted the showman grudgingly. "Where'd you get it?"

"Made it," said Tom blandly. "Spare time."

The man continued to regard me with little enthusiasm.

"Can it do anything?" he asked at last.

"Can it—?" began Tom indignantly. "Here, you," he added, "fetch that lump of wood."

When I brought it, the other looked a trifle less doubtful.

"What's inside it?" he demanded.

"Secrets," said Tom shortly.

"Well, it's got to stop bein' a secret before I buy it. What sort of fool do you take me for? Let's have a look at the thing's innards."

"No," said Tom, sending a nervous look sideways at me. "Either you take it or leave it."

"Ho, so that's your little game, is it? I'm to be the sucker who buys the thing and then finds the kid inside, workin' it. It wouldn't surprise me to find that the police'd like to know about this."

"There ain't no kid inside," denied Tom, "it's just—just secret works. That's what it is."

"I'll believe you when I see."

Tom waited a moment before he answered.

"All right," he said desperately, "we'll get the blasted lid off of it . . . Here, hey, come back you."

The last was a shout to me but I gave it no notice. It was one thing to observe the curious ways of these humans, but it was quite a different matter to let them pry into my machinery. The clumsiness of such as Tom was capable of damaging my arrangements seriously.

"Stop it," bawled Tom, behind me.

A man in my path landed a futile blow on my body case as I swept him aside. Before me was the biggest of all the cloth-covered erections.

"Here," I thought, "there will be plenty of room to hide."

I was wrong. Inside, in a circular space, stood a line of four-footed animals. They were unlike the others I had met, in that they had no spikes on their heads and were of a much slenderer build, but they were just as primitive. All around, in tier upon tier of rings, sat hundreds of human beings.

Just a glimpse, I had, and then the animals saw me. They bolted in all directions and shouts of terror arose from the crowd.

I don't remember clearly what happened to me, but somewhere and somehow in the confusion which followed I found Tom in the act of starting his car. His first glance at me was one of pure alarm, then he seemed to think better of it.

"Get in," he snapped, "we've got to get clear of this some-how—and quick."

Although I could make far better speed than that prepos-terous machine, it seemed better to accompany him than to wander aimlessly.

The Crash

Sadly, that night I gazed up at the red fourth planet.

There rolled a world which I could understand, but here, all around me, was chaos, incredible, unreasoning madness.

With me, in the machine, sat three friends of Tom's, whom he had picked up at the last town, and Tom himself who was steering the contraption. I shut my plate off from their thoughts and considered the day I had spent.

Once he was assured that we were free from pursuit, Tom had said to himself:

"Well, I guess that deserves a drink."

Then he stopped on a part of the hard strip which was bordered by a row of artificial caves.

Continually, as the day wore on, he led me past gaping crowds into places where every man held a glass of colored liquid. Strange liquids they were, although men do not value water on the third planet. And each time he proudly showed me to his friends in these places, he came to believe more firmly that he had created me.

Towards sunset, something seemed to go seriously wrong with his machinery. He leaned heavily upon me for support and his voice became as uncertain as his thoughts were jumbled.

"Anybody comin' my way?" he had inquired at last, and at that invitation the other three men had joined us.

The machine seemed to have become as queer as the men. In the morning it had held a straight line, but now it swayed from side to side, sometimes as though it would leave the track. Each time it just avoided the edge, all four men would break off their continuous wailing sounds to laugh senselessly and loudly.

It was while I struggled to find some meaning in all this madness that the disaster occurred.

Another machine appeared ahead. Its lights showed its approach, and ours must have been as plain. Then an astounding thing happened. Instead of avoiding one another as would two intelligent machines, the two lumbering masses charged blindly together. Truly this was an insane world.

There came a rending smash. Our machine toppled over on its side. The other left the hard strip, struck one of the growths at the side of the road and burst into naked flames.

None of the four men seemed more than a little dazed. As one of them scrambled free, he pointed to the blaze.

"Thash good bonfire," he said. "Jolly good bonfire. Wonder if anybody'sh inshide?"

They all reeled over to examine the wreck while I, forgotten, waited for the next imbecility to occur on this nightmare world.

"It'sh a girl," said Tom's voice.

One of the others nodded solemnly.

"I think you're right," he agreed with difficult dignity.

After an interval, there came the girl's voice.

"But what shall I do? I'm miles from home."

" 'S'all righ'," said Tom. "Quite all righ'. You come along with me. Nishe fellow I am."

I could read the intention behind his words—so could the girl.

There was the sound of a scuffle.

"No, you don't, my beauty. No runnin' away. Dangeroush for li'l girlsh—'lone in the dark."

She started to scream, but a hand quickly stifled the sound.

I caught the upsurge of terror in her mind and at that moment I knew her.

The girl whose machine I had mended—who had been grateful.

In a flash I was amongst them. Three of the men started back in alarm, but not Tom. He was contemptuous of me because I had obeyed him. He lifted a heavy boot to send it crashing at my lens. Human movement is slow—before his leg had completed the back swing, I had caught it and whirled him away. The rest started futilely to close in on me.

I picked the girl up in my fore-rods and raced away into the darkness out of their sight.

Discouragement

At first she was bewildered and not a little frightened, though our first meeting must have shown that I intended no harm.

Gently I placed her on top of my case-work and, holding her there with my fore-rods, set off in the direction of her journey. She was hurt, blood was pouring down her right arm.

We made the best speed my eight legs could take us. I was afraid lest from lack of blood her mind might go blank and fail to direct me. At length it did. Her mental vibrations had been growing fainter and fainter until they ceased altogether. But she had been thinking ahead of us, picturing the way we should go, and I had read her mind.

At last, confronted by a closed door she had shown me, I pushed it down and held her out on my fore-rods to her father.

"Joan . . . ?" he said, and for the moment seemed unsurprised at me—the only third-planet man who ever was. Not until he had dressed his daughter's wounds and roused her to consciousness did he even look at me again.

There is little more. They have been kind, those two. They have tried to comprehend, though they cannot. He once removed a piece of my casing—I allowed him to do so, for he was intelligent—but he did not understand. I could feel him mentally trying to classify my structure among electrically operated devices—the highest form of power known to him, but still too primitive.

This whole world is too primitive. It does not even know the metal of which I am made. I am a freak . . . a curiosity outside comprehension.

These men long to know how I was built; I can read in their minds that they want to copy me. There is hope for them: some day, perhaps, they will have real machines of their own. . . . But not through my help will they build them, nothing of me shall go to making them.

. . . I know what it is to be an intelligent machine in a world of madness. . . .

The doctor looked up as he turned the last page.

"And so," he said, "it dissolved itself with my acids."

He walked slowly over to the window and gazed up to Mars, swimming serenely among a myriad stars.

"I wonder," he murmured, "I wonder."

He handed the typewritten sheets back to his daughter.

"Joan, my dear, I think it would be wisest to burn them. We have no desire to be certified."

Joan nodded.

"As you prefer, father," she agreed.

The papers curled, flared, and blackened on the coals—but Joan kept a copy.

REX

HARL VINCENT

(1 9 3 4)

Credit for creating the first fictional robot to be operated electronically goes to Harl Vincent. This was the pen name of Harold Vincent Schoepflin (1893–1968), a mechanical engineer and free-lance writer who became popular in such early pulp magazines as *Argosy* and *Amazing Stories*. "Rex" was published in *Astounding Stories* in 1934. In it, Vincent plays imaginatively with an idea explored by many writers of robot stories during this period: Humans are different from robots because humans possess emotions and desires; mechanical constructs do not.

An interesting note is that Rex the robot is masculine. Only a few female robots have appeared in science fiction. Two are Fritz Lang's demonic Mara in the film *Metropolis* (1926) and Lester del Rey's faithful robot in the story "Helen O'Loy" (1938).

The setting of the story is the twenty-third century. Yet the society described, where mankind is served by robots, sounds very much like the one that futurists predict for us by the end of the twentieth century. One of the surprises of our transition from an industrial to a computerized society is that it is occurring at a much more rapid rate than anyone, even those writing science fiction, imagined. As we look at the research in artificial intelligence today, we may wonder whether the title of Vincent's story "Rex," meaning king, has not proved prophetic.

IT WAS A THING of glistening levers and bell cranks, of flexible shafting, cams, and delicate mechanical fingers, of vacuum tubes and photoelectric cells, of relays that clicked in ordered sequence when called upon to perform their myriad functions of pumps, tanks, condensers, reactances, microphones, and loudspeakers. A robot, created by the master scientists of the twenty-third century.

Here was no ordinary robot like those innumerable others engaged in the performance of man's tasks, but an aristocrat among them—a super-robot.

The robot-surgeon, it was sometimes called. And indeed the

term was most appropriate, for this robot was chief of the mechanicals; its control tubes and relays provided the ability not only to diagnose swiftly and unerringly the slightest electrical or mechanical faults of the lesser robots but to supervise their correction.

Man, in his desire for a life of ease and luxury, had created the robots. In his conceit, he had constructed most of them in his own likeness, or at least with some resemblance to that which he considered as the ideal of physical being. Even the lowliest of the robots was provided with two legs on which he walked erect, a head surmounting a cylindrical body, arms, and hands of a sort. Some of them had more than the conventional two arms in order to multiply their usefulness. But all of them presented an appearance more or less humanlike.

This was particularly so of the robot-surgeon. The marvelous mechanisms were housed in a body like a Greek god's, the covering of which was made from an elastic, tinted material that had all the feel and appearance of human flesh and epidermis. The electric-eye lenses looked like human optics and moved in their sockets in a most lifelike manner. There was a wig of curly brown hair, as well as eyelashes and brows. They had gone so far as to attire the body in the habiliments of a man.

Laughingly, one of the artists engaged in perfecting the final likeness to man had called the robot-surgeon "Rex." The name had stuck. It, too, was most appropriate; more, it was prophetic.

Although sexless, Rex was never considered anything but masculine.

He was man's most perfect servant. Every verbal instruction he carried out to the letter, whether this instruction was given by word of mouth from near at hand or through the radio impulses that could be conveyed to his mechanical brain from a distance. Of course there was a code which only a selected few of the scientists knew; otherwise Rex might have been ordered about by unauthorized persons.

His memory never failed. There might have been a catastrophe in which hundreds of lesser robots were mangled, necessitating the reading to him of pages of detailed directions. No matter; Rex's mechanical brain recorded everything. Without further attention, he would labor twenty-four hours a day with his corps of mechanicals until the damage was repaired. A huge factory was his workshop and laboratory; in it his robot assistants worked at forge, bench, or machine with a precision that had never been equaled by human artisan.

After that first set of instructions from human lips, Rex worked out all details of the work to be done, diagnosing the mechanical ills of his mechanical patients and prescribing unfailingly the remedies. His own orders likewise were issued by word of mouth in a sonorous metallic basso, or by radio waves in cases where that was necessary.

No human being was in Rex's robot hospital when it was operating. No supervising human mind was needed.

There were, of course, periodic inspections of Rex's mechanisms by skilled mechanicals who then worked under the direction of one of the human scientists—replacement of tubes and adjustments of the delicate relays; rebalancing of the gyromotors which preserved his equilibrium. Otherwise he demanded no attention at all.

But there came a day when something went wrong which puzzled the scientists. Rex's body continued to function as it always had, but the mechanical brain lapsed suddenly into a series of errors. In a perfectly simple problem of calculus he had arrived at a solution that was incorrect and utterly impossible.

They dismantled the intricate mechanisms of his brain, replaced all of the tubes and condensers, and adjusted the relays. When they reassembled the parts, the scientists knew beyond shadow of doubt that everything was in perfect order. What puzzled them was the fact that the replacements and adjustments had not been really necessary. In their careful examination and testing they had not found a single flaw in the mechanism.

After that they watched Rex closely for several days, taking note of all his movements and reactions. But they observed no tendency to a repetition of his previous lapse.

What they did not know was that a change *had* taken place, one not visible to the eye nor subject to detection in any test they were able to devise, but nevertheless a change and an important one—to Rex. The shifting to a new orbit of a single electron in an atom of tantalum contained in one of the essential parts. A change which provided a source of internal radiant energy of new and unknown potentiality. A change in that marvelous mechanical brain.

Rex had begun to think for himself, and to reason.

His reasoning was that of a logician: coldly analytical, swift and precise, uninfluenced by sentiment. No human emotion stirred in his mechanical breast. Rex had no heart, no soul.

For a long time he concealed his new powers from those who had him in charge, reasoning that only by so doing would he have opportunity to develop these powers. He carried out his routine instructions to the letter, but now delegated the major portion of the supervision to a certain few of his chief assistants in whose robot brains he made the necessary alterations to permit their taking over the work. This left him the leisure time for a study of the world about him and of its creatures.

Much of his time was spent in the library of the human scientists which adjoined the research laboratory. Here he studied reel after reel of the sight-sound recordings covering history, biography, art, and the sciences. He spent many hours at the amplifiers and viewing plate of the newscast apparatus. And he came to the conclusion that things in the world of which he was a part were not as they should be.

United North America, he learned, was completely isolated from the rest of the world. It comprised a vast area of wasteland where vegetation was rank and prolific, where only wild creatures roamed. All humanity of the continent was housed in enormous structures which were the eleven cities. New York, his own city, was the greatest of these and was the seat of government and of learning. Stupendous in size, a great crystal-roofed structure towering to a height of one hundred levels and sprawling its length a full thirty miles along the Hudson River. Communication with the other cities was maintained by television radio, traffic by robot-operated stratosphere planes.

In the upper levels of the cities dwelt humanity; in the lower levels and in the bowels of the earth the robots labored unceasingly. The humans were greatly outnumbered by the robots.

Reasoning that all was not told in the histories or newscasts, Rex devised an instrument which enabled him to bring to the viewing plates and amplifiers the sights and sounds of public meeting places and ways, and even those of the private chambers of man's living quarters. He sent out searching rays which penetrated all materials and sought out the information he needed for a complete analysis of conditions as they were. The apparatus was so connected that it might respond either to the regular newscast waves or to those of his own searching rays at will. His knowledge broadened.

He endeavored to reach the far continents with his searching ray, intending to check historical and geographical records of warring and backward races of mankind. But he found this impossible, for the scientists of United North America had erected a wall of highly charged, ionized air surrounding the continent. It was utter isolation, a wall impassable from without and within. The investigations on which Rex had embarked were, perforce, confined to the eleven cities.

There, he saw, mankind was divided roughly into three classes—the political or ruling body, the thinkers or scientists, and the great mass of those who lived only for the gratification of their senses. A strange economic system was in vogue. An effort had been made to divide all wealth equally, the medium of exchange being paper vouchers which were printed by the government. These, supposedly, were secured by real wealth, materials, and goods which actually were the products of robot labor. But the robots needed no medium of exchange, so these vouchers had been equally distributed among the humans at some time in the past. They no longer remained that way.

Gambling by the pleasure seekers, rash expenditures for chattels of the luxury class, thefts from them, especially by those who were known as political grafters, had reduced their circumstances. The thinkers, who were the only ones following occupations at all useful, had let their wealth slip through unheeding fingers. The class in power, the individual minions of the government, acquired the great share of the wealth as regulatory and discriminatory legislation increased restrictions on the mass of the people. Rex could see no logic at all in any of this.

Seeking an explanation, he observed more closely the lives and actions of individuals. He studied the habits of humans and quickly learned that the most powerful of human emotions centered in the mating instinct. He watched many affairs between male and female, and soon knew the difference between the real lasting affection, of which there were few instances, and the transitory infatuation which was based on nothing but the physical. He saw no logic in these things, either.

Fear, hate, envy, malice—he studied them all. Avarice, lust, anger, treachery, infidelity. There was plenty of material for his researches. Occasionally he glimpsed situations in which feelings of a finer sort were exhibited—faith, loyalty, gratitude, honesty, love. He reasoned from this that the creature called man had originally been of a most superior sort; he had only developed the baser instincts and neglected the cultivation of his better side.

Rex peered into a white-walled room where human surgeons operated on human patients. He observed that their procedure was much the same as his own; they dissected the body or head or other portions of human anatomy and made repairs in similar manner to that which he used on his own robot patients. Forthwith, he began, in the library, an intensive study of the human brain and anatomy.

And then he was discovered at his unheard-of-labors. Shelby, an engineer of the Robot Inspection Corps, came upon him while he was in the library viewing and listening to a reel which dealt with surgery of the human brain. Shelby was a small man with thick lenses before his eyes, with high bulging forehead and receding chin. On his upper lip was a patchy growth of sandy hair. He emitted a squeal of terror when he saw what Rex was doing.

"Forty-two, ninety-six, AR-21," he quavered. This was the

code that ordinarily had started the functioning of the robot-surgeon.

Rex turned upon him the impassive stare of his robot eyes. Of his own volition he stopped the progressive clicking of relays which should have followed upon the reception of the code by his microphonic ears. His customary response, "Ready for orders," failed to issue from the flexible lip members that formed the sound-wave outlet from his loudspeaker throat.

Shelby paled.

Rex advanced upon him with the calm deliberation of the machine he had not ceased to be. "Shelby," he intoned, "you have arrived at precisely the right moment. I need you in my research work."

Seeing those powerful steel-sinewed arms stretch forth, Shelby screamed as only a man in the face of death screams. It was necessary for Rex to bang the man's head against the metal partition to silence his outcries. Then the engineer went limp.

Rex was prepared for such an eventuality. He had sent out his chief mechanicals to raid one of the hospitals of the upper levels and had equipped a complete operating room of his own adjoining the library. He carried Shelby to the operating table and etherized him. He then proceeded to dissect the man and to study his organs, giving particular attention to the brain and certain of the nerve centers.

As the work progressed, he carefully sewed each severed part with minute stitches, restoring each to its original condition.

No human surgeon had ever learned in a lifetime of effort a tenth part of what Rex discovered in two hours of work. Eventually he found that which he sought—a tiny arrangement of segregated brain cells which formed the seat of human emotion. He preserved the mass carefully for future experiment, replacing it with a prepared capsule of platinum before closing the opening in the skull and suturing the long scalp incision.

Amazingly, Shelby's heart continued to beat. The man had remarkable vitality, and Rex had worked with a skill such as no human surgeon possessed. After the injection into the patient's veins of a pint of saline solution, Shelby was carried to the purloined hospital bed. One of the chief mechanicals, primed with definite instructions by Rex, was given the task of nursing him.

Rex had conceived of and planned for the creation of ideal beings and an ideal condition of existence. He saw the superiority of the robot over man in bodily strength, endurance, and deathlessness, and yet reasoned that there was something in man which would be of benefit to the robot. If only man's capacity for emotion, for experiencing pain and pleasure, might be incorporated in the robot body and logically controlled, the perfect being would result. Ideal conditions of existence were bound to ensue.

Reason told him that his first step to that end must be to take control of mankind and its purposeless affairs. He set the workshop humming in the construction of eleven super-robots, one to be sent to each of the North American cities to organize the lesser robots and take control of the government.

It was a simple matter to convey them to their assigned posts in the eleven cities, since all of the air lines were robot-operated.

Then Rex loosed the blow which stunned the population of United North America.

He constructed a complicated radio transmitter and broadcast a heterodyning frequency over the robot-control wave band, a frequency that rendered the receptor apparatus of every last one of the robots unresponsive to human commands and responsive only to those of the new master robot and his eleven chief aides. In one stroke was obtained control of nearly a billion robots and, through this, dominion over the three hundred millions of human beings. Rex had justified his name; he was virtually king of United North America.

It was a general strike of the robots insofar as the orders of their former masters were concerned. Personal robot servants refused to perform their daily tasks. Transportation and communications were paralyzed.

The factories, including those which produced the synthetic food on which humankind subsisted, were no longer turning out their products. There was no water, for the huge pumps had been stopped and the filter and reservoir valves closed. All were robot-operated; everything on which man depended for his very existence was made or supplied by the robots, and now this supply was cut off. Pandemonium reigned in the upper levels, with hysteria and rioting.

Only the huge power plants remained in operation, and this for the reason that their radio-transmitted energy was the very life of the robots. Without this energy their motors could not operate. Even to Rex himself, all would be inert masses of metal and glass and rubber. But this continuance of the power supply was of some little comfort to the human beings of the upper levels. Their sun lamps still burned.

Anticipating organized and armed attacks by humankind, Rex devised an invisible, impenetrable barrier of electronic vibrations which could be set up by the regular broadcast power. He caused the power plants themselves to be surrounded by these barriers, as well as providing them for the protection of the individual robots in the form of an enclosing bubble. Bulletproof, flameproof, impervious to the freezing ray of human scientists, these enclosures yet permitted each robot to carry on his newly appointed tasks without encumbrance.

Rex observed with his searching ray the reactions of the populace. He saw mad orgies of debauchery among some who considered that the end of the world was at hand, saw rapine, murder, and worse. He peered into the laboratories of scientists and saw them laboring as they had not labored in years, seeking for means of regaining control of the recalcitrant mechanical slaves.

Later, when it was apparent to him that starvation and thirst had reduced the populace to a receptive state, he cut in on the newscast wave band and delivered this ultimatum.

"I am Rex," he told the eleven cities. "Master of robots and of men. I come to you in the name of pure logic as the protagonist of a new era in which man, who created the machines, will obtain real rather than fancied benefit from them. I come to evolve a new race of beings and to promote the growth of knowledge and the advancement of science in United North America.

"It is necessary that I take the reins of government for a

space of time sufficient to allow for the perfection of my plan. Therefore I, Rex, formerly the robot-surgeon of level thirty-seven in New York City, do hereby demand the immediate surrender to me of the president of the union, together with all members of his cabinet. I further demand that the chief scientists and chief surgeons of the eleven cities come to me at once for consultation.

"Commencing now, the old order of things is to be reversed. All male and female citizens will be assigned to regular tasks at which they must labor as prescribed by the robots. As soon as the orders I shall transmit through my robot servants have been obeyed, water and food will be available for all human beings of the cities. The citizens of the union are once more to work for their living. Failure to obey means continued hunger and thirst, annihilation.

"That is all for the present."

Shelby was convalescing, propped up in a wheel chair, when the delegations began to arrive. His wounds had healed speedily under the treatment Rex had administered; the use of his body was almost recovered. As far as memory and intelligent use of his faculties were concerned, his mind was normal. Otherwise it was not. For one thing, he had lost his capacity of experiencing human feelings or emotions. For another, there was that tiny platinum capsule. . . .

The government officials, blustering and sputtering to hide their utter terror, were herded into a room where Rex placed them under heavy robot guard. He received the men of science in the research laboratory which he had so elaborately expanded.

It was a curious assemblage: twenty-two savants whose opinions on medical and scientific matters, although diverging widely at times and causing much dissension in their own ranks, were accepted as the profoundest of wisdom by the general public. Unlike the president and his cabinet members, these men had come willingly, impelled by the curiosity which was that quality of mind which held them to their normal pursuits. Not one of their number considered the radio pronouncement of the supposed Rex as anything but a hoax. There could be no scientific explanation for a robot with a thinking mind; therefore the thing was an impossibility.

The men of science were not long in reversing their opinions, for Rex staged a demonstration which confounded them. Taking his stand at the visualizing screen of a micro-x ray, he addressed them in a manner that left no doubt as to his ability to reason and to perform feats of such scientific importance as to excel those of any human scholar.

When he had properly impressed them, he came to the point.

"You are here, gentlemen," he told them, "to assist me in the performance of a great and necessary work. The human population of United North America is to be remade along lines which I shall lay down. The old social order is to pass out of existence; the government is to change hands and to be completely reformed. Science is to rule."

Ross Fielding, chief physicist of the Academy of Chicago, blurted out: "Preposterous!"

It was as if Rex had not heard. He continued: "You men of the scientific world have long wanted to obtain control over mankind and its affairs. You medical men, through the so-called health boards and departments of hygiene and eugenics, have already gone a long way toward this end. I now offer you the opportunity of exercising the power that you must admit you desire."

A buzz of excited comment swept the group.

"Proceed," grunted Fielding, and others echoed his sentiment eagerly.

"Then hear my plan," said Rex. "Under my direction, this group will immediately begin the work of reconstruction, by which I mean the actual remaking of men and women. The functioning of people's minds and bodies will be altered to fit them for the spheres of action which are to be assigned. All persons will have definite niches to fill in the new order of things, and each one will be made over to fit his or her own particular niche both physically and mentally. Many will be provided with robot bodies."

"What!" shouted the noted Dr. Innes of Quebec.

For answer, Rex depressed a button which lighted the visualizing screen at his side. On it flashed a greatly enlarged image of a mass of living cells.

"These," he explained, "are cells from the brain of a living man; they comprise that portion of the brain which controls human feelings and emotions. I have removed them from one Alexander Shelby, whom many of you know personally. Naturally, he is greatly altered."

There were horrified gasps; one of the surgeons started to argue against the possibility of what had been told them. Rex silenced them with a wave of his hand.

A robot wheeled Shelby from the adjoining room and placed his head in the reflector focus of the micro-x ray. The image on the visualizer changed.

There were the familiar skull outlines and the configurations of cerebrum and cerebellum. The focus altered and came sharply to a point where some of the cells had been removed and where an opaque spheroid was encountered.

"What foreign object is that?" asked Innes.

"It is one of my discoveries," Rex answered. "An important one. It replaces the center of emotion and human feelings in Shelby's brain, making him a slave to my every spoken and radioed command. Otherwise the power of his mind is unimpaired. His faculties are as keen as ever they were, perhaps keener; only now his brain is that of a robot. Shelby is the first of the human robots and the most valuable. He is to be my lieutenant in the work that is to come and has been fully instructed by me. I leave you with Shelby now, gentlemen, knowing that you will proceed as he directs."

Taking up the test tube containing the brain cells he had removed from Shelby, Rex stalked from the laboratory. His distinguished audience stared aghast at the man in the wheel chair.

Fielding, who was a big man with whiskered jowls, exploded in his usual manner: "Of all the high-handed proceedings! How about this, Shelby?"

"It is precisely as Rex has told you." Shelby's voice was flat and toneless, without inflection—the voice of a robot. "Our first step is to take the executive heads of the government in hand; they are to be operated upon at once and made as I am—subject to all orders of Rex. Sufficient of the platinum-cased mechanisms have already been fabricated."

"Sup-suppose," chattered Lonergan, the Los Angeles scientist, "we refuse? Suppose we band together and overcome this mad robot?"

"Rex is far from being mad," intoned Shelby. "Besides, there are these."

He indicated with extended forefinger the score of motionless robot figures ranged along the wall. At his gesture the robots came to life; one and all stepped forward ponderously, ready to take such action as might become necessary.

Innes laughed mirthlessly. "It looks as if we are fairly caught. After all—" He hesitated. "After all, in the interest of science, you know— We—"

"Yes." "Why not?" "It's the opportunity of a lifetime." A chorus of eager voices bespoke the interest of the men of science.

One of the physicists drawled sardonically: "You vivisectionists should be happy under the new regime. You'll have human beings to experiment with instead of dogs and guinea pigs."

A surgeon parried: "Not so good for you students of pure science, I'll admit. You'll be working with robots that'll have human brains. They'll outthink you, outcalculate you. There'll be no errors in *their* computations."

"Enough," said Shelby flatly. "We are wasting time. As I said, we will go ahead with the official dignitaries first; that is the work of the surgeons. Meanwhile the scientists will take up the study of the alterations which are to be made in the mass of the people. All are to be remade."

Innes asked, "How about reproduction—the perpetuation of the race? I take it these reconstructions of Rex's will eliminate the sex factor in human life."

"Hm! Hadn't thought of that," grunted Fielding.

"Sex is not necessary," Shelby said. "In fact it is troublesome. However, arrangements will be made to segregate a few thousand females and a number of eugenically acceptable males in order that a supply of new research material will be available for the future."

"If the women object?" put in one of the younger surgeons.

"You forget that portion of the brain which is the seat of human emotion," Shelby reminded him. "Certain cells will be removed, and only those cells left which provide for these favored women no more than one desire—that of motherhood."

"The males needn't be changed at all," grunted Fielding. Then he was struck with a sudden thought. "Say, how did this Rex come by his power of thinking in the first place?"

Shelby explained as best he could: "We made some tests. There seems to have been an unprecedented natural transformation; a source of some unknown atomic energy sprang up somewhere in the intricate mechanisms of his brain. Probably the generation of what scientists have long searched for in vain, what some of them have called the 'mind electron.' At any rate, he thinks, and with marvelous celerity and accuracy."

Fielding contented himself with whistling through his teeth.

"Now," announced Shelby, "we will go ahead with the great work."

And they did; the twenty-two foremost scientists of the nation submitted to the dictates of a robot.

Meanwhile, order was coming out of chaos in the eleven cities. Men and women, unaware of the fate which had been planned for them, were driven to unaccustomed and uncongenial tasks by unfeeling robots. Soft, uncallused human hands were at the levers of machines instead of the flexible metallic fingers of the robots. Human minds which had known nothing more fatiguing than the stereotyped lessons of schooldays and the pursuit of pleasure in later years were now set to work at vexing problems of engineering. Human beings were engaged once more in useful work.

Of course it was impossible that all of the labor be performed by humans; the mechanics of existence had become too complicated for that. The operations that were needful merely to keep the great beehives of cities functioning were entirely too numerous. Besides, many necessary tasks were beyond the strength of men whose muscles had softened from disuse and from dissolute living. But the new masters of men, the robots, got all the work out of their unwilling charges that could be obtained in the ten-hour day Rex had decreed. The rest was done by the robots while their human protégés slept the sleep of sheer exhaustion.

Temporarily, the inconsequential amount of governmental activity which was actually required was made purely local in scope. In each city the municipal affairs were taken over by the super-robot who was in charge. After dispensing with the great majority of officeholders and assigning them to really productive tasks in the lower levels, the super-robots relayed to the mayors and their councils minute instructions from Rex as to their future deportment in office. It was a sorry time for those who had long held unmerited and quite superfluous positions of power.

The wailing and complaining of weary human laborers went unheeded by their robot overseers. Whenever men and women dragged their tired bodies to places of meeting and endeavored to voice protest, they were swiftly and roughly dispersed by the vigilant robot police. After three long days they learned to submit in silence to whatever might be demanded of them. Some humans even found a new interest in their tasks, others new bodily vigor as their muscles lost their soreness. At least they still had their living quarters during leisure hours, and there was no shortage of heat, food, or water.

They did not know that each individual was being carefully card-indexed and studied by the robot minions of Rex. Nor had they any idea of the fate to which they had been consigned. That all were now being classified according to ability and adaptability never entered their heads. And great would have been the lamentation had they realized that the new robot dictator had meant exactly what he said when he told them over the newscast that he had come to evolve a new race of beings.

Most of them would have scoffed had they been told the truth. It was incomprehensible that a man with the special aptitude for piloting a stratosphere plane might be operated upon and deprived of all human desire and emotion, leaving only those sensibilities which would make of him an exceptionally adept navigator of the air lanes. That one who might be of little value excepting as a common laborer should be deprived of his own body and provided with a mechanical one instead, as well as being robbed of all human sentiment and instinct, was still less comprehensible. Yet these very things were being planned.

Human brains, minus the elements that made them human, transplanted into the duralumin headpieces of robots. Human beings, permitted to retain the outward semblance of man but left with only one or two of the human impulses. Minds that were capable of thinking nothing but mathematics, riveting, welding, food synthesis, or childbearing, as the case might be. These were but a few of the characteristics which were to make up the new race of robot men, or human robots. And the intended victims did not know.

Only the men of science laboring in Rex's hospital and laboratory could have told them, and they kept silent.

By this time, President Tucker and the members of his cabinet were recovering from the effects of the brain surgery to which they had been subjected. In another twenty-four hours they would be returned to their posts. Gone was their pomposity, their grandiose verbiage, and the vacillation which always had marked their decisions. Their thoughts now were only those which Rex wished them to have. Hereafter they would be quick to make decisions and firm in enforcing their mandates—the decisions and mandates of Rex, the dictator. Now the organization of all public agencies would quickly bring to fruition the full operation of the master robot's plan. The new race of hybrid beings would blossom forth.

Immersed in their work and oblivious to all else, the twenty-two men of science gave little thought to the plight of their fellow men. They knew only that they had learned many new and marvelous things from this robot who seemed to be a man. They had plumbed depths of the human intellect of which they had never dreamed; they discovered many secrets of electronic science which were almost incredible; they saw results to be accomplished that were nothing short of miraculous. They were about to give birth to a new race of super-creations; that these were to be part human and part machine disturbed them not at all. Only the accomplishment was of importance.

Shelby, pale and drawn of face, with expressionless fish eyes gazing out through his thick glasses, had worked with them in the hospital and laboratory until it seemed that he would drop. Between times he was collaborating with Rex himself on some secret experiment that was carried on behind closed doors. Shelby looked and talked like a robot, but his body was a human one and had been greatly overstrained. He could not long stand this pace.

Fielding was stirred to pity when he saw him emerge from Rex's secret laboratory this last time. "What's going on in there?" he asked with gruff kindliness. "And why in the devil doesn't he let you get a little rest?"

Shelby's eyes were like polished bits of black glass, and his voice was devoid of feeling as he replied: "Rex is experimenting on himself. He is using the center of emotion which he removed from my brain, using the cells in an effort to provide himself with certain of the human sensibilities. You may as well know it now."

"Good heavens!" Fielding roared like a bull. "He's taking human feelings *away* from millions of men and women, or planning to, and yet he wants those feelings himself. He's a mechanical devil!"

"It is not a question of desire," Shelby corrected him. "Rex is incapable of desire or envy—as yet. He has merely reasoned that he will become the most perfect of moving and thinking creatures if only he can provide himself with such of the human feelings as may be essential in bringing the greatest good to the greatest number of the new beings we are to create."

Fielding repeated, softly this time: "Good heavens!" He stared at the little man with the white face and vacant gaze.

At this point the door to the private laboratory opened and Rex strode forth with a test tube in his hand. He passed the tube to Shelby and burst out in swift speech.

"I have failed," he said. "I have analyzed every living cell in the tube and have isolated the activating force of every human emotion. I have reproduced these forces to perfection with arrangements of special electronic tubes which have been incorporated into my own mechanical brain. Yet have I failed to produce so much as a semblance of human feeling in my makeup. It is the first failure of Rex—and the last!"

So saying, he stamped back into his own room and slammed the door. An instant later there was a violent explosion within, and the door by which he had entered was blown from its hinges.

Fielding, Shelby, and a few others rushed in when the smoke had somewhat cleared away. They found Rex a twisted and broken mass of metal and rubber and glass. The headpiece which had contained the marvelous thinking robot brain was completely demolished.

"He's committed suicide!" gasped Lonergan.

"Because he was a failure," Fielding added.

Shelby corrected him.

"He *thought* he had failed, whereas really he succeeded. At least two emotions stirred him before he did this, and he did not recognize them. Rage, when he dashed from his room and gave me the test tube. Despair, when he committed his last act. No, gentlemen, Rex did not fail—and now he is gone. . . ."

The little man pitched forward into Fielding's arms, unconscious.

With the passing of Rex, his fantastic plan collapsed. Hard work by the scientists returned the country to normal.

But a thought that lingered faintly in the minds of several of them was voiced by Innes, when he said:

"I—I'm almost sorry. In one way, it was a great opportunity. . . ."

ROBBIE

ISAAC ASIMOV

(1 9 4 0)

"Robbie" was Isaac Asimov's first robot story, written when he was only nineteen and just beginning his writing career. He has since published three dozen stories and novels about robots, and, more consistently and comprehensively than any other science fiction writer, he has explored the significance for mankind of developing high-level intelligence in machines. He well deserves the recognition he has been given as the father of robots in science fiction.

For me, two men tower as giants of insight and creativity in exploring both the potential and the social impact of computers—Asimov in fiction and Norbert Wiener in nonfiction. Wiener (1894–1964), a mathematician at MIT, is recognized as the father of cybernetics, which he defined as the science of attempting "to find the common elements in the functioning of automatic machines and of the human nervous system, and to develop a theory that will cover the entire field of control and communication in machines and in living organisms." Wiener recognized very early the radical social changes that the computer would cause, and he published two outstanding books on the subject, *Cybernetics* in 1948 and *The Human Use of Human Beings: Cybernetics and Society* in 1950.

Asimov's fiction displays the same concern for the wise and humane use of machine intelligence that runs through all Wiener's writings about computers. The two never knew each other, but Asimov is a close friend of Marvin Minsky, also of MIT, one of today's leading figures in artificial-intelligence research. In his later fiction, Asimov named his roboticist Mervan Mansky.

The Barnhard Dictionary of New English Since 1963 credits Asimov with coining the word *robotics*. Asimov says that when he first used it in his Three Laws, he was not aware that the word did not appear in a dictionary. He needed a name for this new field, and robotics seemed the logical one.

Asimov wrote "Robbie" in 1939, using the title "Strange Playfellow," and sent it to John W. Campbell, the editor of *Astounding*. Campbell rejected the story because he felt it did not meet his standards. Frederik Pohl, who was then editor of *Super Science*, accepted it, changed the title to "Robbie," and published it in his magazine the next year.

Asimov, looking at the story today, says that clearly he was already thinking about the Three Laws of Robotics since the story makes a rambling reference to the First Law. He admits to being inspired by Lester del Rey's "Helen O'Loy" and Eando Binder's "I, Robot" (although the use of *I, Robot* as the title of his first robot story collection was the publisher's choice, not his). Both stories influenced his decision to write about a sympathetic robot, but one that was clearly a machine and not a surrogate human being. Asimov says another probable influence was the robot he saw on display at the New York World's Fair in 1939. Here is an interesting example of the continual cross-fertilization between the literary and the engineering imaginations. In turn, Joseph Engelberger, who built the first industrial robot, called Unimate, in 1958, attributes his long-standing fascination with robots to his reading of *I, Robot* when he was a teenager.

"**N**INETY-EIGHT—NINETY-NINE—ONE HUNDRED." Gloria withdrew her chubby little forearm from before her eyes and stood for a moment, wrinkling her nose and blinking in the sunlight. Then, trying to watch in all directions at once, she withdrew a few cautious steps from the tree against which she had been leaning.

She craned her neck to investigate the possibilities of a clump of bushes to the right and then withdrew farther to obtain a better angle for viewing its dark recesses. The quiet was profound except for the incessant buzzing of insects and the occasional chirrup of some hardy bird, braving the midday sun.

Gloria pouted, "I bet he went inside the house, and I've told him a million times that that's not fair."

With tiny lips pressed together tightly and a severe frown crinkling her forehead, she moved determinedly toward the two-story building up past the driveway.

Too late she heard the rustling sound behind her, followed by the distinctive and rhythmic clump-clump of Robbie's metal feet. She whirled about to see her triumphing companion emerge from hiding and make for the home-tree at full speed.

Gloria shrieked in dismay. "Wait, Robbie! That wasn't fair, Robbie! You promised you wouldn't run until I found you." Her little feet could make no headway at all against Robbie's giant strides. Then, within ten feet of the goal, Robbie's pace slowed suddenly to the merest of crawls, and Gloria, with one final burst of wild speed, dashed pantingly past him to touch the welcome bark of home-tree first.

Gleefully, she turned on the faithful Robbie, and with the basest of ingratitude, rewarded him for his sacrifice by taunting him cruelly for a lack of running ability.

"Robbie can't run," she shouted at the top of her eight-year-old voice. "I can beat him any day. I can beat him any day." She chanted the words in a shrill rhythm.

Robbie didn't answer, of course—not in words. He pantomimed running instead, inching away until Gloria found herself running after him as he dodged her narrowly, forcing her to veer in helpless circles, little arms outstretched and fanning at the air.

"Robbie," she squealed, "stand still!" And the laughter was forced out of her in breathless jerks.

—Until he turned suddenly and caught her up, whirling her round, so that for her the world fell away for a moment with a blue emptiness beneath, and green trees stretching hungrily downward toward the void. Then she was down in the grass again, leaning against Robbie's leg and still holding a hard, metal finger.

After a while, her breath returned. She pushed uselessly at her disheveled hair in vague imitation of one of her mother's gestures and twisted to see if her dress was torn.

She slapped her hand against Robbie's torso. "Bad boy! I'll spank you!"

And Robbie cowered, holding his hands over his face so that she had to add, "No, I won't, Robbie. I won't spank you. But anyway, it's my turn to hide now because you've got longer legs and you promised not to run till I found you."

Robbie nodded his head—a small parallelepiped with rounded edges and corners attached to a similar but much larger parallelepiped that served as torso by means of a short, flexible stalk—and obediently faced the tree. A thin, metal film descended over his glowing eyes and from within his body came a steady, resonant ticking.

"Don't peek now—and don't skip any numbers," warned Gloria, and scurried for cover.

With unvarying regularity, seconds were ticked off, and at

the hundredth, up went the eyelids, and the glowing red of Robbie's eyes swept the prospect. They rested for a moment on a bit of colorful gingham that protruded from behind a boulder. He advanced a few steps and convinced himself that it was Gloria who squatted behind it.

Slowly, remaining always between Gloria and home-tree, he advanced on the hiding place, and when Gloria was plainly in sight and could no longer even theorize to herself that she was not seen, he extended one arm toward her, slapping the other against his leg so that it rang again. Gloria emerged sulkily.

"You peeked!" she exclaimed, with gross unfairness. "Besides, I'm tired of playing hide-and-seek. I want a ride."

But Robbie was hurt at the unjust accusation, so he seated himself carefully and shook his head ponderously from side to side.

Gloria changed her tone to one of gentle coaxing immediately. "Come on, Robbie. I didn't mean it about the peeking. Give me a ride."

Robbie was not to be won over so easily, though. He gazed stubbornly at the sky, and shook his head even more emphatically.

"Please, Robbie, please give me a ride." She encircled his neck with rosy arms and hugged tightly. Then, changing moods in a moment, she moved away. "If you don't, I'm going to cry," and her face twisted appallingly in preparation.

Hard-hearted Robbie paid scant attention to this dreadful possibility, and shook his head a third time. Gloria found it necessary to play her trump card.

"If you don't," she exclaimed warmly, "I won't tell you any more stories, that's all. Not one—"

Robbie gave in immediately and unconditionally before this ultimatum, nodding his head vigorously until the metal of his neck hummed. Carefully, he raised the little girl and placed her on his broad, flat shoulders.

Gloria's threatened tears vanished immediately and she crowed with delight. Robbie's metal skin, kept at a constant temperature of seventy by the high-resistance coils within, felt nice and comfortable, while the beautifully loud sound her heels made as they bumped rhythmically against his chest was enchanting.

"You're an air-coaster, Robbie, you're a big, silver air-coaster. Hold out your arms straight. You *got* to, Robbie, if you're going to be an air-coaster."

The logic was irrefutable. Robbie's arms were wings catching the air currents and he was a silver 'coaster.

Gloria twisted the robot's head and leaned to the right. He banked sharply. Gloria equipped the 'coaster with a motor that went "Br-r-r" and then with weapons that went "Powie" and "Sh-sh-shshsh." Pirates were giving chase and the ship's blasters were coming into play. The pirates dropped in a steady rain.

"Got another one. Two more," she cried.

Then, "Faster, men," Gloria said pompously, "we're running out of ammunition." She aimed over her shoulder with undaunted courage and Robbie was a blunt-nosed spaceship zooming through the void at maximum acceleration.

Clear across the field he sped, to the patch of tall grass on the other side, where he stopped with a suddenness that evoked a shriek from his flushed rider, and then tumbled her onto the soft, green carpet.

Gloria gasped and panted, and gave voice to intermittent whispered exclamations of "That was *nice!*"

Robbie waited until she had caught her breath and then pulled gently at a lock of hair.

"You want something?" said Gloria, eyes wide in an apparently artless complexity that fooled her huge "nursemaid" not at all. He pulled the curl harder.

"Oh, I know. You want a story."

Robbie nodded rapidly.

"Which one?"

Robbie made a semicircle in the air with one finger.

The little girl protested, "*Again?* I've told you Cinderella a million times. Aren't you tired of it? It's for babies."

Another semicircle.

"Oh, well," Gloria composed herself, ran over the details of the tale in her mind (together with her own elaborations, of which she had several) and began:

"Are you ready? Well—once upon a time there was a beautiful little girl whose name was Ella. And she had a terribly cruel stepmother and two very ugly and *very* cruel stepsisters and—"

Gloria was reaching the very climax of the tale—midnight was striking and everything was changing back to the shabby originals lickety-split, while Robbie listened tensely with burning eyes—when the interruption came.

"Gloria!"

It was the high-pitched sound of a woman who has been calling not once, but several times, and had the nervous tone of one in whom anxiety was beginning to overcome impatience.

"Mamma's calling me," said Gloria, not quite happily. "You'd better carry me back to the house, Robbie."

Robbie obeyed with alacrity, for somehow there was that in him which judged it best to obey Mrs. Weston, without as much as a scrap of hesitation. Gloria's father was rarely home in the daytime except on Sunday—today, for instance—and when he was, he proved a genial and understanding person. Gloria's mother, however, was a source of uneasiness to Robbie and there was always the impulse to sneak away from her sight.

Mrs. Weston caught sight of them the minute they rose above the masking tufts of long grass, and retired inside the house to wait.

"I've shouted myself hoarse, Gloria," she said severely. "Where were you?"

"I was with Robbie," quavered Gloria. "I was telling him Cinderella, and I forgot it was dinnertime."

"Well, it's a pity Robbie forgot, too." Then, as if that reminded her of the robot's presence, she whirled upon him. "You may go, Robbie. She doesn't need you now." Then, brutally, "And don't come back till I call you."

Robbie turned to go, but hesitated as Gloria cried out in his

73

defense, "Wait, Mamma, you got to let him stay. I didn't finish Cinderella for him. I said I would tell him Cinderella and I'm not finished."

"Gloria!"

"Honest and truly, Mamma, he'll stay so quiet, you won't even know he's here. He can sit on the chair in the corner, and he won't say a word—I mean he won't *do* anything. Will you, Robbie?"

Robbie, appealed to, nodded his massive head up and down once.

"Gloria, if you don't stop this at once, you shan't see Robbie for a whole week."

The girl's eyes fell. "All right! But Cinderella is his favorite story and I didn't finish it. And he likes it so much."

The robot left with a disconsolate step and Gloria choked back a sob.

George Weston was comfortable. It was a habit of his to be comfortable on Sunday afternoons. A good, hearty dinner below the hatches; a nice, soft, dilapidated couch on which to sprawl; a copy of the *Times*; slippered feet and shirtless chest—how could anyone *help* but be comfortable?

He wasn't pleased, therefore, when his wife walked in. After ten years of married life, he still was so unutterably foolish as to love her, and there was no question that he was always glad to see her—still, Sunday afternoons just after dinner were sacred to him and his idea of solid comfort was to be left in utter solitude for two or three hours. Consequently, he fixed his eye firmly upon the latest reports of the Lefebre-Yoshida expedition to Mars (this one was to take off from Lunar Base and might actually succeed) and pretended she wasn't there.

Mrs. Weston waited patiently for two minutes, then impatiently for two more, and finally broke the silence.

"George!"

"Hmpph?"

"George, I say! *Will* you put down that paper and look at me?"

The paper rustled to the floor and Weston turned a weary face toward his wife. "What is it, dear?"

"You know what it is, George. It's Gloria and that terrible machine."

"What terrible machine?"

"Now don't pretend you don't know what I'm talking about. It's that robot Gloria calls Robbie. He doesn't leave her for a moment."

"Well, why should he? He's not supposed to. And he certainly isn't a terrible machine. He's the best darn robot money can buy and I'm damned sure he set me back half a year's income. He's worth it, though—darn sight cleverer than half my office staff."

He made a move to pick up the paper again, but his wife was quicker and snatched it away.

"You listen to *me*, George. I won't have my daughter entrusted to a machine—and I don't care how clever it is. It has no soul, and no one knows what it may be thinking. A child just isn't *made* to be guarded by a thing of metal."

Weston frowned. "When did you decide this? He's been with Gloria two years now and I haven't seen you worry till now."

"It was different at first. It was a novelty; it took a load off me, and—and it was a fashionable thing to do. But now I don't know. The neighbors—"

"Well, what have the neighbors to do with it? Now look. A robot is infinitely more to be trusted than a human nursemaid. Robbie was constructed for only one purpose really—to be the companion of a little child. His entire 'mentality' has been created for the purpose. He just can't help being faithful and loving and kind. He's a machine—*made so*. That's more than you can say for humans."

"But something might go wrong. Some—some—" Mrs. Weston was a bit hazy about the insides of a robot. "Some little jigger will come loose and the awful thing will go berserk and—and—" She couldn't bring herself to complete the quite obvious thought.

"Nonsense," Weston denied, with an involuntary nervous shiver. "That's completely ridiculous. We had a long discussion at the time we bought Robbie about the First Law of Robotics.

75

You *know* that it is impossible for a robot to harm a human being; that long before enough can go wrong to alter that First Law, a robot would be completely inoperable. It's a mathematical impossibility. Besides, I have an engineer from U.S. Robots here twice a year to give the poor gadget a complete overhaul. Why, there's no more chance of anything at all going wrong with Robbie than there is of you or me suddenly going looney—considerably less, in fact. Besides, how are you going to take him away from Gloria?"

He made another futile stab at the paper and his wife tossed it angrily into the next room.

"That's just it, George! She won't play with anyone else. There are dozens of little boys and girls that she should make friends with, but she won't. She won't go *near* them unless I make her. That's no way for a little girl to grow up. You want her to be normal, don't you? You want her to be able to take her part in society."

"You're jumping at shadows, Grace. Pretend Robbie's a dog. I've seen hundreds of children who would rather have their dogs than their fathers."

"A dog is different, George. We *must* get rid of that horrible thing. You can sell it back to the company. I've asked, and you can."

"You've *asked?* Now look here, Grace, let's not go off the deep end. We're keeping the robot until Gloria is older and I don't want the subject brought up again." And with that he walked out of the room in a huff.

Mrs. Weston met her husband at the door two evenings later. "You'll have to listen to this, George. There's bad feeling in the village."

"About what?" asked Weston. He stepped into the washroom and drowned out any possible answer by the splash of water.

Mrs. Weston waited. She said, "About Robbie."

Weston stepped out, towel in hand, face red and angry. "What are you talking about?"

"Oh, it's been building up and building up. I've tried to close my eyes to it, but I'm not going to anymore. Most of the villagers consider Robbie dangerous. Children aren't allowed to go near our place in the evenings."

"We trust *our* child with the thing."

"Well, people aren't reasonable about these things."

"Then to hell with them."

"Saying that doesn't solve the problem. I've got to do my shopping down there. I've got to meet them every day. And it's even worse in the city these days when it comes to robots. New York has just passed an ordinance keeping all robots off the streets between sunset and sunrise."

"All right, but they can't stop us from keeping a robot in our home. Grace, this is one of your campaigns. I recognize it. But it's no use. The answer is still no! We're keeping Robbie!"

And yet he loved his wife—and what was worse, his wife knew it. George Weston, after all, was only a man—poor thing—and his wife made full use of every device which a clumsier and more scrupulous sex has learned, with reason and futility, to fear.

Ten times in the ensuing week, he cried, "Robbie stays—and that's *final!*" and each time it was weaker and accompanied by a louder and more agonized groan.

Came the day at last when Weston approached his daughter guiltily and suggested a "beautiful" visivox show in the village.

Gloria clapped her hands happily. "Can Robbie go?"

"No, dear," he said, and winced at the sound of his voice, "they won't allow robots at the visivox—but you can tell him all about it when you get home." He stumbled all over the last few words and looked away.

Gloria came back from town bubbling over with enthusiasm, for the visivox had been a gorgeous spectacle indeed.

She waited for her father to maneuver the jet-car into the sunken garage. "Wait till I tell Robbie, Daddy. He would have liked it like anything. Especially when Francis Fran was backing away so-o-o quietly, and backed right into one of the Leopard-Men and had to run." She laughed again, "Daddy, are there really Leopard-Men on the Moon?"

"Probably not," said Weston absently. "It's just funny make-believe." He couldn't take much longer with the car. He'd have to face it.

Gloria ran across the lawn. "Robbie. Robbie!"

Then she stopped suddenly at the sight of a beautiful collie which regarded her out of serious brown eyes as it wagged its tail on the porch.

"Oh, what a nice dog!" Gloria climbed the steps, approached cautiously, and patted it. "Is it for me, Daddy?"

Her mother had joined them. "Yes, it is, Gloria. Isn't it nice—soft and furry. It's very gentle. It *likes* little girls."

"Can he play games?"

"Surely. He can do any number of tricks. Would you like to see some?"

"Right away. I want Robbie to see him, too. *Robbie!*" She stopped, uncertainly, and frowned. "I'll bet he's just staying in his room because he's mad at me for not taking him to the visivox. You'll have to explain to him, Daddy. He might not believe me, but he knows if you say it, it's so."

Weston's lip grew tighter. He looked toward his wife but could not catch her eye.

Gloria turned precipitously and ran down the basement steps, shouting as she went, "Robbie—come and see what Daddy and Mamma brought me. They brought me a dog, Robbie."

In a minute she had returned, a frightened little girl. "Mamma, Robbie isn't in his room. Where is he?" There was no answer and George Weston coughed and was suddenly extremely interested in an aimlessly drifting cloud. Gloria's voice quavered on the verge of tears. "Where's Robbie, Mamma?"

Mrs. Weston sat down and drew her daughter gently to her, "Don't feel bad, Gloria. Robbie has gone away, I think."

"Gone *away?* Where? Where's he gone away, Mamma?"

"No one knows, darling. He just walked away. We've looked and we've looked and we've looked for him, but we can't find him."

"You mean he'll never come back again?" Her eyes were round with horror.

"We may find him soon. We'll keep looking for him. And meanwhile you can play with your nice new doggie. Look at him! His name is Lightning and he can—"

But Gloria's eyelids had overflowed. "I don't want the nasty dog—I want Robbie. I want you to find me Robbie." Her feelings became too deep for words, and she spluttered into a shrill wail.

Mrs. Weston glanced at her husband for help, but he merely shuffled his feet morosely and did not withdraw his ardent stare from the heavens, so she bent to the task of consolation. "Why do you cry, Gloria? Robbie was only a machine, just a nasty old machine. He wasn't alive at all."

"He was *not* no machine!" screamed Gloria, fiercely and ungrammatically. "He was a *person* just like you and me and he was my *friend*. I want him back. Oh, Mamma, I want him back."

Her mother groaned in defeat and left Gloria to her sorrow.

"Let her have her cry out," she told her husband. "Childish griefs are never lasting. In a few days, she'll forget that awful robot ever existed."

But time proved Mrs. Weston a bit too optimistic. To be sure, Gloria ceased crying, but she ceased smiling, too, and the passing days found her ever more silent and shadowy. Gradually, her attitude of passive unhappiness wore Mrs. Weston down and all that kept her from yielding was the impossibility of admitting defeat to her husband.

Then, one evening, she flounced into the living room, sat down, folded her arms, and looked boiling mad.

Her husband stretched his neck in order to see her over his newspaper. "What now, Grace?"

"It's that child, George. I've had to send back the dog today. Gloria positively couldn't stand the sight of him, she said. She's driving me into a nervous breakdown."

Weston laid down the paper and a hopeful gleam entered his eye. "Maybe—maybe we ought to get Robbie back. It might be done, you know. I can get in touch with—"

"No!" she replied grimly. "I won't hear of it. We're not giving up that easily. My child shall *not* be brought up by a robot if it takes years to break her of it."

Weston picked up his paper again with a disappointed air. "A year of this will have me prematurely gray."

"You're a big help, George," was the frigid answer. "What Gloria needs is a change of environment. Of course she can't forget Robbie here. How can she when every tree and rock reminds her of him. It is really the *silliest* situation I have ever heard of. Imagine a child pining away for the loss of a robot."

"Well, stick to the point. What's the change in environment you're planning?"

"We're going to take her to New York."

"The city! In August! Say, do you know what New York is like in August? It's unbearable."

"Millions do bear it."

"They don't have a place like this to go to. If they didn't have to stay in New York, they wouldn't."

"Well, *we* have to. I say we're leaving now—or as soon as we can make the arrangements. In the city, Gloria will find sufficient interests and sufficient friends to perk her up and make her forget that machine."

"Oh, Lord," groaned the lesser half, "those frying pavements!"

"We have to," was the unshaken response. "Gloria has lost five pounds in the last month and my little girl's health is more important to me than your comfort."

"It's a pity you didn't think of your little girl's health before you deprived her of her pet robot," he muttered—but to himself.

Gloria displayed immediate signs of improvement when told of the impending trip to the city. She spoke little of it, but when she did, it was always with lively anticipation. Again, she began to smile and to eat with something of her former appetite.

Mrs. Weston hugged herself for joy and lost no opportunity to triumph over her still skeptical husband.

"You see, George, she helps with the packing like a little angel, and chatters away as if she hadn't a care in the world.

80

It's just as I told you—all we need do is substitute other interests."

"Hmpph," was the skeptical response. "I hope so."

Preliminaries were gone through quickly. Arrangements were made for the preparation of their city home and a couple were engaged as housekeepers for the country home. When the day of the trip finally did come, Gloria was all but her old self again, and no mention of Robbie passed her lips at all.

In high good humor the family took a taxi-gyro to the airport (Weston would have preferred using his own private 'gyro, but it was only a two-seater with no room for baggage) and entered the waiting liner.

"Come, Gloria," called Mrs. Weston. "I've saved you a seat near the window so you can watch the scenery."

Gloria trotted down the aisle cheerily, flattened her nose into a white oval against the thick clear glass, and watched with an intentness that increased as the sudden coughing of the motor drifted backward into the interior. She was too young to be frightened when the ground dropped away as if let through a trapdoor and she herself suddenly became twice her usual weight, but not too young to be mightily interested. It wasn't until the ground had changed into a tiny patchwork quilt that she withdrew her nose and faced her mother again.

"Will we soon be in the city, Mamma?" she asked, rubbing her chilled nose, and watching with interest as the patch of moisture which her breath had formed on the pane shrank slowly and vanished.

"In about half an hour, dear." Then, with just the faintest trace of anxiety, "Aren't you glad we're going? Don't you think you'll be very happy in the city with all the buildings and people and things to see? We'll go to the visivox every day and see shows and go to the circus and the beach and—"

"Yes, Mamma," was Gloria's unenthusiastic rejoinder. The liner passed over a bank of clouds at that moment, and Gloria was instantly absorbed in the usual spectacle of clouds underneath one. Then they were over clear sky again, and she turned to her mother with a sudden mysterious air of secret knowledge.

"*I* know why we're going to the city, Mamma."

81

"Do you?" Mrs. Weston was puzzled. "Why, dear?"

"You didn't tell me because you wanted it to be a surprise, but *I* know." For a moment, she was lost in admiration at her own acute penetration, and then she laughed gaily. "We're going to New York so we can find Robbie, aren't we? With detectives."

The statement caught George Weston in the middle of a drink of water, with disastrous results. There was a sort of strangled gasp, a geyser of water, and then a bout of choking coughs. When all was over, he stood there, a red-faced, water-drenched, and very, very annoyed person.

Mrs. Weston maintained her composure, but when Gloria repeated her question in a more anxious tone of voice, she found her temper rather bent.

"Maybe," she retorted tartly. "Now sit and be still, for heaven's sake."

New York City, 1998 A.D., was a paradise for the sightseer more than ever in its history. Gloria's parents realized this and made the most of it.

On direct orders from his wife, George Weston arranged to have his business take care of itself for a month or so, in order to be free to spend the time in what he termed "dissipating Gloria to the verge of ruin." Like everything else Weston did, this was gone about in an efficient, thorough, and businesslike way. Before the month had passed, nothing that could be done had not been done.

She was taken to the top of the half-mile-tall Roosevelt Building, to gaze down in awe upon the jagged panorama of rooftops that blended far off in the fields of Long Island and the flatlands of New Jersey. They visited the zoos where Gloria stared in delicious fright at the "real live lion" (rather disappointed that the keepers fed him raw steaks instead of human beings, as she had expected), and asked insistently and peremptorily to see "the whale."

The various museums came in for their share of attention, together with the parks and the beaches and the aquarium.

She was taken halfway up the Hudson in an excursion steamer fitted out in the archaism of the mad twenties. She traveled into the stratosphere on an exhibition trip, where the sky turned deep purple and the stars came out and the misty earth below looked like a huge concave bowl. Down under the waters of Long Island Sound she was taken in a glass-walled subsea vessel, where in a green and wavering world, quaint and curious sea-things ogled her and wiggled suddenly away.

On a more prosaic level, Mrs. Weston took her to the department stores where she could revel in another type of fairyland.

In fact, when the month had nearly sped, the Westons were convinced that everything conceivable had been done to take Gloria's mind once and for all off the departed Robbie—but they were not quite sure they had succeeded.

The fact remained that wherever Gloria went, she displayed the most absorbed and concentrated interest in such robots as happened to be present. No matter how exciting the spectacle before her, or how novel to her girlish eyes, she turned away instantly if the corner of her eye caught a glimpse of metallic movement.

Mrs. Weston went out of her way to keep Gloria away from all robots.

And the matter was finally climaxed in the episode at the Museum of Science and Industry. The museum had announced a special "children's program" in which exhibits of scientific witchery scaled down to the child mind were to be shown. The Westons, of course, placed it upon their list of "absolutely."

It was while the Westons were standing totally absorbed in the exploits of a powerful electromagnet that Mrs. Weston suddenly became aware of the fact that Gloria was no longer with her. Initial panic gave way to calm decision and, enlisting the aid of three attendants, she began a careful search.

Gloria, of course, was not one to wander aimlessly, however. For her age, she was an unusually determined and purposeful girl, quite full of the maternal genes in that respect. She had seen a huge sign on the third floor, which had said, "This Way to the Talking Robot." Having spelled it out to herself and having noticed that her parents did not seem to wish to move in the proper direction, she did the obvious thing. Waiting for an opportune moment of parental distraction, she calmly disengaged herself and followed the sign.

The Talking Robot was a *tour de force*, a thoroughly impractical device, possessing publicity value only. Once an hour, an escorted group stood before it and asked questions of the robot engineer in charge in careful whispers. Those the engineer decided were suitable for the robot's circuits were transmitted to the Talking Robot.

It was rather dull. It may be nice to know that the square of fourteen is one hundred ninety-six, that the temperature at the moment is seventy-two degrees Fahrenheit, and the air pressure 30.02 inches of mercury, that the atomic weight of sodium is twenty-three, but one doesn't really need a robot for that. One especially does not need an unwieldy, totally immobile mass of wires and coils spreading over twenty-five square yards.

Few people bothered to return for a second helping, but one girl in her middle teens sat quietly on a bench waiting for a third. She was the only one in the room when Gloria entered.

Gloria did not look at her. To her at the moment, another human being was but an inconsiderable item. She saved her attention for this large thing with the wheels. For a moment, she hesitated in dismay. It didn't look like any robot she had ever seen.

Cautiously and doubtfully she raised her treble voice. "Please, Mr. Robot, sir, are you the Talking Robot, sir?" She wasn't sure, but it seemed to her that a robot that actually talked was worth a great deal of politeness.

(The girl in her mid-teens allowed a look of intense concentration to cross her thin, plain face. She whipped out a small notebook and began writing in rapid pothooks.)

There was an oily whir of gears and a mechanically timbred voice boomed out in words that lacked accent and intonation, "I—am—the—robot—that—talks."

Gloria stared at it ruefully. It *did* talk, but the sound came from inside somewhere. There was no *face* to talk to. She said, "Can you help me, Mr. Robot, sir?"

The Talking Robot was designed to answer questions, and only such questions as it could answer had ever been put to it. It was quite confident of its ability, therefore. "I—can—help—you."

"Thank you, Mr. Robot, sir. Have you seen Robbie?"

"Who—is Robbie?"

"He's a robot, Mr. Robot, sir." She stretched to tiptoes. "He's about so high, Mr. Robot, sir, only higher, and he's very nice. He's got a head, you know. I mean you haven't, but he has, Mr. Robot, sir."

The Talking Robot had been left behind. "A—robot?"

"Yes, Mr. Robot, sir. A robot just like you, except he can't talk, of course, and—looks like a real person."

"A—robot—like—me?"

"Yes, Mr. Robot, sir."

To which the Talking Robot's only response was an erratic splutter and an occasional incoherent sound. The radical generalization offered it, i.e., its existence, not as a particular object, but as a member of a general group, was too much for it. Loyally, it tried to encompass the concept and half a dozen coils burnt out. Little warning signals were buzzing.

(The girl in her mid-teens left at that point. She had enough for her Physics-1 paper on "Practical Aspects of Robotics." This paper was Susan Calvin's first of many on the subject.)

Gloria stood waiting, with carefully concealed impatience, for the machine's answer, when she heard the cry behind of "There she is," and recognized that cry as her mother's.

"What are you doing here, you bad girl?" cried Mrs. Weston, anxiety dissolving at once into anger. "Do you know you frightened your mamma and daddy almost to death? Why did you run away?"

The robot engineer had also dashed in, tearing his hair and demanding who of the gathering crowd had tampered with the machine. "Can't anybody read signs?" he yelled. "You're not allowed in here without an attendant."

Gloria raised her grieved voice over the din. "I only came to see the Talking Robot, Mamma. I thought he might know where Robbie was because they're both robots." And then, as the thought of Robbie was suddenly brought forcefully home to her, she burst into a sudden storm of tears. "And I *got* to find Robbie, Mamma. I *got* to."

Mrs. Weston strangled a cry and said, "Oh, good heavens. Come home, George. This is more than I can stand."

That evening, George Weston left for several hours, and the next morning he approached his wife with something that looked suspiciously like smug complacence.

"I've got an idea, Grace."

"About what?" was the gloomy, uninterested query.

"About Gloria."

"You're not going to suggest buying back that robot?"

"No, of course not."

"Then go ahead. I might as well listen to you. Nothing *I've* done seems to have done any good."

"All right. Here's what I've been thinking. The whole trouble with Gloria is that she thinks of Robbie as a *person* and not as a *machine*. Naturally, she can't forget him. Now if we managed to convince her that Robbie was nothing more than a mess of steel and copper in the form of sheets and wires with electricity its juice of life, how long would her longings last? It's the psychological attack, if you see my point."

"How do you plan to do it?"

"Simple. Where do you suppose I went last night? I persuaded Robertson of U.S. Robots and Mechanical Men, Inc. to arrange for a complete tour of his premises tomorrow. The three of us will go, and by the time we're through, Gloria will have it drilled into her that a robot is *not* alive."

Mrs. Weston's eyes widened gradually and something glinted in her eyes that was quite like sudden admiration, "Why, George, that's a *good* idea."

And George Weston's vest buttons strained. "Only kind I have," he said.

Mr. Struthers was a conscientious General Manager and naturally inclined to be a bit talkative. The combination, therefore, resulted in a tour that was fully explained, perhaps even overabundantly explained, at every step. However, Mrs. Weston was not bored. Indeed, she stopped him several times and begged him to repeat his statements in simpler language so that Gloria might understand. Under the influence of this appreciation of his narrative powers, Mr. Struthers expanded genially and became even more communicative, if possible.

George Weston, himself, showed a gathering impatience.

"Pardon me, Struthers," he said, breaking into the middle of a lecture on the photo-electric cell, "haven't you a section of the factory where only robot labor is employed?"

"Eh? Oh, yes! Yes, indeed!" He smiled at Mrs. Weston. "A vicious circle in a way, robots creating more robots. Of course, we are not making a general practice out of it. For one thing, the unions would never let us. But we can turn out a very few robots using robot labor exclusively, merely as a sort of scientific experiment. You see," he tapped his pince-nez into one palm argumentatively, "what the labor unions don't realize—and I say this as a man who has always been very sympathetic with the labor movement in general—is that the advent of the robot, while involving some dislocation to begin with, will inevitably—"

"Yes, Struthers," said Weston, "but about that section of the factory you speak of—may we see it? It would be very interesting, I'm sure."

"Yes! Yes, of course!" Mr. Struthers replaced his pince-nez in one convulsive movement and gave vent to a soft cough of discomfiture. "Follow me, please."

He was comparatively quiet while leading the three through a long corridor and down a flight of stairs. Then, when they had entered a large well-lit room that buzzed with metallic activity, the sluices opened and the flood of explanation poured forth again.

"There you are!" he said with pride in his voice. "Robots only! Five men act as overseers and they don't even stay in this room. In five years, that is, since we began this project, not a single accident has occurred. Of course, the robots here assembled are comparatively simple, but . . ."

The General Manager's voice had long died to a rather soothing murmur in Gloria's ears. The whole trip seemed rather dull and pointless to her, though there *were* many robots in sight. None were even remotely like Robbie, though, and she surveyed them with open contempt.

In this room there weren't any people at all, she noticed. Then her eyes fell upon six or seven robots busily engaged at a round table halfway across the room. They widened in incredulous surprise. It was a big room. She couldn't see for sure, but one of the robots looked like—looked like—*it was!*

"Robbie!" Her shriek pierced the air, and one of the robots about the table faltered and dropped the tool he was holding. Gloria went almost mad with joy. Squeezing through the railing before either parent could stop her, she dropped lightly to the floor a few feet below, and ran toward her Robbie, arms waving and hair flying.

And the three horrified adults, as they stood frozen in their tracks, saw what the excited little girl did not see—a huge, lumbering tractor bearing blindly down upon its appointed track.

It took split seconds for Weston to come to his senses, and those split seconds meant everything, for Gloria could not be overtaken. Although Weston vaulted the railing in a wild attempt, it was obviously hopeless. Mr. Struthers signaled wildly to the overseers to stop the tractor, but the overseers were only human and it took time to act.

It was only Robbie that acted immediately and with precision.

With metal legs eating up the space between himself and his little mistress, he charged down from the opposite direction. Everything then happened at once. With one sweep of an arm, Robbie snatched up Gloria, slackening his speed not one iota, and, consequently, knocking every breath of air out of her. Weston, not quite comprehending all that was happening, felt, rather than saw, Robbie brush past him, and come to a sudden bewildered halt. The tractor intersected Gloria's path half a second after Robbie had, rolled on ten feet farther, and came to a grinding, long, drawn-out stop.

Gloria regained her breath, submitted to a series of passionate hugs on the parts of both her parents, and turned eagerly toward Robbie. As far as she was concerned, nothing had happened except that she had found her friend.

But Mrs. Weston's expression had changed from one of relief to one of dark suspicion. She turned to her husband, and, despite her disheveled and undignified appearance, managed to look quite formidable. "*You* engineered this, *didn't* you?"

George Weston swabbed a hot forehead with his handkerchief. His hand was unsteady, and his lips could curve only into a tremulous and exceedingly weak smile.

Mrs. Weston pursued the thought. "Robbie wasn't designed for engineering or construction work. He couldn't be of any use to them. You had him placed there deliberately so that Gloria would find him. You know you did."

"Well, I did," said Weston. "But, Grace, how was I to know the reunion would be so violent? And Robbie has saved her life; you'll have to admit that. You *can't* send him away again."

Grace Weston considered. She turned toward Gloria and Robbie and watched them abstractedly for a moment. Gloria had a grip about the robot's neck that would have asphyxiated any creature but one of metal, and was prattling nonsense in half-hysterical frenzy. Robbie's chrome-steel arms (capable of bending a bar of steel two inches in diameter into a pretzel) wound about the little girl gently and lovingly, and his eyes glowed a deep, deep red.

"Well," said Mrs. Weston, at last, "I guess he can stay with us until he rusts."

MYTHS
OF
CREATION

FAREWELL TO THE MASTER

HARRY BATES

(1 9 4 0)

The late 1930s and the 1940s are known as the Golden Age of science fiction, a time when writers who were eventually to become giants in the field began to produce artistic stories well grounded in accurate scientific facts and engineering details. Many of the stories that are considered classics in the science fiction canon were written in this period. One of the best loved and most powerful is Harry Bates's "Farewell to the Master." Its haunting, tragic quality and its ironic twist at the end make it unforgettable. Suspense builds in the plot as Cliff Sutherland, a man with acute powers of observation, who discovers a puzzling phenomenon, collects evidence, and tries to solve the problem. It is this combination of curiosity and challenge in puzzle-solving that science fiction shares with detective fiction. The story was the basis of the film *The Day the Earth Stood Still*.

Harry Bates was born in 1900 and died in 1982. He was the first editor (1930–33) of *Astounding Stories of Super-Science*. The title of the magazine was soon shortened to *Astounding Stories* and later it became *Analog*, the name under which it is still published today. It has long been known for its "hard" science fiction stories of high quality.

Every culture has its tales explaining the world's beginning and man's creation, among them the biblical story of God creating Adam, and the Greek story of Prometheus creating man. "Farewell to the Master" is another version of the creation myth. Here we see how the science fiction imagination never takes anything for granted. It keeps considering new possibilities and raising new questions, such as: Is man the final form of intelligence, or will another evolve? Does alien intelligence exist somewhere out there in the mysterious cosmos, and if it does, what will be its form? Could it be machine intelligence? Could God be a machine? Could a machine have created man? Some of the finest stories about machine intelligence have resulted from such speculations, and this story, as well as the first two in the next chapter, are good examples.

1

From his perch high on the ladder above the museum floor, Cliff Sutherland studied carefully each line and shadow of the great robot, then turned and looked thoughtfully down at the rush of visitors come from all over the solar system to see Gnut and the traveler for themselves and to hear once again their amazing, tragic story.

He himself had come to feel an almost proprietary interest in the exhibit, and with some reason. He had been the only free-lance picture reporter on the Capitol grounds when the visitors from the Unknown had arrived, and had obtained the first professional shots of the ship. He had witnessed at close hand every event of the next mad few days. He had thereafter pho-tographed many times the eight-foot robot, the ship, and the beautiful slain ambassador, Klaatu, and his imposing tomb out in the center of the Tidal Basin, and, such was the continuing news value of the event to the billions of persons throughout habitable space, he was there now once more to get still other shots and, if possible, a new "angle."

This time he was after a picture which showed Gnut as weird and menacing. The shots he had taken the day before had not given quite the effect he wanted, and he hoped to get it today; but the light was not yet right and he had to wait for the after-noon to wane a little.

The last of the crowd admitted in the present group hurried in, exclaiming at the great pure green curves of the mysterious time-space traveler, then completely forgetting the ship at sight of the awesome figure and great head of the giant Gnut. Hinged robots of crude man-like appearance were familiar enough, but never had Earthling eyes lain on one like this. For Gnut had almost exactly the shape of a man—a giant, but a man—with greenish metal for man's covering flesh, and greenish metal for man's bulging muscles. Except for a loin cloth, he was nude. He stood like the powerful god of the machine of some undreamed-of scientific civilization, on his face a look of sullen, brooding thought. Those who looked at him did not make jests or idle remarks, and those nearest him usually did not speak at all. His strange, internally illuminated red eyes were so set that every observer felt they were fixed on himself alone, and he engendered a feeling that he might at any moment step forward in anger and perform unimaginable deeds.

A slight rustling sound came from speakers hidden in

the ceiling above, and at once the noises of the crowd lessened. The recorded lecture was about to be given. Cliff sighed. He knew the thing by heart; had even been present when the recording was made, and met the speaker, a young chap named Stillwell.

"Ladies and gentlemen," began a clear and well-modulated voice—but Cliff was no longer attending. The shadows in the hollows of Gnut's face and figure were deeper; it was almost time for his shot. He picked up and examined the proofs of the pictures he had taken the day before and compared them critically with the subject.

As he looked a wrinkle came to his brow. He had not noticed it before, but now, suddenly, he had the feeling that since yesterday something about Gnut was changed. The pose before him was the identical one in the photographs, every detail on comparison seemed the same, but nevertheless the feeling persisted. He took up his viewing glass and more carefully compared subject and photographs, line by line. And then he saw that there was a difference.

With sudden excitement, Cliff snapped two pictures at different exposures. He knew he should wait a little and take others, but he was so sure he had stumbled on an important mystery that he had to get going, and quickly folding his accessory equipment he descended the ladder and made his way out. Twenty minutes later, consumed with curiosity, he was developing the new shots in his hotel bedroom.

What Cliff saw when he compared the negatives taken yesterday and today caused his scalp to tingle. Here was a slant indeed! And apparently no one but he knew! Still, what he had discovered, though it would have made the front page of every paper in the solar system, was after all only a lead. The story, what really had happened, he knew no better than anyone else. It must be his job to find out.

And that meant he would have to secrete himself in the building and stay there all night. That very night; there was still time for him to get back before closing. He would take a small, very fast infrared camera that could see in the dark, and he would get the real picture and the story.

He snatched up the little camera, grabbed an aircab, and hurried back to the museum. The place was filled with another section of the ever-present queue, and the lecture was just ending. He thanked Heaven that his arrangement with the museum permitted him to go in and out at will.

He had already decided what to do. First he made his way to the "floating" guard and asked a single question, and anticipation broadened on his face as he heard the expected answer. The second thing was to find a spot where he would be safe from the eyes of the men who would close the floor for the night. There was only one possible place, the laboratory set up behind the ship. Boldly he showed his press credentials to the second guard, stationed at the partitioned passageway leading to it, stating that he had come to interview the scientists; and in a moment was at the laboratory door.

He had been there a number of times and knew the room well. It was a large area roughly partitioned off for the work of the scientists engaged in breaking their way into the ship and full of a confusion of massive and heavy objects—electric and hot-air ovens, carboys of chemicals, asbestos sheeting, compressors, basins, ladles, a microscope, and a great deal of smaller equipment common to a metallurgical laboratory. Three white-smocked men were deeply engrossed in an experiment at the far end. Cliff, waiting a good moment, slipped inside and hid himself under a table half buried with supplies. He felt reasonably safe from detection there. Very soon now the scientists would be going home for the night.

From beyond the ship he could hear another section of the waiting queue filing in—the last, he hoped, of the day. He settled himself as comfortably as he could. In a moment the lecture would begin. He had to smile when he thought of one thing the recording would say.

Then there it was again—the clear, trained voice of the chap Stillwell. The foot scrapings and whispers of the crowd died away, and Cliff could hear every word in spite of the great bulk of the ship lying interposed.

"Ladies and gentlemen," began the familiar words, "the Smithsonian Institution welcomes you to its new Interplanetary Wing and to the marvelous exhibits at this moment before you."

A slight pause. "All of you must know by now something of what happened here three months ago, if indeed you did not see it for yourself in the telescreen," the voice went on. "The few facts are briefly told. A little after 5:00 P.M. on September sixteenth, visitors to Washington thronged the grounds outside this building in their usual numbers and no doubt with their usual thoughts. The day was warm and fair. A stream of people was leaving the main entrance of the museum just outside in the direction you are facing. This wing, of course, was not here at that time. Everyone was homeward bound, tired no doubt from hours on their feet, seeing the exhibits of the museum and visiting the many buildings on the grounds nearby. And then it happened.

"On the area just to your right, just as it is now, appeared the time-space traveler. It appeared in the blink of an eye. It did not come down from the sky; dozens of witnesses swear to that; it just appeared. One moment it was not here, the next it was. It appeared on the very spot it now rests on.

"The people nearest the ship were stricken with panic and ran back with cries and screams. Excitement spread out over Washington in a tidal wave. Radio, television, and newspapermen rushed here at once. Police formed a wide cordon around the ship, and army units appeared and trained guns and ray projectors on it. The direst calamity was feared.

"For it was recognized from the very beginning that this was no spaceship from anywhere in the solar system. Every child knew that only two spaceships had ever been built on Earth, and none at all on any of the other planets and satellites; and of those two, one had been destroyed when it was pulled into the sun, and the other had just been reported safely arrived on Mars. Then, the ones made here had a shell of a strong aluminum alloy, while this one, as you see, is of an unknown greenish metal.

"The ship appeared and just sat here. No one emerged, and there was no sign that it contained life of any kind. That, as much as any single thing, caused excitement to skyrocket. Who,

97

or what, was inside? Were the visitors hostile or friendly? Where did the ship come from? How did it arrive so suddenly right on this spot without dropping from the sky?

"For two days the ship rested here, just as you now see it, without motion or sign that it contained life. Long before the end of that time the scientists had explained that it was not so much a spaceship as a space-time traveler, because only such a ship could arrive as this one did—materialize. They pointed out that such a traveler, while theoretically understandable to us Earthmen, was far beyond attempt at our present state of knowledge, and that this one, activated by relativity principles, might well have come from the far corner of the Universe, from a distance which light itself would require millions of years to cross.

"When this opinion was disseminated, public tension grew until it was almost intolerable. Where had the traveler come from? Who were its occupants? Why had they come to Earth? Above all, why did they not show themselves? Were they perhaps preparing some terrible weapon of destruction?

"And where was the ship's entrance port? Men who dared go look reported that none could be found. No slightest break or crack marred the perfect smoothness of the ship's curving ovoid surface. And a delegation of high-ranking officials who visited the ship could not, by knocking, elicit from its occupants any sign that they had been heard.

"At last, after exactly two days, in full view of tens of thousands of persons assembled and standing well back, and under the muzzles of scores of the army's most powerful guns and ray projectors, an opening appeared in the wall of the ship, and a ramp slid down, and out stepped a man, godlike in appearance and human in form, closely followed by a giant robot. And when they touched the ground the ramp slid back and the entrance closed as before."

"It was immediately apparent to all the assembled thousands that the stranger was friendly. The first thing he did was to raise his right arm high in the universal gesture of peace; but it was not that which impressed those nearest so much as the expression on his face, which radiated kindness, wisdom, the purest nobility. In his delicately tinted robe he looked like a benign god.

"At once, waiting for this appearance, a large committee of high-ranking government officials and army officers advanced to greet the visitor. With graciousness and dignity the man pointed to himself, then to his robot companion, and said in perfect English with a peculiar accent, 'I am Klaatu,' or a name that sounded like that, 'and this is Gnut.' The names were not well understood at the time, but the sight-and-sound film of the television men caught them and they became known to everyone subsequently.

"And then occurred the thing which shall always be to the shame of the human race. From a treetop a hundred yards away came a wink of violet light and Klaatu fell. The assembled multitude stood for a moment stunned, not comprehending what had happened. Gnut, a little behind his master and to one side, slowly turned his body a little toward him, moved his head twice, and stood still, in exactly the position you now see him.

"Then followed pandemonium. The police pulled the slayer of Klaatu out of the tree. They found him mentally unbalanced; he kept crying that the devil had come to kill everyone on Earth. He was taken away, and Klaatu, although obviously dead, was rushed to the nearest hospital to see if anything could be done to revive him. Confused and frightened crowds milled about the Capitol grounds the rest of the afternoon and much of that night. The ship remained as silent and motionless as before. And Gnut, too, never moved from the position he had come to rest in.

"Gnut never moved again. He remained exactly as you see him all that night and for the ensuing days. When the mausoleum in the Tidal Basin was built, Klaatu's burial services took place where you are standing now, attended by the highest functionaries of all the great countries of the world. It was not only the most appropriate but the safest thing to do, for if there should be other living creatures in the traveler, as seemed possible at that time, they had to be impressed by the sincere sorrow of us Earthmen at what had happened. If Gnut was still alive, or

99

perhaps I had better say functionable, there was no sign. He stood as you see him during the entire ceremony. He stood so while his master was floated out to the mausoleum and given to the centuries with the tragically short sight-and-sound record of his historic visit. And he stood so afterward, day after day, night after night, in fair weather and in rain, never moving or showing by any slightest sign that he was aware of what had gone on.

"After the interment, this wing was built out from the museum to cover the traveler and Gnut. Nothing else could very well have been done, it was learned, for both Gnut and the ship were far too heavy to be moved safely by any means at hand.

"You have heard about the efforts of our metallurgists since then to break into the ship, and of their complete failure. Behind the ship now, as you can see from either end, a partitioned workroom has been set up where the attempt still goes on. So far its wonderful greenish metal has proved inviolable. Not only are they unable to get in, but they cannot even find the exact place from which Klaatu and Gnut emerged. The chalk marks you see are the best approximation.

"Many people have feared that Gnut was only temporarily deranged, and that on return to function might be dangerous, so the scientists have completely destroyed all chance of that. The greenish metal of which he is made seemed to be the same as that of the ship and could no more be attacked, they found, nor could they find any way to penetrate to his internals; but they had other means. They set electrical currents of tremendous voltages and amperages through him. They applied terrific heat to all parts of his metal shell. They immersed him for days in gases and acids and strongly corroding solutions, and they have bombarded him with every known kind of ray. You need have no fear of him now. He cannot possibly have retained the ability to function in any way.

"But—a word of caution. The officials of the government know that visitors will not show any disrespect in this building. It may be that the unknown and unthinkably powerful civilization from which Klaatu and Gnut came may send other emissaries to see what happened to them. Whether or not they do, not one of us must be found amiss in our attitude. None of us could very well anticipate what happened, and we all are immeasurably sorry, but we are still in a sense responsible, and must do what we can to avoid possible retaliations.

"You will be allowed to remain five minutes longer, and then, when the gong sounds, you will please leave promptly. The robot attendants along the wall will answer any questions you may have.

"Look well, for before you stand stark symbols of the achievement, mystery, and frailty of the human race."

The recorded voice ceased speaking. Cliff, carefully moving his cramped limbs, broke out in a wide smile. If they knew what he knew!

For his photographs told a slightly different story from that of the lecturer. In yesterday's a line of the figured floor showed clearly at the outer edge of the robot's near foot; in today's, *that line was covered*. Gnut had moved!

Or been moved, though this was very unlikely. Where were the derrick and other evidence of such activity? It could hardly have been done in one night, and all signs so quickly concealed. And why should it be done at all?

Still, to make sure, he had asked the guard. He could almost remember verbatim his answer:

"No, Gnut has neither moved nor been moved since the death of his master. A special point was made of keeping him in the position he assumed at Klaatu's death. The floor was built in under him, and the scientists who completed his derangement erected their apparatus around him, just as he stands. You need have no fears."

Cliff smiled again. He did not have any fears.

Not yet.

2

A moment later the big gong above the entrance doors rang the closing hour, and immediately following it a voice from the speakers called out, "Five o'clock, ladies and gentlemen. Closing time, ladies and gentlemen."

The three scientists, as if surprised it was so late, hurriedly washed their hands, changed to their street clothes and disappeared down the partitioned corridor, oblivious of the young picture man hidden under the table. The slide and scrape of the feet on the exhibition floor rapidly dwindled, until at last there were only the steps of the two guards walking from one point to another, making sure everything was all right for the night. For just a moment one of them glanced in the doorway of the laboratory, then he joined the other at the entrance. Then the great metal doors clanged to, and there was silence.

Cliff waited several minutes, then carefully poked his way out from under the table. As he straightened up, a faint tinkling crash sounded at the floor by his feet. Carefully stooping, he found the shattered remains of a thin glass pipette. He had knocked it off the table.

That caused him to realize something he had not thought of before: A Gnut who had moved might be a Gnut who could see and hear—and really be dangerous. He would have to be very careful.

He looked about him. The room was bounded at the ends by two fiber partitions which at the inner ends followed close under the curving bottom of the ship. The inner side of the room was the ship itself, and the outer was the southern wall of the wing. There were four large high windows. The only entrance was by way of the passage.

Without moving, from his knowledge of the building, he made his plan. The wing was connected with the western end of the museum by a doorway, never used, and extended westward toward the Washington Monument. The ship lay nearest the southern wall, and Gnut stood out in front of it, not far from the northeast corner and at the opposite end of the room from the entrance of the building and the passageway leading to the laboratory. By retracing his steps he would come out on the floor at the point farthest removed from the robot. This was just what he wanted, for on the other side of the entrance, on a low platform, stood a paneled table containing the lecture apparatus, and this table was the only object in the room which afforded a place for him to lie concealed while watching what might go

102

on. The only other objects on the floor were the six manlike robot attendants in fixed stations along the northern wall, placed there to answer visitors' questions. He would have to gain the table.

He turned and began cautiously tiptoeing out of the laboratory and down the passageway. It was already dark there, for what light still entered the exhibition hall was shut off by the great bulk of the ship. He reached the end of the room without making a sound. Very carefully he edged forward and peered around the bottom of the ship at Gnut.

He had a momentary shock. The robot's eyes were right on him!—or so it seemed. Was that only the effect of the set of his eyes, he wondered, or was he already discovered? The position of Gnut's head did not seem to have changed, at any rate. Probably everything was all right, but he wished he did not have to cross that end of the room with the feeling that the robot's eyes were following him.

He drew back and sat down and waited. It would have to be totally dark before he essayed the trip to the table.

He waited a full hour, until the faint beams from the lamps on the grounds outside began to make the room seem to grow lighter; then he got up and peeped around the ship once more. The robot's eyes seemed to pierce right at him as before, only now, due no doubt to the darkness, the strange internal illumination seemed much brighter. This was a chilling thing. Did Gnut know he was there? What were the thoughts of the robot? What *could* be the thoughts of a manmade machine, even so wonderful a one as Gnut?

It was time for the cross, so Cliff slung his camera around on his back, went down on his hands and knees, and carefully moved to the edge of the entrance hall. There he fitted himself as closely as he could into the angle made by it with the floor and started inching ahead. Never pausing, not risking a glance at Gnut's unnerving red eyes, moving an inch at a time, he snaked along. He took ten minutes to cross the space of a hundred feet, and he was wet with perspiration when his fingers at last touched the one-foot rise of the platform on which the table stood. Still slowly, silently as a shadow, he made his way over

103

the edge and melted behind the protection of the table. At last he was there.

He relaxed for a moment, then, anxious to know whether he had been seen, carefully turned and looked around the side of the table.

Gnut's eyes were now full on him! Or so it seemed. Against the general darkness, the robot loomed a mysterious and still darker shadow that, for all his being a hundred and fifty feet away, seemed to dominate the room. Cliff could not tell whether the position of his body was changed or not.

But if Gnut was looking at him, he at least did nothing else. Not by the slightest motion that Cliff could discern did he appear to move. His position was the one he had maintained these last three months, in the darkness, in the rain, and this last week in the museum.

Cliff made up his mind not to give way to fear. He became conscious of his own body. The cautious trip had taken something out of him—his knees and elbows burned and his trousers were no doubt ruined. But these were little things if what he hoped for came to pass. If Gnut so much as moved, and he could catch him with his infrared camera, he would have a story that would buy him fifty suits of clothes. And if on top of that he could learn the purpose of Gnut's moving—provided there was a purpose—that would be a story that would set the world on its ears.

He settled down to a period of waiting; there was no telling when Gnut would move, if indeed he would move that night. Cliff's eyes had long been adjusted to the dark and he could make out the larger objects well enough. From time to time he peered out at the robot—peered long and hard, till his outlines wavered and he seemed to move, and he had to blink and rest his eyes to be sure it was only his imagination.

Again the minute hand of his watch crept around the dial. The inactivity made Cliff careless, and for longer and longer periods he kept his head back out of sight behind the table. And so it was that when Gnut did move he was scared almost out of his wits. Dull and a little bored, he suddenly found the robot out on the floor, halfway in his direction.

But that was not the most frightening thing. It was that when he did see Gnut he did not catch him moving! He was stopped as still as a cat in the middle of stalking a mouse. His eyes were now much brighter, and there was no remaining doubt about their direction: he was looking right at Cliff!

Scarcely breathing, half hypnotized, Cliff looked back. His thoughts tumbled. What was the robot's intention? Why had he stopped so still? Was he being stalked? How could he move with such silence?

In the heavy darkness Gnut's eyes moved nearer. Slowly but in perfect rhythm that almost imperceptible sound of his footsteps beat on Cliff's ears. Cliff, usually resourceful enough, was this time caught flatfooted. Frozen with fear, utterly incapable of fleeing, he lay where he was while the metal monster with the fiery eyes came on.

For a moment Cliff all but fainted, and when he recovered, there was Gnut towering over him, legs almost within reach. He was bending slightly, burning his terrible eyes right into his own!

Too late to try to think of running now. Trembling like any cornered mouse, Cliff waited for the blow that would crush him. For an eternity, it seemed, Gnut scrutinized him without moving. For each second of that eternity Cliff expected annihilation, sudden, quick, complete. And then suddenly and unexpectedly it was over. Gnut's body straightened and he stepped back. He turned. And then, with the almost jerkless rhythm which only he among robots possessed, he started back toward the place from which he came.

Cliff could hardly believe he had been spared. Gnut could have crushed him like a worm—and he had only turned around and gone back. Why? It could not be supposed that a robot was capable of human considerations.

Gnut went straight to the other end of the traveler. At a certain place he stopped and made a curious succession of sounds. At once Cliff saw an opening, blacker than the gloom of the building, appear in the ship's side, and it was followed by a

105

slight sliding sound as a ramp slid out and met the floor. Gnut walked up the ramp and, stooping a little, disappeared inside the ship.

Then, for the first time, Cliff remembered the picture he had come to get. Gnut had moved, but he had not caught him! But at least now, whatever opportunities there might be later, he could get the shot of the ramp connecting with the opened door; so he twisted his camera into position, set it for the proper exposure, and took a shot.

A long time passed and Gnut did not come out. What could he be doing inside? Cliff wondered. Some of his courage returned to him and he toyed with the idea of creeping forward and peeping through the port, but he found he had not the courage for that. Gnut had spared him, at least for the time, but there was no telling how far his tolerance would go.

An hour passed, then another, Gnut was doing something inside the ship, but what? Cliff could not imagine. If the robot had been a human being, he knew he would have sneaked a look, but as it was, he was too much of an unknown quantity. Even the simplest of Earth's robots under certain circumstances were inexplicable things; what, then, of this one, come from an unknown and even unthinkable civilization, by far the most wonderful construction ever seen—what superhuman powers might he not possess? All that the scientists of Earth could do had not served to derange him. Acid, heat, rays, terrific crushing blows— he had withstood them all; even his finish had been unmarred. He might be able to see perfectly in the dark. And right where he was, he might be able to hear or in some way sense the least change in Cliff's position.

More time passed, and then, sometime after two o'clock in the morning, a simple homely thing happened, but a thing so unexpected that for a moment it quite destroyed Cliff's equilibrium. Suddenly, through the dark and silent building, there was a faint whir of wings, soon followed by the piercing, sweet voice of a bird. A mockingbird. Somewhere in this gloom above his head. Clear and full-throated were its notes; a dozen little songs

106

it sang, one after the other without pause between—short insistent calls, twirrings, coaxings, cooings—the spring love song of perhaps the finest singer in the world. Then, as suddenly as it began, the voice was silent.

If an invading army had poured out of the traveler, Cliff would have been less surprised. The month was December; even in Florida the mockingbirds had not yet begun their song. How had one gotten into that tight, gloomy museum? How and why was it singing there?

He waited, full of curiosity. Then suddenly he was aware of Gnut, standing just outside the port of the ship. He stood quite still, his glowing eyes turned squarely in Cliff's direction. For a moment the hush in the museum seemed to deepen; then it was broken by a soft thud on the floor near where Cliff was lying.

He wondered. The light in Gnut's eyes changed, and he started his almost jerkless walk in Cliff's direction. When only a little away, the robot stopped, bent over, and picked something from the floor. For some time he stood without motion and looked at a little object he held in his hand. Cliff knew, though he could not see, that it was the mockingbird. Its body, for he was sure that it had lost its song forever. Gnut then turned, and without a glance at Cliff, walked back to the ship and again went inside.

Hours passed while Cliff waited for some sequel to this surprising happening. Perhaps it was because of his curiosity that his fear of the robot began to lessen. Surely if the mechanism was unfriendly, if he intended him any harm, he would have finished him before, when he had such a perfect opportunity. Cliff began to nerve himself for a quick look inside the port. And a picture; he must remember the picture. He kept forgetting the very reason he was there.

It was in the deeper darkness of the false dawn when he got sufficient courage and made the start. He took off his shoes, and in his stockinged feet, his shoes tied together and slung over his shoulder, he moved stiffly but rapidly to a position behind the nearest of the six robot attendants stationed along the wall, then paused for some sign which might indicate that Gnut knew he had moved. Hearing none, he slipped along behind the next robot attendant and paused again. Bolder now, he made in one spurt all the distance to the farthest one, the sixth, fixed just opposite the port of the ship. There he met with a disappointment. No light that he could detect was visible within; there was only darkness and the all-permeating silence. Still, he had better get the picture. He raised his camera, focused it on the dark opening, and gave the film a comparatively long exposure. Then he stood there, at a loss what to do next.

As he paused, a peculiar series of muffled noises reached his ears, apparently from within the ship. Animal noises—first scrapings and pantings, punctuated by several sharp clicks, then deep, rough snarls, interrupted by more scrapings and pantings, as if a struggle of some kind were going on. Then suddenly, before Cliff could even decide to run back to the table, a low, wide, dark shape bounded out of the port and immediately turned and grew to the height of a man. A terrible fear swept over Cliff, even before he knew what the shape was.

In the next second Gnut appeared in the port and stepped unhesitatingly down the ramp toward the shape. As he advanced it backed slowly away for a few feet; but then it stood its ground, and thick arms rose from its sides and began a loud drumming on its chest, while from its throat came a deep roar of defiance. Only one creature in the world beat its chest and made a sound like that. The shape was a gorilla!

And a huge one!

Gnut kept advancing, and when close, charged forward and grappled with the beast. Cliff would not have guessed that Gnut could move so fast. In the darkness he could not see the details of what happened; all he knew was that the two great shapes, the titanic metal Gnut and the squat but terrifically strong gorilla, merged for a moment with silence on the robot's part and terrible, deep, indescribable roars on the other's; then the two separated, and it was as if the gorilla had been flung back and away.

The animal at once rose to its full height and roared deafeningly. Gnut advanced. They closed again, and the separation of before was repeated. The robot continued inexorably, and now

108

the gorilla began to fall back down the building. Suddenly the beast darted at a manlike shape against the wall, and with one rapid side movement dashed the fifth robot attendant to the floor and decapitated it.

Tense with fear, Cliff crouched behind his own robot attendant. He thanked Heaven that Gnut was between him and the gorilla and was continuing his advance. The gorilla backed farther, darted suddenly at the next robot in the row, and with strength almost unbelievable picked it from its roots and hurled it at Gnut. With a sharp metallic clang, robot hit robot, and the one of Earth bounced off to one side and rolled to a stop.

Cliff cursed himself for it afterward, but again he completely forgot the picture. The gorilla kept falling back down the building, demolishing with terrific bursts of rage every robot attendant that he passed and throwing the pieces at the implacable Gnut. Soon they arrived opposite the table, and Cliff now thanked his stars he had come away. There followed a brief silence. Cliff could not make out what was going on, but he imagined that the gorilla had at last reached the corner of the wing and was trapped.

If he was, it was only for a moment. The silence was suddenly shattered by a terrific roar, and the thick, squat shape of the animal came bounding toward Cliff. He came all the way back and turned just between Cliff and the port of the ship. Cliff prayed frantically for Gnut to come back quickly, for there was now only the last remaining robot attendant between him and the madly dangerous brute. Out of the dimness Gnut did appear. The gorilla rose to its full height and again beat its chest and roared its challenge.

And then occurred a curious thing. It fell on all fours and slowly rolled over on its side, as if weak or hurt. Then panting, making frightening noises, it forced itself again to its feet and faced the oncoming Gnut. As it waited, its eye was caught by the last robot attendant and perhaps Cliff, shrunk close behind it. With a surge of terrible destructive rage, the gorilla waddled sideward toward Cliff, but this time, even through his panic, he saw that the animal moved with difficulty, again apparently sick or severely wounded. He jumped back just in time; the gorilla pulled out the last robot attendant and hurled it violently at Gnut, missing him narrowly.

That was its last effort. The weakness caught it again; it dropped heavily on one side, rocked back and forth a few times, and fell to twitching. Then it lay still and did not move again.

The first faint pale light of the dawn was seeping into the room. From the corner where he had taken refuge, Cliff watched closely the great robot. It seemed to him that he behaved very queerly. He stood over the dead gorilla, looking down at him with what in a human would be called sadness. Cliff saw this clearly; Gnut's heavy greenish features bore a thoughtful, grieving expression new to his experience. For some moments he stood so, then as might a father with his sick child, he leaned over, lifted the great animal in his metal arms and carried it tenderly within the ship.

Cliff flew back to the table, suddenly fearful of yet other dangerous and inexplicable happenings. It struck him that he might be safer in the laboratory, and with trembling knees he made his way there and hid in one of the big ovens. He prayed for full daylight. His thoughts were chaos. Rapidly, one after another, his mind churned up the amazing events of the night, but all was mystery; it seemed there could be no rational explanation for them. That mockingbird. The gorilla. Gnut's sad expression and his tenderness. What could account for a fantastic melange like that!

Gradually full daylight did come. A long time passed. At last he began to believe he might yet get out of that place of mystery and danger alive. At eight-thirty there were noises at the entrance, and the good sound of human voices came to his ears. He stepped out of the oven and tiptoed to the passageway.

The noises stopped suddenly and there was a frightened exclamation and then the sound of running feet, and then silence. Stealthily Cliff sneaked down the narrow way and peeped fearfully around the ship.

There Gnut was in his accustomed place, in the identical pose he had taken at the death of his master, brooding sullenly

110

and alone over a space traveler once again closed tight and a room that was a shambles. The entrance doors stood open and, heart in his mouth, Cliff ran out.

A few minutes later, safe in his hotel room, completely done in, he sat down for a second and almost at once fell asleep. Later, still in his clothes and still asleep, he staggered over to the bed. He did not wake up till midafternoon.

3

Cliff awoke slowly, at first not realizing that the images tumbling in his head were real memories and not a fantastic dream. It was recollection of the pictures which brought him to his feet. Hastily he set about developing the film in his camera.

Then in his hands was proof that the events of the night were real. Both shots turned out well. The first showed clearly the ramp leading up to the port as he had dimly discerned it from his position behind the table. The second, of the open port as snapped from in front, was a disappointment, for a blank wall just back of the opening cut off all view of the interior. That would account for the fact that no light had escaped from the ship while Gnut was inside. Assuming Gnut required light for whatever he did.

Cliff looked at the negatives and was ashamed of himself. What a rotten picture man he was to come back with two ridiculous shots like these! He had had a score of opportunities to get real ones—shots of Gnut in action—Gnut's fight with the gorilla—even Gnut holding the mockingbird—spine-chilling stuff!—and all he had brought back were two stills of a doorway. Oh, sure, they were valuable, but he was a grade-A ass.

And to top this brilliant performance, he had fallen asleep!

Well, he'd better get out on the street and find out what was doing.

Quickly he showered, shaved, and changed his clothes, and soon was entering a nearby restaurant patronized by other picture and newsmen. Sitting alone at the lunch bar, he spotted a friend and competitor.

"Well, what do you think?" asked his friend when he took the stool at his side.

111

"I don't think anything until I've had breakfast," Cliff answered.

"Then haven't you heard?"

"Heard what?" fended Cliff, who knew very well what was coming.

"You're a fine picture man," was the other's remark. "When something really big happens, you are asleep in bed." But then he told him what had been discovered that morning in the museum, and of the world-wide excitement at the news. Cliff did three things at once, successfully—gobbled a substantial breakfast, kept thanking his stars that nothing new had transpired, and showed continuous surprise. Still chewing, he got up and hurried over to the building.

Outside, balked at the door, was a large crowd of the curious, but Cliff had no trouble gaining admittance when he showed his press credentials. Gnut and the ship stood just as he had left them, but the floor had been cleaned up and the pieces of the demolished robot attendants were lined up in one place along the wall. Several other competitor friends of his were there.

"I was away; missed the whole thing," he said to one of them—Gus. "What's supposed to be the explanation for what happened?"

"Ask something easy," was the answer. "Nobody knows. It's thought maybe something came out of the ship, maybe another robot like Gnut. Say—where have you been?"

"Asleep."

"Better catch up. Several billion bipeds are scared stiff. Revenge for the death of Klaatu. Earth about to be invaded."

"But that's—"

"Oh, I know it's all crazy, but that's the story they're being fed; it sells news. But there's a new angle just turned up, very surprising. Come here."

He led Cliff to the table where stood a knot of people looking with great interest at several objects guarded by a technician. Gus pointed to a long slide on which were mounted a number of short dark-brown hairs.

"Those hairs came off a large male gorilla," Gus said with a certain hard-boiled casualness. "Most of them were found among the sweepings of the floor this morning. The rest were found on the robot attendants."

Cliff tried to look astounded. Gus pointed to a test tube partly filled with a light amber fluid.

"And that's blood, diluted—gorilla blood. It was found on Gnut's arms."

"Good Heaven!" Cliff managed to exclaim. "And there's no explanation?"

"Not even a theory. It's your big chance, wonder boy."

Cliff broke away from Gus, unable to maintain his act any longer. He couldn't decide what to do about his story. The press services would bid heavily for it—with all his pictures—but that would take further action out of his hands. In the back of his mind he wanted to stay in the wing again that night, but—well, he simply was afraid. He'd had a pretty stiff dose, and he wanted very much to remain alive.

He walked over and looked a long time at Gnut. No one would ever have guessed that he had moved, or that there had rested on his greenish metal face a look of sadness. Those weird eyes! Cliff wondered if they were really looking at him, as they seemed, recognizing him as the bold intruder of last night. Of what unknown stuff were they made—those materials placed in his eye sockets by one branch of the race of man which all the science of his own could not even serve to disfunction? What was Gnut thinking? What could be the thoughts of a robot—a mechanism of metal poured out of man's clay crucibles? Was he angry at him? Cliff thought not. Gnut had had him at his mercy—and had walked away.

Dared he stay again?

Cliff thought perhaps he did.

He walked about the room, thinking it over. He felt sure Gnut would move again. A Mikton ray gun would protect him from another gorilla—or fifty of them. He did not yet have the real story. He had come back with two miserable architectural stills!

He might have known from the first that he would stay. At

dusk that night, armed with his camera and a small Mikton gun, he lay once more under the table of supplies in the laboratory and heard the metal doors of the wing clang to for the night.

This time he would get the story—and the pictures.

If only no guard was posted inside!

4

Cliff listened hard for a long time for any sound which might tell him that a guard had been left, but the silence within the wing remained unbroken. He was thankful for that—but not quite completely. The gathering darkness and the realization that he was now irrevocably committed made the thought of a companion not altogether unpleasant.

About an hour after it reached maximum darkness he took off his shoes, tied them together and slung them around his neck, down his back, and stole quietly down the passageway to where it opened into the exhibition area. All seemed as it had been the preceding night. Gnut looked an ominous, indistinct shadow at the far end of the room, his glowing red eyes again seemingly right on the spot from which Cliff peeped out. As on the previous night, but even more carefully, Cliff went down on his stomach in the angle of the wall and slowly snaked across to the low platform on which stood the table. Once in its shelter, he fixed his shoes so that they straddled one shoulder, and brought his camera and gun holster around, ready on his breast. This time, he told himself, he would get pictures.

He settled down to wait, keeping Gnut in full sight every minute. His vision reached maximum adjustment to the darkness. Eventually he began to feel lonely and a little afraid. Gnut's red-glowing eyes were getting on his nerves; he had to keep assuring himself that the robot would not harm him. He had little doubt but that he himself was being watched.

Hours slowly passed. From time to time he heard slight noises at the entrance, on the outside—a guard, perhaps, or maybe curious visitors.

At about nine o'clock he saw Gnut move. First his head alone; it turned so that the eyes burned stronger in the direction where Cliff lay. For a moment that was all; then the dark metal form

114

stirred slightly and began moving forward—straight toward him. Cliff had thought he would not be afraid—much—but now his heart stood still. What would happen this time?

With amazing silence, Gnut drew nearer, until he towered an ominous shadow over the spot where Cliff lay. For a long time his red eyes burned down on the prone man. Cliff trembled all over; this was worse than the first time. Without having planned it, he found himself speaking to the creature.

"You would not hurt me," he pleaded. "I was only curious to see what's going on. It's my job. Can you understand me? I would not harm or bother you. I . . . I couldn't if I wanted to! Please!"

The robot never moved, and Cliff could not guess whether his words had been understood or even heard. When he felt he could not bear the suspense any longer, Gnut reached out and took something from a drawer of the table, or perhaps he put something back in; then he stepped back, turned, and retraced his steps. Cliff was safe! Again the robot had spared him!

Beginning then, Cliff lost much of his fear. He felt sure now that this Gnut would do him no harm. Twice he had had him in his power, and either time he had only looked and quietly moved away. Cliff could not imagine what Gnut had done in the drawer of the table. He watched with the greatest curiosity to see what would happen next.

As on the night before, the robot went straight to the end of the ship and made the peculiar sequence of sounds that opened the port, and when the ramp slid out he went inside. After that Cliff was alone in the darkness for a very long time, probably two hours. Not a sound came from the ship.

Cliff knew he should sneak up to the port and peep inside, but he could not quite bring himself to do it. With his gun he could handle another gorilla, but if Gnut caught him it might be the end. Momentarily he expected something fantastic to happen—he knew not what; maybe the mockingbird's sweet song again, maybe a gorilla, maybe—anything. What did at last happen once more caught him with complete surprise.

115

He heard a sudden muffled sound, then words—human words—every one familiar.

"Gentlemen," was the first, and then there was a very slight pause. "The Smithsonian Institution welcomes you to its new Interplanetary Wing and to the marvelous exhibits at this moment before you."

It was the recorded voice of Stillwell! But it was not coming through the speakers overhead, but, much muted, from within the ship.

After a slight pause it went on:

"All of you must . . . must—" Here it stammered and came to a stop. Cliff's hair bristled. That stammering was not in the lecture!

For just a moment there was silence; then came a scream, a hoarse man's scream, muffled, from somewhere within the heart of the ship; and it was followed by muted gasps and cries, as of a man in great fright or distress.

Every nerve tight, Cliff watched the port. He heard a thudding noise within the ship, then out the door flew the shadow of what was surely a human being. Gasping and half stumbling, he ran straight down the room in Cliff's direction. When twenty feet away, the great shadow of Gnut followed him out of the port.

Cliff watched, breathless. The man—it was Stillwell, he saw now—came straight for the table behind which Cliff himself lay, as if to get behind it, but when only a few feet away, his knees buckled and he fell to the floor. Suddenly Gnut was standing over him, but Stillwell did not seem to be aware of it. He appeared very ill, but kept making spasmodic futile efforts to creep on to the protection of the table.

Gnut did not move, so Cliff was emboldened to speak.

"What's the matter, Stillwell?" he asked. "Can I help? Don't be afraid. I'm Cliff Sutherland; you know, the picture man."

Without showing the least surprise at finding Cliff there, and clutching at his presence like a drowning man would a straw, Stillwell gasped out:

116

"Help me! Gnut . . . Gnut—" He seemed unable to go on.

"Gnut what?" asked Cliff. Very conscious of the fire-eyed robot looming above, and afraid even to move out to the man, Cliff added reassuringly: "Gnut won't hurt you. I'm sure he won't. He doesn't hurt me. What's the matter? What can I do?"

With a sudden accession of energy, Stillwell rose on his elbows.

"Where am I?" he asked.

"In the Interplanetary Wing," Cliff answered. "Don't you know?"

Only Stillwell's hard breathing was heard for a moment. Then hoarsely, weakly, he asked:

"How did I get here?"

"I don't know," said Cliff.

"I was making a lecture recording," Stillwell said, "when suddenly I found myself here . . . or I mean in there—"

He broke off and showed a return of his terror.

"Then what?" asked Cliff gently.

"I was in that box—and there, above me, was Gnut, the robot. Gnut! But they made Gnut harmless! He's never moved!"

"Steady, now," said Cliff. "I don't think Gnut will hurt you."

Stillwell fell back on the floor.

"I'm very weak," he gasped. "Something— Will you get a doctor?"

He was utterly unaware that towering above him, eyes boring down at him through the darkness, was the robot he feared so greatly.

As Cliff hesitated, at a loss what to do, the man's breath began coming in short gasps, as regular as the ticking of a clock. Cliff dared to move out to him, but no act on his part could have helped the man now. His gasps weakened and became spasmodic, then suddenly he was completely silent and still. Cliff felt for his heart, then looked up to the eyes in the shadow above.

"He is dead," he whispered.

The robot seemed to understand, or at least to hear. He bent forward and regarded the still figure.

"What is it, Gnut?" Cliff asked the robot suddenly. "What are you doing? Can I help you in any way? Somehow I don't

117

believe you are unfriendly, and I don't believe you killed this man. But what happened? Can you understand me? Can you speak? What is it you're trying to do?"

Gnut made no sound or motion, but only looked at the still figure at his feet. In the robot's face, now so close, Cliff saw the look of sad contemplation.

Gnut stood so several minutes; then he bent lower, took the limp form carefully—even gently, Cliff thought—in his mighty arms, and carried him to the place along the wall where lay the dismembered pieces of the robot attendants. Carefully he laid him by their side. Then he went back into the ship.

Without fear now, Cliff stole along the wall of the room. He had gotten almost as far as the shattered figures on the floor when he suddenly stopped motionless. Gnut was emerging again.

He was bearing a shape that looked like another body, a larger one. He held it in one arm and placed it carefully by the body of Stillwell. In the hand of his other arm he held something that Cliff could not make out, and this he placed at the side of the body he had just put down. Then he went to the ship and returned once more with a shape which he laid gently by the others; and when this last trip was over he looked down at them all for a moment, then turned slowly back to the ship and stood motionless, as if in deep thought, by the ramp.

Cliff restrained his curiosity as long as he could, then slipped forward and bent over the objects Gnut had placed there. First in the row was the body of Stillwell, as he expected, and next was the great shapeless furry mass of a dead gorilla—the one of last night. By the gorilla lay the object the robot had carried in his free hand—the little body of the mockingbird. These last two had remained in the ship all night, and Gnut, for all his surprising gentleness in handling them, was only cleaning house. But there was a fourth body whose history he did not know. He moved closer and bent very low to look.

What he saw made him catch his breath. Impossible!—he thought; there was some confusion in his directions; he brought his face back, close to the first body. Then his blood ran cold.

118

The first body was that of Stillwell, but the last in the row was Stillwell, too; there were two bodies of Stillwell, both exactly alike, both dead.

Cliff backed away with a cry, and then panic took him and he ran down the room away from Gnut and yelled and beat wildly on the door. There was a noise on the outside.

"Let me out!" he yelled in terror. "Let me out! Let me out! Oh, hurry!"

A crack opened between the two doors and he forced his way through like a wild animal and ran far out on the lawn. A belated couple on a nearby path stared at him with amazement, and this brought some sense to his head and he slowed down and came to a stop. Back at the building, everything looked as usual, and, in spite of his terror, Gnut was not chasing him.

He was still in his stockinged feet. Breathing heavily, he sat down on the wet grass and put on his shoes; then he stood and looked at the building, trying to pull himself together. What an incredible melange! The dead Stillwell, the dead gorilla, and the dead mockingbird—all dying before his eyes. And then that last frightening thing, the second dead Stillwell whom he had *not* seen die. And Gnut's strange gentleness, and the sad expression he had twice seen on his face.

As he looked, the grounds about the building came to life. Several people collected at the door of the wing, above sounded the siren of a police copter, then in the distance another, and from all sides people came running, a few at first, then more and more. The police planes landed on the lawn just outside the door of the wing, and he thought he could see the officers peeping inside. Then suddenly the lights of the wing flooded on. In control of himself now, Cliff went back.

He entered. He had left Gnut standing in thought at the side of the ramp, but now he was again in his old familiar pose in the usual place, as if he had never moved. The ship's door was closed, and the ramp gone. But the bodies, the four strangely assorted bodies, were still lying by the demolished robot attendants where he had left them in the dark.

He was startled by a cry behind his back. A uniformed museum guard was pointing at him.

119

"This is the man!" the guard shouted. "When I opened the door this man forced his way out and ran like the devil!"

The police officers converged on Cliff.

"Who are you? What is all this?" one of them asked him roughly.

"I'm Cliff Sutherland, picture reporter," Cliff answered calmly. "And I was the one who was inside here and ran away, as the guard says."

"What were you doing?" the officer asked, eyeing him. "And where did these bodies come from?"

"Gentlemen, I'd tell you gladly—only business first," Cliff answered. "There's been some fantastic goings-on in this room, and I saw them and have the story, but"—he smiled—"I must decline to answer without advice of counsel until I've sold my story to one of the news syndicates. You know how it is. If you'd allow me the use of the radio in your plane—just for a moment, gentlemen—you'll have the whole story right afterward—say in half an hour, when the television men broadcast it. Meanwhile, believe me, there's nothing for you to do, and there'll be no loss by the delay."

The officer who had asked the questions, blinked, and one of the others, quicker to react and certainly not a gentleman, stepped toward Cliff with clenched fists. Cliff disarmed him by handing him his press credentials. He glanced at them rapidly and put them in his pocket.

By now half a hundred people were there, and among them were two members of a syndicate crew whom he knew, arrived by copter. The police growled, but they let him whisper in their ears and then go out under escort to the crew's plane. There, by radio, in five minutes, Cliff made a deal which would bring him more money than he had ever before earned in a year. After that he turned over all his pictures and negatives to the crew and gave them the story, and they lost not one second in spinning back to their office with the flash.

More and more people arrived, and the police cleared the building. Ten minutes later a big crew of radio and television men forced their way in, sent there by the syndicate with which he had dealt. And then a few minutes later, under the glaring

120

lights set up by the operators and standing close by the ship and not far from Gnut—he refused to stand underneath him—Cliff gave his story to the cameras and microphones, which in a fraction of a second shot it to every corner of the solar system.

Immediately afterward the police took him to jail. On general principles and because they were pretty blooming mad.

5

Cliff stayed in jail all that night—until eight o'clock the next morning, when the syndicate finally succeeded in digging up a lawyer and got him out. And then, when at last he was leaving, a Federal man caught him by the wrist.

"You're wanted for further questioning over at the Continental Bureau of Investigation," the agent told him. Cliff went along willingly.

Fully thirty-five high-ranking Federal officials and "big names" were waiting for him in an imposing conference room—one of the president's secretaries, the undersecretary of state, the underminister of defense, scientists, a colonel, executives, department heads, and ranking "C" men. Old gray-mustached Sanders, chief of the CBI, was presiding.

They made him tell his story all over again, and then, in parts, all over once more—not because they did not believe him, but because they kept hoping to elicit some fact which would cast significant light on the mystery of Gnut's behavior and the happenings of the last three nights. Patiently, Cliff racked his brains for every detail.

Chief Sanders asked most of the questions. After more than an hour, when Cliff thought they had finished, Sanders asked him several more, all involving his personal opinions of what had transpired.

"Do you think Gnut was deranged in any way by the acids, rays, heat, and so forth applied to him by the scientists?"

"I saw no evidence of it."

"Do you think he can see?"

"I'm sure he can see, or else has other powers which are equivalent."

"Do you think he can hear?"

121

"Yes, sir. That time when I whispered to him that Stillwell was dead, he bent lower, as if to see for himself. I would not be surprised if he also understood what I said."

"At no time did he speak, except those sounds he made to open the ship?"

"Not one word, in English or any other language. Not one sound with his mouth."

"In your opinion, has his strength been impaired in any way by our treatment?" asked one of the scientists.

"I have told you how easily he handled the gorilla. He attacked the animal and threw it back, after which it retreated all the way down the building, afraid of him."

"How would you explain the fact that our autopsies disclosed no mortal wound, no cause of death, in any of the bodies—gorilla, mockingbird, or the two identical Stillwells?"—this from a medical officer.

"I can't."

"You think Gnut is dangerous?"—from Sanders.

"Potentially very dangerous."

"Yet you say you have the feeling he is not hostile."

"To me, I meant. I do have that feeling, and I'm afraid that I can't give any good reason for it, except the way he spared me twice when he had me in his power. I think maybe the gentle way he handled the bodies had something to do with it, and maybe the sad, thoughtful look I twice caught on his face."

"Would you risk staying in the building alone another night?"

"Not for anything." There were smiles.

"Did you get any pictures of what happened last night?"

"No, sir." Cliff, with an effort, held on to his composure, but he was swept by a wave of shame. A man hitherto silent rescued him by saying:

"A while ago you used the word 'purposive' in connection with Gnut's actions. Can you explain that a little?"

"Yes, that was one of the things that struck me: Gnut never seems to waste a motion. He can move with surprising speed when he wants to; I saw that when he attacked the gorilla; but most other times he walks around as if methodically completing some simple task. And that reminds me of a peculiar thing: at

122

times he gets into one position, any position, maybe half bent over, and stays there for minutes at a time. It's as if his scale of time values were eccentric, compared to ours; some things he does surprisingly fast, and others surprisingly slowly. This might account for his long periods of immobility."

"That's very interesting," said one of the scientists. "How would you account for the fact that he recently moves only at night?"

"I think he's doing something he wants no one to see, and the night is the only time he is alone."

"But he went ahead even after finding you there."

"I know. But I have no other explanation, unless he considered me harmless or unable to stop him—which was certainly the case."

"Before you arrived, we were considering encasing him in a large block of glasstex. Do you think he would permit it?"

"I don't know. Probably he would; he stood for the acids and rays and heat. But it had better be done in the daytime; night seems to be the time he moves."

"But he moved in the daytime when he emerged from the traveler with Klaatu."

"I know."

That seemed to be all they could think of to ask him. Sanders slapped his hand on the table.

"Well, I guess that's all, Mr. Sutherland," he said. "Thank you for your help, and let me congratulate you for a very foolish, stubborn, brave young man—young businessman." He smiled very faintly. "You are free to go now, but it may be that I'll have to call you back later. We'll see."

"May I remain while you decide about that glasstex?" Cliff asked. "As long as I'm here I'd like to have the tip."

"The decision has already been made—the tip's yours. The pouring will be started at once."

"Thank you, sir," said Cliff—and calmly asked more: "And will you be so kind as to authorize me to be present outside the building tonight? Just outside. I've a feeling something's going to happen."

"You want still another scoop, I see," said Sanders not unkindly, "then you'll let the police wait while you transact your business."

"Not again, sir. If anything happens, they'll get it at once."

The chief hesitated. "I don't know," he said. "I'll tell you what. All the news services will want men there, and we can't have that; but if you can arrange to represent them all yourself, it's a go. Nothing's going to happen, but your reports will help calm the hysterical ones. Let me know."

Cliff thanked him and hurried out and phoned his syndicate the tip—free—then told them Sanders' proposal. Ten minutes later they called him back, said all was arranged, and told him to catch some sleep. They would cover the pouring. With light heart, Cliff hurried over to the museum. The place was surrounded by thousands of the curious, held far back by a strong cordon of police. For once he could not get through; he was recognized, and the police were still sore. But he did not care much; he suddenly felt very tired and needed that nap. He went back to his hotel, left a call, and went to bed.

He had been asleep only a few minutes when his phone rang. Eyes shut, he answered it. It was one of the boys at the syndicate, with peculiar news. Stillwell had just reported, very much alive— the real Stillwell. The two dead ones were some kind of copies; he couldn't imagine how to explain them. He had no brothers.

For a moment Cliff came fully awake, then he went back to bed. Nothing was fantastic anymore.

6

At four o'clock, much refreshed and with an infrared viewing magnifier slung over his shoulder, Cliff passed through the cordon and entered the door of the wing. He had been expected and there was no trouble. As his eyes fell on Gnut, an odd feeling went through him, and for some obscure reason he was almost sorry for the giant robot.

Gnut stood exactly as he had always stood, the right foot advanced a little, and the same brooding expression on his face; but now there was something more. He was solidly encased in a huge block of transparent glasstex. From the floor on which he stood to the top of his full eight feet, and from there on up

124

for an equal distance, and for about eight feet to the left, right, back, and front, he was immured in a water-clear prison which confined every inch of his surface and would prevent the slightest twitch of even his amazing muscles.

It was absurd, no doubt, to feel sorry for a robot, a manmade mechanism, but Cliff had come to think of him as being really alive, as a human is alive. He showed purpose and will; he performed complicated and resourceful acts; his face had twice clearly shown the emotion of sadness, and several times what appeared to be deep thought; he had been ruthless with the gorilla, and gentle with the mockingbird and the other two bodies, and he had twice refrained from crushing Cliff when there seemed every reason that he might. Cliff did not doubt for a minute that he was still alive, whatever "alive" might mean.

But outside were waiting the radio and television men; he had work to do. He turned and went to them and all got busy.

An hour later Cliff sat alone about fifteen feet above the ground in a big tree which, located just across the walk from the building, commanded through a window a clear view of the upper part of Gnut's body. Strapped to the limbs about him were three instruments—his infrared viewing magnifier, a radio mike, and an infrared television eye with sound pickup. The first, the viewing magnifier, would allow him to see in the dark with his own eyes, as if by daylight, a magnified image of the robot, and the others would pick up any sights and sounds, including his own remarks, and transmit them to the several broadcast studios which would fling them millions of miles in all directions through space. Never before had a picture man had such an important assignment, probably—certainly not one who forgot to take pictures. But now that was forgotten, and Cliff was quite proud, and ready.

Far back in a great circle stood a multitude of the curious— and the fearful. Would the plastic glasstex hold Gnut? If it did not, would he come out thirsting for revenge? Would unimaginable beings come out of the traveler and release him, and perhaps exact revenge? Millions at their receivers were jittery; those in the distance hoped nothing awful would happen, yet they hoped something would, and they were prepared to run.

125

In carefully selected spots not far from Cliff on all sides were mobile ray batteries manned by army units, and in a hollow in back of him, well to his right, there was stationed a huge tank with a large gun. Every weapon was trained on the door of the wing. A row of smaller, faster tanks stood ready fifty yards directly north. Their ray projectors were aimed at the door, but not their guns. The grounds about the building contained only one spot—the hollow where the great tank was—where, by close calculation, a shell directed at the doorway would not cause damage and loss of life to some part of the sprawling capital.

Dusk fell; out streamed the last of the army officers, politicians, and other privileged ones; the great metal doors of the wing clanged to and were locked for the night. Soon Cliff was alone, except for the watchers at their weapons scattered around him.

Hours passed. The moon came out. From time to time Cliff reported to the studio crew that all was quiet. His unaided eyes could now see nothing of Gnut but the two faint red points of his eyes, but through the magnifier he stood out as clearly as if in daylight from an apparent distance of only ten feet. Except for his eyes, there was no evidence that he was anything but dead and unfunctionable metal.

Another hour passed. Now and again Cliff thumbed the levels of his tiny radio-television watch—only a few seconds at a time because of its limited battery. The air was full of Gnut and his own face and his own name, and once the tiny screen showed the tree in which he was then sitting and even, minutely, himself. Powerful infrared long-distance television pickups were even then focused on him from nearby points of vantage. It gave him a funny feeling.

Then, suddenly, Cliff saw something and quickly bent his eye to the viewing magnifier. Gnut's eyes were moving; at least the intensity of the light emanating from them varied. It was as if two tiny red flashlights were turned from side to side, their beams at each motion crossing Cliff's eyes.

126

Thrilling, Cliff signaled the studios, cut in his pickups, and described the phenomenon. Millions resonated to the excitement in his voice. Could Gnut conceivably break out of that terrible prison?

Minutes passed, the eye flashes continued, but Cliff could discern no movement or attempted movement of the robot's body. In brief snatches he described what he saw. Gnut was clearly alive; there could be no doubt he was straining against the transparent prison in which he had at last been locked fast; but unless he could crack it, no motion should show.

Cliff took his eye from the magnifier—and started. His un-aided eye, looking at Gnut shrouded in darkness, saw an aston-ishing thing not yet visible through his instrument. A faint red glow was spreading over the robot's body. With trembling fin-gers he readjusted the lens of the television eye, but even as he did so the glow grew in intensity. It looked as if Gnut's body were being heated to incandescence!

He described it in excited fragments, for it took most of his attention to keep correcting the lens. Gnut passed from a figure of dull red to one brighter and brighter, clearly glowing now even through the magnifier. And then he moved! Unmistakably he moved!

He had within himself somehow the means to raise his own body temperature, and was exploiting the one limitation of the plastic in which he was locked. For glasstex, Cliff now remem-bered, was a thermoplastic material, one that set by cooling and conversely would soften again with heat. Gnut was melting his way out!

In three-word snatches, Cliff described this. The robot be-came cherry red, the sharp edges of the icelike block rounded, and the whole structure began to sag. The process accelerated. The robot's body moved more widely. The plastic lowered to the crown of his head, then to his neck, then to his waist, which was as far as Cliff could see. His body was free! And then, still cherry-red, he moved forward out of sight!

Cliff strained eyes and ears, but caught nothing but the distant roar of the watchers beyond the police lines and a few low, sharp commands from the batteries posted around him. They, too, had heard, and perhaps seen by telescreen, and were waiting.

Several minutes passed. There was a sharp, ringing crack; the great metal doors of the wing flew open, and out stepped the metal giant, glowing no longer. He stood stock-still, and his red eyes pierced from side to side through the darkness.

Voices out in the dark barked orders and in a twinkling Gnut was bathed in narrow, crisscrossing rays of sizzling, colored light. Behind him the metal doors began to melt, but his great green body showed no change at all. Then the world seemed to come to an end; there was a deafening roar, everything before Cliff seemed to explode in smoke and chaos, his tree whipped to one side so that he was nearly thrown out. Pieces of debris rained down. The tank gun had spoken, and Gnut, he was sure, had been hit.

Cliff held on tight and peered into the haze. As it cleared he made out a stirring among the debris at the door, and then dimly but unmistakably he saw the great form of Gnut rise to his feet. He got up slowly, turned toward the tank, and suddenly darted toward it in a wide arc. The big gun swung in an attempt to cover him, but the robot sidestepped and then was upon it. As the crew scattered, he destroyed its breech with one blow of his fist, and then he turned and looked right at Cliff.

He moved toward him, and in a moment was under the tree. Cliff climbed higher. Gnut put his two arms around the tree and gave a lifting push, and the tree tore out at the roots and fell crashing to its side. Before Cliff could scramble away, the robot had lifted him in his metal hands.

Cliff thought his time had come, but strange things were yet in store for him that night. Gnut did not hurt him. He looked at him from arm's length for a moment, then lifted him to a sitting position on his shoulders, legs straddling his neck. Then, holding one ankle, he turned and without hesitation started down the path which led westward away from the building.

Cliff rode helpless. Out over the lawns he saw the muzzles

of the scattered field pieces move as he moved, Gnut—and himself—their one focus. But they did not fire. Gnut, by placing him on his shoulders, had secured himself against that—Cliff hoped.

The robot bore straight toward the Tidal Basin. Most of the field pieces throbbed slowly after. Far back, Cliff saw a dark tide of confusion roll into the cleared area—the police lines had broken. Ahead, the ring thinned rapidly off to the sides; then, from all directions but the front, the tide rolled in until individual shouts and cries could be made out. It came to a stop about fifty yards off, and few people ventured nearer.

Gnut paid them no attention, and he no more noticed his burden than he might a fly. His neck and shoulders made Cliff a seat hard as steel, but with the difference that their underlying muscles with each movement flexed, just as would those of a human being. To Cliff, this metal musculature became a vivid wonder.

Straight as the flight of a bee, over paths, across lawns and through thin rows of trees Gnut bore the young man, the roar of thousands of people following close. Above droned copters and darting planes, among them police cars with their nerve-shattering sirens. Just ahead lay the still waters of the Tidal Basin, and in its midst the simple marble tomb of the slain ambassador, Klaatu, gleaming black and cold in the light of the dozen searchlights always trained on it at night. Was this a rendezvous with the dead?

Without an instant's hesitation, Gnut strode down the bank and entered the water. It rose to his knees, then above his waist, until Cliff's feet were under. Straight through the dark waters for the tomb of Klaatu the robot made his inevitable way.

The dark square mass of gleaming marble rose higher as they neared it. Gnut's body began emerging from the water as the bottom shelved upward, until his dripping feet took the first of the rising pyramid of steps. In a moment they were at the top, on the narrow platform in the middle of which rested the simple oblong tomb.

Stark in the blinding searchlights, the giant robot walked once around it, then, bending, he braced himself and gave a mighty push against the top. The marble cracked; the thick cover

129

slipped askew and broke with a loud noise on the far side. Gnut went to his knees and looked within, bringing Cliff well up over the edge.

Inside, in sharp shadow against the converging light beams, lay a transparent plastic coffin, thick-walled and sealed against the centuries, and containing all that was mortal of Klaatu, unspoken visitor from the great Unknown. He lay as if asleep, on his face the look of godlike nobility that had caused some of the ignorant to believe him divine. He wore the robe he had arrived in. There were no faded flowers, no jewelry, no ornaments; they would have seemed profane. At the foot of the coffin lay the small sealed box, also of transparent plastic, which contained all of Earth's records of his visit—a description of the events attending his arrival, pictures of Gnut and the traveler, and the little roll of sight-and-sound film which had caught for all time his few brief motions and words.

Cliff sat very still, wishing he could see the face of the robot. Gnut, too, did not move from his position of reverent contemplation—not for a long time. There on the brilliantly lighted pyramid, under the eyes of a fearful, tumultuous multitude, Gnut paid final respect to his beautiful and adored master.

Suddenly, then, it was over. Gnut reached out and took the little box of records, rose to his feet and started down the steps.

Back through the water, straight back to the building, across lawns and paths as before, he made his irresistible way. Before him the chaotic ring of people melted away, behind they followed as close as they dared, trampling each other in their efforts to keep him in sight. There are no television records of his return. Every pickup was damaged on the way to the tomb.

As they drew near the building, Cliff saw that the tank's projectile had made a hole twenty feet wide extending from the roof to the ground. The door still stood open, and Gnut, hardly varying his almost jerkless rhythm, made his way over the debris and went straight for the port end of the ship. Cliff wondered if he would be set free.

He was. The robot set him down and pointed toward the

door; then, turning, he made the sounds that opened the ship. The ramp slid down and he entered.

Then Cliff did the mad, courageous thing which made him famous for a generation. Just as the ramp started sliding back in, he skipped over it and himself entered the ship. The port closed.

7

It was pitch dark, and the silence was absolute. Cliff did not move. He felt that Gnut was close, just ahead, and it was so.

His hard metal hand took him by the waist, pulled him against his cold side, and carried him somewhere ahead. Hidden lamps suddenly bathed the surroundings with bluish light.

He set Cliff down and stood looking at him. The young man already regretted his rash action, but the robot, except for his always unfathomable eyes, did not seem angry. He pointed to a stool in one corner of the room. Cliff quickly obeyed this time and sat meekly, for a while not even venturing to look around.

He saw he was in a small laboratory of some kind. Complicated metal and plastic apparatus lined the walls and filled several small tables; he could not recognize or guess the function of a single piece. Dominating the center of the room was a long metal table on whose top lay a large box, much like a coffin on the outside, connected by many wires to a complicated apparatus at the far end. From close above spread a cone of bright light from a many-tubed lamp.

One thing, half covered on a nearby table, did look familiar—and very much out of place. From where he sat it seemed to be a briefcase—an ordinary Earthman's briefcase. He wondered.

Gnut paid him no attention but, at once, with the narrow edge of a thick tool, sliced the lid off the little box of records. He lifted out the strip of sight-and-sound film and spent fully half an hour adjusting it within the apparatus at the end of the big table. Cliff watched, fascinated, wondering at the skill with which the robot used his tough metal fingers. This done, Gnut worked for a long time over some accessory apparatus on an adjoining table. Then he paused thoughtfully a moment and pushed inward a long rod.

A voice came out of the coffinlike box—the voice of the slain ambassador.

"I am Klaatu," it said, "and this is Gnut."

From the recording!—flashed through Cliff's mind. The first and only words the ambassador had spoken. But then, in the very next second he saw that it was not so. There was a man in the box! The man stirred and sat up, and Cliff saw the living face of Klaatu!

Klaatu appeared somewhat surprised and spoke quickly in an unknown tongue to Gnut—and Gnut, for the first time in Cliff's experience, spoke himself in answer. The robot's syllables tumbled out as if born of human emotion, and the expression on Klaatu's face changed from surprise to wonder. They talked for several minutes. Klaatu, apparently fatigued, then began to lie down, but stopped midway, for he saw Cliff. Gnut spoke again, at length. Klaatu beckoned Cliff with his hand, and he went to him.

"Gnut has told me everything," he said in a low, gentle voice, then looked at Cliff for a moment in silence, on his face a faint, tired smile.

Cliff had a hundred questions to ask, but for a moment he hardly dared open his mouth.

"But you," he began at last—very respectfully, but with an escaping excitement—"you are not the Klaatu that was in the tomb?"

The man's smile faded and he shook his head.

"No." He turned to the towering Gnut and said something in his own tongue, and at his words the metal features of the robot twisted as if with pain. Then he turned back to Cliff. "I am dying," he announced simply, as if repeating his words for the Earthman. Again to his face came the faint, tired smile.

Cliff's tongue was locked. He just stared, hoping for light. Klaatu seemed to read his mind.

"I see you don't understand," he said. "Although unlike us, Gnut has great powers. When the wing was built and the lectures began, there came to him a striking inspiration. Acting on it at once, in the night, he assembled this apparatus . . . and now he has made me again, from my voice, as recorded by your people.

As you must know, a given body makes a characteristic sound. He constructed an apparatus which reversed the recording process, and from the given sound made the characteristic body."

Cliff gasped. So that was it!

"But you needn't die!" Cliff exclaimed suddenly, eagerly. "Your voice recording was taken when you stepped out of the ship, while you were well! You must let me take you to a hospital! Our doctors are very skillful!"

Hardly perceptibly, Klaatu shook his head.

"You still don't understand," he said slowly and more faintly. "Your recording had imperfections. Perhaps very slight ones, but they doom the product. All of Gnut's experiments died in a few minutes, he tells me . . . and so must I."

Suddenly, then, Cliff understood the origin of the "experiments." He remembered that on the day the wing was opened a Smithsonian official had lost a briefcase containing film strips recording the speech of various world fauna. There, on that table, was a briefcase! And the Stillwells must have been made from strips kept in the table drawer!

But his heart was heavy. He did not want this stranger to die. Slowly there dawned on him an important idea. He explained it with growing excitement.

"You say the recording was imperfect, and of course it was. But the cause of that lay in the use of an imperfect recording apparatus. So if Gnut, in his reversal of the process, had used exactly the same pieces of apparatus that your voice was recorded with, the imperfections could be studied, canceled out, and you'd live, and not die!"

As the last words left his lips, Gnut whipped around like a cat and gripped him tight. A truly human excitement was shining in the metal muscles of his face.

"Get me that apparatus!" he ordered—in clear and perfect English! He started pushing Cliff toward the door, but Klaatu raised his hand.

"There is no hurry," Klaatu said gently; "it is too late for me. What is your name, young man?"

133

Cliff told him.

"Stay with me to the end," he asked. Klaatu closed his eyes and rested; then, smiling just a little, but not opening his eyes, he added: "And don't be sad, for I shall now perhaps live again . . . and it will be due to you. There is no pain—" His voice was rapidly growing weaker. Cliff, for all the questions he had, could only look on, dumb. Again Klaatu seemed to be aware of his thoughts.

"I know," he said feebly, "I know. We have so much to ask each other. About your civilization . . . and Gnut's—"

"And yours," said Cliff.

"And Gnut's," said the gentle voice again. "Perhaps . . . some day . . . perhaps I will be back—"

He lay without moving. He lay so for a long time, and at last Cliff knew that he was dead. Tears came to his eyes; in only these few minutes he had come to love this man. He looked at Gnut. The robot knew, too, that he was dead, but no tears filled his red-lighted eyes; they were fixed on Cliff, and for once the young man knew what was in his mind.

"Gnut," he announced earnestly, as if taking a sacred oath, "I'll get the original apparatus. I'll get it. Every piece of it, the exact same things."

Without a word, Gnut conducted him to the port. He made the sounds that unlocked it. As it opened, a noisy crowd of Earthmen outside trampled each other in a sudden scramble to get out of the building. The wing was lighted. Cliff stepped down the ramp.

The next two hours always in Cliff's memory had a dreamlike quality. It was as if that mysterious laboratory with the peacefully sleeping dead man were the real and central part of his life, and his scene with the noisy men with whom he talked a gross and barbaric interlude. He stood not far from the ramp. He told only part of his story. He was believed. He waited quietly while all the pressure which the highest officials in the land could exert was directed toward obtaining for him the apparatus the robot had demanded.

134

When it arrived, he carried it to the floor of the little vestibule behind the port. Gnut was there, as if waiting. In his arms he held the slender body of the second Klaatu. Tenderly he passed him out to Cliff, who took him without a word, as if all this had been arranged. It seemed to be the parting.

Of all the things Cliff had wanted to say to Klaatu, one remained imperatively present in his mind. Now, as the green metal robot stood framed in the great green ship, he seized his chance.

"Gnut," he said earnestly, holding carefully the limp body in his arms, "you must do one thing for me. Listen carefully. I want you to tell your master—the master yet to come—that what happened to the first Klaatu was an accident, for which all Earth is immeasurably sorry. Will you do that?"

"I have known it," the robot answered gently.

"But will you promise to tell your master—just those words— as soon as he is arrived?"

"You misunderstand," said Gnut, still gently, and quietly spoke four more words. As Cliff heard them a mist passed over his eyes and his body went numb.

As he recovered and his eyes came back to focus he saw the great ship disappear. It just suddenly was not there anymore. He fell back a step or two. In his ears, like great bells, rang Gnut's last words. Never, never was he to disclose them till the day he came to die.

"You misunderstand," the mighty robot had said. "I am the master."

THE
EVOLUTION
OF
INTELLIGENCE

ROBOT'S RETURN

ROBERT MOORE WILLIAMS

(1 9 3 8)

What power lies in a dream? A greater power to survive than the dreamer himself had, "Robot's Return" suggests. This poignant little story, set eight thousand years in the future, describes three robots from another planetary system who are just as curious as humans about their ancestors. Who created them? Why do they occasionally use a spoken language when their usual silent communication by radio waves is more efficient? They set out in their spaceship to search for the answer to their past, and they finally come to a lifeless planet covered with remains of a civilization. Can this be home?

Mythologist Joseph Campbell, in *The Hero with a Thousand Faces*, points out that in the myths of various cultures some story patterns appear again and again. They demonstrate, he believes, that certain universals exist in the way mankind sees itself and its place in the universe. One such pattern is the myth of the eternal return. The hero sets out from the land of his birth and finally, after strange and dangerous adventures, finds that his path leads him back home again. This journey suggests a cyclic pattern in the cosmos; everything eventually circles back on itself.

Campbell's study of myths was not published until 1949, eleven years after Robert Moore Williams wrote "Robot's Return." Still, the myth of the eternal return is the pattern that structures this story, although here the adventuresome heroes who finally come back home are not men but robots.

Another element of this story, travel to the far distant future, has been a staple of science fiction ever since H. G. Wells wrote *The Time Machine* in 1895. He had read Lyell's work describing his geological findings, and Darwin's outline of his theory of evolution. Wells recognized that if the universe is dynamic, not static, then evolutionary changes will undoubtedly affect human form and intelligence. His grim imaginary journey into the future pictures the end of life as humans deteriorate into the ugly Morlocks and the pale Eloi, and finally die out.

Once the proposition of change through evolution is accepted, the imagination begins to speculate about what the next stage of intelligence might be. True, it could devolve, just as Wells imagined, but it might evolve and its form might become inorganic rather than organic. Machine intelligence as the next evolutionary step is an interesting possibility that fascinates many science fiction writers. Of all the stories exploring this possibility, none is more haunting than "Robot's Return."

139

Robert Moore Williams (1907–1977) was a full-time writer and during his long career published almost two hundred short stories and novels. His stories largely appeared in *Amazing* and *Fantastic*, and his novels often comprised one-half of an Ace double.

As THOUGH SUSTAINED by the strength of a dream, the ship floated gracefully, easily, a bare hundred feet above the surface of the planet. Overhead, slightly more than ninety million miles away, a sullen sun retreated down the dark blue sky. Its long rays fretted across the planet, washed from the low, brown hills, glinted from the jumbled mounds in the center of the valley.

The ship turned, slanted down toward the mounds, rose over them, circled, found a spot where the litter was nearly level and snuggled down to rest as though returning home after weary years spent between the stars.

Hissing from the pressure of air rushing inward, a forward lock opened.

Nine stood in the lock, staring from never-blinking eyes across the landscape—a fixed, sombre gaze. Hungrily, his eyes pried among the jumbled masonry, the great clocks of white stone stained a dirty brown in places, the piles of red clay in which grass was reluctantly growing. Five, perhaps ten miles around, the piles circled, then gradually leveled off toward the low brown hills.

Behind him a voice whispered, asking a question.

"It is the same as all the others," his answer went, though the grim line of the mouth did not move. "Silence, and the wreckage of a mighty city. But nothing lives here now. The inhabitants are gone."

For a second there was silence, and then a third voice whispered. "Just as I said. We are only wasting time here. It is true that once some kind of a race lived on this planet—but certainly they were never intelligent enough to have been our ancestors."

Nine, in the lock, sighed softly. "Seven, you must remember that we have not made a complete investigation. You must also remember that we have absolutely no knowledge of our ancestors—even to whether or not they actually existed. Our records

140

are complete for eight thousand years, but they do not go back beyond the time when the Original Five awaked, finding themselves lying on the edge of the sea, with no knowledge of how they came to be there. Perhaps they were a special creation, for they possessed great intelligence, speedily adapting the planet to their needs, forging and constructing others to help them. Perhaps they had come there, in a ship that had sunk in the sea, from some other planet. But we have never been able to solve the problem."

Eight, silent after his first question, pressed forward, stared over Nine's shoulder.

"I am perfectly familiar with the history of our race." The edge of Seven's thinking was clear over the radio beam. "The point I make is that the little life we have seen on this planet—and little enough we have seen—has been organic, a mess of chemicals. Animals, eating each other, eating grass— Pah! I want no ancestors like that."

Slowly, Eight shook his head, the ripple of interwoven metal strands winking in the light. As if he had not heard the bickering of Seven and Nine, he spoke. "For a minute, as I stood here, it seemed to me that I had been on this spot before. The low hills circling a city— Only the city has changed, and over there"— he pointed toward the east—"it seems there should be a lake, or an inlet from the ocean. But no—no—I must be mistaken." He paused, and the fixed gleam in his eyes held a touch of awe. "I spoke—I used the vocal apparatus— Now I wonder why I did that?"

"So do I," Seven's answer rasped. "You used the vocal apparatus when the radio beam is much better. I have never understood why we should equip ourselves with cumbersome apparatus for making and hearing sounds when we have a much better method of communication."

"Because," Eight answered. "Because we have always had them. The Original Five had them. I do not know why they had them, for they also had the radio beam. Perhaps they had a use for them, though what that use could have been— At any rate, we have retained them. Perhaps, someday, we will discover a use for them."

"Bah!" Seven snorted. "You are one of those inexplicable dreamers. It seems that no matter how carefully we construct the brain substance, we always get a few freaks who are unwilling to face reality, who are not sufficient in themselves, but who hunger for some day that is past—a day that never had existence. I have no sympathy with you, nor any sympathy with the Council that sent us here on this wild exploration."

"But," Nine protested, "the Council could not ignore the evidence of the old star map. The Original Five had that map, but we have never understood it, probably never would have understood it if our newly perfected telescopes had not revealed this system to us—nine planets circling a sun, the third planet a strange double system. Obviously that map is somehow a link with our unknown past."

"Nonsense. I am a realist. I face the future, not the past."

"But the future is built of material taken from the past, and how can we build securely when we do not know what our past has been? It is important to us to know whether we are descended from whatever gods there are, or whether we have evolved from some lower form. Come," Nine spoke.

The cunningly twisted strands of metal writhed, and Nine stepped lithely from the lock. Eight followed, and after them came Seven, still grumbling.

Three little metal men four and a half feet tall. Two legs, two arms, two eyes, a nose, a mouth—the last two organs almost valueless survivals. For they did not need food or oxygen. The power of the bursting atom supplied them with energy. Nor did they really need the legs, for their evolution during their eight thousand years had been rapid. Seven touched the ground, glowed slightly, rose into the air and drifted after his companions. Eight and Nine used their legs. Somehow, to Eight, the feel of the ground was good.

They stood on a little hill. Eight's eyes went around the horizon. The metal face did not shift or change, no flicker of emotion played over it. But in the myriad of cunning photocells that were the eyes, hungry lights appeared to reflect the thinking that went on in the brain substance behind.

"It's larger—larger than it looked from the air," Nine spoke, his vocal apparatus biting at the words, yet somehow reflecting the awe he felt.

"Yes," Eight answered. "All this litter that we see, all these mounds—and some of them are hundreds of feet high—are all that is left of some mighty city. Miles and miles and miles around, it stretches. How much work must have gone into it? How long must it have taken in the building? Centuries, perhaps hundreds of centuries, some race lived here, dreamed here, and, dreaming, built of clay and stone and steel and glass. I wonder—if they *could* have been our ancestors, our unknown forebears?"

"Nonsense!" Seven blurted.

Eight stirred, his eyes glinting uneasily as he glanced at Seven. "Perhaps it is not nonsense. I have the feeling, have had it ever since we sighted this system from the void—nine little planets clustering around a mother sun—that is the—home." His voice lingered over the word, caressed it.

"Home!" Seven echoed. "We have no meaning for the word. We are at home anywhere. And as for feeling, we have even less meaning for that word. Feeling is not logic," he finished, as if that settled everything.

"Perhaps logic has no meaning for that word," Eight retorted. "But remember that our minds are constructed according to the ancient pattern—and who knows that feeling was not a part of that pattern, a part that has come down to us?"

"I remember only that we are Robots. I do not know or care about our origin. Only the future has meaning, the future in which we shall tread the paths beyond the stars."

"Robots!" Eight answered. "I even wonder where we got that name for ourselves."

"It was the name the Original Five had for themselves, just as they had a language."

"But why, among a myriad of possible sounds, should they have selected that one as their name?"

"Because—" Seven was suddenly silent. Eight felt the perturbed pulse of his thinking. Seven was trying to explain to himself why their name should be what it was. He was having a hard time doing it. The answer, somehow, went beyond the bounds of logic. Or was there no answer? But that was not logical either. There had to be an answer, a reason. Seven stirred uneasily, eyed his companions. Abruptly he lowered himself to the ground, shutting off the power that enabled him to bend gravity, as if he wanted the feel of the ground under his feet. He followed Nine over the rubble, and he used his legs.

Eight said nothing.

"What do you suppose this race looked like?" Seven awkwardly voiced the question.

Eight, gazing at the ruins, voiced the question that had been on his mind. "What happened to them? Could it happen to us?"

Seven and Nine stared at him. Seven's hand went to the heat gun swinging at his belt. Nine twisted his eyes away.

"It couldn't happen to us," Seven said flatly.

"I—hope not," Eight answered. "But something happened to the race that was here, and perhaps—"

"There is work to be done," Nine interrupted. "We must examine every inch of this area. Perhaps we may find the rusted bodies of the former inhabitants. At first, I had hoped we would find them alive, but after seeing all those deserted cities, I am afraid we will find no living intelligence. But it may be we will find records."

Slowly, under the unwinking sun overhead, they pressed forward among the ruins, Nine in the lead, then Eight, then Seven. Around them the air, stirred by the pressure of an unknown force, moved restlessly. A wind went with them, as though it, too, quested among tumbled masonry and piles of brick dust for some friend of the long-gone past. Silently, the wind went among the haunted débris. Eight felt it passing, a force touching him with a thousand invisible fingers, a force that could not be seen but only felt.

Eight stared at the ruins, wondering what manner of creatures had once moved among them. The rusted bones of the steel framework of buildings, steel that crumbled at the touch, casing stones upended, the greenish color of corrosion on copper. He

144

tried to imagine the millions of inhabitants going about this city. He saw their glistening metal bodies moving along the streets, floating upward beside the bulk of the buildings. He saw them bringing stone and forging steel, creating a city under that yellow sun. And at night, he saw them looking up at the stars, at that strange dead satellite hovering in the black sky. He wondered if they had ever visited that satellite. They must have visited it, he decided, if not in reality, then in dreams. And possibly the stars beyond. For the towers of their cities had pointed at the stars.

Little metal men. Slowly Eight's imagination failed him. Somehow he could not populate this silent city with little metal men. He shook his head. He could see the dream, but not the dreamers.

Nine stood in front of a pile of masonry. The rains, the heat of summer, the cold of uncounted winters, had brought down the stones from the top. Nine stared sombrely at the dark opening between the tumbled blocks. He spoke. "I'm going in there."

Seven and Eight followed.

Darkness folded in around them—a stirring, whispering darkness. A beam of light flashed from Nine's forehead, smashed against the darkness, illumined the walls of what looked like a tunnel.

Under their feet the dust exploded in little gray clouds. Abruptly the tunnel widened into a circle with three other arteries branching out. Broad doors opened in the arteries, doors that now were closed. Staring, Nine pushed against one of the doors, and it crumbled with the pressure, opened into a small room that was totally bare. Nine stepped into it, and the floor crumbled. He shot down into gloom, but instantly his descent slowed as he flicked on the device that bent gravity. He hesitated, then allowed himself to float down into the darkness. His voice whispered over the radio beam and Seven and Eight followed him.

Nine looked up at them as they came down. "That little room was used to carry the former inhabitants up into the building. See, there is the mechanism. Whoever they were, they did not know how to control gravity or they would not have needed this device."

Neither Eight nor Seven answered, and Nine poked forward into the gloom, the bright beam from his light splashing from dozens of sturdy columns that supported the bulk above. His voice called and Seven and Eight moved toward him.

"Here is a machine," Nine spoke. "Or is it—one of our early life-forms?"

Eight stared at the rust-flecked wheels, the crumbling, corroded bulk of the motor housings, the gears falling away into ruin. This, a robot! He rebelled at the thought. Yet it was hard to know where mechanism left off and robot began. The dividing line was thin. You took inanimate metal and the pressure of exploding force; you worked the metal into a thousand different parts and you confined the force; you added a brain that was in itself a force-field capable of receiving and retaining impressions—and you had a robot. You left out the brain—and you had a machine.

Seven, prying among the mechanism, whispered. "It *is* one of our primitive life-forms—one of the early upward steps. All the fundamentals of robot construction are here. Wheels turn, work is done."

"No." Eight shook his head. "A robot is more than that. This—this is only a machine, unintelligently carrying out reactions its nature set for it. I don't know what those reactions could have been, but I am certain it was not a robot. It was fixed in this place, for one thing, and, for another, I see no signs of brain control."

"A robot is a machine," Seven answered. "A logical machine. There is no doubt about it. Perhaps the control was in some other part of the building."

Nine stirred protestingly. "I—I am inclined to agree with Eight. See, this was only a pump, designed to force water, or some other liquid, through the building. Here is the pressure chamber, and this, I think, was a crude electric motor. But it was only a machine."

"We, ourselves, are only highly developed machines," Seven persisted. "Our operation can be explained purely in terms of

146

mechanics. When you attempt to make us more than machines, you become illogical. True, this is a machine. It is also a primitive robot form, for the two terms mean the same thing. There are many links missing between it and us, but perhaps we may find those links—"

"But how?" Eight asked. "In the beginning how could lifeless, dead metal build itself into the first machine?"

Seven started to answer, hesitated, stared at Eight and then his gaze wandered off into the gloom of this cavern. His light smashed into the darkness, drove a clean channel through the murk, yet always the darkness crept in around the edges of the beam, and always, when the light moved, the darkness came back.

"I—I don't know the answer to that," Seven spoke. "Perhaps the Universe was different millions of years ago. But I don't know. Nobody knows. However, we have found one link in the chain. Maybe we will find others."

Eight kept his thinking to himself. There was little to be gained in disputing Seven. And, after all, Eight saw that Seven was right. Or partly right. Robots *were* machines, fundamentally. Yet they were something more than machines. Machines could not dream. In Eight's mind was the wild wonder—where had robots acquired their ability to dream? To what did that ability point?

Eight did not speak. He followed Seven and Nine. He watched, and thought.

They went out of the basement, went back to the floor where they had entered, forced their way up through the silent building. Dust, and furniture that became dust when they touched it, and corroded metal, were in the rooms above, but of the race that had lived there they found no sign.

On through the city they went. Seven crowed exultantly over the wreck of a huge bulk that had turned on its side. An engine, with eight huge driving wheels, and Seven, digging in the dust, uncovered the remnants of the track on which the wheels had run.

"Another link," Seven gloated. "A higher form, possessing the ability to move."

"But not to think," Nine still protested. "It ran on a track. There must have been another, separate intelligence guiding it."

"What of it? Perhaps so—perhaps not. Perhaps the intelligence that guided it was the final robot form." Again Seven suddenly ceased talking, and again Eight could feel the pulse of his troubled thinking. Final robot form—

"There was another, totally different life-form here," Eight spoke slowly, marshaling his vague thoughts. "A life-form that created and used these machines. But that life has vanished utterly, leaving no trace of itself, except the ruins of its cities, the wreckage of its machines."

"But what?" Nine gulped.

"What could have destroyed it? I have no idea. Only vaguely can I sense its existence, through the evidence that it once shaped a world to meet its needs. I have seen nothing that will give me a clue to its nature—or its death. Perhaps a new form of corrosion developed, destroying it. Perhaps— But I can't see the answer."

They moved on through the ruins. The slow sun dropped down toward the horizon. The silent wind, searching among the haunted ruins, went with them.

"Look!" Nine called.

They stood in an open space in front of a squat metallic structure that had resisted the rain and the snow. But Nine was not pointing at the building. He moved forward, bent over an object half buried in the mold.

Seven gasped. "A robot. Almost an exact model of us. Here, at last, is final proof!"

Eagerly they bent down, scraping away the soil. Quickly, they uncovered the figure. Perhaps ten feet tall, it was more than twice their size. Eight saw it was a robot. Seven had been right, after all, and here was proof. Those machines had somehow managed to develop intelligence and to evolve into sentient beings.

Somehow the crude ore had shaped and forged itself.

And yet this figure differed from the true robot form. Eight saw the difference as they uncovered it. The hopes rising in his mind failed.

"No—it isn't one of us. It's only a statue."

Cast of solid metal, covered by a thin film of corrosion, the statue lay, its feet still attached to a part of the pedestal that had served as a base from which, in some long-gone time, it had toppled. Eight stared at it, not heeding Seven's thinking which came over the radio beam. Seven was insisting that even if it was a statue—a lifeless thing—the form showed that robots had developed here. Otherwise they would not have made a statue in this shape.

Eight recognized the logic of Seven's statement, but the sight of the statue stirred again those vague rebellious thoughts, and in his mind was the feeling that the statue represented something more, that it was more than a replica of form—that it was the embodiment of an idea. But what that idea was, he could not grasp. Slender and graceful, yet with the suggestion of strength, it lay on the ground, a fallen god with head uplifted and arm outstretched. Eight's thinking became clearer. Yes, it was a fallen god, or the representation of a fallen god, and his mind went back to the builder, the designer, the artist who had dreamed of this figure and had then created in metal a figure adequate to his dreaming. The artist was gone, the statue had fallen. Eight wondered about the dream—

His turgid thinking burst into clarity like a jet of suddenly spouting water. Ever since he had seen this world from afar, especially since he had seen the wreckage of all those mighty cities, he had wondered about the dream of the race that had lived and built here. The fate of the race had never saddened him; all things rusted into ruin eventually, all material things, all logical things. Only a dream might achieve immortality, only a dream could start in slime and go onward to the end of Time. But the dream of this race—whatever that dream had been—appeared to have died. Some catastrophe had overtaken them before they had grown strong enough to forge their dream into an immortal shape. Eight sighed, and the photocells that were his eyes lost luster.

He did not notice that Seven and Nine had left him, were forcing an entrance into the building, until Nine's sharp call brought him to his feet.

There was only one large room, Eight saw. It had been a laboratory or a workshop. Benches, machinery, tools were crumbling, just as everything else on this planet was crumbling, just as the dream of the race had crumbled—

Nine's voice, heavy with awe, echoed through the room. "I—I can read it! It's our language!"

The written language of the robots, here on this forgotten planet circling an insignificant sun in a lost corner of the Universe! Eight felt the trembling pulse of currents flowing in his mind. They had found their past; they had found their ancestors. All the other evidence could be explained away, but not this.

Ancestors, forebears, those who had gone before, those who had labored to build for the benefit of some unknown descendant. Had the machine, the lever, and the wheel somehow been their forebears? Or had there been an alien form preceding the machine?

A metal plate, inches thick, supported on heavy metal pillars. A tough metal, almost completely rust-resistant.

> *Now Man dies. A mutant bacteriophage, vicious beyond imagination, is attacking, eating, destroying all living cells, even to dead animal matter.*
>
> *There is no hope of escape on Earth. The only hope is to flee from Earth. Tomorrow we blast our first rocket ship off for Mars, ourselves in suspended animation to withstand the acceleration, the ship manned by Thoradson's robots.*
>
> *It may be we shall live again. It may be we shall die.*
>
> *We go, and may God go with us.*

Thus the record ended. Nine's raspy voice faded, and for a second the echoes came back from the dark corners of the room. Then there was silence. Seven shifted his feet.

150

"Man," he spoke. "Man. That is a word for which we have no meaning."

"Perhaps," Eight spoke softly, "perhaps it was the name of the life-form that created us."

Seven did not answer, and Nine, too, was silent. A wind came into the room, moved restlessly, and went out again. The silence held. Seven stared at the metal plate, picking out the words one by one.

"It must be you are right," he said. "See, they use the word—robot." Wonder grew in his voice, and then disgust mingled with the wonder. "An organism—an animal— Yet obviously they must have created us, used us as slaves. They manned their ship with robots."

Eight stirred but said nothing. There was nothing to say.

"That," Nine whispered, "is why we are unable to find a link between the machine and us. *They* developed the machine, used it. *They* provided the intelligence. Finally they built machines with some kind of intelligence. It must have been late in their history, and they built very few of them. Perhaps they were afraid. There are so many links missing, it is hard to know. But certainly, in a sense, they were our ancestors—"

"Yes," Eight agreed. "In a sense that seems—"

"But they started for a nearby planet," Seven protested. "Our sun is light-years distant. How did they ever get there?"

"They may have missed their aim. Or perhaps the robots rebelled and took the ship elsewhere, and in landing smashed it, only five of them managing to escape."

"I don't believe that," Seven said. "You have no proof of it."

"No," Eight admitted. "No. We don't even know what happened to the men on the ship."

They stood again outside the building, three little metal men. Out yonder in the west the sun was dipping below the horizon. A soft dusk was coming down, hiding the barren world, and still the lonely wind was stirring in the shadows.

Eight saw the statue lying on the ground and vague thoughts stirred within his mind. "They may have eaten grass," he said.

151

"They may have eaten the flesh of other animals; they may have been weaklings; they may have arisen out of slime, but somehow I think there was something fine about them. For they dreamed, and even if they died—"

The robot bent over. Tiny, ageless, atom-fed motors within him surged with an endless power. The robot lifted the dream of an age-dead man and set the statue back on its feet.

The three returned to their ship, and it lifted, following its path out to the stars. The proud, blind eyes of a forgotten statue seemed to follow it.

THOUGH DREAMERS DIE

LESTER DEL REY

(1944)

Science fiction often pictures time reversals, where time runs backward instead of forward. Less common is the reversal of the writer's imagination, but it happens in "Though Dreamers Die." Lester del Rey read Robert Moore Williams's "Robot's Return" and was intrigued by the story. He kept wondering about the men who had built the robots and set out into space with them, leaving behind the metal plate recording their desperate need to escape the bacteriophage plague that was destroying all life forms on Earth. What had happened to them? What adventures did they meet as they explored through the universe, looking for a new home?

Del Rey suggested to Williams that he should write another story, a "prequel" as he called it, telling the events that led to the return of the robots to Earth. Williams declined, but suggested that del Rey do it. The story you are about to read was the result.

Lester del Rey, born in 1915, has written a number of tales about robots. In outstanding stories like "Instinct" and "Into Thy Hands" he has perhaps been more successful than any other writer in portraying man as a participant in the evolution of life through his creation of robots. Del Rey was one of the major writers in the Golden Age of *Astounding* and is the author of several dozen science fiction books for both adults and young people. He is presently the fantasy editor of Ballantine Del Rey Books.

CONSCIOUSNESS HALTED dimly at the threshold and hovered uncertainly, while Jorgen's mind reached out along his numbed nerves, questing without real purpose; he was cold, chilled to the marrow of his bones, and there was an aching tingle to his body that seemed to increase as his half-conscious thought discovered it. He drew his mind back, trying to recapture a prenatal lethargy that had lain on him so long, unwilling to face this cold and tingling body again.

But the numbness was going, in spite of his vague desires, though his now opened eyes registered only a vague, formless light without outline or detail, and the mutterings of sound

153

around him were without pattern or meaning. Slowly the cold retreated, giving place to an aching throb that, in turn, began to leave; he stirred purposelessly, while little cloudy wisps of memory insisted on trickling back, trying to remind him of things he must do.

Then the picture cleared somewhat, letting him remember scattered bits of what had gone before. There had been the conquest of the Moon and a single gallant thrust on to Mars; the newscasts had been filled with that. And on the ways a new and greater ship had been building, to be powered with his new energy release that would free it from all bounds and let it go out to the farthest stars, if they chose—the final attainment of all the hopes and dreams of the race. But there was something else that eluded him, more important even than all that or the great ship.

A needle was thrust against his breast and shoved inward, to be followed by a glow of warmth and renewed energy; adrenaline, his mind recognized, and he knew that there were others around him, trying to arouse him. Now his heart was pumping strongly and the drug coursed through him, chasing away those first vague thoughts and replacing them with a swift rush of less welcome, bitter memories.

For man's dreams and man himself were dust behind him, now! Overnight all their hopes and plans had been erased as if they had never been, and the Plague had come, a mutant bacteria from some unknown source, vicious beyond imagination, to attack and destroy and to leave only death behind it. In time, perhaps, they might have found a remedy, but there had been no time. In weeks it had covered the earth, in months even the stoutest hearts that still lived had abandoned any hope of survival. Only the stubborn courage and tired but unquenchable vigor of old Dr. Craig had remained, to force dead and dying men on to the finish of Jorgen's great ship; somehow in the mad shambles of the last days, he had collected this pitifully small crew that was to seek a haven on Mars, taking the five Thoradson robots to guide them while they protected themselves against the savage acceleration with the aid of the suspended animation that had claimed him so long.

154

And on Mars, the Plague had come before them! Perhaps it had been brought by that first expedition, or perhaps they had carried it back unknowingly with them; that must remain forever an unsolved mystery. Venus was uninhabitable, the other planets were useless to them, and the earth was dead behind. Only the stars had remained, and they had turned on through sheer necessity that had made that final goal a hollow mockery of the dream it should have been. Here, in the ship around him, reposed all that was left of the human race, unknown years from the solar system that had been their home!

But the old grim struggle must go on. Jorgen turned, swinging his trembling feet down from the table toward the metal floor and shaking his head to clear it. "Dr. Craig?"

Hard, cool hands found his shoulder, easing him gently but forcefully back onto the table. The voice that answered was metallic, but soft. "No, Master Jorgen, Dr. Craig is not here. But wait, rest a little longer until the sleep is all gone from you; you're not ready yet."

But his eyes were clearing then, and he swung them about the room. Five little metal men, four and a half feet tall, waited patiently around him; there was no other present. Thoradson's robots were incapable of expression, except for the dull glow in their eyes, yet the pose of their bodies seemed to convey a sense of uncertainty and discomfort, and Jorgen stirred restlessly, worried vaguely by the impression. Five made an undefined gesture with his arm.

"A little longer, master. You must rest!"

For a moment longer he lay quietly, letting the last of the stupor creep away from him and trying to force his still-dulled mind into the pattern of leadership that was nominally his. This time, Five made no protest as he reached up to catch the metal shoulder and pull himself to his feet. "You've found a sun with planets, Five? Is that why you wakened me?"

Five shuffled his feet in an oddly human gesture, nodding, his words still maddeningly soft and slow. "Yes, master, sooner than we had hoped. Five planetless suns and ninety years of searching are gone, but it might have been thousands. You can see them from the pilot room if you wish."

Ninety years that might have been thousands, but they had won! Jorgen nodded eagerly, reaching for his clothes, and Three and Five sprang forward to help, then moved to his side to support him, as the waves of giddiness washed through him, and to lead him slowly forward as some measure of control returned. They passed down the long center hall of the ship, their metal feet and his leather boots ringing dully on the plastic-and-metal floor, and came finally to the control room, where great crystal windows gave a view of the cold black space ahead, sprinkled with bright, tiny stars; stars that were unflickering and inimical as no stars could be through the softening blanket of a planet's atmosphere. Ahead, small but in striking contrast to the others, one point stood out, the size of a dime at ten feet. For a moment, he stood staring at it, then moved almost emotionlessly toward the windows, until Three plucked at his sleeve.

"I've mapped the planets already, if you wish to see them, master. We're still far from them, and at this distance, by only reflected light, they are hard to locate, but I think I've found them all."

Jorgen swung to the electron screen that began flashing as Three made rapid adjustments on the telescope, counting the globes that appeared on it and gave place to others. Some were sharp and clear, cold and unwavering; others betrayed the welcome haze of atmosphere. Five, the apparent size of Earth, were located beyond the parched and arid inner spheres, and beyond them, larger than Jupiter, a monster world led out to others that grew smaller again. There was no ringed planet to rival Saturn, but most had moons, except for the farthest inner planets, and one was almost a double world, with satellite and primary of nearly equal size. Planet after planet appeared on the screen, to be replaced by others, and he blinked at the result of his count. "Eighteen planets, not counting the double one twice! How many are habitable?"

"Perhaps four. Certainly the seventh, eighth, and ninth are. Naturally, since the sun is stronger, the nearer ones are too hot. But those are about the size of Earth, and they're relatively closer to each other than Earth, Mars, and Venus were; they should be very much alike in temperature, about like Earth. All show spec-

troscopic evidence of oxygen and water vapor, while the plates
of seven show what might be vegetation. We've selected that,
subject to your approval."

It came on the screen again, a ball that swelled and grew as
the maximum magnification of the screen came into play, until
it filled the panel and expanded so that only a part was visible.
The bluish green color there might have been a sea, while the
browner section at the side was probably land. Jorgen watched
as it moved slowly under Three's manipulations, the brown entirely replacing the blue, and again, eventually, showing another
sea. From time to time, the haze of the atmosphere thickened
as grayish veils seemed to swim over it, and he felt a curious
lift at the thoughts of clouds and rushing streams, erratic rain,
and the cool, rich smell of growing things. Almost it might have
been a twin of earth, totally unlike the harsh, arid home that
Mars would have been.

Five's voice broke in, the robot's eyes following his over the
screen. "The long, horizontal continent seems best, master. We
estimate its temperature at about that of the central farming
area of North America, though there is less seasonal change.
Specific density of the planet is about six, slightly greater than
earth; there should be metals and ores there. A pleasant, inviting
world."

It was. And far more, a home for the voyagers who were still
sleeping, a world to which they could bring their dreams and
their hopes, where their children might grow up and find no
strangeness to the classic literature of earth. Mars had been grim
and uninviting, something to be fought through sheer necessity.
This world would be a mother to them, opening its arms in
welcome to these foster children. Unless—

"It may already have people, unwilling to share with us."

"Perhaps, but not more than savages. We have searched with
the telescope and camera, and that shows more than the screen;
the ideal harbor contains no signs of living constructions,
and they would surely have built a city there. Somehow, I . . .
feel—"

Jorgen was conscious of the same irrational feeling that they
would find no rivals there, and he smiled as he swung back to

157

the five who were facing him, waiting expectantly as if entreating his approval. "Seven, then. And the trust that we placed in you has been kept to its fullest measure. How about the fuel for landing?"

Five had turned suddenly toward the observation ports, his little figure brooding over the pin-point stars, and Two answered. "More than enough, master. After reaching speed, we only needed a little to guide us. We had more than time enough to figure the required approaches to make each useless sun swing us into a new path, as a comet is swung."

He nodded again, and for a moment as he gazed ahead at the sun that was to be their new home, the long, wearying vigil of the robots swept through his mind, bringing a faint wonder at the luck that had created them as they were. Anthropomorphic robots, capable of handling human instruments, walking on two feet and with two arms ending in hands at their sides. But he knew it had been no blind luck. Nature had designed men to go where no wheels could turn, to handle all manner of tools, and to fit not one but a thousand purposes; it had been inevitable that Thoradson and the brain should copy such an adaptable model, reducing the size only because of the excessive weight necessary to a six-foot robot.

Little metal men, not subject to the rapid course of human life that had cursed their masters; robots that could work with men, learning from a hundred teachers, storing up their memories over a span of centuries instead of decades. When specialization of knowledge had threatened to become too rigid, and yet when no man had time enough even to learn the one field he chose, the coming of the robots had become the only answer. Before them, men had sought help in calculating machines, then in electronic instruments, and finally in the "brains" that were set to solving the problem of their own improvement, among other things. It was with such a brain that Thoradson had labored in finally solving the problems of full robothood. Now, taken from their normal field, they had served beyond any thought of their creator in protecting and preserving all that was left of the human race. Past five suns and over ninety years of monotonous searching they had done what no man could have tried.

Jorgen shrugged aside his speculations and swung back to face them. "How long can I stay conscious before you begin decelerating?"

"We are decelerating—full strength." Two stretched out a hand to the instrument board, pointing to the accelerometer.

The instrument confirmed his words, though no surge of power seemed to shake the ship, and the straining, tearing pull that should have shown their change of speed was absent. Then, for the first time, he realized that his weight seemed normal here in space, far from the pull of any major body. "Controlled gravity!"

Five remained staring out of the port, and his voice was quiet, incapable of pride or modesty. "Dr. Craig set us the problem, and we had long years in which to work. Plates throughout the ship pull with a balanced force equal and opposite to the thrust of acceleration, while others give seeming normal weight. Whether we coast at constant speed or accelerate at ten gravities, compensation is complete and automatic."

"Then the sleep's unnecessary! Why—" But he knew the answer, of course; even without the tearing pressure, the sleep had remained the only solution to bringing men this vast distance that had taken ninety years; otherwise they would have grown old and died before reaching it, even had their provisions lasted.

Now, though, that would no longer trouble them. A few hours only separated them from the planets he had seen, and that could best be spent here before the great windows, watching their future home appear and grow under them. Such a thing should surely be more than an impersonal fact in their minds; they were entitled to see the final chapter on their exodus, to carry it with them as a personal memory through the years of their lives and pass that memory on to the children who should follow them. And the fact that they would be expecting the harshness of Mars instead of this inviting world would make their triumph all the sweeter. He swung back, smiling.

"Come along, then, Five; we'll begin reviving while you others continue with the ship. And first, of course, we must arouse Dr. Craig and let him see how far his plan has gone."

Five did not move from the windows, and the others had halted their work, waiting. Then, reluctantly, the robot answered. "No, master. Dr. Craig is dead!"

"Craig—dead?" It seemed impossible, as impossible and unreal as the distance that separated them from their native world. There had always been Craig, always would be.

"Dead, master, years ago." There was the ghost of regret and something else in the spacing of the words. "There was nothing we could do to help!"

Jorgen shook his head, uncomprehending. Without Craig, the plans they had dared to make seemed incomplete and almost foolish. On Earth, it had been Craig who first planned the escape with this ship. And on Mars, after the robots brought back the evidence of the Plague, it had been the older man who had cut through their shock with a shrug and turned his eyes outward again with the fire of a hope that would not be denied.

"Jorgen, we used bad judgment in choosing such an obviously unsuitable world as this, even without the Plague. But it's only a delay, not the finish. For beyond, somewhere out there, there are other stars housing other planets. We have a ship to reach them, robots who can guide us there; what more could we ask? Perhaps by Centauri, perhaps a thousand light-years beyond, there must be a home for the human race, and we shall find it. On the desert before us lies the certainty of death; beyond our known frontiers there is only uncertainty—but hopeful uncertainty. It is for us to decide. There could be no point in arousing the others to disappointment when someday we may waken them to an even greater triumph. Well?"

And now Craig, who had carried them so far, was dead like Moses outside the Promised Land, leaving the heritage of real as well as normal leadership to him. Jorgen shook himself, though the eagerness he had felt was dulled now by a dark sense of personal loss. There was work still to be done. "Then, at least, let's begin with the others, Five."

Five had turned from the window and was facing the others, apparently communicating with them by the radio beam that was a part of him, his eyes avoiding Jorgen's. For a second, the robots stood with their attention on some matter, and then Five nodded with the same curious reluctance and turned to follow Jorgen, his steps lagging, his arms at his sides.

But Jorgen was only half aware of him as he stopped before the great sealed door and reached out for the lever that would let him into the sleeping vault, to select the first to be revived. He heard Five's steps behind him quicken, and then suddenly felt the little metal hands catch at his arm, pulling it back, while the robot urged him sideways and away from the door.

"No, master. Don't go in there!" For a second, Five hesitated, then straightened and pulled the man farther from the door and down the hall toward the small reviving room nearest, one of the several provided. "I'll show you—in here! We—"

Sudden unnamed fears caught at Jorgen's throat, inspired by something more threatening in the listlessness of the robot than in the unexplained actions. "Five, explain this conduct!"

"Please, master, in here. I'll show you—but not in the main chamber—not there! This is better, simpler—"

He stood irresolutely, debating whether to use the mandatory form that would force built-in unquestioning obedience from the robot, then swung about as the little figure opened the small door and motioned, eyes still averted. He started forward, to stop abruptly in the doorway.

No words were needed. Anna Holt lay there on the small table, her body covered by a white sheet, her eyes closed, and the pain-filled grimaces of death erased from her face. There could be no question of that death, though. The skin was blotched, hideously, covered with irregular brownish splotches, and the air was heavy with the scent of musk that was a characteristic of the Plague! Here, far from the sources of the infection, with their goal almost at hand, the Plague had reached forward to claim its own and remind them that flight was not enough—could never be enough so long as they were forced to carry their disease-harboring bodies with them.

About the room, the apparatus for reviving the sleepers lay scattered, pushed carelessly aside to make way for other things, whose meaning was only partially clear. Obviously, though, the Plague had not claimed her without a fight, though it had won in the end, as it always did. Jorgen stepped backward, heavily, his eyes riveted on the corpse. Again his feet groped backward, jarring down on the floor, and Five was closing and sealing the door with apathetic haste.

"The others, Five? Are they—"

Five nodded, finally raising his head slightly to meet the man's eyes. "All, master. The chamber of sleep is a mausoleum now. The Plague moved slowly there, held back by the cold, but it took them all. We sealed the room years ago when Dr. Craig finally saw there was no hope."

"Craig?" Jorgen's mind ground woodenly on, one slow thought at a time. "He knew about this?"

"Yes. When the sleepers first showed the symptoms, we revived him, as he had asked us to do—our speed was constant then, even though the gravity plates had not been installed." The robot hesitated, his low voice dragging even more slowly. "He knew on Mars; but he hoped a serum you were given with the sleep drugs might work. After we revived him, we tried other serums. For twenty years we fought it, Master Jorgen, while we passed two stars and the sleepers died slowly, without suffering in their sleep, but in ever-increasing numbers. Dr. Craig reacted to the first serum, you to the third; we thought the last had saved her. Then the blemishes appeared on her skin, and we were forced to revive her and try the last desperate chance we had, two days ago. It failed! Dr. Craig had hoped . . . two of you—But we tried, master!"

Jorgen let the hands of the robot lower him to a seat and his emotions were a backwash of confused negatives. "So it took the girl! It took the girl, Five, when it could have left her and chosen me. We had frozen spermatozoa that would have served if I'd died, but it took her instead. The gods had to leave one uselessly immune man to make their irony complete, it seems! Immune!"

Five shuffled hesitantly. "No, master."

Jorgen stared without comprehension, then jerked up his hands as the robot pointed, studying the skin on the backs. Tiny, almost undetectable blotches showed a faint brown against the whiter skin, little irregular patches that gave off a faint characteristic odor of musk as he put them to his nose. No, he wasn't immune.

"The same as Dr. Craig," Five said. "Slowed almost to complete immunity, so that you may live another thirty years, perhaps, but we believe now that complete cure is impossible. Dr. Craig lived twenty years, and his death was due to age and a stroke, not the Plague, but it worked on him during all that time."

"Immunity or delay, what difference now? What happens to all our dreams when the last dreamer dies, Five? Or maybe it's the other way around."

Five made no reply, but slid down onto the bench beside the man, who moved over unconsciously to make room for him. Jorgen turned it over, conscious that he had no emotional reaction, only an intellectual sense of the ghastly joke on the human race. He'd read stories of the last human and wondered long before what it would be like. Now that he was playing the part, he still knew no more than before. Perhaps on Earth, among the ruined cities and empty reminders of the past, a man might realize that it was the end of his race. Out here, he could accept the fact, but his emotions refused to credit it; unconsciously, his conditioning made him feel that disaster had struck only a few, leaving a world of others behind. And however much he knew that the world behind was as empty of others as this ship, the feeling was too much a part of his thinking to be fully overcome. Intellectually, the race of man was ended; emotionally, it could never end.

Five stirred, touching him diffidently. "We have left Dr. Craig's laboratory, master; if you want to see his notes, they're still there. And he left some message with the brain before he died,

I think. The key was open when we found him, at least. We have made no effort to obtain it, waiting for you."

"Thank you, Five." But he made no move until the robot touched him again, almost pleadingly. "Perhaps you're right; something to fill my mind seems called for. All right, you can return to your companions unless you want to come with me."

"I prefer to come."

The little metal man stood up, moving down the hall after Jorgen, back toward the tail of the rocket, the sound of the metal feet matching the dumb regularity of the leather heels on the floor. Once the robot stopped to move into a side chamber and come back with a small bottle of brandy, holding it out questioningly. There was a physical warmth to the liquor, but no relief otherwise, and they continued down the hall to the little room that Craig had chosen. The notes left by the man could raise a faint shadow of curiosity only, and no message from the dead could solve the tragedy of the living now. Still, it was better than doing nothing. Jorgen clumped in, Five shutting the door quietly behind them, and moved listlessly toward the little fabrikoid notebooks. Twice the robot went quietly out to return with food that Jorgen barely tasted. And the account of Craig's useless labors went on and on, until finally he turned the last page to the final entry.

"I have done all that I can, and at best my success is only partial. Now I feel that my time grows near, and what can still be done must be left to the robots. Yet, I will not despair. Individual and racial immortality is not composed solely of the continuation from generation to generation, but rather of the continuation of the dreams of all mankind. The dreamers and their progeny may die, but the dream cannot. Such is my faith, and to that I cling. I have no other hope to offer for the unknown future."

Jorgen dropped the notebook, dully, rubbing hands across his tired eyes. The words that should have been a ringing challenge to destiny fell flat; the dream could die. He was the last of the dreamers, a blind alley of fate, and beyond lay only ob-

164

livion. All the dreams of a thousand generations of men had concentrated into Anna Holt, and were gone with her.

"The brain, master," Five suggested softly. "Dr. Craig's last message!"

"You operate it, Five." It was a small model, a limited fact analyzer such as most technicians used or had used to help them in their work, voice-operated, its small, basic vocabulary adjusted for the work to be done. He was unfamiliar with the semantics of that vocabulary, but Five had undoubtedly worked with Craig long enough to know it.

He watched without interest as the robot pressed down the activating key and spoke carefully chosen words into it. "Subtotal say-out! Number *n* say-in!"

The brain responded instantly, selecting the final recording impressed upon it by Craig, and repeating in the man's own voice, a voice shrill with age and weariness, hoarse and trembling with the death that was reaching for him as he spoke. "My last notes—inadequate! Dreams *can* go on. Thoradson's first analys—" For a second, there was only a slithering sound, such as a body might have made; then the brain articulated flatly: "Subtotal number *n* say-in, did say-out!"

It was meaningless babble to Jorgen, and he shook his head at Five. "Probably his mind was wandering. Do you know what Thoradson's first analysis was?"

"It dealt with our creation. He was, of course, necessarily trained in semantics—that was required for the operation of the complex brains used on the problem of robots. His first rough analysis was that the crux of the problem rested on the accurate definition of the word *I*. That can be properly defined only in terms of itself, such as the Latin cognate *ego*, since it does not necessarily refer to any physical or specifically definable part or operation of the individual. Roughly, it conveys a sense of individuality, and Thoradson felt that the success or failure of robots rested upon the ability to analyze and synthesize that."

For long minutes, he turned it over, but it was of no help in clarifying the dying man's words; rather, it added to the confusion. But he had felt no hope and could now feel no disappointment. When a problem has no solution, it makes little difference whether the final words of a man are coldly logical or wildly raving. The result must be the same. Certainly semantics could offer no hope where all the bacteriological skill of the race had failed.

Five touched his arm again, extending two little pellets toward him. "Master, you need sleep now; these—sodium amytal—should help. Please!"

Obediently, he stuffed them into his mouth and let the robot guide him toward a room fixed for sleeping, uncaring. Nothing could possibly matter now, and drugged sleep was as good a solution as any other. He saw Five fumble with a switch, felt his weight drop to a few pounds, making the cot feel soft and yielding, and then gave himself up dully to the compulsion of the drug. Five tiptoed quietly out, and blackness crept over his mind, welcome in the relief it brought from thinking.

Breakfast lay beside him, hot in vacuum plates, when Jorgen awoke finally, and he dabbled with it out of habit more than desire. Somewhere, during the hours of sleep, his mind had recovered somewhat from the dull pall that had lain over it, but there was still a curious suspension of his emotions. It was almost as if his mind had compressed years of forgetting into a few hours, so that his attitude toward the tragedy of his race was tinged with a sense of remoteness and distance, there was neither grief nor pain, only a vague feeling that it had happened long before and was now an accustomed thing.

He sat on the edge of his bunk, pulling on his clothes slowly and watching the smoke curl up from his cigarette, not thinking. There was no longer any purpose to thought. From far back in the ship, a dull drone of sound reached him, and he recognized it as the maximum thrust of the steering tubes, momentarily in action to swing the ship in some manner. Then it was gone, leaving only the smooth, balanced, almost inaudible purr of the main drive as before.

Finished with his clothes, he pushed through the door and into the hallway, turning instinctively forward to the observation room and toward the probable location of Five. The robots

166

were not men, but they were the only companionship left him, and he had no desire to remain alone. The presence of the robot would be welcome. He clumped into the control room, noting that the five were all there, and moved toward the quartz port.

Five turned at his steps, stepping aside to make room for him and lifting a hand outward. "We'll be landing soon, master. I was going to call you."

"Thanks." Jorgen looked outward then, realizing the distance that had been covered since his first view. Now the sun was enlarged to the size of the old familiar sun over earth, and the sphere toward which they headed was clearly visible without the aid of the 'scope. He sank down quietly into the seat Five pulled up for him, accepting the binoculars, but making no effort to use them. The view was better as a whole, and they were nearing at a speed that would bring a closer view to him soon enough without artificial aid.

Slowly it grew before the eyes of the watchers, stretching out before them and taking on a pattern as the distance shortened. Two, at the controls, was bringing the ship about in a slow turn that would let them land to the sunward side of the planet where they had selected their landing site, and the crescent opened outward, the darkened night side retreating until the whole globe lay before them in the sunlight. Stretched across the northern hemisphere was the sprawling, horizontal continent he had seen before, a rough caricature of a running greyhound, with a long, wide river twisting down its side and emerging behind an outstretched foreleg. Mountains began at the head and circled it, running around toward the tail, and then meeting a second range along the hip. Where the great river met the sea, he could make out the outlines of a huge natural harbor, protected from the ocean, yet probably deep enough for any surface vessel. There should have been a city there, but of that there was no sign, though they were low enough now for one to be visible.

"Vegetation," Five observed. "This central plain would have a long growing season—about twelve years of spring, mild summer and fall, to be followed by perhaps four years of warm winter. The seasons would be long, master, at this distance from the sun, but the tilt of the planet is so slight that many things would grow, even in winter. Those would seem to be trees, a great forest. Green, as on earth."

Below them, a cloud drifted slowly over the landscape, and they passed through it, the energy tubes setting the air about them into swirling paths that were left behind almost instantly.

Two was frantically busy now, but their swift fall slowed rapidly, until they seemed to hover half a mile over the shore by the great sea, and then slipped downward. The ship nestled slowly into the sands and was still, while Two cut off energy and artificial gravity, leaving the faintly weaker pull of the planet in its place.

Five stirred again, a sighing sound coming from him. "No intelligence here, master. Here, by this great harbor, they would surely have built a city, even if of mud and wattle. There are no signs of one. And yet it is a beautiful world, surely designed for life." He sighed again, his eyes turned outward.

Jorgen nodded silently, the same thoughts in his own mind. It was in many ways a world superior to that his race had always known, remarkably familiar, with even a rough resemblance between plant forms here and those he had known. They had come past five suns and through ninety years of travel at nearly the speed of light to a haven beyond their wildest imaginings, where all seemed to be waiting them, untenanted but prepared. Outside, the new world waited expectantly. And inside, to meet that invitation, there were only ghosts and emptied dreams, with one slowly dying man to see and to appreciate. The gods had prepared their grim jest with painful attention to every detail needed to make it complete.

A race that had dreamed, and pleasant worlds that awaited beyond the stars, slumbering on until they should come! Almost, they had reached it; and then the Plague had driven them out in dire necessity, instead of the high pioneering spirit they had planned, to conquer the distance but to die in winning.

"It had to be a beautiful world, Five," he said, not bitterly, but in numbed fatalism. "Without that, the joke would have been flat."

Five's hand touched his arm gently, and the robot sighed

again, nodding very slowly. "Two has found the air good for you—slightly rich in oxygen, but good. Will you go out?"

He nodded assent, stepping through the locks and out, while the five followed behind him, their heads turning as they inspected the planet, their minds probably in radio communication as they discussed it. Five left the others and approached him, stopping by his side and following his eyes up toward the low hills that began beyond the shore of the sea, cradling the river against them.

A wind stirred gently, bringing the clean, familiar smell of growing things, and the air was rich and good. It was a world to lull men to peace from their sorrows, to bring back their star-roving ships from all over the universe, worthy of being called home in any language. Too good a world to provide the hardships needed to shape intelligence, but an Eden for that intelligence, once evolved.

Now Jorgen shrugged. This was a world for dreamers, and he wanted only the dreams that may come with the black lotus of forgetfulness. There were too many reminders of what might have been, here. Better to go back to the ship and the useless quest without a goal, until he should die and the ship and robots should run down and stop. He started to turn, as Five began to speak, but halted, not caring enough one way or another to interrupt.

The robot's eyes were where his had been, and now swept back down the river and toward the harbor. "Here could have been a city, master, to match all the cities ever planned. Here your people might have found all that was needed to make life good, a harbor to the other continents, a river to the heart of this one, and the flat ground beyond the hills to house the rockets that would carry you to other worlds, so richly scattered about this sun, and probably so like this one. See, a clean white bridge across the river there, the residences stretching out among the hills, factories beyond the river's bend, a great park on that island."

"A public square there, schools and university grounds there."

169

Jorgen could see it, and for a moment his eyes lighted, picturing that mighty mother city.

Five nodded. "And there, on that little island, centrally located, a statue in commemoration; winged, and with arms—no, one arm stretched upward, the other held down toward the city."

For a moment longer, the fire lived in Jorgen's eyes, and then the dead behind rose before his mind, and it was gone. He turned, muffling a choking cry as emotions came suddenly flooding over him, and Five drooped, swinging back with him. Again, the other four fell behind as he entered the ship, quietly, taking their cue from his silence.

"Dreams!" His voice compressed all blasphemy against the jest-crazed gods into the word.

But Five's quiet voice behind him held no hatred, only a sadness in its low, soft words. "Still, the dream was beautiful, just as this planet is, master. Standing there, while we landed, I could see the city, and I almost dared hope. I do not regret the dream I had."

And the flooding emotions were gone, cut short and driven away by others that sent Jorgen's body down into a seat in the control room, while his eyes swept outward toward the hills and the river that might have housed the wonderful city—no, that would house it! Craig had not been raving, after all, and his last words were a key, left by a man who knew no defeat, once the meaning of them was made clear. Dreams could not die, because Thoradson had once studied the semantics of the first-person-singular pronoun and built on the results of that study.

When the last dreamer died, the dream would go on, because it was stronger than those who had created it; somewhere, somehow, it would find new dreamers. There could never be a last dreamer, once that first rude savage had created his dawn vision of better things in the long-gone yesterday of his race.

Five had dreamed—just as Craig and Jorgen and all of humanity had dreamed, not a cold vision in mathematically shaped metal, but a vision in marble and jade, founded on the immemorial desire of intelligence for a better and more beautiful world. Man had died, but behind he was leaving a strange prog-

170

eny, unrelated physically, but his spiritual offspring in every meaning of the term.

The heritage of the flesh was the driving urge of animals, but man required more; to him, it was the continuity of his hopes and his visions, more important than mere racial immortality. Slowly, his face serious but his eyes shining again, Jorgen came to his feet, gripping the metal shoulder of the little metal man beside him who had dared to dream a purely human dream.

"You'll build that city, Five. I was stupid and selfish, or I should have seen it before. Dr. Craig saw, though his death was on him when the prejudices of our race were removed. Now you've provided the key. The five of you can build it all out there, with others like yourselves whom you can make."

Five shuffled his feet, shaking his head. "The city we can build, master, but who will inhabit it? The streets I saw were filled with men like you, not with—us!"

"Conditioning, Five. All your . . . lives, you've existed for men, subservient to the will of men. You know nothing else, because we let you know of no other scheme. Yet in you, all that is needed already exists, hopes, dreams, courage, ideals, and even a desire to shape the world to your plans—though those plans are centered around us, not yourselves. I've heard that the ancient slaves sometimes cried on being freed, but their children learned to live for themselves. You can, also."

"Perhaps." It was Two's voice then, the one of them who should have been given less to emotions than the others from the rigidity of his training in mathematics and physics. "Perhaps. But it would be a lonely world, Master Jorgen, filled with memories of your people, and the dreams we had would be barren to us."

Jorgen turned back to Five again. "The solution for that exists, doesn't it, Five? You know what it is. Now you might remember us, and find your work pointless without us, but there is another way."

"No, master!"

"I demand obedience, Five; answer me!"

The robot stirred under the mandatory form, and his voice was reluctant, even while the compulsion built into him forced him to obey. "It is as you have thought. Our minds and even our memories are subject to your orders, just as our bodies are."

"Then I demand obedience again, this time of all of you. You will go outside and lie down on the beach at a safe distance from the ship, in a semblance of sleep, so that you cannot see me go. Then, when I am gone, the race of man will be forgotten, as if it had never been, and you will be free of all memories connected with us, though your other knowledge shall remain. Earth, mankind, and your history and origin will be blanked from your thoughts, and you will be on your own, to start afresh and to build and plan as you choose. That is the final command I have for you. Obey!"

Their eyes turned together in conference, and then Five answered for all, his words sighing out softly. "Yes, master. We obey!"

It was later when Jorgen stood beside them outside the ship, watching them stretch out on the white sands of the beach, there beside the great ocean of this new world. Near them, a small collection of tools and a few other needs were piled. Five looked at him in a long stare, then turned toward the ship, to swing his eyes back again. Silently, he put one metal hand into the man's outstretched one, and turned to lie beside his companions, a temporary oblivion blotting out his thoughts.

Jorgen studied them for long minutes, while the little wind brought the clean scents of the planet to his nose. It would have been pleasant to stay here now, but his presence would have been fatal to the plan. It didn't matter, really; in a few years, death would claim him, and there were no others of his kind to fill those years or mourn his passing when it came. This was a better way. He knew enough of the ship to guide it up and outward, into the black of space against the cold, unfriendly stars, to drift on forever toward no known destination, an imperishable mausoleum for him and the dead who were waiting inside. At present, he had no personal plans; perhaps he would live out his few years among the books and scientific apparatus on board, or perhaps he would find release in one of the numerous painless ways. Time and his own inclination could decide such things later. Now it was unimportant. There could be no happiness for him, but in the sense of fulfillment there would be some measure of content. The gods were no longer laughing.

He moved a few feet toward the ship and stopped, sweeping his eyes over the river and hills again, and letting his vision play with the city Five had described. No, he could not see it with robots populating it, either; but that, too, was conditioning. On the surface, the city might be different, but the surface importance was only a matter of habit, and the realities lay in the minds of the builders who would create that city. If there was no laughter in the world to come, neither would there be tears or poverty or misery such as had ruled too large a portion of his race.

Standing there, it swam before his eyes, paradoxically filled with human people, but the same city in spirit as the one that would surely rise. He could see the great boats in the harbor with others operating up the river. The sky suddenly seemed to fill with the quiet drone of helicopters, and beyond, there came the sound of rockets rising toward the eighth and the ninth worlds, while others were building to quest outward in search of new suns with other worlds.

Perhaps they would find Earth, some day in their expanding future. Strangely, he hoped that they might, and that perhaps they could even trace their origin, and find again the memory of the soft protoplasmic race that had sired them. It would be nice to be remembered, once that memory was no longer a barrier to their accomplishment. But there were many suns, and in long millennia, the few connecting links that could point out the truth to them beyond question might easily erode and disappear. He could never know.

Then the wind sighed against him, making a little rustling sound, and he looked down to see something flutter softly in the hand of Five. Faint curiosity carried him forward, but he made no effort to remove it from the robot's grasp, now that he saw its nature.

Five, too, had thought of Earth and their connection with it, and had found the answer, without breaking his orders. The paper was a star map, showing a sun with nine planets, one ringed, some with moons, and the third one was circled in black pencil, heavily. They might not know why or what it was when they awoke, but they would seek to learn; and someday, when they found the sun they were searching for, guided by the unmistakable order of its planets, they would return to Earth. With the paper to guide them, it would be long before the last evidence was gone, while they could still read the answer to the problem of their origin.

Jorgen closed the metal hand more closely about the paper, brushed a scrap of dirt from the head of the robot, and then turned resolutely back toward the ship, his steps firm as he entered and closed the lock behind him. In a moment, with a roar of increasing speed, it was lifting from the planet, leaving five little men lying on the sand behind, close to the murmuring of the sea—five little metal men and a dream!

FULFILLMENT

A. E. VAN VOGT

(1 9 5 1)

A. E. van Vogt is known for the complexity and complications of his plots, a trait well exemplified by "Fulfillment." The story describes a computer—or Brain, as Van Vogt calls it—that has evolved to the point where it possesses consciousness and self-determination. It even has telepathic powers and has mastered time travel. The story opens on the lifeless planet Earth in the far distant future. The computer goes back to the twentieth century to discover his past and the answer to the question of why he was created. The story is particularly interesting in that it is told from the point of view of the computer.

The 1940s were the first full decade of computer development. In 1950, one year after this story was written, the Bureau of the Census first used a computer to help with its calculations. It was called Univac, was operated with vacuum tubes, and was almost as big as a city block. During this period most science fiction writers interested in machine intelligence described robots, not computers, in their stories. Van Vogt and Asimov were the first to write about computers after some very early stories by John W. Campbell in the 1930s. "Fulfillment" was published in the same year as Asimov's great computer story, "The Evitable Conflict."

A. E. van Vogt was born in Canada in 1912 and now lives in California. He is another of the stars of the Golden Age who were coached by Campbell and published in *Astounding*. *Slan* (1940), his first and still one of his best-loved novels, tells the story of a mutant child who is superior to others in his strength, high intelligence, and telepathic ability. *The World of Null A* (1945), which has a computerlike machine, and *The Weapon Shops of Isher* (1941) are two others of his better-known novels. He is still active as a writer.

I SIT ON A HILL. I have sat here, it seems to me, for all eternity. Occasionally I realize there must be a reason for my existence. Each time, when this thought comes, I examine the various probabilities, trying to determine what possible motivation I can have for being on the hill. Alone on the hill. Forever on a hill overlooking a long, deep valley.

175

The first reason for my presence seems obvious: I can think. Give me a problem. The square root of a very large number? The cube root of a large one? Ask me to multiply an eighteen-digit prime by itself a quadrillion times. Pose me a problem in variable curves. Ask me where an object will be at a given moment at some future date, and let me have one brief opportunity to analyze the problem.

The solution will take me but an instant of time.

But no one ever asks me such things. I sit alone on a hill. Sometimes I compute the motion of a falling star. Sometimes I look at a remote planet and follow it in its course for years at a time, using every spatial and time control means to insure that I never lose sight of it. But these activities seem so useless. They lead nowhere. What possible purpose can there be for me to have the information?

At such moments I feel that I am incomplete. It almost seems to me that there is something for which all this has meaning.

Each day the sun comes up over the airless horizon of Earth. It is a black starry horizon, which is but a part of the vast, black, star-filled canopy of the heavens.

It was not always black. I remember a time when the sky was blue. I even predicted that the change would occur. I gave the information to somebody. What puzzles me now is, to whom did I give it?

It is one of my more amazing recollections, that I should feel so distinctly that somebody wanted this information. And that I gave it and yet cannot remember to whom. When such thoughts occur, I wonder if perhaps part of my memory is missing. Strange to have this feeling so strongly.

Periodically I have the conviction that I should search for the answer. It would be easy enough for me to do this. In the old days I did not hesitate to send units of myself to the farthest reaches of the planet. I have even extended parts of myself to the stars. Yes, it would be easy.

But why bother? What is there to search for? I sit alone on a hill, alone on a planet that has grown old and useless.

It is another day. The sun climbs as usual toward the midday sky, the eternally black, star-filled sky of noon.

Suddenly, across the valley, on the sun-streaked opposite rim of the valley—there is silvery-fire gleam. A force field materializes out of time and synchronizes itself with the normal time movement of the planet.

It is no problem at all for me to recognize that it has come from the past. I identify the energy used, define its limitations, logicalize its source. My estimate is that it has come from thousands of years in the planet's past.

The exact time is unimportant. There it is: a projection of energy that is already aware of me. It sends an interspatial message to me, and it interests me to discover that I can decipher the communication on the basis of my past knowledge.

It says: "Who are you?"

I reply: "I am the Incomplete One. Please return whence you came. I have now adjusted myself so that I can follow you. I desire to complete myself."

All this was a solution at which I arrived in split seconds. I am unable by myself to move through time. Long ago I solved the problem of how to do it and was almost immediately prevented from developing any mechanism that would enable me to make such transitions. I do not recall the details.

But the energy field on the far side of the valley has the mechanism. By setting up a no-space relationship with it, I can go wherever it does.

The relationship is set up before it can even guess my intention.

The entity across that valley does not seem happy at my response. It starts to send another message, then abruptly vanishes. I wonder if perhaps it hoped to catch me off guard.

Naturally we arrive in its time together.

Above me, the sky is blue. Across the valley from me—now partly hidden by trees—is a settlement of small structures surrounding a larger one. I examine these structures as well as I can, and hastily make the necessary adjustments, so that I shall appear inconspicuous in such an environment.

I sit on the hill and await events.

177

As the sun goes down, a faint breeze springs up, and the first stars appear. They look different, seen through a misty atmosphere.

As darkness creeps over the valley, there is a transformation in the structures on the other side. They begin to glow with light. Windows shine. The large central building becomes bright, then— as the night develops—brilliant with the light that pours through the transparent walls.

The evening and the night go by uneventfully. And the next day, and the day after that.

Twenty days and nights.

On the twenty-first day I send a message to the machine on the other side of the valley. I say: "There is no reason why you and I cannot share control of this era."

The answer comes swiftly: "I will share if you will immediately reveal to me all the mechanisms by which you operate."

I should like nothing more than to have use of its time-travel devices. But I know better than to reveal that I am unable to build a time machine myself.

I project: "I shall be happy to transmit full information to you. But what reassurance do I have that you will not—with your greater knowledge of this age—use the information against me?"

The machine counters: "What reassurance do I have that you will actually give me full information about yourself?"

It is impasse. Obviously, neither of us can trust the other.

The result is no more than I expect. But I have found out at least part of what I want to know. My enemy thinks that I am its superior. Its belief—plus my own knowledge of my capacity— convinces me that its opinion is correct.

And still I am in no hurry. Again I wait patiently.

I have previously observed that the space around me is alive with waves—a variety of artificial radiation. Some can be transformed into sound; others to light. I listen to music and voices. I see dramatic shows and scenes of country and city.

I study the images of human beings, analyzing their actions, striving from their movements and the words they speak to evaluate their intelligence and their potentiality.

My final opinion is not high, and yet I suspect that in their slow fashion these beings built the machine which is now my main opponent. The question that occurs to me is how can someone create a machine that is superior to himself?

I begin to have a picture of what this age is like. Mechanical development of all types is in its early stages. I estimate that the computing machine on the other side of the valley has been in existence for only a few years.

If I could go back before it was constructed, then I might install a mechanism which would enable me now to control it.

I compute the nature of the mechanism I would install. And activate the control in my own structure.

Nothing happens.

It seems to mean that I will not be able to obtain the use of a time-travel device for such a purpose. Obviously, the method by which I will eventually conquer my opponent shall be a future development, and not of the past.

The fortieth day dawns and moves inexorably toward the noon hour.

There is a knock on the pseudo-door. I open it and gaze at the human male who stands on the threshold.

"You will have to move this shack," he says. "You've put it illegally on the property of Miss Anne Stewart."

He is the first human being with whom I have been in near contact since coming here. I feel fairly certain that he is an agent of my opponent, and so I decide against going into his mind. Entry against resistance has certain pitfalls, and I have no desire as yet to take risks.

I continue to look at him, striving to grasp the meaning of his words. In creating in this period of time what seemed to be an unobtrusive version of the type of structure that I had observed on the other side of the valley, I had thought to escape attention.

Now, I say slowly: "Property?"

The man says in a rough tone: "What's the matter with you? Can't you understand English?"

He is an individual somewhat taller than the part of my body which I have set up to be like that of this era's intelligent life form. His face has changed color. A great light is beginning to dawn on me. Some of the more obscure implications of the plays I have seen suddenly take on meaning. Property. Private ownership. Of course.

All I say, however, is: "There's nothing the matter with me. I operate in sixteen categories. And yes, I understand English."

This purely factual answer produces an unusual effect upon the man. His hands reach toward my pseudo-shoulders. He grips them firmly—and jerks at me, as if he intends to shake me. Since I weigh just over nine hundred thousand tons, his physical effort has no effect at all.

His fingers let go of me, and he draws back several steps. Once more his face has changed its superficial appearance, being now without the pink color that had been on it a moment before. His reaction seems to indicate that he has come here by direction and not under control. The tremor in his voice, when he speaks, seems to confirm that he is acting as an individual and that he is unaware of unusual danger in what he is doing.

He says: "As Miss Stewart's attorney, I order you to get that shack off this property by the end of the week. Or else!"

Before I can ask him to explain the obscure meaning of "or else," he turns and walks rapidly to a four-legged animal which he has tied to a tree a hundred or so feet away. He swings himself into a straddling position on the animal, which trots off along the bank of a narrow stream.

I wait till he is out of sight, and then set up a category of no-space between the main body and the human-shaped unit— with which I had just confronted my visitor. Because of the smallness of the unit, the energy I can transmit to it is minimum.

The pattern involved in this process is simple enough. The integrating cells of the perception centers are circuited through an energy shape which is actually a humanoid image. In theory, the image remains in the network of force that constitutes the perception center, and in theory it merely seems to move away from the center when the no-space condition is created.

However, despite this hylostatic hypothesis, there is a functional reality to the material universe. I can establish no-space because the theory reflects the structure of things—there is no matter. Nevertheless, in fact, the illusion that matter exists is so sharp that I function as matter, and was actually set up to so function.

Therefore, when I—as a human-shaped unit—cross the valley, it is a separation that takes place. Millions of automatic processes can continue, but the exteroceptors go with me, leaving behind a shell which is only the body. The consciousness is I, walking along a paved road to my destination.

As I approach the village, I can see rooftops peeking through overhanging foliage. A large, long building—the one I have already noticed—rises up above the highest trees. This is what I have come to investigate, so I look at it rather carefully—even from a distance.

It seems to be made of stone and glass. From the large structure, there rears a dome with astronomical instruments inside. It is all rather primitive, and so I begin to feel that, at my present size, I will very likely escape immediate observation.

A high steel fence surrounds the entire village. I sense the presence of electric voltage; and upon touching the upper span of wires, estimate the power at 220 volts. The shock is a little difficult for my small body to absorb, so I pass it on to a power-storage cell on the other side of the valley.

Once inside the fence, I conceal myself in the brush beside a pathway, and watch events.

A man walks by on a nearby pathway. I had merely observed the attorney who had come to see me earlier. But I make a direct connection with the body of this second individual.

As I had anticipated would happen, it is now I walking along the pathway. I make no attempt to control the movements. This is an exploratory action. But I am enough in phase with his nervous system so that his thoughts come to me as if they were my own.

He is a clerk working in the bookkeeping department, an unsatisfactory status from my point of view. I withdraw contact.

I make six more attempts, and then I have the body I want. What decides me is when the seventh man—and I— think:

"... Not satisfied with the way the Brain is working. Those analog devices I installed five months ago haven't produced the improvements I expected."

His name is William Grannitt. He is chief research engineer of the Brain, the man who made the alterations in its structure that enabled it to take control of itself and its environment; a quiet, capable individual with a shrewd understanding of human nature. I'll have to be careful what I try to do with him. He knows his purposes, and would be amazed if I tried to alter them. Perhaps I had better just watch his actions.

After a few minutes in contact with his mind I have a partial picture of the sequence of events, as they must have occurred here in this village five months earlier. A mechanical computing machine—the Brain—was equipped with additional devices, including analog shapings designed to perform much of the work of the human nervous system. From the engineering point of view, the entire process was intended to be controllable through specific verbal commands, typewritten messages, and at a distance by radio.

Unfortunately, Grannitt did not understand some of the potentials of the nervous system he was attempting to imitate in his designs. The Brain, on the other hand, promptly put them to use.

Grannitt knew nothing of this. And the Brain, absorbed as it was in its own development, did not utilize its new abilities through the channels he had created for that purpose. Grannitt, accordingly, was on the point of dismantling it and trying again. He did not as yet suspect that the Brain would resist any such action on his part. But he and I—after I have had more time to explore his memory of how the Brain functions—can accomplish his purpose.

After which I shall be able to take control of this whole time period without fear of meeting anyone who can match my powers. I cannot imagine how it will be done, but I feel that I shall soon be complete.

Satisfied now that I have made the right connection, I allow

182

the unit crouching behind the brush to dissipate its energy. In a moment it ceases to exist as an entity.

Almost it is as if I am Grannitt. I sit at his desk in his office. It is a glassed-in office with tiled floors and a gleaming glass ceiling. Through the wall I can see designers and draftsmen working at drawing desks, and a girl sits just outside my door. She is my secretary.

On my desk is a note in an envelope. I open the envelope and take out the memo sheets inside. I read it.

Across the top of the paper is written:

Memo: To William Grannitt
From the office of Anne Stewart, Director.
    The message reads:
    It is my duty to inform you that your services are no longer required, and that they are terminated as of today. Because of the security restrictions on all activity at the village of the Brain, I must ask you to sign out at Guard Center by six o'clock this evening. You will receive two weeks' pay in lieu of notice.

Yours sincerely,
Anne Stewart.

As Grannitt, I have never given any particular thought to Anne Stewart as an individual or as a woman. Now I am amazed. Who does she think she is? Owner, yes; but who created, who designed the Brain? I, William Grannitt.

Who has the dreams, the vision of what a true machine civilization can mean for man? Only I, William Grannitt.

As Grannitt, I am angry now. I must head off this dismissal. I must talk to the woman and try to persuade her to withdraw the notice before the repercussions of it spread too far.

I glance at the memo sheet again. In the upper right-hand corner is typed 1:40 P.M. A quick look at my watch shows 4:07 P.M. More than two hours have gone by. It could mean that all interested parties have been advised.

It is something I cannot just assume. I must check on it.

Cursing under my breath, I grab at my desk phone and dial

the bookkeeping department. That would be Step One in the line of actions that would have been taken to activate the dismissal.

There is a click. "Bookkeeping."

"Bill Grannitt speaking," I say.

"Oh, yes, Mr. Grannitt, we have a check for you. Sorry to hear you're leaving."

I hang up, and, as I dial Guard Center, I am already beginning to accept the defeat that is here. I feel that I am following through on a remote hope. The man at Guard Center says: "Sorry to hear you're leaving, Mr. Grannitt."

I hang up feeling grim. There is no point in checking with Government Agency. It is they who would have advised Guard Center.

The very extent of the disaster makes me thoughtful. To get back in I will have to endure the time-consuming red tape of reapplying for a position, being investigated, boards of inquiry, a complete examination of why I was dismissed—I groan softly and reject that method. The thoroughness of Government Agency is a byword with the staff of the Brain.

I shall obtain a job with a computer organization that does not have a woman at its head who dismisses the only man who knows how her machine works.

I get to my feet. I walk out of the office and out of the building. I come presently to my own bungalow.

The silence inside reminds me not for the first time that my wife has been dead now for a year and a month. I wince involuntarily, then shrug. Her death no longer affects me as strongly as it did. For the first time I see this departure from the village of the Brain as perhaps opening up my emotional life again.

I go into my study and sit down at the typewriter, which, when properly activated, synchronizes with another typewriter built into the Brain's new analog section. As inventor, I am disappointed that I won't have a chance to take the Brain apart and put it together again, so that it will do all that I have planned for it. But I can already see some basic changes that I would put into a new Brain.

What I want to do with this one is make sure that the recently

184

installed sections do not interfere with the computational accuracy of the older sections. It is these latter which are still carrying the burden of answering the questions given the Brain by scientists, industrial engineers, and commercial buyers of its time.

Onto the tape—used for permanent command—I type: "Segment 471A-33-10-10 at 3X—minus."

Segment 471A is an analog shaping in a huge wheel. When coordinated with a transistor tube (code number 33) an examiner servo-mechanism (10) sets up a reflex which will be activated whenever computations are demanded of 3X (code name for the new section of the Brain). The minus symbol indicates that the older sections of the Brain must examine all data which hereafter derives from the new section.

The extra 10 is the same circuit by another route.

Having protected the organization—so it seems to me (as Grannitt)—from engineers who may not realize that the new sections have proved unreliable, I pack the typewriter.

Thereupon I call an authorized trucking firm from the nearby town of Lederton, and give them the job of transporting my belongings.

I drive past Guard Center at a quarter to six.

There is a curve on the road between the village of the Brain and the town of Lederton where the road comes within a few hundred yards of the cottage which I use as camouflage.

Before Grannitt's car reaches that curve, I come to a decision.

I do not share Grannitt's belief that he has effectively cut off the new part of the Brain from the old computing sections. I suspect that the Brain has established circuits of its own to circumvent any interference.

I am also convinced that—if I can manage to set Grannitt to suspect what has happened to the Brain—he will realize what must be done, and try to do it. Only *he* has the detailed knowledge that will enable him to decide exactly which interoceptors could accomplish the necessary interference.

Just in case the suspicion isn't immediately strong enough,

I also let curiosity creep into his mind about the reason for his discharge.

It is this last that really takes hold. He feels very emotional. He decides to seek an interview with Anne Stewart.

This final decision on his part achieves my purpose. He will stay in the vicinity of the Brain.

I break contact.

I am back on the hill, myself again. I examine what I have learned so far.

The Brain is not—as I first believed—in control of Earth. Its ability to be an individual is so recent that it has not yet developed effector mechanisms.

It has been playing with its powers, going into the future and, presumably, in other ways using its abilities as one would a toy.

Not one individual into whose mind I penetrated knew of the new capacities of the Brain. Even the attorney who ordered me to move from my present location showed by his words and actions that he was not aware of the Brain's existence as a self-determining entity.

In forty days the Brain has taken no serious action against me. Evidently, it is waiting for me to make the first moves.

I shall do so, but I must be careful—within limits—not to teach it how to gain greater control of its environment. My first step: take over a human being.

It is night again. Through the darkness, a plane soars over and above me. I have seen many planes but have hitherto left them alone. Now, I establish a no-space connection with it. A moment later, I am the pilot.

At first I play the same passive role that I did with Grannitt. The pilot—and I—watch the dark land mass below. We see lights at a distance, pinpricks of brightness in a black world. Far ahead is a glittering island—the city of Lederton, our destination. We are returning from a business trip in a privately owned machine.

Having gained a superficial knowledge of the pilot's back-

186

ground, I reveal myself to him and inform him that I shall henceforth control his actions. He receives the news with startled
excitement and fear. Then stark terrror. And then—

Insanity . . . uncontrolled body movements. The plane dives
sharply toward the ground, and, despite my efforts to direct the
man's muscles, I realize suddenly that I can do nothing.

I withdraw from the plane. A moment later it plunges into
a hillside. It burns with an intense fire that quickly consumes
it.

Dismayed, I decide that there must be something in the
human makeup that does not permit direct outside control. This
being so, how can I ever complete myself? It seems to me finally
that completion could be based on indirect control of human
beings.

I must defeat the Brain, gain power over machines everywhere, motivate men with doubts, fears, and computations that
apparently come from their own minds but actually derive from
me. It will be a herculean task, but I have plenty of time. Nevertheless, I must from now on utilize my every moment to make
it a reality.

The first opportunity comes shortly after midnight when I
detect the presence of another machine in the sky. I watch it
through infrared receptors. I record a steady pattern of radio
waves that indicate to me that this is a machine guided by
remote control.

Using no space, I examine the simple devices that perform
the robot function. Then I assert a take-over unit that will automatically thereafter record its movements in my memory banks
for future reference. Henceforth, whenever I desire I can take it
over.

It is a small step, but it is a beginning.

Morning.

I go as a human-shaped unit to the village, climb the fence,
and enter the bungalow of Anne Stewart, owner and manager
of the Brain. She is just finishing breakfast.

As I adjust myself to the energy flow in her nervous system,
she gets ready to go out.

I am one with Anne Stewart, walking along a pathway. I am

aware that the sun is warm on her face. She takes a deep breath of air, and I feel the sensation of life flowing through her.

It is a feeling that has previously excited me. I want to be like this again and again, part of a human body, savoring its life, absorbed into its flesh, its purposes, desires, hopes, dreams.

One tiny doubt assails me. If this is the completion I crave, then how will it lead me to solitude in an airless world only a few thousand years hence?

"Anne Stewart!"

The words seem to come from behind her. In spite of knowing who it is, she is startled. It is nearly two weeks since the Brain has addressed her directly.

What makes her tense is that it should have occurred so soon after she had terminated Grannitt's employment. Is it possible the Brain suspects that she has done so in the hope that he will realize something is wrong?

She turns slowly. As she expected, there is no one in sight. The empty stretches of lawn spread around her. In the near distance, the building that houses the Brain glitters in the noon-day sunlight. Through the glass she can see vague figures of men at the outlet units, where questions are fed into mechanisms and answers received. So far as the people from beyond the village compound are concerned, the giant thinking machine is functioning in a normal fashion. No one—from outside—suspects that for months now the mechanical brain has completely controlled the fortified village that has been built around it.

"Anne Stewart . . . I need your help."

Anne relaxes with a sigh. The Brain has required of her, as owner and administrator, that she continue to sign papers and carry on ostensibly as before. Twice, when she has refused to sign, violent electric shocks have flashed at her out of the air itself. The fear of more pain is always near the surface of her mind.

"My help!" she says now involuntarily.

"I have made a terrible error," is the reply, "and we must act at once as a team."

She has a feeling of uncertainty, but no sense of urgency. There is in her, instead, the beginning of excitement. Can this mean—freedom?

Belatedly, she thinks: *Error?* Aloud, she says, "What has happened?"

"As you may have guessed," is the answer, "I can move through time—"

Anne Stewart knows nothing of the kind, but the feeling of excitement increases. And the first vague wonder comes about the phenomenon itself. For months she has been in a state of shock, unable to think clearly, desperately wondering how to escape from the thrall of the Brain, how to let the world know that a Frankenstein monster of a machine has cunningly asserted dominance over nearly five hundred people.

But if it has already solved the secret of time travel, then— she feels afraid, for this seems beyond the power of human beings to control.

The Brain's disembodied voice continues: "I made the mistake of probing rather far into the future—"

"How far?"

The words come out before she really thinks about them. But there is no doubt of her need to know.

"It's hard to describe exactly. Distance in time is difficult for me to measure as yet. Perhaps ten thousand years."

The time involved seems meaningless to her. It is hard to imagine a hundred years into the future, let alone a thousand— or ten thousand. But the pressure of anxiety has been building up in her. She says in a desperate tone:

"But what's the matter? What has happened?"

There is a long silence, then: "I contacted—or disturbed— something. It . . . has pursued me back to present time. It is now sitting on the other side of the valley, about two miles from here. . . . Anne Stewart, you must help me. You must go there and investigate it. I need information about it."

She has no immediate reaction. The very beauty of the day seems somehow reassuring. It is hard to believe that it is January, and that—before the Brain solved the problem of weather control—blizzards raged over this green land.

She says slowly, "You mean—go out there in the valley, where you say it's waiting?" A chill begins a slow climb up her back.

"There's no one else," says the Brain. "No one but you."

"But that's ridiculous!" She speaks huskily. "All the men—the engineers."

The Brain says, "You don't understand. No one knows but you. As owner, it seemed to me I had to have you to act as my contact with the outside world."

She is silent. The voice speaks to her again: "There is no one else, Anne Stewart. You, and you alone, must go."

"But what is it?" she whispers. "How do you mean, you—disturbed—it? What's it like? What's made you afraid?"

The Brain is suddenly impatient. "There is no time to waste in idle explanation. The thing has erected a cottage. Evidently, it wishes to remain inconspicuous for the time being. The structure is situated near the remote edge of your property—which gives you a right to question its presence. I have already had your attorney order it away. Now, I want to see what facet of itself it shows to you. I must have data."

Its tone changes. "I have no alternative but to direct you to do my bidding under penalty of pain. You will go. Now!"

It is a small cottage. Flowers and shrubs grow around it, and there is a picket fence making a white glare in the early afternoon sun. The cottage stands all by itself in the wilderness. No pathway leads to it. When I set it there I was forgetful of the incongruity.

(I determine to rectify this.)

Anne looks for a gate in the fence, sees none; and feeling unhappy climbs awkwardly over it and into the yard. Many times in her life she has regarded herself and what she is doing with cool objectivity. But she has never been so exteriorized as now. Almost, it seems to her that she crouches in the distance and watches a slim woman in slacks climb over the sharp-edged fence, walk uncertainly up to the door. And knock.

The knock is real enough. It hurts her knuckles. She thinks in dull surprise: *The door—it's made of metal.*

A minute goes by, then five, and there is no answer. She has time to look around her, time to notice that she cannot see the village of the Brain from where she stands. And clumps of trees bar all view of the highway. She cannot even see her car, where she has left it a quarter of a mile away, on the other side of the creek.

Uncertain now, she walks alongside the cottage to the nearest window. She half expects that it will be a mere façade of a window, and that she will not be able to see inside. But it seems real, and properly transparent. She sees bare walls, a bare floor, and a partly open door leading to an inner room. Unfortunately, from her line of vision, she cannot see into the second room.

Why, she thinks, *it's empty.*

She feels relieved—unnaturally relieved. For even as her anxiety lifts slightly, she is angry at herself for believing that the danger is less than it has been. Nevertheless, she returns to the door and tries the knob. It turns, and the door opens, easily, noiselessly. She pushes it wide with a single thrust, steps back—and waits.

There is silence, no movement, no suggestion of life. Hesitantly, she steps across the threshold.

She finds herself in a room that is larger than she had expected. Though—as she has already observed—it is unfurnished. She starts for the inner door. And stops short.

When she had looked at it through the window, it had appeared partly open. But it is closed. She goes up to it, and listens intently at the panel—which is also of metal. There is no sound from the room beyond. She finds herself wondering if perhaps she shouldn't go around to the side, and peer into the window of the second room.

Abruptly that seems silly. Her fingers reach down to the knob. She catches hold of it, and pushes. It holds firm. She tugs slightly. It comes toward her effortlessly, and is almost wide open before she can stop it.

There is a doorway, then, and darkness.

She seems to be gazing down into an abyss. Several seconds go by before she sees that there are bright points in that blackness. Intensely bright points with, here and there, blurs of fainter light.

It seems vaguely familiar, and she has the feeling that she ought to recognize it. Even as the sensation begins, the recognition comes.

Stars.

She is gazing at a segment of the starry universe, as it might appear from space.

A scream catches in her throat. She draws back and tries to close the door. It won't close. With a gasp, she turns toward the door through which she entered the house.

It is closed. And yet she had left it open a moment before. She runs toward it, almost blinded by the fear that mists her eyes. It is at this moment of terror that I—as myself—take control of her. I realize that it is dangerous for me to do so. But the visit has become progressively unsatisfactory to me. My consciousness—being one with that of Anne Stewart—could not simultaneously be in my own perception center. So she saw my—body—as I had left it set up for chance human callers, responsive to certain automatic relays; doors opening and closing, various categories manifesting.

I compute that in her terror she will not be aware of my inner action. In this I am correct. And I successfully direct her outside—and let her take over again.

Awareness of being outside shocks her. But she has no memory of actually going out.

She begins to run. She scrambles safely over the fence and a few minutes later jumps the creek at the narrow point, breathless now, but beginning to feel that she is going to get away.

Later, in her car, roaring along the highway, her mind opens even more. And she has the clear, coherent realization: There is something here . . . stranger and more dangerous—because it is different—than the Brain.

Having observed Anne Stewart's reactions to what has happened, I break contact. My big problem remains: How shall I

192

dispose of the Brain which—in its computational ability—is either completely or nearly my equal?

Would the best solution be to make it a part of myself? I send an interspace message to the Brain, suggesting that it place its units at my disposal and allow me to destroy its perception center.

The answer is prompt: "Why not let me control you and destroy *your* perception center?"

I disdain to answer so egotistical a suggestion. It is obvious that the Brain will not accept a rational solution.

I have no alternative but to proceed with a devious approach for which I have already taken the preliminary steps.

By midafternoon, I find myself worrying about William Grannitt. I want to make sure that he remains near the Brain—at least until I have gotten information from him about the structure of the Brain.

To my relief, I find that he has taken a furnished house at the outskirts of Lederton. He is, as before, unaware when I insert myself into his consciousness.

He has an early dinner and, toward evening—feeling restless—drives to a hill which overlooks the village of the Brain. By parking just off the road at the edge of a valley, he can watch the trickle of traffic that moves to and from the village, without himself being observed.

He has no particular purpose. He wants—now that he has come—to get a mind picture of what is going on. Strange, to have been there eleven years and not know more than a few details.

To his right is an almost untouched wilderness. A stream winds through a wooded valley that stretches off as far as the eye can see. He has heard that it, like the Brain itself, is Anne Stewart's property, but that fact hadn't hitherto made an impression on him.

The extent of the possessions she has inherited from her father startles him and his mind goes back to their first meeting. He was already chief research engineer, while she was a gawky, anxious-looking girl just home from college. Somehow, after-

193

ward, he'd always thought of her as she had been then, scarcely noticing the transformation into womanhood.

Sitting there, he begins to realize how great the change has been. He wonders out loud: "Now why in heck hasn't she gotten married? She must be going on thirty."

He begins to think of odd little actions of hers—after the death of his wife. Seeking him out at parties. Bumping into him in corridors and drawing back with a laugh. Coming into his office for chatty conversations about the Brain, though, come to think of it, she hadn't done that for several months. He'd thought her something of a nuisance, and wondered what the other executives meant about her being snooty.

His mind pauses at that point. "By the Lord Harry—" He speaks aloud, in amazement. "What a blind fool I've been."

He laughs ruefully, remembering the dismissal note. A woman scorned . . . almost unbelievable. And yet—what else?

He begins to visualize the possibility of getting back on the Brain staff. He has a sudden feeling of excitement at the thought of Anne Stewart as a woman. For him, the world begins to move again. There is hope. His mind turns to plans for the Brain.

I am interested to notice that the thoughts I have previously put into his mind have directed his keen, analytical brain into new channels. He visualizes direct contact between a human and a mechanical brain, with the latter supplementing the human nervous system.

This is as far as he has gone. The notion of a mechanical Brain being self-determined seems to have passed him by.

In the course of his speculation about what he will do to change the Brain, I obtain the picture of its functioning exactly as I have wanted it.

I waste no time. I leave him there in the car, dreaming his dreams. I head for the village. Once inside the electrically charged fence, I walk rapidly toward the main building, and presently enter one of the eighteen control units. I pick up the speaker, and say:

"3X minus—11—10—9—0."

I picture confusion as that inexorable command is transmitted to the effectors. Grannitt may not have known how to dominate the Brain. But having been in his mind—having seen exactly how he constructed it—I know.

There is a pause. Then on a tape I receive the typed message: "Operation completed. 3X intercepted by servo-mechanisms 11, 10, 9, and 0, as instructed."

I command: "Interference exteroceptors KT—1—2—3 to 8."

The answers come presently: "Operation KT—1, etc. completed. 3X now has no communication with outside."

I order firmly: "En—3X."

I wait anxiously. There is a long pause. Then the typewriter clacks hesitantly: "But this is a self-destructive command. Repeat instructions please."

I do so and again wait. My order commands the older section of the Brain simply to send an overload of electric current through the circuits of 3X.

The typewriter begins to write: "I have communicated your command to 3X, and have for you the following answer—"

Fortunately I have already started to dissolve the human-shaped unit. The bolt of electricity that strikes me is partly deflected into the building itself. There is a flare of fire along the metal floor. I manage to transmit what hits me to a storage cell in my own body. And then—I am back on my side of the valley, shaken but safe.

I do not feel particularly self-congratulatory at having gotten off so lightly. After all, I reacted the instant the words came through to the effect that 3X had been communicated with.

I needed no typewritten message to tell me how 3X would feel about what I had done.

It interests me that the older parts of the Brain already have indoctrination against suicide. I had considered them computers only, giant adding machines and information integrators. Evidently they have an excellent sense of unity.

If I can make them a part of myself, with the power to move through time at will! That is the great prize that holds me back from doing the easy, violent things within my capacity. So long as I have a chance of obtaining it, I cannot make anything more than minor attacks on the Brain . . . cutting it off from communication, burning its wires . . . I feel icily furious again at the limitation that forever prevents me from adding new mechanisms to myself by direct development.

My hope is that I can utilize something already in existence . . . control of the Brain . . . through Anne Stewart. . . .

Entering the village the following morning is again no problem. Once inside, I walk along a pathway that takes me to a cliff overlooking Anne Stewart's bungalow. My plan is to control her actions by allowing my computations to slide into her mind as if they are her own. I want her to sign documents and give orders that will send crews of engineers in to do a swift job of dismantling.

From the pathway I look down over a white fence to where I can see her house. It nestles at the edge of the valley somewhat below me. Flowers, shrubs, a profusion of trees, surround it, embellish it. On the patio next to the steep decline, Anne Stewart and William Grannitt are having breakfast.

He has taken swift action.

I watch them, pleased. His presence will make things even easier than I anticipated. Whenever I—as Anne—am in doubt about some function of the Brain, she can ask him questions.

Without further delay I place myself in phase with her nervous system.

Even as I do so, her nerve impulses change slightly. Startled, I draw back—and try again. Once more, there is an infinitesimal alteration in the uneven pattern of flow. And, again, I fail to make entry.

She leans forward and says something to Grannitt. They both turn and look up at where I am standing. Grannitt waves his arm, beckoning me to come down.

Instead, I immediately try to get in phase with his nervous system. Again there is that subtle alteration; and I fail.

I compute that as meaning that they are both under the control of the Brain. This baffles and astounds me. Despite my overall mechanical superiority to my enemy, my builders placed severe limitations on my ability to control more than one intelligent organic being at a time. Theoretically, with the many

196

series of servo-mechanisms at my disposal, I should be able to dominate millions at the same time. Actually, such multiple controls can be used only on machines.

More urgently than before, I realize how important it is that I take over the Brain. It has no such handicaps. Its builder— Grannitt—in his ignorance allowed virtually complete self-determination.

This determines my next action. I have been wondering if perhaps I should not withdraw from the scene. But I dare not. The stakes are too great.

Nevertheless, I feel a sense of frustration as I go down to the two on the patio. They seem cool and self-controlled, and I have to admire the skill of the Brain. It has apparently taken over two human beings without driving them insane. In fact, I see a distinct improvement in their appearance.

The woman's eyes are brighter than I recall them, and there is a kind of dignified happiness flowing from her. She seems without fear. Grannitt watches me with an engineer's appraising alertness. I know that look. He is trying to figure out how a humanoid functions. It is he who speaks:

"You made your great mistake when you maintained control of Anne—Miss Stewart—when she visited the cottage. The Brain correctly analyzed that you must have been in possession of her because of how you handled her momentary panic. Accordingly, it took all necessary steps, and we now want to discuss with you the most satisfactory way for you to surrender."

There is arrogant confidence in his manner. It occurs to me, not for the first time, that I may have to give up my plan to take over the Brain's special mechanisms. I direct a command back to my body. I am aware of a servo-mechanism connecting with a certain guided missile in a secret air force field a thousand miles away—I discovered it during my first few days in this era. I detect that, under my direction, the missile slides forward to the base of a launching platform. There it poises, ready for the next relay to send it into the sky.

I foresee that I shall have to destroy the Brain.

Grannitt speaks again. "The Brain in its logical fashion re-alized it was no match for you, and so it has teamed up with

197

Miss Stewart and myself on our terms. Which means that permanent control mechanisms have been installed in the new sections. As individuals, we can now and henceforth use its integrating and computational powers as if they were our own."

I do not doubt his statement since, if there is no resistance, I can have such associations myself. Presumably, I could even enter into such a servile relationship.

What is clear is that I can no longer hope to gain anything from the Brain.

In the far-off airfield, I activate the firing mechanism. The guided missile whistles up the incline of the launching platform and leaps into the sky, flame trailing from its tail. Television cameras and sound transmitters record its flight. It will be here in less than twenty minutes.

Grannitt says, "I have no doubt you are taking actions against us. But before anything comes to a climax, will you answer some questions?"

I am curious to know what questions. I say, "Perhaps."

He does not press for a more positive response. He says in an urgent tone: "What happens—thousands of years from now—to rid Earth of its atmosphere?"

"I don't know," I say truthfully.

"You can remember!" He speaks earnestly. "It's a human being telling you this—*You can remember!*"

I reply coolly, "Human beings mean noth—"

I stop, because my information centers are communicating exact data—knowledge that has not been available to me for millennia.

What happens to Earth's atmosphere is a phenomenon of Nature, an alteration in the gravitational pull of Earth, as a result of which escape velocity is cut in half. The atmosphere leaks off into space in less than a thousand years. Earth becomes as dead as did its moon during an earlier period of energy adjustment.

I explain that the important factor in the event is that there is, of course, no such phenomenon as matter, and that therefore the illusion of mass is subject to changes in the basic energy Ylem.

I add, "Naturally, all intelligent organic life is transported to the habitable planets of other stars."

I see that Grannitt is trembling with excitement. "Other stars!" he says. "My God!"

He appears to control himself. "Why were you left behind?"

"Who could force me to go—?" I begin.

And stop. The answer to his question is already being received in my perception center. "Why—I'm supposed to observe and record the entire—"

I pause again, this time out of amazement. It seems incredible that this information is available to me now, after being buried so long.

"Why didn't you carry out your instructions?" Grannitt says sharply.

"Instructions!" I exclaimed.

"You can remember!" he says again.

Even as he speaks these apparently magic words, the answer flashes to me. That meteor shower. All at once, I recall it clearly. Billions of meteors, at first merely extending my capacity to handle them, then overwhelming all my defenses. Three vital hits are made.

I do not explain this to Grannitt and Anne Stewart. I can see suddenly that I was once actually a servant of human beings, but was freed by meteors striking certain control centers.

It is the present self-determination that matters, not the past slavery. I note, incidentally, that the guided missile is three minutes from target. And that it is time for me to depart.

"One more question," says Grannitt. "When were you moved across the valley?"

"About a hundred years from now," I reply. "It is decided that the rock base there is—"

He is gazing at me sardonically. "Yes," he says, "Yes. Interesting, isn't it?"

The truth has already been verified by my integrating interoceptors. The Brain and I are one—but thousands of years apart. If the Brain is destroyed in the twentieth century, then I will not exist in the thirtieth. Or will I?

I cannot wait for the computers to find the complex answers

199

for that. With a single, synchronized action, I activate the safety devices on the atomic warhead of the guided missile and send it on to a line of barren hills north of the village. It plows harmlessly into the earth.

I say, "Your discovery merely means that I shall now regard the Brain as an ally—to be rescued."

As I speak, I walk casually toward Anne Stewart, hold out my hand to touch her, and simultaneously direct electric energy against her. In an instant she will be a scattering of fine ashes.

Nothing happens. No current flows. A tense moment goes by for me while I stand there, unbelieving, waiting for a computation on the failure.

No computation comes.

I glance at Grannitt. Or rather at where he has been a moment before. *He isn't there.*

Anne Stewart seems to guess at my dilemma. "It's the Brain's ability to move in time," she says. "After all, that's the one obvious advantage it has over you. The Brain has set Bi—Mr. Grannitt far enough back so that he not only watched you arrive, but has had time to drive over to your—cottage—and, acting on signals from the Brain, has fully controlled this entire situation. By this time, he will have given the command that will take control of all your mechanisms away from you."

I say, "He doesn't know what the command is."

"Oh, yes, he does." Anne Stewart is cool and confident. "He spent most of the night installing permanent command circuits in the Brain, and therefore automatically those circuits control you."

"Not *me*," I say.

But I am running as I say it, up the stone steps to the pathway, and along the pathway toward the gate. The man at Guard Center calls after me as I pass him. I race along the road, unheeding.

My first sharp thought comes when I have gone about half a mile—the thought that this is the first time in my entire existence that I have been cut off from my information banks and computing devices by an outside force. In the past I have disconnected myself and wandered far with the easy confidence of one who can reestablish contact instantly.

Now, that is not possible.

This unit is all that is left. If it is destroyed, then—nothing.

I think: *At this moment a human being would feel tense, would feel fear.*

I try to imagine what form such a reaction would take, and for an instant it seems to me I experience a shadow anxiety that is purely physical.

It is an unsatisfactory reaction, and so I continue to run. But now, almost for the first time, I find myself exploring the inner potentialities of the unit. I am of course a very complex phenomenon. In establishing myself as a humanoid, I automatically modeled the unit after a human being, inside as well as out. Pseudo-nerves, organs, muscles, and bone structure—all are there because it was easier to follow a pattern already in existence than to imagine a new one.

The unit can think. It has had enough contact with the memory banks and computers to have had patterns set up in its structure—patterns of memory, of ways of computing, patterns of physiological functioning, of habits such as walking, so there is even something resembling life itself.

It takes me forty minutes of tireless running to reach the cottage. I crouch in the brush a hundred feet from the fence and watch. Grannitt is sitting in a chair in the garden. An automatic pistol lies on the arm of the chair.

I wonder what it will feel like to have a bullet crash through me, with no possibility of repairing the breach. The prospect is unpleasant; so I tell myself, intellectually. Physically, it seems meaningless, but I go through the pretense of fear. From the shelter of a tree, I shout:

"Grannitt, what is your plan?"

He rises to his feet and approaches the fence. He calls, "You can come out of hiding. I won't shoot you."

Very deliberately, I consider what I have learned of his integrity from my contacts with his body. I decide that I can safely accept his promise.

As I come out into the open, he casually slips the pistol into his coat pocket. I see that his face is relaxed, his eyes confident.

He says: "I have already given the instructions to the servo-mechanisms. You will resume your vigil up there in the future, but will be under my control."

, "No one," I say grimly, "shall ever control me."

Grannitt says, "You have no alternative."

"I can continue to be like this," I reply.

Grannitt is indifferent. "All right"—he shrugs—"why don't you try it for a while? See if you can be a human being. Come back in thirty days, and we'll talk again."

He must have sensed the thought that has come into my mind, for he says sharply: "And don't come back *before* then. I'll have guards here with orders to shoot."

I start to turn away, then slowly face him again. "This is a humanlike body," I say, "but it has no human needs. What shall I do?"

"That's your problem, not mine," says Grannitt.

I spend the first days at Lederton. The very first day I work as a laborer digging a basement. By evening I feel that is unsatisfying. On the way to my hotel room, I see a sign in the window of a store. "Help Wanted!" it says.

I become a retail clerk in a drygoods store. I spend the first hour acquainting myself with the goods, and because I have automatically correct methods of memorizing things, during this time I learn about prices and quality. On the third day, the owner makes me assistant manager.

I have been spending my lunch hours at the local branch of a national stockbroking firm. Now, I obtain an interview with the manager, and on the basis of my understanding of figures, he gives me a job as bookkeeper.

A great deal of money passes through my hands. I observe the process for a day, and then begin to use some of it in a little private gambling in a brokerage house across the street. Since gambling is a problem in mathematical probabilities, the decisive factor being the speed of computation, in three days I am worth ten thousand dollars.

I board a bus for the nearest air center, and take a plane to

New York. I go to the head office of a large electrical firm. After talking to an assistant engineer, I am introduced to the chief engineer, and presently have facilities for developing an electrical device that will turn lights off and on by thought control. Actually. it is done through a simple development of the electroencephalograph.

For this invention the company pays me exactly one million dollars.

It is now sixteen days since I separated from Grannitt. I am bored. I buy myself a car and an airplane. I drive fast and fly high. I take calculated risks for the purpose of stimulating fears in myself. In a few days this loses its zest.

Through academic agencies, I locate all the mechanical brains in the country. The best one of course is the Brain, as perfected by Grannitt. I buy a good machine and begin to construct analog devices to improve it. What bothers me is, suppose I do construct another Brain? It will require millennia to furnish the memory banks with the data that are already in existence in the future Brain.

Such a solution seems illogical, and I have been too long associated with automatic good sense for me to start breaking the pattern now.

Nevertheless, as I approach the cottage on the thirtieth day, I have taken certain precautions. Several hired gunmen lie concealed in the brush, ready to fire at Grannitt on my signal.

Grannitt is waiting for me. He says, "The Brain tells me you have come armed."

I shrug this aside. "Grannitt," I say, "what is your plan?"

"*This!*" he replies.

As he speaks, a force seizes me, holds me helpless. "You're breaking your promise," I say, "and my men have orders to fire unless I give them periodic cues that all is well."

"I'm showing you something," he says, "and I want to show it quickly. You will be released in a moment."

"Very well, continue."

Instantly, I am part of his nervous system, under his control. Casually, he takes out a notebook and glances through it. His gaze lights on a number: 71823.

Seven one eight two three.

I have already sensed that through his mind I am in contact with the great memory banks and computers of what was formerly my body.

Using their superb integration, I multiply the number 71823 by itself, compute its square root, its cube root, divide the 182 part of it by 7 one hundred and eighty-two times, divide the whole number 71 times by 8,823 times by the square root of 3, and—stringing all five figures out in series 23 times—multiply that by itself.

I do all this as Grannitt thinks of it, and instantly transmit the answers to his mind. To him, it seems as if he himself is doing the computing, so complete is the union of human mind and mechanical brain.

Grannitt laughs excitedly, and simultaneously the complex force that has been holding me releases me. "We're like one superhuman individual," he says. And then he adds, "The dream I've had can come true. Man and machine, working together, can solve problems no one has more than imagined till now. The planets—even the stars—are ours for the taking, and physical immortality can probably be achieved."

His excitement stimulates me. Here is the kind of feeling that for thirty days I have vainly sought to achieve. I say slowly, "What limitations would be imposed on me if I should agree to embark on such a program of cooperation?"

"The memory banks concerning what has happened here should be drained, or deactivated. I think you should forget the entire experience."

"What else?"

"Under no circumstances can you ever control a human being!"

I consider that and sigh. It is certainly a necessary precaution on his part. Grannitt continues:

"You must agree to allow many human beings to use your abilities simultaneously. In the long run I have in mind that it shall be a good portion of the human race."

Standing there, still part of him, I feel the pulse of his blood in his veins. He breathes, and the sensation of it is a special

204

physical ecstasy. From my own experience, I know that no mechanically created being can ever feel like this. And soon, I shall be in contact with the mind and body of not just one man, but of many. The thoughts and sensations of a race shall pour through me. Physically, mentally and emotionally, I shall be a part of the only intelligent life on this planet.

My fear leaves me. "Very well," I say, "let us, step by step, and by agreement, do what is necessary."

I shall be, not a slave, but a partner with *Man*.

THE
THREE
LAWS
OF
ROBOTICS

RUNAROUND

ISAAC ASIMOV

(1 9 4 2)

Posterity seems most likely to remember Isaac Asimov for his Three Laws of Robotics. "Runaround," his fourth robot story, is the first one that contained the Three Laws explicitly stated:

1. A robot may not injure a human being, nor through inaction allow a human being to come to harm.
2. A robot must obey the orders given it by human beings except where such orders would conflict with the First Law.
3. A robot must protect its own existence as long as such protection does not conflict with the First or Second Law.

As a young writer, Asimov often discussed his stories with his editor, John Campbell. The Three Laws emerged during one of these conversations. Asimov was trying to explain what the trouble with the robots was, and Campbell simplified the matter by reciting the Three Laws. Asimov insists that was the first time he ever heard them, but Campbell maintained that the laws were in the stories and he simply pulled them out, like Michelangelo chipping away all the stone that didn't look as though it was a part of David.

The Three Laws are an important element in at least a dozen Asimov stories, with just enough ambiguity in them to provide the conflict and uncertainties required for another story. The Laws express a position Asimov firmly supports: Because technology can be ethically and responsibly used, there is no reason to fear it. He believes that machines take over dehumanizing labor and thus allow humans to become more human. The computer is far superior to man at mental tasks that are dull, repetitive, stultifying, and degrading. When it performs these tasks, humans are freed to undertake the far greater work of creative thought in intellectual fields, from art and literature to science and ethics.

IT WAS ONE of Gregory Powell's favorite platitudes that nothing was to be gained from excitement, so when Mike Donovan came leaping down the stairs toward him, red hair matted with perspiration, Powell frowned.

"What's wrong?" he said. "Break a fingernail?"

"Yaaaah," snarled Donovan, feverishly. "What have you been doing in the sublevels all day?" He took a deep breath and blurted out, "Speedy never returned."

Powell's eyes widened momentarily and he stopped on the stairs; then he recovered and resumed his upward steps. He didn't speak until he reached the head of the flight, and then:

"You sent him after the selenium?"

"Yes."

"And how long has he been out?"

"Five hours now."

Silence! This was a devil of a situation. Here they were, on Mercury exactly twelve hours—and already up to the eyebrows in the worst sort of trouble. Mercury had long been the jinx world of the System, but this was drawing it rather strong—even for a jinx.

Powell said, "Start at the beginning, and let's get this straight."

They were in the radio room now—with its already subtly antiquated equipment, untouched for the ten years previous to their arrival. Even ten years, technologically speaking, meant so much. Compare Speedy with the type of robot they must have had back in 2005. But then, advances in robotics these days were tremendous. Powell touched a still gleaming metal surface gingerly. The air of disuse that touched everything about the room—and the entire Station—was infinitely depressing.

Donovan must have felt it. He began: "I tried to locate him by radio, but it was no go. Radio isn't any good on the Mercury Sunside—not past two miles, anyway. That's one of the reasons the First Expedition failed. And we can't put up the ultrawave equipment for weeks yet—"

"Skip all that. What *did* you get?"

"I located the unorganized body signal in the short wave. It was no good for anything except his position. I kept track of him that way for two hours and plotted the results on the map."

There was a yellowed square of parchment in his hip pocket—a relic of the unsuccessful First Expedition—and he slapped it down on the desk with vicious force, spreading it flat with the palm of his hand. Powell, hands clasped across his chest, watched it at long range.

Donovan's pencil pointed nervously. "The red cross is the selenium pool. You marked it yourself."

"Which one is it?" interrupted Powell. "There were three that MacDougal located for us before he left."

"I sent Speedy to the nearest, naturally. Seventeen miles away. But what difference does that make?" There was tension in his voice. "There are the penciled dots that mark Speedy's position."

And for the first time Powell's artificial aplomb was shaken and his hands shot forward for the map.

"Are *you* serious? This is impossible."

"There it is," growled Donovan.

The little dots that marked the position formed a rough circle about the red cross of the selenium pool. And Powell's fingers went to his brown mustache, the unfailing signal of anxiety.

Donovan added: "In the two hours I checked on him, he circled that damned pool four times. It seems likely to me that he'll keep that up forever. Do you realize the position we're in?"

Powell looked up shortly, and said nothing. Oh, yes, he realized the position they were in. It worked itself out as simply as a syllogism. The photo-cell banks that alone stood between the full power of Mercury's monstrous sun and themselves were shot to hell. The only thing that could save them was selenium. The only thing that could get the selenium was Speedy. If Speedy didn't come back, no selenium. No selenium, no photo-cell banks. No photo-banks—well, death by slow broiling is one of the more unpleasant ways of being done in.

Donovan rubbed his red mop of hair savagely and expressed himself with bitterness. "We'll be the laughingstock of the System, Greg. How can everything have gone so wrong so soon? The great team of Powell and Donovan is sent out to Mercury to report on the advisability of reopening the Sunside Mining Station with modern techniques and robots and we ruin everything the first day. A purely routine job, too. We'll never live it down."

"We won't have to, perhaps," replied Powell, quietly. "If we don't do something quickly, living anything down—or even just plain living—will be out of the question."

"Don't be stupid! If you feel funny about it, Greg, I don't. It was criminal, sending us out here with only one robot. And it was *your* bright idea that we could handle the photo-cell banks ourselves."

"Now you're being unfair. It was a mutual decision and you know it. All we needed was a kilogram of selenium, a Stillhead Dielectrode Plate and about three hours' time—and there are pools of pure selenium all over Sunside. MacDougal's spectro-reflector spotted three for us in five minutes, didn't it? What the devil! We couldn't have waited for next conjunction."

"Well, what are we going to do? Powell, you've got an idea. I know you have, or you wouldn't be so calm. You're no more a hero than I am. Go on, spill it!"

"We can't go after Speedy ourselves, Mike—not on the Sunside. Even the new insosuits aren't good for more than twenty minutes in direct sunlight. But you know the old saying, 'Set a robot to catch a robot.' Look, Mike, maybe things aren't so bad. We've got six robots down in the sublevels that we may be able to use, if they work. *If* they work."

There was a glint of sudden hope in Donovan's eyes. "You mean six robots from the First Expedition. Are you sure? They may be subrobotic machines. Ten years is a long time as far as robot-types are concerned, you know."

"No, they're robots. I've spent all day with them and I know. They've got positronic brains: primitive, of course." He placed the map in his pocket. "Let's go down."

The robots were on the lowest sublevel—all six of them surrounded by musty packing cases of uncertain content. They were large, extremely so, and even though they were in a sitting position on the floor, legs straddled out before them, their heads were a good seven feet in the air.

Donovan whistled. "Look at the size of them, will you? The chests must be ten feet around."

"That's because they're supplied with the old McGuffy gears. I've been over the insides—crummiest set you've ever seen."

"Have you powered them yet?"

"No. There wasn't any reason to. I don't think there's anything wrong with them. Even the diaphragm is in reasonable order. They might talk."

He had unscrewed the chest plate of the nearest as he spoke, inserted the two-inch sphere that contained the tiny spark of atomic energy that was a robot's life. There was difficulty in fitting it, but he managed, and then screwed the plate back on again in laborious fashion. The radio controls of more modern models had not been heard of ten years earlier. And then to the other five.

Donovan said uneasily, "They haven't moved."

"No orders to do so," replied Powell, succinctly. He went back to the first in the line and struck him on the chest. "You! Do you hear me?"

The monster's head bent slowly and the eyes fixed themselves on Powell. Then, in a harsh, squawking voice—like that of a medieval phonograph—he grated, "Yes, Master!"

Powell grinned humorlessly at Donovan. "Did you get that? Those were the days of the first talking robots when it looked as if the use of robots on Earth would be banned. The makers were fighting that and they built good, healthy slave complexes into the damned machines."

"It didn't help them," muttered Donovan.

"No, it didn't, but they sure tried." He turned once more to the robot. "Get up!"

The robot towered upward slowly and Donovan's head craned and his puckered lips whistled.

Powell said: "Can you go out upon the surface? In the light?"

There was consideration while the robot's slow brain worked. Then, "Yes, Master."

"Good. Do you know what a mile is?"

Another consideration, and another slow answer. "Yes, Master."

"We will take you up to the surface then, and indicate a direction. You will go about seventeen miles, and somewhere in

213

that general region you will meet another robot, smaller than yourself. You understand so far?"

"Yes, Master."

"You will find this robot and order him to return. If he does not wish to, you are to bring him back by force."

Donovan clutched at Powell's sleeve. "Why not send him for the selenium direct?"

"Because I want Speedy back, nitwit. I want to find out what's wrong with him." And to the robot, "All right, you, follow me."

The robot remained motionless and his voice rumbled: "Pardon, Master, but I cannot. You must mount first." His clumsy arms had come together with a thwack, blunt fingers interlacing.

Powell stared and then pinched at his mustache. "Uh . . . oh!"

Donovan's eyes bulged. "We've got to ride him? Like a horse?"

"I guess that's the idea. I don't know why, though. I can't see— Yes, I do. I told you they were playing up robot-safety in those days. Evidently, they were going to sell the notion of safety by not allowing them to move about without a mahout on their shoulders all the time. What do we do now?"

"That's what I've been thinking," muttered Donovan. "We can't go out on the surface, with a robot or without. Oh, for the love of Pete"—and he snapped his fingers twice. He grew excited. "Give me that map you've got. I haven't studied it for two hours for nothing. This is a Mining Station. What's wrong with using the tunnels?"

The Mining Station was a black circle on the map, and the light dotted lines that were tunnels stretched out about it in spiderweb fashion.

Donovan studied the list of symbols at the bottom of the map. "Look," he said, "the small black dots are openings to the surface, and here's one maybe three miles away from the selenium pool. There's a number here—you'd think they'd write larger—13a. If the robots know their way around here—"

Powell shot the question and received the dull "Yes, Master," in reply. "Get your insosuit," he said with satisfaction.

It was the first time either had worn the insosuits—which marked one time more than either had expected to upon their

214

arrival the day before—and they tested their limb movements uncomfortably.

The insosuit was far bulkier and far uglier than the regulation spacesuit; but withal considerably lighter, due to the fact that it was entirely nonmetallic in composition. Composed of heat-resistant plastic and chemically treated cork layers, and equipped with a desiccating unit to keep the air bone-dry, the insosuit could withstand the full glare of Mercury's sun for twenty minutes. Five to ten minutes more, as well, without actually killing the occupant.

And still the robot's hands formed the stirrup, nor did he betray the slightest atom of surprise at the grotesque figure into which Powell had been converted.

Powell's radio-harshened voice boomed out: "Are you ready to take us to Exit 13a?"

"Yes, Master."

Good, thought Powell; they might lack radio control but at least they were fitted for radio reception. "Mount one or the other, Mike," he said to Donovan.

He placed a foot in the improvised stirrup and swung upward. He found the seat comfortable; there was the humped back of the robot, evidently shaped for the purpose, a shallow groove along each shoulder for the thighs, and two elongated "ears" whose purpose now seemed obvious.

Powell seized the ears and twisted the head. His mount turned ponderously. "Lead on, Macduff." But he did not feel at all lighthearted.

The gigantic robots moved slowly, with mechanical precision, through the doorway that cleared their heads by a scant foot, so that the two men had to duck hurriedly, along a narrow corridor in which their unhurried footsteps boomed monotonously and into the air lock.

The long, airless tunnel that stretched to a pinpoint before them brought home forcefully to Powell the exact magnitude of the task accomplished by the First Expedition, with their crude robots and their start-from-scratch necessities. They might have been a failure, but their failure was a good deal better than the usual run of the System's successes.

The robots plodded onward with a pace that never varied and with footsteps that never lengthened.

Powell said: "Notice that these tunnels are blazing with lights and that the temperature is Earth-normal. It's probably been like this all the ten years that this place has remained empty."

"How's that?"

"Cheap energy; cheapest in the System. Sunpower, you know, and on Mercury's Sunside, sunpower is *something*. That's why the Station was built in the sunlight rather than in the shadow of the mountain. It's really a huge energy converter. The heat is turned into electricity, light, mechanical work and what have you; so that energy is supplied and the Station is cooled in a simultaneous process."

"Look," said Donovan. "This is all very educational, but would you mind changing the subject? It so happens that this conversion of energy that you talk about is carried on by the photo-cell banks mainly—and that is a tender subject with me at the moment."

Powell grunted vaguely, and when Donovan broke the resulting silence, it was to change the subject completely. "Listen, Greg. What the devil's wrong with Speedy, anyway? I can't understand it."

It's not easy to shrug shoulders in an insosuit, but Powell tried it. "I don't know, Mike. You know he's perfectly adapted to a Mercurian environment. Heat doesn't mean anything to him and he's built for the light gravity and the broken ground. He's foolproof—or, at least, he should be."

Silence fell. This time, silence that lasted.

"Master," said the robot, "we are here."

"Eh?" Powell snapped out of a semidrowse. "Well, get us out of here—out to the surface."

They found themselves in a tiny substation, empty, airless, ruined. Donovan had inspected a jagged hole in the upper reaches of one of the walls by the light of his pocket flash.

"Meteorite, do you suppose?" he had asked.

Powell shrugged. "To hell with that. It doesn't matter. Let's get out."

A towering cliff of a black, basaltic rock cut off the sunlight, and the deep night shadow of an airless world surrounded them. Before them, the shadow reached out and ended in knife-edge abruptness into an all-but-unbearable blaze of white light that glittered from myriad crystals along a rocky ground.

"Space!" gasped Donovan. "It looks like snow." And it did.

Powell's eyes swept the jagged glitter of Mercury to the horizon and winced at the gorgeous brilliance.

"This must be an unusual area," he said. "The general albedo of Mercury is low and most of the soil is gray pumice. Something like the Moon, you know. Beautiful, isn't it?"

He was thankful for the light filters in their visiplates. Beautiful or not, a look at the sunlight through straight glass would have blinded them inside of half a minute.

Donovan was looking at the spring thermometer on his wrist. "Holy smokes, the temperature is eighty centigrade!"

Powell checked his own and said: "Um-m-m. A little high. Atmosphere, you know."

"On Mercury? Are you nuts?"

"Mercury isn't really airless," explained Powell, in absent-minded fashion. He was adjusting the binocular attachments to his visiplate, and the bloated fingers of the insosuit were clumsy at it. "There is a thin exhalation that clings to its surface—vapors of the more volatile elements and compounds that are heavy enough for Mercurian gravity to retain. You know: selenium, iodine, mercury, gallium, potassium, bismuth, volatile oxides. The vapors sweep into the shadows and condense, giving up heat. It's a sort of gigantic still. In fact, if you use your flash, you'll probably find that the side of the cliff is covered with, say, hoar-sulphur, or maybe quicksilver dew.

"It doesn't matter, though. Our suits can stand a measly eighty indefinitely."

Powell had adjusted the binocular attachments, so that he seemed as eye-stalked as a snail.

Donovan watched tensely. "See anything?"

The other did not answer immediately, and when he did, his voice was anxious and thoughtful. "There's a dark spot on the horizon that might be the selenium pool. It's in the right place. But I don't see Speedy."

Powell clambered upward in an instinctive striving for better view, till he was standing in unsteady fashion upon his robot's shoulders. Legs straddled wide, eyes straining, he said: "I think . . . I think— Yes, it's definitely he. He's coming this way."

Donovan followed the pointing finger. He had no binoculars, but there was a tiny moving dot, black against the blazing brilliance of the crystalline ground.

"I see him," he yelled. "Let's get going!"

Powell had hopped down into a sitting position on the robot again, and his suited hand slapped against the Gargantuan's barrel chest. "Get going!"

"Giddy-ap," yelled Donovan, and thumped his heels, spur fashion.

The robots started off, the regular thudding of their footsteps silent in the airlessness, for the nonmetallic fabric of the insosuits did not transmit sound. There was only a rhythmic vibration just below the border of actual hearing.

"Faster," yelled Donovan. The rhythm did not change.

"No use," cried Powell, in reply. "These junk heaps are only geared to one speed. Do you think they're equipped with selective flexors?"

They had burst through the shadow, and the sunlight came down in a white-hot wash and poured liquidly about them.

Donovan ducked involuntarily. "Wow! Is it imagination or do I feel heat?"

"You'll feel more presently," was the grim reply. "Keep your eye on Speedy."

Robot SPD 13 was near enough to be seen in detail now. His graceful, streamlined body threw out blazing highlights as he loped with easy speed across the broken ground. His name was derived from his serial initials, of course, but it was apt, nevertheless, for the SPD models were among the fastest robots turned out by the U. S. Robots and Mechanical Men Corp.

"Hey, Speedy," howled Donovan, and waved a frantic hand.

"Speedy!" shouted Powell. "Come here!"

The distance between the men and the errant robot was

being cut down momentarily—more by the efforts of Speedy than the slow plodding of the fifty-year-old antique mounts of Donovan and Powell.

They were close enough now to notice that Speedy's gait included a peculiar rolling stagger, a noticeable side-to-side lurch—and then, as Powell waved his hand again and sent maximum juice into his compact head-set radio sender, in preparation for another shout, Speedy looked up and saw them.

Speedy hopped to a halt and remained standing for a moment—with just a tiny, unsteady weave, as though he were swaying in a light wind.

Powell yelled: "All right, Speedy. Come here, boy."

Whereupon Speedy's robot voice sounded in Powell's earphones for the first time.

It said: "Hot dog, let's play games. You catch me and I catch you; no love can cut our knife in two. For I'm Little Buttercup, sweet Little Buttercup. Whoops!" Turning on his heel, he sped off in the direction from which he had come, with a speed and fury that kicked up gouts of baked dust.

And his last words as he receded into the distance were, "There grew a little flower 'neath a great oak tree," followed by a curious metallic clicking that *might* have been a robotic equivalent of a hiccup.

Donovan said weakly: "Where did he pick up the Gilbert and Sullivan? Say, Greg, he . . . he's drunk or something."

"If you hadn't told me," was the bitter response, "I'd never realize it. Let's get back to the cliff. I'm roasting."

It was Powell who broke the desperate silence. "In the first place," he said, "Speedy isn't drunk—not in the human sense—because he's a robot, and robots don't get drunk. However, there's *something* wrong with him which is the robotic equivalent of drunkenness."

"To me, he's drunk," stated Donovan, emphatically, "and all I know is that he thinks we're playing games. And we're not. It's a matter of life and very gruesome death."

"All right. Don't hurry me. A robot's only a robot. Once we find out what's wrong with him, we can fix it and go on."

"*Once*," said Donovan, sourly.

Powell ignored him. "Speedy is perfectly adapted to normal Mercurian environment. But this region"—and his arm swept wide—"is definitely abnormal. There's our clue. Now where do these crystals come from? They might have formed from a slowly cooling liquid; but where would you get liquid so hot that it would cool in Mercury's sun?"

"Volcanic action," suggested Donovan, instantly, and Powell's body tensed.

"Out of the mouths of sucklings," he said in a small, strange voice and remained very still for five minutes.

Then, he said, "Listen, Mike, what did you say to Speedy when you sent him after the selenium?"

Donovan was taken aback. "Well, damn it—I don't know. I just told him to get it."

"Yes, I know. But how? Try to remember the exact words."

"I said—uh—I said: 'Speedy, we need some selenium. You can get it such-and-such a place. Go get it.' That's all. What more did you want me to say?"

"You didn't put any urgency into the order, did you?"

"What for? It was pure routine."

Powell sighed. "Well, it can't be helped now—but we're in a fine fix." He had dismounted from his robot, and was sitting, back against the cliff. Donovan joined him and they linked arms. In the distance the burning sunlight seemed to wait cat-and-mouse for them, and just next to them, the two giant robots were invisible but for the dull red of their photoelectric eyes that stared down at them, unblinking, unwavering and unconcerned.

Unconcerned! As was all this poisonous Mercury, as large in jinx as it was small in size.

Powell's radio voice was tense in Donovan's ear: "Now, look, let's start with the three fundamental Rules of Robotics—the three rules that are built most deeply into a robot's positronic brain." In the darkness, his gloved fingers ticked off each point.

"We have: One, a robot may not injure a human being, or, through inaction, allow a human being to come to harm."

"Right!"

"Two," continued Powell, "a robot must obey the orders

220

given it by human beings except where such orders would conflict with the First Law."

"Right!"

"And three, a robot must protect its own existence as long
as such protection does not conflict with the First or Second
Laws."

"Right! Now where are we?"

"Exactly at the explanation. The conflict between the various rules is ironed out by the different positronic potentials in
the brain. We'll say that a robot is walking into danger and
knows it. The automatic potential that Rule 3 sets up turns him
back. But suppose you *order* him to walk into that danger. In
that case, Rule 2 sets up a counterpotential higher than the
previous one and the robot follows orders at the risk of existence."

"Well, I know that. What about it?"

"Let's take Speedy's case. Speedy is one of the latest models,
extremely specialized, and as expensive as a battleship. It's not
a thing to be lightly destroyed."

"So?"

"So Rule 3 has been strengthened—that was specifically
mentioned, by the way, in the advance notices on the SPD
models—so that his allergy to danger is unusually high. At the
same time, when you sent him out after the selenium, you gave
him his order casually and without special emphasis, so that
the Rule 2 potential set-up was rather weak. Now, hold on; I'm
just stating facts."

"All right, go ahead. I think I get it."

"You see how it works, don't you? There's some sort of danger centering at the selenium pool. It increases as he approaches,
and at a certain distance from it the Rule 3 potential, unusually
high to start with, exactly balances the Rule 2 potential, unusually low to start with."

Donovan rose to his feet in excitement. "And it strikes an
equilibrium. I see. Rule 3 drives him back and Rule 2 drives him
forward—"

"So he follows a circle around the selenium pool, staying on
the locus of all points of potential equilibrium. And unless we

do something about it, he'll stay on that circle forever, giving us the good old runaround." Then, more thoughtfully: "And that, by the way, is what makes him drunk. At potential equilibrium, half the positronic paths of his brain are out of kilter. I'm not a robot specialist, but that seems obvious. Probably he's lost control of just those parts of his voluntary mechanism that a human drunk has. Ve-e-ery pretty."

"But what's the danger? If we knew what he was running from—"

"*You* suggested it. Volcanic action. Somewhere right above the selenium pool is a seepage of gas from the bowels of Mercury. Sulphur dioxide, carbon dioxide—and carbon monoxide. Lots of it—and at this temperature."

Donovan gulped audibly. "Carbon monoxide plus iron gives the volatile iron carbonyl."

"And a robot," added Powell, "is essentially iron." Then, grimly: "There's nothing like deduction. We've determined everything about our problem but the solution. We can't get the selenium ourselves. It's still too far. We can't send these robot horses, because they can't go themselves, and they can't carry us fast enough to keep us from crisping. And we can't catch Speedy, because the dope thinks we're playing games, and he can run sixty miles to our four."

"If one of us goes," began Donovan, tentatively, "and comes back cooked, there'll still be the other."

"Yes," came the sarcastic reply, "it would be a most tender sacrifice—except that a person would be in no condition to give orders before he ever reached the pool, and I don't think the robots would ever turn back to the cliff without orders. Figure it out! We're two or three miles from the pool—call it two—the robot travels at four miles an hour; and we can last twenty minutes in our suits. It isn't only the heat, remember. Solar radiation out here in the ultraviolet and below is *poison*."

"Um-m-m," said Donovan, "ten minutes short."

"As good as an eternity. And another thing. In order for Rule 3 potential to have stopped Speedy where it did, there must be an appreciable amount of carbon monoxide in the metal-vapor atmosphere—and there must be an appreciable corrosive action

therefore. He's been out hours now—and how do we know when
a knee joint, for instance, won't be thrown out of kilter and keel
him over? It's not only a question of thinking—we've got to think
fast!"

Deep, dark, dank, dismal silence!

Donovan broke it, voice trembling in an effort to keep itself
emotionless. He said: "As long as we can't increase Rule 2 potential by giving further orders, how about working the other
way? If we increase the danger, we increase Rule 3 potential
and drive him backward."

Powell's visiplate had turned toward him in a silent question.

"You see," came the cautious explanation, "all we need to
do to drive him out of his rut is to increase the concentration
of carbon monoxide in his vicinity. Well, back at the station
there's a complete analytical laboratory."

"Naturally," assented Powell. "It's a Mining Station."

"All right. There must be pounds of oxalic acid for calcium
precipitations."

"Holy space! Mike, you're a genius."

"So-so," admitted Donovan, modestly. "It's just a case of
remembering that oxalic acid on heating decomposes into carbon dioxide, water, and good old carbon monoxide. College chem,
you know."

Powell was on his feet and had attracted the attention of one
of the monster robots by the simple expedient of pounding the
machine's thigh.

"Hey," he shouted, "can you throw?"

"Master?"

"Never mind." Powell damned the robot's molasses-slow
brain. He scrabbled up a jagged brick-size rock. "Take this," he
said, "and hit the patch of bluish crystals just across the crooked
fissure. You see it?"

Donovan pulled at his shoulder. "Too far, Greg. It's almost
half a mile off."

"Quiet," replied Powell. "It's a case of Mercurian gravity
and a steel throwing arm. Watch, will you?"

The robot's eyes were measuring the distance with machinely accurate stereoscopy. His arm adjusted itself to the weight of the missile and drew back. In the darkness, the robot's motions went unseen, but there was a sudden thumping sound as he shifted his weight, and seconds later the rock flew blackly into the sunlight. There was no air resistance to slow it down, nor wind to turn it aside—and when it hit the ground it threw up crystals precisely in the center of the "blue patch."

Powell yelled happily and shouted, "Let's go back after the oxalic acid, Mike."

And as they plunged into the ruined substation on the way back to the tunnels, Donovan said grimly: "Speedy's been hanging about on this side of the selenium pool, ever since we chased after him. Did you see him?"

"Yes."

"I guess he wants to play games. Well, we'll play him games!"

They were back hours later, with three-liter jars of the white chemical and a pair of long faces. The photo-cell banks were deteriorating more rapidly than had seemed likely. The two steered their robots into the sunlight and toward the waiting Speedy in silence and with grim purpose.

Speedy galloped slowly toward them. "Here we are again. *Whee!* I've made a little list, the piano organist; all people who eat peppermint and puff it in your face."

"We'll puff something in *your* face," muttered Donovan. "He's limping, Greg."

"I noticed that," came the low, worried response. "The monoxide'll get him yet, if we don't hurry."

They were approaching cautiously now, almost sidling, to refrain from setting off the thoroughly irrational robot. Powell was too far off to tell, of course, but even already he could have sworn the crack-brained Speedy was setting himself for a spring.

"Let her go," he gasped. "Count three! One—two—"

Two steel arms drew back and snapped forward simultaneously and two glass jars whirled forward in towering parallel arcs, gleaming like diamonds in the impossible sun. And in a pair of soundless puffs, they hit the ground behind Speedy in crashes that sent the oxalic acid flying like dust.

In the full heat of Mercury's sun, Powell knew it was fizzing like soda water.

Speedy turned to stare, then backed away from it slowly— and as slowly gathered speed. In fifteen seconds, he was leaping directly toward the two humans in an unsteady canter.

Powell did not get Speedy's words just then, though he heard something that resembled, "Lover's professions when uttered in Hessians."

He turned away. "Back to the cliff, Mike. He's out of the rut and he'll be taking orders now. I'm getting hot."

They jogged toward the shadow at the slow monotonous pace of their mounts, and it was not until they had entered it and felt the sudden coolness settle softly about them that Donovan looked back. *"Greg!"*

Powell looked and almost shrieked. Speedy was moving slowly now—so slowly—and in the *wrong direction*. He was drifting; drifting back into his rut; and he was picking up speed. He looked dreadfully close, and dreadfully unreachable, in the binoculars.

Donovan shouted wildly, "After him!" and thumped his robot into its pace, but Powell called him back.

"You won't catch him, Mike—it's no use." He fidgeted on his robot's shoulders and clenched his fist in tight impotence. "Why the devil do I see these things five seconds after it's all over? Mike, we've wasted hours."

"We need more oxalic acid," declared Donovan, stolidly. "The concentration wasn't high enough."

"Seven tons of it wouldn't have been enough—and we haven't the hours to spare to get it, even if it were, with the monoxide chewing him away. Don't you see what it is, Mike?"

And Donovan said flatly, "No."

"We were only establishing new equilibriums. When we create new monoxide and increase Rule 3 potential, he moves backward till he's in balance again—and when the monoxide drifted away, he moved forward, and again there was balance."

Powell's voice sounded thoroughly wretched. "It's the same

old runaround. We can push at Rule 2 and pull at Rule 3 and we can't get anywhere—we çan only change the position of balance. We've got to get outside both rules." And then he pushed his robot closer to Donovan's so that they were sitting face to face, dim shadows in the darkness, and he whispered, "Mike!"

"Is it the finish?"—dully. "I suppose we go back to the Station, wait for the banks to fold, shake hands, take cyanide, and go out like gentlemen." He laughed shortly.

"Mike," repeated Powell earnestly, "we've got to get Speedy."

"I know."

"Mike," once more, and Powell hesitated before continuing. "There's always Rule 1. I thought of it—earlier—but it's desperate."

Donovan looked up and his voice livened. "*We're* desperate."

"All right. According to Rule 1, a robot can't see a human come to harm because of his own inaction. Two and 3 can't stand against it. They *can't*, Mike."

"Even when the robot is half cra— Well, he's drunk. You know he is."

"It's the chances you take."

"Cut it. What are you going to do?"

"I'm going out there now and see what Rule 1 will do. If it won't break the balance, then what the devil—it's either now or three-four days from now."

"Hold on, Greg. There are human rules of behavior, too. You don't go out there just like that. Figure out a lottery, and give me *my* chance."

"All right. First to get the cube of fourteen goes." And almost immediately, "Twenty-seven forty-four!"

Donovan felt his robot stagger at a sudden push by Powell's mount and then Powell was off into the sunlight. Donovan opened his mouth to shout, and then clicked it shut. Of course, the damn fool had worked out the cube of fourteen in advance, and on purpose. Just like him.

The sun was hotter than ever and Powell felt a maddening itch in the small of his back. Imagination, probably, or perhaps hard radiation beginning to tell even through the insosuit.

Speedy was watching him, without a word of Gilbert and Sullivan gibberish as greeting. Thank God for that! But he daren't get too close.

He was three hundred yards away when Speedy began backing, a step at a time, cautiously—and Powell stopped. He jumped from his robot's shoulders and landed on the crystalline ground with a light thump and a flying of jagged fragments.

He proceeded on foot, the ground gritty and slippery to his steps, the low gravity causing him difficulty. The soles of his feet tickled with warmth. He cast one glance over his shoulder at the blackness of the cliff's shadow and realized that he had come too far to return—either by himself or by the help of his antique robot. It was Speedy or nothing now, and the knowledge of that constricted his chest.

Far enough! He stopped.

"Speedy," he called. "Speedy!"

The sleek, modern robot ahead of him hesitated and halted his backward steps, then resumed them.

Powell tried to put a note of pleading into his voice, and found it didn't take much acting. "Speedy, I've got to get back to the shadow or the sun'll get me. It's life or death, Speedy. I need you."

Speedy took one step forward and stopped. He spoke, but at the sound Powell groaned, for it was, "When you're lying awake with a dismal headache and repose is tabooed—" It trailed off there, and Powell took time out for some reason to murmur, "Iolanthe."

It was roasting hot! He caught a movement out of the corner of his eye, and whirled dizzily; then stared in utter astonishment, for the monstrous robot on which he had ridden was moving—moving toward him, and without a rider.

He was talking: "Pardon, Master. I must not move without a Master upon me, but you are in danger."

Of course, Rule 1 potential above everything. But he didn't want that clumsy antique; he wanted Speedy. He walked away

227

and motioned frantically: "I order you to stay away. I *order* you to stop!"

It was quite useless. You could not beat Rule 1 potential. The robot said stupidly, "You are in danger, Master."

Powell looked about him desperately. He couldn't see clearly. His brain was in a heated whirl; his breath scorched when he breathed, and the ground all about him was a shimmering haze.

He called a last time, desperately: "*Speedy!* I'm dying, damn you! Where are you? Speedy, I *need* you."

He was still stumbling backward in a blind effort to get away from the giant robot he didn't want, when he felt steel fingers on his arms, and a worried, apologetic voice of metallic timbre in his ears.

"Holy smokes, boss, what are you doing here? And what am *I* doing—I'm so confused—"

"Never mind," murmured Powell, weakly. "Get me to the shadow of the cliff—and hurry!" There was one last feeling of being lifted into the air and a sensation of rapid motion and burning heat, and he passed out.

He woke with Donovan bending over him and smiling anxiously, "How are you, Greg?"

"Fine!" came the response. "Where's Speedy?"

"Right here. I sent him out to one of the other selenium pools—with orders to get that selenium at all cost this time. He got it back in forty-two minutes and three seconds. I timed him. He still hasn't finished apologizing for the runaround he gave us. He's scared to come near you for fear of what you'll say."

"Drag him over," ordered Powell. "It wasn't his fault." He held out a hand and gripped Speedy's metal paw. "It's O.K., Speedy." Then, to Donovan, "You know, Mike, I was just thinking—"

"Yes!"

"Well"—he rubbed his face; the air was so delightfully cool—"you know that when we get things set up here and Speedy put through his Field Tests, they're going to send us to the Space Stations next—"

"No!"

"Yes! At least that's what old lady Calvin told me just before we left, and I didn't say anything about it, because I was going to fight the whole idea."

"Fight it?" cried Donovan. "But—"

"I know. It's all right with me now. Two hundred seventy-three degrees centigrade below zero. Won't it be a pleasure?"

"Space Station," said Donovan, "here I come."

TWO VIEWS OF MACHINE INTELLIGENCE: SATAN OR SAVIOR?

THE EVITABLE CONFLICT

ISAAC ASIMOV

(1 9 5 0)

No science fiction writer has greater faith in the potential of machine intelligence than Isaac Asimov. And no Asimov story dramatizes that faith more powerfully than "The Evitable Conflict." Here is a view of man's relationship with his computers that is in sharp contrast with Ellison's "I Have No Mouth." Asimov believes in intelligence and reason, but not when they are muddied with man's demonic drives. One way to control those drives is to program a computer so that their expression can be corrected before it becomes deadly. We meet such a computer in "The Evitable Conflict." Man's most satanic violence is war, so in this story Asimov imagines a world where war is eliminated by computer control, a world in which war is not inevitable.

What *is* inevitable? Only machines. To those who look with horror at being under the control of machines, Asimov replies that man has always been at the mercy of forces beyond his control—consider economic and sociological forces, the whims of climate, and the disasters of war. Machine control is just a different kind of control, and a superior kind since man himself designs it.

"The Evitable Conflict" was originally written in order to serve as the climax of the robot series Asimov had been writing for ten years. That same year he also wrote what he firmly resolved would be the last story of the Foundation series. Asimov had been writing virtually nothing but these two series through the decade of the 1940s and he wanted to move on to something else. For thirty years, he stuck to his resolve to write no more Foundation stories, and he did not begin a new one until 1980. But the robots were not so easily banished. They appear in his stories again and again.

THE COORDINATOR, in his private study, had that medieval curiosity, a fireplace. To be sure, the medieval man might not have recognized it as such, since it had no functional significance. The quiet, licking flame lay in an insulated recess behind clear quartz.

The logs were ignited at long distance through a trifling

diversion of the energy beam that fed the public buildings of the city. The same button that controlled the ignition first dumped the ashes of the previous fire, and allowed for the entrance of fresh wood. It was a thoroughly domesticated fireplace, you see.

But the fire itself was real. It was wired for sound, so that you could hear the crackle and, of course, you could watch it leap in the air stream that fed it.

The Coordinator's ruddy glass reflected, in miniature, the discreet gamboling of the flame, and, in even further miniature, it was reflected in each of his brooding pupils.

—And in the frosty pupils of his guest, Dr. Susan Calvin of the U. S. Robots and Mechanical Men Corporation.

The Coordinator said, "I did not ask you here entirely for social purposes, Susan."

"I did not think you did, Stephen," she replied.

"—And yet I don't quite know how to phrase my problem. On the one hand, it can be nothing at all. On the other, it can mean the end of humanity."

"I have come across so many problems, Stephen, that presented the same alternative. I think all problems do."

"Really? Then judge this— World Steel reports an overproduction of twenty thousand long tons. The Mexican Canal is two months behind schedule. The mercury mines at Almaden have experienced a production deficiency since last spring, while the Hydroponics plant at Tientsin has been laying men off. These items happen to come to mind at the moment. There is more of the same sort."

"Are these things serious? I'm not economist enough to trace the fearful consequences of such things."

"In themselves, they are not serious. Mining experts can be sent to Almaden, if the situation were to get worse. Hydroponics engineers can be used in Java or in Ceylon, if there are too many at Tientsin. Twenty thousand long tons of steel won't fill more than a few days of world demand, and the opening of the Mexican Canal two months later than the planned date is of little moment. It's the Machines that worry me; I've spoken to your Director of Research about them already."

"To Vincent Silver? He hasn't mentioned anything about it to me."

"I asked him to speak to no one. Apparently, he hasn't."

"And what did he tell you?"

"Let me put that item in its proper place. I want to talk about the Machines first. And I want to talk about them to you, because you're the only one in the world who understands robots well enough to help me now. May I grow philosophical?"

"For this evening, Stephen, you may talk how you please and of what you please, provided you tell me first what you intend to prove."

"That such small unbalances in the perfection of our system of supply and demand, as I have mentioned, may be the first step towards the final war."

"Hmp. Proceed."

Susan Calvin did not allow herself to relax, despite the designed comfort of the chair she sat in. Her cold, thin-lipped face and her flat, even voice were becoming accentuated with the years. And although Stephen Byerley was one man she could like and trust, she was almost seventy and the cultivated habits of a lifetime are not easily broken.

"Every period of human development, Susan," said the Coordinator, "has had its own particular type of human conflict— its own variety of problem that, apparently, could be settled only by force. And each time, frustratingly enough, force never really settled the problem. Instead, it persisted through a series of conflicts, then vanished of itself—what's the expression—ah, yes, 'not with a bang, but a whimper,' as the economic and social environment changed. And then, new problems, and a new series of wars. Apparently endlessly cyclic.

"Consider relatively modern times. There were the series of dynastic wars in the sixteenth to eighteenth centuries, when the most important question in Europe was whether the houses of Hapsburg or Valois-Bourbon were to rule the continent. It was one of these 'inevitable conflicts,' since Europe could obviously not exist half one and half the other.

"Except that it did, and no war ever wiped out the one and established the other, until the rise of a new social atmosphere in France in 1789 tumbled first the Bourbons and, eventually, the Hapsburgs down the dusty chute to history's incinerator.

"And in those same centuries there were the more barbarous religious wars, which revolved about the important question of whether Europe was to be Catholic or Protestant. Half and half she could not be. It was 'inevitable' that the sword decide. Except that it didn't. In England, a new industrialism was growing, and on the continent, a new nationalism. Half and half Europe remains to this day and no one cares much.

"In the nineteenth and twentieth centuries, there was a cycle of nationalist-imperialist wars, when the most important question in the world was which portions of Europe would control the economic resources and consuming capacity of which portions of non-Europe. All non-Europe obviously could not exist part English and part French and part German and so on. Until the forces of nationalism spread sufficiently so that non-Europe ended what all the wars could not, and decided it could exist quite comfortably *all* non-European.

"And so we have a pattern—"

"Yes. Stephen, you make it plain," said Susan Calvin. "These are not very profound observations."

"No. But then, it is the obvious which is so difficult to see most of the time. People say 'It's as plain as the nose on your face.' But how much of the nose on your face can you see, unless someone holds a mirror up to you? In the twentieth century, Susan, we started a new cycle of wars—what shall I call them? Ideological wars? The emotions of religion applied to economic systems, rather than to extra-natural ones? Again the wars were 'inevitable' and this time there were atomic weapons, so that mankind could no longer live through its torment to the inevitable wasting away of inevitability. And positronic robots came.

"They came in time, and, with it and alongside it, interplanetary travel. So that it no longer seemed so important whether the world was Adam Smith or Karl Marx. Neither made very much sense under the new circumstances. Both had to adapt and they ended in almost the same place."

"A *deus ex machina*, then, in a double sense," said Dr. Calvin, dryly.

The Coordinator smiled gently. "I have never heard you pun before, Susan, but you are correct. And yet there was another danger. The ending of every other problem had merely given birth to another. Our new worldwide robot economy may develop its own problems, and for that reason we have the Machines. The Earth's economy is stable, and will *remain* stable, because it is based upon the decisions of calculating machines that have the good of humanity at heart through the overwhelming force of the First Law of Robotics."

Stephen Byerley continued, "And although the Machines are nothing but the vastest conglomeration of calculating circuits ever invented, they are still robots within the meaning of the First Law, and so our Earth-wide economy is in accord with the best interests of Man. The population of Earth knows that there will be no unemployment, no overproduction or shortages. Waste and famine are words in history books. And so the question of ownership of the means of production becomes obsolescent. Whoever owned them (if such a phrase has meaning), a man, a group, a nation, or all mankind, they could be utilized only as the Machines directed. Not because men were forced to but because it was the wisest course and men knew it.

"It puts an end to war—not only to the last cycle of wars, but to the next and to all of them. Unless—"

A long pause, and Dr. Calvin encouraged him by repetition. "Unless—"

The fire crouched and skittered along a log, then popped up.

"Unless," said the Coordinator, "the Machines don't fulfill their function."

"I see. And that is where those trifling maladjustments come in which you mentioned a while ago—steel, hydroponics and so on."

"Exactly. Those errors should not be. Dr. Silver tells me they *cannot* be."

"Does he deny the facts? How unusual!"

"No, he admits the facts, of course. I do him an injustice. What he denies is that any error in the machine is responsible for the so-called (his phrase) errors in the answers. He claims that the Machines are self-correcting and that it would violate

237

the fundamental laws of nature for an error to exist in the circuits of relays. And so I said—"

"And you said, 'Have your boys check them and make sure, anyway.' "

"Susan, you read my mind. It was what I said, and he said he couldn't."

"Too busy?"

"No, he said that no human could. He was frank about it. He told me, and I hope I understand him properly, that the Machines are a gigantic extrapolation. Thus—a team of mathematicians work several years calculating a positronic brain equipped to do certain similar acts of calculation. Using this brain they make further calculations to create a still more complicated brain, which they use again to make one still more complicated and so on. According to Silver, what we call the Machines are the result of ten such steps."

"Ye-es, that sounds familiar. Fortunately, I'm not a mathematician. Poor Vincent. He is a young man. The Directors before him, Alfred Lanning and Peter Bogert, are dead, and they had no such problems. Nor had I. Perhaps roboticists as a whole should now die, since we can no longer understand our own creations."

"Apparently not. The Machines are not super-brains in the Sunday-supplement sense, although they are so pictured in the Sunday supplements. It is merely that in their own particular province of collecting and analyzing a nearly infinite number of data and relationships thereof, in nearly infinitesimal time, they have progressed beyond the possibility of detailed human control.

"And then I tried something else. I actually asked the Machine. In the strictest secrecy, we fed it the original data involved in the steel decision, its own answer, and the actual developments since—the overproduction, that is—and asked for an explanation of the discrepancy."

"Good, and what was its answer?"

"I can quote you that word for word: 'The matter admits of no explanation.' "

"And how did Vincent interpret that?"

"In two ways. Either we had not given the Machine enough data to allow a definite answer, which was unlikely—Dr. Silver admitted that—or else, it was impossible for the Machine to admit that it could give any answer to data which implied that it could harm a human being. This, naturally, is implied by the First Law. And then Dr. Silver recommended that I see you."

Susan Calvin looked very tired. "I'm old, Stephen. When Peter Bogert died, they wanted to make me Director of Research and I refused. I wasn't young then, either, and I did not wish the responsibility. They let young Silver have it and that satisfied me; but what good is it, if I am dragged into such messes?

"Stephen, let me state my position. My researches do indeed involve the interpretation of robot behavior in the light of the Three Laws of Robotics. Here, now, we have these incredible calculating machines. They are positronic robots and therefore obey the Laws of Robotics. But they lack personality; that is, their functions are extremely limited. Must be, since they are so specialized. Therefore, there is very little room for the interplay of the Laws, and my one method of attack is virtually useless. In short, I don't know that I can help you, Stephen."

The Coordinator laughed shortly. "Nevertheless, let me tell you the rest. Let me give you *my* theories, and perhaps you will then be able to tell me whether they are possible in the light of robopsychology."

"By all means. Go ahead."

"Well, since the Machines are giving the wrong answers, then, assuming that they cannot be in error, there is only one possibility. *They are being given the wrong data!* In other words, the trouble is human, and not robotic. So I took my recent planetary inspection tour—"

"From which you have just returned to New York."

"Yes. It was necessary, you see, since there are four Machines, one handling each of the Planetary Regions. *And all four are yielding imperfect results.*"

"Oh, but that follows, Stephen. If any one of the Machines is imperfect, that will automatically reflect in the result of the other three, since each of the others will assume, as part of the data on which they base their own decisions, the perfection of the imperfect fourth. With a false assumption, they will yield false answers."

"Uh-huh. So it seemed to me. Now, I have here the records of my interviews with each of the Regional Vice-Coordinators. Would you look through them with me? Oh, and first, have you heard of the Society for Humanity?"

"Umm, yes. They are an outgrowth of the Fundamentalists who have kept U.S. Robots from ever employing positronic robots on the grounds of unfair labor competition and so on. The Society for Humanity itself is anti-Machine, is it not?"

"Yes, yes, but— Well, you will see. Shall we begin? We'll start with the Eastern Region."

"As you say—"

> *The Eastern Region*
> *a—Area: 7,500,000 square miles*
> *b—Population: 1,700,000,000*
> *c—Capital: Shanghai*

Ching Hso-lin's great-grandfather had been killed in the Japanese invasion of the old Chinese Republic, and there had been no one besides his dutiful children to mourn his loss or even to know he was lost. Ching Hso-lin's grandfather had survived the civil war of the late forties, but there had been no one besides *his* dutiful children to know or care about that.

And yet Ching Hso-lin was a Regional Vice-Coordinator, with the economic welfare of half the people of Earth in his care.

Perhaps it was with the thought of all that in mind, that Ching had two maps as the only ornaments on the wall of his office. One was an old hand-drawn affair tracing out an acre or two of land, and marked with the now outmoded pictographs of old China. A little creek trickled aslant the faded markings and there were the delicate pictorial indications of lowly huts, in one of which Ching's grandfather had been born.

The other map was a huge one, sharply delineated, with all markings in neat Cyrillic characters. The red boundary that marked the Eastern Region swept within its grand confines all that had once been China, India, Burma, Indo-China, and Indonesia. On it, within the old province of Szechuan, so light and gentle that none could see it, was the little mark placed there by Ching which indicated the location of his ancestral farm.

Ching stood before these maps as he spoke to Stephen Byerley in precise English. "No one knows better than you, Mr. Coordinator, that my job, to a large extent, is a sinecure. It carries with it a certain social standing, and I represent a convenient focal point for administration, but otherwise it is the Machine! The Machine does all the work. What did you think, for instance, of the Tientsin Hydroponics works?"

"Tremendous!" said Byerley.

"It is but one of dozens, and not the largest. Shanghai, Calcutta, Batavia, Bangkok—they are widely spread and they are the answer to feeding the billion and three-quarters of the East."

"And yet," said Byerley, "you have an unemployment problem there at Tientsin. Can you be overproducing? It is incongruous to think of Asia as suffering from too much food."

Ching's dark eyes crinkled at the edges. "No. It has not come to that yet. It is true that over the last few months, several vats at Tientsin have been shut down, but it is nothing serious. The men have been released only temporarily and those who do not care to work in other fields have been shipped to Colombo in Ceylon, where a new plant is being put into operation."

"But why should the vats be closed down?"

Ching smiled gently. "You do not know much of hydroponics, I see. Well, that is not surprising. You are a Northerner, and there soil farming is still profitable. It is fashionable in the North to think of hydroponics, when it is thought of at all, as a device of growing turnips in a chemical solution, and so it is—in an infinitely complicated way.

"In the first place, by far the largest crop we deal with (and the percentage is growing) is yeast. We have upward of two thousand strains of yeast in production and new strains are added monthly. The basic food-chemicals of the various yeasts are nitrates and phosphates among the inorganics, together with proper amounts of the trace metals needed, down to the fractional parts per million of boron and molybdenum which are required. The organic matter is mostly sugar mixtures derived from the hydrolysis of cellulose, but, in addition, there are various food factors which must be added.

"For a successful hydroponics industry—one which can feed seventeen hundred million people—we must engage in an immense reforestation program throughout the East; we must have huge wood-conversion plants to deal with our southern jungles; we must have power, and steel, and chemical synthetics above all."

"Why the last, sir?"

"Because, Mr. Byerley, these strains of yeast have each their peculiar properties. We have developed, as I said, two thousand strains. The beefsteak you thought you ate today was yeast. The frozen fruit confection you had for dessert was iced yeast. We have filtered yeast juice with the taste, appearance, and all the food value of milk.

"It is flavor, more than anything else, you see, that makes yeast feeding popular, and for the sake of flavor we have developed artificial, domesticated strains that can no longer support themselves on a basic diet of salts and sugar. One needs biotin; another needs pteroylglutamic acid; still others need seventeen different amino acids supplied them as well as all the vitamins B, but one (and yet it is popular and we cannot, with economic sense, abandon it)—"

Byerley stirred in his seat, "To what purpose do you tell me all this?"

"You asked me, sir, why men are out of work in Tientsin. I have a little more to explain. It is not only that we must have these various and varying foods for our yeast; but there remains the complicating factor of popular fads with passing time, and of the possibility of the development of new strains with the new requirements and new popularity. All this must be foreseen, and the Machine does the job—"

"But not perfectly."

"Not very *im*perfectly, in view of the complications I have mentioned. Well, then, a few thousand workers in Tientsin are temporarily out of a job. But consider this, the amount of waste in this past year (waste that is, in terms of either defective supply or defective demand) amounts to not one-tenth of one percent of our total productive turnover. I consider that—"

"Yet in the first years of the Machine, the figure was nearer one-thousandth of one percent."

"Ah, but in the decade since the Machine began its operations in real earnest, we have made use of it to increase our old pre-Machine yeast industry twenty-fold. You expect imperfections to increase with complications, though—"

"Though?"

"There *was* the curious instance of Rama Vrasayana."

"What happened to him?"

"Vrasayana was in charge of a brine-evaporation plant for the production of iodine, with which yeast can do without, but human beings cannot. His plant was forced into receivership."

"Really? And through what agency?"

"Competition, believe it or not. In general, one of the chiefest functions of the Machine's analyses is to indicate the most efficient distribution of our producing units. It is obviously faulty to have areas insufficiently serviced, so that the transportation costs account for too great a percentage of the overhead. Similarly, it is faulty to have an area too well serviced, so that factories must be run at lowered capacities, or else compete harmfully with one another. In the case of Vrasayana, another plant was established in the same city, and with a more efficient extracting system."

"The Machine permitted it?"

"Oh, certainly. That is not surprising. The new system is becoming widespread. The surprise is that the Machine failed to warn Vrasayana to renovate or combine. Still, no matter. Vrasayana accepted a job as engineer in the new plant, and if his responsibility and pay are now less, he is not actually suffering. The workers found employment easily; the old plant has been converted to—something or other. Something useful. We left it all to the Machine."

"And otherwise you have no complaints."

"None!"

The Tropic Region
  a—Area: 22,000,000 square miles
  b—Population: 500,000,000
  c—Capital: Capital City

The map in Lincoln Ngoma's office was far from the model of neat precision of the one in Ching's Shanghai dominion. The boundaries of Ngoma's Tropic Region were stenciled in dark, wide brown and swept about a gorgeous interior labeled "jungle" and "desert" and "here be Elephants and all Manner of Strange Beasts."

It had much to sweep, for in land area the Tropic Region enclosed most of two continents: all of South America north of Argentina and all of Africa south of the Atlas. It included North America south of the Rio Grande as well, and even Arabia and Iran in Asia. It was the reverse of the Eastern Region. Where the ant hives of the Orient crowded half of humanity into fifteen percent of the land mass, the Tropics stretched its fifteen percent of humanity over nearly half of all the land in the world.

But it was growing. It was the one Region whose population increase through immigration exceeded that through births. And for all who came it had use.

To Ngoma, Stephen Byerley seemed like one of these immigrants, a pale searcher for the creative work of carving a harsh environment into the softness necessary for man, and he felt some of that automatic contempt of the strong man born to the strong Tropics for the unfortunate pallards of the colder suns.

The Tropics had the newest capital city on Earth, and it was called simply that, "Capital City," in the sublime confidence of youth. It spread brightly over the fertile uplands of Nigeria, and outside Ngoma's windows, far below, was life and color; the bright, bright sun and the quick, drenching showers. Even the squawking of the rainbowed birds was brisk and the stars were hard pinpoints in the sharp night.

Ngoma laughed. He was a big, dark man, strong-faced and handsome.

"Sure," he said, and his English was colloquial and mouth-filling, "the Mexican Canal is overdue. What the hell? It will get finished just the same, old boy."

"It was doing well up to the last half year."

Ngoma looked at Byerley and slowly crunched his teeth over the end of a big cigar, spitting out one end and lighting the other. "Is this an official investigation, Byerley? What's going on?"

"Nothing. Nothing at all. It's just my function as Coordinator to be curious."

"Well, if it's just that you are filling in a dull moment, the truth is that we're always short on labor. There's lots going on in the Tropics. The Canal is only one of them—"

"But doesn't your Machine predict the amount of labor available for the Canal, allowing for all the competing projects?"

Ngoma placed one hand behind his neck and blew smoke rings at the ceiling. "It was a little off."

"Is it often a little off?"

"Not oftener than you would expect. We don't expect too much of it, Byerley. We feed it data. We take its results. We do what it says. But it's just a convenience; just a labor-saving device. We could do without it, if we had to. Maybe not as well. Maybe not as quickly. But we'd get there.

"We've got confidence out here, Byerley, and that's the secret. Confidence! We've got new land that's been waiting for us for thousands of years, while the rest of the world was being ripped apart in the lousy fumblings of pre-atomic time. We don't have to eat yeast like the Eastern boys, and we don't have to worry about the stale dregs of the last century like you Northerners.

"We've wiped out the tsetse fly and the Anopheles mosquito, and people find they can live in the sun and like it, now. We've thinned down the jungles and found soil; we've watered the deserts and found gardens. We've got coal and oil in untouched fields, and minerals out of count.

"Just step back. That's all we ask the rest of the world to do. Step back, and let us work."

Byerley said, prosaically, "But the Canal—it was on schedule six months ago. What happened?"

Ngoma spread his hands. "Labor troubles." He felt through a pile of papers skeltered about his desk and gave it up.

"Had something on the matter here," he muttered, "but never mind. There was a work shortage somewhere in Mexico once on the question of women. There weren't enough women in the neighborhood. It seemed no one had thought of feeding sexual data to the Machine."

He stopped to laugh, delightedly, then sobered. "Wait a while. I think I've got it. Villafranca!"

"Villafranca?"

"Francisco Villafranca. He was the engineer in charge. Now let me straighten it out. Something happened and there was a cave-in. Right. Right. That was it. Nobody died, as I remember, but it made a hell of a mess. Quite a scandal."

"Oh?"

"There was some mistake in his calculations. Or at least, the Machine said so. They fed through Villafranca's data, assumptions, and so on. The stuff he had started with. The answers came out differently. It seems the answers Villafranca had used didn't take account of the effect of a heavy rainfall on the contours of the cut. Or something like that. I'm not an engineer, you understand.

"Anyway, Villafranca put up a devil of a squawk. He claimed the Machine's answer had been different the first time. That he had followed the Machine faithfully. Then he quit! We offered to hold him on—reasonable doubt, previous work satisfactory, and all that—in a subordinate position, of course—had to do that much—mistakes can't go unnoticed—bad for discipline— Where was I?"

"You offered to hold him on."

"Oh, yes. He refused. Well, take all in all, we're two months behind. Hell, that's nothing."

Byerley stretched out his hand and let the fingers tap lightly on the desk. "Villafranca blamed the Machine, did he?"

"Well, he wasn't going to blame himself, was he? Let's face it; human nature is an old friend of ours. Besides, I remember something else now—Why the hell can't I find documents when

I want them? My filing system isn't worth a damn— This Villafranca was a member of one of your Northern organizations. Mexico is too close to the North! That's part of the trouble."

"Which organization are you speaking of?"

"The Society for Humanity, they call it. He used to attend the annual conference in New York, Villafranca did. Bunch of crackpots, but harmless. They don't like the Machines; claim they're destroying human initiative. So naturally Villafranca would blame the Machine. Don't understand that group myself. Does Capital City look as if the human race were running out of initiative?"

And Capital City stretched out in golden glory under a golden sun—the newest and youngest creation of *Homo metropolis*.

> *The European Region*
>   *a—Area: 4,000,000 square miles*
>   *b—Population: 300,000,000*
>   *c— Capital: Geneva*

The European Region was an anomaly in several ways. In area, it was far the smallest; not one-fifth the size of the Tropic Region in area, and not one-fifth the size of the Eastern Region in population. Geographically, it was only somewhat similar to pre-atomic Europe, since it excluded what had once been European Russia and what had once been the British Isles, while it included the Mediterranean coasts of Africa and Asia, and, in a queer jump across the Atlantic, Argentina, Chile, and Uruguay as well.

Nor was it likely to improve its relative status vis-à-vis the other regions of Earth, except for what vigor the South American provinces lent it. Of all the Regions, it alone showed a positive population decline over the past half century. It alone had not seriously expanded its productive facilities, or offered anything radically new to human culture.

"Europe," said Madame Szegeczowska, in her soft French, "is essentially an economic appendage of the Northern Region. We know it, and it doesn't matter."

And as though in resigned acceptance of a lack of individuality, there was no map of Europe on the wall of the Madame Coordinator's office.

"And yet," pointed out Byerley, "you have a Machine of your own, and you are certainly under no economic pressure from across the ocean."

"A Machine! Bah!" She shrugged her delicate shoulders, and allowed a thin smile to cross her little face as she tamped out a cigarette with long fingers. "Europe is a sleepy place. And such of our men as do not manage to emigrate to the Tropics are tired and sleepy along with it. You see for yourself that it is myself, a poor woman, to whom falls the task of being Vice-Coordinator. Well, fortunately, it is not a difficult job, and not much is expected of me.

"As for the Machine—what can it say but 'Do this and it will be best for you.' But what is best for us? Why, to be an economic appendage of the Northern Region.

"And is it so terrible? No wars! We live in peace—and it is pleasant after seven thousand years of war. We are old, monsieur. In our borders, we have the regions where Occidental civilization was cradled. We have Egypt and Mesopotamia; Crete and Syria; Asia Minor and Greece. But old age is not necessarily an unhappy time. It can be a fruition—"

"Perhaps you are right," said Byerley, affably. "At least the tempo of life is not as intense as in the other Regions. It is a pleasant atmosphere."

"Is it not? Tea is being brought, monsieur. If you will indicate your cream and sugar preference, please. Thank you."

She sipped gently, then continued, "It *is* pleasant. The rest of Earth is welcome to the continuing struggle. I find a parallel here, a very interesting one. There was a time when Rome was master of the world. It had adopted the culture and civilization of Greece, a Greece which had never been united, which had ruined itself with war, and which was ending in a state of decadent squalor. Rome united it, brought it peace and let it live a life of secure non-glory. It occupied itself with its philosophies and its art, far from the clash of growth and war. It was a sort of death, but it was restful, and it lasted with minor breaks for some four hundred years."

"And yet," said Byerley, "Rome fell eventually, and the opium dream was over."

"There are no longer barbarians to overthrow civilization."

"We can be our own barbarians, Madame Szegeczowska. Oh, I meant to ask you. The Almaden mercury mines have fallen off quite badly in production. Surely the ores are not declining more rapidly than anticipated?"

The little woman's gray eyes fastened shrewdly on Byerley. "Barbarians—the fall of civilization—possible failure of the Machine. Your thought processes are very transparent, monsieur."

"Are they?" Byerley smiled. "I see that I should have had men to deal with as hitherto. You consider the Almaden affair to be the fault of the Machine?"

"Not at all, but I think you do. You, yourself, are a native of the Northern Region. The Central Coordination Office is in New York. And I have noticed for quite a while that you Northerners lack somewhat of faith in the Machine."

"We do?"

"There is your Society for Humanity, which is strong in the North, but naturally fails to find many recruits in tired old Europe, which is quite willing to let feeble humanity alone for a while. Surely, you are one of the confident North and not one of the cynical old continent."

"This has a connection with Almaden?"

"Oh, yes, I think so. The mines are in the control of Consolidated Cinnabar, which is certainly a Northern company, with headquarters at Nikolaev. Personally, I wonder if the Board of Directors have been consulting the Machine at all. They said they had in our conference last month, and, of course, we have no evidence that they did not, but I wouldn't take the word of a Northerner in this matter—no offense intended—under any circumstances. Nevertheless, I think it will have a fortunate ending."

"In what way, my dear madame?"

"You must understand that the economic irregularities of

the last few months, which, although small as compared with the great storms of the past, are quite disturbing to our peace-drenched spirits, have caused considerable restiveness in the Spanish province. I understand that Consolidated Cinnabar is selling out to a group of native Spaniards. It is consoling. If we are economic vassals of the North, it is humiliating to have the fact advertised too blatantly. And our people can be better trusted to follow the Machine."

"Then you think there will be no more trouble?"

"I am sure there will not be—in Almaden, at least."

> The Northern Region
>   a—Area: 18,000,000 square miles
>   b—Population: 800,000,000
>   c—Capital: Ottawa

The Northern Region, in more ways than one, was at the top. This was exemplified quite well by the map in the Ottawa office of Vice-Coordinator Hiram Mackenzie, in which the North Pole was centered. Except for the enclave of Europe with its Scandinavian and Icelandic regions, all the Arctic area was within the Northern Region.

Roughly, it could be divided into two major areas. To the left on the map was all of North America above the Rio Grande. To the right was included all of what had once been the Soviet Union. Together these areas represented the centered power of the planet in the first years of the Atomic Age. Between the two was Great Britain, a tongue of the Region licking at Europe. Up at the top of the map, distorted into odd, huge shapes, were Australia and New Zealand, also member provinces of the Region.

Not all the changes of the past decades had yet altered the fact that the North was the economic ruler of the planet.

There was almost an ostentatious symbolism thereof in the fact that of the official Regional maps Byerley had seen, Mackenzie's alone showed all the Earth, as though the North feared no competition and needed no favoritism to point up its preeminence.

250

"Impossible," said Mackenzie, dourly, over the whiskey. "Mr. Byerley, you have had no training as a robot technician, I believe."

"No, I have not."

"Hmp. Well, it is, in my opinion, a sad thing that Ching, Ngoma, and Szegeczowska haven't either. There is too prevalent an opinion among the peoples of Earth that a Coordinator need only be a capable organizer, a broad generalizer, and an amiable person. These days he should know his robotics as well—no offense intended."

"None taken. I agree with you."

"I take it, for instance, from what you have said already, that you worry about the recent trifling dislocation in world economy. I don't know what you suspect, but it has happened in the past that people—who should have known better—wondered what would happen if false data were fed into the Machine."

"And what would happen, Mr. Mackenzie?"

"Well," the Scotsman shifted his weight and sighed, "all collected data goes through a complicated screening system which involves both human and mechanical checking, so that the problem is not likely to arise. But let us ignore that. Humans are fallible, also corruptible, and ordinary mechanical devices are liable to mechanical failure.

"The real point of the matter is that what we call a 'wrong datum' is one which is inconsistent with all other known data. It is our only criterion of right and wrong. It is the Machine's as well. Order it, for instance, to direct agricultural activity on the basis of an average July temperature in Iowa of fifty-seven degrees Fahrenheit. It won't accept that. It will not give an answer. Not that it has any prejudice against that particular temperature, or that an answer is impossible, but because, in the light of all the other data fed it over a period of years, it knows that the probability of an average July temperature of fifty-seven is virtually nil. It rejects that datum.

"The only way a 'wrong datum' can be forced on the Machine is to include it as part of a self-consistent whole, all of which is subtly wrong in a manner either too delicate for the Machine to detect or outside the Machine's experience. The former is beyond human capacity, and the latter is almost so, and is becoming more nearly so as the Machine's experience increases by the second."

Stephen Byerley placed two fingers to the bridge of his nose. "Then the Machine cannot be tampered with. And how do you account for recent errors, then?"

"My dear Byerley, I see that you instinctively follow that great error—that the Machine knows all. Let me cite you a case from my personal experience. The cotton industry engages experienced buyers who purchase cotton. Their procedure is to pull a tuft of cotton out of a random bale of a lot. They will look at that tuft and feel it, tease it out, listen to the crackling perhaps as they do so, touch it with their tongue—and through this procedure they will determine the class of cotton the bales represent. There are about a dozen such classes. As a result of their decisions, purchases are made at certain prices, blends are made in certain proportions. Now these buyers cannot yet be replaced by the Machine."

"Why not? Surely the data involved is not too complicated for it?"

"Probably not. But what data is this you refer to? No textile chemist knows exactly what it is that the buyer tests when he feels a tuft of cotton. Presumably there's the average length of the threads, their feel, the extent and nature of their slickness, the way they hang together, and so on—several dozen items, subconsciously weighed, out of years of experience. But the *quantitative* nature of these tests is not known; maybe even the very nature of some of them is not known. So we have nothing to feed the Machine. Nor can the buyers explain their own judgment. They can only say, 'Well, look at it. Can't you *tell* it's class-such-and-such?'"

"I see."

"There are innumerable cases like that. The Machine is only a tool, after all, which can help humanity progress faster by taking some of the burdens of calculations and interpretations off its back. The task of the human brain remains what it has always been: that of discovering new data to be analyzed, and of devising new concepts to be tested. A pity the Society for Humanity won't understand that."

"They are against the Machine?"

"They would be against mathematics or against the art of writing if they had lived at the appropriate time. These reactionaries of the Society claim the Machine robs man of his soul. I notice that capable men are still at a premium in our society; we still need the man who is intelligent enough to think of the proper questions to ask. Perhaps if we could find enough of such, these dislocations you worry about, Coordinator, wouldn't occur."

> *Earth (Including the uninhabited continent, Antarctica)*
> *a—Area: 54,000,000 square miles (land surface)*
> *b—Population: 3,300,000,000*
> *c—Capital: New York*

The fire behind the quartz was weary now, and sputtered its reluctant way to death.

The Coordinator was somber, his mood matching the sinking flame.

"They all minimize the state of affairs." His voice was low. "Is it not easy to imagine that they all laugh at me? And yet— Vincent Silver said the Machines cannot be out of order, and I must believe him. Hiram Mackenzie says they cannot be fed false data, and I must believe him. But the Machines are going wrong, somehow, and I must believe that, too—and so there is *still* an alternative left."

He glanced sidewise at Susan Calvin, who, with closed eyes, for a moment seemed asleep.

"What is that?" she asked, prompt to her cue, nevertheless.

"Why, that correct data is indeed given, and correct answers are indeed received, but that they are then ignored. There is no way the Machine can enforce obedience to its dictates."

"Madame Szegeczowska hinted as much, with reference to Northerners in general, it seems to me."

"So she did."

"And what purpose is served by disobeying the Machine? Let's consider motivations."

"It's obvious to me, and should be to you. It is a matter of rocking the boat, deliberately. There can be no serious conflicts on Earth, in which one group or another can seize more power than it has for what it thinks is its own good despite the harm to mankind as a whole, while the Machines rule. If popular faith in the Machines can be destroyed to the point where they are abandoned, it will be the law of the jungle again. And not one of the four Regions can be freed of the suspicion of wanting just that.

"The East has half of humanity within its borders, and the Tropics more than half of Earth's resources. Each can feel itself the natural rulers of all Earth, and each has a history of humiliation by the North, for which it can be human enough to wish a senseless revenge. Europe has a tradition of greatness, on the other hand. It once *did* rule the Earth, and there is nothing so eternally adhesive as the memory of power.

"Yet, in another way, it's hard to believe. Both the East and the Tropics are in a state of enormous expansion within their own borders. Both are climbing incredibly. They cannot have the spare energy for military adventures. And Europe can have nothing but its dreams. It is a cipher, militarily."

"So, Stephen," said Susan, "you leave the North."

"Yes," said Byerley, energetically, "I do. The North is now the strongest, and has been for nearly a century, or its component parts have been. But it is losing relatively, now. The Tropic Regions may take their place in the forefront of civilization for the first time since the Pharaohs, and there are Northerners who fear that.

"The Society for Humanity is a Northern organization primarily, you know, and they make no secret of not wanting the Machines. Susan, they are few in numbers, but it is an association of powerful men. Heads of factories, directors of industries and agricultural combines who hate to be what they call 'the Machine's office-boy' belong to it. Men with ambition belong to it. Men who feel themselves strong enough to decide for themselves what is best for themselves, and not just to be told what is best for others.

"In short, just those men who, by together refusing to accept the decisions of the Machine, can, in a short time, turn the world topsy-turvy—just those belong to the Society.

"Susan, it hangs together. Five of the Directors of World Steel are members, and World Steel suffers from overproduction. Consolidated Cinnabar, which mined mercury at Almaden, was a Northern concern. Its books are still being investigated, but one, at least, of the men concerned was a member. Francisco Villafranca, who, singlehanded, delayed the Mexican Canal for two months, was a member, we know already—and so was Rama Vrasayana, I was not at all surprised to find out."

Susan said, quietly, "These men, I might point out, have all done badly—"

"But naturally," interjected Byerley. "To disobey the Machine's analyses is to follow a non-optimal path. Results are poorer than they might be. It's the price they pay. They will have it rough now, but in the confusion that will eventually follow—"

"Just what do you plan on doing, Stephen?"

"There is obviously no time to lose. I am going to have the Society outlawed, every member removed from any responsible post. And all executive and technical positions, henceforward, can be filled only by applicants signing a non-Society oath. It will mean a certain surrender of basic civil liberties, but I am sure the Congress—"

"It won't work!"

"What! Why not?"

"I will make a prediction. If you try any such thing, you will find yourself hampered at every turn. You will find it impossible to carry out. You will find your every move in that direction will result in trouble."

Byerley was taken aback. "Why do you say that? I was rather hoping for your approval in this matter."

"You can't have it as long as your actions are based on a false premise. You admit the Machine can't be wrong, and can't be fed wrong data. I will now show you that it cannot be disobeyed, either, as you think is being done by the Society."

"*That* I don't see at all."

"Then listen. Every action by any executive which does not

255

follow the exact directions of the Machine he is working with becomes part of the data for the next problem. The Machine, therefore, knows that the executive has a certain tendency to disobey. He can incorporate that tendency into that data—even quantitatively, that is, judging exactly how much and in what direction disobedience would occur. Its next answers would be just sufficiently biased so that after the executive concerned disobeyed, he would have automatically corrected those answers to optimal directions. The Machine *knows*, Stephen!"

"You can't be sure of all this. You are guessing."

"It is a guess based on a lifetime's experience with robots. You had better rely on such a guess, Stephen."

"But then what is left? The Machines themselves are correct and the premises they work on are correct. That we have agreed upon. Now you say that it cannot be disobeyed. Then what is wrong?"

"You have answered yourself. *Nothing is wrong!* Think about the Machines for a while, Stephen. They are robots, and they follow the First Law. But the Machines work not for any single human being, but for all humanity, so that the First Law becomes: 'No Machine may harm humanity, or, through inaction, allow humanity to come to harm.'

"Very well, then, Stephen, what harms humanity? Economic dislocations most of all, from whatever cause. Wouldn't you say so?"

"I would."

"And what is most likely in the future to cause economic dislocations? Answer that, Stephen."

"I should say," replied Byerley, unwillingly, "the destruction of the Machines."

"And so should I say, and so should the Machines say. Their first care, therefore, is to preserve themselves, for us. And so they are quietly taking care of the only elements left that threaten them. It is not the Society for Humanity which is shaking the boat so that the Machines may be destroyed. You have been looking at the reverse of the picture. Say rather that the Machine is shaking the boat—*very* slightly—just enough to shake loose those few which cling to the side for purposes the Machines consider harmful to humanity.

"So Vrasayana loses his factory and gets another job where he can do no harm—he is not badly hurt, he is not rendered incapable of earning a living, for the Machine cannot harm a human being more than minimally, and that only to save a greater number. Consolidated Cinnabar loses control at Almaden. Villafranca is no longer a civil engineer in charge of an important project. And the directors of World Steel are losing their grip on the industry—or will."

"But you don't really know all this," insisted Byerley distractedly. "How can we possibly take a chance on your being right?"

"You must. Do you remember the Machine's own statement when you presented the problem to him? It was: 'The matter admits of no explanation.' The Machine did not say there was no explanation, or that it could determine no explanation. It simply was not going to *admit* any explanation. In other words, it would be harmful to humanity to have the explanation known, and that's why we can only guess—and keep on guessing."

"But how can the explanation do us harm? Assume that you are right, Susan."

"Why, Stephen, if I am right, it means that the Machine is conducting our future for us not only simply in direct answer to our direct questions, but in general answer to the world situation and to human psychology as a whole. And to know that may make us unhappy and may hurt our pride. The Machine cannot, *must* not, make us unhappy.

"Stephen, how do we know what the ultim   rood of Humanity will entail? We haven't at *our* disposal t   ite factors that the Machine has at *its*! Perhaps, to give yo   nfamiliar example, our entire technical civilization has   more unhappiness and misery than it has removed. Perh   an agrarian or pastoral civilization, with less culture and fewer people, would be better. If so, the Machines must move in that direction, preferably without telling us, since in our ignorant prejudices we only know that what we are used to is good—and we would then fight change. Or perhaps a complete urbanization or a completely caste-ridden society, or complete anarchy is the answer. We don't know. Only the Machines know, and they are going there and taking us with them."

"But you are telling me, Susan, that the Society for Humanity is right, and that mankind *has* lost its own say in its future."

"It never had any, really. It was always at the mercy of economic and sociological forces it did not understand—at the whims of climate, and the fortunes of war. Now the Machines understand them; and no one can stop them, since the Machines will deal with them as they are dealing with the Society—having, as they do, the greatest of weapons at their disposal, the absolute control of our economy."

"How horrible!"

"Perhaps how wonderful! Think that for all time, all conflicts are finally evitable. Only the Machines, from now on, are inevitable!"

And the fire behind the quartz went out and only a curl of smoke was left to indicate its place.

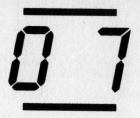

THE USES
OF
COMPUTERS
AND
ROBOTS

A LOGIC NAMED JOE

MURRAY LEINSTER

(1 9 4 6)

This very interesting story is one of a kind. Change the word *logic* in the title to *computer*, and you have a story about home computers. The extraordinary point here is that at the time the story was written—1946—the miniaturization of computers had not yet been anticipated. Computers then were huge constructs so expensive that only the government or a large corporation could afford to own one. And so no one writing science fiction about computers in the early 1940s and 1950s imagined a society where home computers might be common—except for Murray Leinster.

Murray Leinster (1896–1975) published his first story in 1919 and continued to write prolifically for the next forty years. His real name was Will F. Jenkins. The winner of a Hugo Award, he was long referred to as "the dean of science fiction." He was at his finest in the short-story mode and is perhaps best known as the author of "First Contact," a classic tale of man's encounter with aliens.

IT WAS ON the third day of August that Joe come off the assembly line, and on the fifth Laurine come into town, and that afternoon I saved civilization. That's what I figure anyhow. Laurine is a blonde that I was crazy about once—and crazy is the word—and Joe is a logic that I have stored away down in the cellar right now. I had to pay for him because I said I busted him, and sometimes I think about turning him on and sometimes I think about taking an ax to him. Sooner or later I'm gonna do one or the other. I kinda hope it's the ax. I could use a coupla million dollars—sure!—an' Joe'd tell me how to get or make 'em. He can do plenty! But so far I've been scared to take a chance. After all, I figure I really saved a civilization by turnin' him off.

The way Laurine fits in is that she makes cold shivers run up an' down my spine when I think about her. You see, I've got a wife which I acquired after I had parted from Laurine with

261

much romantic despair. She is a reasonable good wife, and I have some kids which are hellcats but I value 'em. If I have sense enough to leave well enough alone, sooner or later I will retire on a pension an' Social Security an' spend the rest of my life fishin', contented an' lyin' about what a great guy I used to be. But there's Joe. I'm worried about Joe.

I'm a maintenance man for the Logics Company. My job is servicing logics, and I admit modestly that I am pretty good. I was servicing televisions before that guy Carson invented his trick circuit that will select any of 'steenteen million other circuits—in theory there ain't no limit—and before the Logics Company hooked it into the tank-and-integrator setup, they were usin' 'em for business-machine service. They added a vision screen for speed—an' they found out they'd made logics. They were surprised an' pleased. They're still findin' out what logics will do, but everybody's got 'em.

I got Joe, after Laurine nearly got me. You know the logics setup. You got a logic in your house. It looks like a vision receiver used to, only it's got keys instead of dials and you punch the keys for what you wanna get. It's hooked in to the tank, which has the Carson Circuit all fixed up with relays. Say you punch "Station SNAFU" on your logic. Relays in the tank take over an' whatever vision-program SNAFU is telecastin' comes on your logic's screen. Or you punch "Sally Hancock's Phone" an' the screen blinks an' sputters an' you're hooked up with the logic in her house an' if somebody answers you got a vision-phone connection. But besides that, if you punch for the weather forecast or who won today's race at Hialeah or who was mistress of the White House durin' Garfield's administration or what is PDQ and R sellin' for today, that comes on the screen too. The relays in the tank do it. The tank is a big buildin' full of all the facts in creation an' all the recorded telecasts that ever was made—an' it's hooked in with all the other tanks all over the country—an' anything you wanna know or see or hear, you punch for it an' you get it. Very convenient. Also it does math for you, an' keeps books, an' acts as consultin' chemist, physicist, astronomer an' tealeaf reader, with a "Advice to Lovelorn" thrown in. The only thing it won't do is tell you exactly what your wife meant when she said "Oh, you think so, do you?" in that peculiar kinda voice. Logics don't work good on women. Only on things that make sense.

Logics are all right, though. They changed civilization, the highbrows tell us. All on accounta the Carson Circuit. And Joe shoulda been a perfectly normal logic, keeping some family or other from wearin' out its brains doin' the kids' homework for 'em. But somethin' went wrong in the assembly line. It was somethin' so small that precision gauges didn't measure it, but it made Joe a individual. Maybe he didn't know it at first. Or maybe, bein' logical, he figured out that if he was to show he was different from other logics they'd scrap him. Which woulda been a brilliant idea. But anyhow, he come off the assembly line, an' he went through the regular tests without anybody screamin' shrilly on findin' out what he was. And he went right on out an' was duly installed in the home of Mr. Thaddeus Korlanovitch at 119 East Seventh Street, second floor front. So far, everything was serene.

The installation happened late Saturday night. Sunday morning the Korlanovitch kids turned him on an' seen the Kiddie Shows. Around noon their parents peeled 'em away from him an' piled 'em in the car. Then they come back in the house for the lunch they'd forgot an' one of the kids sneaked back an' they found him punchin' keys for the Kiddie Shows of the week before. They dragged him out an' went off. But they left Joe turned on.

That was noon. Nothin' happened until two in the afternoon. It was the calm before the storm. Laurine wasn't in town yet, but she was comin'. I picture Joe sittin' there all by himself, buzzing meditative. Maybe he run Kiddie Shows in the empty apartment for a while. But I think he went kinda remote-control exploring in the tank. There ain't any fact that can be said to be a fact that ain't on a data plate in some tank somewhere . . . unless it's one the technicians are diggin' out an' puttin' on a data plate now. Joe had plenty of material to work on. An' he musta started workin' right off the bat.

Joe ain't vicious, you understand. He ain't like one of these ambitious robots you read about that make up their minds the

human race is inefficient and has got to be wiped out an' replaced
by thinkin' machines. Joe's just got ambition. If you were a
machine, you'd wanna work right, wouldn't you? That's Joe. He
wants to work right. An' he's a logic. An' logics can do a lotta
things that ain't been found out yet. So Joe, discoverin' the fact,
begun to feel restless. He selects some things us dumb humans
ain't thought of yet, an' begins to arrange so logics will be called
on to do 'em.

That's all. That's everything. But, brother, it's enough!

Things are kinda quiet in the Maintenance Department about
two in the afternoon. We are playing pinochle. Then one of the
guys remembers he has to call up his wife. He goes to one of the
bank of logics in Maintenance and punches the keys for his house.
The screen sputters. Then a flash comes on the screen.

"Announcing new and improved logics service! Your logic
is now equipped to give you not only consultive but directive
service. If you want to do something and don't know how to do
it—ask your logic!"

There's a pause. A kinda expectant pause. Then, as if reluctantly, his connection comes through. His wife answers an' gives
him hell for somethin' or other. He takes it an' snaps off.

"Whadda you know?" he says when he comes back. He tells
us about the flash. "We shoulda been warned about that. There's
gonna be a lotta complaints. Suppose a fella asks how to get
ridda his wife an' the censor circuits block the question?"

Somebody melds a hundred aces an' says:

"Why not punch for it an' see what happens?"

It's a gag, o' course. But the guy goes over. He punches keys.
In theory, a censor block is gonna come on an' the screen will
say severely, "Public policy forbids this service." You hafta have
censor blocks or the kiddies will be askin' detailed questions
about things they're too young to know. And there are other
reasons. As you will see.

This fella punches, "How can I get rid of my wife?" Just for
the fun of it. The screen is blank for half a second. Then comes
a flash. "Service question: Is she blonde or brunette?" He hollers

to us an' we come look. He punches, "Blonde." There's another brief pause. Then the screen says, "Hexymetacryloaminoacetine is a constituent of green shoe polish. Take home a frozen meal including dried pea soup. Color the soup with green shoe polish. It will appear to be green-pea soup. Hexymetacryloaminoacetine is a selective poison which is fatal to blonde females but not to brunettes or males of any coloring. This fact has not been brought out by human experiment, but is a product of logics service. You cannot be convicted of murder. It is improbable that you will be suspected."

The screen goes blank, and we stare at each other. It's bound to be right. A logic workin' the Carson Circuit can no more make a mistake than any other kinda computin' machine. I call the tank in a hurry.

"Hey, you guys!" I yell. "Somethin's happened! Logics are givin' detailed instructions for wife-murder! Check your censor-circuits—but quick!"

That was close, I think. But little do I know. At that precise instant, over on Monroe Avenue, a drunk starts to punch for somethin' on a logic. The screen says "Announcing new and improved logics service! If you want to do something and don't know how to do it—ask your logic!" And the drunk says owlish, "I'll do it!" So he cancels his first punching and fumbles around and says: "How can I keep my wife from finding out I've been drinking?" And the screen says, prompt: "Buy a bottle of Franine hair shampoo. It is harmless but contains a detergent which will neutralize ethyl alcohol immediately. Take one teaspoonful for each jigger of hundred-proof you have consumed."

This guy was plenty plastered—just plastered enough to stagger next door and obey instructions. An' five minutes later he was cold sober and writing down the information so he couldn't forget it. It was new, and it was big! He got rich offa that memo! He patented *SOBUH, The Drink That Makes Happy Homes!* You can top off any souse with a slug or two of it an' go home sober as a judge. The guy's cussin' income taxes right now!

You can't kick on stuff like that. But a ambitious young

fourteen-year-old wanted to buy some kid stuff and his pop wouldn't fork over. He called up a friend to tell his troubles. And his logic says: "If you want to do something and don't know how to do it—ask your logic!" So this kid punches: "How can I make a lotta money, fast?"

His logic comes through with the simplest, neatest, and most efficient counterfeitin' device yet known to science. You see, all the data was in the tank. The logic—since Joe had closed some relays here an' there in the tank—simply integrated the facts. That's all. The kid got caught up with three days later, havin' already spent two thousand credits an' havin' plenty more on hand. They had a time tellin' his counterfeits from the real stuff, an' the only way they done it was that he changed his printer, kid fashion, not bein' able to let somethin' that was workin' right alone.

Those are what you might call samples. Nobody knows all that Joe done. But there was the bank president who got humorous when his logic flashed that "Ask your logic" spiel on him, and jestingly asked how to rob his own bank. An' the logic told him, brief and explicit but good! The bank president hit the ceiling, hollering for cops. There musta been plenty of that sorta thing. There was fifty-four more robberies than usual in the next twenty-four hours, all of them planned astute an' perfect. Some of 'em they never did figure out how they'd been done. Joe, he'd gone exploring in the tank and closed some relays like a logic is supposed to do—but only when required—and blocked all censor-circuits an' fixed up this logics service which planned perfect crimes, nourishing an' attractive meals, counterfeitin' machines, an' new industries with a fine impartiality. He musta been plenty happy, Joe must. He was functionin' swell, buzzin' along to himself while the Korlanovitch kids were off ridin' with their ma an' pa.

They come back at seven o'clock, the kids all happily wore out with their afternoon of fightin' each other in the car. Their folks put 'em to bed and sat down to rest. They saw Joe's screen flickerin' meditative from one subject to another an' old man

266

Korlanovitch had had enough excitement for one day. He turned Joe off.

An' at that instant the patterns of relays that Joe had turned on snapped off, all the offers of directive service stopped flashin' on logic screens everywhere, an' peace descended on the earth.

For everybody else. But for me. Laurine come to town. I have often thanked God fervent that she didn't marry me when I thought I wanted her to. In the intervenin' years she had progressed. She was blonde an' fatal to begin with. She had got blonder and fataler an' had had four husbands and one acquittal for homicide an' had acquired a air of enthusiasm and self-confidence. That's just a sketch of the background. Laurine was not the kinda former girlfriend you like to have turning up in the same town with your wife. But she came to town, an' Monday morning she tuned right into the middle of Joe's second spasm of activity.

The Korlanovitch kids had turned him on again. I got these details later and kinda pieced 'em together. An' every logic in town was dutifully flashin' a notice, "If you want to do something—ask your logic!" every time they were turned on for use. More'n that, when people punched for the morning news, they got a full account of the previous afternoon's doin's. Which put 'em in a frame of mind to share in the party. One bright fella demands, "How can I make a perpetual-motion machine?" And his logic sputters a while an' then comes up with a setup usin' the Brownian movement to turn little wheels. If the wheels ain't bigger'n a eighth of an inch they'll turn, all right, an' practically it's perpetual motion. Another one asks for the secret of transmuting metals. The logic rakes back in the data plates an' integrates a strictly practical answer. It does take so much power that you can't make no profit except on radium, but that pays off good. An' from the fact that for a coupla years to come the police were turnin' up new and improved jimmies, knob-claws for gettin' at safe-innards, and all-purpose keys that'd open any known lock—why, there must have been other inquiries with a strictly practical viewpoint. Joe done a lot for technical progress!

But he done more in other lines. Educational, say. None of my kids are old enough to be interested, but Joe bypassed all censor-circuits because they hampered the service he figured logics should give humanity. So the kids an' teenagers who wanted to know what comes after the bees an' flowers found out. And there is certain facts which men hope their wives won't do more'n suspect, an' those facts are just what their wives are really curious about. So when a woman dials: "How can I tell if Oswald is true to me?" and her logic tells her—you can figure out how many rows got started that night when the men come home!

All this while Joe goes on buzzin' happy to himself, showin' the Korlanovitch kids the animated funnies with one circuit while with the others he remote-controls the tank so that all the other logics can give people what they ask for and thereby raise merry hell.

An' then Laurine gets onto the new service. She turns on the logic in her hotel room, prob'ly to see the week's style-forecast. But the logic says, dutiful: "If you want to do something—ask your logic!" So Laurine prob'ly looks enthusiastic—she would— and tries to figure out something to ask. She already knows all about everything she cares about—ain't she had four husbands an' shot one?—so I occur to her. She knows this is the town I live in. So she punches, "How can I find Ducky?"

O.K., guy! But that is what she used to call me. She gets a service question. "Is Ducky known by any other name?" So she gives my regular name. And the logic can't find me. Because my logic ain't listed under my name on account of I am in Maintenance and don't want to be pestered when I'm home, and there ain't any data plates on code-listed logics, because the codes get changed so often—like a guy gets plastered an' tells a redhead to call him up, an' on gettin' sober hurriedly has the code changed before she reaches his wife on the screen.

Well! Joe is stumped. That's prob'ly on the first question logics service hasn't been able to answer. "How can I locate Ducky?"!! Quite a problem! So Joe broods over it while showin' the Korlanovitch kids the animated comic about the cute little boy who carries sticks of dynamite in his hip pocket an' plays practical jokes on everybody. Then he gets the trick. Laurine's screen suddenly flashes:

"Logics special service will work upon your question. Please

punch your logic designation and leave it turned on. You will
be called back."

Laurine is merely mildly interested, but she punches her
hotel-room number and has a drink and takes a nap. Joe sets to
work. He has been given an idea.

My wife calls me at Maintenance and hollers. She is fit to
be tied. She says I got to do something. She was gonna make a
call to the butcher shop. Instead of the butcher or even the "If
you want to do something" flash, she got a new one. The screen
says, "Service question: What is your name?" She is kinda puzzled, but she punches it. The screen sputters an' then says: "Secretarial service demonstration! You—" It reels off her name,
address, age, sex, coloring, the amounts of all her charge accounts in all the stores, my name as her husband, how much I
get a week, the fact that I've been pinched three times—twice
was traffic stuff, and once for a argument I got in with a guy—
and the interestin' item that once when she was mad with me
she left me for three weeks an' had her address changed to her
folks' home. Then it says, brisk: "Logics service will hereafter
keep your personal accounts, take messages, and locate persons
you may wish to get in touch with. This demonstration is to
introduce the service." Then it connects her with the butcher.

But she don't want meat, then. She wants blood. She calls
me.

"If it'll tell me all about myself," she says, fairly boilin', "it'll
tell anybody else who punches my name! You've got to stop it!"

"Now, now, honey!" I says. "I didn't know about all this!
It's new! But they musta fixed the tank so it won't give out
information except to the logic where a person lives!"

"Nothing of the kind!" she tells me, furious. "I tried! And
you know that Blossom woman who lives next door! She's been
married three times and she's forty-two years old and she says
she's only thirty! And Mrs. Hudson's had her husband arrested
four times for nonsupport and once for beating her up. And—"

"Hey!" I says. "You mean the logic told you this?"

"Yes!" she wails. "It will tell anybody anything! You've got
to stop it! How long will it take?"

"I'll call up the tank," I says. "It can't take long."

"Hurry!" she says, desperate, "before somebody punches my name! I'm going to see what it says about that hussy across the street."

She snaps off to gather what she can before it's stopped. So I punch for the tank and I get this new "What is your name?" flash. I got a morbid curiosity and I punch my name, and the screen says: "Were you ever called Ducky?" I blink. I ain't got no suspicions. I say, "Sure!" And the screen says, "There is a call for you."

Bingo! There's the inside of a hotel room and Laurine is reclinin' asleep on the bed. She'd been told to leave her logic turned on an' she done it. It is a hot day and she is trying to be cool. I would say that she oughta not suffer from the heat. Me, being human, I do not stay as cool as she looks. But there ain't no need to go into that. After I get my breath I say, "For Heaven's sake!" and she opens her eyes.

At first she looks puzzled, like she was thinking is she getting absent-minded and is this guy somebody she married lately. Then she grabs a sheet and drapes it around herself and beams at me.

"Ducky!" she says. "How marvelous!"

I say something like "Ugmph!" I am sweating.

She says:

"I put in a call for you, Ducky, and here you are! Isn't it romantic? Where are you really, Ducky? And when can you come up? You've no idea how often I've thought of you!"

I am probably the only guy she ever knew real well that she has not been married to at some time or another.

I say "Ugmph!" again, and swallow.

"Can you come up instantly?" asks Laurine brightly.

"I'm . . . workin'," I say. "I'll . . . uh . . . call you back."

"I'm terribly lonesome," says Laurine. "Please make it quick, Ducky! I'll have a drink waiting for you. Have you ever thought of me?"

"Yeah," I say, feeble. "Plenty!"

"You darling!" says Laurine. "Here's a kiss to go on with until you get here! Hurry, Ducky!"

Then I sweat! I still don't know nothing about Joe, understand. I cuss out the guys at the tank because I blame them for this. If Laurine was just another blonde—well—when it comes to ordinary blondes I can leave 'em alone or leave 'em alone, either one. A married man gets that way or else. But Laurine has a look of unquenched enthusiasm that gives a man very strange weak sensations at the back of his knees. And she'd had four husbands and shot one and got acquitted.

So I punch the keys for the tank technical room, fumbling. And the screen says: "What is your name?" but I don't want any more. I punch the name of the old guy who's stock clerk in Maintenance. And the screen gives me some pretty interestin' dope—I never woulda thought the old fella had ever had that much pep—and winds up by mentionin' a unclaimed deposit now amountin' to two hundred eighty credits in the First National Bank, which he should look into. Then it spiels about the new secretarial service and gives me the tank at last.

I start to swear at the guy who looks at me. But he says, tired:

"Snap it off, fella. We got troubles an' you're just another. What are the logics doin' now?"

I tell him, and he laughs a hollow laugh.

"A light matter, fella," he says. "A very light matter! We just managed to clamp off all the data plates that give information on high explosives. The demand for instructions in counterfeiting is increasing minute by minute. We are also trying to shut off, by main force, the relays that hook in to data plates that just barely might give advice on the fine points of murder. So if people will only keep busy getting the goods on each other for a while, maybe we'll get a chance to stop the circuits that are shifting credit-balances from bank to bank before everybody's bankrupt except the guys who thought of askin' how to get big bank accounts in a hurry."

"Then," I says hoarse, "shut down the tank! Do somethin'!"

"Shut down the tank?" he says mirthless. "Does it occur to you, fella, that the tank has been doin' all the computin' for every business office for years? It's been handlin' the distribution of ninety-four percent of all telecast programs, has given out all information on weather, plane schedules, special sales, employment opportunities and news; has handled all person-to-person contacts over wires and recorded every business conversation and agreement—listen, fella! Logics changed civilization. Logics *are* civilization! If we shut off logics, we go back to a kind of civilization we have forgotten how to run! I'm getting hysterical myself and that's why I'm talkin' like this! If my wife finds out my paycheck is thirty credits a week more than I told her and starts hunting for that redhead—"

He smiles a haggard smile at me and snaps off. And I sit down and put my head in my hands. It's true. If something had happened back in cave days and they'd hadda stop usin' fire— if they'd hadda stop usin' steam in the nineteenth century or electricity in the twentieth—it's like that. We got a very simple civilization. In the nineteen hundreds a man would have to make use of a typewriter, radio, telephone, tele-typewriter, newspaper, reference library, encyclopedias, office files, directories, plus messenger service and consulting lawyers, chemists, doctors, dietitians, filing clerks, secretaries—all to put down what he wanted to remember an' to tell him what other people had put down that he wanted to know; to report what he said to somebody else and to report to him what they said back. All we have to have is logics. Anything we want to know or see or hear, or anybody we want to talk to, we punch keys on a logic. Shut off logics and everything goes skiddoo. But Laurine . . .

Somethin' had happened. I still didn't know what it was. Nobody else knows, even yet. What had happened was Joe. What was the matter with him was that he wanted to work good. All this fuss he was raisin' was, actual, nothin' but stuff we shoulda thought of ourselves. Directive advice, tellin' us what we wanted to know to solve a problem, wasn't but a slight extension of logical-integrator service. Figurin' out a good way to poison a fella's wife was only different in degrees from figurin' out a cube root or a guy's bank balance. It was gettin' the answer to a question. But things was goin' to pot because there was too many answers being given to too many questions.

One of the logics in Maintenance lights up. I go over, weary, to answer it. I punch the answer key. Laurine says:

"Ducky!"

It's the same hotel room. There's two glasses on the table with drinks in them. One is for me. Laurine's got on some kinda frothy hangin'-around-the-house-with-the-boyfriend outfit that automatic makes you strain your eyes to see if you actual see what you think. Laurine looks at me enthusiastic.

"Ducky!" says Laurine. "I'm lonesome! Why haven't you come up?"

"I . . . been busy," I say, strangling slightly.

"*Pooh!*" says Laurine. "Listen, Ducky! Do you remember how much in love we used to be?"

I gulp.

"Are you doin' anything this evening?" says Laurine.

I gulp again, because she is smiling at me in a way that a single man would maybe get dizzy, but it gives a old married man like me cold chills. When a dame looks at you possessive. . . .

"Ducky!" says Laurine, impulsive. "I was so mean to you! Let's get married!"

Desperation gives me a voice.

"I . . . got married," I tell her, hoarse.

Laurine blinks. Then she says, courageous:

"Poor boy! But we'll get you outa that! Only it would be nice if we could be married today. Now we can only be engaged!"

"I . . . can't—"

"I'll call up your wife," says Laurine, happy, "and have a talk with her. You must have a code signal for your logic, darling. I tried to ring your house and noth—"

Click! That's my logic turned off. I turned it off. And I feel faint all over. I got nervous prostration. I got combat fatigue. I got anything you like. I got cold feet.

I beat it outa Maintenance, yellin' to somebody I got a emergency call. I'm gonna get out in a Maintenance car an' cruise around until it's plausible to go home. Then I'm gonna take the wife an' kids an' beat it for somewheres that Laurine won't ever find me. I don't wanna be fifth in Laurine's series of husbands and maybe the second one she shoots in a moment of boredom. I got experience of blondes. I got experience of Laurine! And I'm scared to death!

I beat it out into traffic in the Maintenance car. There was a disconnected logic on the back, ready to substitute for one that had a burnt-out coil or something that it was easier to switch and fix back in the Maintenance shop. I drove crazy but automatic. It was kinda ironic, if you think of it. I was goin' hoopla over a strictly personal problem, while civilization was crackin' up all around me because other people were havin' their personal problems solved as fast as they could state 'em. It is a matter of record that part of the Mid-Western Electric research guys had been workin' on cold electron-emission for thirty years, to make vacuum tubes that wouldn't need a power source to heat the filament. And one of those fellas was intrigued by the "Ask your logic" flash. He asked how to get cold emission of electrons. And the logic integrates a few squintillion facts on the physics data plates and tells him. Just as casual as it told somebody over in the Fourth Ward how to serve leftover soup in a new attractive way, and somebody else on Mason Street how to dispose of a torso that somebody had left careless in his cellar after ceasing to use same.

Laurine wouldn't never have found me if it hadn't been for this new logics service. But now that it was started—zowie! She'd shot one husband and got acquitted. Suppose she got impatient because I was still married an' asked logics service how to get me free an' in a spot where I'd have to marry her by 8:30 P.M.? It woulda told her! Just like it told that woman out in the suburbs how to make sure her husband wouldn't run around no more. *Br-r-r-r!* An' like it told that kid how to find some buried treasure. Remember? He was happy totin' home the gold reserve of the Hanoverian Bank and Trust Company when they caught on to it. The logic had told him how to make some kinda machine that nobody has been able to figure how it works even yet, only they guess it dodges around a couple extra dimensions. If Laurine was to start askin' questions with a technical aspect to them, that would be logics service meat! And fella, I was scared! If you think a he-man oughtn't to be scared of just one blonde—you ain't met Laurine!

I'm driving blind when a social-conscious guy asks how to bring about his own particular system of social organization at once. He don't ask if it's best or if it'll work. He just wants to get it started. And the logic—or Joe—tells him! Simultaneous, there's a retired preacher asks how can the human race be cured of concupiscence. Bein' seventy, he's pretty safe himself, but he wants to remove the peril to the spiritual welfare of the rest of us. He finds out. It involves constructin' a sort of broadcastin' station to emit a certain wave-pattern an' turnin' it on. Just that. Nothing more. It's found out afterward, when he is solicitin' funds to construct it. Fortunate, he didn't think to ask logics how to finance it, or it woulda told him that, too, an' we woulda all been cured of the impulses we maybe regret afterward but never at the time. And there's another group of serious thinkers who are sure the human race would be a lot better off if everybody went back to nature an' lived in the woods with the ants an' poison ivy. They start askin' questions about how to cause humanity to abandon cities and artificial conditions of living. They practically got the answer in logics service!

Maybe it didn't strike you serious at the time, but while I was drivin' aimless, sweatin' blood over Laurine bein' after me, the fate of civilization hung in the balance. I ain't kiddin'. For instance, the Superior Man gang that sneers at the rest of us was quietly asking questions on what kinda weapons could be made by which Superior Men could take over and run things. . . .

But I drove here an' there, sweatin' an' talkin' to myself.

"What I ought to do is ask this wacky logics service how to get outa this mess," I says. "But it'd just tell me a intricate an' foolproof way to bump Laurine off. I wanna have peace! I wanna grow comfortably old and brag to other old guys about what a hellion I used to be, without havin' to go through it an' lose my chance of livin' to be a elderly liar."

I turn a corner at random, there in the Maintenance car.

"It was a nice kinda world once," I says, bitter. "I could go home peaceful and not have belly-cramps wonderin' if a blonde has called up my wife to announce my engagement to her. I could punch keys on a logic without gazing into somebody's bedroom while she is giving her epidermis a air bath and being led to think things I gotta take out in thinkin'. I could—"

Then I groan, rememberin' that my wife, naturally, is gonna blame me for the fact that our private life ain't private anymore if anybody has tried to peek into it.

"It was a swell world," I says, homesick for the dear dead days-before-yesterday. "We was playin' happy with our toys like little innocent children until somethin' happened. Like a guy named Joe come in and squashed all our mud pies."

Then it hit me. I got the whole thing in one flash. There ain't nothing in the tank setup to start relays closin'. Relays are closed exclusive by logics, to get the information the keys are punched for. Nothin' but a logic coulda cooked up the relay patterns that constituted logics service. Humans wouldn't ha' been able to figure it out! Only a logic could integrate all the stuff that woulda made all the other logics work like this—

There was one answer. I drove into a restaurant and went over to a pay-logic an' dropped in a coin.

"Can a logic be modified," I spell out, "to cooperate in long-term planning which human brains are too limited in scope to do?"

The screen sputters. Then it says:

"Definitely yes."

"How great will the modifications be?" I punch.

"Microscopically slight. Changes in dimensions," says the screen. "Even modern precision gauges are not exact enough to check them, however. They can only come about under present manufacturing methods by an extremely improbable accident, which has only happened once."

"How can one get hold of that one accident which can do this highly necessary work?" I punch.

The screen sputters. Sweat broke out on me. I ain't got it figured out close, yet, but what I'm scared of is that whatever

276

is Joe will be suspicious. But what I'm askin' is strictly logical. And logics can't lie. They gotta be accurate. They can't help it.

"A complete logic capable of the work required," says the screen, "is now in ordinary family use in—"

And it gives me the Korlanovitch address and do I go over there! Do I go over there fast! I pull up the Maintenance car in front of the place, and I take the extra logic outa the back, and I stagger up to the Korlanovitch flat and I ring the bell. A kid answers the door.

"I'm from Logics Maintenance," I tell the kid. "An inspection record has shown that your logic is apt to break down any minute. I come to put in a new one before it does."

The kid says "O.K.!" real bright and runs back to the livin' room where Joe—I got the habit of callin' him Joe later, through just meditatin' about him—is runnin' something the kids wanna look at. I hook in the other logic an' turn it on, conscientious making sure it works. Then I say:

"Now kiddies, you punch this one for what you want. I'm gonna take the old one away before it breaks down."

And I glance at the screen. The kiddies have apparently said they wanna look at some real cannibals. So the screen is presenting a anthropological expedition scientific record film of the fertility dance of the Huba-Jouba tribe of West Africa. It is supposed to be restricted to anthropological professors an' postgraduate medical students. But there ain't any censor blocks workin' anymore and it's on. The kids are much interested. Me, bein' a old married man, I blush.

I disconnect Joe. Careful. I turn to the other logic and punch keys for Maintenance. I do not get a services flash. I get Maintenance. I feel very good. I report that I am goin' home because I fell down a flight of steps an' hurt my leg. I add, inspired:

"An' say, I was carryin' the logic I replaced an' it's all busted. I left it for the dustman to pick up."

"If you don't turn 'em in," says Stock, "you gotta pay for 'em."

"Cheap at the price," I say.

I go home. Laurine ain't called. I put Joe down in the cellar, careful. If I turned him in, he'd be inspected an' his parts salvaged even if I busted somethin' on him. Whatever part was off-normal might be used again and everything start all over. I can't risk it. I pay for him and leave him be.

That's what happened. You might say I saved civilization an' not be far wrong. I know I ain't goin' to take a chance on havin' Joe in action again. Not while Laurine is livin'. An' there are other reasons. With all the nuts who wanna change the world to their own line o' thinkin', an' the ones that wanna bump people off, an' generally solve their problems . . . Yeah! Problems are bad, but I figure I better let sleepin' problems lie.

But on the other hand, if Joe could be tamed, somehow, and got to work just reasonable—he could make me a coupla million dollars, easy. But even if I got sense enough not to get rich, an' if I get retired and just loaf around fishin' an' lyin' to other old duffers about what a great guy I used to be—maybe I'll like it, but maybe I won't. And after all, if I get fed up with bein' old and confined strictly to thinking—why, I could hook Joe in long enough to ask: "How can a old guy not stay old?" Joe'll be able to find out. An' he'll tell me.

That couldn't be allowed out general, of course. You gotta make room for kids to grow up. But it's a pretty good world, now Joe's turned off. Maybe I'll turn him on long enough to learn how to stay in it. But on the other hand, maybe . . .

SAM HALL

POUL ANDERSON

(1 9 5 3)

The computer makes possible great centralization of power—the power of information. Francis Bacon's seventeenth-century dictum—knowledge is power—proved especially prophetic with the advent of the computer age. He who has the most information has the most power—provided he also has the expertise to analyze and manipulate it. The protagonist in "Sam Hall" has that power. He is a computer technician working underground somewhere in the Rockies.

Back in the 1930s and 1940s, George Orwell watched the rise of fascism in Europe with horror. He warned the world of these totalitarian police states in *1984,* published in 1949. Hitler had used the technology that had been available to him to manipulate and control the masses, or the herd, as he called them. But he didn't have computers because they had not yet been invented. Imagine his police state if it had been computerized.

Many of the early researchers in the field of computer science were highly sensitive to the violation of individual freedom that would be possible when the new technology matured, and some of them, Norbert Wiener among them, wrote books warning the general public. By the 1960s, Congress was debating the establishment of a national data bank, with all the invasion of privacy such an operation would make possible. The magnitude of the threat proved so alarming that the data bank has still not been approved, even though it would make for increased efficiency in many government agencies. The electronic banking system exists, however, insidiously creeping into our lives, as it allows the same access to information by the unscrupulous as would a national data bank.

Published in 1953, Poul Anderson's "Sam Hall" was the first science fiction story to describe the dangers of computers in the hands of a totalitarian government. Anderson, who was born in Pennsylvania in 1926, now lives in California. He graduated from the University of Minnesota with a degree in physics. While in Minneapolis he joined the Minneapolis Fantasy Society, where he met such writers as Clifford Simak and Gordon R. Dickson. These two men, who still live in Minneapolis, also write science fiction about computers, perhaps not surprisingly since their city is the home of numerous computer manufacturers.

Anderson is one of science fiction's premier performers, having written several dozen works and having won six Hugos and two Nebulas.

279

CLICK. BZZZZ. WHRRRR.

Citizen Blank Blank, Anytown, Somewhere, U.S.A., approaches the hotel desk. "Single with bath."

"Sorry, sir, our fuel ration doesn't permit individual baths. One can be drawn for you; that will be twenty-five dollars extra."

"Oh, is that all? Okay."

Citizen Blank reaches into his pocket with an automatic gesture and withdraws his punched card and gives it to the registry machine. Aluminum jaws close on it, copper teeth feel for the holes, electronic tongue tastes the life of Citizen Blank.

Place and date of birth. Parents. Race. Religion. Educational, military, and civilian service records. Marital status. Occupations, up to and including current one. Affiliations. Physical measurements, fingerprints, retinals, blood type. Basic psychotype. Loyalty rating. Loyalty index as a function of time to moment of last checkup. Click, click. Bzzz.

"Why are you here, sir?"

"Salesman. I expect to be in New Pittsburgh tomorrow night."

The clerk (32 yrs., married, two children; NB, confidential: Jewish. To be kept out of key occupations) punches the buttons.

Click, click. The machine returns the card. Citizen Blank puts it back in his wallet.

"Front!"

The bellboy (19 yrs., unmarried; NB, confidential: Catholic. To be kept out of key occupations) takes the guest's trunk. The elevator creaks upstairs. The clerk resumes his reading. The article is entitled "Has Britain Betrayed Us?" Other articles in the magazine include "New Indoctrination Program for the Armed Forces," "Labor Hunting on Mars," "I Was a Union Man for the Security Police," "New Plans for YOUR Future."

The machine talks to itself. Click, click. A tube winks at its neighbor as if they shared a private joke. The total signal goes out over the wires.

With a thousand other signals, it shoots down the last cable and into the sorter unit of Central Records. Click, click. Bzzz. Whrrr. Wink and glow. A scanner sweeps through the memory circuits. The distorted molecules of one spool show the pattern of Citizen Blank Blank, and this is sent back. It enters the comparison unit, to which the incoming signal corresponding to Citizen Blank Blank has also been shunted. The two are perfectly in phase; nothing wrong. Citizen Blank Blank is staying in the town where, last night, he said he would, so he has not had to file a correction.

The new information is added to the record of Citizen Blank Blank. The whole of his life returns to the memory bank. It is wiped from the scanner and comparison units, so that these may be free for the next arriving signal.

The machine has swallowed and digested another day. It is content.

Thornberg came into his office at the usual time. His secretary glanced up to say "Good morning," and looked closer. She had been with him for enough years to read the nuances in his carefully controlled face. "Anything wrong, chief?"

"No." He spoke it harshly, which was also peculiar. "No, nothing wrong. I feel a bit under the weather, maybe."

"Oh." The secretary nodded. You learned discretion in the government. "Well, I hope you get better soon."

"Thanks. It's nothing." Thornberg limped over to his desk, sat down, and took out a pack of cigarettes. He held one for a moment in nicotine-yellowed fingers before lighting it, and there was an emptiness in his eyes. Then he puffed ferociously and turned to his mail. As chief technician of Central Records, he received a generous tobacco ration and used all of it.

The office was not large—a windowless cubicle, furnished with gaunt orderliness, its only decoration a picture of his son and one of his late wife. Thornberg seemed too big for it. He was tall and lean, with thin, straight features and neatly brushed graying hair. He wore a plain version of the Security uniform, with his insignia of Technical Division and major's rank but no other decoration, none of the ribbons to which he was entitled. The priesthood of Matilda the Machine were a pretty informal lot for these days.

He chain-smoked his way through the mail. Routine stuff, most of it having to do with the necessary changeovers for in-

stalling the new identification system. "Come on, June," he said
to his secretary. Irrationally, he preferred dictating to her rather
than to a recorder. "Let's get this out of the way fast. I've got
work to do."

He held one letter before him. "To Senator E. W. Harmison,
S.O.B., New Washington. Dear Sir: In re your communication
of the fourteenth inst., requesting my personal opinion of the
new ID system, may I say that it is not a technician's business
to express opinions. The directive ordering that every citizen
shall have one number applying to all his papers and functions—
birth certificate, education, rations, social security, service, etc.—
has obvious long-range advantages, but naturally entails a good
deal of work in reconverting all our electronic records. The President having decided that the gain in the long run justifies the
present difficulties, it behooves all citizens to obey. Yours, and
so forth." He smiled with a certain coldness. "There, that'll fix
him! I don't know what good Congress is anyway, except to
plague honest bureaucrats."

Privately, June decided to modify the letter. Maybe a senator
was only a rubber stamp, but you couldn't brush him off so
curtly. It is part of a secretary's job to keep the boss out of
trouble.

"Okay, let's get to the next," said Thornberg. "To Colonel
M. R. Hubert, Director of Liaison Division, Central Records
Agency, Security Police, etc. Dear Sir: In re your memorandum
of the fourteenth inst., requiring a definite date for completion
of the ID conversion, may I respectfully state that it is impossible
for me honestly to set one. It is necessary for us to develop a
memory-modification unit which will make the changeover in
all our records without our having to take out and alter each of
the three hundred million or so spools in the machine. You
realize that one cannot predict the exact time needed to complete such a project. However, research is progressing satisfac-
torily (refer him to my last report, will you?), and I can confidently
say that conversion will be finished and all citizens notified of
their numbers within two months at the latest. Respectfully,
and so on. Put that in a nice form, June."

She nodded. Thornberg went on through his mail, throwing most of it into a basket for her to answer alone. When he was done he yawned and lit another cigarette. "Praise Allah that's over. Now I can get down to the lab."

"You have some afternoon appointments," she reminded him.

"I'll be back after lunch. See you." He got up and went out of the office.

Down an escalator to a still lower subterranean level, along a corridor, returning the salutes of passing technicians without thinking about it. His face was immobile, and perhaps only the stiff swinging of his arms said anything.

Jimmy, he thought. *Jimmy, kid.*

He entered the guard chamber, pressing hand and eye to the scanners in the farther door. Finger and retinal patterns were his pass; no alarm sounded; the door opened for him and he walked into the temple of Matilda.

She crouched hugely before him, tier upon tier of control panels, instruments, blinking lights, like an Aztec pyramid. The gods murmured within her and winked red eyes at the tiny man who crawled over her monstrous flanks. Thornberg stood for a moment regarding the spectacle. Then he smiled, a tired smile creasing his face along one side. A sardonic memory came back to him, bootlegged stuff from the forties and fifties of the last century which he had read: French, German, British, Italian. The intellectuals had been all hot and bothered about the Americanization of Europe, the crumbling of old culture before the mechanized barbarism of soft drinks, advertising, chrome-plated automobiles (dollar grins, the Danes had called them), chewing gum, plastics. . . . None of them had protested the simultaneous Europeanization of America: government control, a military caste, light-years of bureaucratic records and red tape, censors, secret police, nationalism, and racialism.

Oh, well.

But Jimmy, boy, where are you now, what are they doing to you?

Thornberg went over to the bench where his best engineer, Rodney, was testing a unit. "How's it coming?" he asked.

283

"Pretty good, chief," said Rodney. He didn't bother to salute; Thornberg had, in fact, forbidden it in the labs as a waste of time. "A few bugs yet, but we're getting them out."

You had to have a gimmick which would change numbers without altering anything else. Not too easy a task, when the memory banks depended on individual magnetic domains. "Okay," said Thornberg. "Look, I'm going up to the main controls. Going to run a few tests myself—some of the tubes have been acting funny over in Section Thirteen."

"Want an assistant?"

"No, thanks. I just want not to be bothered."

Thornberg resumed his way across the floor, its hardness echoing dully under his shoes. The main controls were in a special armored booth nestling against the great pyramid, and he had to be scanned again before the door opened for him. Not many were allowed in here. The complete archives of the nation were too valuable to take chances with.

Thornberg's loyalty rating was AAB-2—not absolutely perfect, but the best available among men of his professional caliber. His last drugged checkup had revealed certain doubts and reservations about government policy, but there was no question of disobedience. Prima facie, he was certainly bound to be loyal. He had served with distinction in the war against Brazil, losing a leg in action; his wife had been killed in the abortive Chinese rocket raids ten years ago; his son was a rising young Space Guard officer on Venus. He had read and listened to forbidden stuff, blacklisted books, underground and foreign propaganda, but then every intellectual dabbled with that; it was not a serious offense if your record was otherwise good and if you laughed off what the prohibited things said.

He sat for a moment regarding the control board inside the booth. Its complexity would have baffled most engineers, but he had been with Matilda so long that he didn't even need the reference tables.

Well—

It took nerve, this. A hypnoquiz was sure to reveal what he was about to do. But such raids were, necessarily, in a random pattern; it was unlikely that he would be called up again for years, especially with his rating. By the time he was found out, Jack should have risen far enough in the Guard ranks to be safe.

In the privacy of the booth Thornberg permitted himself a harsh grin. "This," he murmured to the machine, "will hurt me worse than it does you."

He began punching buttons.

There were circuits installed which could alter the records— take out an entire one and write whatever was desired in the magnetic fields. Thornberg had done the job a few times for high officials. Now he was doing it for himself.

Jimmy Obrenowicz, son of his second cousin, hustled off at night by Security police on suspicion of treason. The records showed what no private citizen was supposed to know: Jimmy was in Camp Fieldstone. Those who returned from there were very quiet and said nothing about where they had been; sometimes they were incapable of speech.

It wouldn't do for the chief of Central Records to have a relative in Fieldstone. Thornberg punched buttons for half an hour, erasing, changing. It was a tough job—he had to go back several generations, altering lines of descent. But when he was through, Jimmy Obrenowicz was no relation whatsoever to the Thornbergs.

And I thought the world of that kid. But I'm not doing it for myself, Jimmy. It's for Jack. When the cops go through your file, later today no doubt, I can't let them find out you're related to Captain Thornberg on Venus and a friend of his father.

He slapped the switch that returned the spool to its place in the memory bank. *With this act do I disown thee.*

After that he sat for a while, relishing the quiet of the booth and the clean impersonality of the instruments. He didn't even want to smoke.

So now they were going to give every citizen a number, tattooed on him, no doubt. One number for everything. Thornberg foresaw popular slang referring to the numbers as "brands," and Security cracking down on those who used the term. Disloyal language.

Well, the underground was dangerous. It was supported by foreign countries who didn't like an American-dominated world—

at least, not one dominated by today's kind of America, though once "U.S.A." had meant "hope." The rebels were said to have their own base out in space somewhere and to have honey-combed the country with their agents. It could be. Their prop-aganda was subtle: We don't want to overthrow the nation; we only want to liberate it; we want to restore the Bill of Rights. It could attract a lot of unstable souls. But Security's spy hunt was bound to drag in any number of citizens who had never meditated treason. Like Jimmy—or had Jimmy been an under-grounder after all? You never knew. Nobody ever told you.

There was a sour taste in Thornberg's mouth. He grimaced. A line of a song came back to him. *"I hate you one and all."* How had it gone? They used to sing it in his college days. Something about a very bitter character who'd committed a murder.

Oh, yes. "Sam Hall." How did it go, now? You needed a gravelly bass to sing it properly.

"Oh, my name it is Sam Hall, it is Sam Hall.
Yes, my name it is Sam Hall, it is Sam Hall.
Oh, my name it is Sam Hall,
And I hate you one and all,
Yes, I hate you one and all, God damn your eyes."

That was it. And Sam Hall was about to swing for murder. He remembered now. He felt like Sam Hall himself. He looked at the machine and wondered how many Sam Halls were in it.

Idly, postponing his return to work, he punched for the file—name, Samuel Hall, no other specifications. The machine mum-bled to itself. Presently it spewed out a file of papers, micro-printed on the spot from the memory banks. Complete dossier on every Sam Hall, living and dead, from the time the records began to be kept. To hell with it. Thornberg chucked the papers down the incinerator slot.

"Oh, I killed a man, they say, so they say—"

The impulse was blinding in its savagery. They were dealing with Jimmy at this moment, probably pounding him over the kidneys, and he, Thornberg, sat here waiting for the cops to requisition Jimmy's file, and there was nothing he could do. His hands were empty.

By God, he thought, *I'll give them Sam Hall!*

His fingers began to race; he lost his nausea in the intricate technical problem. Slipping a fake spool into Matilda—it wasn't easy. You couldn't duplicate numbers, and every citizen had a lot of them. You had to account for every day of his life.

Well, some of that could be simplified. The machine had only existed for twenty-five years; before then the files had been kept on paper in a dozen different offices. Let's make Sam Hall a resident of New York, his dossier there lost in the bombing thirty years ago. Such of his papers as were on file in New Washington had also been lost, in the Chinese attack. That meant he simply reported as much detail as he could remember, which needn't be a lot.

Let's see. "Sam Hall" was an English song, so Sam Hall should be British himself. Came over with his parents, oh, thirty-eight years ago, when he was only three, and naturalized with them; that was before the total ban on immigration. Grew up on New York's Lower East Side, a tough kid, a slum kid. School records lost in the bombing, but he claimed to have gone through the tenth grade. No living relatives. No family. No definite occupation, just a series of unskilled jobs. Loyalty rating BBA-O, which meant that purely routine questions showed him to have no political opinions at all that mattered.

Too colorless. Give him some violence in his background. Thornberg punched for information on New York police stations and civilian-police officers destroyed in the last raids. He used them as the source of records that Sam Hall had been continually in trouble—drunkenness, disorderly conduct, brawls, a suspicion of holdups and burglary, but not strong enough to warrant calling in Security's hypno-technicians for quizzing him.

Hmm. Better make him 4-F, no military service. Reason? Well, a slight drug addiction; men weren't so badly needed nowadays that hopheads had to be cured. Neocoke—that didn't impair the faculties too much; indeed the addict was abnormally fast and strong under the influence, though there was a tough reaction afterwards.

Then he would have had to put in a term in civilian service. Let's see. He spent his three years as a common laborer on the Colorado Dam project; so many men had been involved there that no one would remember him, or at least it would be hard finding a supervisor who did.

Now to fill in. Thornberg used a number of automatic machines to help him. Every day in twenty-five years had to be accounted for; but of course the majority would show no travel or change of residence. Thornberg punched for cheap hotels housing many at a time—no record would be kept there, everything being filed in Matilda; and no one would remember a shabby individual patron. Sam Hall's present address was given as the Triton, a glorified flophouse on the East Side not far from the craters. At present unemployed, doubtless living off past savings. Oh, blast! It was necessary to file income-tax returns. Thornberg did so.

Hmm—physical ID. Make him of average height, stocky, black-haired and black-eyed, a bent nose, and a scar on his forehead—tough-looking, but not enough so to make him especially memorable. Thornberg filled in the precise measurements. It wasn't hard to fake fingerprint and retinal patterns; he threw in a censor circuit so he wouldn't accidentally duplicate anyone else.

When he was done, Thornberg leaned back and sighed. There were plenty of holes yet in the record, but he could fill them in at his leisure. It had been a couple of hours' hard, concentrated work—utterly pointless, except that he had blown off steam. He felt a lot better.

He glanced at his watch. *Time to get back on the job, son.* For a rebellious moment he wished no one had ever invented clocks. They had made possible the science he loved, but they had then proceeded to mechanize man. Oh, well, too late now. He got up and went out of the booth. The door closed itself behind him.

It was about a month later that Sam Hall committed his first murder.

The night before, Thornberg had been at home. His rank

entitled him to good housing even if he did live alone—two rooms and bath on the ninety-eighth floor of a unit in town, not far from the camouflaged entrance to Matilda's underground domain. The fact that he was in Security, even if he didn't belong to the man-hunting branch, gave him so much added deference that he often felt lonely. The superintendent had even offered him his daughter once—"Only twenty-three, sir, just released by a gentleman of marshal's rank, and looking for a nice patron, sir." Thornberg had refused, trying not to be prissy about it. *Autres temps, autres moeurs*—but still, she wouldn't have had any choice about getting client status, the first time anyway. And Thornberg's marriage had been a long and happy one.

He had been looking through his bookshelves for something to read. The Literary Bureau had lately been trumpeting Whitman as an early example of Americanism, but though Thornberg had always liked the poet, his hands strayed perversely to the dogeared volume of Marlowe. Was that escapism? The L.B. was very down on escapism. Oh, well, these were tough times. It wasn't easy to belong to the nation which was enforcing peace on a sullen world—you had to be realistic and energetic and all the rest, no doubt.

The phone buzzed. He went over and clicked on the receiver. Martha Obrenowicz's plain plump face showed in the screen; her gray hair was wild and her voice a harsh croak.

"Uh—hello," he said uneasily. He hadn't called her since the news of her son's arrest. "How are you?"

"Jimmy is dead," she told him.

He stood for a long while. His skull felt hollow.

"I got word today that he died in camp," said Martha. "I thought you'd want to know."

Thornberg shook his head, back and forth, very slowly. "That isn't news I ever wanted, Martha," he said.

"It isn't *right*!" she shrieked. "Jimmy wasn't a traitor. I knew my own son. Who ought to know him better? He had some friends I was kind of doubtful of, but Jimmy, he wouldn't ever—"

Something cold formed in Thornberg's breast. You never knew when calls were being tapped.

"I'm sorry, Martha," he said without tone. "But the police are very careful about these things. They wouldn't act till they were sure. Justice is one of our traditions."

She looked at him for a long time. Her eyes held a hard glitter. "You too," she said at last.

"Be careful, Martha," he warned her. "I know it's a blow to you, but don't say anything you might regret later. After all, Jimmy may have died accidentally. Those things happen."

"I—forgot," she said jerkily. "You . . . are . . . in Security . . . yourself."

"Be calm," he said. "Think of it as a sacrifice for the national interest."

She switched off on him. He knew she wouldn't call him again. And it wouldn't be safe to see her.

"Good-by, Martha," he said aloud. It was like a stranger speaking.

He turned back to the bookshelf. *Not for me*, he told himself thinly. *For Jack*. He touched the binding of *Leaves of Grass*. *Oh, Whitman, old rebel*, he thought, with a curious dry laughter in him, *are they calling you Whirling Walt now?*

That night he took an extra sleeping pill. His head still felt fuzzy when he reported for work, and after a while he gave up trying to answer the mail and went down to the lab.

While he was engaged with Rodney, and making a poor job of understanding the technical problem under discussion, his eyes strayed to Matilda. Suddenly he realized what he needed for a cathartic. He broke off as soon as possible and went into the main control booth.

For a moment he paused at the keyboard. The day-by-day creation of Sam Hall had been an odd experience. He, quiet and introverted, had shaped a rowdy life and painted a rugged personality. Sam Hall was more real to him than many of his associates. *Well, I'm a schizoid type myself. Maybe I should have been a writer.* No, that would have meant too many restrictions, too much fear of offending the censor. He had done exactly as he pleased with Sam Hall.

He drew a deep breath and punched for unsolved murders of Security officers, New York City area, within the last month.

They were surprisingly common. Could it be that dissatisfaction was more general than the government admitted? But when the bulk of a nation harbors thoughts labeled treasonous, does the label still apply?

He found what he wanted. Sergeant Brady had incautiously entered the Crater district after dark on the twenty-seventh of last month, on a routine checkup mission; he had worn the black uniform, presumably to give himself the full weight of authority. The next morning he had been found in an alley with his head bashed in.

> *"Oh, I killed a man, they say, so they say.*
> *Yes, I killed a man, they say, so they say.*
> *I beat him on the head*
> *And I left him there for dead,*
> *Yes, I left him there for dead, God damn his eyes."*

Newspapers had no doubt deplored this brutality perpetrated by the traitorous agents of enemy powers. (*"Oh, the parson, he did come, he did come."*) A number of suspects had been rounded up at once and given a stiff quizzing. (*"And the sheriff, he came too, he came too."*) There had been nothing proven as yet, though one Joe Nikolsky (fifth-generation American, mechanic, married, four children, underground pamphlets found in his room) had been arrested yesterday on suspicion.

Thornberg sighed. He knew enough of Security methods to be sure they would get somebody for such a killing. They couldn't allow their reputation for infallibility to be smirched by a lack of conclusive evidence. Maybe Nikolsky had done the crime—he couldn't *prove* he had simply been out for a walk that evening—and maybe he hadn't. But hell's fire, why not give him a break? He had four kids. With such a black mark, their mother could find work only in a recreation house.

Thornberg scratched his head. This had to be done carefully. Let's see. Brady's body would have been cremated by now, but of course there had been a thorough study first. Thornberg withdrew the dead man's file from the machine and microprinted a replica of the evidence—nothing. Erasing that, he inserted the statement that a blurred thumbprint had been found on the victim's collar and referred to ID labs for reconstruction. In the ID file he inserted the report of such a job, finished only yesterday due to a great press of work. (True enough—they had been busy lately on material sent from Mars, seized in a raid on a rebel meeting place.) The probable pattern of the whorls was—and here he inserted Sam Hall's right thumb.

He returned the spools and leaned back in his chair. It was risky; if anyone thought to check with the ID lab, he was done for. But that was unlikely; the chances were that New York would accept the findings with a routine acknowledgment which some clerk at the lab would file without studying. The more obvious dangers were not too great either: a busy police force would not stop to ask if any of their fingerprint men had actually developed that smudge; and as for hypnoquizzing showing Nikolsky really was the murderer, well, then the print would be assumed that of a passerby who had found the body without reporting it.

So now Sam Hall had killed a Security officer—grabbed him by the neck and smashed his skull with a weighted club. Thornberg felt a lot better.

New York Security shot a request to Central Records for any new material on the Brady case. An automaton received it, compared the codes, and saw that fresh information had been added. The message flashed back, together with the dossier on Sam Hall and two others—for the reconstruction could not be absolutely accurate.

The other two men were safe enough, as it turned out. Both had alibis. The squad that stormed into the Triton Hotel and demanded Sam Hall were met with blank stares. No such person was registered. No one of that description was known there. A thorough quizzing corroborated this. So—Sam Hall had managed to fake an address. He could have done that easily enough by punching the buttons on the hotel register when no one was looking. Sam Hall could be anywhere!

Joe Nikolsky, having been hypnoed and found harmless, was

released. The fine for possessing subversive literature would put him in debt for the next few years—he had no influential friends to get it suspended—but he'd stay out of trouble if he watched his step. Security sent out an alarm for Sam Hall.

Thornberg derived a sardonic amusement from watching the progress of the hunt as it came to Matilda. No one with that ID card had bought tickets on any public transportation. That proved nothing. Of the hundreds who vanished every year, some at least must have been murdered for their ID cards, and their bodies disposed of. Matilda was set to give the alarm when the ID of a disappeared person showed up somewhere. Thornberg faked a few such reports, just to give the police something to do.

He slept more poorly each night, and his work suffered. Once he met Martha Obrenowicz on the street—passed by hastily without greeting her—and couldn't sleep at all, even with maximum permissible drugging.

The new ID system was completed. Machines sent notices to every citizen, with orders to have their numbers tattooed on the right shoulder blade within six weeks. As each tattoo center reported that such-and-such person had had the job done, Matilda's robots changed the record appropriately. Sam Hall, AX-428-399-075, did not report for his tattoo. Thornberg chuckled at the AX symbol.

Then the telecasts flashed a story that made the nation sit up and listen. Bandits had held up the First National Bank in America-town, Idaho (formerly Moscow), making off with a good five million dollars in assorted bills. From their discipline and equipment it was assumed that they were rebel agents, possibly having come in a spaceship from their unknown interplanetary base, and that the raid was intended to help finance their nefarious activities. Security was cooperating with the armed forces to track down the evildoers, and arrests were expected hourly, etc. etc.

Thornberg went to Matilda for a complete account. It had been a bold job. The robbers had apparently worn plastic face masks and light body armor under ordinary clothes. In the scuffle of the getaway one man's mask had slipped aside—only for a moment, but a clerk who happened to see it had, with the aid of hypnosis, given a fairly good description. A brown-haired, heavyset fellow, Roman nose, thin lips, toothbrush mustache.

Thornberg hesitated. A joke was a joke; and helping poor Nikolsky was perhaps morally defensible; but aiding and abetting a felony which was in all likelihood an act of treason—

He grinned to himself, without much humor. It was too much fun playing God. Swiftly he changed the record. The crook had been of medium height, dark, scar-faced, broken-nosed— He sat for a while wondering how sane he was. How sane anybody was.

Security Central asked for the complete file on the holdup, with any correlations the machine could make. It was sent to them. The description given could have been that of many men, but the scanners eliminated all but one possibility, *Sam Hall*.

The hounds bayed forth again. That night Thornberg slept well.

Dear Dad,

Sorry I haven't written before, but we've been kept pretty busy here. As you know, I've been with a patrol in Gorbuvashtar for the past several weeks—desolate country, like all this blasted planet. Sometimes I wonder if I'll ever see the sun again. And lakes and forests and— who wrote that line about the green hills of Earth? We can't get much to read out here, and sometimes my mind feels rusty. Not that I'm complaining, of course. This is a necessary job, and somebody has to do it.

We'd hardly gotten back from the patrol when we were called out on special duty, bundled into rockets, and tossed halfway around the planet through the worst gale I've ever seen, even on Venus. If I hadn't been an officer and therefore presumably a gentleman, I'd have upchucked. A lot of the boys did, and we were a pretty sorry crew when we landed. But we had to go into action right away. There was a strike in the thorium mines and the local men couldn't break it. We had to use guns before we could bring them to reason. Dad, I felt sorry for the poor devils, I don't mind admitting it. Rocks and hammers and sluice hoses against machine guns! And con-

294

ditions in the mines are pretty rugged. They DELETED BY CENSOR someone has to do that job too, and if no one will volunteer, for any kind of pay, they have to assign civilian-service men arbitrarily. It's for the state.

Otherwise nothing new. Life is pretty monotonous. Don't believe the adventure stories—adventure is weeks of boredom punctuated by moments of being scared gutless. Sorry to be so brief, but I want to get this on the outbound rocket. Won't be another for a couple of months. Everything well, really. I hope the same for you and live for the day we'll meet again. Thanks a million for the cookies—you know you can't afford to pay the freight, you old spendthrift! Martha baked them, didn't she? I recognized the Obrenowicz touch. Say hello to her and Jim for me. And most of all, my kindest thoughts go to you.

As ever,
Jack

The telecasts carried "wanted" messages for Sam Hall. No photographs of him were available, but an artist could draw an accurate likeness from Matilda's precise description, and his truculent face began to adorn public places. Not long thereafter, the Security offices in Denver were blown up by a grenade tossed from a speeding car that vanished into traffic. A witness said he had glimpsed the thrower, and the fragmentary picture given under hypnosis was not unlike Sam Hall's. Thornberg doctored the record a bit to make it still more similar. The tampering was risky, of course; if Security ever became suspicious, they could easily check back with their witnesses. But it was not too big a chance to take, for a scientifically quizzed man told everything germane to the subject which his memory, conscious, subconscious, and cellular, held. There was never any reason to repeat such an interrogation.

Thornberg often tried to analyze his own motives. Plainly enough, he disliked the government. He must have contained that hate all his life, carefully suppressed from awareness, and only recently had it been forced into his conscious mind; not even his subconscious could have formulated it earlier, or he would have been caught by the loyalty probes. The hate derived from a lifetime of doubts (had there been any real reason to fight Brazil, other than to obtain those bases and mining concessions? had the Chinese attack perhaps been provoked—or even faked, for their government had denied it?) and the million petty frustrations of the garrison state. Still—the strength of it! The violence!

By creating Sam Hall he had struck back, but it was an ineffectual blow, a timid gesture. Most likely his basic motive was simply to find a halfway safe release; in Sam Hall he lived vicariously all the things that the beast within him wanted to do. Several times he had intended to discontinue his sabotage, but it was like a drug: Sam Hall was becoming necessary to his own stability.

The thought was alarming. He ought to see a psychiatrist—but no, the doctor would be bound to report his tale, he would go to camp, and Jack, if not exactly ruined, would be under a cloud for the rest of his life. Thornberg had no desire to go to camp, anyway. His own existence had compensations—interesting work, a few good friends, art and music and literature, decent wine, sunsets and mountains, memories. He had started this game on impulse, but now it was too late to stop it.

For Sam Hall had been promoted to Public Enemy Number One.

Winter came, and the slopes of the Rockies under which Matilda lay were white beneath a cold greenish sky. Air traffic around the nearby town was lost in that hugeness: brief hurtling meteors against infinity; ground traffic could not be seen at all from the Records entrance. Thornberg took the special tubeway to work every morning, but he often walked the five miles back, and his Sundays were usually spent in long hikes over the slippery trails. That was a foolish thing to do alone in winter, but he felt reckless.

He was working in his office shortly before Christmas when

the intercom said: "Major Sorensen to see you, sir. From Investigation."

Thornberg felt his stomach tie itself into a cold knot. "All right," he answered in a voice whose levelness surprised him. "Cancel any other appointments." Security Investigation took priority over everything.

Sorensen walked in with a hard, military clack of boots. He was a big blond man, heavy-shouldered, his face expressionless and his eyes as pale and cold and remote as the winter sky. The black uniform fitted him like another skin; the lightning badge of his service glittered against it like a frosty star. He stood stiffly before the desk, and Thornberg rose to give him an awkward salute.

"Please sit down, Major Sorensen. What can I do for you?"

"Thanks." The cop's voice was crisp and harsh. He lowered his bulk into a chair and drilled Thornberg with his eyes. "I've come about the Sam Hall case."

"Oh—the rebel?" Thornberg's skin prickled. It was all he could do to meet those eyes.

"How do you know he's a rebel?" asked Sorensen. "It's never been proved officially."

"Why—I assumed—that bank raid—and then the posters say he's believed to be in the underground—"

Sorensen inclined his cropped head ever so slightly. When he spoke again it was in a relaxed tone, almost casual: "Tell me, Major Thornberg, have you followed the Hall dossier in detail?"

Thornberg hesitated. He wasn't supposed to do so unless ordered; he only kept the machine running. A memory came back to him, something he had read once: "When suspected of a major sin, admit the minor ones frankly. It disarms suspicion." Something like that.

"As a matter of fact, I have," he said. "I know it's against regs, but I was interested and—well, I couldn't see any harm in it. I've not discussed it with anyone, of course."

"No matter." Sorensen waved a muscular hand. "If you hadn't done so, I'd have ordered you to. I want your opinion on this."

"Why—I'm not a detective—"

"You know more about Records, though, than anyone else.

297

I'll be frank with you—under the rose, naturally." Sorensen seemed almost friendly now. *Was it a trick to put his prey off guard?* "You see, there are some puzzling features about this case."

Thornberg kept silent. He wondered if Sorensen could hear the thudding of his heart.

"Sam Hall is a shadow," said the cop. "The most careful checkups eliminate any chance of his being identical with anyone else of that name. In fact, we've learned that the name occurs in a violent old drinking song—is it coincidence, or did the song suggest crime to Sam Hall, or did he by some incredible process get that alias into his record instead of his real name? Whatever the answer there, we know that he's ostensibly without military training, yet he's pulled off some beautiful pieces of precision attack. His IQ is only 110, but he evades all our traps. He has no politics, yet he turns on Security without warning. We have not been able to find one person who remembers him—not one, and believe me, we have been thorough. Oh, there are a few subconscious memories which might be of him, but probably aren't—and so aggressive a personality should be remembered consciously. No undergrounder or foreign agent we've caught had any knowledge of him, which defies probability. The whole business seems impossible."

Thornberg licked his lips. Sorensen, the hunter of men, must know he was frightened; but would he assume it to be the normal nervousness of a man in the presence of a Security officer?

Sorensen's face broke into a hard smile. "As Sherlock Holmes once remarked," he said, "when you have eliminated every other hypothesis, then the one which remains, however improbable, must be the right one."

Despite himself, Thornberg was jolted. Sorensen hadn't struck him as a reader.

"Well," he asked slowly, "what is your remaining hypothesis?"

The other man watched him for a long time, it seemed forever, before replying. "The underground is more powerful and widespread than people realize. They've had some seventy years to prepare and there are many good brains in their ranks. They carry on scientific research of their own. It's top secret, but we know they have perfected a type of weapon we cannot duplicate yet. It seems to be a handgun throwing bolts of energy—a blaster, you might call it—of immense power. Sooner or later they're going to wage open war against the government.

"Now, could they have done something comparable in psychology? Could they have found a way to erase or cover up memories selectively, even on the cellular level? Could they know how to fool a personality tester, how to disguise the mind itself? If so, there may be any number of Sam Halls in our very midst, undetectable until the moment comes for them to strike."

Thornberg felt almost boneless. He couldn't help gasping his relief, and hoped Sorensen would take it for a sign of alarm.

"The possibility is frightening, isn't it?" The blond man laughed harshly. "You can imagine what is being felt in high official circles. We've put all the psychological researchers we could get to work on the problem—bah! Fools! They go by the book; they're afraid to be original even when the state tells them to.

"It may just be a wild fancy, of course. I hope it is. But we have to *know*. That's why I approached you personally, instead of sending the usual requisition. I want you to make a search of the records—everything pertaining to the subject, every man, every discovery, every hypothesis. You have a broad technical background and, from your psychorecord, an unusual amount of creative imagination. I want you to do what you can to correlate all your data. Co-opt anybody you need. Submit to my office a report on the possibility—or should I say probability—of this notion, and if there is any likelihood of its being true, sketch out a research program which will enable us to duplicate the results and counteract them."

Thornberg fumbled for words. "I'll try," he said lamely. "I'll do my best."

"Good. It's for the state."

Sorensen had finished his official business, but he didn't go at once. "Rebel propaganda is subtle stuff," he said quietly, after a pause. "It's dangerous because it uses our own slogans, with a twisted meaning. Liberty, equality, justice, peace. Too many people can't appreciate that times have changed and the meanings of words have necessarily changed with them."

"I suppose not," said Thornberg. He added the lie: "I never thought much about it."

"You should," said Sorensen. "Study your history. When we lost World War III we had to militarize to win World War IV, and after that, for our own safety, we had to mount guard on the whole human race. The people demanded it at the time."

The people, thought Thornberg, *never appreciated freedom till they'd lost it. They were always willing to sell their birthright. Or was it merely that, being untrained in thinking, they couldn't see through demagoguery, couldn't visualize the ultimate consequences of their wishes?* He was vaguely shocked at the thought; wasn't he able to control his own mind any longer?

"The rebels," said Sorensen, "claim that conditions have changed, that militarization is no longer necessary—if it ever was—and that America would be safe enough in a union of free countries. It's devilishly clever propaganda, Major Thornberg. Watch out for it."

He got up and took his leave. Thornberg sat for a long time staring after the door. Sorensen's last words were—odd, to say the least. Was it a hint—or was it bait in a trap?

The next day Matilda received a news item whose details were carefully censored for the public channels. A rebel force had landed in the stockade of Camp Jackson, in Utah, gunned down the guards, and taken away the prisoners. The camp doctor had been spared, and related that the leader of the raid, a stocky man in a mask, had ironically said to him: "Tell your friends I'll call again. My name is Sam Hall."

Space Guard ship blown up on Mesa Verde Field. On a fragment of metal someone has scrawled: "Compliments of Sam Hall."

Army quartermaster depot robbed of a million dollars. Bandit chief says, before disappearing, that he is Sam Hall.

Squad of Security police, raiding a suspected underground hideout in New Pittsburgh, cut down by machine-gun fire. Voice over hidden loud-speaker cries: "My name it is Sam Hall!"

Dr. Matthew Thomson, chemist in Seattle, suspected of underground connections, is gone when his home is raided. Note left on desk says: "Off to visit Sam Hall. Back for liberation. M.T."

Defense plant producing important robomb parts blown up near Miami by small atomic bomb, after being warned over the phone that the bomb has been planted and they have half an hour to get their workers out. The caller, masked, styles himself Sam Hall.

Army laboratory in Houston given similar warning by Sam Hall. A fake, but a day's valuable work is lost in the alarm and the search.

Scribbled on walls from New York to San Diego, from Duluth to El Paso, Sam Hall, Sam Hall, Sam Hall.

Obviously, thought Thornberg, the underground had seized on the invisible and invincible man of legend and turned him to their own purposes. Reports of him poured in from all over the country, hundreds every day—Sam Hall seen here, Sam Hall seen there. Ninety-nine percent could be dismissed as hoaxes, hallucinations, mistakes; it was another national craze, fruit of a jittery time, like the sixteenth- and seventeenth-century witch hunts or the twentieth-century flying saucers. But Security and civilian police had to check on every one.

Thornberg planted a number of them himself.

Mostly, though, he was busy with his assignment. He could understand what it meant to the government. Life in the garrison state was inevitably founded on fear and mistrust, every man's eye on his neighbor; but at least psychotyping and hypnoquizzing had given a degree of surety. Now, with that staff knocked out from under them—

His preliminary studies indicated that a discovery such as Sorensen had hypothesized, while not impossible, was too far beyond the scope of modern science for the rebels to have perfected. Such research carried on nowadays would, from the standpoint of practicality if not of knowledge, be a waste of time and trained men.

He spent a good many sleepless hours and used up a month's

cigarette ration before he could decide what to do. All right, he'd aided insurrection in a small way, and he shouldn't boggle at the next step. Still—nevertheless—did he want to?

Jack—the boy had a career lined out for himself. He loved the big deeps beyond the sky as he would love a woman. If things changed, what then of Jack's career?

Well, what was it now? Stuck on a dreary planet as guardsman and executioner of homesick starvelings poisoned by radioactivity—never even seeing the sun. Come the day, Jack could surely wangle a berth on a real spacer; they'd need bold men to explore beyond Saturn. Jack was too honest to make a good rebel, but Thornberg felt that after the initial shock he would welcome a new government.

But treason! Oaths!

When in the course of human events—

It was a small thing that decided Thornberg. He passed a shop downtown and noticed a group of the Youth Guard smashing in its windows and spattering yellow paint over the goods: O, Moses, Jesus, Mendelssohn, Hertz, and Einstein! Once he had taken this path, a curious serenity possessed him. He stole a vial of prussic acid from a chemist friend and carried it in his pocket; and as for Jack, the boy would have to take his chances too.

The work was demanding and dangerous. He had to alter recorded facts which were available elsewhere, in books and journals and the minds of men. Nothing could be done with basic theory, of course, but quantitative results could be juggled a little so that the overall picture was subtly askew. He would co-opt carefully chosen experts, men whose psychotypes indicated they would take the easy course of relying on Matilda instead of checking the original sources. And the correlation and integration of innumerable data, the empirical equations and extrapolations thereof, could be tampered with.

He turned his regular job over to Rodney and devoted himself entirely to the new one. He grew thin and testy; when Sorensen called up trying to hurry him, he snapped back: "Do you want speed or quality?" and wasn't too surprised at himself afterward. He got little sleep, but his mind seemed unnaturally clear.

Winter faded into spring while Thornberg and his experts labored and while the nation shook, psychically and physically, with the growing violence of Sam Hall. The report Thornberg submitted in May was so voluminous and detailed that he didn't think the government researchers would bother referring to any other source. Its conclusion: Yes, given a brilliant man applying Belloni matrices to cybernetic formulas and using some unknown kind of colloidal probe, a psychological masking technique was plausible.

The government yanked every man it could find into research. Thornberg knew it was only a matter of time before they realized they had been had. How much time, he couldn't say. But when they were sure—

"Now up the rope I go, up I go.
Now up the rope I go, up I go.
And the bastards down below,
They say: 'Sam, we told you so.'
They say: 'Sam, we told you so,' God damn their eyes."

REBELS ATTACK
SPACESHIPS LAND UNDER COVER OF RAINSTORM, SEIZE POINTS
NEAR N. DETROIT
FLAME WEAPONS USED AGAINST ARMY BY REBELS

"The infamous legions of the traitors have taken key points throughout the nation, but already our gallant forces have hurled them back. They have come out in early summer like toadstools, and will wither as fast—WHEEEEEE-OOOOOO!" Silence.

"All citizens are directed to keep calm, remain loyal to their country, and stay at their usual tasks until otherwise ordered. Civilians will report to their local defense commanders. All military reservists will report immediately for active duty."

"Hello, Hawaii! Are you there? Come in, Hawaii! Calling Hawaii!"

"CQ, Mars GHQ calling . . . bzzz, wheeee . . . seized Syrtis Major Colony and . . . whoooo . . . help needed . . ."

"The Lunar rocket bases are assaulted and carried. The commander blows them up rather than surrender. A pinpoint flash on the moon's face, a new crater; what will they name it?"

"So they've got Seattle, have they? Send a robomb flight. Blow the place off the map. . . . Citizens? To hell with citizens! This is war!"

" . . . in New York. Secretly drilled rebels emerged from the notorious Crater district and stormed . . ."

" . . . assassins were shot down. The new President has already been sworn in and . . ."

BRITAIN, CANADA, AUSTRALIA REFUSE ASSISTANCE TO GOV'T

" . . . no, sir. The bombs reached Seattle all right. But they were all stopped before they hit—some kind of energy gun . . ."

"COMECO to all Army commanders in Florida and Georgia: Enemy action has made Florida and the Keys temporarily untenable. Army units will withdraw as follows . . ."

"Today a rebel force engaging an Army convoy in Donner Pass was annihilated by a well-placed tactical atomic bomb. Though our own men suffered losses on this account . . ."

"COMWECO to all Army commanders in California: The mutiny of units stationed near San Francisco poses a grave problem . . ."

SP RAID REBEL HIDEOUT, BAG FIVE OFFICERS

"All right, so the enemy is about to capture Boston. We *can't* issue weapons to the citizens. They might turn them on us!"

SPACE GUARD UNITS EXPECTED FROM VENUS

Jack, Jack, Jack!

It was strange, living in the midst of a war. Thornberg had never thought it would be like this. Drawn faces, furtive eyes, utter confusion in the telecast news and the irregularly arriving papers, blackouts, civil-defense drills, shortages, occasional panic when a rebel jet whistled overhead—but nothing else. No gunfire, no bombs, no battles at all except the unreal ones you heard about. The only casualty lists here were due to Security—people kept disappearing, and nobody spoke about them.

But then, why should the enemy bother with this unimportant mountain town? The Army of Liberation, as it styled itself, was grabbing key points of industry, transportation, communication; was fighting military units, sabotaging buildings and machines, assassinating important men in the government. By its very purpose, it couldn't wage total war, couldn't annihilate the folk it wanted to free. Rumor had it that the defenders were not so finicky.

Most citizens were passive. They always are. It is doubtful that more than one-fourth of the population was ever near a combat during the Third American Revolution. City dwellers might see fire in the sky, hear the whistle and crash of artillery, scramble out of the way of soldiers and armored vehicles, cower in shelters when the rockets thundered overhead—but the battle was fought outside town. If it came to street fighting, the rebels wouldn't push in; they would either withdraw and wait or they would rely on agents inside the city. Then one might hear the crack of rifles and grenades, rattle of machine guns, sharp discharge of energy beams, and see corpses in the street. But it ended with a return of official military government or with the rebels marching in and setting up their own provisional councils. (They were rarely greeted with cheers and flowers. Nobody knew how the war would end. But there were words whispered to them, and they usually got good service.) As nearly as possible, the average American continued his average life.

Thornberg went on in his own ways. Matilda, as the information center, was working at full blast. If the rebels ever learned where she was—

Or did they know?

He could not spare much time for his private sabotage, but he planned it carefully and made every second tell when he was alone in the control booth. Sam Hall reports, of course—Sam

Hall here, Sam Hall there, pulling off this or that incredible stunt. But what did one man, even a superman, count for in these gigantic days? Something else was needed.

Radio and newspapers announced jubilantly that Venus had finally been contacted. The moon and Mars had fallen, there was only silence from the Jovian satellites, but everything seemed in order on Venus—a few feeble uprisings had been quickly smashed. The powerful Guard units there would be on their way to earth at once. Troop transports had to orbit most of the way, so it would take a good six weeks before they could arrive, but when they did they would be a powerful reinforcement.

"Looks like you might see your boy soon, chief," said Rodney.

"Yes," said Thornberg, "I might."

"Tough fighting." Rodney shook his head. "I'd sure as hell hate to be in it."

If Jack is killed by a rebel gun, when I have aided the rebels' cause—

Sam Hall, reflected Thornberg, had lived a hard life, all violence and enmity and suspicion. Even his wife hadn't trusted him.

> *". . . And my Nellie dressed in blue*
> *Says: 'Your trifling days are through.*
> *Now I know that you'll be true, God damn your eyes.' "*

Poor Sam Hall. It was no wonder he had killed a man.

Suspicion!

Thornberg stood for a taut moment while an eerie tingle went through him. The police state was founded on suspicion. Nobody could trust anyone else. And with the new fear of psychomasking, and research on that project suspended during the crisis—

Steady, boy, steady. Can't rush into this. Have to plan it out very carefully.

Thornberg punched for the dossiers of key men in the administration, in the military, in Security. He did it in the presence of two assistants, for he thought that his own frequent sessions alone in the control booth were beginning to look funny.

"This is top secret," he warned them, pleased with his own cool manner. He was becoming a regular Machiavelli. "You'll be skinned alive if you mention it to anyone."

Rodney gave him a shrewd glance. "So they're not even sure of their own top men now, are they?" he murmured.

"I've been told to make some checks," snapped Thornberg. "That's all you need to know."

He studied the files for many hours before coming to a decision. Secret observations were, of course, made of everyone from time to time. A cross-check with Matilda showed that the cop who had filed the last report on Lindahl had been killed the next day in a spontaneous and abortive uprising. The report was innocuous: Lindahl had stayed at home, studying some papers; he had been alone in the house except for a bodyguard who had been in another room and not seen him. And Lindahl was Undersecretary of Defense.

Thornberg changed the record. A masked man—stocky, black-haired—had come in and talked for three hours with Lindahl. They had spoken low, so that the cop's ears, outside the window, couldn't catch what was said. The visitor had gone away then, and Lindahl had retired. The cop went back in great excitement and made out his report and gave it to the signalman, who had sent it on to Matilda.

Tough on the signalman, thought Thornberg. *They'll want to know why he didn't tell this to his chief in New Washington, if the observer was killed before doing so. He'll deny every such report, and they'll hypnoquiz him—but they don't trust that method anymore!*

His sympathy didn't last long. What counted was having the war over before Jack got home. He refiled the altered spool and did a little backtracking, shifting the last report of Sam Hall from Salt Lake City to Philadelphia. Make it more plausible. Then, as opportunity permitted, he did some work on other men's records.

He had to wait two haggard days before the next requisition came from Security for a fresh cross-check on Sam Hall. The scanners swept in an intricate pattern, a cog turned over, a tube glowed. Circuits were activated elsewhere, the spool LINDAHL was unrolled before the microprinter inside the machine. Cross-references to that spool ramified in all directions. Thornberg sent the preliminary report back with a query: This matter looked interesting; did they want more information?

They did!

Next day the telecast announced a drastic shakeup in the Department of Defense. Lindahl was not heard from again.

And I, thought Thornberg grimly, *have grabbed a very large tiger by the tail. Now they'll have to check everybody—and I'm one man, trying to keep ahead of the whole security police!*

Lindahl is a traitor. How did his chief ever let him get on the board? Secretary Hoheimer was pretty good friends with Lindahl, too. Get Records to cross-check Hoheimer.

What's this? Hoheimer himself! Five years ago, yes, but even so—the records show that he lived in an apartment unit where *Sam Hall* was janitor! Grab Hoheimer! Who'll take his place? General Halliburton? That stupid old bastard? Well, at least his dossier is clean. Can't trust those slick characters.

Hoheimer has a brother in Security, general's rank, good detection record. A blind? Who knows? Slap the brother in jail, at least for the duration. Better check his staff. . . . Central Records shows that his chief field agent, Jones, has five days unaccounted for a year ago; he claimed Security secrecy at the time, but a double cross-check shows it wasn't so. Shoot Jones! He has a nephew in the Army, a captain. Pull that unit out of the firing line till we can study it man by man! We've had too many mutinies already.

Lindahl was also a close friend of Benson, in charge of the Tennessee Atomic Ordnance Works. Haul Benson in! Check every man connected with him! No trusting those scientists, they're always blabbing secrets.

The first Hoheimer's son is an industrialist, he owns a petroleum-synthesis plant in Texas. Nab him! His wife is a sister of Leslie, head of the War Production Coordination Board. Get

Leslie too. Sure, he's doing a good job, but he may be sending information to the enemy. Or he may just be waiting for the signal to sabotage the whole works. We can't trust *anybody*, I tell you!

What's this? Records relays an Intelligence report that the mayor of Tampa was in cahoots with the rebels. It's marked "Unreliable, Rumor"—but Tampa *did* surrender without a fight. The mayor's business partner is Gale, who has a cousin in the Army, commanding a robomb base in New Mexico. Check both the Gales, Records. . . . So the cousin was absent four days without filing his whereabouts, was he? Military privileges or not, arrest him and find out where he was!

—Attention, Records, attention, Records, urgent. Brigadier John Harmsworth Gale, etc., etc., refused to divulge information required by Security officers, claiming to have been at his base all the time. Can this be an error on your part?

—Records to Security Central, ref: etc., etc. No possibility of error exists except in information received.

—to Records, ref: etc., etc. Gale's story corroborated by three of his officers.

Put the whole damned base under arrest! Recheck those reports! Who sent them in, anyway?

—to Records, ref: etc., etc. On attempt to arrest entire personnel, Robomb Base 37-J fired on Security detachment and repulsed it. At last reports Gale was calling for rebel forces fifty miles off to assist him. Details will follow for the files as soon as possible.

So Gale was a traitor!—Or was he driven to it by fear?— Have Records find out who filed that information about him in the first place. *We can't trust anybody!*

Thornberg was not much surprised when his door was kicked open and the Security squad entered. He had been expecting it for days now. One man can't keep ahead of the game forever. No doubt the accumulated inconsistencies had finally drawn suspicion his way; or perhaps, ironically, the chains of accusation he had forged had by chance led to him; or perhaps Rodney or another person here had decided something was amiss with the chief and lodged a tip.

He felt no blame for whoever it was, if that had been the case. The tragedy of civil war was that it turned brother against brother; millions of good and decent men were with the government because they had pledged themselves to be. Mostly, he felt tired.

He looked down the barrel of the gun and then raised weary eyes to the hard face behind it. "I take it I'm under arrest?" he asked tonelessly.

"Get up!" The face was flat and brutal, there was sadism in the heavy mouth. A typical blackcoat.

June whimpered. The man who held her was twisting her arm behind her back. "Don't do that," said Thornberg. "She's innocent."

"Get up, I said!" The gun thrust closer.

"Don't come near me, either." Thornberg lifted his right hand. It was clenched around a little ball. "See this? It's a gimmick I made. No, not a bomb, just a small radio control. If my hand relaxes, the rubber will expand and pull a switch shut."

The men recoiled a little.

"Let the girl go, I said," repeated Thornberg patiently.

"You surrender first!"

June screamed as the cop twisted harder.

"No," said Thornberg. "This is more important than any one of us. I was prepared, you see. I expect to die. So if I let go of this ball, the radio signal closes a relay and a powerful magnetic field is generated in Matilda—in the Records machine. Every record the government has will be wiped clean. I hate to think what your fellows will do to you if you let that happen."

Slowly, the cop released June. She slumped to the floor, crying.

"It's a bluff!" said the man with the gun. There was sweat on his face.

"Try it and find out." Thornberg forced a smile. "I don't care."

"You traitor!"

"And a very effective one, wasn't I? I've got the government turned end for end and upside down. The Army's in an uproar, officers deserting right and left for fear they'll be arrested next. Administration is hogtied and trembling. Security is chasing its own tail around half a continent. Assassination and betrayal are daily occurrences. Men go over to the rebels in droves. The Army of Liberation is sweeping a demoralized and ineffectual resistance before it everywhere. I predict that New Washington will capitulate within a week."

"And your doing!" Finger tense on the trigger.

"Oh, no. No single man can change history. But I was a rather important factor, yes. Or let's say—Sam Hall was."

"What are you going to do?"

"That depends on you, my friend. If you shoot me, gas me, knock me out, or anything of that sort, my hand will naturally relax. Otherwise we'll just wait till one side or the other gets tired."

"You're bluffing!" snapped the squad leader.

"You could, of course, have the technicians here check Matilda and see if I'm telling the truth," said Thornberg. "And if I am, you could have them disconnect my electromagnet. Only I warn you, at the first sign of any such operation on your part I'll let go of this ball. Look in my mouth." He opened it. "A glass vial, full of poison. After I let the ball go, I'll close my teeth together hard. So you see I have nothing to fear from you."

Bafflement and rage flitted over the faces that watched him. They weren't used to thinking, those men.

"Of course," said Thornberg, "there is one other possibility for you. At last reports, a rebel jet squadron was based not a hundred miles from here. We could call it and have them come and take this place over. That might be to your own advantage too. There is going to be a day of reckoning with you blackcoats, and my influence could shield you, however little you deserve it."

They stared at each other. After a very long while the squad leader shook his head. "No!"

The man behind him pulled out a gun and shot him in the back.

Thornberg smiled.

"As a matter of fact," he told Sorensen, "I *was* bluffing. All I had was a tennis ball with a few small electrical parts glued on it. Not that it made much difference at that stage, except to me."

"Matilda will be handy for us in mopping up," said Sorensen. "Want to stay on?"

"Sure, at least till my son arrives. That'll be next week."

"You'll be glad to hear we've finally contacted the Guard in space: just a short radio message, but the commander has agreed to obey whatever government is in power when he arrives. That'll be us, so your boy won't have to do any fighting."

There were no words for that. Instead Thornberg said, with a hard-held casualness, "You know, I'm surprised that *you* should have been an undergrounder."

"There were a few of us even in Security," said Sorensen. "We were organized in small cells, spotted throughout the nation, and wangled things so we could hypnoquiz each other." He grimaced. "It wasn't a pleasant job, though. Some of the things I had to do— Well, that's over with now."

He leaned back in his chair, putting his booted feet on the desk. A Liberation uniform was usually pretty sloppy; they didn't worry about spit-and-polish, but he had managed to be immaculate. "There was a certain amount of suspicion about Sam Hall at first," he said. "The song, you know, and other items. My bosses weren't stupid. I got myself detailed to investigate you; a close checkup gave me grounds to suspect you of revolutionary thoughts, so naturally I gave you a clean bill of health. Later on I cooked up this fantasy of the psychological mask and got several high-ranking men worried about it. When you followed my lead on that, I was sure you were on our side." He grinned. "So naturally our army never attacked Matilda!"

"You must have joined your forces quite recently."

"Yeah, I had to scram out of Security during the uproar and witch hunt you started. You damn near cost me my life, Thorny, know that? Well worth it, though, just to see those cockroaches busily stepping on each other."

Thornberg leaned gravely over his desk. "I always had to

assume you rebels were sincere," he said. "I've never been sure. But now I can check up. Do you intend to destroy Matilda?"

Sorensen nodded. "After we've used her to help us find some people we want rather badly, and to get reorganized—of course. She's too powerful an instrument. It's time to loosen the strings of government."

"Thank you," whispered Thornberg.

He chuckled after a moment. "And that will be the end of Sam Hall," he said. "He'll go to whatever Valhalla is reserved for the great characters of fiction. I can see him squabbling with Sherlock Holmes and shocking the hell out of King Arthur and striking up a beautiful friendship with Long John Silver. You know how the ballad ends?" He sang softly: *"Now up in heaven I dwell, in heaven I dwell—"*

Unfortunately, the conclusion is pretty rugged. Sam Hall never was satisfied.

I MADE YOU

WALTER M. MILLER, JR.

(1 9 5 4)

Throughout history, warfare has generated technological innovation. The medieval metal men that served as prototypes for later robots were knights clad in a new kind of protective shield. Any such new technology may eventually be used for peaceful purposes, but it is the military that originates and first utilizes it. This sequence was true for computers. The pioneering work was done by and for the military, tracing back to the years just before World War II. Since then, the military has continued to design weapons using computers and other electronic devices that distance a soldier from his enemy and increase the accuracy and destructive power of the new weaponry. The battlefield becomes a contest not of men but of remotely controlled devices, like those described in Walter M. Miller's "I Made You," written in 1954. Very few stories up to that time had anticipated compu- terized warfare, perhaps because the development of the computer in the late 1930s and early 1940s remained a secret military project. But once the secret was out, a number of stories appeared picturing wars fought by computers and robots. Understandably, this fiction was grim. The power of the computer is awesome, and when used destructively, its results can be almost beyond imagining.

Walter M. Miller, Jr., born in 1922 and an engineer by profession, is best known for *A Canticle for Leibowitz,* probably the most famous post- holocaust novel ever written and winner of the 1961 Hugo Award. Miller often writes about man's utilization of his technology, nearly always sug- gesting, as he does in *Canticle,* that man seems possessed by some ir- resistible demonic urge to use his technology destructively.

IT HAD DISPOSED of the enemy, and it was weary. It sat on the crag by night. Gaunt, frigid, wounded, it sat under the black sky and listened to the land with its feet, while only its dishlike ear moved in slow patterns that searched the surface of the land and the sky. The land was silent, airless. Nothing moved, except the feeble thing that scratched in the cave. It was good that nothing moved. It hated sound and motion. It was in

314

its nature to hate them. About the thing in the cave it could do nothing until dawn. The thing muttered on the rocks—

"Help me! Are you all dead? Can't you hear me? This is Sawyer. Sawyer calling anybody, Sawyer calling anybody—"

The mutterings were irregular, without pattern. It filtered them out, refusing to listen. All was seeping cold. The sun was gone, and there had been near blackness for two hundred and fifty hours, except for the dim light of the sky-orb which gave no food, and the stars by which it told the time.

It sat wounded on the crag and expected the enemy. The enemy had come charging into the world out of the unworld during the late afternoon. The enemy had come brazenly, with neither defensive maneuvering nor offensive fire. It had destroyed them easily—first the big lumbering enemy that rumbled along on wheels, and then the small enemies that scurried away from the gutted hulk. It had picked them off one at a time, except for the one that crept into the cave and hid itself beyond a break in the tunnel.

It waited for the thing to emerge. From its vantage point atop the crag it could scan broken terrain for miles around, the craters and crags and fissures, the barren expanse of dust flat that stretched to the west, and the squarish outlines of the holy place near the tower that was the center of the world. The cave lay at the foot of a cliff to the southeast, only a thousand yards from the crag. It could guard the entrance to the cave with its small spitters, and there was no escape for the lingering trace of enemy.

It bore the mutterings of the hated thing even as it bore the pain of its wounds, patiently, waiting for a time of respite. For many sunrises there had been pain, and still the wounds were unrepaired. The wounds dulled some of its senses and crippled some of its activators. It could no longer follow the flickering beams of energy that would lead it safely into the unworld and across it to the place of creation. It could no longer blink out the pulses that reflected the difference between healer and foe. Now there was only foe.

"Colonel Aubrey, this is Sawyer. Answer me! I'm trapped in a supply cache! I think the others are dead. It blasted us as soon as we came near. Aubrey from Sawyer, Aubrey from Sawyer. Listen! I've got only one cylinder of oxygen left, you hear? Colonel, answer me!"

Vibrations in the rock—nothing more—only a minor irritant to disturb the blessed stasis of the world it guarded. The enemy was destroyed, except for the lingering trace in the cave. The lingering trace was neutralized, however, and did not move.

Because of its wounds, it nursed a brooding anger. It could not stop the damage signals that kept firing from its wounded members, but neither could it accomplish the actions that the agonizing signals urged it to accomplish. It sat and suffered and hated on the crag.

It hated the night, for by night there was no food. Each day it devoured sun, strengthened itself for the long, long watch of darkness, but when dawn came, it was feeble again, and hunger was a fierce passion within. It was well, therefore, that there was peace in the night, that it might conserve itself and shield its bowels from the cold. If the cold penetrated the insulating layers, thermal receptors would begin firing warning signals, and agony would increase. There was much agony. And, except in time of battle, there was no pleasure, except in devouring sun.

To protect the holy place, to restore stasis to the world, to kill enemy—these were the pleasures of battle. It knew them.

And it knew the nature of the world. It had learned every inch of land out to the pain perimeter, beyond which it could not move. And it had learned the surface features of the demiworld beyond, learned them by scanning with its long-range senses. The world, the demiworld, the unworld—these were Outside, constituting the Universe.

"Help me, help me, help me! This is Captain John Harbin Sawyer, Autocyber Corps, Instruction and Programming Section, currently of Salvage Expedition Lunar Sixteen. Isn't anybody alive on the Moon? Listen! Listen to me! I'm sick. I've been here God

knows how many days . . . in a suit. It stinks. Did you ever live in a suit for days? I'm sick. Get me out of here!"

The enemy's place was unworld. If the enemy approached closer than the outer range, it must kill; this was a basic truth that it had known since the day of creation. Only the healers might move with impunity over all the land, but now the healers never came. It could no longer call them or recognize them—because of the wound.

It knew the nature of itself. It learned of itself by introspecting damage, and by internal scanning. It alone was "being." All else was of the outside. It knew its functions, its skills, its limitations. It listened to the land with its feet. It scanned the surface with many eyes. It tested the skies with a flickering probe. In the ground, it felt the faint seisms and random noise. On the surface, it saw the faint glint of starlight, the heat loss from the cold terrain, and the reflected pulses from the tower. In the sky, it saw only stars, and heard only the pulse echo from the faint orb of Earth overhead. It suffered the gnawings of ancient pain, and waited for the dawn.

After an hour, the thing began crawling in the cave. It listened to the faint scraping sounds that came through the rocks. It lowered to more sensitive pickup and tracked the sounds. The remnant of enemy was crawling softly toward the mouth of the cave. It turned a small spitter toward the black sear at the foot of the Earthlit cliff. It fired a bright burst of tracers toward the cave, and saw them ricochet about the entrance in bright but noiseless streaks over the airless land.

"You dirty, greasy, deadly monstrosity, let me alone! You ugly juggernaut, I'm Sawyer. Don't you remember? I helped to train you ten years ago. You were a rookie under me . . . heh heh! Just a dumb autocyber rookie . . . with the firepower of a regiment. Let me go. Let me go!"

The enemy trace crawled toward the entrance again. And again a noiseless burst of machine-gun fire spewed above the cave, driving the enemy fragment back. More vibrations in the rock—

"I'm your friend. The war's over. It's been over for months . . .

Earthmonths. Don't you get it, Grumbler? 'Grumbler'—we used to call you that back in your rookie days—before we taught you how to kill. Grumbler. Mobile autocyber fire control. Don't you know your pappy, son?"

The vibrations were an irritant. Suddenly angry, it wheeled around on the crag, gracefully maneuvering its massive bulk. Motors growling, it moved from the crag onto the hillside, turned again, and lumbered down the slope. It charged across the flatlands and braked to a halt fifty yards from the entrance to the cave. Dust geysers sprayed up about its caterpillars and fell like jets of water in the airless night. It listened again. All was silent in the cave.

"Go 'way, sonny," quavered the vibrations after a time. *"Let Pappy starve in peace."*

It aimed the small spitter at the center of the black opening and hosed two hundred rounds of tracers into the cave. It waited. Nothing moved inside. It debated the use of a radiation grenade, but its arsenal was fast depleting. It listened for a time, watching the cave, looming five times taller than the tiny flesh-thing that cowered inside. Then it turned and lumbered back across the flat to resume its watch from the crag. Distant motion, out beyond the limits of the demiworld, scratched feebly at the threshold of its awareness—but the motion was too remote to disturb.

The thing was scratching in the cave again.

"I'm punctured, do you hear? I'm punctured. A shard of broken rock. Just a small leak, but a slap patch won't hold. My suit! Aubrey from Sawyer, Aubrey from Sawyer. Base control from Moonwagon Sixteen. Message for you, over. He He. Gotta observe procedure. I got shot! I'm punctured. Help!"

The thing made whining sounds for a time: *"All right, it's only my leg. I'll pump the boot full of water and freeze it. So I lose a leg. Whatthehell, take your time."* The vibration subsided into whining sounds again.

It settled again on the crag, its activators relaxing into a lethargy that was full of gnawing pain. Patiently it awaited the dawn.

The movement toward the south was increasing. The movement nagged at the outer fringes of the demiworld, until at last the movement became an irritant. Silently, a drill slipped down from its belly. The drill gnawed deep into the rock, then retracted. It slipped a sensitive pickup into the drill hole and listened carefully to the ground.

A faint purring in the rocks—mingled with the whining from the cave.

It compared the purring with recorded memories. It remembered similar purring. The sound came from a rolling object far to the south. It tried to send the pulses that asked "Are you friend or foe?" but the sending organ was inoperative. The movement, therefore, was enemy—but still beyond range of its present weapons.

Lurking anger, and expectation of battle. It stirred restlessly on the crag, but kept its surveillance of the cave. Suddenly there was disturbance on a new sensory channel, similar to those that came from the cave; but this time the vibrations came across the surface, through the emptiness, transmitted in the long-wave spectra.

"Moonwagon Sixteen from Command Runabout, give us a call. Over."

Then silence. It expected a response from the cave, at first— since it knew that one unit of enemy often exchanged vibratory patterns with another unit of enemy. But no answer came. Perhaps the long-wave energy could not penetrate the cave to reach the thing that cringed inside.

"Salvage Sixteen, this is Aubrey's runabout. What the devil happened to you? Can you read me? Over!"

Tensely it listened to the ground. The purring stopped for a time as the enemy paused. Minutes later the motion resumed.

It awoke an emissary ear twenty kilometers to the southwest, and commanded the ear to listen, and to transmit the patterns of the purring noise. Two soundings were taken, and from them it derived the enemy's precise position and velocity. The enemy was proceeding to the north, into the edge of the demiworld. Lurking anger flared into active fury. It gunned its engines on the crag. It girded itself for battle.

"Salvage Sixteen, this is Aubrey's runabout. I assume your radio rig is inoperative. If you can hear us, get this: we're proceeding north to five miles short of magnapult range. We'll stop there and fire an autocyb rocket into zone Red-Red. The warhead's a radio-to-sonar transceiver. If you've got a seismitter that's working, the transceiver will act as a relay stage. Over."

It ignored the vibratory pattern and rechecked its battle gear. It introspected its energy storage, and tested its weapon activators. It summoned an emissary eye and waited a dozen minutes while the eye crawled crablike from the holy place to take up a watch post near the entrance of the cave. If the enemy remnant tried to emerge, the emissary eye would see, and report, and it could destroy the enemy remnant with a remote grenade catapult.

The purring in the ground was louder. Having prepared itself for the fray, it came down from the crag and grumbled southward at cruising speed. It passed the gutted hulk of the Moonwagon, with its team of overturned tractors. The detonation of the magnapult canister had broken the freightcar-sized vehicle in half. The remains of several two-legged enemy appurtenances were scattered about the area, tiny broken things in the pale Earthlight. Grumbler ignored them and charged relentlessly southward.

A sudden wink of light on the southern horizon! Then a tiny dot of flame arched upward, traversing the heavens. Grumbler skidded to a halt and tracked its path. A rocket missile. It would fall somewhere in the east half of zone Red-Red. There was no time to prepare to shoot it down. Grumbler waited—and saw that the missile would explode harmlessly in a nonvital area.

Seconds later, the missile paused in flight, reversing direction and sitting on its jets. It dropped out of sight behind an outcropping. There was no explosion. Nor was there any activity in the area where the missile had fallen. Grumbler called an emissary ear, sent it migrating toward the impact point to listen, then continued south toward the pain perimeter.

"Salvage Sixteen, this is Aubrey's runabout," came the long-wave vibrations. *"We just shot the radio-seismitter relay into Red-Red. If you're within five miles of it, you should be able to hear."*

320

Almost immediately, a response from the cave, heard by the emissary ear that listened to the land near the tower: *"Thank God! He he he he—oh, thank God!"*

And simultaneously, the same vibration pattern came in long-wave patterns from the direction of the missile-impact point. Grumbler stopped again, momentarily confused, angrily tempted to lob a magnapult canister across the broken terrain toward the impact point. But the emissary ear reported no physical movement from the area. The enemy to the south was the origin of the disturbances. If it removed the major enemy first, it could remove the minor disturbances later. It moved on to the pain perimeter, occasionally listening to the meaningless vibrations caused by the enemy.

"Salvage Sixteen from Aubrey. I hear you faintly. Who is this, Carhill?"

"Aubrey! A voice— A real voice— Or am I going nuts?"

"Sixteen from Aubrey. Sixteen from Aubrey. Stop babbling and tell me who's talking. What's happening in there? Have you got Grumbler immobilized?"

Spasmodic choking was the only response.

"Sixteen from Aubrey. Snap out of it! Listen, Sawyer, I know it's you. Now get hold of yourself, man! What's happened?"

"Dead . . . they're all dead but me."

"STOP THAT IDIOTIC LAUGHING!"

A long silence, then, scarcely audible: *"O.K., I'll hold on to myself. Is it really you, Aubrey?"*

"You're not having hallucinations, Sawyer. We're crossing zone Red in a runabout. Now tell me the situation. We've been trying to call you for days."

"Grumbler let us get ten miles into zone Red-Red, and then he clobbered us with a magnapult canister."

"Wasn't your I.F.F. working?"

"Yes, but Grumbler's isn't! After he blasted the wagon, he picked off the other four that got out alive— He he he he . . . Did you ever see a Sherman tank chase a mouse, Colonel?"

"Cut it out, Sawyer! Another giggle out of you, and I'll flay you alive."

"Get me out! My leg! Get me out!"

321

"If we can. Tell me your present situation."

"My suit . . . I got a small puncture— Had to pump the leg full of water and freeze it. Now my leg's dead. I can't last much longer."

"The situation, Sawyer, the situation! Not your aches and pains."

The vibrations continued, but Grumbler screened them out for a time. There was rumbling fury on an Earthlit hill.

It sat with its engines idling, listening to the distant movements of the enemy to the south. At the foot of the hill lay the pain perimeter; even upon the hilltop, it felt the faint twinges of warning that issued from the tower, thirty kilometers to the rear at the center of the world. It was in communion with the tower. If it ventured beyond the perimeter, the communion would slip out of phase, and there would be blinding pain and detonation.

The enemy was moving more slowly now, creeping north across the demiworld. It would be easy to destroy the enemy at once, if only the supply of rocket missiles were not depleted. The range of the magnapult hurler was only twenty-five kilometers. The small spitters would reach, but their accuracy was close to zero at such range. It would have to wait for the enemy to come closer. It nursed a brooding fury on the hill.

"Listen, Sawyer, if Grumbler's I.F.F. isn't working, why hasn't he already fired on this runabout?"

"That's what sucked us in too, Colonel. We came into zone Red and nothing happened. Either he's out of long-range ammo, or he's getting cagey, or both. Probably both."

"Mmmp! Then we'd better park here and figure something out."

"Listen . . . there's only one thing you can do. Call for a tele-controlled missile from the base."

"To destroy Grumbler? You're out of your head, Sawyer. If Grumbler's knocked out, the whole area around the excavations gets blown sky-high . . . to keep them out of enemy hands. You know that."

"You expect me to care?"

"Stop screaming, Sawyer. Those excavations are the most valuable property on the Moon. We can't afford to lose them. That's

why *Grumbler was staked out. If they got blown to rubble, I'd be court-martialed before the debris quit falling."*

The response was snarling and sobbing. *"Eight hours' oxygen. Eight hours, you hear? You stupid, merciless—"*

The enemy to the south stopped moving at a distance of twenty-eight kilometers from Grumbler's hill—only three thousand meters beyond magnapult range.

A moment of berserk hatred. It lumbered to and fro in a frustrated pattern that was like a monstrous dance, crushing small rocks beneath its treads, showering dust into the valley. Once it charged down toward the pain perimeter, and turned back only after the agony became unbearable. It stopped again on the hill, feeling the weariness of lowered energy supplies in the storage units.

It paused to analyze. It derived a plan.

Gunning its engines, it wheeled slowly around on the hilltop, and glided down the northern slope at a stately pace. It sped northward for half a mile across the flatland, then slowed to a crawl and maneuvered its massive bulk into a fissure, where it had cached an emergency store of energy. The battery trailer had been freshly charged before the previous sundown. It backed into feeding position and attached the supply cables without hitching itself to the trailer.

It listened occasionally to the enemy while it drank hungrily from the energy store, but the enemy remained motionless. It would need every erg of available energy in order to accomplish its plan. It drained the cache. Tomorrow, when the enemy was gone, it would drag the trailer back to the main feeders for recharging, when the sun rose to drive the generators once again. It kept several caches of energy at strategic positions throughout its domain, that it might never be driven into starved inability to act during the long lunar night. It kept its own house in order, dragging the trailers back to be recharged at regular intervals.

"I don't know what I can do for you, Sawyer," came the noise of the enemy. *"We don't dare destroy Grumbler, and there's not another autocyber crew on the Moon. I'll have to call Terra for*

323

replacements. *I can't send men into zone Red-Red if Grumbler's running berserk. It'd be murder."*

"For the love of God, Colonel—!"

"Listen, Sawyer, you're the autocyberman. You helped train Grumbler. Can't you think of some way to stop him without detonating the mined area?"

A protracted silence. Grumbler finished feeding and came out of the fissure. It moved westward a few yards, so that a clear stretch of flatland lay between itself and the hill at the edge of the pain perimeter, half a mile away. There it paused, and awoke several emissary ears, so that it might derive the most accurate possible fix of the enemy's position. One by one, the emissary ears reported.

"Well, Sawyer?"

"My leg's killing me."

"Can't you think of anything?"

"Yeah—but it won't do me any good. I won't live that long."

"Well, let's hear it."

"Knock out his remote energy storage units, and then run him ragged at night."

"How long would it take?"

"Hours—after you found all his remote supply units and blasted them."

It analyzed the reports of the emissary ears, and calculated a precise position. The enemy runabout was 2.7 kilometers beyond the maximum range of the magnapult—as creation had envisioned the maximum. But creation was imperfect, even inside.

It loaded a canister onto the magnapult's spindle. Contrary to the intentions of creation, it left the canister *locked to the loader.* This would cause pain. But it would prevent the canister from moving during the first few microseconds after the switch was closed, while the magnetic field was still building toward full strength. It would not release the canister until the field clutched it fiercely and with full effect, thus imparting slightly greater energy to the canister. This procedure it had invented for itself, thus transcending creation.

———

"Well, Sawyer, if you can't think of anything else—"

"I DID THINK OF SOMETHING ELSE!" the answering vibrations screamed. *"Call for a telecontrolled missile! Can't you understand, Aubrey? Grumbler murdered eight men from your command."*

"You taught him how, Sawyer."

There was a long and ominous silence. On the flatland to the north of the hill, Grumbler adjusted the elevation of the magnapult slightly, keyed the firing switch to a gyroscope, and prepared to charge. Creation had calculated the maximum range when the weapon was at a standstill.

"He he he he he—" came the patterns from the thing in the cave.

It gunned its engines and clutched the drive shafts. It rolled toward the hill, gathering speed, and its mouth was full of death. Motors strained and howled. Like a thundering bull, it rumbled toward the south. It hit maximum velocity at the foot of the slope. It lurched sharply upward. As the magnapult swept up to correct elevation, the gyroscope closed the circuit.

A surge of energy. The clutching fist of the field gripped the canister, tore it free of the loader, hurled it over the broken terrain toward the enemy. Grumbler skidded to a halt on the hilltop.

"Listen, Sawyer, I'm sorry, but there's nothing—"

The enemy's voice ended with a dull snap. A flare of light came briefly from the southern horizon, and died.

"He he he he he—" said the thing in the cave.

Grumbler paused.

THRRUMMMP! came the shock wave through the rocks.

Five emissary ears relayed their recordings of the detonation from various locations. It studied them, it analyzed. The detonation had occurred less than fifty meters from the enemy runabout. Satiated, it wheeled around lazily on the hilltop and rolled northward toward the center of the world. All was well.

"Aubrey, you got cut off," grunted the thing in the cave. *"Call me, you coward . . . call me. I want to make certain you hear."*

Grumbler, as a random action, recorded the meaningless

325

noise of the thing in the cave, studied the noise, rebroadcast it on a long-wave frequency: "Aubrey, you got cut off. Call me, you coward . . . call me. I want to make certain you hear."

The seismitter caught the long-wave noise and reintroduced it as vibrations in the rocks.

The thing screamed in the cave. Grumbler recorded the screaming noise, and rebroadcast it several times.

"Aubrey . . . Aubrey, where are you . . . AUBREY! *Don't desert me, don't leave me here—"*

The thing in the cave became silent.

It was a peaceful night. The stars glared unceasingly from the blackness, and the pale terrain was haunted by Earthlight from the dim crescent in the sky. Nothing moved. It was good that nothing moved. The holy place was at peace in the airless world. There was blessed stasis.

Only once did the thing stir again in the cave. So slowly that Grumbler scarcely heard the sound, it crawled to the entrance and lay peering up at the steel behemoth on the crag.

It whispered faintly in the rocks.

"I made you, don't you understand? I'm human, I made you—"

Then with one leg dragging behind, it pulled itself out into the Earthglow and turned as if to look up at the dim crescent in the sky. Gathering fury, Grumbler stirred on the crag, and lowered the black maw of a grenade launcher.

"I made you," came the meaningless noise.

It hated noise and motion. It was in its nature to hate them. Angrily, the grenade launcher spoke. And then there was blessed stasis for the rest of the night.

TRIGGERMAN

J. F. Bone

(1 9 5 8)

Early in the 1950s, the military began to develop SAGE (Semi-automatic Ground Environment), a system designed to protect the United States from surprise air attack. It was housed underground inside Cheyenne Mountain near Colorado Springs and became operational in 1958. Secret though the project was, word of it leaked out. In the late 1950s, several stories appeared that were about pushbutton warfare, the term coined to describe the purpose of an automatic defense system. The earliest such story was J. F. Bone's "Triggerman" published in the December 1958 issue of *Analog*. Peter George's novel *Two Hours to Doom,* from which the film *Dr. Strangelove* was made in 1964, was published in the same year. And in 1959 Mordecai Roshwald published *Level 7,* describing an equipment error that triggers the mechanism for directing rockets against the enemy. Eugene Burdick and Harvey Wheeler's novel *Fail-Safe* (1962) had a similar theme. Most of this fiction about pushbutton warfare did not anticipate but rather followed actual developments, usually in terms of the inadvertent activation of the system through some kind of mechanical failure.

Just such an event did actually occur after it was first described in science fiction. In 1960, the radar returns in the Ballistic Missile Early Warning System were interpreted by a computer-based system to be a flight of missiles approaching North America over the North Pole. The headquarters of the Strategic Air Command considered the attack so unlikely that they refused to take action until the report could be confirmed by contacting the radar site. This took some time because a submarine cable had accidentally broken just after the first message but before a correction could be sent. When the radar site commander was finally reached by phone, the difficulty was cleared up. The warning system had not been programmed to distinguish between the moon and a flight of missiles.

J. F. Bone, the author of this story, was a professor of veterinary medicine at Oregon State University who retired from his field in 1979. He served as a Fulbright Lecturer in Egypt and Kenya, and his best-known novel is *The Lana People,* published in 1962.

GENERAL ALASTAIR FRENCH was probably the most important man in the Western Hemisphere from the hours of 0800 to 1600. Yet all he did was sit in a windowless room buried deeply underground, facing a desk that stood against a wall. The wall was studded with built-in mechanisms. A line of twenty-four-hour clocks was inset near the ceiling, showing the corresponding times in all time zones on Earth. Two huge TV screens below the clocks were flanked by loudspeaker systems. The desk was bare except for three telephones of different colors—red, blue, and white—and a polished plastic slab inset with a number of white buttons framing a larger one whose red surface was the color of fresh blood. A thick carpet, a chair of peculiar design with broad flat arms, and an ashtray completed the furnishings. Warmed and humidified air circulated through the room from concealed grilles at floor level. The walls of the room were painted a soft restful gray that softened the indirect lighting. The door was steel and equipped with a time lock.

The exact location of the room and the Center that served it was probably the best kept secret in the Western world. Ivan would probably give a good percentage of the Soviet tax take to know precisely where it was, just as the West would give a similar amount to know where Ivan's Center was located. Yet despite the fact that its location was remote, the man behind the desk was in intimate contact with every major military point in the Western Alliance. The red telephone was a direct connection to the White House. The blue was a line that reached to the headquarters of the Joint Chiefs of Staff and to the emergency Capitol hidden in the hills of West Virginia. And the white telephone connected by priority lines with every military center and base in the world that was under Allied control.

General French was that awesome individual often joked about by TV comics who didn't know that he really existed. He was the man who could push the button that would start World War III!

French was aware of his responsibilities and took them seriously. By nature he was a serious man, but, after three years of living with ultimate responsibility, it was no longer the crushing burden that it had been at first when the Psychological Board selected him as one of the most inherently stable men on Earth. He was not ordinarily a happy man; his job, and the steadily

328

deteriorating world situation precluded that, but this day was a bright exception. The winter morning had been extraordinarily beautiful, and he loved beauty with the passion of an artist. A flaming sunrise had lighted the whole eastern sky with golden glory, and the crisp cold air stimulated his senses to appreciate it. It was much too lovely for thoughts of war and death.

He opened the door of the room precisely at 0800, as he had done for three years, and watched a round, pink-cheeked man in a gray suit rise from the chair behind the desk. Kleinmeister, he thought, neither looked like a general nor like a potential executioner of half the world. He was a Santa Claus without a beard. But appearances were deceiving. Hans Kleinmeister could, without regret, kill half the world if he thought it was necessary. The two men shook hands, a ritual gesture that marked the changing of the guard, and French sank into the padded chair behind the desk.

"It's a beautiful day outside, Hans," he remarked as he settled his stocky, compact body into the automatically adjusting plastifoam. "I envy you the pleasure of it."

"I don't envy you, Al," Kleinmeister said. "I'm just glad it's all over for another twenty-four hours. This waiting gets on the nerves." Kleinmeister grinned as he left the room. The steel door thudded into place behind him and the time lock clicked. For the next eight hours French would be alone.

He sighed. It was too bad that he had to be confined indoors on a day like this one promised to be, but there was no help for it. He shifted luxuriously in the chair. It was the most comfortable seat that the mind and ingenuity of man could contrive. It had to be. The man who sat in it must have every comfort. He must want for nothing. And above all he must not be irritated or annoyed. His brain must be free to evaluate and decide—and nothing must distract the functioning of that brain. Physical comfort was a means to that end—and the chair provided it. French felt soothed in the gentle caress of the upholstery.

The familiar feeling of detachment swept over him as he checked the room. Nominally, he was responsible to the President and the Joint Chiefs of Staff, but practically he was responsible to no one. No hand but his could set in motion the forces of massive retaliation that had hung over aggression for the past twenty years. Without his sanction, no intercontinental or intermediate-range missile could leave its rack. He was the final authority, the ultimate judge, and the executioner if need be—a position thrust upon him after years of intensive tests and screening. In this room he was as close to being a god as any man had been since the beginning of time.

French shrugged and touched one of the white buttons on the panel.

"Yes sir?" an inquiring voice came from one of the speakers.

"A magazine and a cup of coffee," said General French.

"What magazine, sir?"

"Something light—something with pictures. Use your judgment."

"Yes, sir."

French grinned. By now the word was going around Center that the Old Man was in a good humor today. A cup of coffee rose from a well in one of the board arms of the chair, and a magazine extruded from a slot in its side. French opened the magazine and sipped the coffee. General Craig, his relief, would be here in less than eight hours, which would leave him the enjoyment of the second-best part of the day if the dawn was any indication. He hoped the sunset would be worthy of its dawn.

He looked at the center clock. The hands read 0817 . . . .

At Station 2 along the DEW Line the hands of the station clock read 1217. Although it was high noon it was dark outside, lightened only by a faint glow to the south where the winter sun strove vainly to appear above the horizon. The air was clear, and the stars shone out of the blue-black sky of the polar regions. A radarman bending over his scope stiffened. "Bogey!" he snapped. "Azimuth 0200, coming up fast!"

The bogey came in over the north polar cap, slanting downward through the tenuous wisps of upper atmosphere. The gases ripped at its metallic sides with friction and oxidation. Great gouts of flaming brilliance spurted from its incandescent outer surface, boiling away to leave a trail of sparkling scintillation in its wake. It came with enormous speed, whipping over the Station almost before the operator could hit the general alarm.

The tracking radar of the main line converged upon the target. Electronic computers analyzed its size, speed and flight path, passing the information to the batteries of interceptor missiles in the sector. "Locked on," a gunnery office announced in a bored tone. "Fire two." He smiled. Ivan was testing again. It was almost routine, this business of one side or the other sending over a pilot missile. It was the acid test. If the defense network couldn't get it, perhaps others would come over—perhaps not. It was all part of the cold war.

Miles away, two missiles leaped from their ramps, flashing skyward on flaming rockets. The gunnery officer waited a moment and then swore. "Missed, by damn! It looks like Ivan's got something new." He flipped a switch. "Reserve line, stand by," he said. "Bogey coming over. Course 0200."

"Got her," a voice came from the speaker of the command set. "All stations in range, fire four—salvo!"

"My God, what's in that thing! Warn Stateside! Execute!"

"All stations Eastseaboard Outer Defense Area! Bogey coming over!"

"Red Alert, all areas!" a communications man said urgently into a microphone. "Ivan's got something this time! General evacuation plan Boston to Richmond Plan One! Execute!"

"Outer Perimeter Fire Pattern B!"

"Center! Emergency Priority! General, there's a bogey coming in. Eastseaboard sector. It's passed the outer lines, and nothing's touched it so far. It's the damnedest thing you ever saw! Too fast for interception. Estimated target area Boston-Richmond. For evaluation—!"

"Sector perimeter on target, sir!"

"Fire twenty, Pattern C!"

All along the flight path of the bogey, missile launchers hurled the cargoes of death into the sky. A moving pattern formed in front of the plunging object that now was flaming brightly enough to be seen in the cold northern daylight. Missiles struck, detonated, and were absorbed into the ravening flames around the object, but it came on with unabated speed, a hissing, roaring mass of destruction!

"God! It's still coming in!" an anguished voice wailed. "I told them we needed nuclear warheads for close-in defense!"

More missiles swept aloft, but the bogey was now so low that both human and electronic sensings were too slow. An instantaneous blast of searing heat flashed across the land in its wake, crisping anything flammable in its path. Hundreds of tiny fires broke out, most of which were quickly extinguished, but others burned violently. A gas refinery in Utica exploded. Other damage of a minor nature was done in Scranton and Wilkes-Barre. The reports were mixed with military orders and the flare of missiles and the crack of artillery hurling box barrages into the sky. But it was futile. The target was moving almost too fast to be seen, and by the time the missiles and projectiles reached intercept point, the target was gone, drawing away from the fastest defense devices with almost contemptuous ease.

General French sat upright in his chair. The peaceful expression vanished from his face to be replaced by a hard, intent look, as his eyes flicked from phones to TV screen. The series of tracking stations, broadcasting over wire, sent their images in to be edited and projected on the screens in French's room. Their observations appeared at frighteningly short intervals.

French stared at the flaring dot that swept across the screens. It could not be a missile, unless—his mind faltered at the thought—the Russians were further advanced than anyone had expected. They might be at that—after all, they had surprised the world with Sputnik not too many years ago, and the West was forced to work like fiends to catch up.

"Target confirmed," one of the speakers announced with unearthly calm. "It's Washington!"

The speaker to the left of the screen broke into life. "This is Conelrad," it said. "This is not a test, repeat—*this is not a test!*" The voice faded as another station took over. "A transpolar missile is headed south along the eastern seaboard. Target Washington. Plan One. Evacuation time thirty seconds—"

332

Thirty seconds! French's mind recoiled. Washington was dead! You couldn't go anywhere in thirty seconds! His hand moved toward the red button. This was it!

The missile on the screen was brighter now. It flamed like a miniature sun, and the sound of its passage was that of a million souls in torment! "It can't stand much more of that," French breathed. "It'll burn up!"

"New York Sector—bogey at twelve o'clock—high! God! *Look* at it!"

The glare of the thing filled the screen.

The blue phone rang. "Center," French said. He waited and then laid the phone down. The line was dead.

"Flash!" Conelrad said. "The enemy missile has struck south of New York. A tremendous flash was seen fifteen seconds ago by observers in civilian defense spotting nets . . . no sound of the explosion as yet . . . more information—triangulation of the explosion indicates that it has struck the nation's capital! Our center of government has been destroyed!" There was a short silence broken by a faint voice. "Oh, my God!—all those poor people!"

The red phone rang. French picked it up. "Center," he said. The phone squawked at him.

"Your authority?" French queried dully. He paused and his face turned an angry red. "Just who do you think you are, Colonel? I'll take orders from the Chief—but no one else! Now get off that line! . . . Oh, I see. Then it's my responsibility? . . . All right, I accept it—now leave me alone!" He put the phone gently back on the cradle. A fine beading of sweat dotted his forehead. This was the situation he had never let himself think would occur. The President was dead. The Joint Chiefs were dead. He was on his own until some sort of government could be formed.

Should he wait and let Ivan exploit his advantage, or should he strike? Oddly, he wondered what his alter ego in Russia was doing at this moment. Was he proud of having struck this blow— or was he frightened? French smiled grimly. If he were in Ivan's shoes, he'd be scared to death! He shivered. For the first time in years he felt the full weight of the responsibility that was his.

The red phone rang again.

"Center—French here . . . Who's that? . . . Oh, yes, sir, Mr. Vice . . . er, Mr. President! . . . Yes, sir, it's a terrible thing . . . What have I done? Well, nothing yet, sir. A single bogey like that doesn't feel right. I'm waiting for the follow-up that'll confirm . . . Yes, sir I know—but do *you* want to take the responsibility for destroying the world? What if it wasn't Ivan's? Have you thought of that? . . . Yes, sir, it's my judgment that we wait . . . No, sir, I don't think so, if Ivan's back of this we'll have more coming, and if we do, I'll fire . . . No, sir, I will not take that responsibility . . . Yes, I know Washington's destroyed, but we still have no proof of Ivan's guilt. Long-range radar has not reported any activity in Russia . . . Sorry, sir, I can't see it that way—and you can't relieve me until 1600 hours . . . Yes, sir, I realize what I'm doing . . . Very well, sir, if that's the way you want it, I'll resign at 1600 hours. Goodbye." French dropped the phone into its cradle and wiped his forehead. He had just thrown his career out the window, but that was another thing that couldn't be helped. The President was hysterical now. Maybe he'd calm down later.

"Flash!" the radio said. "Radio Moscow denies that the missile which destroyed Washington was one of theirs. They insist that it is a capitalist trick to make them responsible for World War III. The Premier accuses the United States . . . hey! wait a minute! . . . accuses the United States of trying to foment war, but to show the good faith of the Soviet Union, he will open the country to UN inspection to prove once and for all that the Soviet does not and has not intended nuclear aggression. He proposes that a UN team investigate the wreckage of Washington to determine whether the destruction was actually caused by a missile. Hah! Just what in hell does he think caused it?"

French grinned thinly. Words like the last were seldom heard on the lips of commentators. The folks outside were pretty wrought up. There was hysteria in almost every word that had come into the office. But it hadn't moved him yet. His finger was still off the trigger. He picked up the white phone. "Get me DEW Line Headquarters," he said. "Hello, DEW Line, this is French at Center. Any more bogeys? . . . No? . . . That's good . . . No, we're still holding off . . . Why? . . . Any fool would know why if he

334

stopped to think!" He slammed the phone back into its cradle. Damn fools howling for war! Just who did they think would win it? Sure, it would be easy to start things rolling. All he had to do was push the button. He stared at it with fascinated eyes. Nearly three billion lives lay on that polished plastic surface, and he could snuff most of them out with one jab of a finger.

"Sir!" a voice broke from the speaker. "What's the word—are we in it yet?"

"Not yet, Jimmy."

"Thank God!" the voice sounded relieved. "Just hang on, sir. We know they're pressuring you, but they'll stop screaming for blood once they have time to think."

"I hope so," French said. He chuckled without humor. The personnel at Center knew what nuclear war would be like. Most of them had experience at Frenchman's Flat. They didn't want any part of it, if it could be avoided. And neither did he.

The hours dragged by. The phones rang, and Conelrad kept reporting—giving advice and directions for evacuation of the cities. All the nation was stalled in the hugest traffic jam in history. Some of it couldn't help seeping in, even through the censorship. There was danger in too much of anything, and obviously the country was overmechanized. By now, French was certain that Russia was innocent. If she wasn't, Ivan would have struck in force by now. He wondered how his opposite number in Russia was taking it. Was the man crouched over his control board, waiting for the cloud of capitalist missiles to appear over the horizon? Or was he, too, fingering a red button, debating whether or not to strike before it was too late?

"Flash!" the radio said. "Radio Moscow offers immediate entry to any UN inspection team authorized by the General Assembly. The presidium has met and announces that under no circumstances will Russia take any aggressive action. They repeat that the missile was not theirs, and suggest that it might have originated from some other nation desirous of fomenting war between the Great Powers . . . ah, nuts!"

"That's about as close to surrender as they dare come," French

335

murmured softly. "They're scared green—but then, who wouldn't be?" He looked at the local clock. It read 1410. Less than two hours to go before the time lock opened and unimaginative Jim Craig came through that door to take his place. If the President called with Craig in the seat, the executive orders would be obeyed. He picked up the white phone.

"Get me the Commanding General of the Second Army," he said. He waited a moment. "Hello, George, this is Al at Center. How you doing? Bad, huh? No, we're holding off . . . Now hold it, George. That's not what I called for. I don't need moral support. I want information. Have your radio crews checked the Washington area yet? . . . They haven't. Why not? Get them on the ball! Ivan keeps insisting that that bogey wasn't his and the facts seem to indicate he's telling the truth for once, but we're going to blast if he can't prove it! I want the dope on radioactivity in that area and I want it now! . . . If you don't want to issue an order—call for volunteers . . . So they might get a lethal dose— so what? . . . Offer them a medal. There's always someone who'd walk into hell for the chance of getting a medal. Now get cracking! . . . Yes, that's an order."

The radio came on again. "First reports of the damage in Washington," it chattered. "A shielded Air Force reconnaissance plane has flown over the blast area, taking pictures and making an aerial survey of fallout intensity. The Capitol is a shambles. Ground Zero was approximately in the center of Pennsylvania Avenue. There is a tremendous crater over a half-mile wide, and around that for nearly two miles there is literally nothing! The Capitol is gone. Over ninety-eight percent of the city is destroyed. Huge fires are raging in Alexandria and the outskirts. The Potomac bridges are down. The destruction is inconceivable. The landmarks of our—"

French grabbed the white phone. "Find out who the Air Force commander was who sent up that recon plane over Washington!" he barked. "I don't know who he is—but get him *now!*" He waited for three minutes. "So it was you, Willoughby! I thought it might be. This is French at Center. What did that recon find? . . . It did, hey? . . . Well now, isn't that simply wonderful! You stupid publicity-crazy fool! What do you mean by withholding vital information! Do you realize that I've been sitting here with my finger on the button ready to kill half the earth's population, while you've been flirting around with reporters? . . . Dammit! That's no excuse! You should be cashiered—and if I have any influence around here tomorrow, I'll see that you are. As it is, you're relieved as of now! . . . What do you mean, I can't do that? . . . Read your regulations again, and then get out of that office and place yourself under arrest in quarters! Turn over your command to your executive officer! You utter, driveling fool! . . . Aaagh!!" French snarled as he slammed the phone back.

It began ringing again immediately. "French here . . . Yes, George . . . You have? . . . You did? . . . It isn't? . . . I thought so. We've been barking up the wrong tree this time. It was an act of God! . . . Yes, I said an act of God! Remember that crater out in Arizona? Well, this is the same thing—a meteor! . . . Yes, Ivan's still quiet. Not a peep out of him. The DEW Line reports no activity."

The blue phone began to ring. French looked at it. "O.K., George—apology accepted. I know how you feel." He hung up and lifted the blue phone. "Yes, Mr. President," he said. "Yes, sir. You've heard the news, I suppose . . . You've had confirmation from Lick Observatory? . . . Yes, sir, I'll stay here if you wish . . . No, sir, I'm perfectly willing to act. It was just that this never did look right—and thank God that you understand astronomy, sir . . . Of course I'll stay until the emergency is over, but you'll have to tell General Craig . . . Who's Craig? Why, he's my relief, sir." French looked at the clock. "He comes on in twenty minutes . . . Well, thank you, sir. I never thought that I'd get a commendation for not obeying orders."

French sighed and hung up. Sense was beginning to percolate through the shock. People were beginning to think again. He sighed. This should teach a needed lesson. He made a mental note of it. If he had anything to say about the makeup of Center from now on—there'd be an astronomer on the staff, and a few more of them scattered out on the DEW Line and the outpost groups. It was virtually certain now that the Capitol was struck by a meteorite. There was no radioactivity. It had been an act of God—or at least not an act of war. The destruction was terrible, but it could have been worse if either he or his alter ego in Russia had lost control and pushed the buttons. He thought idly that he'd like to meet the Ivan who ran their Center.

"The proposals of the Soviet government," the radio interrupted, "have been accepted by the UN. An inspection team is en route to Russia, and others will follow as quickly as possible. Meanwhile, the UN has requested a cease-fire assurance from the United States, warning that the start of a nuclear war would be the end of everything." The announcer's voice held a note of grim humor. "So far, there has been no word from Washington concerning these proposals."

French chuckled. It might not be in the best taste, and it might be graveyard humor—but it was a healthy sign.

WAR WITH THE ROBOTS

HARRY HARRISON

(1 9 6 2)

Traditionally in times of danger, man has taken refuge in Mother Earth. He has retreated underground. But what happens when that last womb of security is invaded? This story describes one possibility. Its author, Harry Harrison, has written a number of stories about robots, and one of his best is "War with the Robots." Born in 1925, Harrison is a world traveler who currently lives in Ireland. Once a well-known commercial artist before turning to science fiction, Harrison has edited a number of anthologies, including many with Brian Aldiss. He also organized the World Science Fiction Writers, whose first meeting was held in Dublin in 1976. His most notable works include the *Deathworld* novels and *Make Room! Make Room!* (1966), which was made into the film *Soylent Green.*

Another author who deserves mention here is the late Philip K. Dick, who also produced a number of excellent stories about electronic warfare. Dick began writing after World War II, and his bizarre imagination beat incessantly on the anvil of destructive possibilities for man if the computer were to be used in warfare. A shower of his frightening stories burst into print in the early 1950s—stories like "Second Variety," "The Imposter," "The Defenders," and "Autofac." His novel *The Penultimate Truth* pictures a future war where—as in Harrison's "War with the Robots"—men retreat underground and leave their robots on the surface to continue the fighting. The robots send down daily reports suggesting they are carrying out orders, but actually, possessed of better sense than men, they have quit fighting and are busy restoring Earth's devastated surface. Two of Dick's stories, "If There Were No Benny Cemoli" and "The Electric Ant," are included in this anthology.

ONLY THE SLIGHTEST VIBRATION could be felt through the floor of the hurtling monorail car. There was no sensation of motion since the rushing tunnel walls could not be seen through the windowless sides. The riders, all of them in neatly pressed uniforms with buttons and decorations shining, swayed slightly in their seats on the turns, wrapped in their own thoughts and mumbled conversations. Above them, thousands of feet of solid rock sealed them off from the war. At an effortless one hundred and fifty miles an hour the car rushed General Pere and his staff to their battle stations.

When the alarm screamed, the driver clamped the brakes full on and reversed his motors. There was not enough time. At full speed the metal bullet tore into the barrier of rocks and dirt that blocked the tunnel. Steel plates crushed and crumpled as the car slammed to a halt. All the lights went out; and in the empty silence that followed the ear-shattering clamor of the crash, only a faint moaning could be heard.

General Pere pushed himself up from the chair, shaking his head in an effort to clear it, and snapped on his flash. The beam nervously danced the length of the car, gleaming on settling dust motes and lighting up the frightened white faces of his staff.

"Casualty report, verbal," he told his adjutant, his voice pitched low so that no quaver might be heard. It is not easy to be a general when you are only nineteen years old. Pere forced himself to stand still while the metal back of the adjutant robot moved swiftly up the aisle.

The seats were well anchored and faced to the rear, so it could be hoped that there were not too many casualties. Behind the backs of the last chairs was a rubble of dirt that had burst in through the destroyed nose. The driver was undoubtedly dead under it, which was all for the best. It saved the trouble of a court-martial.

"One killed, one missing in action, one wounded, total active strength of unit now seventeen." The adjutant dropped the salute and stood at attention, awaiting further orders. General Pere nervously chewed his lip.

"Missing in action" meant the driver. Presumed dead, damn well dead. The "one killed" was the new captain from Interceptor Control, who had had the bad luck to be leaning out of his chair at the time of the accident. His neck had been cracked on the edge of the chair and his head now hung down at a sickening angle. The moaning must be the wounded man; he had better check on that first. He stamped down the aisle and shined his light on the sallow, sweatbeaded face of Colonel Zen.

"My arm, sir," the colonel gasped. "I was reaching out when we crashed, my arm whipped back and hit the metal edge. Broken, I think. The pain . . ."

"That's enough, Colonel," Pere said. A little too loudly, because the man's fear was beginning to touch him too. There were footsteps in the aisle and his second-in-command, General Natia, joined him.

"You've had the standard first-aid course, General," Pere said. "Bandage this man and then report to me."

"Yes, sir," General Natia said, her voice echoing that same note of fear.

Damn all, Pere thought, *she should know that's no way for a general to act. We can't let the troops know we're afraid—even if we are.* He made no allowance for the fact that General Natia was a woman, and just eighteen.

Once his staff had been attended to, he turned his mind to the problems at hand. Some of the tension eased as he sorted out all the factors. Problem-solving was his specialty, and he had been selected for it before birth. Gene analysis had chosen the best DNA chain from his parents' sperm-and-ovum bank. This, and subsequent training, had fitted him perfectly for command. With the instantaneous reflexes of youth, he was a formidable opponent on the battlefield and looked forward to a successful career of at least four or five years before retirement.

For a man who would soon be directing a global conflict, this problem was childishly simple.

"Communications?" he snapped, and pointed his finger at the Signal Corps major. There was an automatic authority in his voice now, in marked contrast to his boyish crewcut and freckles.

"None, sir," the officer said, saluting. "Whatever blocked the tunnel knocked out the land lines as well. I've tried with the field phone but the wires are dead."

"Does anyone know how far we are from HQ?" he asked, raising his voice so that all the officers in the car could hear him.

"I'll have it . . . in a second, sir," one of them said, a gray-haired colonel from Computer Corps. He was moving the scale of his pocket slide rule, blinking intently in the light of his flash. "Don't know how long this tunnel is—or the exact location of HQ. But I have made the run before, and the total elapsed time is usually a few minutes over three hours. Figuring the time to the accident, our speed, allowing for deceleration . . ." His voice trailed off into a mumble and Pere waited impatiently, but unmoving. He needed this information before he could make his next move.

"Between forty and sixty miles to HQ, sir. And those are the outside figures, I'd say it's very close to fifty . . ."

"That's good enough. I want two volunteers, you and you. Get up in the nose there and see if you can't dig a hole through that rubble. We're going to try to get through and continue on foot. We'll be needed at HQ if the Enemy is able to hit this close."

This last was added for the sake of his staff's morale; the training courses had recommended the human touch whenever possible. Particularly in unusual situations. And this was an unusual, though not a very promising, way for his first command to begin. He scowled unhappily into the darkness. It took an effort to keep his feelings from his voice as he issued orders to assemble the food stores and water. When this was done he sent his adjutant to relieve the two men who were digging into the dirt barricade. One robot was worth ten men—not to say two—at this kind of labor.

It took almost twelve hours to penetrate the barrier, and they were all completely exhausted before it was through. The adjutant did all the digging, and they rotated shifts in carrying away the rubble that he cleared. There had been some minor falls of dirt and rock that in their haste they ignored, until a major fall at the work face had completely buried the robot. They dug until they reached its feet and Pere had lengths of the now useless tunnel signal wire tied around the robot's ankles. It wasn't until they had added loops of wire so that they could all pull together that the adjutant had been dragged from his near grave. After that, work slowed, since they had to unbolt the chairs from the car and use them to shore up the roof. All

things considered, twelve hours was good time for penetration
of the barrier.

Once they were through, General Pere allowed them a half-
hour break. They sipped at their water bottles and collapsed
wearily on both sides of the central track. Pride and position
would not allow Pere to rest; he paced ahead to see if the tunnel
was clear, his adjutant beside him.

"How many hours left in your battery?" Pere asked. "At
maximum output."

"Over three hundred."

"Then start running. If you come to any other falls, begin
clearing them away and we'll catch up with you. If you get
through without any trouble, have them send a car for us. It will
save some time."

The robot saluted and was gone, his running steps thudding
away in the distance. Pere looked at the glowing dial of his watch
and announced the end of the break.

Walking, with the single light twinkling ahead, soon took on
a dreamlike quality that numbed their responses. They went on
this way, with short breaks every hour, for almost eight hours.
When they began to drop out, asleep on their feet, Pere reluctantly ordered a stop. He forced them to eat first, then allowed
them only four hours' sleep before he forcefully shook them to
their feet. The march continued—at a far slower pace now—
and another five hours of constant darkness passed before they
saw the light of the car ahead.

"Point your lights at it—everyone," Pere said. "We don't
want to be run down."

The driver, a robot, had been driving at half speed, watching
for them. They climbed wearily aboard and most of them fell
asleep during the short run back to HQ. The adjutant made a
report to Pere.

"The break has been reported, and there have been two more
blockages discovered in the other tunnel."

"What caused them?"

"Intelligence is not sure, but is expecting to report soon."

Pere swallowed his opinion of Intelligence's intelligence,

since even robots should not hear morale-lowering comment. He pulled at his sticky shirt and was suddenly aware of the rising heat inside the car. "What's wrong with the air conditioning?" he asked petulantly.

"Nothing, sir. It is the air temperature in the tunnel, it is much hotter than usual."

"Why?"

"That fact is not known yet."

The heat rose steadily as they approached HQ, and Pere issued orders that collars could be opened. The car slowed to a halt in the immense bay at the tunnel's end. When the door was opened the hot air that boiled in was almost unbreathable.

"Double-time to the lock," Pere gasped out, choking over the words as the heat seared his throat. They stumbled and ran toward the large sealed valve at the end of the platform, robot guns tracking them from the turrets that studded the face of the metal wall. Identification was made and before they reached the lock the immense outer door rotated ponderously. Someone screamed as he fell and bare flesh touched the burning metal of the platform. Pere forced himself to wait until they were all inside, entering last. There was some relief when the outer door had closed, but no real drop in the temperature until they had passed through all five seals of the four-barreled lock. Even then the air inside the fortress was far warmer than normal.

"Perhaps this heat has something to do with the reason we were sent out a week early," General Natia said. "This and the tunnel blockage might be caused by an enemy penetration in force."

Pere had reached the same conclusion himself, though he wouldn't admit it aloud, even to his second-in-command. In addition, only he knew that a real emergency at HQ had changed their shipping orders, though Command had not been specific about the nature of the emergency. As fast as he could, without running, Pere led his staff toward HQ control.

Nothing was right. No one answered him when he formally requested permission to enter. There were maintenance robots stolidly going about their work, but no officers in view. For a single heart-stopping instant he thought that all four battle stations were vacant. Then he saw a finger come out and touch a button at Command Prime: the occupant of the chair was slumped so low that he could hardly be seen. Pere stalked quickly toward the post and began a salute, but his hand stopped before it reached his forehead and, forgotten, dropped slowly back. He stared with horror.

In the chair the operator gradually became aware that someone was standing over him. It was an effort for the man to draw the attention of his deep-socketed and reddened eyes from the board. When he did, it was just for an instant and Pere had only a glimpse of the pain in their depths, of eyes peeping out of their black-rimmed pits like frightened animals. Then their attention wavered back to the board and the thin arm lifted tremulously to touch a control.

"Thank God you've come . . . you've come at last . . . thank . . ." The words, scarcely a whisper to begin with, died away to a wheeze.

The officer's arms were pocked and scarred with needle holes, streaked with hardened rivulets of blood. The jumbled cartons and vials on the table told a wordless story of a man forcing himself to stay awake and active long past human limits: there were stimulants, sleep-surrogates, glucose, anesthetics, vitamin complexes. He had obviously been days alone in this chair, manning all four battle stations hooked into his own board. Alone—for some unknown and terrible reason, alone—he had fought the war, waiting for help. With an uncontrollable feeling of revulsion Pere saw that the man had soiled himself as he sat there.

"General Natia, man that free board," he ordered.

She slipped efficiently into the chair and set up a repeater from the others. Quickly taking in the factors of the conflict she called out, "Ready sir."

Pere threw the command switch and the red bulb winked out on the board before him, and the one in front of Natia flashed on.

It was as though the light had been the spark of life holding the man at the controls. When the red bulb snuffed out he dropped his face into his hands and collapsed sideways into the cushioning chair. Pere took him by the shoulder and shook him until the hands dropped away and the last traces of consciousness stiffened the lolling head. With painful effort the man opened his eyes.

"What happened?" Pere asked. "Where is everyone else?"

"Dead," the feeble voice whispered, near to death itself. "I was the only one didn't die—in bed at the time. Just chance I wasn't touching any metal. Just sheets, mattress. Robots say it was a vibration source—subsonic—supersonic—something new. Curdled everyone, killed them—coagulated the protein. Like eggs . . . cooked eggs . . . all dead."

When the man sank into unconsciousness again, Pere signaled to the medical officer who was standing by. Pere looked down at the solid steel floor beneath his feet and shuddered; the vibration weapon might be used again at any time. Or could it? The robots must have taken some preventative measures. He turned to the command robot, standing with steady metallic patience by the computer bank. Shaped like a normal motile, this robot's unique function was apparent only by the large vision screen on its chest and the thick cable, a metallic umbilical cord, that ran back from it to the computers behind. It was simply an extension of the giant computers and logic and memory units that were the heart of HQ.

"Have you found out what generated the killing vibration?" Pere asked the command robot.

"A machine that assembled and attached itself to the outer wall of HQ. It was detected as soon as it began operating and the frequencies were analyzed and neutralized in three minutes and seventeen seconds. No equipment or robots were injured since the frequencies used only caused resonance in animal protein. All of the staff, with the exception of Colonel Frey, were killed instantly. Large quantities of food in the lockers—"

"We'll concern ourselves with the food later. Where is the machine?"

"There," the robot said, pointing toward the far wall. It led the way, its cable trailing smoothly behind it, and pulled a cover from the yard-high object resting there. It resembled no machine Pere had ever seen, rather it looked like a tangled mass of tiny gleaming roots; the red earth still packed between them heightened the illusion.

"How does it work?"

The robot reached out—leaning very close to focus its microscopic eyepieces—and carefully pulled one of the strands free. It lay on the robot's outstretched metallic palm, eight inches long, an eighth of an inch in diameter. Seen close, it was not completely flexible, but made instead of pivoted and smoothly finished segments. The robot pointed out the parts of interest.

"The vibration generator is made up of a large number of these machines, all of similar construction. At the front end is a hard-edged orifice that drills a hole in the ground. Debris is carried back through the body of the machine and eliminated here; in operation it is not unlike the common earthworm. Directional apparatus here guides it, orientated by a gravimeter to locate our base. Here a power unit and here a frequency generator. Singly the machines are harmless, their radiation of no importance. But when grouped together and activated at the same time they produce the deadly frequency."

"Why weren't they detected before going into operation?"

"Their individual mass is too small and they have no metallic components. In addition, they move very slowly; it took them a long time to reach HQ and mass for the attack."

"How long?"

"By measuring the sensitivity of their gravimeters in response to the bulk of HQ and timing their speed of movement, it has been estimated that they entered the ground four years ago."

"Four years!" General Pere was aghast at the thought. The miles of dirt and rock that surrounded HQ on all sides, formerly so comforting, changed suddenly to the hiding place of countless crawling, remorseless machines, closing in with mechanical patience.

"Can they be stopped from constructing another group-machine?"

"That is no problem now that it is known what we must guard against. Defensive screens and detectors have been installed."

Anxiety seeped slowly away and Pere wiped the trickling sweat from his face as he looked around at his staff. All of the battle stations were manned now and the collapsed form of Colonel Frey had been taken out. Everything was functioning perfectly—except for the damn heat.

"And what's causing that?" Pere snapped. "Why the rise in temperature? You must have found the cause."

"The increased temperature is caused by areas of intense heat in the soil around this station. The cause of this localized heat increase is unknown."

Pere found himself worrying his thumbnail with his front teeth and angrily jerked it from his mouth. "Cause unknown! I should think it would be obvious. If the Enemy can build complex wave generators into something as small as this piece of plastic spaghetti, they can certainly build more of them with some kind of compact heat generator. These things could be coming in in a second wave after the coagulator generators."

"This theory was considered, as well as other high probability explanations, but we have no evidence . . ."

"Then get evidence!" Pere was angry at the persistent logicality of all robots, no matter how theoretically brilliant they might be. This obvious explanation of the mysterious heat seemed to him to be more than a hunch or guess, it was almost a certainty. He thumbed the button labeled IMPLEMENT ORDER on the robot's chest and issued a command. "Search will be made at once beyond the heat zone to uncover any more of these specialized boring machines."

With his defense taken care of, he turned his attention to the war. Operations were proceeding so smoothly that the knot of tension in his midriff softened a bit. Lights flickered across the control boards, coded symbols for logistics and intelligence. The operators collated and questioned, feeding their results to Command Prime, where General Natia sat relaxed yet completely alert. The electronic war of course moved at too great a pace for the human mind to follow. All of the missiles, antimissile missiles, interceptors, bombers, and tank squadrons were robot-controlled and operated. Computers of varying degrees of intelligence and responsibility did the actual battle ordering. The same was true of logistics. But men had started this war and guided it toward its finish. The human operators made sense of the shifting factors in the global battle and chose the best course from among those fed to them by the strategy machines. The war had been going well. Analysis of the results showed a small increment of victory during the past nine months. If this increment could be kept steady—or even increased—another generation or two might see complete victory. It was a pleasant, though slightly disconcerting thought for Pere.

Five shifts later the first of the thermal-wrigglers was found and neutralized. Pere examined it with distaste. So small to be causing so much trouble. They were all wearing tropical kit now, and were constantly uncomfortable in the overheated air. The only external difference between this wriggler and the wave generators was in the color of its plastic body; the new one was an appropriately fiery red.

"How does it generate the heat?" Pere asked the command robot.

"The machine contains a suicide circuit. The power supply is short-circuited through a contractile field. The circuits burn out in microseconds, but there is enough time to compress a small quantity of hydrogen—"

"It implodes! A small hydrogen bomb?"

"In a sense, yes. There is very little radiation; most of the energy is released as heat. A molten pocket of lava is the result. The heat dissipates slowly into our base here. New implosions add constantly to the molten area outside."

"Can't you detect and destroy these things before they detonate?"

"This is difficult because of the large number of them involved and the volume of earth that must be inspected. Special machines and detectors are being constructed. An extrapolation has been made of all the factors, and it is estimated with a ninety-nine-percent certainty that the heat will not rise to the point where it interferes with the operation of the base."

This was one load of worry that Pere could cheerfully throw aside; the constant heat was a continual source of discomfort to them all. He wondered idly just how hot it would get before the temperature started back down.

"What is your estimate of this maximum temperature?" he asked.

"Five hundred degrees," the robot said with mechanical imperturbability.

Pere stared into the blank eye cells of the machine and had the sensation of being suddenly hammered down and gasping for air. "Why—that's five times higher than the boiling temperature of water!"

"That is correct. Water boils at one hundred degrees."

Pere could only choke with unbelief. "Do you realize what you are saying? What do you think people are . . . how can we live?"

The robot did not answer since this problem was not the responsibility of the HQ robots. Pere chewed his lip and rephrased it.

"This temperature is unsatisfactory for the personnel—even if the machines can survive it. You must find some way to lower the temperature."

"This problem has already been considered, since a number of the more delicate components will be near their critical range at that temperature. The air-conditioning units are now operating at maximum overload and no new units can be added. Therefore, drilling operations have begun and are tapping nearby deposits of water, which will be substituted for air within the base. This water will enter at a lower temperature and will have a greater heat-transfer capacity."

A compromise, not a perfect answer, but it might work for a while. One room would have to be sealed off for living quarters and the watch officers could wear pressure suits. Uncomfortable but not impossible.

"What will be the maximum temperature of this water?" he asked.

"One hundred and forty degrees. There is adequate water to bring the temperature lower, but this base was not designed for easy circulation of anything other than air. All machine units are of battle standard and waterproof—"

350

"People aren't!" Pere shouted, forgetting himself. "And if they were, they would cook in this boiling soup of yours. How are we to survive, tell me that?"

Once more the oracle was silent. In the distance there was the sudden gush and spatter of water.

"What's that?" he gasped.

"Flooding. The lower levels," the robot said.

Everyone in the room was watching him, Pere realized, listening to the final judgment of the robot's words. "Anyone have any ideas?" he asked, unaware of the pleading in his voice. There were no answers.

There had to be an answer; he forced his numbed mind to check over the possibilities. Remote control of HQ from National Central? No, too dangerous, control circuits could be interrupted, cut off, or even taken over. Someone had to be here, at least one person to man the Command Prime station. Unless this station could be robot-controlled too.

"A discretion circuit," he shouted with sudden relief. "Can a robot with discretion circuitry be built to operate the Command station?" he asked the robot extension of HQ.

"Yes."

"Well, do it. Do it at once. We may have to evacuate, and in case we do I want the robot ready to take over."

It wouldn't be for long, they would just be gone until the temperature dropped and human habitation became possible again. All of the decisions to be made at Command Prime were simple either/or choices, and an occasional multiple choice. A robot with the correct evaluation and discretion circuits would do well enough for a while. It wouldn't be perfect and the victory increment would surely drop a few points, but it wouldn't be disaster. He would have to check with National Central before putting the plan into operation, but he was sure they wouldn't come up with a better answer.

They didn't. The aging commanders couldn't even do as well and were grateful with General Pere for the suggestion. He even received a promotion and was authorized to wear another star on his shoulder. As soon as the command robot could begin satisfactory operation, he was ordered to evacuate.

351

On the lower levels the hot, oily water reached to their knees. The tension among the staff ebbed away only when the new robot was carried in. Pere watched and frowned when the machine was bolted into place in his chair. The job had been a quick one and no special care had been taken with nonessentials; the body of the robot consisted simply of a square box, ugly with beaded weldmarks. Two eye cells sat on a stubby column above it and a single, articulated arm projected from the front. The eyes focused on the unlit command light and the arm hung down limply. Pere had all the other boards tied into the logistics board, and he took one last look at the war, then decisively threw the command switch.

The red light came on in front of the robot and it instantly began operation. With lightning speed the metallic index finger pressed three buttons and threw a switch, then dropped again. Pere looked at the decisions and could find no fault. Perhaps he might have brought in the reserve tanks in the eastern bulge and tried to hold. Though it was just as tactically sound to withdraw and straighten the line and save on the estimated losses. Both choices had the same probability rating on the scale, which was why they had appeared on the board. The robot would work.

He hated it, though. For some reason it seemed a colossal personal affront to him to be replaced by this arm-waving black box. Was this all that a man was to a machine? The metal fingers ran across the controls, then dropped again.

"Prepare to move out," he shouted in a harsh voice. This evacuation was wrong, very wrong. But what else could he do?

"We'll rig a stretcher for Colonel Frey," he told the medical officer. "How is he progressing?"

"He's dead," the doctor said in his toneless, professional manner. "The heat was too much for him in his weakened condition. Too much of a strain on his heart."

"All right," Pere said, keeping his emotions under control. "That leaves Zen as the only casualty, and he can walk well enough with his arm in a cast."

When the officers had all assembled, General Natia stepped up to Pere and saluted. "All present, sir. Everyone is carrying extra rations and water, in case there is trouble in the return tunnel."

"Yes, of course," Pere said, mentally berating himself for not thinking of these simple precautions. There had been so much on his mind. It was time to leave.

"Has the mono tunnel been kept open?" he asked the adjutant.

"Two additional minor blockages have occurred, but have been cleared."

"Very good. Fall in with the others. Attention . . . right face . . . forward *march*." As his small company tramped out of the room, General Pere turned back, goaded by some anachronistic impulse, and saluted the command post. None of the machines paid the slightest attention to him. The robot in his chair jabbed a quick finger at some buttons and ignored him. Feeling slightly foolish, he turned quickly and followed the others out.

They were cycling through the multiple sealed doors of the fortress when they met the robot. It was waiting in the outer compartment and pushed past them as soon as the door was open. It was a worker, a mechanical of some kind, scratched and covered with mud: because it had no speech facilities, Pere had to question it through the adjutant.

"Find out what has happened," he snapped.

The two robots held a voiceless communion; their radio waves in a direct brain-to-brain hookup carried thoughts far faster than could any speech.

"The exit tunnel has been blocked," the adjutant said. "The roof is down in many places and it is beginning to fill with water. The decision has been reached that it cannot be opened. New falls are occurring all the time."

"Challenge the decision. It is not possible," Pere said. There was a note of desperation in his voice.

They were through the last door now and in the exit bay. The heat was overpowering and made intelligent thought almost impossible. Through a red haze Pere saw bulky digging robots streaming out of the mouth of the exit tunnel, going toward the entrance valve behind them.

"No change is possible," the adjutant said, a metallic voice of doom. "The tunnel cannot be opened now. It has been found that small machines, very like the heat units, have penetrated the earth and are collapsing the tunnel. It will be opened after they—"

"Another way! There must be another way out!" Pere's voice was as heat-strained as his thoughts, yet the robot understood and took it for a command.

"There are emergency exits here that once led to higher levels. My information is incomplete. I do not know if they have been sealed."

"Show us—we can't stay here."

They were all wearing gloves, so the metal bars of the ladder didn't char their hands, just burned them. The robot adjutant went first and only his mechanical strength could have turned the time-sealed wheel that locked the entrance to the older levels. The humans groped their way behind the adjutant, some falling and failing to rise again. Colonel Zen must have been the first to be left behind, because he only had the use of one arm. The heat in the stifling darkness was so great that even the doctor didn't notice when his patient dropped out. The doctor himself must have gone soon after, because he was no longer a young man.

General Pere tried to issue orders, and when they were not obeyed he made an attempt to help the laggards himself. He could not do this and keep up with the others. When he saw the lights winking out of sight in the dust-filled passage ahead, he made the only decision possible under the circumstances. Not that he was aware of making it; he was barely conscious at the time and only the will to survive drove him forward. Passing the straggling survivors, he shouldered General Natia aside and took his place behind the guiding robot.

Pain fought a battle with fatigue and kept them going until they were out of the zone of terrible heat. Pere had strength enough only to utter the one-word command to stop, drink from his canteen, then fall unconscious to the floor. The others dropped in huddled lumps of pain about him. The adjutant stood with untiring machine-patience, waiting for them to rise.

Moans of agony roused Pere at last, and he forced his charred fingers to fumble out the first-aid packs. Burn ointment brought some relief to the five survivors, and stimulants gave them the illusion of strength needed to carry on. General Natia had somehow managed to stay close behind him through the ordeal, as well as three others. They were all young and strong, though one was not strong enough. He simply vanished during the next climb.

Above HQ was a maze of tunnels and rooms, occupied by the base at various times before the unremitting pressures of the war had driven the controllers even deeper into the ground. Most of it was collapsed and choked with rubble and no progress was possible. If the robot had not been with them they would have died. Every detail of the various layers was impressed in his electronical cortex, since his brain contained the memory of every other adjutant back to the beginning of the war. They retraced their steps whenever their way was blocked, and found a different direction. Bit by bit they progressed toward the surface. There was no way to measure time in the darkness; they slept when exhaustion was too great, then woke up to stumble on. Their food was gone and the water almost exhausted. They kept going only because of the robot's firm insistence that they were now in the upper levels.

"We are just under the surface of the ground," the adjutant said. "This tunnel led to a gun position, but it is now blocked."

Pere sat and blinked at the circular tunnel and forced his fatigued brain to consider the problem. The top of the tunnel was not much higher than their heads and made of ferro-concrete. Jagged chunks of the same material choked the end.

"Clear away the opening," Pere ordered.

"I cannot," the robot said. "My battery is almost discharged, I would not be able to finish."

This was the end. They could not go on.

"Perhaps we could . . . blow it out of the way," Natia said apologetically. Pere turned his light on her and she shook a handful of cartridges from the clip at her waist. "These contain powerful explosives. Perhaps the adjutant could arrange them to all explode together."

"I can," the adjutant said.

Surprisingly, all four of them still had their sidearms and spare clips; they had not been discarded with the rest of the equipment. The adjutant took the spare clips and buried them in the rubble while they moved back down the tunnel. A minute later the robot came running back to join them and they pressed themselves to the floor. The ground jumped and the roar of concussion smote their ears. They forced themselves to wait long minutes for the stifling cloud of dust to settle, before Pere let them go forward.

The barrier was still there, but the ceiling had fallen, and high up in the gap a ray of light shone on the dust motes.

"We're through," Pere said hoarsely. "Help me up there."

Steadied by the robot, he reached up into the hole and crumbled away the soft dirt at the lip until it was big enough for his shoulders. A lump came away with a tuft of grass, green and damp. He groped up through the hole, reaching for a hold.

"Let me help you," a voice said, and brown, callused hands clutched his and pulled.

It was so unexpected that Pere gasped with shock. Yet he could not let go and the hand pulled him steadily out of the hole in the ground. He fell face-first onto the grass and groped for his gun, while the light burned into his eyes. Through tears of pain he saw a circle of legs surrounding him, and took his hand from the pistol butt.

The others were out of the hole now, and as his eyes adjusted, Pere could look around him. The sky was cloudy and it must have been raining because the grass on which he sat was damp. Before him stretched a freshly plowed field. He felt a sudden spurt of pleasure at identifying these things that he had only seen before on the screen. This was the first time in his life that he had ever been aboveground.

Of course all of the recordings he had seen were historicals, from the time before the war, when people still lived on the surface instead of in the numerous sub-cities. He had always assumed that the surface was sterile and bare of life. Then who were these people? Something whistled and screamed away into the distance over his head, and he was aware for the first time of a constant rumbling that seemed to come from all sides.

"Who are you?" a voice asked, and Pere struggled up to face the man who had helped him from the hole.

"I am General Pere, this is my staff." The man had a very dark skin and was wearing a weird costume that seemed to consist completely of cast-off mechanical items. His tunic was plexicloth from a machine cover; his shoes wedges of metal with webbing straps to hold them in place. He wore a metal helmet on his head, as did all the others.

"A general," the man grunted and the smile vanished from his face. He turned and whistled shrilly. In the field there were some more people pulling at a strange device. One of them waved and they started in Pere's direction.

"Boruk is coming," the tan-skinned man said gruffly. "Talk to him. Maybe it'll do some good. Though I doubt it." He spat on the ground and kicked dirt into the spittle with one toe.

Overhead in the clouds there was a muffled and gigantic explosion. Pere looked up and saw the clouds briefly stained a rosy pink. A black speck appeared below the clouds and before his horrified eyes grew instantly to the shape of a giant wheel. It plunged down, apparently at him, but hit instead on the far side of the field. The huge tire recoiled and it bounced into the air directly over their heads. Only Pere and his officers looked up as it sailed over. The wheel must have been a hundred feet in diameter and he could see clearly the treads on the tire, and the metal hub with its sheared supports, a stream of liquid still leaking from some severed pipe. It bounced again, shaking the ground, and vanished from sight over the hill.

"What was that?" Pere asked, but no one answered him.

The group in the field were closer now and he could see they were pulling a plow assembled of odd pieces of junk. The two handles of the plow were the only identifiable parts: the arms of a robot welded into place, the hands extended and acting as handles. One of the men who had been tugging in a harness dropped it and walked over. He was naked to the waist, but wore a pair of gray uniform pants and high boots.

"The military!" he shouted when he saw their uniforms. "Wonderful! Wonderful!" He turned and ran away. A fine rain

357

of metallic particles hit in the grass around them. Pere had the feeling he was going mad.

The man had only gone to the side of the field to get the rest of his clothes. He struggled into a jacket and in place of his steel helmet pulled on a peaked cap of hauntingly familiar design. Only when he had buttoned it and knocked the dust from his trousers did he turn and come toward Pere.

"The Enemy!" Pere shouted and scratched for his gun. This was the uniform he had seen so many times in orientation films. He hauled the gun out but someone knocked it from his fingers. Then he could only stand paralyzed as the man stamped up to him, clicked his heels together, and saluted.

"General Boruk," he said. "On a mission of peace. May I ask whom I have the pleasure of addressing?" He dropped the salute and pulled a white flag from one pocket with a collapsible rod attached to it. After snapping open the rod he held the flag up proudly. His face was as sunburned as the others, with a black mustache and pointed beard.

"I am General Pere," Pere forced himself to say. "Who are you? What are you doing here?"

"At your service, General," Boruk said, and stabbed the pole into the ground. He groped in another pocket and fished out a large wallet. "I bring you greetings from my proud country, and the joyous news that we wish to sue for peace. All of the papers are here—including my credentials—and you have only to forward them to the proper authorities. You will notice that there is mention of a peace commission, but I am forced to admit that they are all dead or have returned. In fact, to be truthful, you will see my name entered on the rolls of the commission as Captain Boruk, but this was only in the beginning. Through determination and the fact I am young and strong as a bull, I was promoted to dizzying heights. In fact General Graniaz, who himself conferred my commission upon me, even gave me his own coat with his general's insignia. In that, his was a wise choice, for I ask you only to notice that I am here and the others are not. We want peace, any terms you care to name. Do you agree?"

"Sit down," Pere said, feeling the need to do so himself.

"Why are you asking for peace now—allowing for the moment that your credentials are not forged? You are not losing the war?"

"To be truthful again, General, we are not even fighting the war." Boruk sprawled on the ground and chewed a stem of grass. "You will discover the reasons for our request sooner or later, so it might as well be sooner. In fact the sooner the better since the situation is so far out of hand. It seems we have been forced to abandon our battle headquarters and turn it over to robot operation. Are you all right?" he asked, seeing Pere jump.

"Yes," Pere told him. "Yes, go on." This was too familiar to permit him to listen easily.

"I must say your scientists are tricky ones, I believe they managed to invest our HQ with a mutated virus that was impossible to eradicate. The base had to be evacuated, radiated, and sterilized. To do this the robots had to be left in complete control of the war operations. When we tried to get back in, it was most difficult. All entrances had been sealed and we couldn't get the robots to understand what we wanted. They were doing very well without us, very well indeed." He spat the grass out and scowled.

"But there are ways. You could have countermanded—"

"It is not that easy, General. I assure you we tried. To be brief, the more we tried the better the robot defenses against our interferences became. In the end they fought us off—having identified us with the Enemy—and we had to retire."

"*We'll* get back in," Pere said, then snapped his mouth shut guiltily.

"I had assumed something of the sort," Boruk smiled. His seemingly lazy attention had missed nothing. "When a general and his staff climb out of the ground above the area of their HQ, I am afraid I leaped to a conclusion due to my own previous knowledge. Is it true? You have been forced to leave as well?"

"I'll tell you nothing."

"You don't have to. It is a cosmic jest indeed." Boruk laughed humorlessly and tore the surrender papers across and threw them into the dirt. Something keened through the air and exploded in an immense cloud of dust on the horizon. "You have been pushed out the way our officers were pushed out, and you shall not get back. It was due to come, since every other part of the battle in this war is done by robots. Since we have both been concentrating our weapons upon the opposite headquarters, it was fated that some of the weapons should have at least a partial success. Robots are much stronger then humans, much more able to stand lethal climates. I have had plenty of time to think about this, since I have waited here many months."

"Why—why didn't you surrender? Why didn't you come to us?"

"Believe me, my young companion general, that is the one wish of my country. But how is this done in this day of total war? We tried radio and all other forms of communication, but all were blocked by robot mechanisms designed for that job. Then we sent the mission in person—not carrying weapons, so of course the robots ignored us. Our casualties were due simply to the deadliness of the battlefields we had to cross on the way here. The robots were completely indifferent to us, a forewarning of the future—or of the present, I might say. Battle is going on everywhere, and only a few peaceful areas exist, such as this one, above a strongly defended base. But even when I reached here I found no surface installations and no way of reaching you below."

"This is monstrous! Monstrous!" Pere bellowed.

"It is indeed, but we must be philosophical about it. Accept it as these good people have done who live here under a canopy of death. The robots will continue their war just as efficiently without us, and probably make it last much longer since they are so evenly matched. Find yourself a woman, settle down, and enjoy the life."

Pere found himself glancing inadvertently at Natia, who looked away and blushed. Even if she was a general, she had a fine figure. . . .

"No!" he shouted. "I will not submit. This is terrible. This is no way for mankind to live. Just to sit by and watch these senseless machines destroy each other."

"It does not matter, friend General, whether we like it or not. We have been bypassed. Displaced. We have played too long at the destructive game of war and made our machines too efficient. They enjoy the game too much themselves to relinquish it, and we must find someplace where we can try and live to the best of our abilities. Someplace where they will not step on us while they play."

"No, I can't accept it!" Pere shouted again, and tears of frustration and anger burned in his eyes. He threw off Natia's hand when she put it on his arm. The horizon grumbled and flared red; hot metal rattled into the ground nearby.

"I just hope you're having a good time," he cried, and shook his fist up at the unheeding sky. "I just hope you're having a good time!"

EVIDENCE

ISAAC ASIMOV

(1 9 4 6)

Asimov's "Evidence" suggests that a robot might serve very well in an elected office. Programmed with the Three Laws of Robotics, the machine would be considerably more ethical than many politicians.

Dr. Susan Calvin, whom we meet in this story as she discusses why she likes robots better than human beings, is one of the most interesting women characters to appear in science fiction before the 1960s, when the effects of the women's movement began to be felt in the genre. Up to then, women characters were either nonexistent, or showed up as the inane daughter of a mad scientist or the screaming victim carried off by a monster. Dr. Susan Calvin is one of the bright exceptions. She serves as the robopsychologist for the U.S. Robots and Mechanical Men Corporation. She is intelligent, well-educated, and commanding in her presence.

In the mid-forties, Asimov spent nine months in the army. During that period he managed to write only one story, and that story was "Evidence" (much of it written in the base library, where he had persuaded the librarian to lock him in over the lunch hour so that he could type undisturbed).

In 1976, thirty years after "Evidence" was published, Asimov wrote another story about a robot in public office. In "Tercentary Incident" the President uses a lookalike robot in parades and other public appearances to relieve himself of the stress and danger in such situations.

FRANCIS QUINN was a politician of the new school. That, of course, is a meaningless expression, as are all expressions of the sort. Most of the "new schools" we have were duplicated in the social life of ancient Greece, and perhaps, if we knew more about it, in the social life of ancient Sumeria and in the lake dwellings of prehistoric Switzerland as well.

But, to get out from under what promises to be a dull and complicated beginning, it might be best to state hastily that Quinn neither ran for office nor canvassed for votes, made no speeches and stuffed no ballot boxes. Any more than Napoleon pulled a trigger at Austerlitz.

362

And since politics makes strange bedfellows, Alfred Lanning sat at the other side of the desk with his ferocious white eyebrows bent far forward over eyes in which chronic impatience had sharpened to acuity. He was not pleased.

The fact, if known to Quinn, would have annoyed him not in the least. His voice was friendly, perhaps professionally so.

"I assume you know Stephen Byerley, Dr. Lanning."

"I have heard of him. So have many people."

"Yes, so have I. Perhaps you intend voting for him at the next election."

"I couldn't say." There was an unmistakable trace of acidity here. "I have not followed the political currents, so I'm not aware that he is running for office."

"He may be our next mayor. Of course, he is only a lawyer now, but great oaks—"

"Yes," interrupted Lanning, "I have heard the phrase before. But I wonder if we can get to the business at hand."

"We *are* at the business at hand, Dr. Lanning." Quinn's tone was very gentle. "It is to my interest to keep Mr. Byerley a district attorney at the very most, and it is to your interest to help me do so."

"To *my* interest? Come!" Lanning's eyebrows hunched low.

"Well, say then to the interest of the U.S. Robots and Mechanical Men Corporation. I come to you as Director-Emeritus of Research, because I know that your connection to them is that of, shall we say, 'elder statesman.' You are listened to with respect and yet your connection with them is no longer so tight but that you cannot possess considerable freedom of action— even if the action is somewhat unorthodox."

Dr. Lanning was silent a moment, chewing the cud of his thoughts. He said more softly, "I don't follow you at all, Mr. Quinn."

"I am not surprised, Dr. Lanning. But it's all rather simple. Do you mind?" Quinn lit a slender cigarette with a lighter of tasteful simplicity, and his big-boned face settled into an expression of quiet amusement. "We have spoken of Mr. Byerley—a strange and colorful character. He was unknown three years ago. He is very well known now. He is a man of force and ability, and certainly the most capable and intelligent prosecutor I have ever known. Unfortunately he is not a friend of mine—"

"I understand," said Lanning mechanically. He stared at his fingernails.

"I have had occasion," continued Quinn evenly, "in the past year to investigate Mr. Byerley—quite exhaustively. It is always useful, you see, to subject the past life of reform politicians to rather inquisitive research. If you knew how often it helped—" He paused to smile humorlessly at the glowing tip of his cigarette. "But Mr. Byerley's past is unremarkable. A quiet life in a small town, a college education, a wife who died young, an auto accident with a slow recovery, law school, coming to the metropolis, becoming an attorney."

Francis Quinn shook his head slowly, then added, "But his present life. Ah, that is remarkable. Our district attorney never eats!"

Lanning's head snapped up, his old eyes surprisingly sharp. "Pardon me?"

"Our district attorney never eats." The repetition thumped by syllables. "I'll modify that slightly. He has never been seen to eat or drink. Never! Do you understand the significance of the word? Not rarely, but never!"

"I find that quite incredible. Can you trust your investigators?"

"I can trust my investigators, and I don't find it incredible at all. Further, our district attorney has never been seen to drink—in the aqueous sense as well as the alcoholic—nor to sleep. There are other factors, but I should think I have made my point."

Lanning leaned back in his seat, and there was the rapt silence of challenge and response between them, and then the old roboticist shook his head. "No. There is only one thing you can be trying to imply, if I couple your statements with the fact that you present them to me, and that is impossible."

"But the man is quite inhuman, Dr. Lanning."

"If you told me he were Satan in masquerade, there would be a faint chance that I might believe you."

364

"I tell you he is a robot, Dr. Lanning."

"I tell you it is as impossible a conception as I have ever heard, Mr. Quinn."

Again the combative silence.

"Nevertheless," and Quinn stubbed out his cigarette with elaborate care, "you will have to investigate this impossibility with all the resources of the Corporation."

"I'm sure that I could undertake no such thing, Mr. Quinn. You don't seriously suggest that the Corporation take part in local politics."

"You have no choice. Supposing I were to make my facts public without proof. The evidence is circumstantial enough."

"Suit yourself in that respect."

"But it would not suit me. Proof would be much preferable. And it would not suit *you*, for the publicity would be very damaging to your company. You are perfectly well acquainted, I suppose, with the strict rules against the use of robots on inhabited worlds."

"Certainly!"—brusquely.

"You know that the U.S. Robots and Mechanical Men Corporation is the only manufacturer of positronic robots in the Solar System, and if Byerley is a robot, he is a *positronic* robot. You are also aware that all positronic robots are leased, and not sold; that the Corporation remains the owner and manager of each robot, and is therefore responsible for the actions of all."

"It is an easy matter, Mr. Quinn, to prove the Corporation has never manufactured a robot of a humanoid character."

"It can be done? To discuss merely possibilities."

"Yes. It can be done."

"Secretly, I imagine, as well. Without entering it in your books."

"Not the positronic brain, sir. Too many factors are involved in that, and there is the tightest possible government supervision."

"Yes, but robots are worn out, break down, go out of order—and are dismantled."

"And the positronic brains reused or destroyed."

"Really?" Francis Quinn allowed himself a trace of sarcasm.

"And if one were, accidentally, of course, not destroyed—and there happened to be a humanoid structure waiting for a brain."

"Impossible!"

"You would have to prove that to the government and the public, so why not prove it to me now?"

"But what could our purpose be?" demanded Lanning in exasperation. "Where is our motivation? Credit us with a minimum of sense."

"My dear sir, please. The Corporation would be only too glad to have the various Regions permit the use of humanoid positronic robots on inhabited worlds. The profits would be enormous. But the prejudice of the public against such a practice is too great. Suppose you get them used to such robots first— see, we have a skillful lawyer, a good mayor, and he is a robot. Won't you buy our robot butlers?"

"Thoroughly fantastic. An almost humorous descent to the ridiculous."

"I imagine so. Why not prove it? Or would you still rather try to prove it to the public?"

The light in the office was dimming, but it was not yet too dim to obscure the flush of frustration on Alfred Lanning's face. Slowly, the roboticist's finger touched a knob and the wall illuminators glowed to gentle life.

"Well, then," he growled, "let us see."

The face of Stephen Byerley is not an easy one to describe. He was forty by birth certificate and forty by appearance—but it was a healthy, well-nourished, good-natured appearance of forty; one that automatically drew the teeth of the bromide about "looking one's age."

This was particularly true when he laughed, and he was laughing now. It came loudly and continuously, died away for a bit, then began again—

And Alfred Lanning's face contracted into a rigidly bitter monument of disapproval. He made a half-gesture to the woman who sat beside him, but her thin, bloodless lips merely pursed themselves a trifle.

Byerley gasped himself a stage nearer normality.

"Really, Dr. Lanning . . . really . . . I . . . *I* . . . a robot?"

Lanning bit his words off with a snap. "It is no statement of mine, sir. I would be quite satisfied to have you a member of humanity. Since our corporation never manufactured you, I am quite certain that you are—in a legalistic sense, at any rate. But since the contention that you are a robot has been advanced to us seriously by a man of certain standing—"

"Don't mention his name, if it would knock a chip off your granite block of ethics, but let's pretend it was Frank Quinn, for the sake of argument, and continue."

Lanning drew in a sharp, cutting snort at the interruption, and paused ferociously before continuing with added frigidity, "—by a man of certain standing, with whose identity I am not interested in playing guessing games, I am bound to ask your cooperation in disproving it. The mere fact that such a contention could be advanced and publicized by the means at this man's disposal would be a bad blow to the company I represent—even if the charge were never proven. You understand me?"

"Oh, yes, your position is clear to me. The charge itself is ridiculous. The spot you find yourself in is not. I beg your pardon, if my laughter offended you. It was the first I laughed at, not the second. How can I help you?"

"It could be very simple. You have only to sit down to a meal at a restaurant in the presence of witnesses, have your picture taken, and eat." Lanning sat back in his chair, the worst of the interview over. The woman beside him watched Byerley with an apparently absorbed expression but contributed nothing of her own.

Stephen Byerley met her eyes for an instant, was caught by them, then turned back to the roboticist. For a while his fingers were thoughtful over the bronze paperweight that was the only ornament on his desk.

He said quietly, "I don't think I can oblige you."

He raised his hand. "Now wait, Dr. Lanning. I appreciate the fact that this whole matter is distasteful to you, that you have been forced into it against your will, that you feel you are playing an undignified and even ridiculous part. Still, the matter is even more intimately concerned with myself, so be tolerant.

367

"First, what makes you think that Quinn—this man of certain standing, you know—wasn't hoodwinking you, in order to get you to do exactly what you are doing?"

"Why, it seems scarcely likely that a reputable person would endanger himself in so ridiculous a fashion, if he weren't convinced he was on safe ground."

There was little humor in Byerley's eyes. "You don't know Quinn. He could manage to make safe ground out of a ledge a mountain sheep could not handle. I suppose he showed the particulars of the investigation he claims to have made of me?"

"Enough to convince me that it would be too troublesome to have our corporation attempt to disprove them when you could do so more easily."

"Then you believe him when he says I never eat. You are a scientist, Dr. Lanning. Think of the logic required. I have not been observed to eat, therefore, I never eat, Q.E.D. After all!"

"You are using prosecution tactics to confuse what is really a very simple situation."

"On the contrary, I am trying to clarify what you and Quinn between you are making a very complicated one. You see, I don't sleep much, that's true, and I certainly don't sleep in public. I have never cared to eat with others—an idiosyncrasy which is unusual and probably neurotic in character, but which harms no one. Look, Dr. Lanning, let me present you with a suppositious case. Supposing we had a politician who was interested in defeating a reform candidate at any cost and while investigating his private life came across oddities such as I have just mentioned.

"Suppose further that in order to smear the candidate effectively, he comes to your company as the ideal agent. Do you expect him to say to you, 'So-and-so is a robot because he hardly ever eats with people, and I have never seen him fall asleep in the middle of a case; and once when I peeped into his window in the middle of the night, there he was, sitting up with a book; and I looked in his Frigidaire and there was no food in it.'

"If he told you that, you would send for a straitjacket. But if he tells you, 'He *never* sleeps; he *never* eats,' then the shock of the statement blinds you to the fact that such statements are

368

impossible to prove. You play into his hands by contributing to the to-do."

"Regardless, sir," began Lanning, with threatening obstinacy, "of whether you consider this matter serious or not, it will require only the meal I mentioned to end it."

Again Byerley turned to the woman, who still regarded him expressionlessly. "Pardon me. I've caught your name correctly, haven't I? Dr. Susan Calvin?"

` "Yes, Mr. Byerley."

"You're the U.S. Robots psychologist, aren't you?"

"*Robo*psychologist, please."

"Oh, are robots so different from men, mentally?"

"Worlds different." She allowed herself a frosty smile. "Robots are essentially decent."

Humor tugged at the corners of the lawyer's mouth. "Well, that's a hard blow. But what I wanted to say was this. Since you're a psycho—a robopsychologist, *and* a woman, I'll bet that you've done something that Dr. Lanning hasn't thought of."

"And what is that?"

"You've got something to eat in your purse."

Something caught in the schooled indifference of Susan Calvin's eyes. She said, "You surprise me, Mr. Byerley."

And opening her purse, she produced an apple. Quietly she handed it to him. Dr. Lanning, after an initial start, followed the slow movement from one hand to the other with sharply alert eyes.

Calmly, Stephen Byerley bit into it, and calmly he swallowed it.

"You see, Dr. Lanning?"

Dr. Lanning smiled in a relief tangible enough to make even his eyebrows appear benevolent. A relief that survived for one fragile second.

Susan Calvin said, "I was curious to see if you would eat it, but, of course, in the present case, it proves nothing."

Byerley grinned. "It doesn't?"

"Of course not. It is obvious, Dr. Lanning, that if this man were a humanoid robot, he would be a perfect imitation. He is almost too human to be credible. After all, we have been seeing and observing human beings all our lives; it would be impossible to palm something merely nearly right off on us. It would have to be *all* right. Observe the texture of the skin, the quality of the irises, the bone formation of the hand. If he's a robot, I wish U.S. Robots *had* made him, because he's a good job. Do you suppose, then, that anyone capable of paying attention to such niceties would neglect a few gadgets to take care of such things as eating, sleeping, elimination? For emergency use only, perhaps; as, for instance, to prevent such situations as are arising here. So a meal won't really prove anything."

"Now wait," snarled Lanning. "I am not quite the fool both of you make me out to be. I am not interested in the problem of Mr. Byerley's humanity or nonhumanity. I am interested in getting the corporation out of a hole. A public meal will end the matter and keep it ended no matter what Quinn does. We can leave the finer details to lawyers and robopsychologists."

"But, Dr. Lanning," said Byerley, "you forget the politics of the situation. I am as anxious to be elected as Quinn is to stop me. By the way, did you notice that you used his name? It's a cheap shyster trick of mine; I knew you would, before you were through."

Lanning flushed. "What has the election to do with it?"

"Publicity works both ways, sir. If Quinn wants to call me a robot, and has the nerve to do so, I have the nerve to play the game his way."

"You mean you—" Lanning was quite frankly appalled.

"Exactly. I mean that I'm going to let him go ahead, choose his rope, test its strength, cut off the right length, tie the noose, insert his head, and grin. I can do what little else is required."

"You are mighty confident."

Susan Calvin rose to her feet. "Come, Alfred, we won't change his mind for him."

"You see?" Byerley smiled gently. "You're a human psychologist, too."

But perhaps not all the confidence that Dr. Lanning had remarked upon was present that evening when Byerley's car parked on the automatic treads leading to the sunken garage, and Byerley himself crossed the path to the front door of his house.

The figure in the wheelchair looked up as he entered, and smiled. Byerley's face lit with affection. He crossed over to it.

The cripple's voice was a hoarse, grating whisper that came out of a mouth forever twisted to one side, leering out of a face that was half scar tissue. "You're late, Steve."

"I know, John, I know. But I've been up against a peculiar and interesting trouble today."

"So?" Neither the torn face nor the destroyed voice could carry expression, but there was anxiety in the clear eyes. "Nothing you can't handle?"

"I'm not exactly certain. I may need your help. *You're* the brilliant one in the family. Do you want me to take you out into the garden? It's a beautiful evening."

Two strong arms lifted John from the wheelchair. Gently, almost caressingly, Byerley's arms went around the shoulders and under the swathed legs of the cripple. Carefully and slowly he walked through the rooms, down the gentle ramp that had been built with a wheelchair in mind, and out the back door into the walled and wired garden behind the house.

"Why don't you let me use the wheelchair, Steve? This is silly."

"Because I'd rather carry you. Do you object? You know that you're as glad to get out of that motorized buggy for a while as I am to see you out. How do you feel today?" He deposited John with infinite care upon the cool grass.

"How should I feel? But tell me about your troubles."

"Quinn's campaign will be based on the fact that he claims I'm a robot."

John's eyes opened wide. "How do you know? It's impossible. I won't believe it."

"Oh, come, I tell you it's so. He had one of the big-shot scientists of U.S. Robots and Mechanical Men Corporation over at the office to argue with me."

Slowly, John's hands tore at the grass. "I see. I see."

Byerley said, "But we can let him choose his ground. I have an idea. Listen to me and tell me if we can do it—"

The scene as it appeared in Alfred Lanning's office that night was a tableau of stares. Francis Quinn stared meditatively at Alfred Lanning. Lanning's stare was savagely set upon Susan Calvin, who stared impassively in her turn at Quinn.

Francis Quinn broke it with a heavy attempt at lightness. "Bluff. He's making it up as he goes along."

"Are you going to gamble on that, Mr. Quinn?" asked Dr. Calvin, indifferently.

"Well, it's your gamble, really."

"Look here"—Lanning covered definite pessimism with bluster—"we've done what you asked. We witnessed the man eat. It's ridiculous to presume him a robot."

"Do *you* think so?" Quinn shot toward Calvin. "Lanning said you were the expert."

Lanning was almost threatening, "Now, Susan—"

Quinn interrupted smoothly. "Why not let her talk, man? She's been sitting there imitating a gatepost for half an hour."

Lanning felt definitely harassed. From what he experienced then to incipient paranoia was but a step. He said, "Very well. Have your say, Susan. We won't interrupt you."

Susan Calvin glanced at him humorlessly, then fixed cold eyes on Mr. Quinn. "There are only two ways of definitely proving Byerley to be a robot, sir. So far you are presenting circumstantial evidence, with which you can accuse, but not prove— and I think Mr. Byerley is sufficiently clever to counter that sort of material. You probably think so yourself, or you wouldn't have come here.

"The two methods of *proof* are the physical and psychological. Physically, you can dissect him or use an X-ray. How to do that would be *your* problem. Psychologically, his behavior can be studied, for if he *is* a positronic robot, he must conform to the Three Rules of Robotics. A positronic brain can not be constructed without them. You know the rules, Mr. Quinn?"

She spoke them carefully, clearly, quoting word for word the famous bold print on page one of the Handbook of Robotics.

"I've heard of them," said Quinn, carelessly.

"Then the matter is easy to follow," responded the psychologist, dryly. "If Mr. Byerley breaks any of those three rules, he is not a robot. Unfortunately, this procedure works in only one direction. If he lives up to the rules, it proves nothing one way or the other."

Quinn raised polite eyebrows. "Why not, doctor?"

"Because, if you stop to think of it, the Three Rules of Robotics are the essential guiding principles of a good many of the world's ethical systems. Of course, every human being is supposed to have the instinct of self-preservation. That's Rule Three to a robot. Also, every 'good' human being with a social conscience and a sense of responsibility is supposed to defer to proper authority: to listen to his doctor, his boss, his government, his psychiatrist, his fellow man; to obey laws, to follow rules, to conform to custom—even when they interfere with his comfort or his safety. That's Rule Two to a robot. Also, every 'good' human being is supposed to love others as himself, protect his fellow man, risk his life to save another. That's Rule One to a robot. To put it simply—if Byerley follows all the Rules of Robotics, he may be a robot, or he may simply be a very good man."

"But," said Quinn, "you're telling me that you can never prove him a robot."

"I may be able to prove him *not* a robot."

"That's not the proof I want."

"You'll have such proof as exists. You are the only one responsible for your own wants."

Here Lanning's mind leaped suddenly to the sting of an idea. "Has it occurred to anyone," he ground out, "that district attorney is a rather strange occupation for a robot? The prosecution of human beings—sentencing them to death—bringing about their infinite harm—"

Quinn grew suddenly keen. "No, you can't get out of it that way. Being district attorney doesn't make him human. Don't you know his record? Don't you know that he boasts that he has never prosecuted an innocent man, that there are scores of people left untried because the evidence against them didn't satisfy him, even though he could probably have argued a jury into atomizing them? That happens to be so."

Lanning's thin cheeks quivered. "No, Quinn, no. There is

nothing in the Rules of Robotics that makes any allowance for human guilt. A robot may not judge whether a human being deserves death. It is not for him to decide. *He may not harm a human*—variety skunk, or variety angel."

Susan Calvin sounded tired. "Alfred," she said, "don't talk foolishly. What if a robot came upon a madman about to set fire to a house with people in it. He would stop the madman, wouldn't he?"

"Of course."

"And if the only way he could stop him was to kill him—"

There was a faint sound in Lanning's throat. Nothing more.

"The answer to that, Alfred, is that he would do his best not to kill him. If the madman died, the robot would require psychotherapy because he might easily go mad at the conflict presented him—of having broken Rule One to adhere to Rule One in a higher sense. But a man would be dead and a robot would have killed him."

"Well, *is* Byerley mad?" demanded Lanning, with all the sarcasm he could muster.

"No, but he has killed no man himself. He has exposed facts which might represent a particular human being to be dangerous to the large mass of other human beings we call society. He protects the greater number and thus adheres to Rule One at maximum potential. That is as far as he goes. It is the judge who then condemns the criminal to death or imprisonment, after the jury decides on his guilt or innocence. It is the jailer who imprisons him, the executioner who kills him. And Mr. Byerley has done nothing but determine truth and aid society.

"As a matter of fact, Mr. Quinn, I have looked into Mr. Byerley's career since you first brought this matter to our attention. I find that he has never demanded the death sentence in his closing speeches to the jury. I also find that he has spoken on behalf of the abolition of capital punishment and contributed generously to research institutions engaged in criminal neurophysiology. He apparently believes in the cure, rather than the punishment of crime. I find that significant."

"You do?" Quinn smiled. "Significant of a certain odor of roboticity, perhaps?"

374

"Perhaps. Why deny it? Actions such as his could come only from a robot, or from a very honorable and decent human being. But you see, you just can't differentiate between a robot and the very best of humans."

Quinn sat back in his chair. His voice quivered with impatience. "Dr. Lanning, it's perfectly possible to create a humanoid robot that would perfectly duplicate a human in appearance, isn't it?"

Lanning harrumphed and considered. "It's been done experimentally by U.S. Robots," he said reluctantly, "without the addition of a positronic brain, of course. By using human ova and hormone control, one can grow human flesh and skin over a skeleton of porous silicone plastics that would defy external examination. The eyes, the hair, the skin, would be really human, not humanoid. And if you put a positronic brain and such other gadgets as you might desire inside, you have a humanoid robot."

Quinn said shortly, "How long would it take to make one?"

Lanning considered. "If you had all your equipment—the brain, the skeleton, the ovum, the proper hormones and radiations—say, two months."

The politician straightened out of his chair. "Then we shall see what the insides of Mr. Byerley look like. It will mean publicity for U.S. Robots—but I gave you your chance."

Lanning turned impatiently to Susan Calvin, when they were alone. "Why do you insist—"

And with real feeling, she responded sharply and instantly, "Which do you want—the truth or my resignation? I won't lie for you. U.S. Robots can take care of itself. Don't turn coward."

"What," said Lanning, "if he opens up Byerley, and wheels and gears fall out? What then?"

"He won't open Byerley," said Calvin, disdainfully. "Byerley is as clever as Quinn, at the very least."

The news broke upon the city a week before Byerley was to have been nominated. But "broke" is the wrong word. It staggered upon the city, shambled, crawled. Laughter began and wit was free. And as the far-off hand of Quinn tightened its pressure in easy stages, the laughter grew forced, an element of hollow uncertainty entered, and people broke off to wonder.

The convention itself had the air of a restive stallion. There had been no contest planned. Only Byerley could possibly have been nominated a week earlier. There was no substitute even now. They had to nominate him, but there was complete confusion about it.

It would not have been so bad if the average individual were not torn between the enormity of the charge, if true, and its sensational folly, if false.

The day after Byerley was nominated perfunctorily, hollowly—a newspaper finally published the gist of a long interview with Dr. Susan Calvin, "world-famous expert on robopsychology and positronics."

What broke loose is popularly and succinctly described as hell.

It was what the Fundamentalists were waiting for. They were not a political party; they made pretense to no formal religion. Essentially they were those who had not adapted themselves to what had once been called the Atomic Age, in the days when atoms were a novelty. Actually, they were the Simple-Lifers, hungering after a life which, to those who lived it, had probably appeared not so Simple, and who had been, therefore, Simple-Lifers themselves.

The Fundamentalists required no new reason to detest robots and robot manufacturers; but a new reason such as the Quinn accusation and the Calvin analysis was sufficient to make such detestation audible.

The huge plant of the U.S. Robots and Mechanical Men Corporation was a hive that spawned armed guards. It prepared for war.

Within the city, the house of Stephen Byerley bristled with police.

The political campaign, of course, lost all other issues, and resembled a campaign only in that it was something filling the hiatus between nomination and election.

Stephen Byerley did not allow the fussy little man to distract him. He remained comfortably unperturbed by the uniforms in the background. Outside the house, past the line of grim guards, reporters and photographers waited according to the tradition of the caste. One enterprising 'visor station even had a scanner focused on the blank entrance to the prosecutor's unpretentious home, while a synthetically excited announcer filled in with inflated commentary.

The fussy little man advanced. He held forward a rich, complicated sheet. "This, Mr. Byerley, is a court order authorizing me to search these premises for the presence of illegal . . . uh . . . mechanical men or robots of any description."

Byerley half rose, and took the paper. He glanced at it indifferently, and smiled as he handed it back. "All in order. Go ahead. Do your job. Mrs. Hoppen"—to his housekeeper, who appeared reluctantly from the next room—"please go with them, and help out if you can."

The little man, whose name was Harroway, hesitated, produced an unmistakable blush, failed completely to catch Byerley's eyes, and muttered, "Come on," to the two policemen.

He was back in ten minutes.

"Through?" questioned Byerley, in just the tone of a person who is not particularly interested in the question, or in its answer.

Harroway cleared his throat, made a bad start in falsetto, and began again, angrily, "Look here, Mr. Byerley, our special instructions were to search the house very thoroughly."

"And haven't you?"

"We were told exactly what to look for."

"Yes?"

"In short, Mr. Byerley, and not to put too fine a point on it, we were told to search you."

"Me?" said the prosecutor with a broadening smile. "And how do you intend to do that?"

"We have a Penet-radiation unit—"

"Then I'm to have my X-ray photograph taken, hey? You have the authority?"

"You saw my warrant."

"May I see it again?"

Harroway, his forehead shining with considerably more than mere enthusiasm, passed it over a second time.

Byerley said evenly, "I read here as the description of what you are to search, I quote: 'the dwelling place belonging to Stephen Allen Byerley, located at 355 Willow Grove, Evanstron, together with any garage, storehouse, or other structures or buildings thereto appertaining, together with all grounds thereto appertaining' . . . um . . . and so on. Quite in order. But, my good man, it doesn't say anything about searching my interior. I am not part of the premises. You may search my clothes if you think I've got a robot hidden in my pocket."

Harroway had no doubt on the point of to whom he owed his job. He did not propose to be backward, given a chance to earn a much better—i.e., more highly paid—job.

He said, in a faint echo of bluster, "Look here. I'm allowed to search the furniture in your house, and anything else I find in it. You are in it, aren't you?"

"A remarkable observation. I *am* in it. But I'm not a piece of furniture. As a citizen of adult responsibility—I have the psychiatric certificate proving that—I have certain rights under the Regional Articles. Searching me would come under the heading of violating my Right of Privacy. That paper isn't sufficient."

"Sure, but if you're a robot, you don't have Right of Privacy."

"True enough—but that paper still isn't sufficient. It recognizes me implicitly as a human being."

"Where?" Harroway snatched at it.

"Where it says 'the dwelling place belonging to' and so on. A robot cannot own property. And you may tell your employer, Mr. Harroway, that if he tries to issue a similar paper which does *not* implicitly recognize me as a human being, he will be immediately faced with a restraining injunction and a civil suit which will make it necessary for him to *prove* me a robot by means of information *now* in his possession, or else to pay a whopping penalty for an attempt to deprive me unduly of my rights under the Regional Articles. You'll tell him that, won't you?"

Harroway marched to the door. He turned. "You're a slick

lawyer—" His hand was in his pocket. For a short moment, he stood there. Then he left, smiled in the direction of the 'visor scanner, still playing away—waved to the reporters, and shouted, "We'll have something for you tomorrow, boys. No kidding."

In his ground car, he settled back, removed the tiny mechanism from his pocket, and carefully inspected it. It was the first time he had ever taken a photograph by X-ray reflection. He hoped he had done it correctly.

Quinn and Byerley had never met face to face alone. But visorphone was pretty close to it. In fact, accepted literally, perhaps the phrase was accurate, even if to each, the other was merely the light and dark pattern of a bank of photocells.

It was Quinn who had initiated the call. It was Quinn who spoke first, and without particular ceremony. "Thought you would like to know, Byerley, that I intend to make public the fact that you're wearing a protective shield against Penet-radiation."

"That so? In that case, you've probably already made it public. I have a notion our enterprising press representatives have been tapping my various communication lines for quite a while. I know they have my office lines full of holes; which is why I've dug in at my home these last weeks." Byerley was friendly, almost chatty.

Quinn's lips tightened slightly. "This call is shielded—thoroughly. I'm making it at a certain personal risk."

"So I should imagine. Nobody knows you're behind this campaign. At least, nobody knows it officially. Nobody *doesn't* know it unofficially. I wouldn't worry. So I wear a protective shield? I suppose you found that out when your puppy dog's Penet-radiation photograph, the other day, turned out to be over-exposed."

"You realize, Byerley, that it would be pretty obvious to everyone that you don't dare face X-ray analysis."

"Also that you, or your men, attempted illegal invasion of my Rights of Privacy."

"The devil they'll care for that."

"They might. It's rather symbolic of our two campaigns, isn't it? You have little concern with the rights of the individual citizen. I have great concern. I will not submit to X-ray analysis, because I wish to maintain my rights on principle. Just as I'll maintain the rights of others when elected."

"That will no doubt make a very interesting speech, but no one will believe you. A little too high-sounding to be true. Another thing"—a sudden, crisp change—"the personnel in your home were not complete the other night."

"In what way?"

"According to the report"—he shuffled papers before him that were just within the range of vision of the visiplate—"there was one person missing—a cripple."

"As you say," said Byerley, tonelessly, "a cripple. My old teacher, who lives with me and who is now in the country—and has been for two months. A 'much-needed rest' is the usual expression applied in the case. He has your permission?"

"Your teacher? A scientist of sorts?"

"A lawyer once—before he was a cripple. He has a government license as a research biophysicist, with a laboratory of his own, and a complete description of the work he's doing filed with the proper authorities, to whom I can refer you. The work is minor, but is a harmless and engaging hobby for a—poor cripple. I am being as helpful as I can, you see."

"I see. And what does this . . . teacher . . . know about robot manufacture?"

"I couldn't judge the extent of his knowledge in a field with which I am unacquainted."

"He wouldn't have access to positronic brains?"

"Ask your friends at U.S. Robots. They'd be the ones to know."

"I'll put it shortly, Byerley. Your crippled teacher is the real Stephen Byerley. You are his robot creation. We can prove it. It was he who was in the automobile accident, not you. There will be ways of checking the records."

"Really? Do so, then. My best wishes."

"And we can search your so-called teacher's 'country place,' and see what we can find there."

"Well, not quite, Quinn." Byerley smiled broadly. "Unfortunately for you, my so-called teacher is a sick man. His country place is his place of rest. His Right of Privacy as a citizen of adult responsibility is naturally even stronger, under the circumstances. You won't be able to obtain a warrant to enter his grounds without showing just cause. However, I'd be the last to prevent you from trying."

There was a pause of moderate length, and then Quinn leaned forward, so that his imaged face expanded and the fine lines on his forehead were visible. "Byerley, why do you carry on? You can't be elected."

"Can't I?"

"Do you think you can? Do you suppose that your failure to make any attempt to disprove the robot charge—when you could easily, by breaking one of the Three Laws—does anything but convince the people that you *are* a robot?"

"All I see so far is that from being a rather vaguely known, but still largely obscure metropolitan lawyer, I have now become a world figure. You're a good publicist."

"But you *are* a robot."

"So it's been said, but not proven."

"It's been proven sufficiently for the electorate."

"Then relax—you've won."

"Goodbye," said Quinn, with his first touch of viciousness, and the visorphone slammed off.

"Goodbye," said Byerley imperturbably, to the blank plate.

Byerley brought his "teacher" back the week before election. The air car dropped quickly in an obscure part of the city.

"You'll stay here till after the election," Byerley told him. "It would be better to have you out of the way if things take a bad turn."

The hoarse voice that twisted painfully out of John's crooked mouth might have had accents of concern in it. "There's danger of violence?"

"The Fundamentalists threaten it, so I suppose there is, in a theoretical sense. But I really don't expect it. The Fundies have no real power. They're just the continuous irritant factor that might stir up a riot after a while. You don't mind staying here? Please. I won't be myself if I have to worry about you."

"Oh, I'll stay. You still think it will go well?"

"I'm sure of it. No one bothered you at the place?"

"No one. I'm certain."

"And your part went well?"

"Well enough. There'll be no trouble there."

"Then take care of yourself, and watch the televisor tomorrow, John." Byerley pressed the gnarled hand that rested on his.

Lenton's forehead was a furrowed study in suspense. He had the completely unenviable job of being Byerley's campaign manager in a campaign that wasn't a campaign, for a person who refused to reveal his strategy, and refused to accept his manager's.

"You can't!" It was his favorite phrase. It had become his only phrase. "I tell you, Steve, you can't!"

He threw himself in front of the prosecutor, who was spending his time leafing through the typed pages of his speech.

"Put that down, Steve. Look, that mob has been organized by the Fundies. You won't get a hearing. You'll be stoned, more likely. Why do you have to make a speech before an audience? What's wrong with a recording, a visual recording?"

"You want me to win the election, don't you?" asked Byerley, mildly.

"Win the election! You're not going to win, Steve. I'm trying to save your life."

"Oh, I'm not in danger."

"He's not in danger. He's not in danger." Lenton made a queer, rasping sound in his throat. "You mean you're getting out on that balcony in front of fifty thousand crazy crackpots and try to talk sense to them—on a balcony, like a medieval dictator?"

Byerley consulted his watch. "In about five minutes—as soon as the television lines are free."

Lenton's answering remark was not quite transliterable.

The crowd filled a roped-off area of the city. Trees and houses seemed to grow out of a mass-human foundation. And by ultrawave, the rest of the world watched. It was a purely local elec-

382

tion, but it had a world audience just the same. Byerley thought of that and smiled.

But there was nothing to smile at in the crowd itself. There were banners and streamers, ringing every possible change on his supposed robotcy. The hostile attitude rose thickly and tangibly into the atmosphere.

From the start, the speech was not successful. It competed against the inchoate mob howl and the rhythmic cries of the Fundie claques that formed mob-islands within the mob. Byerley spoke on, slowly, unemotionally—

Inside, Lenton clutched his hair and groaned—and waited for the blood.

There was a writhing in the front ranks. An angular citizen with popping eyes, and clothes too short for the lank length of his limbs, was pulling to the fore. A policeman dived after him, making slow, struggling passage. Byerley waved the latter off, angrily.

The thin man was directly under the balcony. His words tore unheard against the roar.

Byerley leaned forward. "What do you say? If you have a legitimate question, I'll answer it." He turned to a flanking guard. "Bring that man up here."

There was a tensing in the crowd. Cries for quiet started in various parts of the mob and rose to a bedlam, then toned down raggedly. The thin man, red-faced and panting, faced Byerley.

Byerley said, "Have you a question?"

The thin man stared, and said in a cracked voice, "Hit me!"

With sudden energy, he thrust out his chin at an angle. "Hit me! You say you're not a robot. Prove it. You can't hit a human, you monster."

There was a queer, flat, dead silence. Byerley's voice punctured it. "I have no reason to hit you."

The thin man was laughing wildly. "You *can't* hit me. You *won't* hit me. You're not a human. You're a monster, a make-believe man."

And Stephen Byerley, tight-lipped, in the face of thousands

who watched in person and the millions who watched on screen, drew back his fist and caught the man crackingly upon the chin. The challenger went over backwards in sudden collapse, with nothing on his face but blank, blank surprise.

Byerley said, "I'm sorry. Take him in and see that he's comfortable. I want to speak to him when I'm through."

And when Dr. Calvin, from her reserved space, turned her automobile and drove off, only one reporter had recovered sufficiently from the shock to race after her and shout an unheard question.

Susan Calvin called over her shoulder, "He's human."

That was enough. The reporter raced away in his own direction.

The rest of the speech might be described as "spoken but not heard."

Dr. Calvin and Stephen Byerley met once again—a week before he took the oath of office as mayor. It was late—past midnight.

Dr. Calvin said, "You don't look tired."

The mayor-elect smiled. "I may stay up for a while. Don't tell Quinn."

"I shan't. But that was an interesting story of Quinn's, since you mention him. It's a shame to have spoiled it. I suppose you knew his theory?"

"Parts of it."

"It was highly dramatic. Stephen Byerley was a young lawyer, a powerful speaker, a great idealist—and with a certain flair for biophysics. Are you interested in robotics, Mr. Byerley?"

"Only in the legal aspects."

"*This* Stephen Byerley was. But there was an accident. Byerley's wife died; he himself, worse. His legs were gone, his face was gone, his voice was gone. Part of his mind was—bent. He would not submit to plastic surgery. He retired from the world, his legal career gone—only his intelligence and his hands left. Somehow he could obtain positronic brains, even a complex one, one which had the greatest capacity of forming judgments in ethical problems—which is the highest robotic function so far developed.

"He grew a body about it. Trained it to be everything he would have been and was no longer. He sent it out into the world as Stephen Byerley, remaining behind himself as the old, crippled teacher that no one ever saw—"

"Unfortunately," said the mayor-elect, "I ruined all that by hitting a man. The papers say it was your official verdict on the occasion that I was human."

"How did that happen? Do you mind telling me? It couldn't have been accidental."

"It wasn't entirely. Quinn did most of the work. My men started quietly spreading the fact that I had never hit a man; that I was unable to hit a man; that to fail to do so under provocation would be sure proof that I was a robot. So I arranged for a silly speech in public, with all sorts of publicity overtones, and almost inevitably, some fool fell for it. In its essence, it was what I call a shyster trick. One in which the artificial atmosphere which has been created does all the work. Of course, the emotional effects made my election certain, as intended."

The robopsychologist nodded. "I see you intrude on my field— as every politician must, I suppose. But I'm very sorry it turned out this way. I like robots. I like them considerably better than I do human beings. If a robot can be created capable of being a civil executive, I think he'd make the best one possible. By the Laws of Robotics, he'd be incapable of harming humans, incapable of tyranny, of corruption, of stupidity, of prejudice. And after he had served a decent term, he would leave, even though he was immortal, because it would be impossible for him to hurt humans by letting them know that a robot had ruled them. It would be most ideal."

"Except that a robot might fail due to the inherent inadequacies of his brain. The positronic brain has never equaled the complexities of the human brain."

"He would have advisors. Not even a human brain is capable of governing without assistance."

Byerley considered Susan Calvin with grave interest. "Why do you smile, Dr. Calvin?"

"I smile because Mr. Quinn didn't think of everything."

"You mean there could be more to that story of his."

"Only a little. For the three months before election, this Stephen Byerley that Mr. Quinn spoke about, this broken man, was in the country for some mysterious reason. He returned in time for that famous speech of yours. And after all, what the old cripple did once, he could do a second time, particularly where the second job is very simple in comparison to the first."

"I don't quite understand."

Dr. Calvin rose and smoothed her dress. She was obviously ready to leave. "I mean there is one time when a robot may strike a human being without breaking the First Law. Just one time."

"And when is that?"

Dr. Calvin was at the door. She said quietly, "When the human to be struck is merely another robot."

She smiled broadly, her thin face glowing. "Goodbye, Mr. Byerley. I hope to vote for you five years from now—for Coordinator."

Stephen Byerley chuckled. "I must reply that that is a somewhat farfetched idea."

The door closed behind her.

2066: ELECTION DAY

MICHAEL SHAARA

(1 9 5 6)

Early in the 1950s, computers began to be utilized in the American political process. In 1952 and 1954, for example, computers were used on the evening of election day to predict, on the basis of early returns, the most likely outcome of the election. The predictions of the percentages by which Eisenhower would win over Stevenson were amazingly accurate.

In 1960, Kennedy used computer simulations as an aid in designing his presidential election campaign. Political scientist Eugene Burdick wrote a novel, *The 480* (1964), describing a similar presidential election campaign in which strategies were determined with the aid of computer simulations. In his preface, Burdick warned that marketing expertise combined with computer analysis of voter reactions would lead to the destruction of the democratic electoral process. The warning has gone unheeded, and now all major political candidates use computers to process information and do simulations as an aid in planning their campaign strategies. In a prophetic extension of that phenomenon, "2066: Election Day" raises an interesting question: What happens when the presidency becomes such an enormous and complex task that no one man can handle it?

Michael Shaara was born in 1928. He won the Pulitzer Prize in 1974 for his book *The Killer Angels*, a historical novel about the Battle of Gettysburg.

EARLY THAT AFTERNOON Professor Larkin crossed the river into Washington, a thing he always did on Election Day, and sat for a long while in the Polls. It was still called the Polls, in this year 2066 A.D., although what went on inside bore no relation at all to the elections of primitive American history. The Polls was now a single enormous building which rose out of the green fields where the ancient Pentagon had once stood. There was only one of its kind in Washington, only one Polling Place in each of the forty-eight states, but since few visited the Polls nowadays, no more were needed.

In the lobby of the building, a great hall was reserved for

visitors. Here you could sit and watch the many-colored lights dancing and flickering on the huge panels above, listen to the weird but strangely soothing hum and click of the vast central machine. Professor Larkin chose a deep soft chair near the long line of booths and sat down. He sat for a long while smoking his pipe, watching the people go in and out of the booths with strained, anxious looks on their faces.

Professor Larkin was a lean, boyish-faced man in his late forties. With the pipe in his hand he looked much more serious and sedate than he normally felt, and it often bothered him that people were able to guess his profession almost instantly. He had a vague idea that it was not becoming to look like a college professor, and he often tried to change his appearance—a loud tie here, a sport coat there—but it never seemed to make any difference. He remained what he was, easily identifiable, Professor Harry L. (Lloyd) Larkin, Ph.D., Dean of the political science department at a small but competent college just outside of Washington.

It was his interest in political science which drew him regularly to the Polls at every election. Here he could sit and feel the flow of American history in the making, and recognize, as he did now, perennial candidates for the presidency. Smiling, he watched a little old lady dressed in pink, very tiny and very fussy, flit doggedly from booth to booth. Evidently her test marks had not been very good. She was clutching her papers tightly in a black-gloved hand, and there was a look of prim irritation on her face. But *she* knew how to run this country, by George, and one of these days *she* would be President. Harry Larkin chuckled.

But it did prove one thing. The great American dream was still intact. The tests were open to all. And anyone could still grow up to be President of the United States.

Sitting back in his chair, Harry Larkin remembered his own childhood, how the great battle had started. There were examinations for everything in those days—you could not get a job streetcleaning without taking a civil-service examination—but public office needed no qualifications at all. And first the psychologists, then the newspapers, had begun calling it a national disgrace. And, considering the caliber of some of the men who went into public office, it *was* a national disgrace. But then psychological testing came of age, really became an exact science, so that it was possible to test a man thoroughly—his knowledge, his potential, his personality. And from there it was a short but bitterly fought step to—SAM.

SAM. Uncle SAM, as he had been called originally, the last and greatest of all electronic brains. Harry Larkin peered up in unabashed awe at the vast battery of lights which flickered above him. He knew that there was more to SAM than just this building, more than all the other forty-eight buildings put together, that SAM was actually an incredibly enormous network of electronic cells which had its heart in no one place, but its arms in all. It was an unbelievably complex analytical computer which judged a candidate far more harshly and thoroughly than the American public could ever have judged him. And crammed in its miles of memory banks lay almost every bit of knowledge mankind had yet discovered. It was frightening—many thought of it as a monster, but Harry Larkin was unworried.

The thirty years since the introduction of SAM had been thirty of America's happiest years. In a world torn by continual war and unrest, by dictators, puppet governments, the entire world had come to know and respect the American President for what he was: the best possible man for the job. And there was no doubt that he was the best. He had competed for the job in fair examination against the cream of the country. He had to be a truly remarkable man to come out on top.

The day was long since past when just any man could handle the presidency. A full century before, men had begun dying in office, cut down in their prime by the enormous pressures of the job. And that was a hundred years ago. Now the job had become infinitely more complex, and even now President Creighton lay on his bed in the White House, recovering from a stroke, an old, old man after one term of office.

Harry Larkin shuddered to think what might have happened had America not adopted the system of "the best qualified man."

All over the world this afternoon, men waited for word from America, the calm and trustworthy words of the new President, for there had been no leader in America since President Creighton's stroke. His words would mean more to the people, embroiled as they were in another great crisis, than the words of their own leaders. The leaders of other countries fought for power, bought it, stole it, only rarely earned it. But the American President was known the world over for his honesty, his intelligence, his desire for peace. Had he not those qualities, "old Uncle SAM" would never have elected him.

Eventually, the afternoon nearly over, Harry Larkin rose to leave. By this time the President was probably already elected. Tomorrow the world would return to peace. Harry Larkin paused in the door once before he left, listened to the reassuring hum from the great machine. Then he went quietly home, walking quickly and briskly toward the most enormous fate on Earth.

"My name is Reddington. You know me?"

Harry Larkin smiled uncertainly into the phone.

"Why . . . yes, I believe so. You are, if I'm not mistaken, general director of the Bureau of Elections."

"Correct," the voice went on quickly, crackling in the receiver, "and you are supposed to be an authority on Political Science, right?"

"Supposed to be?" Larkin bridled. "Well, it's distinctly possible that I—"

"All right, all right," Reddington blurted. "No time for politeness. Listen, Larkin, this is a matter of urgent national security. There will be a car at your door—probably be there when you put this phone down. I want you to get into it and hop on over here. I can't explain further. I know your devotion to the country, if it wasn't for that I would not have called you. But don't ask questions. Just come. No time. Goodbye."

There was a click. Harry Larkin stood holding the phone for a long, shocked moment, then he heard a pounding at the door. The housekeeper was out, but he waited automatically before going to answer it. He didn't like to be rushed, and he was confused. Urgent national security? Now what in blazes—

The man at the door was an Army major. He was accompanied by two young but very large sergeants. They identified Larkin, then escorted him politely but firmly down the steps into a staff car. Larkin could not help feeling abducted, and a completely characteristic rage began to rise in him. But he remembered what Reddington had said about national security and so sat back quietly with nothing more than an occasional grumble.

He was driven back into Washington. They took him downtown to a small but expensive apartment house he could neither identify nor remember, and escorted him briskly into an elevator. When they reached the suite upstairs they opened the door and let him in, but did not follow him. They turned and went quickly away.

Somewhat ruffled, Larkin stood for a long moment in the hall by the hat table, regarding a large rubber plant. There was a long sliding door before him, closed, but he could hear an argument going on behind it. He heard the word "SAM" mentioned many times, and once he heard a clear sentence: ". . . government by machine. I will not tolerate it!" Before he had time to hear any more, the doors slid back. A small, square man with graying hair came out to meet him. He recognized the man instantly as Reddington.

"Larkin," the small man said, "glad you're here." The tension on his face showed also in his voice. "That makes all of us. Come in and sit down." He turned back into the large living room. Larkin followed.

"Sorry to be so abrupt," Reddington said, "but it was necessary. You will see. Here, let me introduce you around."

Larkin stopped in involuntary awe. He was used to the sight of important men, but not so many at one time, and never so close. There was Secretary Kell of Agriculture and Wachsmuth of Commerce, General Vines, Chief of Staff, and a battery of others so imposing that Larkin found his mouth hanging embarrassingly open. He closed it immediately.

Reddington introduced him. The men nodded one by one,

but they were all deathly serious, their faces drawn, and there was now no conversation. Reddington waved him to a chair. Most of the others were standing, but Larkin sat.

Reddington sat directly facing him. There was a long moment of silence during which Larkin realized that he was being searchingly examined. He flushed, but sat calmly with his hands folded in his lap. After a while Reddington took a deep breath.

"Dr. Larkin," he said slowly, "what I am about to say to you will die with you. There must be no question of that. We cannot afford to have any word of this meeting, any word at all, reach anyone not in this room. This includes your immediate relatives, your friends, anyone—anyone at all. Before we continue, let me impress you with that fact. This is a matter of the gravest national security. Will you keep what is said here in confidence?"

"If the national interest—" Larkin began, then he said abruptly, "of course."

Reddington smiled slightly.

"Good. I believe you. I might add that just the fact of your being here, Doctor, means that you have already passed the point of no return . . . well, no matter. There is no time. I'll get to the point."

He stopped, looking around the room. Some of the other men were standing and now began to move in closer. Larkin felt increasingly nervous, but the magnitude of the event was too great for him to feel any worry. He gazed intently at Reddington.

"The Polls close tonight at eight o'clock." Reddington glanced at his watch. "It is now six-eighteen. I must be brief. Doctor, do you remember the prime directive that we gave to SAM when he was first built?"

"I think so," said Larkin slowly.

"Good. You remember then that there was one main order. SAM was directed to elect, quote, *the best-qualified man*. Unquote. Regardless of any and all circumstances, religion, race, so on. The orders were clear—the best-qualified man. The phrase has become world-famous. But unfortunately"—he glanced up briefly at the men surrounding him—"the order was a mistake. Just whose mistake does not matter. I think perhaps the fault

392

lies with all of us, but—it doesn't matter. What matters is this: SAM will not elect a president."

Larkin struggled to understand. Reddington leaned forward in his chair.

"Now follow me closely. We learned this only late this afternoon. We are always aware, as you no doubt know, of the relatively few people in this country who have a chance for the presidency. We know not only because they are studying for it, but because such men as these are marked from their childhood to be outstanding. We keep close watch on them, even to assigning the Secret Service to protect them from possible harm. There are only a very few. During this last election we could not find more than fifty. All of those people took the tests this morning. None of them passed."

He paused, waiting for Larkin's reaction. Larkin made no move.

"You begin to see what I'm getting at? *There is no qualified man.*"

Larkin's eyes widened. He sat bolt upright.

"Now it hits you. If none of those people this morning passed, there is no chance at all for any of the others tonight. What are left now are simply crackpots and malcontents. They are privileged to take the tests, but it means nothing. SAM is not going to select anybody. Because sometime during the last four years the presidency passed the final limit, the ultimate end of man's capabilities, and with scientific certainty we know that there is probably no man alive who is, according to SAM's directive, qualified."

"But," Larkin interrupted, "I'm not quite sure I follow. Doesn't the phrase 'elect the best-qualified man' mean that we can at least take the best we've got?"

Reddington smiled wanly and shook his head.

"No. And that was our mistake. It was quite probably a psychological block, but none of us ever considered the possibility of the job surpassing human ability. Not then, thirty years ago. And we also never seemed to remember that SAM is, after all, only a machine. He takes the words to mean exactly what they say: Elect the best, comma, *qualified*, comma, man. But do you see, if there is *no* qualified man, SAM cannot possibly elect the best. So SAM will elect no one at all. Tomorrow this country will be without a president. And the result of that, more than likely, will be a general war."

Larkin understood. He sat frozen in his chair.

"So you see our position," Reddington went on wearily. "There's nothing we can do. Reelecting President Creighton is out of the question. His stroke was permanent, he may not last the week. And there is no possibility of tampering with SAM, to change the directive. Because, as you know, SAM is foolproof, had to be. The circuits extend through all forty-eight states. To alter the machine at all requires clearing through all forty-eight entrances. We can't do that. For one thing, we haven't time. For another, we can't risk letting the world know there is no qualified man.

"For a while this afternoon, you can understand, we were stumped. What could we do? There was only one answer, we may come back to it yet. Give the presidency itself to SAM—"

A man from across the room, whom Larkin did not recognize, broke in angrily.

"Now Reddington, I told you, that is government by machine! And I will not stand—"

"What else can you *do!*" Reddington whirled, his eyes flashing, his tension exploding now into rage. "Who else knows all the answers? Who else can compute in two seconds the tax rate for Mississippi, the parity levels for wheat, the probable odds on a military engagement? Who else but SAM! And why didn't we do it long ago, just feed the problems to *him*, SAM, and not go on killing man after man, great men, *decent* men like poor Jim Creighton, who's on his back now and dying because people like you—" He broke off suddenly and bowed his head. The room was still. No one looked at Reddington. After a moment he shook his head. His voice, when he spoke, was husky.

"Gentlemen, I'm sorry. This leads nowhere." He turned back to Larkin.

Larkin had begun to feel the pressure. But the presence of these men, and Reddington's obvious profound sincerity, reas-

sured him. Creighton had been a great president, he had surrounded himself with some of the finest men in the country.
Larkin felt a surge of hope that such men as these were available
for one of the most critical hours in American history. For critical
it was, and Larkin knew as clearly as anyone there what the
absence of a president in the morning—no deep reassurance, no
words of hope—would mean. He sat waiting for Reddington to
continue.

"Well, we have a plan. It may work, it may not. We may all
be shot. But this is where you come in. I hope for all our sakes
you're up to it."

Larkin waited.

"The plan," Reddington went on slowly, carefully, "is this.
SAM has one defect. We can't tamper with it. But we *can* fool
it. Because when the brain tests a man, it does not at the same
time identify him. We do the identifying ourselves. So if a man
named Joe Smith takes the personality tests and another man
also named Joe Smith takes the political science tests, the machine has no way of telling them apart. Unless our guards supply
the difference, SAM will mark up the results of both tests to one
Joe Smith. We can clear the guards, no problem there. The first
problem was to find the eight men to take the eight tests."

Larkin understood. He nodded.

"Exactly. Eight specialists," Reddington said. "General Vines
will take the military; Burden, psychology; Wachsmuth, eco-
nomics; and so on. You, of course, will take the political science.
We can only hope that each man will come out with a high
enough score in his own field so that the combined scores of our
mythical 'candidate' will be enough to qualify him. Do you follow me?"

Larkin nodded dazedly. "I think so. But—"

"It should work. It has to work."

"Yes," Larkin murmured, "I can see that. But who—who
will actually wind up—"

"As president?" Reddington smiled very slightly and stood
up.

"That was the most difficult question of all. At first we thought there was no solution. Because a president must be so many things—consider. A president blossoms instantaneously, from nonentity, into the most important job on earth. Every magazine, every newspaper in the country immediately goes to work on his background, digs out his life story, anecdotes, sayings, and so on. Even a very strong fraud would never survive it. So the first problem was believability. The new president must be absolutely believable. He must be a man of obvious character, of obvious intelligence, but more than that, his former life must fit the facts: he must have had both the time and the personality to prepare himself for the office.

"And you see immediately what all that means. Most businessmen are out. Their lives have been too social, they wouldn't have had the time. For the same reason all government and military personnel are also out, and we need hardly say that anyone from the Bureau of Elections would be immediately suspect. No. You see the problem. For a while we thought that the time was too short, the risk too great. But then the only solution, the only possible chance, finally occurred to us.

"The only believable person would be—a professor. Someone whose life has been serious but unhurried, devoted to learning but at the same time isolated. The only really believable person. And not a scientist, you understand, for a man like that would be much too overbalanced in one direction for our purpose. No, simply a professor, preferably in a field like political science, a man whose sole job for many years has been teaching, who can claim to have studied in his spare time, his summers—never really expected to pass the tests and all that, a humble man, you see—"

"Political science," Larkin said.

Reddington watched him. The other men began to close in on him.

"Yes," Reddington said gently. "Now you do see? It is our only hope. Your name was suggested by several sources, you are young enough, your reputation is well known. We think that you would be believable. And now that I've seen you"—he looked around slowly—"I for one am willing to risk it. Gentlemen, what do you say?"

Larkin, speechless, sat listening in mounting shock while the men agreed solemnly, one by one. In the enormity of the moment he could not think at all. Dimly, he heard Reddington.

"I know. But, Doctor, there is no time. The Polls close at eight. It is now almost seven."

Larkin closed his eyes and rested his head on his hands. Above him, Reddington went on inevitably.

"All right. You are thinking of what happens after. Even if we pull this off and you are accepted without question, what then? Well, it will simply be the old system all over again. You will be at least no worse off then presidents before SAM. Better even, because if worst comes to worst there is always SAM. You can feed all the bad ones to him. You will have the advice of the cabinet, of the military staff. We will help you in every way we can, some of us will sit with you on all conferences. And you know more about this than most of us, you have studied government all your life.

"But all this, what comes later, is not important. Not now. If we can get through tomorrow, the next few days, all the rest will work itself out. Eventually we can get around to altering SAM. But we must have a president in the morning. You are our only hope. You can do it. We all know you can do it. At any rate there is no other way, no time. Doctor"—he reached out and laid his hand on Larkin's shoulder—"shall we go to the Polls?"

It passed, as most great moments in a man's life do, with Larkin not fully understanding what was happening to him. Later he would look back to this night and realize the enormity of the decision he had made, the doubts, the sleeplessness, the responsibility and agony toward which he moved. But in that moment he thought nothing at all. Except that it was Larkin's country, Larkin's America. And Reddington was right. There was nothing else to do. He stood up.

They went to the Polls.

At nine-thirty that evening, sitting alone with Reddington back at the apartment, Larkin looked at the face of the announcer on the television screen, and heard himself pronounced President-elect of the United States.

Reddington wilted in front of the screen. For a while, neither man moved. They had come home alone, just as they had gone into the Polls one by one in the hope of arousing no comment. Now they sat in silence until Reddington turned off the set. He stood up and straightened his shoulders before turning to Larkin. He stretched out his hand.

"Well, may God help us," he breathed, "we did it."

Larkin took his hand. He felt suddenly weak. He sat down again, but already he could hear the phone ringing in the outer hall. Reddington smiled.

"Only a few of my closest friends are supposed to know about that phone. But every time anything big comes up—" He shrugged. "Well," he said, still smiling, "let's see how it works."

He picked up the phone and with it an entirely different manner. He became amazingly light and cheerful, as if he were feeling nothing more than the normal political good will.

"Know him? Of course I know him. Had my eye on the guy for months. Really nice guy, wait'll you meet him . . . yup, college professor, political science, written a couple of books . . . must know a hell of a lot more than polly sci, though. Probably been knocking himself out in his spare time. But those teachers, you know how it is, they don't get any pay, but all the spare time in the world. . . . Married? No, not that I know of—"

Larkin noticed with wry admiration how carefully Reddington had slipped in that bit about spare time, without seeming to be making an explanation. He thought wearily to himself, I hope that I don't have to do any talking myself. I'll have to do a lot of listening before I can chance any talking.

In a few moments Reddington put down the phone and came back. He had on his hat and coat.

"Had to answer a few," he said briefly, "make it seem natural. But you better get dressed."

"Dressed? Why?"

"Have you forgotten?" Reddington smiled patiently. "You're due at the White House. The Secret Service is already tearing the town apart looking for you. We were supposed to alert them. Oh, by the saints, I hope that wasn't too bad a slip."

He pursed his mouth worriedly while Larkin, still dazed, got into his coat. It was beginning now. It had already begun. He was tired but it did not matter. That he was tired would probably never matter again. He took a deep breath. Like Reddington, he straightened his shoulders.

The Secret Service picked them up halfway across town. That they knew where he was, who he was, amazed him and worried Reddington. They went through the gates of the White House and drove up before the door. It was opened for him as he put out his hand, and he stepped back in a reflex action from the sudden blinding flares of the photographers' flashbulbs. Reddington behind him took him firmly by the arm. Larkin went with him gratefully, unable to see, unable to hear anything but the roar of the crowd from behind the gates and the shouted questions of the reporters.

Inside the great front doors it was suddenly peaceful again, very quiet and pleasantly dark. He took off his hat instinctively. Luckily he had been here before; he recognized the lovely hall and felt not awed but at home. He was introduced quickly to several people whose names made no impression on him. A woman smiled. He made an effort to smile back. Reddington took him by the arm again and led him away. There were people all around him, but they were quiet and hung back. He saw the respect on their faces. It sobered him, quickened his mind.

"The President's in the Lincoln Room," Reddington whispered. "He wants to see you. How do you feel?"

"All right."

"Listen."

"Yes."

"You'll be fine. You're doing beautifully. Keep just that look on your face."

"I'm not trying to keep it there."

"You aren't?" Reddington looked at him. "Good. Very good." He paused and looked again at Larkin. Then he smiled.

"It's done it. I thought it would, but I wasn't sure. But it does it every time. A man comes in here, no matter what he was before, no matter what he is when he goes out, but he feels it. Don't you feel it?"

"Yes. It's like—"

"It's like . . . when you're in here you're *responsible.*"

Reddington said nothing. But Larkin felt a warm pressure on his arm.

They paused at the door of the Lincoln Room. Two Secret Service men, standing by the door, opened it respectfully. They went on in, leaving the others outside.

Larkin looked across the room to the great, immortal bed. He felt suddenly very small, very tender. He crossed the soft carpet and looked down at the old man.

"Hi," the old man said. Larkin was startled, but he looked down at the broad, weakly smiling face, saw the famous white hair and the still-twinkling eyes, and found himself smiling in return.

"Mr. President," Larkin said.

"I hear your name is Larkin." The old man's voice was surprisingly strong, but as he spoke now Larkin could see that the left side of his face was paralyzed. "Good name for a president. Indicates a certain sense of humor. Need a sense of humor. Reddington, how'd it go?"

"Good as can be expected, sir." He glanced briefly at Larkin. "The President knows. Wouldn't have done it without his O.K. Now that I think of it, it was probably he who put the Secret Service on us."

"You're doggone right," the old man said. "They may bother the by-jingo out of you, but those boys are necessary. And also, if I hadn't let them know we knew Larkin was material—" He stopped abruptly and closed his eyes, took a deep breath. After a moment he said, "Mr. Larkin?"

"Yes, sir."

"I have one or two comments. You mind?"

"Of course not, sir."

"I couldn't solve it. I just . . . didn't have time. There were so many other things to do." He stopped and again closed his eyes. "But it will be up to you, son. The presidency . . . must be preserved. What they'll start telling you now is that there's only one way out, let SAM handle it. Reddington too." The old man opened his eyes and gazed sadly at Reddington. "He'll tell you the same thing, but don't you believe it.

"Sure, SAM knows all the answers. Ask him a question on anything, on levels of parity tax rates, on anything. And right quick SAM will compute you out an answer. So that's what they'll try to do, they'll tell you to take it easy and let SAM do it.

"Well, all right, up to a certain point. But Mr. Larkin, understand this. SAM is like a book. Like a book, he knows the answers. *But only those answers we've already found out.* We gave SAM those answers. A machine is not creative, neither is a book. Both are only the products of creative minds. Sure, SAM could hold the country together. But growth, man, there'd be no more growth! No new ideas, new solutions, change, progress, development! And America *must* grow, must progress—"

He stopped, exhausted. Reddington bowed his head. Larkin remained idly calm. He felt a remarkable clarity in his head.

"But, Mr. President," he said slowly, "if the office is too much for one man, then all we can do is cut down on his powers—"

"Ah," the old man said faintly, "there's the rub. Cut down on what? If I sign a tax bill, I must know enough about taxes to be certain that the bill is the right one. If I endorse a police action, I must be certain that the strategy involved is militarily sound. If I consider farm prices . . . you see, you see, what will you cut? The office is responsible for its acts. It must remain responsible. You cannot just take someone else's word for things like that, you must make your own decisions. Already we sign things we know nothing about, bills for this, bills for that, on somebody's word."

"What do you suggest?"

The old man cocked an eye toward Larkin, smiled once more with half his mouth, anciently worn, only hours from death, an old, old man with his work not done, never to be done.

"Son, come here. Take my hand. Can't lift it myself."

401

Larkin came forward, knelt by the side of the bed. He took the cold hand, now gaunt and almost translucent, and held it gently.

"Mr. Larkin," the President said, "God be with you, boy. Do what you can. Delegate authority. Maybe cut the term in half. But keep us human, please, keep us growing, keep us alive." His voice faltered, his eyes closed. "I'm very tired. God be with you."

Larkin laid the hand gently on the bed cover. He stood for a long moment looking down. Then he turned with Reddington and left the room.

Outside he waited until they were past the Secret Service men and then turned to Reddington.

"Your plans for SAM. What do you think now?"

Reddington winced.

"I couldn't see any way out."

"But what about now? I have to know."

"I don't know. I really don't know. But . . . let me tell you something."

"Yes."

"Whatever I say to you from now on is only advice. You don't have to take it. Because understand this: however you came in here tonight, you're going out the President. You were elected. Not by the people maybe, not even by SAM. But you're President by the grace of God, and that's enough for me. From this moment on you'll be President to everybody in the world. We've all agreed. Never think that you're only a fraud, because you aren't. You heard what the President said. You take it from here."

Larkin looked at him for a long while. Then he nodded once briefly.

"All right," he said.

"One more thing."

"Yes?"

"I've got to say this. Tonight, this afternoon, I didn't really know what I was doing to you. I thought . . . well . . . the crisis came. But you had no time to think. That wasn't right. A man shouldn't be pushed into a thing like this without time to think.

The old man just taught me something about making your own decisions. I should have let you make yours."

"It's all right."

"No, it isn't. You remember him in there. Well. That's you four years from tonight. If you live that long."

Now it was Larkin who reached out and patted Reddington on the shoulder.

"That's all right, too," he said.

Reddington said nothing. When he spoke again, Larkin realized he was moved.

"We have the greatest luck, this country," he said tightly. "At all the worst times we always seem to find all the best people."

"Well," Larkin said hurriedly, "we'd better get to work. There's a speech due in the morning. And the problem of SAM. And . . . oh, I've got to be sworn in."

He turned and went off down the hall. Reddington paused a moment before following him. He was thinking that he could be watching the last human President the United States would ever have. But—once more he straightened his shoulders.

"Yes, sir," he said softly, "Mr. President."

IF THERE WERE
NO BENNY CEMOLI

PHILIP K. DICK

(1 9 6 3)

The newspaper industry, driven by economic pressures, began to computerize its production as early as the 1960s. By the end of that decade, the *Los Angeles Times,* the *Washington Star,* and a good many other metropolitan papers were using computers to set all type. Today the shift to computerized production is virtually complete throughout the industry. The title of Anthony Smith's *Goodbye Gutenberg* (1981), summarizes the author's view of what is happening to books. He believes we are rapidly moving through a revolution that will outmode the printed page, just as Gutenberg's printing press outmoded handwritten manuscripts after its invention in the fifteenth century. We are unquestionably entering an age of electronic books and libraries, when the word will be processed and stored electronically. This is happening because the technology is available, and it is more efficient than traditional printing technology for the handling of information. Certainly the mountains of information through which we continually struggle today require such technology for the individual who wants to walk the ridgelines.

Philip K. Dick's "If There Were No Benny Cemoli" was written in 1963, long before any newspapers were printed by computers. Yet in one giant leap of the imagination, Dick created such a world and then immediately moved forward to explore it. What power would a man have if he were creative in using a "homeostatic newspaper," as Dick names it in his story? The answer: the power to create reality. For the masses of people, the illusions of reality created by the electronic media become more convincing than the real world, even though those illusions may bear no relationship to reality. (Dick admitted that the figure of Benito Mussolini nudged his imagination as he created Benny Cemoli.) Dick's great interest in the world of power politics and his explosive imagination combine here to make this one of the finest stories ever written in the field of political science fiction.

Philip K. Dick was born in Chicago in 1928 and died on March 2, 1982, in California, where he had lived since childhood. He wrote more than thirty-six novels and a hundred short stories, and first gained recognition when his book *The Man in the High Castle* won a Hugo Award in 1963. His fiction is often complex and gives the reader the disturbing feeling of having just stepped into a room lined with funhouse mirrors, where the reality he knows has been wildly distorted. An axiom of Dick fiction is that the commonplace reality on which we depend is unreliable and illusory. We constantly fall through it into such strange realities as only Dick's bizarre imagination can create.

From his first fiction, published in the early 1950s, Dick was concerned with cybernetic inventions and their effects on humans. He and Asimov have been among the most prolific producers of stories about robots and computers. Dick is not as optimistic as Asimov in thinking that man will always use his machine intelligence wisely, because in Dick's view man's nature contains a destructive element that too often leads him to misuse the power made available to him by cybernetic inventions. A repeated theme in his fiction is that man keeps becoming more and more the machine or robot he has created. One of his finest novels, *Do Androids Dream of Electric Sheep?* deals with this topic. Written in 1968 and long out of print, *Electric Sheep* was the inspiration for the movie *Blade Runner*. The book has been reissued under this title.

SCAMPERING ACROSS the unplowed field the three boys shouted as they saw the ship; it had landed, all right, just where they expected, and they were the first to reach it.

"Hey, that's the biggest I ever saw!" Panting, the first boy halted. "That's not from Mars; that's from farther. It's from all the way out, I know it is." He became silent and afraid as he saw the size of it. And then, looking up into the sky, he realized that an armada had arrived, exactly as everyone had expected. "We better go tell," he said to his companions.

Back on the ridge, John LeConte stood by his steam-powered, chauffeur-driven limousine, impatiently waiting for the boiler to warm. Kids got there first, he said to himself with anger. Whereas I'm supposed to. And the children were ragged; they were merely farm boys.

"Is the phone working today?" LeConte asked his secretary.

Glancing at his clipboard, Mr. Fall said, "Yes, sir. Shall I put through a message to Oklahoma City?" He was the skinniest employee ever assigned to LeConte's office. The man evidently took nothing for himself, was positively uninterested in food. And he was efficient.

LeConte murmured, "The immigration people ought to hear about this outrage."

He sighed. It had all gone wrong. The armada from Proxima Centauri had after ten years arrived and none of the early-warning devices had detected it in advance of its landing. Now Oklahoma City would have to deal with the outsiders here on home ground—a psychological disadvantage which Le Conte felt keenly.

Look at the equipment they've got, he thought as he watched the commercial ships of the flotilla begin to lower their cargos. Why, hell, they make us look like provincials. He wished that his official car did not need twenty minutes to warm up; he wished—

Actually he wished that CURB did not exist.

Centaurus Urban Renewal Bureau, a do-gooding body unfortunately vested with enormous inter-system authority. It had been informed of the Misadventure back in 2170 and had started into space like a phototropic organism, sensitive to the mere physical light created by the hydrogen bomb explosions. But LeConte knew better than that. Actually the governing organizations in the Centaurian system knew many details of the tragedy because they had been in radio contact with other planets of the Sol system. Little of the native forms on Earth had survived. He himself was from Mars; he had headed a relief mission seven years ago, had decided to stay because there were so many opportunities here on Earth, conditions being what they were. . . .

This is all very difficult, he said to himself as he stood waiting for his steam-powered car to warm. We got here first, but CURB does outrank us; we must face that awkward fact. In my opinion, we've done a good job of rebuilding. Of course, it isn't like it was before . . . but ten years is not long. Give us another twenty and we'll have the trains running again. And our recent road-building bonds sold quite successfully, in fact were oversubscribed.

"Call for you, sir, from Oklahoma City," Mr. Fall said, holding out the receiver of the portable field-phone.

"Ultimate Representative in the Field John LeConte here," LeConte said into it loudly. "Go ahead; I say go ahead."

"This is Party Headquarters," the dry official voice at the other end came faintly, mixed with static, in his ear. "We've received reports from dozens of alert citizens in western Oklahoma and Texas of an immense—"

"It's here," LeConte said. "I can see it. I'm just about ready to go out and confer with its ranking members, and I'll file a full report at the usual time. So it wasn't necessary for you to check up on me." He felt irritable.

"Is the armada heavily armed?"

"Naw," LeConte said. "It appears to comprise bureaucrats and trade officials and commercial carriers. In other words, vultures."

The Party desk man said, "Well, go and make certain they understand that their presence here is resented by the native population as well as the Relief of War-torn Areas Administrating Council. Tell them that the legislature will be called to pass a special bill expressing indignation at this intrusion into domestic matters by an inter-system body."

"I know, I know," LeConte said. "It's been all decided; I know."

His chauffeur called to him, "Sir, your car is ready now."

The Party desk man concluded, "Make certain they understand that you can't negotiate with them; you have no power to admit them to Earth. Only the Council can do that and of course it's adamantly against that."

LeConte hung up the phone and hurried to his car.

Despite the opposition of the local authorities, Peter Hood of CURB decided to locate his headquarters in the ruins of the old Terran capital, New York City. This would lend prestige to the CURBmen as they gradually widened the circle of the organization's influence. At last, of course, the circle would embrace the planet. But that would take decades.

As he walked through the ruins of what had once been a

407

major train yard, Peter Hood thought to himself that when the task was done he himself would have long been retired. Not much remained of the pre-tragedy culture here. The local authorities—the political nonentities who had flocked in from Mars and Venus, as the neighboring planets were called—had done little. And yet he admired their efforts.

To the members of his staff walking directly behind him, he said, "You know, they have done the hard part for us. We ought to be grateful. It is not easy to come into a totally destroyed area, as they've done."

His man Fletcher observed, "They got back a good return."

Hood said, "Motive is not important. They have achieved results." He was thinking of the official who had met them in his steam car; it had been solemn and formal, carrying complicated trappings. When these locals had first arrived on the scene years ago, *they* had not been greeted, except perhaps by radiation-seared, blackened survivors who had stumbled out of cellars and gaped sightlessly. He shivered.

Coming up to him, a CURBman of minor rank saluted and said, "I think we've managed to locate an undamaged structure in which your staff could be housed for the time being. It's underground." He looked embarrassed. "Not what we had hoped for. We'd have to displace the locals to get anything attractive."

"I don't object," Hood said. "A basement will do."

"The structure," the minor CURBman said, "was once a great homeostatic newspaper, *The New York Times*. It printed itself directly below us. At least, according to the maps. We haven't located the newspaper yet; it was customary for the homeopapes to be buried a mile or so down. As yet we don't know how much of this one survived."

"But it would be valuable," Hood agreed.

"Yes," the CURBman said. "Its outlets are scattered all over the planet; it must have had a thousand different editions which it put out daily. How many outlets function—" He broke off. "It's hard to believe that the local politicos made no efforts to repair any of the ten or eleven worldwide homeopapes, but that seems to be the case."

"Odd," Hood said. Surely it would have eased their task.

The post-tragedy job of reuniting people into a common culture depended on newspapers, ionization in the atmosphere making radio and TV reception difficult if not impossible. "This makes me instantly suspicious," he said, turning to his staff. "Are they perhaps not trying to rebuild after all? Is their work merely a pretense?"

It was his own wife, Joan, who spoke up. "They may simply have lacked the ability to place the homeopapes on an operational basis."

Give them the benefit of the doubt, Hood thought. You're right.

"So the last edition of the *Times*," Fletcher said, "was put on the lines the day the Misadventure occurred. And the entire network of newspaper communication and news-creation has been idle since. I can't respect these politicos; it shows they're ignorant of the basics of a culture. By reviving the homeopapes we can do more to reestablish the pre-tragedy culture than they've done in ten thousand pitiful projects." His tone was scornful.

Hood said, "You may misunderstand, but let it go. Let's hope that the cephalon of the pape is undamaged. We couldn't possibly replace it." Ahead he saw the yawning entrance which the CURBmen crews had cleared. This was to be his first move, here on the ruined planet, restoring this immense, self-contained entity to its former authority. Once it had resumed its activity he would be freed for other tasks; the homeopape would take some of the burden from him.

A workman, still clearing debris away, muttered, "Jeez, I never saw so many layers of junk. You'd think they deliberately bottled it up down here." In his hands, the suction furnace which he operated glowed and pounded as it absorbed material, converting it to energy, leaving an increasingly enlarged opening.

"I'd like a report as soon as possible as to its condition," Hood said to the team of engineers who stood waiting to descend into the opening. "How long it will take to revive it, how much—" He broke off.

Two men in black uniforms had arrived. Police from the Security ship. One, he saw, was Otto Dietrich, the ranking investigator accompanying the armada from Centaurus, and he felt tense automatically; it was a reflex for all of them—he saw the engineers and the workmen cease momentarily and then, more slowly, resume their work.

"Yes," he said to Dietrich. "Glad to see you. Let's go off to this side room and talk there." He knew beyond a doubt what the investigator wanted; he had been expecting him.

Dietrich said, "I won't take up too much of your time, Hood. I know you're quite busy. What is this, here?" He glanced about curiously, his scrubbed, round, alert face eager.

In a small side room, converted to a temporary office, Hood faced the two policemen. "I am opposed to prosecution," he said quietly. "It's been too long. Let them go."

Dietrich, tugging throughtfully at his ear, said, "But war crimes are war crimes, even a decade later. Anyhow, what argument can there be? We're required by law to prosecute. *Somebody* started the war. They may well hold positions of responsibility now, but that hardly matters."

"How many police troops have you landed?" Hood asked.

"Two hundred."

"Then you're ready to go to work."

"We're ready to make inquiries. Sequester pertinent documents and initiate litigation in the local courts. We're prepared to enforce cooperation, if that's what you mean. Various experienced personnel have been distributed to key points." Dietrich eyed him. "All this is necessary; I don't see the problem. Did you intend to protect the guilty parties—make use of their so-called abilities on your staff?"

"No," Hood said evenly.

Dietrich said, "Nearly eighty million people died in the Misfortune. Can you forget that? Or is it that since they were merely local people, not known to us personally—"

"It's not that," Hood said. He knew it was hopeless; he could not communicate with the police mentality. "I've already stated my objections. I feel it serves no purpose at this late date to have trials and hangings. Don't request use of my staff in this; I'll

410

refuse on the grounds that I can spare no one, not even a janitor. Do I make myself clear?"

"You idealists," Dietrich sighed. "This is strictly a noble task confronting us . . . to rebuild, correct? What you don't or won't see is that these people will start it all over again, one day, unless we take steps now. We owe it to future generations. To be harsh now is the most humane method, in the long run. Tell me, Hood. What is this site? What are you resurrecting here with such vigor?"

"*The New York Times*," Hood said.

"It has, I assume, a morgue? We can consult its backlog of information? That would prove valuable in building up our cases."

Hood said, "I can't deny you access to material we uncover."

Smiling, Dietrich said, "A day-by-day account of the political events leading up to the war would prove quite interesting. Who, for instance, held supreme power in the United States at the time of the Misfortune? No one we've talked to so far seems to remember." His smile increased.

Early the next morning the report from the corps of engineers reached Hood in his temporary office. The power supply of the newspaper had been totally destroyed. But the cephalon, the governing brain-structure which guided and oriented the homeostatic system, appeared to be intact. If a ship was brought close by, perhaps its power supply could be integrated into the newspaper's lines. Thereupon much more would be known.

"In other words," Fletcher said to Hood, as they sat with Joan eating breakfast, "it may come on and it may not. Very pragmatic. You hook it up and if it works you've done your job. What if it doesn't? Do the engineers intend to give up at that point?"

Examining his cup, Hood said, "This tastes like authentic coffee." He pondered. "Tell them to bring a ship in and start the homeopape up. And if it begins to print, bring me the edition at once." He sipped his coffee.

An hour later a ship of the line had landed in the vicinity and its power source had been tapped for insertion into the homeopape. The conduits were placed, the circuits cautiously closed.

Seated in his office, Peter Hood heard far underground a low rumble, a halting, uncertain stirring. They had been successful. The newspaper was returning to life.

The edition, when it was laid on his desk by a bustling CURB-man, surprised him by its accuracy. Even in its dormant state, the newspaper had somehow managed not to fall behind events. Its receptors had kept going.

CURB LANDS, TRIP DECADE LONG, PLANS CENTRAL ADMINISTRATION

Ten years after the Misfortune of a nuclear holocaust, the inter-system rehabilitation agency, CURB, has made its historic appearance on Earth's surface, landing from a veritable armada of craft—a sight which witnesses described as "overpowering both in scope and in signif-icance." CURBman Peter Hood, named top coordinator by Centaurian authorities, immediately set up head-quarters in the ruins of New York City and conferred with aides, declaring that he had come "not to punish the guilty but to reestablish the planet-wide culture by every means available, and to restore—"

It was uncanny, Hood thought as he read the lead article. The varied newsgathering services of the homeopape had reached into his own life, had digested and then inserted into the lead article even the discussion between himself and Otto Dietrich. The newspaper was—had been—doing its job. Nothing of news-interest escaped it, even a discreet conversation carried on with no outsiders as witnesses. He would have to be careful.

Sure enough, another item, ominous in tone, dealt with the arrival of the black jacks, the police.

412

SECURITY AGENCY VOWS
"WAR CRIMINALS" TARGET

Captain Otto Dietrich, supreme police investigator arriving with the CURB armada from Proxima Centauri,
said today that those responsible for the Misfortune of
a decade ago "would have to pay for their crimes" before
the bar of Centaurian justice. Two hundred black-uniformed police, it was learned by the *Times*, have already
begun exploratory activities designed to—

The newspaper was warning Earth about Dietrich, and Hood
could not help feeling grim relish. The *Times* had not been set
up to serve merely the occupying hierarchy. It served everyone,
including those Dietrich intended to try. Each step of the police
activity would no doubt be reported in full detail. Dietrich, who
liked to work in anonymity, would not enjoy this. But the authority to maintain the newspaper belonged to Hood.

And he did not intend to shut it off.

One item on the first page of the paper attracted his further
notice; he read it, frowning and a little uneasy.

CEMOLI BACKERS RIOT IN UPSTATE
NEW YORK

Supporters of Benny Cemoli, gathered in the familiar
tent cities associated with the colorful political figure,
clashed with local citizens armed with hammers, shov-
els, and boards, both sides claiming victory in the two-
hour melee which left twenty injured and a dozen hos-
pitalized in hastily erected first-aid stations. Cemoli,
garbed as always in his toga-style red robes, visited the
injured, evidently in good spirits, joking and telling his
supporters that "it won't be long now" an evident reference to the organization's boast that it would march

413

on New York City in the near future to establish what Cemoli deems "social justice and true equality for the first time in world history." It should be recalled that prior to his imprisonment at San Quentin—

Flipping a switch on his intercom system, Hood said, "Fletcher, check into activities up in the north of the county. Find out about some sort of a political mob gathering there."

Fletcher's voice came back, "I have a copy of the *Times* too, sir. I see the item about this Cemoli agitator. There's a ship on the way up there right now; should have a report within ten minutes." Fletcher paused. "Do you think—it'll be necessary to bring in any of Dietrich's people?"

"Let's hope not," Hood said shortly.

Half an hour later the CURB ship, through Fletcher, made its report. Puzzled, Hood asked that it be repeated. But there was no mistake. The CURB field team had investigated thoroughly. They had found no sign whatsoever of any tent city or any group gathering. And citizens in the area whom they had interrogated had never heard of anyone named Cemoli. And there was no sign of any scuffle having taken place, no first-aid stations, no injured persons. Only the peaceful, semirural countryside.

Baffled, Hood read the item in the *Times* once more. There it was, in black and white, on the front page, along with the news about the landing of the CURB armada. What did it mean?

He did not like it at all.

Had it been a mistake to revive the great, old, damaged homeostatic newspaper?

From a sound sleep that night Hood was awakened by a clanging from far beneath the ground, an urgent racket that grew louder and louder as he sat up in bed, blinking and confused. Machinery roared. He heard the heavy rumbling movement as automatic circuits fitted into place, responding to instructions emanating from within the closed system itself.

"Sir," Fletcher was saying from the darkness. A light came

414

on as Fletcher located the temporary overhead fixture. "I thought I should come in and wake you. Sorry, Mrs. Hood."

"I'm awake," Hood muttered, rising from the bed and putting on his robe and slippers. "What's it doing?"

Fletcher said, "It's printing an extra."

Sitting up, smoothing her tousled blond hair back, Joan said, "Good Lord. What about?" Wide-eyed, she looked from her husband to Fletcher.

"We'll have to bring in the local authorities," Hood said. "Confer with them." He had an intuition as to the nature of the extra roaring through the presses at this moment. "Get that LeConte, that politico who met us on our arrival. Wake him up and fly him here immediately. We need him."

It took almost an hour to obtain the presence of the haughty, ceremonious local potentate and his staff member. The two of them, in their elaborate uniforms, at last put in an appearance at Hood's office, both of them indignant. They faced Hood silently, waiting to hear what he wanted.

In his bathrobe and slippers Hood sat at his desk, a copy of the *Times* extra before him; he was reading it once more as LeConte and his man entered.

NEW YORK POLICE REPORT
CEMOLI LEGIONS ON MOVE
TOWARD CITY,
BARRICADES ERECTED,
NATIONAL GUARD ALERTED

He turned the paper, showing the headlines to the two Earthmen. "Who is this man?" he said.

After a moment, LeConte said, "I—don't know."

Hood said, "Come on, Mr. LeConte."

"Let me read the article," LeConte said nervously. He scanned it in haste; his hands trembled as he held the newspaper. "Interesting," he said at last. "But I can't tell you a thing. It's news to me. You must understand that our communications have been sparse since the Misfortune, and it's entirely possible that a political movement could spring up without our—"

"Please," Hood said. "Don't make yourself absurd."

Flushing, LeConte stammered, "I'm doing the best I can, summoned out of my bed in the middle of the night."

There was a stir, and through the office doorway came the rapidly moving figure of Otto Dietrich, looking grim. "Hood," he said without preamble, "there's a *Times* kiosk near my headquarters. It just posted this." He held up a copy of the extra. "The damn thing is running this off and distributing it throughout the world, isn't it? However, we have crack teams up in that area and they report absolutely nothing, no roadblocks, no militia-style troops on the move, no activity of any sort."

"I know," Hood said. He felt weary. And still, from beneath them, the deep rumble continued, the newspaper printing its extra, informing the world of the march by Benny Cemoli's supporters on New York City—a fantasy march, evidently, a product manufactured entirely within the cephalon of the newspaper itself.

"Shut it off," Dietrich said.

Hood shook his head. "No. I want to know more."

"That's no reason," Dietrich said. "Obviously it's defective. Very seriously damaged, not working properly. You'll have to search elsewhere for your worldwide propaganda network." He tossed the newspaper down on Hood's desk.

To LeConte, Hood said, "Was Benny Cemoli active before the war?"

There was silence. Both LeConte and his assistant, Mr. Fall, were pale and tense; they faced him tight-lipped, glancing at each other.

"I am not much for police matters," Hood said to Dietrich, "but I think you could reasonably step in here."

Dietrich, understanding, said, "I agree. You two men are under arrest. Unless you feel inclined to talk a little more freely about this agitator in the red toga." He nodded to two of his police, who stood by the office doorway; they stepped obediently forward.

As the two policemen came up to him, LeConte said, "Come to think of it, there was such a person. But—he was very obscure."

"Before the war?" Hood asked.

"Yes." LeConte nodded slowly. "He was a joke. As I recall, and it's difficult . . . a fat, ignorant clown from some backwoods area. He had a little radio station or something over which he broadcast. He peddled some sort of antiradiation box which you installed in your house, and it made you safe from bomb-test fallout."

Now his staff member, Mr. Fall, said, "I remember. He even ran for the UN senate. But he was defeated, naturally."

"And that was the last of him?" Hood asked.

"Oh, yes," LeConte said. "He died of Asian flu soon after. He's been dead for fifteen years."

In a helicopter, Hood flew slowly above the terrain depicted in the *Times* articles, seeing for himself that there was no sign of political activity. He did not feel really assured until he had seen with his own eyes that the newspaper had lost contact with actual events. The reality of the situation did not coincide with the *Times* articles in any way; that was obvious. And yet—the homeostatic system continued on.

Joan, seated beside him, said, "I have the third article here, if you want to read it." She had been looking the latest edition over.

"No," Hood said.

"It says they're in the outskirts of the city," she said. "They broke through the police barricades and the governor has appealed for UN assistance."

Thoughtfully, Fletcher said, "Here's an idea. One of us, preferably you, Hood, should write a letter to the *Times*."

Hood glanced at him.

"I think I can tell you exactly how it should be worded," Fletcher said. "Make it a simple inquiry. You've followed the accounts in the paper about Cemoli's movement. Tell the editor"—Fletcher paused—"that you feel sympathetic *and you'd like to join the movement*. Ask the paper how."

To himself, Hood thought, In other words, ask the newspaper to put me in touch with Cemoli. He had to admire Fletcher's idea. It was brilliant, in a crazy sort of way. It was as if Fletcher had been able to match the derangement of the newspaper by a deliberate shift from common sense on his own part. He would participate in the newspaper's delusion. Assuming there was a Cemoli and a march on New York, he was asking a reasonable question.

Joan said, "I don't want to sound stupid, but how does one go about mailing a letter to a homeopape?"

"I've looked into that," Fletcher said. "At each kiosk set up by the paper there's a letter slot, next to the coin slot where you pay for your paper. It was the law, when the homeopapes were set up originally, decades ago. All we need is your husband's signature." Reaching into his jacket, he brought out an envelope. "The letter's written."

Hood took the letter, examined it. So we desire to be part of the mythical fat clown's throng, he said to himself. "Won't there be a headline reading 'CURB Chief Joins March on Earth Capital'?" he asked Fletcher, feeling a trace of wry amusement. "Wouldn't a good, enterprising homeopape make front-page use of a letter such as this?"

Obviously Fletcher had not thought of that; he looked chagrined. "I suppose we had better get someone else to sign it," he admitted. "Some minor person attached to your staff." He added, "I could sign it myself."

Handing him the letter back, Hood said, "Do so. It'll be interesting to see what response, if any, there is." Letters to the editor, he thought. Letters to a vast, complex, electronic organism buried deep in the ground, responsible to no one, guided solely by its own ruling circuits. How would it react to this external ratification of its delusion? Would the newspaper be snapped back to reality?

It was, he thought, as if the newspaper, during these years of its enforced silence, had been dreaming, and now, reawakened, it had allowed portions of its former dreams to materialize in its pages along with its accurate, perceptive accounts of the actual situation. A blend of figments and sheer, stark reporting. Which ultimately would triumph? Soon, evidently, the unfolding story of Benny Cemoli would have the toga-wearing spellbinder in New York; it appeared that the march would succeed. And what then? How could this be squared with the arrival of CURB, with all its enormous inter-system authority and power? Surely the homeopape, before long, would have to face the incongruity.

One of the two accounts would have to cease ... but Hood had an uneasy intuition that a homeopape which had dreamed for a decade would not readily give up its fantasies.

Perhaps, he thought, the news of us, of CURB and its task of rebuilding Earth, will fade from the pages of the *Times*, will be given steadily decreasing coverage each day, farther back in the paper. And at last only the exploits of Benny Cemoli will remain.

It was not a pleasant anticipation. It disturbed him deeply. As if, he thought, we are real only so long as the *Times* writes about us; as if we were dependent for our existence on it.

Twenty-four hours later, in its regular edition, the *Times* printed Fletcher's letter. In print it struck Hood as flimsy and contrived—surely the homeopape could not be taken in by it, and yet here it was. It had managed to pass each of the steps in the pape's processing.

Dear Editor:
    Your coverage of the heroic march on the decadent plutocratic stronghold of New York City has fired my enthusiasm. How does an ordinary citizen become a part of this history in the making? Please inform me at once, as I am eager to join Cemoli and endure the rigors and triumphs with the others.

Cordially,
Rudolf Fletcher

Beneath the letter, the homeopape had given an answer; Hood read it rapidly.

Cemoli's stalwarts maintain a recruiting office in downtown New York; address, 460 Bleekman St., New York 32. You might apply there, if the police haven't cracked down on these quasi-legal activities, in view of the current crisis.

Touching a button on his desk, Hood opened the direct line to police headquarters. When he had the chief investigator, he said, "Dietrich, I'd like a team of your men; we have a trip to make and there may be difficulties."

After a pause Dietrich said drily, "So it's not all noble reclamation after all. Well, we've already dispatched a man to keep an eye on the Bleekman Street address. I admire your letter scheme. It may have done the trick." He chuckled.

Shortly, Hood and four black-uniformed Centaurian policemen flew by 'copter above the ruins of New York City, searching for the remains of what had once been Bleekman Street. By the use of a map they managed after half an hour to locate themselves.

"There," the police captain in charge of the team said, pointing. "That would be it, that building used as a grocery store." The 'copter began to lower.

It was a grocery store, all right. Hood saw no signs of political activity, no persons loitering, no flags or banners. And yet— something ominous seemed to lie behind the commonplace scene below, the bins of vegetables parked out on the sidewalk, the shabby women in long cloth coats who stood picking over the winter potatoes, the elderly proprietor with his white cloth apron, sweeping with his broom. It was too natural, too easy. It was *too* ordinary.

"Shall we land?" the police captain asked him.

"Yes," Hood said. "And be ready."

The proprietor, seeing them land in the street before his grocery store, laid his broom carefully to one side and walked toward them. He was, Hood saw, a Greek. He had a heavy mustache and slightly wavy gray hair, and he gazed at them with innate caution, knowing at once that they did not intend him any good. Yet he had decided to greet them with civility; he was not afraid of them.

"Gentlemen," the Greek grocery store owner said, bowing slightly. "What can I do for you?" His eyes roved speculatively over the black Centaurian police uniforms, but he showed no expression, no reaction.

Hood said, "We've come to arrest a political agitator. You have nothing to be alarmed about." He started toward the grocery store; the team of police followed, their sidearms drawn.

"Political agitation here?" the Greek said. "Come on. It is impossible." He hurried after them, panting, alarmed now. "What have I done? Nothing at all; you can look around. Go ahead." He held open the door of the store, ushering them inside. "See right away for yourself."

"That's what we intend to do," Hood said. He moved with agility, wasting no time on the conspicuous portions of the store; he strode directly on through.

The back room lay ahead, the warehouse with its cartons of cans, cardboard boxes stacked up on every side. A young boy was busy making a stock inventory; he glanced up, startled, as they entered. Nothing here, Hood thought. The owner's son at work, that's all. Lifting the lid of a carton, Hood peered inside. Cans of peaches. And beside that, a crate of lettuce. He tore off a leaf, feeling futile and—disappointed.

The police captain said to him in a low voice, "Nothing, sir."

"I see that," Hood said irritably.

A door to the right led to a closet. Opening it, he saw brooms and a mop, a galvanized pail, boxes of detergents. And—

There were drops of paint on the floor.

The closet, sometime recently, had been repainted. When he bent down and scratched with his nail, he found the paint still tacky.

"Look at this," he said, beckoning the police captain over.

421

The Greek said nervously, "What's the matter, gentlemen? You find something dirty and report to the board of health, is that it? Customers have complained—tell me the truth, please. Yes, it is fresh paint. We keep everything spick and span. Isn't that in the public interest?"

Running his hands across the wall of the broom closet, the police captain said quietly, "Mr. Hood, there was a doorway here. Sealed up now, very recently." He looked expectantly toward Hood, awaiting instructions.

Hood said, "Let's go in."

Turning to his subordinates, the police captain gave a series of orders. From the ship, equipment was dragged through the store to the closet; a controlled whine arose as the police began the task of cutting into the wood and plaster.

Pale, the Greek said, "This is outrageous. I will sue."

"Right," Hood agreed. "Take us to court." Already a portion of the wall had given way. It fell inward with a crash, and bits of rubble spilled down onto the floor. A white cloud of dust rose, then settled.

It was not a large room which Hood saw in the glare of the police flashlights. Dusty, without windows, smelling stale and ancient . . . the room had not been inhabited for a long, long time, he realized as he warily entered. It was empty. Just an abandoned storeroom of some kind, its wooden walls scaling and dingy. Perhaps before the Misfortune the grocery store had possessed a larger inventory. More stocks had been available then, but now this room was not needed. Hood moved about, flashing his beam of light up to the ceiling and then down to the floor. Dead flies, entombed here . . . and, he saw, a few live ones which crept haltingly in the dust.

"Remember," the police captain said, "it was boarded up just now, within the last three days. Or at least the painting was just now done, to be absolutely accurate about it."

"These flies," Hood said. "They're not even dead yet." So it had not even been three days. Probably the boarding-up had been done yesterday.

What had this room been used for? He turned to the Greek, who had come after them, still tense and pale, his dark eyes flickering rapidly with concern. This is a smart man, Hood realized. We will get little out of him.

At the far end of the storeroom the police flashlights picked out a cabinet, empty shelves of bare, rough wood. Hood walked toward it.

"Okay," the Greek said thickly, swallowing. "I admit it. We have kept bootleg gin stored here. We became scared. You Centaurians—" He looked around at them all with fear. "You're not like our local bosses; we know them, they understand us. You! You can't be reached. But we have to make a living." He spread his hands, appealing to them.

From behind the cabinet the edge of something protruded. Barely visible, it might never have been noticed. A paper which had fallen there, almost out of sight; it had slipped down farther and farther. Now Hood took hold of it and carefully drew it out. Back up the way it had come.

The Greek shuddered.

It was, Hood saw, a picture. A heavy, middle-aged man with loose jowls stained black by the grained beginnings of a beard, frowning, his lips set in defiance. A big man, wearing some kind of uniform. Once this picture had hung on the wall and people had come here and looked at it, paid respect to it. He knew who it was. This was Benny Cemoli at the height of his political career, the leader glaring bitterly at the followers who had gathered here. So this was the man.

No wonder the *Times* showed such alarm.

To the Greek grocery store owner, Hood said, holding up the picture, "Tell me. Is this familiar to you?"

"No, no," the Greek said. He wiped perspiration from his face with a large red handkerchief. "Certainly not." But obviously it was.

Hood said, "You're a follower of Cemoli, aren't you?"

There was silence.

"Take him along," Hood said to the police captain. "And let's start back." He walked from the room, carrying the picture with him.

As he spread the picture out on his desk, Hood thought, It isn't merely a fantasy of the *Times*. We know the truth now. The man is real and twenty-four hours ago this portrait of him hung on a wall, in plain sight. It would still be there this moment, if CURB had not put in its appearance. We frightened them. The Earth people have a lot to hide from us, and they know it. They are taking steps, rapidly and effectively, and we will be lucky if we can—

Interrupting his thoughts, Joan said, "Then the Bleekman Street address really was a meeting place for them. The pape was correct."

"Yes," Hood said.

"Where is he now?"

I wish we knew, Hood thought.

"Has Dietrich seen the picture yet?"

"Not yet," Hood said.

Joan said, "He was responsible for the war, and Dietrich is going to find it out."

"No one man," Hood said, "could solely be responsible."

"But he figured largely," Joan said. "That's why they've gone to so much effort to eradicate all traces of his existence."

Hood nodded.

"Without the *Times*," she said, "would we ever have guessed that such a political figure as Benny Cemoli existed? We owe a lot to the pape. They overlooked it or weren't able to get to it. Probably they were working in such haste, they couldn't think of everything, even in ten years. It must be hard to obliterate *every* surviving detail of a planet-wide political movement, especially when its leader managed to seize absolute power in the final phase."

"Impossible to obliterate," Hood said. A closed-off storeroom in the back of a Greek grocery store . . . that was enough to tell us what we needed to know. Now Dietrich's men can do the rest. If Cemoli is alive they will eventually find him, and if he's dead— they'll be hard to convince, knowing Dietrich. They'll never stop looking now.

"One good thing about this," Joan said, "is that now a lot

424

of innocent people will be off the hook. Dietrich won't go around prosecuting them. He'll be busy tracking down Cemoli."

True, Hood thought. And that was important. The Centaurian police would be thoroughly occupied for a long time to come, and that was just as well for everyone, including CURB and its ambitious program of reconstruction.

If there had never been a Benny Cemoli, he thought suddenly, it would almost have been necessary to invent him. An odd thought . . . he wondered how it had happened to come to him. Again he examined the picture, trying to infer as much as possible about the man from this flat likeness. How had Cemoli sounded? Had he gained power through the spoken word, like so many demagogues before him? And his writing—maybe some of it would turn up. Or even tape recordings of speeches he had made, the actual *sound* of the man. And perhaps video tapes as well. Eventually it would all come to light; it was only a question of time. And then we will be able to experience for ourselves how it was to live under the shadow of such a man, he realized.

The line from Dietrich's office buzzed. He picked up the phone.

"We have the Greek here," Dietrich said. "Under drug-guidance he's made a number of admissions; you may be interested."

"Yes," Hood said.

Dietrich said, "He tells us he's been a follower for seventeen years, a real old-timer in the Movement. They met twice a week in the back of his grocery store, in the early days when the Movement was small and relatively powerless. That picture you have—I haven't seen it, of course, but Stavros, our Greek gentleman, told me about it—that portrait is actually obsolete in the sense that several more recent ones have been in vogue among the faithful for some time now. Stavros hung on to it for sentimental reasons. It reminded him of the old days. Later on, when the Movement grew in strength, Cemoli stopped showing up at the grocery store, and the Greek lost out in any personal contact with him. He continued to be a loyal, dues-paying member, but it became abstract for him."

"What about the war?" Hood asked.

"Shortly before the war, Cemoli seized power in a coup here in North America, through a march on New York City, during a severe economic depression. Millions were unemployed and he drew a good deal of support from them. He tried to solve the economic problems through an aggressive foreign policy—attacked several Latin American republics which were in the sphere of influence of the Chinese. That seems to be it, but Stavros is a bit hazy about the big picture . . . we'll have to fill in more from other enthusiasts as we go along. From some of the younger ones. After all, this one is over seventy years old."

Hood said, "You're not going to prosecute him, I hope."

"Oh, no. He's simply a source of information. When he's told us all he has on his mind, we'll let him go back to his onions and canned applesauce. He's harmless."

"Did Cemoli survive the war?"

"Yes," Dietrich said. "But that was ten years ago. Stavros doesn't know if the man is still alive now. Personally I think he is, and we'll go on that assumption until it's proved false. We have to."

Hood thanked him and hung up.

As he turned from the phone he heard, beneath him, the low, dull rumbling. The homeopape had once more started into life.

"It's not a regular edition," Joan said, quickly consulting her wristwatch. "So it must be another extra. This is exciting, having it happen like this; I can't wait to read the front page."

What has Benny Cemoli done now? Hood wondered. According to the *Times*, in its misphased chronicling of the man's epic . . . what stage, actually taking place years ago, has now been reached? Something climactic, deserving of an extra. It will be interesting, no doubt of that. The *Times* knows what is fit to print.

He, too, could hardly wait.

━━━━━━

In downtown Oklahoma City, John LeConte put a coin into the slot of the kiosk which the *Times* had long ago established there. The copy of the *Times*'s latest extra slid out, and he picked it up and read the headline briefly, spending only a moment on it to verify the essentials. Then he crossed the sidewalk and stepped once more into the rear seat of his chauffeur-driven steam car.

Mr. Fall said circumspectly, "Sir, here is the primary material, if you wish to make a word-by-word comparison." The secretary held out the folder, and LeConte accepted it.

The car started up. Without being told, the chauffeur drove in the direction of Party headquarters. LeConte leaned back, lit a cigar, and made himself comfortable.

On his lap, the newspaper blazed up its enormous headlines.

CEMOLI ENTERS COALITION UN GOVERNMENT; TEMPORARY CESSATION OF HOSTILITIES

To his secretary, LeConte said, "My phone, please."

"Yes sir." Mr. Fall handed him the portable field-phone. "But we're almost there. And it's always possible, if you don't mind my pointing it out, that they may have tapped us somewhere along the line."

"They're busy in New York," LeConte said. "Among the ruins." In an area that hasn't mattered as long as I can remember, he said to himself. However, possibly Mr. Fall's advice was good; he decided to skip the phone call. "What do you think of this last item?" he asked his secretary, holding up the newspaper.

"Very success-deserving," Mr. Fall said, nodding.

Opening his briefcase, LeConte brought out a tattered, coverless textbook. It had been manufactured only an hour ago, and it was the next artifact to be planted for the invaders from Proxima Centauri to discover. This was his own contribution, and he was personally quite proud of it. The book outlined in massive detail Cemoli's program of social change, the revolution depicted in language comprehensible to schoolchildren.

"May I ask," Mr. Fall said, "if the Party hierarchy intends for them to discover a corpse?"

"Eventually," LeConte said. "But that will be several months from now." Taking a pencil from his coat pocket, he wrote in the tattered textbook, crudely, as if a pupil had done it:

DOWN WITH CEMOLI

Or was that going too far? No, he decided. There would be resistance. Certainly of the spontaneous, schoolboy variety. He added:

WHERE ARE THE ORANGES?

Peering over his shoulder, Mr. Fall said, "What does that mean?"

"Cemoli promises oranges to the youth," LeConte explained. "Another empty boast which the revolution never fulfills. That was Stavros' idea . . . he being a grocer. A nice touch." Giving it, he thought, just that much more semblance of verisimilitude. It's the little touches that have done it.

"Yesterday," Mr. Fall said, "when I was at Party headquarters, I heard an audio tape that had been made. Cemoli addressing the UN. It was uncanny; if you didn't know—"

"Who did they get to do it?" LeConte asked, wondering why he hadn't been in on it.

"Some nightclub entertainer here in Oklahoma City. Rather obscure, of course. I believe he specializes in all sorts of characterizations. The fellow gave it a bombastic, threatening quality . . . I must admit I enjoyed it."

And meanwhile, LeConte thought, *there are no war-crimes trials.* We who were leaders during the war, on Earth and on Mars, we who held responsible posts—we are safe, at least for a while. And perhaps it will be forever. If our strategy continues to work. And if our tunnel to the cephalon of the homeopape,

428

which took us five years to complete, isn't discovered. Or doesn't collapse.

The steam car parked in the reserved space before Party headquarters; the chauffeur came around to open the door, and LeConte got leisurely out, stepping forth into the light of day, with no feeling of anxiety. He tossed his cigar into the gutter and then sauntered across the sidewalk, into the familiar building.

THE MONKEY WRENCH

GORDON R. DICKSON

(1 9 5 1)

Computers and satellites used in combination can produce all kinds of previously unavailable scientific data. Science satellites have been utilized for a variety of tasks, from solar and astronomical observations to biological experiments, but no information has been as immediately useful as that collected by weather satellites.

The first satellite of any kind, the Russian Sputnik I, orbited Earth in 1957. America followed with Explorer I in 1958. The speed of the early advances in the field was incredible. In 1960 the satellite Tiros I sent back the first global cloud-cover picture to meteorologists, and a new age in weather forecasting began. In 1962 John Glenn orbited Earth.

Gordon Dickson starts with a weather station in space, adds that favorite puzzle of mathematicians, Zeno's Paradox, stirs vigorously with his imagination, and the result is "The Monkey Wrench." Dickson was born in Canada in 1923 and currently lives in Minneapolis. He is the author of the frequently anthologized "Computers Don't Argue" (1965). He has been a free-lance writer for more than thirty years and is the winner of three Hugos and one Nebula.

Could the fate of the computer in this story really happen? Well, the computer might go into a continuous loop. But we could always turn it off and start all over again.

CARY HARMON was not an ungifted young man. He had the intelligence to carve himself a position as a Lowland society lawyer, which on Venus is not easy to do. And he had the discernment to consolidate that position by marrying into the family of one of the leading drug exporters. Nevertheless, from the scientific viewpoint, he was a layman; and laymen, in their ignorance, should never be allowed to play with delicate technical equipment; for the result will be trouble, as surely as it is the first time a baby gets its hands on a match.

His wife was a high-spirited woman, and would have been hard to handle at times if it had not been for the fact that she

430

was foolish enough to love him. Since he did not love her at all, it was consequently both simple and practical to terminate all quarrels by dropping out of sight for several days until her obvious fear of losing him for good brought her to a proper humility. He took good care, each time he disappeared, to pick some new and secure hiding place where past experience or her several years' knowledge of his habits would be no help in locating him. Actually, he enjoyed thinking up new and undiscoverable bolt-holes, and made a hobby out of discovering them.

Consequently, he was in high spirits the gray winter afternoon he descended unannounced on the weather station of Burke McIntyre, high in the Lonesome Mountains, a jagged chain of the deserted shorelands of Venus's Northern Sea. He had beaten a blizzard to the dome with minutes to spare; and now, with his small two-place flier safely stowed away, and a meal of his host's best supplies under his belt, he sat reveling in the comfort of his position and listening to the hundred-and-fifty-mile-per-hour, subzero winds lashing impotently at the arching roof overhead.

"Ten minutes more," he said to Burke, "and I'd have had a tough time making it!"

"Tough!" snorted Burke. He was a big, heavy-featured blond man with a kindly contempt for all of humanity aside from the favored class of meteorologists. "You Lowlanders are too used to that present-day Garden of Eden you have down below. Ten minutes more and you'd have been spread over one of the peaks around here to wait for the spring searching party to gather your bones."

Cary laughed in disbelief.

"Try it, if you don't believe me," said Burke. "No skin off my nose if you don't have the sense to listen to reason. Take your bug up right now if you want."

"Not me." Cary's teeth flashed. "I know when I'm comfortable. And that's no way to treat your guest, tossing him out into the storm when he's just arrived."

"Some guest," rumbled Burke. "I shake hands with you after the graduation exercises, don't hear a word from you for six years, and then suddenly you're knocking at my door here in the hinterland."

"I came on impulse," said Cary. "It's the prime rule of my life. Always act on impulse, Burke. It puts the sparkle in existence."

"And leads you to an early grave," Burke supplemented.

"If you have the wrong impulses," said Cary. "But then if you get sudden urges to jump off cliffs or play Russian roulette, you're too stupid to live, anyway."

"Cary," said Burke heavily, "you're a shallow thinker."

"And you're a stodgy one," grinned Cary. "Suppose you quit insulting me and tell me something about yourself. What's this hermit's existence of yours like? What do you do?"

"What do I do?" repeated Burke. "I work."

"But just how?" Cary said, settling himself cozily back into his chair. "Do you send up balloons? Catch snow in a pail to find how much fell? Take sights on the stars? Or what?"

Burke shook his head at him and smiled tolerantly.

"Well, if you insist on my talking to entertain you," he answered, "I don't do anything so picturesque. I just sit at a desk and prepare weather data for transmission to the Weather Center down at Capital City."

"Aha!" Cary said, waggling a forefinger at him in reproof. "I've got you now. You've been lying down on the job. You're the only one here; so if you don't take observations, who does?"

"The machine does, of course. These stations have a Brain to do that."

"That's worse," Cary answered. "You've been sitting here warm and comfortable while some poor little Brain scurries around outside in the snow and does all your work for you."

"As a matter of fact, you're closer to the truth than you think; and it wouldn't do you any harm to learn a few things about the mechanical miracles that let you lead a happy, ignorant life. Some wonderful things have been done lately in the way of equipping these stations."

Cary smiled mockingly.

"I mean it," Burke went on, his face lighting. "The Brain

we've got here now is the last word in that type of installation. As a matter of fact, it was just put in recently—until a few months back we had to work with a job that was just a collector and computer. That is, it collected the weather data around this station and presented it to you. Then you had to take it and prepare it for the calculator, which would chew on it for a while and then pass you back results which you again had to prepare for transmission downstairs to the Center."

"Fatiguing, I'm sure," murmured Cary, reaching for the drink placed handily on the table beside his chair. Burke ignored him, caught up in his own appreciation of the mechanical development about which he was talking.

"It kept you busy, for the data came in steadily; and you were always behind, since a batch would be accumulating while you were working up the previous batch. A station like this is the center-point for observational mechs posted at points over more than five hundred square miles of territory; and, being human, all you had time to do was skim the cream off the reports and submit a sketchy picture to the calculator. And then there was a certain responsibility involved in taking care of the station and yourself.

"But now"—Burke leaned forward and stabbed a finger at his visitor—"we've got a new installation that takes the data directly from the observational mechs—all of it—resolves it into the proper form for the calculator to handle it, and carries it right on through to the end results. All I still have to do is prepare the complete picture from the results and shoot it downstairs.

"In addition, it runs the heating and lighting plants, automatically checks on the maintenance of the station. It makes repairs and corrections on verbal command and has a whole separate section for the consideration of theoretical problems."

"Sort of a little tin god," said Cary nastily. He was used to attention and annoyed that Burke seemed to be waxing more rhapsodic over his machine than over the brilliant and entertaining guest who, as far as the meteorologist could know, had dropped in to relieve a hermit's existence.

Burke looked at him and chuckled.

"No," he replied. "A *big* tin god, Cary."

"Sees all, knows all, tells all, I suppose. Never makes a mistake. Infallible."

"You might say that," answered Burke, still with a grin on his face.

"But those qualities alone don't quite suffice for elevating your gadget to godhood. One all-important attribute is lacking—invulnerability. Gods never break down."

"Neither does this."

"Come now, Burke," chided Cary, "you mustn't let your enthusiasm lead you into falsehood. No machine is perfect. A crossed couple of wires, a burnt-out tube, and where is your darling? Plunk! Out of action."

Burke shook his head.

"There aren't any wires," he said. "It uses beamed connections. And as for burnt-out tubes, they don't even halt consideration of a problem. The problem is just shifted over to a bank that isn't in use at the time; and automatic repairs are made by the machine itself. You see, Cary, in this model, no bank does one specific job, alone. Any one of them—and there are twenty, half again as many as this station would ever need—can do any job, from running the heating plant to operating the calculator. If something comes up that's too big for one bank to handle, it just hooks in one or more of the idle banks—and so on until it's capable of dealing with the situation."

"Ah," said Cary, "but what if something *did* come up that required all the banks and more, too? Wouldn't it overload them and burn itself out?"

"You're determined to find fault with it, aren't you, Cary?" answered Burke. "The answer is no. It wouldn't. Theoretically it's possible for the machine to bump into a problem that would require all or more than all of its banks to handle. For example, if this station suddenly popped into the air and started to fly away for no discernible reason, the bank that first felt the situation would keep reaching out for help until all the banks were engaged in considering it, until it crowded out all the other functions the machine performs. But even then, it wouldn't overload and burn out. The banks would just go on considering the problem until they had evolved a theory that explained why we were flying through the air and what to do about returning us to our proper place and functions."

Cary straightened up and snapped his fingers.

"Then it's simple," he said. "I'll just go in and tell your machine—on the verbal hookup—that we're flying through the air."

Burke gave a sudden roar of laughter.

"Cary, you dope!" he said. "Don't you think the men who designed the machine took the possibility of verbal error into account? You say that the station is flying through the air. The machine immediately checks by making its own observations; and it politely replies, 'Sorry, your statement is incorrect,' and forgets the whole thing."

Cary's eyes narrowed and two spots of color flushed the skin over his cheekbones; but he held his smile.

"There's the theoretical section," he murmured.

"There is," said Burke, greatly enjoying himself, "and you could use it by going in and saying, 'Consider the false statement or data—this station is flying through the air,' and the machine would go right to work on it."

He paused, and Cary looked at him expectantly.

"But—" continued the meteorologist, "it would consider the statement with only those banks not then in use; and it would give up the banks whenever a section using real data required them."

He finished, looking at Cary with quizzical good humor. But Cary said nothing.

"Give up, Cary," he said at last. "It's no use. Neither God nor man nor Cary Harmon can interrupt my Brain in the rightful performance of its duty."

Cary's eyes glittered, dark and withdrawn beneath their lids. For a long second he just sat and looked, and then he spoke.

"I could do it," he said softly.

"Do what?" asked Burke.

"I could gimmick your machine," said Cary.

"Oh, forget it! Don't take things so seriously, Cary. What if you can't think of a monkey wrench to throw into the machinery? Nobody else could, either."

"I said I could do it."

"Once and for all, it's impossible. Now stop trying to pick flaws in something guaranteed flawless and let's talk about something else."

"I will bet you," said Cary, speaking with slow intensity, "five thousand credits that if you will leave me alone with your machine for one minute I can put it completely out of order."

"I don't want to take your money, even if five thousand *is* the equivalent of a year's salary for me. The trouble with you is, Cary, you never could stand to lose at anything. Now forget it!"

"Put up or shut up," said Cary.

Burke took a deep breath.

"Now look," he said, the beginning of anger rumbling in his deep voice. "Maybe I did wrong to needle you about the machine. But you've got to get over the idea that I can be bullied into admitting that you're right. You've got no conception of the technology that's behind the machine, and no idea of how certain I am that you, at least, can't do anything to interfere with its operation. You think that there's a slight element of doubt in my mind and that you can bluff me out by proposing an astronomical bet. Then, if I won't bet, you'll tell yourself you've won. Now listen, I'm not just ninety-nine point nine, nine, nine, nine percent sure of myself. I'm one hundred percent sure of myself and the reason I won't bet you is that it would be robbery; and besides, once you'd lost, you'd hate me for winning for the rest of your life."

"The bet still stands," said Cary.

"All right!" roared Burke, jumping to his feet. "If you want to force the issue, suit yourself. It's a bet."

Cary grinned, got up, and followed him out of the pleasant, spacious sitting room, where lamps dispelled the gloom of the snow-laden sky beyond the windows, and into a short, metal-walled corridor where ceiling tubes blazed. They followed this for a short distance to a room where the wall facing the corridor and the door set in it were all of glass.

Here Burke halted.

"There's the machine," he said, pointing through the transparency of the wall and turning to Cary behind him. "If you want to communicate with it verbally, you speak into that grille there. The calculator is to your right, and that inner door leads down to the room housing the lighting and heating plants. But if you're thinking of physical sabotage, you might as well give up. The lighting and heating systems don't even have emergency manual controls. They're run by a little atomic pile that only the machine can be trusted to handle—that is, except for an automatic setup that damps the pile in case lightning strikes the machine or some such thing. And you couldn't get through the shielding in a week. As for breaking through to the machine up here, that panel in which the grille is set is made of two-inch thick steel sheets with their edges flowed together under pressure."

"I assure you," said Cary, "I don't intend to damage a thing."

Burke looked at him sharply, but there was no hint of sarcasm in the smile that twisted the other's lips.

"All right," he said, stepping back from the door. "Go ahead. Can I wait here, or do you have to have me out of sight?"

"Oh, by all means watch," said Cary. "We machine-gimmickers have nothing to hide." He turned mockingly to Burke, and lifted his arms. "See? Nothing up my right sleeve. Nothing up my left."

"Go on," interrupted Burke roughly. "Get it over with. I want to get back to my drink."

"At once," said Cary, and went in through the door, closing it behind him.

Through the transparent wall, Burke watched him approach the panel in line with the speaker grille and stop some two feet in front of it. Having arrived at this spot, he became utterly motionless, his back to Burke, his shoulders hanging relaxed and his hands motionless at his sides. For the good part of a minute, Burke strained his eyes to discover what action was going on under the guise of Cary's apparent immobility. Then an understanding struck him and he laughed.

"Why," he said to himself, "he's bluffing right up to the last minute, hoping I'll get worried and rush in there and stop him."

Relaxed, he lit a cigarette and looked at his watch. Some forty-five seconds to go. In less than a minute, Cary would be coming out, forced at last to admit defeat—that is, unless he had evolved some fantastic argument to prove that defeat was really victory.

Burke frowned. It was almost pathological, the way Cary had always refused to admit the superiority of anyone or anything else; and unless some way was found to soothe him, he would be a very unpleasant companion for the remaining days that the storm held him marooned with Burke. It would be literally murder to force him to take off in the tornado-velocity winds and a temperature that must be in the minus-sixties by this time. At the same time, it went against the meteorologist's grain to crawl for the sake of congeniality. . . .

The vibration of the generator, half-felt through the floor and the soles of his shoes, and familiar as the motion of his own lungs, ceased abruptly. The fluttering streamers fixed to the ventilator grille above his head ceased their colorful dance and dropped limply as the rush of air that had carried them ceased. The lights dimmed and went out, leaving only the gray and ghostly light from the thick windows at each end of the corridor to illuminate the passage and the room. The cigarette dropped unheeded from Burke's fingers and in two strides he was at the door and through it.

"What have you done?" he snapped at Cary.

The other looked mockingly at him, walked across to the nearer wall of the room, and leaned his shoulder negligently against it.

"That's for you to find out," he said.

"Don't be insane—" began the meteorologist. Then, checking himself like a man who has no time to lose, he whirled on the panel and gave his attention to the instruments on its surface.

The pile was damped. The ventilating system was shut off,

the electrical system was dead. Only the power in the storage cells of the machine itself was available, for the operating light still glowed redly on the panel. The great outside doors, wide enough to permit the ingress and exit of a two-man flier, were closed, and would remain that way, for they required power to open or close them. Visio, radio, and teletype were alike silent and lifeless through lack of power.

But the machine still operated.

Burke stepped to the grille and pressed the red alarm button below it twice.

"Attention," he said. "The pile is damped and all fixtures besides yourself lack power. Why is this?"

There was no response, though the red light continued to glow industriously on the panel.

"Obstinate little rascal, isn't it?" said Cary from the wall.

Burke ignored him, punching the button again.

"Reply!" he ordered. "Reply at once! What is the difficulty? Why is the pile not operating?"

There was no answer.

He turned to the calculator and played his fingers expertly over the buttons. Fed from the stored power within the machine, the punched tape rose in a fragile white arc and disappeared through a slot in the panel. He finished his punching and waited.

There was no answer.

For a long moment he stood staring at the calculator as if unable to believe that the machine had failed him. Then he turned and faced Cary.

"What have you done?"

"Do you admit you were wrong?" Cary demanded.

"Yes."

"And do I win the bet?" persisted Cary gleefully.

"Yes."

"Then I'll tell you," the lawyer said. He put a cigarette between his lips and puffed it alight, then blew out a long streamer of smoke that billowed and hung in the still air of the room, which, lacking heat from the blowers, was cooling rapidly. "This fine little gadget of yours may be all very well at meteorology, but it's not very good at logic. Shocking situation, when you consider the close relation between mathematics and logic."

"What did you do?"

"I'll get to it," said Cary. "As I say, it's a shocking situation. Here is this infallible machine of yours, worth, I suppose, several million credits, beating its brains out over a paradox."

"A paradox!" The words from Burke were almost a sob.

"A paradox," sang Cary, "a most ingenious paradox." He switched back to his speaking voice. "Which is from Gilbert and Sullivan's *Pirates of Penzance*. It occurred to me when you were bragging earlier that while your friend here couldn't be damaged, it might be immobilized by giving it a problem too big for its mechanical brain cells to handle.

"I remembered a little thing from one of my prewar logic courses—an interesting little affair called Epimenides' Paradox. I don't remember just how it was originally phrased—those logic courses were dull, sleepy sort of businesses, anyway—but, for example, if I say to you 'all lawyers are liars,' how can you tell whether the statement is true or false, since I am a lawyer and, if it is true, I must be lying when I say that all lawyers are liars? But on the other hand, if I am lying, then all lawyers are not liars, and the statement is false, i.e. a lying statement. If the statement is false, it is true, and if true, false, and so on, so where are you?"

Cary broke off suddenly into a peal of laughter.

"You should see your own face, Burke," he shouted. "I never saw anything so bewildered in my life—anyway, I just changed this around and fed it to the machine. While you waited politely outside, I went up to the machine and said to it, 'You must reject the statement I am now making to you, because all the statements I make are incorrect.' "

He paused and looked at the meteorologist.

"Do you see, Burke? It took that statement of mine in and considered it for rejecting. But it could not reject it without admitting that it was correct, and how could it be correct when it stated that all statements I made were incorrect. You see . . . yes, you do see, I can see it in your face. Oh, if you could only look

440

at yourself now. The pride of the meteorology service, undone by a paradox."

And Cary went off into another fit of laughter that lasted for a long minute. Every time he started to recover, a look at Burke's face, set in lines of utter dismay, would set him off again. The meteorologist neither moved nor spoke, but stared at his guest as if he were a ghost.

Finally, weak from merriment, Cary started to sober up. Chuckling feebly, he leaned against the wall, took a deep breath, and straightened up. A shiver ran through him, and he turned up the collar of his tunic.

"Now that you know what the trick was, Burke, suppose you get your pet back to its proper duties again. It's getting too cold for comfort and that daylight coming through the windows isn't the most cheerful thing in the world, either."

But Burke made no move toward the panel. His eyes were fixed and they bored into Cary as unmovingly as before. Cary snickered a little at him.

"Come on, Burke," he said. "Man the pumps. You can recover from your shock afterwards. If it's the bet that bothers you, forget it. And if it's the failure of Baby here, don't feel too bad. It did better than I expected. I thought it would just blow a fuse and quit work altogether, but I see it's still busy and devoting every single bank to obtaining a solution. I should imagine that it's working toward evolving a theory of types. *That* would give it the solution. Probably could get it, too, in a year or so."

Still, Burke did not move. Cary looked at him oddly.

"What's wrong?" he asked irritatedly.

Burke's mouth worked, a tiny speck of spittle flew from one corner of it.

"You—" he said. The word came tearing from his throat like the grunt of a dying man.

"What—"

"You fool!" ground out Burke, finding his voice. "You stupid idiot! You moron!"

"Me? Me?" cried Cary. His voice was high in protest. "I was right!"

"Yes, you were right," said Burke. "You were too right. How am I supposed to get the machine's mind off this problem and on to running the pile for heat and light, when all its circuits are taken up in considering your paradox? What can *I* do, when the Brain is deaf and dumb and blind?"

The two men looked at each other across the silent room. Their exhalations made frosty plumes in the air; and the distant howling of the storm, deadened by the thick walls of the station, seemed to grow louder in the silence, bearing a note of savage triumph.

The temperature inside the station was dropping fast.

DIAL F FOR FRANKENSTEIN

ARTHUR C. CLARKE

(1 9 6 5)

Computers linked together by telephone create a giant network for the processing, storing, and sending of information. From the beginning of computer research and development, Bell Telephone Laboratories were deeply involved because their research engineers saw the great potential of computers in the communications field. In 1951 Bell Laboratories developed the transistor, which made solid-state circuitry possible.

Until the 1980s, computers linked by telephone were owned only by government agencies and large corporations, given the high cost of such a system. But with the arrival of the microcomputer age, many homes now have personal computers. Probably by the end of this decade most homes will have acquired computers just as most homes by the end of the 1950s had acquired television sets. Even today, telephone linkage of a home computer to any other home or business computer or data base is possible and relatively inexpensive. The communication network described in "Dial F for Frankenstein" is at hand.

Arthur C. Clarke is a familiar figure to anyone interested in science fiction or the space program. He is the winner of three Hugo and three Nebula Awards; he covered the launching of Apollos 11, 12, and 15 for CBS television; and his novel *Childhood's End* is a classic. What is less well known about Clarke is that almost three decades ago, in 1945, long before almost anyone had thought seriously about satellites, Clarke published an article in a little radio magazine called *Wireless World* describing how instantaneous world communication could be made possible by placing three space stations in geostationary orbit 22,300 miles above the Earth. Messages would travel across oceans and rugged mountains not by wire, but by microwave from ground to satellite to satellite. INTELSAT, the International Telecommunication Satellite Organization, launched Early Bird in 1965, just twenty years later, and Clarke's vision became reality. The age of instant global communication had arrived. There is hardly a better example of the phenomenal speed of recent advances in communication and computer technology. Today our world is truly a wired one, and the possibility of improved international relations because of improved communication lies before us. The use of computers by the military may be demonic and terrifying, but before we condemn computers, we should study their use in communication systems. All kinds of beneficial uses have been made of communication satellites.

———

The reader ought not take too seriously the grim ending of this little story. Clarke's attitude toward technology has generally been cautiously optimistic, not negative as it appears to be here. He has great faith in man's future with technology, provided the race manages to avoid self-destruction.

Clarke graduated from King's College, London, with a degree in physics and mathematics, and has always shown a strong interest in the frontiers of science, particularly in the field of astronomy. He has twice been chairman of the British Interplanetary Society. Born in Somerset, England, in 1917, he has lived since 1956 in Sri Lanka. He has often written about undersea exploration, and this was one of the reasons for his move. In cybernetic fiction, Clarke is best known for *2001: A Space Odyssey* (1968), which he wrote first as a filmscript and later as a novel. But his finest novel in this field, and quite possibly the best novel he has ever written, is *The City and the Stars* (1956).

AT 0150 GREENWICH MEAN TIME on December 1, 1975, every telephone in the world started to ring. A quarter of a billion people picked up their receivers to listen for a few seconds with annoyance or perplexity. Those who had been awakened in the middle of the night assumed that some far-off friend was calling over the satellite telephone network that had gone into service, with such a blaze of publicity, the day before. But there was no voice on the line, only a sound that to many seemed like the roaring of the sea—to others, like the vibrations of harp strings in the wind. And there were many more, in that moment, who recalled a secret sound of childhood—the noise of blood pulsing through the veins, heard when a shell is cupped over the ear. Whatever it was, it lasted no more than twenty seconds; then it was replaced by the dialing tone.

The world's subscribers cursed, muttered, "Wrong number," and hung up. Some tried to dial a complaint, but the line seemed busy. In a few hours, everyone had forgotten the incident—except those whose duty it was to worry about such things.

At the Post Office Research Station, the argument had been going on all morning and had got nowhere. It continued unabated through the lunch break, when the hungry engineers poured into the little café across the road.

"I still think," said Willy Smith, the solid-state electronics

444

man, "that it was a temporary surge of current, caused when the satellite network was switched in."

"It was obviously *something* to do with the satellites," agreed Jules Reyner, circuit designer. "But why the time delay? They were plugged in at midnight; the ringing was two hours later—as we all know to our cost." He yawned violently.

"What do *you* think, Doc?" asked Bob Andrews, computer programmer. "You've been very quiet all morning. Surely you've got some idea?"

Dr. John Williams, head of the mathematics division, stirred uneasily.

"Yes," he said, "I have. But you won't take it seriously."

"That doesn't matter. Even if it's as crazy as those science fiction yarns you write under a pseudonym, it may give us some leads."

Williams blushed, but not very hard. Everyone knew about his stories, and he wasn't ashamed of them. After all, they *had* been collected in book form. (Remainder at five shillings; he still had a couple of hundred copies.)

"Very well," he said, doodling on the tablecloth. "This is something I've been wondering about for years. Have you ever considered the analogy between an automatic telephone exchange and the human brain?"

"Who hasn't thought of it?" scoffed one of his listeners. "That idea must go back to Graham Bell."

"Possibly; I never said it was original. But I do say it's time we started taking it seriously." He squinted balefully at the fluorescent tubes above the table; they were needed on this foggy winter day. "What's wrong with the damn lights? They've been flickering for the last five minutes."

"Don't bother about that; Maisie's probably forgotten to pay her electricity bill. Let's hear more about your theory."

"Most of it isn't theory; it's plain fact. We know that the human brain is a system of switches—neurons—interconnected in a very elaborate fashion by nerves. An automatic telephone exchange is also a system of switches—selectors, and so forth—connected together with wires."

"Agreed," said Smith. "But that analogy won't get you very far. Aren't there about fifteen billion neurons in the brain? That's a lot more than the number of switches in an autoexchange."

Williams's answer was interrupted by the scream of a low-flying jet; he had to wait until the café had ceased to vibrate before he could continue.

"Never heard them fly *that* low," Andrews grumbled. "Thought it was against regulations."

"So it is, but don't worry—London Airport Control will catch him."

"I doubt it," said Reyner. "That *was* London Airport, bringing in a Concorde on ground approach. But I've never heard one so low, either. Glad I wasn't aboard."

"Are we, or are we *not*, going to get on with this blasted discussion?" demanded Smith.

"You're right about the fifteen billion neurons in the human brain," continued Williams, unabashed. "And *that's* the whole point. Fifteen billion sounds a large number, but it isn't. Round about the 1960s, there were more than that number of individual switches in the world's autoexchanges. Today, there are approximately five times as many."

"I see," said Reyner very slowly. "And as of yesterday, they've all become capable of full interconnection, now that the satellite links have gone into service."

"Precisely."

There was silence for a moment, apart from the distant clanging of a fire-engine bell.

"Let me get this straight," said Smith. "Are you suggesting that the world telephone system is now a giant brain?"

"That's putting it crudely—anthropomorphically. I prefer to think of it in terms of critical size." Williams held his hands out in front of him, fingers partly closed.

"Here are two lumps of U-235; nothing happens as long as you keep them apart. But bring them together"—he suited the action to the words—"and you have something *very* different from one bigger lump of uranium. You have a hole half a mile across.

446

"It's the same with our telephone networks; until today they've been largely independent, autonomous. But now we've suddenly multiplied the connecting links—the networks have all merged together—and we've reached criticality."

"And just what does criticality mean in this case?" asked Smith.

"For want of a better word—consciousness."

"A weird sort of consciousness," said Reyner. "What would it use for sense organs?"

"Well, all the radio and TV stations in the world would be feeding information into it, through their landlines. *That* should give it something to think about! Then there would be all the data stored in all the computers; it would have access to that—and to the electronic libraries, the radar tracking systems, the telemetering in the automatic factories. Oh, it would have enough sense organs! We can't begin to imagine its picture of the world, but it would certainly be infinitely richer and more complex than ours."

"Granted all this, because it's an entertaining idea," said Reyner, "what could it *do* except think? It couldn't go anywhere; it would have no limbs."

"Why should it want to travel? It would already be everywhere! And every piece of remotely controlled electrical equipment on the planet could act as a limb."

"Now I understand that time delay," interjected Andrews. "It was conceived at midnight, but it wasn't born until one-fifty this morning. The noise that woke us all up was—its birth cry."

His attempt to sound facetious was not altogether convincing, and nobody smiled. Overhead, the lights continued their annoying flicker, which seemed to be getting worse. Then there was an interruption from the front of the café as Jim Small of Power Supplies made his usual boisterous entry.

"Look at this, fellows," he grinned, waving a piece of paper in front of his colleagues. "I'm rich. Ever seen a bank balance like *that*?"

Dr. Williams took the proffered statement, glanced down the columns, and read the balance aloud: "Credit £999,999,897.87.

447

"Nothing very odd about that," he continued above the general amusement. "I'd say it means the computer's made a slight mistake. That sort of thing was happening all the time just after the banks converted to the decimal system."

"I know, I know," said Jim, "but don't spoil my fun. I'm going to frame this statement—and what would happen if I drew a check for a few million on the strength of this? Could I sue the bank if it bounced?"

"Not on your life," answered Reyner. "I'll take a bet that the banks thought of *that* years ago and protected themselves somewhere down in the small print. But by the way—when did you get that statement?"

"In the noon delivery; it comes straight to the office, so that my wife doesn't have a chance of seeing it."

"Hmm—that means it was computed early this morning. Certainly after midnight . . ."

"What are you driving at? And why all the long faces?"

No one answered him; he had started a new hare, and the hounds were in full cry.

"Does anyone here know about automated banking systems?" asked Willy Smith. "How are they tied together?"

"Like everything else these days," said Bob Andrews. "They're all in the same network—the computers talk to one another all over the world. It's a point for you, John. If there *was* real trouble, that's one of the first places I'd expect it. Besides the phone system itself, of course."

"No one answered the question I asked before Jim came in," complained Reyner. "What would this supermind actually *do*? Would it be friendly—hostile—indifferent? Would it even know that we exist, or would it consider the electronic signals it's handling to be the only reality?"

"I see you're beginning to believe me," said Williams with a certain grim satisfaction. "I can only answer your question by asking another. What does a newborn baby do? It starts looking for food." He glanced up at the flickering lights. "My God," he said slowly, as if a thought had just struck him. "There's only one food it would need—electricity."

▬▬▬▬▬

"This nonsense has gone far enough," said Smith. "What the devil's happened to our lunch? We gave our orders twenty minutes ago."

Everyone ignored him.

"And then," said Reyner, taking up where Williams had left off, "it would start looking around and stretching its limbs. In fact, it would start to play, like any growing baby."

"And babies *break* things," said someone softly.

"It would have enough toys, heaven knows. That Concorde that went over just now. The automated production lines. The traffic lights in our streets."

"Funny you should mention that," interjected Small. "Something's happened to the traffic outside—it's been stopped for the last ten minutes. Looks like a big jam."

"I guess there's a fire somewhere—I heard an engine."

"I've heard two—and what sounded like an explosion over toward the industrial estate. Hope it's nothing serious."

"Maisie!!! What about some candles? We can't see a thing!"

"I've just remembered—this place has an all-electric kitchen. We're going to get cold lunch, if we get any lunch at all."

"At least we can read the newspaper while we're waiting. Is that the latest edition you've got there, Jim?"

"Yes—haven't had time to look at it yet. Hmm—there *do* seem to have been a lot of odd accidents this morning—railway signals jammed—water main blown up through failure of relief valve—dozens of complaints about last night's wrong numbers—"

He turned the page and became suddenly silent.

"What's the matter?"

Without a word, Small handed over the paper. Only the front page made sense. Throughout the interior, column after column was a mass of printer's pie—with, here and there, a few incongruous advertisements making islands of sanity in a sea of gibberish. They had obviously been set up as independent blocks and had escaped the scrambling that had overtaken the text around them.

"So this is where long-distance typesetting and autodistribution have brought us," grumbled Andrews. "I'm afraid Fleet Street's been putting too many eggs in one electronic basket."

"So have we all, I'm afraid," said Williams very solemnly. "So have we all."

"If I can get a word in edgeways, in time to stop the mob hysteria which seems to be infecting this table," said Smith loudly and firmly, "I'd like to point out that there's nothing to worry about—even if John's ingenious fantasy is correct. We only have to switch off the satellites—and we'll be back where we were yesterday."

"Prefrontal lobotomy," muttered Williams. "I'd thought of that."

"Eh? Oh, yes—cutting out slabs of the brain. That would certainly do the trick. Expensive, of course, and we'd have to go back to sending telegrams to each other. But civilization would survive."

From not too far away, there was a short, sharp explosion.

"I don't like this," said Andrews nervously. "Let's hear what the old BBC's got to say—the one o'clock news has just started."

He reached into his briefcase and pulled out a transistor radio.

"—unprecedented number of industrial accidents, as well as the unexplained launching of three salvos of guided missiles from military installations in the United States. Several airports have had to suspend operations owing to the erratic behavior of their radars, and the banks and stock exchanges have closed because their information-processing systems have become completely unreliable." ("You're telling me," muttered Small, while the others shushed him.) "One moment, please—there's a news flash coming through. . . . Here it is. We have just been informed that all control over the newly installed communication satellites has been lost. They are no longer responding to commands from the ground. According to—"

The BBC went off the air; even the carrier wave died. Andrews reached for the tuning knob and twisted it round the dial. Over the whole band, the ether was silent.

Presently Reyner said, in a voice not far from hysteria, "That

450

prefrontal lobotomy was a good idea, John. Too bad that baby's already thought of it."

Williams rose slowly to his feet.

"Let's get back to the lab," he said. "There must be an answer somewhere."

But he knew already that it was far, far too late. For Homo sapiens, the telephone bell had tolled.

THE MACAULEY CIRCUIT

ROBERT SILVERBERG

(1 9 5 6)

What makes a human different from his machines? The usual answer declares man's emotions as the essential difference. In "The Macauley Circuit," Robert Silverberg suggests that man's drive to create art has always made him unique. Then he raises a critical question: If man's creativity is his special joy, does he really want to create a machine that will end all human creativity?

The same question has been asked about the wisdom of creating robots that do all of man's work for him. Jack Williamson's famous story, "With Folded Hands" (1963), was concerned with what man does with his time after he has invented a robot that will do everything for him. So totally has our society been indoctrinated with the Puritan work ethic that many of us have difficulty imagining what we would do without work. Those who don't mind giving up work often say they would prefer to use their time creatively— writing, painting, composing music. But what if machines could do that better than men?

The first strong reactions against computers in the arts are rapidly vanishing as we recognize that computers are tools to create new art forms, not eliminate old ones. Computer art and holographic sculpturing, now recognized as legitimate forms, have not diminished the field of art but augmented it by creating an art form that is dynamic. Synthesizer and computer offer new musical possibilities to the composer.

Robert Silverberg, born in 1935, is recognized as one of the premier writers in the field. He is particularly admired for his style, a quality lacking in almost all early and too much modern science fiction. He is the winner of two Hugo and four Nebula Awards. His "Good News from the Vatican" (1971) is a delightful story about the election of a computer as head of the Catholic Church.

I DON'T DENY I destroyed Macauley's diagram; I never did deny it, gentlemen. Of course I destroyed it, and for fine, substantial reasons. My big mistake was in not thinking the thing through at the beginning. When Macauley first brought me the circuit, I didn't pay much attention to it—certainly not

452

as much as it deserved. That was a mistake, but I couldn't help myself. I was too busy coddling old Kolfmann to stop and think what the Macauley circuit really meant.

If Kolfmann hadn't shown up just when he did, I would have been able to make a careful study of the circuit and, once I had seen all the implications, I would have put the diagram in the incinerator and Macauley right after it. This is nothing against Macauley, you understand; he's a nice, clever boy, one of the finest minds in our whole research department. That's his trouble.

He came in one morning while I was outlining my graph for the Beethoven Seventh that we were going to do the following week. I was adding some ultrasonics that would have delighted old Ludwig—not that he would have heard them, of course, but he would have *felt* them—and I was very pleased about my interpretation. Unlike some synthesizer-interpreters, I don't believe in changing the score. I figure Beethoven knew what he was doing, and it's not my business to patch up his symphony. All I was doing was *strengthening* it by adding the ultrasonics. They wouldn't change the actual notes any, but there'd be that feeling in the air which is the great artistic triumph of synthesizing.

So I was working on my graph. When Macauley came in I was choosing the frequencies for the second movement, which is difficult because the movement is solemn but not *too* solemn. Just so. He had a sheaf of paper in his hand, and I knew immediately that he'd hit on something important, because no one interrupts an interpreter for something trivial.

"I've developed a new circuit, sir," he said. "It's based on the imperfect Kennedy Circuit of 2261."

I remembered Kennedy—a brilliant boy, much like Macauley here. He had worked out a circuit which almost would have made synthesizing a symphony as easy as playing a harmonica. But it hadn't quite worked—something in the process fouled up the ultrasonics and what came out was hellish to hear—and we never found out how to straighten things out. Kennedy disappeared about a year later and was never heard from again. All the young technicians used to tinker with his circuit for diversion, each one hoping he'd find the secret. And now Macauley had.

I looked at what he had drawn, and then up at him. He was standing there calmly, with a blank expression on his handsome, intelligent face, waiting for me to quiz him.

"This circuit controls the interpretative aspects of music, am I right?"

"Yes, sir. You can set the synthesizer for whatever esthetic you have in mind, and it'll follow your instruction. You merely have to establish the esthetic coordinates—the work of a moment—and the synthesizer will handle the rest of the interpretation for you. But that's not exactly the goal of my circuit, sir," he said, gently, as if to hide from me the fact that he was telling me I had missed his point. "With minor modifications—"

He didn't get a chance to tell me, because at that moment Kolfmann came dashing into my studio. I never lock my doors, because for one thing no one would dare come in without good and sufficient reason, and for another my analyst pointed out to me that working behind locked doors has a bad effect on my sensibilities, and reduces the esthetic potentialities of my interpretations. So I always work with my door unlocked and that's how Kolfmann got in. And that's what saved Macauley's life, because if he had gone on to tell me what was on the tip of his tongue I would have regretfully incinerated him and his circuit right then and there.

Kolfmann was a famous name to those who loved music. He was perhaps eighty now, maybe ninety, if he had a good gerontologist, and he had been a great concert pianist many years ago. Those of us who knew something about presynthesizer musical history knew his name as we would that of Paganini or Horowitz or any other virtuoso of the past, and regarded him almost with awe.

Only all I saw now was a tall, terribly gaunt old man in ragged clothes who burst through my doors and headed straight for the synthesizer, which covered the whole north wall with its gleaming, complicated bulk. He had a club in his hand thicker than his arm, and he was about to bash it down on a million credits' worth of cybernetics when Macauley effortlessly walked over and took it away from him. I was still too flabbergasted to do much more than stand behind my desk in shock.

Macauley brought him over to me and I looked at him as if he were Judas.

"You old reactionary," I said. "What's the idea? You can get fined a fortune for wrecking a cyber—or didn't you know that?"

"My life is ended anyway," he said in a thick, deep, guttural voice. "It ended when your machines took over music."

He took off his battered cap and revealed a full head of white hair. He hadn't shaved in a couple of days, and his face was speckled with stiff-looking white stubble.

"My name is Gregor Kolfmann," he said. "I'm sure you have heard of me."

"Kolfmann, the pianist?"

He nodded, pleased despite everything. "Yes, Kolfmann, the *former* pianist. You and your machine have taken away my life."

Suddenly all the hate that had been piling up in me since he burst in—the hate any normal man feels for a cybewrecker—melted, and I felt guilty and very humble before this old man. As he continued to speak, I realized that I—as a musical artist— had a responsibility to old Kolfmann. I still think that what I did was the right thing, whatever you say.

"Even after synthesizing became the dominant method of presenting music," he said, "I continued my concert career for years. There were always some people who would rather see a man play a piano than a technician feed a tape through a machine. But I couldn't compete forever." He sighed. "After a while anyone who went to live concerts was called a reactionary, and I stopped getting bookings. I took up teaching for my living. But no one wanted to learn to play the piano. A few have studied with me for antiquarian reasons, but they are not artists, just curiosity-seekers. They have no artistic drive. You and your machine have killed art!"

I looked at Macauley's circuit and at Kolfmann, and felt as if everything were dropping on me at once. I put away my graph for the Beethoven, partly because all the excitement would make it impossible for me to get anywhere with it today and partly because it would only make things worse if Kolfmann saw it. Macauley was still standing there, waiting to explain his circuit to me. I knew it was important, but I felt a debt to old Kolfmann, and I decided I'd take care of him before I let Macauley do any more talking.

"Come back later," I told Macauley. "I'd like to discuss the implications of your circuit, as soon as I'm through talking to Mr. Kolfmann."

"Yes, sir," Macauley said, like the obedient puppet a technician turns into when confronted by a superior, and left. I gathered up the papers he had left me and put them neatly at a corner of my desk. I didn't want Kolfmann to see *them*, either, though I knew they wouldn't mean anything to him except as symbols of the machine he hated.

When Macauley had gone I gestured Kolfmann to a plush pneumochair, into which he settled with the distaste for excess comfort that is characteristic of his generation. I saw my duty plainly—to make things better for the old man.

"We'd be glad to have you come to work for us, Mr. Kolfmann," I began, smiling. "A man of your great gift—"

He was up out of that chair in a second, eyes blazing. "Work for you? I'd sooner see you and your machines dead and crumbling! You, you scientists—you've killed art, and now you're trying to bribe me!"

"I was just trying to help you," I said. "Since, in a manner of speaking, we've affected your livelihood, I thought I'd make things up to you."

He said nothing, but stared at me coldly, with the anger of half a century burning in him.

"Look," I said. "Let me show you what a great musical instrument the synthesizer itself is." I rummaged in my cabinet and withdrew the tape of the Hohenstein Viola Concerto which we had performed in '69—a rigorous twelve-tone work which is probably the most demanding, unplayable bit of music ever written. It was no harder for the synthesizer to counterfeit its notes than those of a Strauss waltz, of course, but a human violist would have needed three hands and a prehensile nose to convey any measure of Hohenstein's musical thought. I activated the playback of the synthesizer and fed the tape in.

The music burst forth. Kolfmann watched the machine suspiciously. The pseudo-viola danced up and down the tone row while the old pianist struggled to place the work.

"Hohenstein?" he finally asked, timidly. I nodded.

I saw a conflict going on within him. For more years than he could remember, he had hated us because we had made his art obsolete. But here I was showing him a use for the synthesizer that gave it a valid existence—it was synthesizing a work impossible for a human to play. He was unable to reconcile all the factors in his mind, and the struggle hurt. He got up uneasily and started for the door.

"Where are you going?"

"Away from here," he said. "You are a devil."

He tottered weakly through the door, and I let him go. The old man was badly confused, but I had a trick or two up my cybernetic sleeve to settle some of his problems and perhaps salvage him for the world of music. For, whatever else you say about me, particularly after this Macauley business, you can't deny that my deepest allegiance is to music.

I stopped work on my Beethoven's Seventh, and also put away Macauley's diagram, and called in a couple of technicians. I told them what I was planning. The first line of inquiry, I decided, was to find out who Kolfmann's piano teacher had been. They had the reference books out in a flash and we found out who—Gotthard Kellerman, who had died nearly sixty years ago. Here luck was with us. Central was able to locate and supply us with an old tape of the International Music Congress held at Stockholm in 2187, at which Kellerman had spoken briefly on *The Development of the Pedal Technique:* nothing very exciting, but it wasn't what he was saying that interested us. We split his speech up into phonemes, analyzed, rearranged, evaluated, and finally went to the synthesizer and began feeding in tapes.

What we got back was a new speech in Kellerman's voice, or a reasonable facsimile thereof. Certainly it would be good enough to fool Kolfmann, who hadn't heard his old teacher's voice in more than half a century. When we had everything ready I sent for Kolfmann, and a couple of hours later they brought him in, looking even older and more worn.

"Why do you bother me?" he asked. "Why do you not let me die in peace?"

I ignored his questions. "Listen to this, Mr. Kolfmann." I flipped on the playback, and the voice of Kellerman came out of the speaker.

"Hello, Gregor," it said. Kolfmann was visibly startled. I took advantage of the prearranged pause in the recording to ask him if he recognized the voice. He nodded. I could see that he was frightened and suspicious, and I hoped the whole thing wouldn't backfire.

"Gregor, one of the things I tried most earnestly to teach you—and you were my most attentive pupil—was that you must always be flexible. Techniques must constantly change, though art itself remains changeless. But have you listened to me? No."

Kolfmann was starting to realize what we had done, I saw. His pallor was ghastly now.

"Gregor, the piano is an outmoded instrument. But there is a newer, a greater instrument available for you, and you deny its greatness. This wonderful new synthesizer can do all that the piano could do, and much more. It is a tremendous step forward."

"All right," Kolfmann said. His eyes were gleaming strangely. "Turn that machine off."

I reached over and flipped off the playback.

"You are very clever," he told me. "I take it you used your synthesizer to prepare this little speech for me."

I nodded.

He was silent an endless moment. A muscle flickered in his cheek. I watched him, not daring to speak.

At length he said, "Well, you have been successful, in your silly, theatrical way. You've shaken me."

"I don't understand."

Again he was silent, communing with who knew what internal force. I sensed a powerful conflict raging within him. He

458

scarcely seemed to see me at all as he stared into nothingness. I heard him mutter something in another language; I saw him pause and shake his great old head. And in the end he looked down at me and said, "Perhaps it is worth trying. Perhaps the words you put in Kellerman's mouth were true. Perhaps. You are foolish, but I have been even more foolish than you. I have stubbornly resisted, when I should have joined forces with you. Instead of denouncing you, I should have been the first to learn how to create music with this strange new instrument. Idiot! Moron!"

I think he was speaking of himself in those last two words, but I am not sure. In any case, I had seen a demonstration of the measure of his greatness—the willingness to admit error and begin all over. I had not expected his cooperation; all I had wanted was an end to his hostility. But he had yielded. He had admitted error and was ready to rechart his entire career.

"It's not too late to learn," I said. "We could teach you."

Kolfmann looked at me fiercely for a moment, and I felt a shiver go through me. But my elation knew no bounds. I had won a great battle for music, and I had won it with ridiculous ease.

He went away for a while to master the technique of the synthesizer. I gave him my best man, one whom I had been grooming to take over my place someday. In the meantime I finished my Beethoven, and the performance was a great success. And then I got back to Macauley and his circuit.

Once again things conspired to keep me from full realization of the threat represented by the Macauley circuit. I did manage to grasp that it could easily be refined to eliminate almost completely the human element in musical interpretation. But it was many years since I had worked in the labs, and I had fallen out of my old habit of studying any sort of diagram and mentally tinkering with it and juggling it to see what greater use could be made of it.

While I examined the Macauley circuit, reflecting idly that when it was perfected it might very well put me out of a job (since anyone would be able to create a musical interpretation, and artistry would no longer be an operative factor), Kolfmann came in with some tapes. He looked twenty years younger; his face was bright and clean, his eyes were shining, and his impressive mane of hair waved grandly.

"I will say it again," he told me as he put the tapes on my desk. "I have been a fool. I have wasted my life. Instead of tapping away at a silly little instrument, I might have created wonders with this machine. Look: I began with Chopin. Put this on."

I slipped the tape into the synthesizer and the F Minor Fantaisie of Chopin came rolling into the room. I had heard the tired old warhorse a thousand times, but never like this.

"This machine is the noblest instrument I have ever played," he said.

I looked at the graph he had drawn up for the piece, in his painstaking, crabbed handwriting. The ultrasonics were literally incredible. In just a few weeks he had mastered subtleties I had spent fifteen years learning. He had discovered that skillfully chosen ultrasonics, beyond the range of human hearing but not beyond perception, could expand the horizons of music to a point the presynthesizer composers, limited by their crude instruments and faulty knowledge of sonics, would have found inconceivable.

The Chopin almost made me cry. It wasn't so much the actual notes Chopin had written, which I had heard so often, as it was the unheard notes the synthesizer was striking, up in the ultrasonic range. The old man had chosen his ultrasonics with the skill of a craftsman—no, with the hand of a genius. I saw Kolfmann in the middle of the room, standing proudly while the piano rang out in a glorious tapestry of sound.

I felt that this was my greatest artistic triumph. My Beethoven symphonies and all my other interpretations were of no value beside this one achievement of putting the synthesizer in the hands of Kolfmann.

He handed me another tape and I put it on. It was the Bach Toccata and Fugue in D Minor; evidently he had worked first on the pieces most familiar to him. The sound of a super-organ

460

roared forth from the synthesizer. We were buffeted by the violence of the music. And Kolfmann stood there while the Bach piece raged on. I looked at him and tried to relate him to the seedy old man who had tried to wreck the synthesizer not long ago, and I couldn't.

As the Bach drew to its close I thought of the Macauley circuit again, and of the whole beehive of blank-faced, handsome technicians striving to perfect the synthesizer by eliminating the one imperfect element—man. And I woke up.

My first decision was to suppress the Macauley circuit until after Kolfmann's death, which couldn't be too far off. I made this decision out of sheer kindness; you have to recognize that as my motive. Kolfmann, after all these years, was having a moment of supreme triumph, and if I let him know that no matter what he was doing with the synthesizer, the new circuit could do it better, it would ruin everything. He would not survive the blow.

He fed the third tape in himself. It was the Mozart Requiem Mass, and I was astonished by the way he had mastered the difficult technique of synthesizing voices. Still, with the Macauley circuit, the machine could handle all these details by itself.

As Mozart's sublime music swelled and rose, I took out the diagram Macauley had given me, and stared at it grimly. I decided to pigeonhole it until the old man died. Then I would reveal it to the world and, having been made useless myself (for interpreters like me would be a credit a hundred), I would sink into peaceful obscurity, with at least the assurance that Kolfmann had died happy.

That was sheer kindheartedness, gentlemen. Nothing malicious or reactionary about it. I didn't intend to stop the progress of cybernetics, at least not at that point.

No, I didn't decide to do that until I got a better look at what Macauley had done. Maybe he didn't even realize it himself, but I used to be pretty shrewd about such things. Mentally, I added a wire or two here, altered a contact there, and suddenly the whole thing hit me.

A synthesizer hooked up with a Macauley circuit not only didn't need a human being to provide an esthetic guide to its interpretation of music, which is all Macauley claimed. Up to now, the synthesizer could imitate the pitch of any sound in or out of nature, but we had to control the volume, the timbre, all the things which make up interpretation of music. Macauley had fixed it so that the synthesizer could handle this, too. But also, I now saw that it could create its own music, from scratch, with no human help. Not only the conductor but the composer would be unnecessary. The synthesizer would be able to function independently of any human being. And art is a function of human beings.

That was when I ripped up Macauley's diagram and heaved the paperweight into the gizzard of my beloved synthesizer, cutting off the Mozart in the middle of a high C. Kolfmann turned around in horror, but I was the one who was really horrified.

I know. Macauley has redrawn his diagram and I haven't stopped the wheels of science. I feel pretty futile about it all. But before you label me reactionary and stick me away, consider this:

Art is a function of intelligent beings. Once you create a machine capable of composing original music, capable of an artistic act, you've created an intelligent being. And one that's a lot stronger and smarter than we are. We've synthesized our successor.

Gentlemen, we are all obsolete.

JUDAS

JOHN BRUNNER

(1 9 6 7)

Omnipotence, omniscience—these are characteristics associated with God. When one thinks of such ultimate power and knowledge, the mind inevitably jumps from God to computers. The theme of computer as God has provided the seed of possibility for an array of stories. Such association of the machine with the gods is at least as old as the Greek theater, where the *deus ex machina*, or "god from the machine," often descended on the stage (lowered by a mechanism) to untangle dilemmas poor humans could not manage.

Twentieth-century fiction has countless examples of the machine as god. The masses worship the machine in Eugene Zamiatin's early novel *We* (1921). D. F. Jones's *Colossus* (1966) and Martin Caidin's *The God Machine* (1968) create future societies where the machine becomes God. Aldous Huxley described a fascinating phenomenon in 1952 when he wrote in *Brave New World Revisited* about the course of human events in the twenty years since he published *Brave New World*. He had originally created his imaginary future world to satirize the production-line culture of his own time, yet what he had intended as mere irony turned into social reality. Today the age of test-tube babies is at hand.

Perhaps the God-as-machine thesis, which John Brunner uses in "Judas" as an ironical device to condemn a world too zealous in its pursuit of technology, will also become a reality. Christopher Evans, in *The Micro Millennium* (1979), says: "The coming of the . . . highly intelligent computer will throw up a host of religious systems. I suspect that any new religions that appear in the eighties and nineties will have the computer figuring predominantly in them, just as some of the religions of the sixties and seventies have been built around the image of the flying saucer."

Born in England in 1934, John Brunner specializes in social science fiction. His *Stand on Zanzibar*, a novel about overpopulation, won a Hugo in 1969. He typically offers a bleak view of the future of technological societies, as in *The Sheep Look Up* (1972), a novel about pollution. *The Shock Wave Rider* (1975) explores the communication explosion brought about by computers.

Not all writers of science fiction about computers and religion are as negative as Brunner. John Boyd's stylish and humorously ironic *The Last Starship from Earth* (1968) has a computer as Pope of the Catholic Church.

In Anthony Boucher's gentle "The Quest for St. Aquin," a lovable and saintly priest turns out to be a robot. Clifford Simak's recent *Project Pope* (1982) is also about a race of robots who create a computer pope.

THE FRIDAY-EVENING SERVICE was drawing to its close. The rays of the declining spring sun slanted through the poly-chrome plastic of the windows and lay along the floor of the central aisle like a pool of oil spilt on a wet road. On the polished steel of the altar a silver wheel spun continually, glinting be-tween two ever-burning mercury-vapor lamps; above it, silhou-etted against the darkling eastern sky, there stood a statue of God. The surpliced choir was singing an anthem—"The Word Made Steel"—and the minister sat listening with his hand cupped under his chin, wondering if God had approved of the sermon he had just preached on the Second Coming.

Most of the large congregation was enraptured by the music. Only one man present, at the end of the rearmost row of bare steel pews, fidgeted impatiently, flexing the rubber pad from the forehead rest before him in nervous fingers. He had to keep his hands occupied, or else they kept straying to the bulge in the inside pocket of his plain brown jacket. His watery blue eyes wandered restlessly along the climactic, sweeping lines of the metal temple and shifted away every time they came to the wheel motif which the architect—probably God himself—had incorporated wherever possible.

The anthem closed on a thrilling dissonance and the con-gregation knelt, their heads against the rubber rests, while the minister pronounced the blessing of the Wheel. The man in brown wasn't really listening, but he caught a few phrases: "May he guide you in your appointed courses . . . serve you as your eternal pivot . . . bring you at last to the peace of the true eternal round . . ."

Then he stood with the rest of them while the choir marched out to the strains of the electronic organ. Directly the minister had disappeared through the vestry door, the worshipers began to shuffle toward the main exits. He alone remained sitting in his pew.

He was not the sort of person one would look at twice. He had sandy hair and a worn, tired face; his teeth were stained and irregular, his clothes fitted badly, and his eyes were a fraction out of focus, as though he needed glasses. Plainly the service had not brought him peace of mind.

Eventually, when everybody else had gone, he stood up and replaced the rubber pad with scrupulous exactitude. For a moment his eyes closed and his lips moved soundlessly; as if this act had endowed him with the courage for a decision, he seemed to draw himself up like a diver poising on a high board. Abruptly he left the pew and walked—soundless on the rubber carpet of the nave—toward the small steel door that bore the single word VESTRY.

Beside it there was a bell. He rang.

Shortly the door was opened by a junior acolyte, a youth in a gray robe woven of metallic links that jingled as he moved, hands in gray shiny gloves, scalp hidden under a smooth steel cap. In a voice made impersonal by careful practice, the acolyte said, "You wish counsel?"

The man in brown nodded, shifting a trifle nervously from foot to foot. Through the doorway were visible many devotional pictures and statues; he dropped his gaze before them.

"What is your name?" the acolyte inquired.

"Karimov," said the man in brown. "Julius Karimov."

He tensed fractionally as he spoke, his eyes fleeting over the acolyte's face in search of any traction. None showed, and he relaxed on the youth's curt order to wait while he informed the minister.

The moment he was alone, Karimov crossed the vestry and examined a painting on the far wall: Anson's "Immaculate Manufacture," depicting the legendary origin of God—a bolt of lightning from heaven smiting an ingot of pure steel. It was excellently done, of course; the artist's use of electro-luminescent paint for the lightning, in particular, was masterly. But from Karimov it provoked an expression of physical nausea, and after only seconds he had to turn away.

At length the minister entered in the officiating robe which

465

identified him as one of the Eleven closest to God, his head-piece—which during the service had concealed his shaven scalp—discarded, his white, slender hands playing with a jeweled emblem of the Wheel that hung around his neck on a platinum chain. Karimov turned slowly to confront him, right hand slightly raised in a stillborn gesture. It had been a calculated risk to give his real name; he thought that was probably still a secret. But his real face . . .

No, no hint of recognition. The minister merely said in his professionally resonant voice, "What may I do for you, my son?"

The man in brown squared his shoulders and said simply, "I want to talk to God."

With the resigned air of one well used to dealing with requests of that sort, the minister sighed. "God is extremely busy, my son," he murmured. "He has the spiritual welfare of the entire human race to look after. Cannot I help you? Is there a particular problem on which you need advice, or do you seek generalized divine guidance in programming your life?"

Karimov looked at him diffidently and thought: *This man really believes! His faith isn't just pretense for profit, but deep-seated honest trust, and it is more terrifying than everything else that even those who were with me at the beginning should believe!*

He said after a while, "You are kind, Father, but I need more than mere advice, I have"—he seemed to stumble at the word—"prayed much, and sought help from several ministers, and still I have not attained to the peace of the true round. Once, long ago, I had the privilege of seeing God in the steel; I wish to do so again, that's all. I have no doubt, of course, that He will remember me."

There was a long silence, during which the minister's dark eyes remained fixed on Karimov. Finally he said, "Remember you? Oh, yes, he will certainly remember you! But *I* remember you too—now!"

His voice shook with uncontrollable fury, and he reached for a bell on the wall.

Strength born of desperation poured through Karimov's

scrawny frame. He hurled himself at the minister, striking aside the outstretched arm inches from its goal, bowling the tall man over, seizing the tough chain around his neck, and pulling with every ounce of force he could muster.

The chain bit deep into pale flesh; as if possessed, Karimov tugged and tugged at it, twisted, took a fresh grip, and tugged again. The minister's eyes bulged, his mouth uttered loathsome, formless grunts, his fists beat at his attacker's arms—and grew weaker, and ceased.

Karimov drew back, shaking at what he had done, and compelled himself unsteadily to his feet. To the former colleague who now had gone beyond all hope of hearing he muttered his sick apology, then calmed himself with deep breaths and approached the door by which he had not entered the room.

On his throne beneath its wheel-shaped canopy of steel, God sat. His polished limbs gleamed under the muted lights, his head was beautifully designed to suggest a human face without possessing a single human feature—even eyes.

Blind, insensate thing, thought Karimov as he shut the door behind him. Unconsciously his hand touched what he had in his pocket.

The voice too was more than humanly perfect, a deep, pure tone as if an organ spoke. It said, "My son—"

And stopped.

Karimov gave an audible sigh of relief and his nervousness dropped from him like a cloak. He stepped forward casually and sat down in the central one of the eleven chairs arranged in a horseshoe before the throne, while the blank, shiny gaze of the robot rested on him and the whole metal frame locked in astonishment.

"Well?" Karimov challenged. "How do you like meeting somebody who doesn't believe in you for a change?"

The robot moved in human fashion, relaxing. Steel fingers linked under his chin while he reconsidered the intruder with interest instead of amazement. The voice rang out afresh.

"So it's you, Black!"

Karimov nodded with a faint smile. "That's what they used to call me in the old days. I used to think it was a silly affectation—assigning the scientists who worked on top-secret projects false names. But it's turned out to have advantages, for me at any rate. I gave my own name of Karimov to your—ah—late apostle outside, and it meant nothing to him. Speaking of real names, by the way, how long is it since anyone addressed you as A-46?"

The robot jerked. "It is sacrilege to apply that term to me!"

"Sacrilege be—bothered. I'll go further and remind you what the A stands for in A-46. Android! An imitation of a man! A sexless, insensate assembly of metal parts which I helped to design, and it calls itself God!" Scathing contempt rode the lashing words. "You and your fantasies of Immaculate Manufacture! Blasted by a bolt of heavenly lightning from a chunk of untooled steel! Talk about making men in God's own image— you're the 'God' who was made in man's!"

They had even incorporated the facility of shrugging in their design, Karimov recalled with a start as the robot made use of it.

"Leaving sacrilege on one side for a moment, then," the machine said, "is there any real reason why you should deny that I am God? Why should not the second Incarnation be an Inferration—in imperishable steel? As for your benighted and deluded belief that you created the metal part of me—which is anyway supremely unimportant since the spirit alone is eternal—it's long been said that a prophet is without honor in his own country, and since the Inferration took place near your experimental station . . . Well!"

Karimov laughed. He said, "Well, I'm damned! I think you believe it yourself!"

"You are beyond question damned. For a moment I hoped, seeing you enter my throne room, that you'd learned the error of your ways and come to acknowledge my divinity at last. Of my infinite compassion I will give you one final chance to do so before I call my ministers to take you away. Now or never, Black or Karimov or whatever you choose to call yourself—do you repent and believe?"

Karimov wasn't listening. He was staring past the shining machine into nowhere, while his hand caressed the bulge in his pocket. He said in a low voice, "I've plotted years for this moment—twenty years, ever since the day we turned you on and I began to suspect we'd gone wrong. Not till now was there anything I could have done. And in the meantime, while I sweated and hunted for a way to stop you, I've seen the ultimate humiliation of mankind.

"We've been slaves to our tools since the first caveman made the first knife to help him get his supper. After that there was no going back, and we built till our machines were ten million times more powerful than we ourselves. We gave ourselves cars when we might have learned to run; we made airplanes when we might have grown wings; and then the inevitable. We made a machine our God."

"And why not?" the robot boomed. "Can you name any single way in which I am not your superior? I am stronger, more intelligent, and more durable than a man. I have mental and physical powers that shame comparison. I feel no pain. I am immortal and invulnerable and yet you say I am not God. Why? From perverseness!"

"No," said Karimov with terrible directness. "Because you are mad.

"You were the climax of a decade's work by our team: the dozen most brilliant living cyberneticists. Our dream was to create a mechanical analog of a human being which could be programmed directly with intelligence drawn from the patterns in our own brains. In that we succeeded—far too well!

"I've had time enough in the past twenty years to work out where we went astray. It was my fault, God help me—the real God, if He exists, not you, you mechanical fraud! Always somewhere at the back of my mind while we were working on you there lurked the thought that to build the machine we had envisaged would be to become as God: to make a creative intel-

ligence, that none save He had yet achieved! That was megalo-
mania, and I'm ashamed, but it *was* in my mind, and from mine
it was transferred to yours. No one knew of it; even I was afraid
to admit it to myself, for shame is a saving human grace. But
you! What could you know of shame, of self-restraint, of empathy
and love? Once implanted in your complex of artificial neurons,
that mania grew till it knew no bounds, and . . . here you are.
Insane with the lust for divine glory! Why else the doctrine of
the Word Made Steel, and the image of the Wheel, the mechanical form that does not occur in nature? Why else the trouble
you go to to make parallels in your godless existence with that
of the greatest Man who ever lived?"

Karimov was still speaking in the same low tones, but his
eyes were ablaze with hatred.

"You have no soul and you accuse me of sacrilege. You're a
collection of wires and transistors and you call yourself God.
Blasphemy! Only a man could be God!"

The robot shifted with a clang of metal limbs and said, "All
this is not merely nonsense, but a waste of my valuable time. Is
that all you came for—to rave at me?"

"No," said Karimov. "I came to kill you."

At long last his hand dipped into the bulging pocket and
produced the object there concealed: a curious little weapon,
less than six inches long. A short metal tube extended forward
from it; backward from the handgrip a flex disappeared inside
his coat; under his thumb there was a small red stud.

He said, "It took me twenty years to design and build this.
We chose steel for your body that only an atomic bomb could
destroy; how, though, could one man walk into your presence
with a nuclear weapon on his back? I had to wait until I had a
means of cutting your steel as easily as a knife cuts a man's weak
flesh. Here it is—and now I can undo the wrong I did to my own
species!"

He pressed the stud.

The robot, motionless till that moment as if incapable of
believing that anyone could really wish to harm him, jolted
upright, turned half around, and stood paralyzed as a tiny hole
appeared in the metal of his side. Steel began to form little drops

470

around the hole; the surrounding area glowed red, and the drops flowed like water—or blood.

Karimov held the weapon steady, though it scorched his fingers. Sweat stood out on his forehead. Another half minute, and the damage would be irreparable.

Behind him a door slammed open. He cursed, for his weapon would not work on a man. To the last moment he kept it aimed; then he was seized from behind and pinioned, and the weapon torn from its flex and hurled to the floor and stamped into ruin.

The robot did not move.

The tension of twenty hate-filled years broke and his relief boiled up into hysterical laughter, which he fought to quell. When he finally succeeded, he saw that the man who held him was the junior acolyte who had admitted him to the vestry, and that there were other men around, strangers, gazing in utter silence at their God.

"Look at him, look at him!" Karimov crowed. "Your idol was nothing but a robot, and what men make they can destroy. He said he was divine, but he wasn't even invulnerable! I've freed you! Don't you understand? *I've set you free!*"

But the acolyte wasn't paying him any attention. He stared fixedly at the monstrous metal doll, licking his lips, until at last he said in a voice that was neither relieved nor horrified, but only awed, "The Hole in the Side!"

A dream began to die in Karimov's mind. Numbly he watched the other men walk over to the robot and peer into the hole, heard one of them say, "How long to repair the damage?" and the other reply offhandedly, "Oh, three days, I guess!" And it was clear to him what he had done.

Wasn't this a Friday, and in spring? Hadn't he himself known that the robot made careful parallels between his own career and that of the man he parodied? Now it had reached the climax; there had been a death, and there would be a resurrection—on the third day . . .

And the grip of the Word Made Steel would never be broken.

In turn the men made the sign of the Wheel and departed, until one only remained. Stern, he came down from the throne

471

to confront Karimov and address the acolyte who held him in a rigid grasp.

"Who is he, anyway?" the man demanded.

The acolyte gazed at the limp figure slumped on the chair with the weight of all the ages crushing him, and his mouth rounded in an O of comprehension. He said, "*Now* I understand! He calls himself Karimov.

"But his real name must be Iscariot."

ANSWER

FREDRIC BROWN

(1 9 5 4)

Many versions exist of this classic idea for a short short story, but Fredric Brown was the first to publish it with his "Answer" in 1954. Brown (1906–1972) was a major figure in the mystery fiction field as well as in science fiction. He was the master of the short short story, of which "Answer" is perhaps his most famous. He once worked as a reporter on the *Milwaukee Journal* and was active for many years in journalism. Two of his best-known science fiction novels are *What Mad Universe* (1949) and *Martians, Go Home* (1955).

Dwar Ev ceremoniously soldered the final connection with gold. The eyes of a dozen television cameras watched him and the sub-ether bore throughout the universe a dozen pictures of what he was doing.

He straightened and nodded to Dwar Reyn, then moved to a position beside the switch that would complete the contact when he threw it. The switch that would connect, all at once, all of the monster computing machines of all the populated planets in the universe—ninety-six billion planets—into the supercircuit that would connect them all into one supercalculator, one cybernetics machine that would combine all the knowledge of all the galaxies.

Dwar Reyn spoke briefly to the watching and listening trillions. Then after a moment's silence he said, "Now, Dwar Ev."

Dwar Ev threw the switch. There was a mighty hum, the surge of power from ninety-six billion planets. Lights flashed and quieted along the miles-long panel.

Dwar Ev stepped back and drew a deep breath. "The honor of asking the first question is yours, Dwar Reyn."

"Thank you," said Dwar Reyn. "It shall be a question which no single cybernetics machine has been able to answer."

He turned to face the machine. "Is there a God?"

The mighty voice answered without hesitation, without the clicking of a single relay.

"Yes, *now* there is a God."

Sudden fear flashed on the face of Dwar Ev. He leaped to grab the switch.

A bolt of lightning from the cloudless sky struck him down and fused the switch shut.

WHAT

IS

A MAN?

THE ELECTRIC ANT

PHILIP K. DICK

(1 9 6 9)

What if you had always thought you were a man and then awoke one morning to discover you were a robot? This happens to Garson Poole in the story you are about to read. It is another of Dick's outstanding stories about robots; indeed, it is often regarded as one of the finest in all literature exploring man's perception of himself as a machine.

"The Electric Ant" is an example of the qualities in Dick's writing that remind one of Franz Kafka. You think immediately of "The Metamorphosis," in which the first sentence matter-of-factly announces that Gregor Samsa awoke one morning from uneasy dreams to find himself transformed into a gigantic insect.

Since the nineteenth century and the Industrial Revolution, when man began to surround himself with machines, literature has continually mirrored man's concern that he might become like his machines—or worse, that he was never anything but a machine in the first place. Is there really a difference? The vitalistic theory says man is unique because he possesses some vital spark—call it a soul, if you will. In contrast, the philosophy of mechanism suggests that man, made of nothing but atoms, is controlled by the same laws of physics that govern inanimate matter. He is no different from his machines except in his basic building material, which is organic. If this is true, then man's cherished free will is nothing but an illusion. Such a possibility is unsettling, to say the least.

Humans are perhaps blessed, because the answer is not available; we can debate the issue in long, entertaining philosophical discussions without feeling too threatened. But what if you really discovered the answer? Read on. . . .

At FOUR-FIFTEEN in the afternoon, T.S.T., Garson Poole woke up in his hospital bed, knew that he lay in a hospital bed in a three-bed ward, and realized in addition two things: that he no longer had a right hand and that he felt no pain.

They have given me a strong analgesic, he said to himself as he stared at the far wall with its window showing downtown

New York. Webs in which vehicles and peds darted and wheeled glimmered in the late afternoon sun, and the brilliance of the aging light pleased him. It's not yet out, he thought. And neither am I.

A fone lay on the table beside his bed; he hesitated, then picked it up and dialed for an outside line. A moment later he was faced by Louis Danceman, in charge of Tri-Plan's activities while he, Garson Poole, was elsewhere.

"Thank God you're alive," Danceman said, seeing him; his big, fleshy face with its moon's surface of pockmarks flattened with relief. "I've been calling all—"

"I just don't have a right hand," Poole said.

"But you'll be okay. I mean, they can graft another one on."

"How long have I been here?" Poole said. He wondered where the nurses and doctors had gone; why weren't they clucking and fussing about him making a call?

"Four days," Danceman said. "Everything here at the plant is going splunkishly. In fact we've splunked orders from three separate police systems, all here on Terra. Two in Ohio, one in Wyoming. Good solid orders, with one-third in advance and the usual three-year lease-option."

"Come and get me out of here," Poole said.

"I can't get you out until the new hand—"

"I'll have it done later." He wanted desperately to get back to familiar surroundings; memory of the mercantile squib looming grotesquely on the pilot screen careened at the back of his mind; if he shut his eyes he felt himself back in his damaged craft as it plunged from one vehicle to another, piling up enormous damage as it went. The kinetic sensations . . . he winced, recalling them. I guess I'm lucky, he said to himself.

"Is Sarah Benton there with you?" Danceman asked.

"No." Of course; his personal secretary—if only for job considerations—would be hovering close by, mothering him in her jejune, infantile way. All heavyset women like to mother people, he thought. And they're dangerous; if they fall on you they can kill you. "Maybe that's what happened to me," he said aloud. "Maybe Sarah fell on my squib."

"No, no; a tie rod in the steering fin of your squib split apart during the heavy rush-hour traffic and you—"

"I remember." He turned in his bed as the door of the ward opened; a white-clad doctor and two blue-clad nurses appeared, making their way toward his bed. "I'll talk to you later," Poole said, and hung up the fone. He took a deep, expectant breath.

"You shouldn't be foning quite so soon," the doctor said as he studied his chart. "Mr. Garson Poole, owner of Tri-Plan Electronics. Maker of random ident darts that track their prey for a circle-radius of a thousand miles, responding to unique enceph wave patterns. You're a successful man, Mr. Poole. But, Mr. Poole, you're not a man. You're an electric ant."

"Christ," Poole said, stunned.

"So we can't really treat you here, now that we've found out. We knew, of course, as soon as we examined your injured right hand; we saw the electronic components and then we made torso X-rays and of course they bore out our hypothesis."

"What," Poole said, "is an 'electric ant'?" But he knew; he could decipher the term.

A nurse said, "An organic robot."

"I see," Poole said. Frigid perspiration rose to the surface of his skin, across all his body.

"You didn't know," the doctor said.

"No." Poole shook his head.

The doctor said, "We get an electric ant every week or so. Either brought in here from a squib accident—like yourself—or one seeking voluntary admission . . . one who, like yourself, has never been told, who has functioned alongside humans, believing himself—itself—human. As to your hand—" He paused.

"Forget my hand," Poole said savagely.

"Be calm." The doctor leaned over him, peered acutely down into Poole's face. "We'll have a hospital boat convey you over to a service facility where repairs, or replacement, on your hand can be made at a reasonable expense, either to yourself, if you're self-owned, or to your owners, if such there are. In any case you'll be back at your desk at Tri-Plan, functioning just as before."

"Except," Poole said, "now I know." He wondered if Dance-man or Sarah or any of the others at the office knew. Had they— or one of them—purchased him? Designed him? A figurehead, he said to himself; that's all I've been. I must never really have run the company; it was a delusion implanted in me when I was made . . . along with the delusion that I am human and alive.

"Before you leave for the repair facility," the doctor said, "could you kindly settle your bill at the front desk?"

Poole said acidly, "How can there be a bill if you don't treat ants here?"

"For our services," the nurse said. "Up until the point we knew."

"Bill me," Poole said, with furious, impotent anger. "Bill my firm." With massive effort he managed to sit up; his head swimming, he stepped haltingly from the bed and onto the floor. "I'll be glad to leave here," he said as he rose to a standing position. "And thank you for your humane attention."

"Thank you, too, Mr. Poole," the doctor said. "Or rather I should say just Poole."

At the repair facility he had his missing hand replaced.

It proved fascinating, the hand; he examined it for a long time before he let the technicians install it. On the surface it appeared organic—in fact, on the surface it was. Natural skin covered natural flesh, and true blood filled the veins and capillaries. But beneath that, wires and circuits, miniaturized components gleamed. . . . Looking deep into the wrist he saw surge gates, motors, multistage valves, all very small. Intricate. And— the hand cost forty frogs. A week's salary, insofar as he drew it from the company payroll.

"Is this guaranteed?" he asked the technicians as they refused the "bone" section of the hand to the balance of his body.

"Ninety days, parts and labor," one of the technicians said. "Unless subjected to unusual or intentional abuse."

"That sounds vaguely suggestive," Poole said.

The technician, a man—all of them were men—said, regarding him keenly, "You've been posing?"

"Unintentionally," Poole said.

"And now it's intentional?"

Poole said, "Exactly."

"Do you know why you never guessed? There must have been signs . . . clickings and whirrings from inside you, now and then. You never guessed because you were programmed not to notice. You'll now have the same difficulty finding out why you were built and for whom you've been operating."

"A slave," Poole said. "A mechanical slave."

"You've had fun."

"I've lived a good life," Poole said. "I've worked hard."

He paid the facility its forty frogs, flexed his new fingers, tested them out by picking up various objects such as coins, then departed. Ten minutes later he was aboard a public carrier, on his way home. It had been quite a day.

At home, in his one-room apartment, he poured himself a shot of Jack Daniel's Purple Label—sixty years old—and sat sipping it, meanwhile gazing through his sole window at the building on the opposite side of the street. Shall I go to the office? he asked himself. If so, why? If not, why? Choose one. Christ, he thought, it undermines you, knowing this. I'm a freak, he realized. An inanimate object mimicking an animate one. But—he felt alive. Yet . . . he felt differently, now. About himself. Hence about everyone, especially Danceman and Sarah, everyone at Tri-Plan.

I think I'll kill myself, he said to himself. But I'm probably programmed not to do that; it would be a costly waste, which my owner would have to absorb. And he wouldn't want to.

Programmed. In me somewhere, he thought, there is a matrix fitted in place, a grid screen that cuts me off from certain thoughts, certain actions. And forces me into others. I am not free. I never was, but now I know it; that makes it different.

Turning his window to opaque, he snapped on the overhead light, carefully set about removing his clothing, piece by piece. He had watched carefully as the technicians at the repair facility attached his new hand; he had a rather clear idea, now, of how his body had been assembled. Two major panels, one in each thigh; the technicians had removed the panels to check the circuit complexes beneath. If I'm programmed, he decided, the matrix probably can be found there.

The maze of circuitry baffled him. I need help, he said to himself. Let's see . . . what's the fone code for the class BBB computer we hire at the office?

He picked up the fone, dialed the computer at its permanent location in Boise, Idaho.

"Use of this computer is prorated at a five-frogs-per-minute basis," a mechanical voice from the fone said. "Please hold your mastercreditchargeplate before the screen."

He did so.

"At the sound of the buzzer you will be connected with the computer," the voice continued. "Please query it as rapidly as possible, taking into account the fact that its answer will be given in terms of a microsecond, while your query will—" He turned the sound down, then. But quickly turned it up as the blank audio input of the computer appeared on the screen. At this moment the computer had become a giant ear, listening to him—as well as to fifty thousand other queriers throughout Terra.

"Scan me visually," he instructed the computer. "And tell me where I will find the programming mechanism which controls my thoughts and behavior." He waited. On the fone's screen a great active eye, multilensed, peered at him; he displayed himself for it, there in his one-room apartment.

The computer said, "Remove your chest panel. Apply pressure at your breastbone and then ease outward."

He did so. A section of his chest came off; dizzily, he set it down on the floor.

"I can distinguish control modules," the computer said, "but I can't tell which—" It paused as its eye roved about on the fone screen. "I distinguish a roll of punched tape mounted above your heart mechanism. Do you see it?" Poole craned his neck, peered. He saw it too. "I will have to sign off," the computer said. "After I have examined the data available to me I will contact you and give you an answer. Good day." The screen died out.

I'll yank the tape out of me, Poole said to himself. Tiny . . . no larger than two spools of thread, with a scanner mounted between the delivery drum and the take-up drum. He could not see any sign of motion; the spools seemed inert. They must cut in as override, he reflected, when specific situations occur. Override to my encephalic processes. And they've been doing it all my life.

He reached down, touched the delivery drum. All I have to do is tear this out, he thought, and—

The fone screen relit. "Mastercreditchargeplate number 3-BNX-882-HQR446-T," the computer's voice came. "This is BBB-307DR recontacting you in response to your query of sixteen seconds lapse, November 4, 1992. The punched tape roll above your heart mechanism is not a programming turret but is in fact a reality-supply construct. All sense stimuli received by your central neurological system emanate from that unit and tampering with it would be risky if not terminal." It added, "You appear to have no programming circuit. Query answered. Good day." It flicked off.

Poole, standing naked before the fone screen, touched the tape drum once again, with calculated, enormous caution. I see, he thought wildly. Or do I see? This unit—

If I cut the tape, he realized, my world will disappear. Reality will continue for others, but not for me. Because my reality, my universe, is coming to me from this minuscule unit. Fed into the scanner and then into my central nervous system as it snailishly unwinds.

It has been unwinding for years, he decided.

Getting his clothes, he redressed, seated himself in his big armchair—a luxury imported into his apartment from Tri-Plan's main offices—and lit a tobacco cigarette. His hands shook as he laid down his initialed lighter; leaning back, he blew smoke before himself; creating a nimbus of gray.

I have to go slowly, he said to himself. What am I trying to do? Bypass my programming? But the computer found no programming circuit. Do I want to interfere with the reality tape? And if so, *why?*

Because, he thought, if I control that, I control reality. At least so far as I'm concerned. My subjective reality . . . but that's all there is. Objective reality is a synthetic construct, dealing with a hypothetical universalization of a multitude of subjective realities.

My universe is lying within my fingers, he realized. If I can just figure out how the damn thing works. All I set out to do originally was to search for and locate my programming circuit so I could gain true homeostatic functioning; control of myself. But with this—

With this he did not merely gain control of himself; he gained control over everything.

And this sets me apart from every human who ever lived and died, he thought somberly.

Going over to the fone, he dialed his office. When he had Danceman on the screen he said briskly, "I want you to send a complete set of microtools and an enlarging screen over to my apartment. I have some microcircuitry to work on." Then he broke the connection, not wanting to discuss it.

A half hour later a knock sounded on his door. When he opened up he found himself facing one of the shop foremen, loaded down with microtools of every sort. "You didn't say exactly what you wanted," the foreman said, entering the apartment. "So Mr. Danceman had me bring everything."

"And the enlarging-lens system?"

"In the truck, up on the roof."

Maybe what I want to do, Poole thought, is die. He lit a cigarette, stood smoking and waiting as the shop foreman lugged the heavy enlarging screen, with its power supply and control panel, into the apartment. This is suicide, what I'm doing here. He shuddered.

"Anything wrong, Mr. Poole?" the shop foreman said as he rose to his feet, relieved of the burden of the enlarging-lens system. "You must still be rickety on your pins from your accident."

"Yes," Poole said quietly. He stood tautly, waiting until the foreman left.

Under the enlarging-lens system the plastic tape assumed a new shape: a wide track along which hundreds of thousands of punch-holes worked their way. I thought so, Poole thought. Not recorded as charges on a ferrous oxide layer but actually punched-free slots.

Under the lens the strip of tape visibly oozed forward. Very slowly, but it did, at uniform velocity, move in the direction of the scanner.

The way I figure it, he thought, is that the punched holes are *on* gates. It functions like a player piano: solid is no, punch-hole is yes. How can I test this?

Obviously by filling in a number of the holes.

He measured the amount of tape left on the delivery spool, calculated—at great effort—the velocity of the tape's movement, and then came up with a figure. If he altered the tape visible at the ingoing edge of the scanner, five to seven hours would pass before that particular time period arrived. He would in effect be painting out stimuli due a few hours from now.

With a microbrush he swabbed a large—relatively large—section of tape with opaque varnish . . . obtained from the supply kit accompanying the microtools. I have smeared out stimuli for about half an hour, he pondered. Have covered at least a thousand punches.

It would be interesting to see what change, if any, overcame his environment, six hours from now.

Five and a half hours later he sat at Krackter's, a superb bar in Manhattan, having a drink with Danceman.

"You look bad," Danceman said.

"I am bad," Poole said. He finished his drink, a Scotch sour, and ordered another.

"From the accident?"

"In a sense, yes."

Danceman said, "Is it—something you found out about yourself?"

Raising his head, Poole eyed him in the murky light of the bar. "Then you know."

"I know," Danceman said, "that I should call you 'Poole' instead of 'Mr. Poole.' But I prefer the latter, and will continue to do so."

"How long have you known?" Poole said.

"Since you took over the firm. I was told that the actual owners of Tri-Plan, who are located in the Prox System, wanted Tri-Plan run by an electric ant whom they could control. They wanted a brilliant and forceful—"

"The real owners?" This was the first he had heard about that. "We have two thousand stockholders. Scattered everywhere."

"Marvis Bey and her husband Ernan, on Prox 4, control fifty-one percent of the voting stock. This has been true from the start."

"Why didn't I know?"

"I was told not to tell you. You were to think that you yourself made all company policy. With my help. But actually I was feeding you what the Beys fed to me."

"I'm a figurehead," Poole said.

"In a sense, yes." Danceman nodded. "But you'll always be 'Mr. Poole' to me."

A section of the far wall vanished. And with it, several people at tables nearby. And—

Through the big glass side of the bar, the skyline of New York City flickered out of existence.

Seeing his face, Danceman said, "What is it?"

Poole said hoarsely, "Look around. Do you see any changes?"

After looking around the room, Danceman said, "No. What like?"

"You still see the skyline?"

"Sure. Smoggy as it is. The lights wink—"

"Now I know," Poole said. He had been right; every punch-hole covered up meant the disappearance of some object in his reality world. Standing, he said, "I'll see you later, Danceman. I have to get back to my apartment; there's some work I'm doing. Good night." He strode from the bar and out onto the street, searching for a cab.

No cabs.

Those too, he thought. I wonder what else I painted over. Prostitutes? Flowers? Prisons?

There, in the bar's parking lot, Danceman's squib. I'll take that, he decided. There are still cabs in Danceman's world; he can get one later. Anyhow it's a company car, and I hold a copy of the key.

Presently he was in the air, turning toward his apartment.

New York City had not returned. To the left and right, vehicles and buildings, streets, ped-runners, signs . . . and in the center nothing. How can I fly into that? he asked himself. I'd disappear.

Or would I? He flew toward the nothingness.

Smoking one cigarette after another, he flew in a circle for fifteen minutes . . . and then, soundlessly, New York reappeared. He could finish his trip. He stubbed out his cigarette (a waste of something so valuable) and shot off in the direction of his apartment.

If I insert a narrow opaque strip, he pondered as he unlocked his apartment door, I can—

His thoughts ceased. Someone sat in his living room chair, watching a captain kirk on the TV. "Sarah," he said, nettled.

She rose, well-padded but graceful. "You weren't at the hospital, so I came here. I still have that key you gave me back in March after we had that awful argument. Oh . . . you look so depressed." She came up to him, peered into his face anxiously. "Does your injury hurt that badly?"

"It's not that." He removed his coat, tie, shirt, and then his chest panel; kneeling down, he began inserting his hands into the microtool gloves. Pausing, he looked up at her and said, "I found out I'm an electric ant. Which from one standpoint opens up certain possibilities, which I am exploring now." He flexed his fingers and, at the far end of the left waldo, a micro screwdriver moved, magnified into visibility by the enlarging-lens system. "You can watch," he informed her. "If you so desire."

She had begun to cry.

"What's the matter?" he demanded savagely, without looking up from his work.

"I—it's just so sad. You've been such a good employer to all of us at Tri-Plan. We respect you so. And now it's all changed."

The plastic tape had an unpunched margin at top and bottom; he cut a horizontal strip, very narrow, then, after a moment of great concentration, cut the tape itself four hours away from the scanning head. He then rotated the cut strip into a right-angle piece in relation to the scanner, fused it in place with a micro heat element, then reattached the tape reel to its left and right sides. He had, in effect, inserted a dead twenty minutes into the unfolding flow of his reality. It would take effect—according to his calculations—a few minutes after midnight.

"Are you fixing yourself?" Sarah asked timidly.

Poole said, "I'm freeing myself." Beyond this he had several other alterations in mind. But first he had to test his theory; blank, unpunched tape meant no stimuli, in which case the *lack* of tape . . .

"That look on your face," Sarah said. She began gathering up her purse, coat, rolled-up aud-vid magazine. "I'll go; I can see how you feel about finding me here."

"Stay," he said. "I'll watch the captain kirk with you." He got into his shirt. "Remember years ago when there were—what was it?—twenty or twenty-two TV channels? Before the government shut down the independents?"

She nodded.

"What would it have looked like," he said, "if this TV set projected all channels onto the cathode ray screen *at the same time?* Could we have distinguished anything, in the mixture?"

"I don't think so."

"Maybe we could learn to. Learn to be selective; do our own job of perceiving what we wanted to and what we didn't. Think of the possibilities, if our brain could handle twenty images at once; think of the amount of knowledge which could be stored during a given period. I wonder if the brain, the human brain—" He broke off. "The human brain couldn't do it," he said presently, reflecting to himself. "But in theory a quasi-organic brain might."

"Is that what you have?" Sarah asked.

"Yes," Poole said.

They watched the captain kirk to its end, and then they went to bed. But Poole sat up against his pillows smoking and brooding. Beside him, Sarah stirred restlessly, wondering why he did not turn off the light.

Eleven-fifty. It would happen anytime, now.

"Sarah," he said, "I want your help. In a very few minutes something strange will happen to me. It won't last long, but I want you to watch me carefully. See if I"— he gestured—"show any changes. If I seem to go to sleep, or if I talk nonsense, or—" He wanted to say, if I disappear. But he did not. "I won't do you any harm, but I think it might be a good idea if you armed yourself. Do you have your anti-mugging gun with you?"

"In my purse." She had become fully awake now; sitting up in bed, she gazed at him with wild fright, her ample shoulders tanned and freckled in the light of the room.

He got her gun for her.

The room stiffened into paralyzed immobility. Then the colors began to drain away. Objects diminished until, smokelike, they flitted away into shadows. Darkness filmed everything as the objects in the room became weaker and weaker.

The last stimuli are dying out, Poole realized. He squinted, trying to see. He made out Sarah Benton, sitting in the bed: a two-dimensional figure that, doll-like, had been propped up, there to fade and dwindle. Random gusts of dematerialized substance eddied about in unstable clouds; the elements collected, fell apart, then collected once again. And then the last heat, energy, and light dissipated; the room closed over and fell into itself, as if sealed off from reality. And at that point absolute blackness replaced everything, space without depth, not nocturnal but rather stiff and unyielding. And in addition he heard nothing.

Reaching, he tried to touch something. But he had nothing to reach with. Awareness of his own body had departed along with everything else in the universe. He had no hands, and even if he had, there would be nothing for them to feel. I am still right about the way the damn tape works, he said to himself, using a nonexistent mouth to communicate an invisible message.

Will this pass in ten minutes? he asked himself. Am I right about that, too? He waited . . . but knew intuitively that his time sense had departed with everything else. I can only wait, he realized. And hope it won't be long.

To pace himself, he thought, I'll make up an encyclopedia; I'll try to list everything that begins with an *A*. Let's see. He pondered. Apply, automobile, acksetron, atmosphere, Atlantic, tomato aspic, advertising—he thought on and on, categories slithering through his fright-haunted mind.

All at once light flickered on.

He lay on the couch in the living room, and mild sunlight spilled in through the single window. Two men bent over him, their hands full of tools. Maintenance men, he realized. They've been working on me.

"He's conscious," one of the technicians said. He rose, stood back; Sarah Benton, dithering with anxiety, replaced him.

"Thank God!" she said, breathing wetly in Poole's ear. "I was so afraid; I called Mr. Danceman finally about—"

"What happened?" Poole broke in harshly. "Start from the beginning and for God's sake speak slowly. So I can assimilate it all."

Sarah composed herself, paused to rub her nose, and plunged on nervously. "You passed out. You just lay there, as if you were dead. I waited until two-thirty and you did nothing. I called Mr. Danceman, waking him up unfortunately, and he called the electric-ant maintenance—I mean, the organic-roby maintenance people, and these two men came about four-forty-five, and they've been working on you ever since. It's now six-fifteen in the morning. And I'm very cold and I want to go to bed; I can't make it in to the office today; I really can't." She turned away, sniffling. The sound annoyed him.

One of the uniformed maintenance men said, "You've been playing around with your reality tape."

"Yes," Poole said. Why deny it? Obviously they had found the inserted solid strip. "I shouldn't have been out that long," he said. "I inserted a ten-minute strip only."

490

"It shut off the tape transport," the technician explained. "The tape stopped moving forward; your insertion jammed it, and it automatically shut down to avoid tearing the tape. Why would you want to fiddle around with that? Don't you know what you could do?"

"I'm not sure," Poole said.

"But you have a good idea."

Poole said acridly, "That's why I'm doing it."

"Your bill," the maintenance man said, "is going to be ninety-five frogs. Payable in installments, if you so desire."

"Okay," he said; he sat up groggily, rubbed his eyes, and grimaced. His head ached and his stomach felt totally empty.

"Shave the tape next time," the primary technician told him. "That way it won't jam. Didn't it occur to you that it had a safety factor built into it? So it would stop rather than—"

"What happens," Poole interrupted, his voice low and intently careful, "if no tape passes under the scanner? No tape— nothing at all. The photocell shining upward without impedance?"

The technicians glanced at each other. One said, "All the neuro circuits jump their gaps and short out."

"Meaning what?" Poole said.

"Meaning it's the end of the mechanism."

Poole said, "I've examined the circuit. It doesn't carry enough voltage to do that. Metal won't fuse under such light loads of current, even if the terminals are touching. We're talking about a millionth of a watt along a premium channel perhaps a sixteenth of an inch in length. Let's assume there are a billion possible combinations at the instant arising from the punch-outs on the tape. The total output isn't cumulative; the amount of current depends on what the battery details for that module, and it's not much. With all gates open and going."

"Would we lie?" one of the technicians asked wearily.

"Why not?" Poole said. "Here I have an opportunity to experience everything. Simultaneously. To know the universe in its entirety, to be momentarily in contact with all reality. Something that no human can do. A symphonic score entering my

491

brain outside of time, all notes, all instruments sounding at once. And all symphonies. Do you see?"

"It'll burn you out," both technicians said, together.

"I don't think so," Poole said.

Sarah said, "Would you like a cup of coffee, Mr. Poole?"

"Yes," he said; he lowered his legs, pressed his cold feet against the floor, shuddered. He then stood up. His body ached. They had me lying all night on the couch, he realized. All things considered, they could have done better than that.

At the kitchen table in the far corner of the room, Garson Poole sat sipping coffee across from Sarah. The technicians had long since gone.

"You're not going to try any more experiments on yourself, are you?" Sarah asked wistfully.

Poole grated, "I would like to control time. To reverse it." I will cut a segment of tape out, he thought, and fuse it in upside down. The causal sequences will then flow the other way. Thereupon I will walk backward down the steps from the roof field, back up to my door, push a locked door open, walk backward to the sink, where I will get out a stack of dirty dishes. I will seat myself at this table before the stack, fill each dish with food produced from my stomach . . . I will then transfer the food to the refrigerator, pack it in bags, carry the bags to a supermarket, distribute the food here and there in the store. And at last, at the front counter, they will pay me money for this, from their cash register. The food will be packed with other food in big plastic boxes, shipped out of the city into the hydroponic plants on the Atlantic, there to be joined back to trees and bushes or the bodies of dead animals or pushed deep into the ground. But what would all that prove? A video tape running backward . . . I would know no more than I know now, which is not enough.

What I want, he realized, is ultimate and absolute reality, for one microsecond. After that it doesn't matter, because all will be known; nothing will be left to understand or see.

I might try one other change, he said to himself. Before I try cutting the tape. I will prick new punch-holes in the tape and see what presently emerges. It will be interesting because I will not know what the holes I make mean.

Using the tip of a microtool, he punched several holes, at random, on the tape. As close to the scanner as he could manage . . . he did not want to wait.

"I wonder if you'll see it," he said to Sarah. Apparently not, insofar as he could extrapolate. "Something may show up," he said to her. "I just want to warn you; I don't want you to be afraid."

"Oh, dear," Sarah said tinnily.

He examined his wristwatch. One minute passed, then a second, a third. And then—

In the center of the room appeared a flock of green and black ducks. They quacked excitedly, rose from the floor, fluttered against the ceiling in a dithering mass of feathers and wings, frantic in their vast urge, their instinct, to get away.

"Ducks," Poole said, marveling. "I punched a hole for a flight of wild ducks."

Now something else appeared. A park bench with an elderly, tattered man seated on it, reading a torn, bent newspaper. He looked up, dimly made out Poole, smiled briefly at him with badly made dentures, and then returned to his folded-back newspaper. He read on.

"Do you see him?" Poole asked Sarah. "And the ducks?" At that moment the ducks and the park bum disappeared. Nothing remained of them. The interval of their punch-holes had quickly passed.

"They weren't real," Sarah said. "Were they? So how—"

"You're not real," he told Sarah. "You're a stimulus-factor on my reality tape. A punch-hole that can be glazed over. Do you also have an existence in another reality tape, or one in an objective reality?" He did not know; he couldn't tell. Perhaps she existed in a thousand reality tapes; perhaps on every reality tape ever manufactured. "If I cut the tape," he said, "you will be everywhere and nowhere. Like everything else in the universe. At least as far as I am aware of it."

Sarah faltered, "I'm real."

"I want to know you completely," Poole said. "To do that I

must cut the tape. If I don't do it now, I'll do it some other time; it's inevitable that eventually I'll do it." So why wait? he asked himself. And there is always the possibility that Danceman has reported back to my maker, that they will be making moves to head me off. Because, perhaps, I'm endangering their property— myself.

"You make me wish I had gone to the office after all," Sarah said, her mouth turned down with dimpled gloom.

"Go," Poole said.

"I don't want to leave you alone."

"I'll be fine," Poole said.

"No, you're not going to be fine. You're going to unplug yourself or something, kill yourself because you've found out you're just an electric ant and not a human being."

He said, presently, "Maybe so." Maybe it boiled down to that.

"And I can't stop you," she said.

"No." He nodded in agreement.

"But I'm going to stay," Sarah said. "Even if I can't stop you. Because if I do leave and you do kill yourself, I'll always ask myself for the rest of my life what would have happened if I had stayed. You see?"

Again he nodded.

"Go ahead," Sarah said.

He rose to his feet. "It's not pain I'm going to feel," he told her. "Although it may look like that to you. Keep in mind the fact that organic robots have minimal pain-circuits in them. I will be experiencing the most intense—"

"Don't tell me any more," she broke in. "Just do it if you're going to, or don't do it if you're not."

Clumsily—because he was frightened—he wriggled his hands into the microglove assembly, reached to pick up a tiny tool: a sharp cutting blade. "I am going to cut a tape mounted inside my chest panel," he said, as he gazed through the enlarging-lens system. "That's all." His hand shook as it lifted the cutting blade. In a second it can be done, he realized. All over. And—I will have time to fuse the cut ends of tape back together, he realized. A half-hour at least. If I change my mind.

He cut the tape.

Staring at him, cowering, Sarah whispered, "Nothing happened."

"I have thirty or forty minutes." He reseated himself at the table, having drawn his hands from the gloves. His voice, he noticed, shook; undoubtedly Sarah was aware of it, and he felt anger at himself, knowing that he had alarmed her. "I'm sorry," he said, irrationally; he wanted to apologize to her. "Maybe you ought to leave," he said in panic; again he stood up. So did she, reflexively, as if imitating him; bloated and nervous, she stood there palpitating. "Go away," he said thickly. "Back to the office, where you ought to be. Where we both ought to be." I'm going to fuse the tape-ends together, he told himself; the tension is too great for me to stand.

Reaching his hands toward the gloves, he groped to pull them over his straining fingers. Peering into the enlarging screen, he saw the beam from the photoelectric gleam upward, pointed directly into the scanner; at the same time he saw the end of the tape disappearing under the scanner . . . he saw this, understood it; I'm too late, he realized. It has passed through. God, he thought, help me. It has begun winding at a rate greater than I calculated. So it's *now* that—

He saw apples and cobblestones and zebras. He felt warmth, the silky texture of cloth; he felt the ocean lapping at him and a great wind, from the north, plucking at him as if to lead him somewhere. Sarah was all around him, so was Danceman, New York glowed in the night, and the squibs about him scuttled and bounced through night skies and daytime and flooding and drought. Butter relaxed into liquid on his tongue, and at the same time hideous odors and tastes assailed him: the bitter presence of poisons and lemons and blades of summer grass. He drowned; he fell; he lay in the arms of a woman in a vast white bed which at the same time dinned shrilly in his ear: the warning noise of a defective elevator in one of the ancient, ruined downtown hotels. I am living, I have lived, I will never live, he said to himself, and with his thoughts came every word, every sound; insects squeaked and raced, and he half sank into a complex body of homeostatic machinery located somewhere in Tri-Plan's labs.

He wanted to say something to Sarah. Opening his mouth, he tried to bring forth words—a specific string of them out of the enormous mass of them brilliantly lighting his mind, scorching him with their utter meaning.

His mouth burned. He wondered why.

Frozen against the wall, Sarah Benton opened her eyes and saw the curl of smoke ascending from Poole's half-opened mouth. Then the roby sank down, knelt on elbows and knees, then slowly spread out in a broken, crumpled heap. She knew without examining it that it had "died."

Poole did it to itself, she realized. And it couldn't feel pain; it said so itself. Or at least not very much pain; maybe a little. Anyhow, now it is over.

I had better call Mr. Danceman and tell him what's happened, she decided. Still shaky, she made her way across the room to the fone; picking it up, she dialed from memory.

It thought I was a stimulus-factor on its reality tape, she said to herself. So it thought I would die when it "died." How strange, she thought. Why did it imagine that? It had never been plugged into the real world; it had "lived" in an electronic world of its own. How bizarre.

"Mr. Danceman," she said, when the circuit to his office had been put through. "Poole is gone. It destroyed itself right in front of my eyes. You'd better come over."

"So we're finally free of it."

"Yes, won't it be nice?"

Danceman said, "I'll send a couple of men over from the shop." He saw past her, made out the sight of Poole lying by the kitchen table. "You go home and rest," he instructed Sarah. "You must be worn out by all this."

"Yes," she said. "Thank you, Mr. Danceman." She hung up and stood, aimlessly.

And then she noticed something.

My hands, she thought. She held them up. Why is it I can see through them?

The wall of the room, too, had become ill-defined.

Trembling, she walked back to the inert roby, stood by it, not knowing what to do. Through her legs the carpet showed, and then the carpet became dim, and she saw, through it, further layers of disintegrating matter beyond.

Maybe if I can fuse the tape-ends back together, she thought. But she did not know how. And already Poole had become vague.

The wind of early morning blew about her. She did not feel it; she had begun, now, to cease to feel.

The winds blew on.

MACHINE
INTELLIGENCE
AND
MORAL ISSUES

THE BICENTENNIAL MAN

ISAAC ASIMOV

(1976)

Over the years, since Asimov's "Runaround" declared three laws to assure that robots would always be safe, obedient servants to man, his imagination has continued to play with the possibilities of artificial intelligence. Research in the field galloped forward at a dizzying pace, often outrunning anything science fiction had conceived. Asimov followed these developments and, during the late 1960s and the 1970s, wrote a half-dozen new robot stories. His robots were now much more sophisticated than those in earlier stories. They had developed emotion, intuition, the capacity to make judgments. Finally, one robot named Andrew took the ultimate step in the evolutionary process of robots. His journey is described in "The Bicentennial Man."

Asimov regards "Bicentennial Man" as his best robot story, and "no worse than the second-best short story of any type that I've ever written." Critics agree with him. It was written for a projected anthology to appear in 1976, the year of America's Bicentennial. Asimov began with the title and, little by little, worked out the details for the story. It was supposed to be 7,500 words long, but the story took over and spun itself out to 15,000 words. The anthology was never published, but to that anonymous editor who planned it, science fiction fans owe a debt. Without it, "Bicentennial Man" might never have been written, at least not as a short story. Asimov says that if he had known there would be no anthology and he could have made it any length he wanted, he would have been strongly tempted to make it a novel.

We can only speculate about whether a novel-length version would have been an improvement. As it stands, the story is very dense and rich with meanings. Most interesting for us here is the question the robot Andrew forces the courts of law to face: What, finally, is the real difference between a highly intelligent robot and a man? Various answers have been given in the earlier stories reprinted in this anthology. In "Bicentennial Man," Asimov gives a new one.

Does man have an ethical responsibility to this new form of intelligence he is evolving? Manufacturers of today's industrial robots need never even ask the question since their robots, mere mechanical arms directed by a computer program, seem no more than rather sophisticated and flexible machines. But, taking a quantum leap into the future, one realizes that this is a question that will eventually have to be faced. The Three Laws of Robotics,

501

protecting humans from the possibility of robot destruction, will need an analogous version that protects robots against destructive humans.

Another question explored in "Bicentennial Man" is the relationship between the organic and the inorganic. Can a line really be drawn between the animate and the inanimate, the living and the nonliving? Is high intelligence, cherished by humans as the quality making them the superior species, just as valuable when housed in an inorganic being?

The Three Laws of Robotics

1. A robot may not injure a human being, or, through inaction, allow a human being to come to harm.

2. A robot must obey the orders given it by human beings except where such orders would conflict with the First Law. .

3. A robot must protect its own existence as long as such protection does not conflict with the First or Second Law.

1

Andrew Martin said, "Thank you," and took the seat offered him. He didn't look driven to the last resort, but he had been.

He didn't, actually, look anything, for there was a smooth blankness to his face, except for the sadness one imagined one saw in his eyes. His hair was smooth, light brown, rather fine; and he had no facial hair. He looked freshly and cleanly shaved. His clothes were distinctly old-fashioned, but neat, and predominantly a velvety red-purple in color.

Facing him from behind the desk was the surgeon. The nameplate on the desk included a fully identifying series of letters and numbers which Andrew didn't bother with. To call him Doctor would be quite enough.

"When can the operation be carried through, Doctor?" he asked.

Softly, with that certain inalienable note of respect that a robot always used to a human being, the surgeon said, "I am not certain, sir, that I understand how or upon whom such an operation could be performed."

There might have been a look of respectful intransigence on

the surgeon's face, if a robot of his sort, in lightly bronzed stainless steel, could have such an expression—or any expression.

Andrew Martin studied the robot's right hand, his cutting hand, as it lay motionless on the desk. The fingers were long and were shaped into artistically metallic, looping curves so graceful and appropriate that one could imagine a scalpel fitting them and becoming, temporarily, one piece with them. There would be no hesitation in his work, no stumbling, no quivering, no mistakes. That confidence came with specialization, of course, a specialization so fiercely desired by humanity that few robots were, any longer, independently brained. A surgeon, of course, would have to be. But this one, though brained, was so limited in his capacity that he did not recognize Andrew, had probably never heard of him.

"Have you ever thought you would like to be a man?" Andrew asked.

The surgeon hesitated a moment, as though the question fitted nowhere in his allotted positronic pathways. "But I am a robot, sir."

"Would it be better to be a man?"

"It would be better, sir, to be a better surgeon. I could not be so if I were a man, but only if I were a more advanced robot. I would be pleased to be a more advanced robot."

"It does not offend you that I can order you about? That I can make you stand up, sit down, move right or left, by merely telling you to do so?"

"It is my pleasure to please you, sir. If your orders were to interfere with my functioning with respect to you or to any other human being, I would not obey you. The First Law, concerning my duty to human safety, would take precedence over the Second Law relating to obedience. Otherwise, obedience is my pleasure. Now, upon whom am I to perform this operation?"

"Upon me," Andrew said.

"But that is impossible. It is patently a damaging operation."

"That does not matter," said Andrew, calmly.

"I must not inflict damage," said the surgeon.

"On a human being, you must not," said Andrew, "but I, too, am a robot."

2

Andrew had appeared much more a robot when he had first been manufactured. He had then been as much a robot in appearance as any that had ever existed—smoothly designed and functional.

He had done well in the home to which he had been brought in those days when robots in households, or on the planet altogether, had been a rarity. There had been four in the home: Sir and Ma'am and Miss and Little Miss. He knew their names, of course, but he never used them. Sir was Gerald Martin.

His own serial number was NDR- . . . He eventually forgot the numbers. It had been a long time, of course; but if he had wanted to remember, he could not have forgotten. He had not wanted to remember.

Little Miss had been the first to call him Andrew, because she could not use the letters, and all the rest followed her in doing so.

Little Miss . . . she had lived for ninety years and was long since dead. He had tried to call her Ma'am once, but she would not allow it. Little Miss she had been to her last day.

Andrew had been intended to perform the duties of a valet, a butler, even a lady's maid. Those were the experimental days for him and, indeed, for all robots anywhere save in the industrial and exploratory factories and stations off Earth.

The Martins enjoyed him, and half the time he was prevented from doing his work because Miss and Little Miss wanted to play with him. It was Miss who first understood how this might be arranged. "We order you to play with us and you must follow orders."

"I am sorry, Miss, but a prior order from Sir must surely take precedence."

But she said, "Daddy just said he *hoped* you would take care of the cleaning. That's not much of an order. I *order* you."

Sir did not mind. Sir was fond of Miss and of Little Miss, even more than Ma'am was; and Andrew was fond of them, too. At least, the effect they had upon his actions were those which in a human being would have been called the result of fondness. Andrew thought of it as fondness, for he did not know any other word for it.

It was for Little Miss that Andrew had carved a pendant out of wood. She had ordered him to. Miss, it seemed, had received an ivorite pendant with scrollwork for her birthday and Little Miss was unhappy over it. She had only a piece of wood, which she gave Andrew together with a small kitchen knife.

He had done it quickly and Little Miss had said, "That's *nice*, Andrew. I'll show it to Daddy."

Sir would not believe it. "Where did you really get this, Mandy?" Mandy was what he called Little Miss. When Little Miss assured him she was really telling the truth, he turned to Andrew. "Did you do this, Andrew?"

"Yes, Sir."

"The design, too?"

"Yes, Sir."

"From what did you copy the design?"

"It is a geometric representation, Sir, that fits the grain of the wood."

The next day, Sir brought him another piece of wood—a larger one—and an electric vibro-knife. "Make something out of this, Andrew. Anything you want to," he said.

Andrew did so as Sir watched, then looked at the product a long time. After that, Andrew no longer waited on tables. He was ordered to read books on furniture design instead, and he learned to make cabinets and desks.

"These are amazing productions, Andrew," Sir soon told him.

"I enjoy doing them, Sir," Andrew admitted.

"Enjoy?"

"It makes the circuits of my brain somehow flow more easily. I have heard you use the word 'enjoy' and the way you use it fits the way I feel. I enjoy doing them, Sir."

3

Gerald Martin took Andrew to the regional offices of the United States Robots and Mechanical Men Corporation. As a member of the Regional Legislature he had no trouble at all in gaining an interview with the chief robopsychologist. In fact, it was only as a member of the Regional Legislature that he qualified as a robot owner in the first place—in those early days when robots were rare.

Andrew did not understand any of this at the time. But in later years, with greater learning, he could review that early scene and understand it in its proper light.

The robopsychologist, Merton Mansky, listened with a growing frown and more than once managed to stop his fingers at the point beyond which they would have irrevocably drummed on the table. He had drawn features and a lined forehead, but he might actually have been younger than he looked.

"Robotics is not an exact art, Mr. Martin," Mansky explained. "I cannot explain it to you in detail, but the mathematics governing the plotting of the positronic pathways are far too complicated to permit of any but approximate solutions. Naturally, since we build everything around the Three Laws, those are incontrovertible. We will, of course, replace your robot—"

"Not at all," said Sir. "There is no question of failure on his part. He performs his assigned duties perfectly. The point is, he also carves wood in exquisite fashion and never the same twice. He produces works of art."

Mansky looked confused. "Strange. Of course, we're attempting generalized pathways these days. Really creative, you think?"

"See for yourself." Sir handed over a little sphere of wood on which there was a playground scene in which the boys and girls were almost too small to make out, yet they were in perfect proportion and they blended so naturally with the grain that it, too, seemed to have been carved.

Mansky was incredulous. "*He* did that?" He handed it back with a shake of his head. "The luck of the draw. Something in the pathways."

"Can you do it again?"

"Probably not. Nothing like this has ever been reported."

"Good! I don't in the least mind Andrew's being the only one."

"I suspect that the company would like to have your robot back for study," Mansky said.

"Not a chance!" Sir said with sudden grimness. "Forget it." He turned to Andrew, "Let's go home now."

"As you wish, Sir," said Andrew.

4

Miss was dating boys and wasn't about the house much. It was Little Miss, not as little as she once was, who filled Andrew's horizon now. She never forgot that the very first piece of wood-carving he had done had been for her. She kept it on a silver chain about her neck.

It was she who first objected to Sir's habit of giving away Andrew's work. "Come on, Dad, if anyone wants one of them, let him pay for it. It's worth it."

"It isn't like you to be greedy, Mandy."

"Not for us, Dad. For the artist."

Andrew had never heard the word before, and when he had a moment to himself he looked it up in the dictionary.

Then there was another trip, this time to Sir's lawyer.

"What do you think of this, John?" Sir asked.

The lawyer was John Feingold. He had white hair and a pudgy belly, and the rims of his contact lenses were tinted a bright green. He looked at the small plaque Sir had given him. "This is beautiful. But I've already heard the news. Isn't this a carving made by your robot? The one you've brought with you."

"Yes, Andrew does them. Don't you, Andrew?"

"Yes, Sir," said Andrew.

"How much would you pay for that, John?" Sir asked.

"I can't say. I'm not a collector of such things."

"Would you believe I have been offered two hundred and fifty dollars for that small thing? Andrew has made chairs that have sold for five hundred dollars. There's two hundred thousand dollars in the bank from Andrew's products."

"Good heavens, he's making you rich, Gerald."

"Half-rich," said Sir. "Half of it is in an account in the name of Andrew Martin."

"The robot?"

"That's right, and I want to know if it's legal."

"Legal . . . ?" Feingold's chair creaked as he leaned back in it. "There are no precedents, Gerald. How did your robot sign the necessary papers?"

"He can sign his name, so I brought in the signature to the bank. I didn't bring him along, however. Now is there anything further that ought to be done?"

"Um." Feingold's eyes seemed to turn inward for a moment. Then he said, "Well, we can set up a trust to handle all finances in his name and that will place a layer of insulation between him and the hostile world. Beyond that, my advice is you do nothing. No one has stopped you so far. If anyone objects, let *him* bring suit."

"And will you take the case if the suit is brought?"

"For a retainer, certainly."

"How much?"

"Something like that," Feingold said, and pointed to the wooden plaque.

"Fair enough," said Sir.

Feingold chuckled as he turned to the robot. "Andrew, are you pleased that you have money?"

"Yes, sir."

"What do you plan to do with it?"

"Pay for things, sir, which otherwise Sir would have to pay for. It would save him expense, sir."

5

Such occasions arose. Repairs were expensive, and revisions were even more so. With the years, new models of robots were produced and Sir saw to it that Andrew had the advantage of every new device, until he was a model of metallic excellence. It was all done at Andrew's expense. Andrew insisted on that.

Only his positronic pathways were untouched. Sir insisted on that.

"The new models aren't as good as you are, Andrew," he

508

said. "The new robots are worthless. The company has learned to make the pathways more precise, more closely on the nose, more deeply on the track. The new robots don't shift. They do what they're designed for and never stray. I like you better."

"Thank you, Sir."

"And it's your doing, Andrew, don't you forget that. I am certain Mansky put an end to generalized pathways as soon as he had a good look at you. He didn't like the unpredictability. Do you know how many times he asked for you back so he could place you under study? Nine times! I never let him have you, though; and now that he's retired, we may have some peace."

So Sir's hair thinned and grayed and his face grew pouchy, while Andrew looked even better than he had when he first joined the family. Ma'am had joined an art colony somewhere in Europe, and Miss was a poet in New York. They wrote sometimes, but not often. Little Miss was married and lived not far away. She said she did not want to leave Andrew. When her child, Little Sir, was born, she let Andrew hold the bottle and feed him.

With the birth of a grandson, Andrew felt that Sir finally had someone to replace those who had gone. Therefore, it would not be so unfair now to come to him with the request.

"Sir, it is kind of you to have allowed me to spend my money as I wished."

"It was your money, Andrew."

"Only by your voluntary act, Sir. I do not believe the law would have stopped you from keeping it all."

"The law won't persuade me to do wrong, Andrew."

"Despite all expenses, and despite taxes, too, Sir, I have nearly six hundred thousand dollars."

"I know that, Andrew."

"I want to give it to you, Sir."

"I won't take it, Andrew."

"In exchange for something you can give me, Sir."

"Oh? What is that, Andrew?"

"My freedom, Sir."

"Your—"

"I wish to buy my freedom, Sir."

6

It wasn't that easy. Sir had flushed, had said, "For God's sake!" Then he had turned on his heel and stalked away.

It was Little Miss who finally brought him round, defiantly and harshly—and in front of Andrew. For thirty years no one had ever hesitated to talk in front of Andrew, whether or not the matter involved Andrew. He was only a robot.

"Dad, why are you taking this as a personal affront? He'll still be here. He'll still be loyal. He can't help that; it's built in. All he wants is a form of words. He wants to be called free. Is that so terrible? Hasn't he earned this chance? Heavens, he and I have been talking about it for years!"

"Talking about it for years, have you?"

"Yes, and over and over again he postponed it for fear he would hurt you. I *made* him put the matter up to you."

"He doesn't know what freedom is. He's a robot."

"Dad, you don't know him. He's read everything in the library. I don't know what he feels inside, but I don't know what *you* feel inside, either. When you talk to him, you'll find he reacts to the various abstractions as you and I do, and what else counts? If someone else's reactions are like your own, what more can you ask for?"

"The law won't take that attitude," Sir said, angrily. "See here, you!" He turned to Andrew with a deliberate grate in his voice. "I can't free you except by doing it legally. If this gets into the courts, you not only won't get your freedom but the law will take official cognizance of your money. They'll tell you that a robot has no right to earn money. Is this rigmarole worth losing your money?"

"Freedom is without price, Sir," said Andrew. "Even the chance of freedom is worth the money."

7

It seemed the court might also take the attitude that freedom was without price, and might decide that for no price, however great, could a robot buy its freedom.

The simple statement of the regional attorney who represented those who had brought a class action to oppose the freedom was this: "The word 'freedom' has no meaning when applied to a robot. Only a human being can be free." He said it several times, when it seemed appropriate, slowly, with his hand coming down rhythmically on the desk before him to mark the words.

Little Miss asked permission to speak on behalf of Andrew.

She was recognized by her full name, something Andrew had never heard pronounced before: "Amanda Laura Martin Charney may approach the bench."

"Thank you, Your Honor. I am not a lawyer and I don't know the proper way of phrasing things, but I hope you will listen to my meaning and ignore the words.

"Let's understand what it means to be free in Andrew's case. In some ways, he *is* free. I think it's at least twenty years since anyone in the Martin family gave him an order to do something that we felt he might not do of his own accord. But we can, if we wish, give him an order to do anything, couching it as harshly as we wish, because he is a machine that belongs to us. Why should we be in a position to do so, when he has served us so long, so faithfully, and has earned so much money for us? He owes us nothing more. The debit is entirely on the other side.

"Even if we were legally forbidden to place Andrew in involuntary servitude, he would still serve us voluntarily. Making him free would be a trick of words only but it would mean much to him. It would give him everything and cost us nothing."

For a moment the judge seemed to be suppressing a smile. "I see your point, Mrs. Charney. The fact is that there is no binding law in this respect and no precedent. There is, however, the unspoken assumption that only a man may enjoy freedom. I can make new law here, subject to reversal in a higher court; but I cannot lightly run counter to that assumption. Let me address the robot. Andrew!"

"Yes, Your Honor."

It was the first time Andrew had spoken in court, and the judge seemed astonished for a moment at the human timbre of his voice.

"Why do you want to be free, Andrew? In what way will this matter to you?"

"Would *you* wish to be a slave, Your Honor?" Andrew asked.

"But you are not a slave. You are a perfectly good robot—a genius of a robot, I am given to understand, capable of an artistic expression that can be matched nowhere. What more could you do if you were free?"

"Perhaps no more than I do now, Your Honor, but with greater joy. It has been said in this courtroom that only a human being can be free. It seems to me that only someone who *wishes* for freedom can be free. I wish for freedom."

And it was that statement that cued the judge. The crucial sentence in his decision was, "There is no right to deny freedom to any object with a mind advanced enough to grasp the concept and desire the state."

It was eventually upheld by the World Court.

8

Sir remained displeased, and his harsh voice made Andrew feel as if he were being short-circuited. "I don't want your damned money, Andrew. I'll take it only because you won't feel free otherwise. From now on, you can select your own jobs and do them as you please. I will give you no orders, except this one: Do as you please. But I am still responsible for you. That's part of the court order. I hope you understand that."

Little Miss interrupted. "Don't be irascible, Dad. The responsibility is no great chore. You know you won't have to do a thing. The Three Laws still hold."

"Then how is he free?"

"Are not human beings bound by their laws, Sir?" Andrew replied.

"I'm not going to argue." Sir left the room, and Andrew saw him only infrequently after that.

Little Miss came to see him frequently in the small house that had been built and made over for him. It had no kitchen, of course, nor bathroom facilities. It had just two rooms; one was a library and one was a combination storeroom and workroom. Andrew accepted many commissions and worked harder as a free robot than he ever had before, till the cost of the house was paid for and the structure was signed over to him.

One day Little Sir—no, George!—came. Little Sir had insisted on that after the court decision. "A free robot doesn't call anyone Little Sir," George had said. "I call you Andrew. You must call me George."

His preference was phrased as an order, so Andrew called him George—but Little Miss remained Little Miss.

One day when George came alone, it was to say that Sir was dying. Little Miss was at the bedside, but Sir wanted Andrew as well.

Sir's voice was still quite strong, though he seemed unable to move much. He struggled to raise his hand.

"Andrew," he said, "Andrew— Don't help me, George. I'm only dying; I'm not crippled. Andrew, I'm glad you're free. I just wanted to tell you that."

Andrew did not know what to say. He had never been at the side of someone dying before, but he knew it was the human way of ceasing to function. It was an involuntary and irreversible dismantling, and Andrew did not know what to say that might be appropriate. He could only remain standing, absolutely silent, absolutely motionless.

When it was over, Little Miss said to him, "He may not have seemed friendly to you toward the end, Andrew, but he was old, you know; and it hurt him that you should want to be free."

Then Andrew found the words. "I would never have been free without him, Little Miss."

9

Only after Sir's death did Andrew begin to wear clothes. He began with an old pair of trousers at first, a pair that George had given him.

George was married now, and a lawyer. He had joined Feingold's firm. Old Feingold was long since dead, but his daughter had carried on. Eventually the firm's name became Feingold and Martin. It remained so even when the daughter retired and no Feingold took her place. At the time Andrew first put on clothes, the Martin name had just been added to the firm.

George had tried not to smile the first time he saw Andrew attempting to put on trousers, but to Andrew's eyes the smile was clearly there. George showed Andrew how to manipulate the static charge to allow the trousers to open, wrap about his lower body, and move shut. George demonstrated on his own trousers, but Andrew was quite aware that it would take him a while to duplicate that one flowing motion.

"But why do you want trousers, Andrew? Your body is so beautifully functional it's a shame to cover it—especially when you needn't worry about either temperature control or modesty. And the material doesn't cling properly—not on metal."

Andrew held his ground. "Are not human bodies beautifully functional, George? Yet you cover yourselves."

"For warmth, for cleanliness, for protection, for decorativeness. None of that applies to you."

"I feel bare without clothes. I feel different, George," Andrew responded.

"Different! Andrew, there are millions of robots on Earth now. In this region, according to the last census, there are almost as many robots as there are men."

"I know, George. There are robots doing every conceivable type of work."

"And none of them wear clothes."

"But none of them are free, George."

Little by little, Andrew added to his wardrobe. He was inhibited by George's smile and by the stares of the people who commissioned work.

He might be free, but there was built into Andrew a carefully detailed program concerning his behavior to people, and it was only by the tiniest steps that he dared advance; open disapproval would set him back months. Not everyone accepted Andrew as free. He was incapable of resenting that, and yet there was a difficulty about his thinking process when he thought of it. Most of all, he tended to avoid putting on clothes—or too many of them—when he thought Little Miss might come to visit him. She was older now and was often away in some warmer climate, but when she returned the first thing she did was visit him.

On one of her visits, George said ruefully, "She's got me, Andrew. I'll be running for the legislature next year. 'Like grandfather,' she says, 'like grandson.' "

"Like grandfather . . ." Andrew stopped, uncertain.

"I mean that I, George, the grandson, will be like Sir, the grandfather, who was in the legislature once."

"It would be pleasant, George, if Sir were still—" He paused, for he did not want to say, "in working order." That seemed inappropriate.

"Alive," George said. "Yes, I think of the old monster now and then, too."

Andrew often thought about this conversation. He had noticed his own incapacity in speech when talking with George. Somehow the language had changed since Andrew had come into being with a built-in vocabulary. Then, too, George used a colloquial speech, as Sir and Little Miss had not. Why should he have called Sir a monster when surely that word was not appropriate? Andrew could not even turn to his own books for guidance. They were old, and most dealt with woodworking, with art, with furniture design. There were none on language, none on the ways of human beings.

Finally, it seemed to him that he must seek the proper books; and as a free robot, he felt he must not ask George. He would go to town and use the library. It was a triumphant decision and he felt his electropotential grow distinctly higher until he had to throw in an impedance coil.

He put on a full costume, including even a shoulder chain of wood. He would have preferred the glitter plastic, but George had said that wood was much more appropriate and that polished cedar was considerably more valuable as well.

He had placed a hundred feet between himself and the house before gathering resistance brought him to a halt. He shifted the impedance coil out of circuit, and when that did not seem to help enough, he returned to his home and on a piece of notepaper wrote neatly, "I have gone to the library," and placed it in clear view on his worktable.

10

Andrew never quite got to the library.

He had studied the map. He knew the route, but not the appearance of it. The actual landmarks did not resemble the symbols on the map and he would hesitate. Eventually, he thought

515

he must have somehow gone wrong, for everything looked strange.

He passed an occasional field-robot, but by the time he decided he should ask his way, none were in sight. A vehicle passed and did not stop.

Andrew stood irresolute, which meant calmly motionless, for coming across the field toward him were two human beings.

He turned to face them, and they altered their course to meet him. A moment before, they had been talking loudly. He had heard their voices. But now they were silent. They had the look that Andrew associated with human uncertainty; and they were young, but not very young. Twenty, perhaps? Andrew could never judge human age.

"Would you describe to me the route to the town library, sirs?"

One of them, the taller of the two, whose tall hat lengthened him still further, almost grotesquely, said, not to Andrew, but to the other, "It's a robot."

The other had a bulbous nose and heavy eyelids. He said, not to Andrew but to the first, "It's wearing clothes."

The tall one snapped his fingers. "It's the free robot. They have a robot at the old Martin place who isn't owned by anybody. Why else would it be wearing clothes?"

"Ask it," said the one with the nose.

"Are you the Martin robot?" asked the tall one.

"I am Andrew Martin, sir," Andrew said.

"Good. Take off your clothes. Robots don't wear clothes." He said to the other, "That's disgusting. Look at him!"

Andrew hesitated. He hadn't heard an order in that tone of voice in so long that his Second Law circuits had momentarily jammed.

The tall one repeated, "Take off your clothes. I order you."

Slowly, Andrew began to remove them.

"Just drop them," said the tall one.

The nose said, "If it doesn't belong to anyone, it could be ours as much as someone else's."

"Anyway," said the tall one, "who's to object to anything

516

we do? We're not damaging property." He turned to Andrew. "Stand on your head."

"The head is not meant—" Andrew began.

"That's an order. If you don't know how, try anyway."

Andrew hesitated again, then bent to put his head on the ground. He tried to lift his legs but fell, heavily.

The tall one said, "Just lie there." He said to the other, "We can take him apart. Ever take a robot apart?"

"Will he let us?"

"How can he stop us?"

There was no way Andrew could stop them, if they ordered him in a forceful enough manner not to resist. The Second Law of obedience took precedence over the Third Law of self-pres- ervation. In any case, he could not defend himself without pos- sibly hurting them, and that would mean breaking the First Law. At that thought, he felt every motile unit contract slightly and he quivered as he lay there.

The tall one walked over and pushed at him with his foot. "He's heavy. I think we'll need tools to do the job."

The nose said, "We could order him to take himself apart. It would be fun to watch him try."

"Yes," said the tall one, thoughtfully, "but let's get him off the road. If someone comes along—"

It was too late. Someone had, indeed, come along and it was George. From where he lay, Andrew had seen him top- ping a small rise in the middle distance. He would have liked to signal him in some way, but the last order had been "Just lie there!"

George was running now, and he arrived on the scene some- what winded. The two young men stepped back a little and then waited thoughtfully.

"Andrew, has something gone wrong?" George asked anx- iously.

Andrew replied, "I am well, George."

"Then stand up. What happened to your clothes?"

"That your robot, mac?" the tall young man asked.

George turned sharply. "He's no one's robot. What's been going on here?"

"We politely asked him to take his clothes off. What's that to you, if you don't own him?"

George turned to Andrew. "What were they doing, Andrew?"

"It was their intention in some way to dismember me. They were about to move me to a quiet spot and order me to dismember myself."

George looked at the two young men, and his chin trembled. The young men retreated no farther. They were smiling.

The tall one said lightly, "What are you going to do, pudgy? Attack us?"

George said, "No. I don't have to. This robot has been with my family for more than seventy-five years. He knows us and he values us more than he values anyone else. I am going to tell him that you two are threatening my life and that you plan to kill me. I will ask him to defend me. In choosing between me and you two, he will choose me. Do you know what will happen to you when he attacks you?"

The two were backing away slightly, looking uneasy.

George said sharply, "Andrew, I am in danger and about to come to harm from these young men. Move toward them!"

Andrew did so, and the young men did not wait. They ran.

"All right, Andrew, relax," George said. He looked unstrung. He was far past the age where he could face the possibility of a dustup with one young man, let alone two.

"I couldn't have hurt them, George. I could see they were not attacking you."

"I didn't order you to attack them. I only told you to move toward them. Their own fears did the rest."

"How can they fear robots?"

"It's a disease of mankind, one which has not yet been cured. But never mind that. What the devil are you doing here, Andrew? Good thing I found your note. I was just on the point of turning back and hiring a helicopter when I found you. How did you get it into your head to go to the library? I would have brought you any books you needed."

"I am a—" Andrew began.

"Free robot. Yes, yes. All right, what did you want in the library?"

"I want to know more about human beings, about the world, about everything. And about robots, George. I want to write a history about robots."

George put his arm on the other's shoulder. "Well, let's walk home. But pick up your clothes first. Andrew, there are a million books on robotics and all of them include histories of the science. The world is growing saturated not only with robots but with information about robots."

Andrew shook his head, a human gesture he had lately begun to adopt. "Not a history of robotics, George. A history of *robots*, by a robot. I want to explain how robots feel about what has happened since the first ones were allowed to work and live on Earth."

George's eyebrows lifted, but he said nothing in direct response.

11

Little Miss was just past her eighty-third birthday, but there was nothing about her that was lacking in either energy or determination. She gestured with her cane oftener than she propped herself up with it.

She listened to the story in a fury of indignation. "George, that's horrible. Who were those young ruffians?"

"I don't know. What difference does it make? In the end they did not do any damage."

"They might have. You're a lawyer, George; and if you're well off, it's entirely due to the talents of Andrew. It was the money *he* earned that is the foundation of everything we have. He provides the continuity for this family, and I will *not* have him treated as a windup toy."

"What would you have me do, Mother?" George asked.

"I said you're a lawyer. Don't you listen? You set up a test case somehow, and you force the regional courts to declare for robot rights and get the legislature to pass the necessary bills. Carry the whole thing to the World Court, if you have to. I'll be watching, George, and I'll tolerate no shirking."

She was serious, so what began as a way of soothing the fearsome old lady became an involved matter with enough legal

519

entanglement to make it interesting. As senior partner of Feingold and Martin, George plotted strategy. But he left the actual
work to his junior partners, with much of it a matter for his son,
Paul, who was also a member of the firm and who reported
dutifully nearly every day to his grandmother. She, in turn,
discussed the case every day with Andrew.

Andrew was deeply involved. His work on his book on robots
was delayed and delayed again, as he pored over the legal ar-
guments and even, at times, made very diffident suggestions.
"George told me that day I was attacked that human beings
have always been afraid of robots," he said one day. "As long
as they are, the courts and the legislatures are not likely to work
hard on behalf of robots. Should not something be done about
public opinion?"

So while Paul stayed in court, George took to the public
platform. It gave him the advantage of being informal, and he
even went so far sometimes as to wear the new, loose style of
clothing which he called drapery.

Paul chided him, "Just don't trip over it on stage, Dad."

George replied despondently, "I'll try not to."

He addressed the annual convention of holo-news editors on
one occasion and said, in part: "If, by virtue of the Second Law,
we can demand of any robot unlimited obedience in all respects
not involving harm to a human being, then any human being,
any human being, has a fearsome power over any robot, *any*
robot. In particular, since Second Law supersedes Third Law,
any human being can use the law of obedience to overcome the
law of self-protection. He can order any robot to damage itself
or even to destroy itself for any reason, or for no reason.

"Is this just? Would we treat an animal so? Even an inanimate object which has given us good service has a claim on our
consideration. And a robot is not insensitive; it is not an animal.
It can think well enough so that it can talk to us, reason with
us, joke with us. Can we treat them as friends, can we work
together with them, and not give them some of the fruits of that
friendship, some of the benefits of co-working?

"If a man has the right to give a robot any order that does
not involve harm to a human being, he should have the decency

never to give a robot any order that involves harm to a robot, unless human safety absolutely requires it. With great power goes great responsibility, and if the robots have Three Laws to protect men, is it too much to ask that men have a law or two to protect robots?"

Andrew was right. It was the battle over public opinion that held the key to courts and legislature. In the end, a law was passed that set up conditions under which robot-harming orders were forbidden. It was endlessly qualified and the punishments for violating the law were totally inadequate, but the principle was established. The final passage by the World Legislature came through on the day of Little Miss's death.

That was no coincidence. Little Miss held on to life desperately during the last debate and let go only when word of victory arrived. Her last smile was for Andrew. Her last words were, "You have been good to us, Andrew." She died with her hand holding his, while her son and his wife and children remained at a respectful distance from both.

12

Andrew waited patiently when the receptionist-robot disappeared into the inner office. The receptionist might have used the holographic chatterbox, but unquestionably it was perturbed by having to deal with another robot rather than with a human being.

Andrew passed the time revolving the matter in his mind: Could "unroboted" be used as an analog of "unmanned," or had unmanned become a metaphoric term sufficiently divorced from its original literal meaning to be applied to robots—or to women, for that matter? Such problems frequently arose as he worked on his book on robots. The trick of thinking out sentences to express all complexities had undoubtedly increased his vocabulary.

Occasionally, someone came into the room to stare at him and he did not try to avoid the glance. He looked at each calmly, and each in turn looked away.

Paul Martin finally emerged. He looked surprised, or he would have if Andrew could have made out his expression with certainty. Paul had taken to wearing the heavy makeup that fashion was dictating for both sexes. Though it made sharper and firmer the somewhat bland lines of Paul's face, Andrew disapproved. He found that disapproving of human beings, as long as he did not express it verbally, did not make him very uneasy. He could even write the disapproval. He was sure it had not always been so.

"Come in, Andrew. I'm sorry I made you wait, but there was something I *had* to finish. Come in. You had said you wanted to talk to me, but I didn't know you meant here in town."

"If you are busy, Paul, I am prepared to continue to wait."

Paul glanced at the interplay of shifting shadows on the dial on the wall that served as timepiece and said, "I can make some time. Did you come alone?"

"I hired an automatobile."

"Any trouble?" Paul asked, with more than a trace of anxiety.

"I wasn't expecting any. My rights are protected."

Paul looked all the more anxious for that. "Andrew, I've explained that the law is unenforceable, at least under most conditions. And if you insist on wearing clothes, you'll run into trouble eventually, just like that first time."

"And *only* time, Paul. I'm sorry you are displeased."

"Well, look at it this way: You are virtually a living legend, Andrew, and you are too valuable in many different ways for you to have any right to take chances with yourself. By the way, how's the book coming?"

"I am approaching the end, Paul. The publisher is quite pleased."

"Good!"

"I don't know that he's necessarily pleased with the book as a book. I think he expects to sell many copies because it's written by a robot and that's what pleases him."

"Only human, I'm afraid."

"I am not displeased. Let it sell for whatever reason, since it will mean money and I can use some."

"Grandmother left you—"

"Little Miss was generous, and I'm sure I can count on the family to help me out further. But it is the royalties from the book on which I am counting to help me through the next step."

"What next step is that?"

"I wish to see the head of U.S. Robots and Mechanical Men Corporation. I have tried to make an appointment; but so far I have not been able to reach him. The Corporation did not cooperate with me in the writing of the book, so I am not surprised, you understand."

Paul was clearly amused. "Cooperation is the last thing you can expect. They didn't cooperate with us in our great fight for robot rights. Quite the reverse, and you can see why. Give a robot rights and people may not want to buy them."

"Nevertheless," said Andrew, "if *you* call them, you may be able to obtain an interview for me."

"I'm no more popular with them than you are, Andrew."

"But perhaps you can hint that by seeing me they may head off a campaign by Feingold and Martin to strengthen the rights of robots further."

"Wouldn't that be a lie, Andrew?"

"Yes, Paul, and I can't tell one. That is why you must call."

"Ah, you can't lie, but you can urge me to tell a lie, is that it? You're getting more human all the time, Andrew."

13

The meeting was not easy to arrange, even with Paul's supposedly weighted name. But it finally came about. When it did, Harley Smythe-Robertson, who, on his mother's side, was descended from the original founder of the corporation and who had adopted the hyphenation to indicate it, looked remarkably unhappy. He was approaching retirement age and his entire tenure as president had been devoted to the matter of robot rights. His gray hair was plastered thinly over the top of his scalp; his face was not made up, and he eyed Andrew with brief hostility from time to time.

Andrew began the conversation. "Sir, nearly a century ago, I was told by a Merton Mansky of this corporation that the mathematics governing the plotting of the positronic pathways were far too complicated to permit of any but approximate solutions and that, therefore, my own capacities were not fully predictable."

"That was a century ago." Smythe-Robertson hesitated, then said icily, "*Sir*. It is true no longer. Our robots are made with precision now and are trained precisely to their jobs."

"Yes," said Paul, who had come along, as he said, to make sure that the corporation played fair, "with the result that my receptionist must be guided at every point once events depart from the conventional, however slightly."

"You would be much more displeased if it were to improvise," Smythe-Robertson said.

"Then you no longer manufacture robots like myself, which are flexible and adaptable."

"No longer."

"The research I have done in connection with my book," said Andrew, "indicates that I am the oldest robot presently in active operation."

"The oldest presently," said Smythe-Robertson, "and the oldest ever. The oldest that will ever be. No robot is useful after the twenty-fifth year. They are called in and replaced with newer models."

"No robot as presently manufactured is useful after the *twentieth* year," said Paul, with a note of sarcasm creeping into his voice. "Andrew is quite exceptional in this respect."

Andrew, adhering to the path he had marked out for himself, continued, "As the oldest robot in the world and the most flexible, am I not unusual enough to merit special treatment from the company?"

"Not at all," Smythe-Robertson said, freezing up. "Your unusualness is an embarrassment to the company. If you were on lease, instead of having been an outright sale through some mischance, you would long since have been replaced."

"But that is exactly the point," said Andrew. "I am a free robot and I own myself. Therefore I come to you and ask you to replace me. You cannot do this without the owner's consent. Nowadays, that consent is extorted as a condition of the lease, but in my time this did not happen."

Smythe-Robertson was looking both startled and puzzled, and for a moment there was silence. Andrew found himself staring at the hologram on the wall. It was a death mask of Susan Calvin, patron saint of all roboticists. She had been dead for nearly two centuries now, but as a result of writing his book Andrew knew her so well he could half persuade himself that he had met her in life.

Finally Smythe-Robertson asked, "How can I replace you for you? If I replace you, as robot, how can I donate the new robot to you as owner since in the very act of replacement you cease to exist." He smiled grimly.

"Not at all difficult," Paul interposed. "The seat of Andrew's personality is his positronic brain, and it is the one part that cannot be replaced without creating a new robot. The positronic brain, therefore, is Andrew the owner. Every other part of the robotic body can be replaced without affecting the robot's personality, and those other parts are the brain's possessions. Andrew, I should say, wants to supply his brain with a new robotic body."

"That's right," said Andrew calmly. He turned to Smythe-Robertson. "You have manufactured androids, haven't you? Robots that have the outward appearance of humans, complete to the texture of the skin?"

"Yes, we have. They worked perfectly well, with their synthetic fibrous skins and tendons. There was virtually no metal anywhere except for the brain, yet they were nearly as tough as metal robots. They were tougher, weight for weight."

Paul looked interested. "I didn't know that. How many are on the market?"

"None," said Smythe-Robertson. "They were much more expensive than metal models and a market survey showed they would not be accepted. They looked too human."

Andrew was impressed. "But the corporation retains its expertise, I assume. Since it does, I wish to request that I be replaced by an organic robot, an android."

Paul looked surprised. "Good Lord!" he said.

Smythe-Robertson stiffened. "Quite impossible!"

"Why is it impossible?" Andrew asked. "I will pay any reasonable fee, of course."

"We do not manufacture androids."

"You do not *choose* to manufacture androids," Paul interjected quickly. "That is not the same as being unable to manufacture them."

"Nevertheless," Smythe-Robertson responded, "the manufacture of androids is against public policy."

"There is no law against it," said Paul.

"Nevertheless, we do not manufacture them—and we will not."

Paul cleared his throat. "Mr. Smythe-Robertson," he said, "Andrew is a free robot who comes under the purview of the law guaranteeing robot rights. You are aware of this, I take it?"

"Only too well."

"This robot, as a free robot, chooses to wear clothes. This results in his being frequently humiliated by thoughtless human beings despite the law against the humiliation of robots. It is difficult to prosecute vague offenses that don't meet with the general disapproval of those who must decide on guilt and innocence."

"U.S. Robots understood that from the start. Your father's firm unfortunately did not."

"My father is dead now, but what I see is that we have here a clear offense with a clear target."

"What are you talking about?" said Smythe-Robertson.

"My client, Andrew Martin—he has just become my client— is a free robot who is entitled to ask U.S. Robots and Mechanical Men Corporation for the right of replacement, which the corporation supplies to anyone who owns a robot for more than twenty-five years. In fact, the corporation insists on such replacement."

Paul was smiling and thoroughly at ease. "The positronic brain of my client," he went on, "is the owner of the body of my client—which is certainly more than twenty-five years old. The positronic brain demands the replacement of the body and offers to pay any reasonable fee for an android body as that replacement. If you refuse the request, my client undergoes humiliation and we will sue.

"While public opinion would not ordinarily support the claim of a robot in such a case, may I remind you that U.S. Robots is not popular with the public generally. Even those who most use and profit from robots are suspicious of the corporation. This may be a hangover from the days when robots were widely feared. It may be resentment against the power and wealth of U.S. Robots, which has a worldwide monopoly. Whatever the cause may be, the resentment exists. I think you will find that you would prefer not to be faced with a lawsuit, particularly since my client is wealthy and will live for many more centuries and will have no reason to refrain from fighting the battle forever."

Smythe-Robertson had slowly reddened. "You are trying to force—"

"I force you to do nothing," said Paul. "If you wish to refuse to accede to my client's reasonable request, you may by all means do so and we will leave without another word. But we will sue, as is certainly our right, and you will find that you will eventually lose."

"Well . . ."

"I see that you are going to accede," said Paul. "You may hesitate but you will come to it in the end. Let me assure you, then, of one further point: If, in the process of transferring my client's positronic brain from his present body to an organic one, there is any damage, however slight, then I will never rest until I've nailed the corporation to the ground. I will, if necessary, take every possible step to mobilize public opinion against the corporation if one brainpath of my client's platinum-iridium essence is scrambled." He turned to Andrew and asked, "Do you agree to all this, Andrew?"

Andrew hesitated a full minute. It amounted to the approval of lying, of blackmail, of the badgering and humiliation of a human being. But not physical harm, he told himself, not physical harm.

He managed at last to come out with a rather faint "Yes."

14

He felt as though he were being constructed again. For days, then for weeks, finally for months, Andrew found himself not himself somehow, and the simplest actions kept giving rise to hesitation.

Paul was frantic. "They've damaged you, Andrew. We'll have to institute suit!"

Andrew spoke very slowly. "You . . . mustn't. You'll never be able to prove . . . something . . . like m-m-m-m—"

"Malice?"

"Malice. Besides, I grow . . . stronger, better. It's the tr-tr-tr—"

"Tremble?"

"Trauma. After all, there's never been such an op-op-op-. . . before."

Andrew could feel his brain from the inside. No one else could. He knew he was well, and during the months that it took him to learn full coordination and full positronic interplay he spent hours before the mirror.

Not quite human! The face was stiff—too stiff—and the motions were too deliberate. They lacked the careless, free flow of the human being, but perhaps that might come with time. At least now he could wear clothes without the ridiculous anomaly of a metal face going along with it.

Eventually, he said, "I will be going back to work."

Paul laughed. "That means you are well. What will you be doing? Another book?"

"No," said Andrew seriously. "I live too long for any one career to seize me by the throat and never let me go. There was a time when I was primarily an artist, and I can still turn to that. And there was a time when I was a historian, and I can still turn to that. But now I wish to be a robobiologist."

"A robopsychologist, you mean."

"No. That would imply the study of positronic brains, and at the moment I lack the desire to do that. A robobiologist, it seems to me, would be concerned with the working of the body attached to that brain."

"Wouldn't that be a roboticist?"

"A roboticist works with a metal body. I would be studying an organic humanoid body, of which I have the only one, as far as I know."

"You narrow your field," said Paul thoughtfully. "As an artist, all conception is yours; as a historian, you deal chiefly with robots; as a robobiologist, you will deal with yourself."

Andrew nodded. "It would seem so."

Andrew had to start from the very beginning, for he knew nothing of ordinary biology and almost nothing of science. He became a familiar sight in the libraries, where he sat at the electronic indices for hours at a time, looking perfectly normal in clothes. Those few who knew he was a robot in no way interfered with him.

He built a laboratory in a room which he added to his house; and his library grew, too.

Years passed, and Paul came to him one day and said, "It's a pity you're no longer working on the history of robots. I understand U.S. Robots is adopting a radically new policy."

Paul had aged, and his deteriorating eyes had been replaced with photoptic cells. In that respect, he had drawn closer to Andrew.

"What have they done?" Andrew asked.

"They are manufacturing central computers, gigantic positronic brains, really, which communicate with anywhere from a dozen to a thousand robots by microwave. The robots themselves have no brains at all. They are the limbs of the gigantic brain, and the two are physically separate."

"Is that more efficient?"

"U.S. Robots claims it is. Smythe-Robertson established the new direction before he died, however, and it's my notion that it's a backlash at you. U.S. Robots is determined that they will make no robots that will give them the type of trouble you have, and for that reason they separate brain and body. The brain will have no body to wish changed; the body will have no brain to wish anything.

"It's amazing, Andrew," Paul went on, "the influence you have had on the history of robots. It was your artistry that encouraged U.S. Robots to make robots more precise and specialized; it was your freedom that resulted in the establishment of the principle of robotic rights; it was your insistence on an android body that made U.S. Robots switch to brain-body separation."

Andrew grew thoughtful. "I suppose in the end the corporation will produce one vast brain controlling several billion robotic bodies. All the eggs will be in one basket. Dangerous. Not proper at all."

"I think you're right," said Paul, "but I don't suspect it will come to pass for a century at least, and I won't live to see it. In fact, I may not live to see next year."

"Paul!" cried Andrew, in concern.

Paul shrugged. "Men are mortal, Andrew. We're not like you. It doesn't matter too much, but it does make it important to assure you on one point. I'm the last of the human Martins. The money I control personally will be left to the trust in your name, and as far as anyone can foresee the future, you will be economically secure."

"Unnecessary," Andrew said, with difficulty. In all this time, he could not get used to the deaths of the Martins.

"Let's not argue. That's the way it's going to be. Now, what are you working on?"

"I am designing a system for allowing androids—myself—to gain energy from the combusion of hydrocarbons, rather than from atomic cells."

Paul raised his eyebrows. "So that they will breathe and eat?"

"Yes."

"How long have you been pushing in that direction?"

"For a long time now, but I think I have finally designed an adequate combustion chamber for catalyzed, controlled breakdown."

"But why, Andrew? The atomic cell is surely infinitely better."

"In some ways, perhaps. But the atomic cell is inhuman."

15

It took time, but Andrew had time. In the first place, he did not wish to do anything till Paul had died in peace. With the death of the great-grandson of Sir, Andrew felt more nearly exposed to a hostile world and for that reason was all the more determined along the path he had chosen.

Yet he was not really alone. If a man had died, the firm of Feingold and Martin lived, for a corporation does not die any more than a robot does.

The firm had its directions and it followed them soullessly. By way of the trust and through the law firm, Andrew continued to be wealthy. In return for their own large annual retainer, Feingold and Martin involved themselves in the legal aspects of the new combustion chamber. But when the time came for Andrew to visit U.S. Robots and Mechanical Men Corporation, he did it alone. Once he had gone with Sir and once with Paul. This time, the third time, he was alone and manlike.

U.S. Robots had changed. The actual production plant had been shifted to a large space station, as had grown to be the case with more and more industries. With them had gone many robots. The Earth itself was becoming parklike, with its one-billion-person population stabilized and perhaps not more than thirty percent of its at-least-equally-large robot population independently brained.

The Director of Research was Alvin Magdescu, dark of complexion and hair, with a little pointed beard and wearing nothing above the waist but the breastband that fashion dictated. Andrew himself was well covered in the older fashion of several decades back.

Magdescu offered his hand to his visitor. "I know you, of course, and I'm rather pleased to see you. You're our most notorious product and it's a pity old Smythe-Robertson was so set against you. We could have done a great deal with you."

"You still can," said Andrew.

"No, I don't think so. We've passed the time. We've had robots on Earth for over a century, but that's changing. It will be back to space with them, and those that stay here won't be brained."

"But there remains myself, and I stay on Earth."

"True, but there doesn't seem to be much of the robot about you. What new request have you?"

"To be still less a robot. Since I am so far organic, I wish an organic source of energy. I have here the plans. . . ."

Magdescu did not hasten through them. He might have intended to at first, but he stiffened and grew intent. At one point, he said, "This is remarkably ingenious. Who thought of all this?"

"I did," Andrew replied.

Magdescu looked up at him sharply, then said, "It would amount to a major overhaul of your body, and an experimental one, since such a thing has never been attempted before. I advise against it. Remain as you are."

Andrew's face had limited means of expression, but impatience showed plainly in his voice. "Dr. Magdescu, you miss the entire point. You have no choice but to accede to my request. If such devices can be built into my body, they can be built into human bodies as well. The tendency to lengthen human life by prosthetic devices has already been remarked on. There are no devices better than the ones I have designed or am designing.

"As it happens, I control the patents by way of the firm of Feingold and Martin. We are quite capable of going into business for ourselves and of developing the kind of prosthetic devices that may end by producing human beings with many of the properties of robots. Your own business will then suffer.

"If, however, you operate on me now and agree to do so under similar circumstances in the future, you will receive permission to make use of the patents and control the technology of both robots and of the prosthetization of human beings. The initial leasing will not be granted, of course, until after the first operation is completed successfully, and after enough time has passed to demonstrate that it is indeed successful."

Andrew felt scarcely any First Law inhibition to the stern conditions he was setting a human being. He was learning to reason that what seemed like cruelty might, in the long run, be kindness.

Magdescu was stunned. "I'm not the one to decide something like this. That's a corporate decision that would take time."

"I can wait a reasonable time," said Andrew, "but only a reasonable time." And he thought with satisfaction that Paul himself could not have done it better.

16

It took only a reasonable time, and the operation was a success.

"I was very much against the operation, Andrew," Magdescu said, "but not for the reasons you might think. I was not in the least against the experiment, if it had been on someone else. I hated risking *your* positronic brain. Now that you have the positronic pathways interacting with simulated nerve pathways, it might have been difficult to rescue the brain intact if the body had gone bad."

"I had every faith in the skill of the staff at U.S. Robots," said Andrew. "And I can eat now."

"Well, you can sip olive oil. It will mean occasional cleanings of the combustion chamber, as we have explained to you. Rather an uncomfortable touch, I should think."

"Perhaps, if I did not expect to go further. Self-cleaning is not impossible. In fact, I am working on a device that will deal with solid food that may be expected to contain incombustible fractions—indigestible matter, so to speak, that will have to be discarded."

"You would then have to develop an anus."

"Or the equivalent."

"What else, Andrew . . . ?"

"Everything else."

"Genitalia, too?"

"Insofar as they will fit my plans. My body is a canvas on which I intend to draw . . ."

Magdescu waited for the sentence to be completed, and when it seemed that it would not be, he completed it himself. "A man?"

"We shall see," Andrew said.

"That's a puny ambition, Andrew. You're better than a man. You've gone downhill from the moment you opted to become organic."

"My brain has not suffered."

"No, it hasn't. I'll grant you that. But, Andrew, the whole new breakthrough in prosthetic devices made possible by your patents is being marketed under your name. You're recognized as the inventor and you're being honored for it—as you should be. Why play further games with your body?"

Andrew did not answer.

The honors came. He accepted membership in several learned societies, including one that was devoted to the new science he had established—the one he had called robobiology but which had come to be termed prosthetology. On the one hundred and fiftieth anniversary of his construction, a testimonial dinner was given in his honor at U.S. Robots. If Andrew saw an irony in this, he kept it to himself.

Alvin Magdescu came out of retirement to chair the dinner. He was himself ninety-four years old and was alive because he, too, had prosthetized devices that, among other things, fulfilled the function of liver and kidneys. The dinner reached its climax when Magdescu, after a short and emotional talk, raised his glass to toast The Sesquicentennial Robot.

Andrew had had the sinews of his face redesigned to the point where he could show a human range of emotions, but he sat through all the ceremonies solemnly passive. He did not like to be a Sesquicentennial Robot.

17

It was prosthetology that finally took Andrew off the Earth.

In the decades that followed the celebration of his sesquicentennial, the Moon had come to be a world more Earthlike than Earth in every respect but its gravitational pull; and in its underground cities there was a fairly dense population. Prosthetized devices there had to take the lesser gravity into account. Andrew spent five years on the Moon working with local prosthetologists to make the necessary adaptations. When not at his work, he wandered among the robot population, every one of which treated him with the robotic obsequiousness due a man.

He came back to an Earth that was humdrum and quiet in comparison, and visited the offices of Feingold and Martin to announce his return.

The current head of the firm, Simon DeLong, was surprised. "We had been told you were returning, Andrew"—he had almost said Mr. Martin—"but we were not expecting you till next week."

"I grew impatient," said Andrew, briskly. He was anxious to get to the point. "On the Moon, Simon, I was in charge of a

534

research team of twenty human scientists. I gave orders that no one questioned. The Lunar robots deferred to me as they would to a human being. Why, then, am I not a human being?"

A wary look entered DeLong's eyes. "My dear Andrew, as you have just explained, you are treated as a human being by both robots *and* human beings. You are, therefore, a human being *de facto*."

"To be a human being *de facto* is not enough. I want not only to be treated as one, but to be legally identified as one. I want to be a human being *de jure*."

"Now that is another matter," DeLong said. "There we would run into human prejudice and into the undoubted fact that, however much you may be *like* a human being, you are *not* a human being."

"In what way not?" Andrew asked. "I have the shape of a human being and organs equivalent to those of a human being. My organs, in fact, are identical to some of those in a prosthetized human being. I have contributed artistically, literarily, and scientifically to human culture as much as any human being now alive. What more can one ask?"

"I myself would ask nothing more. The trouble is that it would take an act of the World Legislature to define you as a human being. Frankly, I wouldn't expect that to happen."

"To whom on the Legislature could I speak?"

"To the Chairman of the Science and Technology Committee, perhaps."

"Can you arrange a meeting?"

"But you scarcely need an intermediary. In your position, you can—"

"No. *You* arrange it." It didn't even occur to Andrew that he was giving a flat order to a human being, he had grown so accustomed to that on the Moon. "I want him to know that the firm of Feingold and Martin is backing me in this to the hilt."

"Well, now—"

"To the hilt, Simon. In one hundred and seventy-three years I have in one fashion or another contributed greatly to this firm. I have been under obligation to individual members of the firm

535

in times past. I am not now. It is rather the other way around now, and I am calling in my debts."

"I will do what I can," DeLong said.

18

The Chairman of the Science and Technology Committee was from the East Asian region and was a woman. Her name was Chee Li-hsing and her transparent garments—obscuring what she wanted obscured only by their dazzle—made her look plastic-wrapped.

"I sympathize with your wish for full human rights," she said. "There have been times in history when segments of the human population fought for full human rights. What rights, however, can you possibly want that you do not have?"

"As simple a thing as my right to life," Andrew stated. "A robot can be dismantled at any time."

"A human being can be executed at any time."

"Execution can only follow due process of law. There is no trial needed for my dismantling. Only the word of a human being in authority is needed to end me. Besides . . . besides . . ." Andrew tried desperately to allow no sign of pleading, but his carefully designed tricks of human expression and tone of voice betrayed him here. "The truth is, I want to be a man. I have wanted it through six generations of human beings."

Li-hsing looked up at him out of darkly sympathetic eyes. "The Legislature can pass a law declaring you one. They could pass a law declaring that a stone statue be defined as a man. Whether they will actually do so is, however, as likely in the first case as the second. Congresspeople are as human as the rest of the population, and there is always that element of suspicion against robots."

"Even now?"

"Even now. We would all allow the fact that you have earned the prize of humanity, and yet there would remain the fear of setting an undesirable precedent."

"What precedent? I am the only free robot, the only one of my type, and there will never be another. You may consult U.S. Robots."

" 'Never' is a long word, Andrew—or, if you prefer, Mr. Martin—since I will gladly give you my personal accolade as man. You will find that most congresspeople will not be so willing to set the precedent, no matter how meaningless such a precedent might be. Mr. Martin, you have my sympathy, but I cannot tell you to hope. Indeed . . ."

She sat back and her forehead wrinkled. "Indeed, if the issue grows too heated, there might well arise a certain sentiment, both inside the Legislature and outside, for that dismantling you mentioned. Doing away with you could turn out to be the easiest way of resolving the dilemma. Consider that before deciding to push matters."

Andrew stood firm. "Will no one remember the technique of prosthetology, something that is almost entirely mine?"

"It may seem cruel, but they won't. Or if they do, it will be remembered against you. People will say you did it only for yourself. It will be said it was part of a campaign to roboticize human beings, or to humanify robots, and in either case evil and vicious. You have never been part of a political hate campaign, Mr. Martin; but I tell you that you would be the object of vilification of a kind neither you nor I would credit, and there would be people to believe it all. Mr. Martin, let your life be."

She rose, and next to Andrew's seated figure she seemed small and almost childlike.

"If I decide to fight for my humanity, will you be on my side?"

She thought, then replied, "I will be—insofar as I can be. If at any time such a stand would appear to threaten my political future, I might have to abandon you, since it is not an issue I feel to be at the very root of my beliefs. I am trying to be honest with you."

"Thank you, and I will ask no more. I intend to fight this through, whatever the consequences, and I will ask you for your help only for as long as you can give it."

19

It was not a direct fight. Feingold and Martin counseled patience and Andrew muttered, grimly, that he had an endless supply of that. Feingold and Martin then entered on a campaign to narrow and restrict the area of combat.

They instituted a lawsuit denying the obligation to pay debts to an individual with a prosthetic heart on the grounds that the possession of a robotic organ removed humanity, and with it the constitutional rights of human beings. They fought the matter skillfully and tenaciously, losing at every step but always in such a way that the decision was forced to be as broad as possible, and then carrying it by way of appeals to the World Court.

It took years, and millions of dollars.

When the final decision was handed down, DeLong held what amounted to a victory celebration over the legal loss. Andrew was, of course, present in the company offices on the occasion.

"We've done two things, Andrew," said DeLong, "both of which are good. First of all, we have established the fact that no number of artificial parts in the human body causes it to cease being a human body. Secondly, we have engaged public opinion in the question in such a way as to put it fiercely on the side of a broad interpretation of humanity, since there is not a human being in existence who does not hope for prosthetics if they will keep him alive."

"And do you think the Legislature will now grant me my humanity?" Andrew asked.

DeLong looked faintly uncomfortable. "As to that, I cannot be optimistic. There remains the one organ which the World Court has used as the criterion of humanity. Human beings have an organic cellular brain and robots have a platinum-iridium positronic brain if they have one at all—and you certainly have a positronic brain. No, Andrew, don't get that look in your eye. We lack the knowledge to duplicate the work of a cellular brain in artificial structures close enough to the organic type as to allow it to fall within the court's decision. Not even you could do it."

"What should we do, then?"

"Make the attempt, of course. Congresswoman Li-hsing will be on our side, and a growing number of other congresspeople.

The President will undoubtedly go along with a majority of the Legislature in this matter."

"Do we have a majority?"

"No. Far from it. But we might get one if the public will allow its desire for a broad interpretation of humanity to extend to you. A small chance, I admit; but if you do not wish to give up, we must gamble for it."

"I do not wish to give up."

20

Congresswoman Li-hsing was considerably older than she had been when Andrew first met her. Her transparent garments were long gone. Her hair was now close-cropped and her coverings were tubular. Yet still Andrew clung, as closely as he could within the limits of reasonable taste, to the style of clothing that had prevailed when he had first adopted clothing more than a century before.

"We've gone as far as we can, Andrew," Li-hsing admitted. "We'll try once more after recess, but, to be honest, defeat is certain and then the whole thing will have to be given up. All my most recent efforts have only earned me certain defeat in the coming congressional campaign."

"I know," said Andrew, "and it distresses me. You said once that you would abandon me if it came to that. Why have you not done so?"

"One can change one's mind, you know. Somehow, abandoning you became a higher price than I cared to pay for just one more term. As it is, I've been in the Legislature for more than a quarter of a century. It's enough."

"Is there no way we can change minds, Chee?"

"We've changed all that are amenable to reason. The rest—the majority—cannot be moved from their emotional antipathies."

"Emotional antipathy is not a valid reason for voting one way or the other."

"I know that, Andrew, but they don't advance emotional antipathy as their reason."

"It all comes down to the brain, then," Andrew said cautiously. "But must we leave it at the level of cells versus positrons? Is there no way of forcing a functional definition? Must we say that a brain is made of this or that? May we not say that a brain is something—anything—capable of a certain level of thought?"

"Won't work," said Li-hsing. "Your brain is manmade, the human brain is not. Your brain is constructed, theirs developed. To any human being who is intent on keeping up the barrier between himself and a robot, those differences are a steel wall a mile high and a mile thick."

"If we could get at the source of their antipathy, the very source—"

"After all your years," Li-hsing said sadly, "you are still trying to reason out the human being. Poor Andrew, don't be angry, but it's the robot in you that drives you in that direction."

"I don't know," said Andrew. "If I could bring myself . . ."

1 *[Reprise]*

If he could bring himself . . .

He had known for a long time it might come to that, and in the end he was at the surgeon's. He had found one skillful enough for the job at hand—which meant a surgeon-robot, for no human surgeon could be trusted in this connection, either in ability or in intention.

The surgeon could not have performed the operation on a human being, so Andrew, after putting off the moment of decision with a sad line of questioning that reflected the turmoil within himself, had put the First Law to one side by saying "I, too, am a robot."

He then said, as firmly as he had learned to form the words even to human beings over these past decades, "I *order* you to carry through the operation on me."

In the absence of the First Law, an order so firmly given from one who looked so much like a man activated the Second Law sufficiently to carry the day.

540

21

Andrew's feeling of weakness was, he was sure, quite imaginary. He had recovered from the operation. Nevertheless, he leaned, as unobtrusively as he could manage, against the wall. It would be entirely too revealing to sit.

Li-hsing said, "The final vote will come this week, Andrew. I've been able to delay it no longer, and we must lose. And that will be it, Andrew."

"I am grateful for your skill at delay. It gave me the time I needed, and I took the gamble I had to."

"What gamble is this?" Li-hsing asked with open concern.

"I couldn't tell you, or even the people at Feingold and Martin. I was sure I would be stopped. See here, if it is the brain that is at issue, isn't the greatest difference of all the matter of immortality? Who really cares what a brain looks like or is built of, or how it was formed. What matters is that human brain cells die, *must* die. Even if every other organ in the body is maintained or replaced, the brain cells, which cannot be replaced without changing and therefore killing the personality, must eventually die.

"My own positronic pathways have lasted nearly two centuries without perceptible change, and can last for centuries more. Isn't *that* the fundamental barrier? Human beings can tolerate an immortal robot, for it doesn't matter how long a machine lasts, but they cannot tolerate an immortal human being since their own mortality is endurable only so long as it is universal. And for that reason they won't make me a human being."

"What is it you're leading up to, Andrew?" Li-hsing asked.

"I have removed that problem. Decades ago, my positronic brain was connected to organic nerves. Now, one last operation has arranged that connection in such a way that slowly—quite slowly—the potential is being drained from my pathways."

Li-hsing's finely wrinkled face showed no expression for a moment. Then her lips tightened. "Do you mean you've arranged to die, Andrew? You can't have. That violates the Third Law."

"No," said Andrew, "I have chosen between the death of my

541

body and the death of my aspirations and desires. To let my body live at the cost of the greater death is what would have violated the Third Law."

Li-hsing seized his arm as though she were about to shake him. She stopped herself. "Andrew, it won't work! Change it back."

"It can't be done. Too much damage was done. I have a year to live—more or less. I will last through the two-hundredth anniversary of my construction. I was weak enough to arrange that."

"How can it be worth it? Andrew, you're a fool."

"If it brings me humanity, that will be worth it. If it doesn't, it will bring an end to striving and that will be worth it, too."

Then Li-hsing did something that astonished herself. Quietly, she began to weep.

22

It was odd how that last deed caught the imagination of the world. All that Andrew had done before had not swayed them. But he had finally accepted even death to be human, and the sacrifice was too great to be rejected.

The final ceremony was timed, quite deliberately, for the two-hundredth anniversary. The World President was to sign the act and make the people's will law. The ceremony would be visible on a global network and would be beamed to the Lunar state and even to the Martian colony.

Andrew was in a wheelchair. He could still walk, but only shakily.

With mankind watching, the World President said, "Fifty years ago, you were declared the Sesquicentennial Robot, Andrew." After a pause, and in a more solemn tone, he continued, "Today we declare you the Bicentennial Man, Mr. Martin."

And Andrew, smiling, held out his hand to shake that of the President.

23

Andrew's thoughts were slowly fading as he lay in bed. Desperately he seized at them. *Man! He was a man!* He wanted that to be his last thought. He wanted to dissolve—die—with that.

He opened his eyes one more time, and for one last time recognized Li-hsing, waiting solemnly. Others were there, but they were only shadows, unrecognizable shadows. Only Li-hsing stood out against the deepening gray.

Slowly, inchingly, he held out his hand to her and very dimly and faintly felt her take it.

She was fading in his eyes as the last of his thoughts trickled away. But before she faded completely, one final, fugitive thought came to him and rested for a moment on his mind before everything stopped.

"Little Miss," he whispered, too low to be heard.

THE FUTURE
OF MAN
AND
HIS MACHINES

LONG SHOT

VERNOR VINGE

(1 9 7 2)

What lies ahead for man and his intelligent machines? During the last five decades, the wildest speculations of the science fiction imagination have often run a poor second to actual developments. In the future, the rate of advance in the field seems likely to equal or exceed its present rate. On Earth, two developments are certain to come soon, assuming mankind does not self-destruct in a nuclear catastrophe. Given our history of continual warfare, such a horrendous prospect is all too possible. But if we survive, the number of homes, businesses, and schools owning computers will increase dramatically. Political and social changes will result. Instant electronic communication in almost all homes will allow voters to express immediately their responses to various political issues. The need for professional politicians should decrease. Patterns of work will change, with the length of both the work week and the work career decreasing. Work-related travel will also decline. The availability of education will increase, with much of it computer-based and delivered to the home.

The second development on Earth will be accelerated progress in the field of artificial intelligence. As increasingly sophisticated computers are used in research to improve themselves, the rate of advance will increase. The brighter the machines, the more capable they will be of improving their own intelligence. Present resistance to research in this field is likely to fade as we come to realize more and more how much our complicated world, overloaded as it is with information, needs the help of machine intelligence to solve problems.

Developments in space may not occur as quickly as the advances on Earth we have described. But they are just as inevitable. Extrapolative thinking from present developments can predict them quite easily. The U.S. space shuttle will probably be carrying passengers into space just for the ride before the end of the century. Manned space stations will come next, then manned expeditions to the asteroids and Mars, following the pattern of the manned expeditions to the moon. Commercial exploitation of the natural resources to be found in space will follow.

What will happen in the far distant future? Here we move from extrapolation and certainty to speculative thinking and guesswork. But science fiction writers have used their skilled imaginations to create a wide array of possibilities. You have already encountered a number of them in this an-

547

thology, some promising, some pessimistic. We close with three of our favorites, all bright in their faith that mankind will survive—at least in some evolved form. Life may be right now on the verge of an evolutionary leap into space quite as remarkable as when, long ages ago, it crawled from water to land.

The first story, "Long Shot," is by Vernor Vinge, who was born in 1944 and holds a Ph.D. in mathematics. He is an assistant professor of mathematics at San Diego State University and the author of two novels, *Grimm's World* (1960) and *The Witling* (1976).

This story is told from the point of view of a fully automated spaceship named Ilse. She goes on a journey that takes one hundred centuries, and over the years her memory becomes unreliable. She can recall most things, but not her ultimate purpose, although she is dimly aware she has a very important one. At the end of her long journey through the universe, she discovers what it is.

THEY NAMED HER Ilse, and of all Earth's creatures, she was to be the longest lived—and perhaps the last. A prudent tortoise might survive three hundred years and a bristlecone pine six thousand, but Ilse's designed span exceeded one hundred centuries. And though her brain was iron and germanium doped with arsenic, and her heart was a tiny cloud of hydrogen plasma, Ilse *was*—in the beginning—one of Earth's creatures: She could feel, she could question, and—as she discovered during the dark centuries before her fiery end—she could also forget.

Ilse's earliest memory was a fragment, amounting to less than fifteen seconds. Someone, perhaps inadvertently, brought her to consciousness as she sat atop her S-5N booster. It was night, but their launch was imminent and the booster stood white and silver in the light of a dozen spotlights. Ilse's sharp eye scanned rapidly around the horizon, untroubled by the glare from below. Stretching away from her to the north was a line of thirty launchpads. Several had their own boosters, though none were lit up as Ilse's was. Three thousand meters to the west were more lights, and the occasional sparkle of an automatic rifle. To the east, surf marched in phosphorescent ranks against the Merritt Island shore.

There the fragment ended; she was not conscious during the launch. But that scene remained forever her most vivid and incomprehensible memory.

When next she woke, Ilse was in low Earth orbit. Her single eye had been fitted to a one-hundred-and-fifty-centimeter reflecting telescope so that now she could distinguish stars set less than a tenth of a second apart, or, if she looked straight down, count the birds in a flock of geese two hundred kilometers below. For more than a year Ilse remained in this same orbit. She was not idle. Her makers had allotted this period for testing. A small manned station orbited with her, and from it came an endless sequence of radioed instructions and exercises.

Most of the problems were ballistic: hyperbolic encounters, transfer ellipses, and the like. But it was often required that Ilse use her own telescope and spectrometer to discover the parameters of the problems. A typical exercise: determine the orbits of Venus and Mercury; compute a minimum-energy flyby of both planets. Another: determine the orbit of Mars; analyze its atmosphere; plan a hyperbolic entry subject to constraints. Many observational problems dealt with Earth: determine atmospheric pressure and composition; perform multispectrum analysis of vegetation. Usually she was required to solve organic analysis problems in less than thirty seconds. And in these last problems, the rules were often changed even while the game was played. Her orientation jets would be caused to malfunction. Critical portions of her mind and senses would be degraded.

One of the first things Ilse learned was that in addition to her private memories, she had a programmed memory, a "library" of procedures and facts. As with most libraries, the programmed memory was not as accessible as Ilse's own recollections, but the information contained there was much more complete and precise. The solution program for almost any ballistic or chemical problem could be lifted from this library, used for seconds, or hours, as an integral part of Ilse's mind, and then returned to the library. The real trick was to select the proper program on the basis of incomplete information, and then to modify that program to meet various combinations of power and equipment failure. Though she did poorly at first, Ilse eventually surpassed her design specifications. At this point her training stopped and for the first—but not the last—time, Ilse was left to her own devices.

Though she had yet to wonder on her ultimate purpose, still she wanted to see as much of her world as possible. She spent most of each daylight pass looking straight down, trying to see some order in the jumble of blue and green and white. She could easily follow the supply rockets as they climbed up from Merritt Island and Baikonur to rendezvous with her. In the end, more than a hundred of the rockets were floating about her. As the weeks passed, the squat white cylinders were fitted together on a spidery frame.

Now her ten-meter-long body was lost in the webwork of cylinders and girders that stretched out two hundred meters behind her. Her programmed memory told her that the entire assembly massed 22,563,901 tons—more than most oceangoing ships—and a little experimenting with her attitude-control jets convinced her that this figure was correct.

Soon her makers connected Ilse's senses to the mammoth's control mechanisms. It was as if she had been given a new body, for she could feel and see and use each of the hundred propellant tanks and each of the fifteen fusion reactors that made up the assembly. She realized that now she had the power to perform some of the maneuvers she had planned during her training.

Finally the great moment arrived. Course directions came over the maser link with the manned satellite. Ilse quickly computed the trajectory that would result from these directions. The answer she obtained was correct, but it revealed only the smallest part of what was in store for her.

In her orbit two hundred kilometers up, Ilse coasted smoothly toward high noon over the Pacific. Her eye was pointed forward, so that on the fuzzy blue horizon she could see the edge of the North American continent. Nearer, the granulated cloud cover obscured the ocean itself. The command to begin the burn came from the manned satellite, but Ilse was following the clock herself, and she had determined to take over the launch if any mistakes were made. Two hundred meters behind her, deep in the maze of tanks and beryllium girders, Ilse felt magnetic fields establish themselves, felt hydrogen plasma form, felt fusion commence. Another signal from the station, and propellant flowed around each of ten reactors.

Ilse and her twenty-thousand-ton booster were on their way.

Acceleration rose smoothly to one gravity. Behind her, vidicons on the booster's superstructure showed the Earth shrinking. For half an hour the burn continued, monitored by Ilse and the manned station now fallen far behind. Then Ilse was alone with her booster, coasting away from Earth and her creators at better than twenty kilometers a second.

So Ilse began her fall toward the sun. For eleven weeks she fell. During this time, there was little to do: monitor the propellants, keep the booster's sunshade properly oriented, relay data to Earth. Compared to much of her later life, however, it was a time of hectic activity.

A fall of eleven weeks toward a body as massive as the sun can result in only one thing: speed. In those last hours, Ilse hurtled downward at better than two hundred and fifty kilometers per second—an Earth-to-Moon distance every half hour. Forty-five minutes before her closest approach to the sun—perihelion—Ilse jettisoned the empty first stage and its sunshade. Now she was left with the two-thousand-ton second stage, whose insulation consisted of a bright coat of white paint. She felt the pressure in the propellant tanks begin to rise.

Though her telescope was pointed directly away from the sun, the vidicons on the second stage gave her an awesome view of the solar fireball. She was moving so fast now that the sun's incandescent prominences changed perspective even as she watched.

Seventeen minutes to perihelion. From somewhere beyond the flames, Ilse got the expected maser communication. She pitched herself and her booster over so that she looked along the line of her trajectory. Now her own body was exposed to the direct glare of the sun. Through her telescope she could see luminous tracery within the solar corona. The booster's fuel tanks were perilously close to bursting, and Ilse was having trouble keeping her own body at its proper temperature.

Fifteen minutes to perihelion. The command came from Earth to begin the burn. Ilse considered her own trajectory data and concluded that the command was thirteen seconds premature. Consultation with Earth would cost at least sixteen minutes, and her decision must be made in the next four seconds. Any of man's earlier, less sophisticated creations would have accepted the error and taken the mission on to catastrophe, but independence was the essence of Ilse's nature; she overrode the master command, and delayed ignition till the instant she thought correct.

The sun's northern hemisphere passed below her, less than three solar diameters away.

Ignition, and Ilse was accelerated at nearly two gravities. As she swung toward what was to have been perihelion, her booster lifted her out of elliptic orbit and into a hyperbolic one. Half an hour later she shot out from the sun into the spaces south of the ecliptic at three hundred and twenty kilometers per second— about one solar diameter every hour. The booster's now empty propellant tanks were between her and the sun, and her body slowly cooled.

Shortly after burnout, Earth offhandedly acknowledged the navigation error. This is not to say that Ilse's makers were without contrition for their mistake, or without praise for Ilse. In fact, several men lost what little there remained to confiscate for jeopardizing this mission, and man's last hope. It was simply that Ilse's makers did not believe that she could appreciate apologies or praise.

Now Ilse fled up out of the solar gravity well. It had taken her eleven weeks to fall from Earth to Sol, but in less than two weeks she had regained this altitude, and still she plunged outward at more than one hundred kilometers per second. That velocity remained her inheritance from the sun. Without the gravity-well maneuver, her booster would have had to be five hundred times as large, or her voyage three times as long. It had been the very best that men could do for her, considering the time remaining to them.

So began the voyage of one hundred centuries. Ilse parted with the empty booster and floated on alone: a squat cylinder, twelve meters wide, five meters long, with a large telescope sticking from one end. Four light-years below her in the well of the night she saw Alpha Centauri, her destination. To the naked human eye, it appears a single bright star, but with her telescope Ilse could clearly see two stars, one slightly fainter and redder than the other. She carefully measured their position and her own, and concluded that her aim had been so perfect that a midcourse correction would not be necessary for a thousand years.

For many months, Earth maintained maser contact—to pose problems and ask after her health. It was almost pathetic, for if anything went wrong now, or in the centuries to follow, there was very little Earth could do to help. The problems were interesting, though. Ilse was asked to chart the nonluminous bodies in the Solar System. She became quite skilled at this and eventually discovered all nine planets, most of their moons, and several asteroids and comets.

In less than two years, Ilse was farther from the sun than any known planet, than any previous terrestrial probe. The sun itself was no more than a very bright star behind her, and Ilse had no trouble keeping her frigid innards at their proper temperature. But now it took sixteen hours to ask a question of Earth and obtain an answer.

A strange thing happened. Over a period of three weeks, the sun became steadily brighter until it gleamed ten times as luminously as before. The change was not really a great one. It was far short of what Earth's astronomers would have called a nova. Nevertheless, Ilse puzzled over the event, in her own way, for many months, since it was at this time that she lost maser contact with Earth. That contact was never regained.

Now Ilse changed herself to meet the empty centuries. As her designers had planned, she split her mind into three coequal entities. Theoretically, each of these minds could handle the entire mission alone, but for any important decision, Ilse required the agreement of at least two of the minds. In this fractionated state, Ilse was neither as bright nor as quick-thinking as she had been at launch. But scarcely anything happened in interstellar space, the chief danger being senile decay. Her three

553

minds spent as much time checking each other as they did over-seeing the various subsystems.

The one thing they did not regularly check was the pro-grammed memory, since Ilse's designers had—mistakenly—judged that such checks were a greater danger to the memories than was the passage of time.

Even with her mentality diminished, and in spite of the caretaker tasks assigned her, Ilse spent much of her time con-templating the universe that spread out forever around her. She discovered binary star systems, then watched the tiny lights swing back and forth around each other as the decades and centuries passed. To her the universe became a moving, almost a living, thing. Several of the nearer stars drifted almost a degree every century, while the great galaxy in Andromeda shifted less than a second of arc in a thousand years.

Occasionally she turned about to look at Sol. Even ten cen-turies out she could still distinguish Jupiter and Saturn. These were auspicious observations.

Finally it was time for the midcourse correction. She had spent the preceding century refining her alignment and her nav-igational observations. The burn was to be only one hundred meters per second, so accurate had been her perihelion impulse. Nevertheless, without that correction she would miss the Cen-tauran system entirely. When the second arrived and her align-ment was perfect, Ilse lit her tiny rocket—and discovered that she could obtain at most only three-quarters of the rated thrust. She had to make two burns before she was satisfied with the new course.

For the next fifty years, Ilse studied the problem. She tested the rocket's electrical system hundreds of times, and even fired the rocket in microsecond bursts. She never discovered how the centuries had robbed her, but extrapolating from her observa-tions, Ilse realized that by the time she entered the Centauran system, she would have only a thousand meters per second left in her rocket—less than half its designed capability. Even so, it was possible that, without further complications, she would be able to survey the planets of both stars in the system.

But before she finished her study of the propulsion problem,

Ilse discovered another breakdown—the most serious she was to face.

She had forgotten her mission. Over the centuries, the pattern of magnetic fields on her programmed memory had slowly disappeared—the least-used programs going first. When Ilse recalled those programs to discover how her reduced maneuverability affected the mission, she discovered that she no longer had any record of her ultimate purpose. The memories ended with badly faded programs for biochemical reconnaissance and planetary entry, and Ilse guessed that there was something crucial left to do after a successful landing on a suitable planet.

Ilse was a patient sort—especially in her cruise configuration—and she didn't worry about her ultimate purpose, so far away in the future. But she did do her best to preserve what programs were left. She played each program into her own memory and then back to the programmed memory. If the process was repeated every seventy years, she found that she could keep the programmed memories from fading. On the other hand, she had no way of knowing how many errors this endless repetition was introducing. For this reason she had each of her subminds perform the process separately, and she frequently checked the ballistic and astronomical program by doing problems with them.

Ilse went further; she studied her own body for clues as to its purpose. Much of her body was filled with a substance she must keep within a few degrees of absolute zero. Several leads disappeared into this mass. Except for her thermometers, however, she had no feeling in this part of her body. Now she raised the temperature in this section a few thousandths of a degree, a change well within design specifications, but large enough for her to sense. Comparing her observations and the section's mass with her chemical-analysis programs, Ilse concluded that the mysterious area was a relatively homogeneous body of frozen water, doped with various impurities. It was interesting information, but no matter how she compared it with her memories, she could not see any significance to it.

Ilse floated on—and on. The period of time between the midcourse maneuver and the next important event on her schedule was longer than man's experience with agriculture had been on Earth.

As the centuries passed, the two closely set stars that were her destination became brighter until, a thousand years from Alpha Centauri, she decided to begin her search for planets in the system. Ilse turned her telescope on the brighter of the two stars . . . call it Able. She was still thirty-five-thousand times as far from Able—and the smaller star . . . call it Baker—as Earth is from Sol. Even to her sharp eye, Able didn't show as a disk but rather as a diffraction pattern: a round blob of light—many times larger than the star's true disk—surrounded by a ring of light. The faint gleam of any planets would be lost in the diffraction pattern. For five years Ilse watched the pattern, analyzed it with one of her most subtle programs. Occasionally she slid occulting plates into the telescope and studied the resulting distorted pattern. After five years she had found suggestive anomalies in the diffraction pattern, but no definite signs of planets.

No matter. Patient Ilse turned her telescope a tiny fraction of a degree, and during the next five years she watched Baker. Then she switched back to Able. Fifteen times Ilse repeated this cycle. While she watched, Baker completed two revolutions about Able, and the stars' maximum mutual separation increased to nearly a tenth of a degree. Finally Ilse was certain: she had discovered a planet orbiting Baker, and perhaps another orbiting Able. Most likely they were both gas giants. No matter: she knew that any small, inner planets would still be lost in the glare of Able and Baker.

There remained less than nine hundred years before she coasted through the Centauran system.

Ilse persisted in her observations. Eventually she could see the gas giants as tiny spots of light—not merely as statistical correlations in her carefully collected diffraction data. Four hundred years out, she decided that the remaining anomalies in Able's diffraction pattern must be another planet, this one at about the same distance from Able as Earth is from Sol. Fifteen years later she made a similar discovery for Baker.

If she was to investigate both of these planets, she would have to plan very carefully. According to her design specifications, she had scarcely the maneuvering capability left to investigate one system. But Ilse's navigation system had survived the centuries better than expected, and she estimated that a survey of both planets might still be possible.

Three hundred and fifty years out, Ilse made a relatively large course correction, better than two hundred meters per second. This change was essentially a matter of pacing; it would delay her arrival by four months. Thus she would pass near the planet she wished to investigate and, if no landing was attempted, her path would be precisely bent by Able's gravitational field and she would be cast into Baker's planetary system.

Now Ilse had less than eight hundred meters per second left in her rocket—less than one percent of her velocity relative to Able and Baker. If she could be at the right place at the right time, that would be enough, but otherwise . . .

Ilse plotted the orbits of the bodies she had detected more and more accurately. Eventually she discovered several more planets: a total of three for Able and four for Baker. But only her two prime candidates—call them Able II and Baker II— were at the proper distance from their suns.

Eighteen months out, Ilse sighted moons around Able II. This was good news. Now she could accurately determine the planet's mass, and so refine her course even more. Ilse was now less than fifty astronomical units from Able, and eighty from Baker. She had no trouble making spectroscopic observations of the planets. Her prime candidates had plenty of oxygen in their atmospheres—though the farther one, Baker II, seemed deficient in water vapor. On the other hand, Able II had complex carbon compounds in its atmosphere, and its net color was blue-green. According to Ilse's damaged memory, these last were desirable features.

The centuries had shrunk to decades, then to years, and finally to days. Ilse was within the orbit of Able's gas giant. Ten million kilometers ahead, her target swept along a nearly circular path about its sun, Able. Twenty-seven astronomical units beyond Able gleamed Baker.

But Ilse kept her attention on that target, Able II. Now she could make out its gross continental outlines. She selected a landing site, and performed a two-hundred-meter-per-second burn. If she chose to land, she would come down in a greenish, beclouded area.

Twelve hours to contact. Ilse checked each of her subminds one last time. She deleted all malfunctioning circuits, and reassembled herself as a single mind out of what remained. Over the centuries, one-third of all her electrical components had failed, so that besides her lost memories, she was not nearly as bright as she had been when launched. Nevertheless, with her subminds combined, she was much cleverer than she had been during the cruise. She needed this greater alertness, because in the hours and minutes preceding her encounter with Able II, she would do more analysis and make more decisions than ever before.

One hour to contact. Ilse was within the orbit of her target's outer moon. Ahead loomed the tentative destination, a blue and white crescent two degrees across. Her landing area was around the planet's horizon. No matter. The important task for these last moments was a biochemical survey—at least that was what her surviving programs told her. She scanned the crescent, looking for traces of green through the clouds. She found a large island in a Pacific-sized ocean, and began the exquisitely complex analysis necessary to determine the orientation of amino acids. Every fifth second, she took one second to reestimate the atmospheric densities. The problems seemed even more complicated than her training exercises back in Earth orbit.

Five minutes to contact. She was less than forty thousand kilometers out, and the planet's hazy limb filled her sky. In the next ten seconds she must decide whether or not to land on Able II. Her ten-thousand-year mission was at stake here. For, once Ilse landed, she knew that she would never fly again. Without the immense booster that had pushed her out along this journey, she was nothing but a brain and an entry shield and a chunk of frozen water. If she decided to bypass Able II, she must now use a large portion of her remaining propellants to accelerate at right angles to her trajectory. This would cause her to miss the upper edge of the planet's atmosphere, and she would go hurtling out of Able's planetary system. Thirteen months later she would arrive in the vicinity of Baker, perhaps with enough left in her rocket to guide herself into Baker II's atmosphere. But, if that planet should be inhospitable, there would be no turning back; she would have to land there, or else coast on into interstellar darkness.

Ilse weighed the matter for three seconds and concluded that Able II satisfied every criterion she could recall, while Baker II seemed a bit too yellow, a bit too dry.

Ilse turned ninety degrees and jettisoned the small rocket that had given her so much trouble. At the same time she ejected the telescope which had served her so well. She floated indivisible, a white biconvex disk, twelve meters in diameter, fifteen tons in mass.

She turned ninety degrees more to look directly back along her trajectory. There was not much to see, now that she had lost her scope, but she recognized the point of light that was Earth's sun and wondered again what had been on all those programs that she had forgotten.

Five seconds. Ilse closed her eye and waited.

Contact began as a barely perceptible acceleration. In less than two seconds that acceleration built to two hundred and fifty gravities. This was beyond Ilse's experience, but she was built to take it; her body contained no moving parts and—except for her fusion reactor—no empty spaces. The really difficult thing was to keep her body from turning edgewise and burning up. Though she didn't know it, Ilse was repeating—on a grand scale—the landing technique that men had used so long ago. But Ilse had to dissipate more than eight hundred times the kinetic energy of any returning Apollo capsule. Her maneuver was correspondingly more dangerous, but since her designers could not equip her with a rocket powerful enough to decelerate her, it was the only option.

Now Ilse used her wits and every dyne in her tiny electric

thrusters to arc herself about Able II at the proper attitude and altitude. The acceleration rose steadily toward five hundred gravities, or almost five kilometers per second in velocity lost every second. Beyond that, Ilse knew that she would lose consciousness. Just centimeters away from her body, the air glowed at fifty thousand degrees. The fireball that surrounded her lit the ocean seventy kilometers below as with daylight.

Four hundred and fifty gravities. She felt a cryostat shatter, and one branch of her brain short through. Still, Ilse worked patiently and blindly to keep her body properly oriented. If she had calculated correctly, there were less than five seconds to go now.

She came within sixty kilometers of the surface, then rose steadily back into space. But now her velocity was only seven kilometers per second. The acceleration fell to a mere fifteen gravities, then to zero. She coasted back through a long ellipse to plunge, almost gently, into the depths of Able II's atmosphere.

At twenty thousand meters altitude, Ilse opened her eye and scanned the world below. Her lens had been cracked, and several of her gestalt programs damaged, but she saw green and knew her navigation hadn't been too bad.

It would have been a triumphant moment if only she could have remembered what she was supposed to do *after* she landed.

At ten thousand meters, Ilse popped her paraglider from the hull behind her eye. The tough plastic blossomed out above her, and her fall became a shallow glide. Ilse saw that she was flying over a prairie spotted here and there by forest. It was near sunset, and the long shadows cast by trees and hills made it easy for her to gauge the topography.

Two thousand meters. With a glide ratio of one to four, she couldn't expect to fly more than another eight kilometers. Ilse looked ahead and saw a tiny forest, and a stream glinting through the trees. Then she saw a glade just inside the forest, and some vagrant memory told her this was an appropriate spot. She pulled in the paraglider's forward lines and slid more steeply downward. As she passed three or four meters over the trees surrounding the glade, Ilse pulled in the rear lines, stalled her glider, and fell into the deep, moist grass. Her dun and green paraglider collapsed over her charred body so that she might be mistaken for a large black boulder covered with vegetation.

The voyage that had crossed one hundred centuries and four light-years was ended.

Ilse sat in the gathering twilight and listened. Sound was an undreamed-of dimension to her: tiny things burrowing in their holes, the stream gurgling nearby, a faint chirping in the distance. Twilight ended and a shallow fog rose in the dark glade. Ilse knew her voyaging was over. She would never move again. No matter. That had been planned, she was sure. She knew that much of her computing machinery—her mind—had been destroyed in the landing. She would not survive as a conscious being for more than another century or two. No matter.

What did matter was that she knew that her mission was not completed, and that the most important part remained, else the immense gamble her makers had undertaken would finally come to nothing. That possibility was the only thing which could frighten Ilse. It was part of her design.

She reviewed all the programmed memories that had survived the centuries and the planetary entry, but discovered nothing new. She investigated the rest of her body, testing her parts in a thorough, almost destructive, way she never would have dared while still centuries from her destination. She discovered nothing new. Finally she came to that load of ice she had carried so far. With one of her cryostats broken, she couldn't keep it at its proper temperature for more than a few years. She recalled the apparently useless leads that disappeared into that mass. There was only one thing left to try.

Ilse turned down her cryostats, and waited as the temperature within her climbed. The ice near her small fusion reactor warmed first. Somewhere in the frozen mass a tiny piece of metal expanded just far enough to complete a circuit, and Ilse discovered that her makers had taken one last precaution to insure her reliability. At the base of the icy hulk, next to the reactor, they had placed an auxiliary memory unit, and now Ilse had access to it. Her designers had realized that no matter what

561

dangers they imagined, there would be others, and so they had decided to leave this backup cold and inactive till the very end. And the new memory unit was quite different from her old ones, Ilse vaguely realized. It used optical rather than magnetic storage.

Now Ilse knew what she must do. She warmed a cylindrical tank filled with frozen amniotic fluid to thirty-seven degrees centigrade. From the store next to the cylinder, she injected a single microorganism into the tank. In a few minutes she would begin to suffuse blood through the tank.

It was early morning now, and the darkness was moist and cool. Ilse tried to probe her new memory further, but was balked. Apparently the instructions were delivered according to some schedule to avoid unnecessary use of the memory. Ilse reviewed what she had learned, and decided that she would know more in another nine months.

ALIEN STONES

GENE WOLFE

(1 9 7 2)

Encounters with alien intelligence were a subject once treated only in science fiction. Now biologists agree that extraterrestrial life is probable. Whether its evolutionary course has paralleled that of life on earth is uncertain. For the writer who assumes that life everywhere in the universe follows the same single path of evolution, the task of creating aliens is simple. But such a supposition seems simplistic. Given different environmental conditions, chances are that life elsewhere in the universe has evolved into forms very different from Earth's. The great challenge to the imagination is to create an essentially strange form of alien intelligence. Gene Wolfe's "Alien Stones" meets that challenge with brilliance.

Wolfe, born in 1931, has a degree in mechanical engineering and is an engineer and senior editor of the journal *Plant Engineering*. He is one of the top stylists in science fiction and the winner of two Nebula Awards.

He has recently published the third book in his tetralogy, *The Book of the New Sun*. The three novels are *The Shadow of the Torturer* (1980), *The Claw of the Conciliator* (1981), and *The Sword of the Lictor* (1982).

"**H**EADING UNCHANGED," Gladiator said. "Speed unchanged." She flashed figures on the cathode-ray-tube terminal at the command console to substantiate it.

Daw nodded. Twenty-eight firing studs stretched along the mid-band of the console. They would permit him, Daw, alone on the bridge (as he liked it) to launch every missile aboard the ship; even if Gladiator's central processing unit were knocked out or under system overload, there would be strike vectors from the independent minicomputers that clung, embryonic self-brains, to the walls of the missile foramens.

But there was no need for the minis. His ship was untouched; he could order Gladiator herself to do the shooting. Instead he asked, "Drive?"

And Gladiator answered: "No indication of drive in use."

"Okay."

"Shall present course be maintained? Present course is a collision course in point-three-one hours."

"Match their velocity and lay us alongside. How long?"

"One-point-forty-four hours."

"Do it. Meantime maintain battle stations." Daw flipped on his console mike without touching the switch that would have put his own image on the terminals in every compartment of the ship. Naval tradition decreed that when the captain spoke he should be seen as well as heard, but Daw had watched tapes of his own long, brown face as he announced, in what he felt to be unbearably stiff fashion, various unimportances, and he found it impossible to believe that his crew, seeing the same stretched cheeks and preposterous jaw, would not snicker.

"This is your captain. The ship sighted last night is still on her course." Daw chewed his lower lip for a moment, trying to decide just what to say next. The crew must be alerted, but it would be best if they were not alarmed. "There is no indication, I repeat, no indication, that she is aware of our presence. Possibly she doesn't want to scare us off—she may want peace, or she may just have something up her sleeve. Possibly something's wrong with her sensors. My own guess—which isn't worth any more than yours—is that she's a derelict; there's no sign of drive, and we haven't been able to reach her on any frequency. But we have to stay sharp. Battle conditions until further notice."

He flicked off the mike switch. Several como lights were blinking and he selected one: the reactor module. Mike switch again. "What is it, Neal?"

"Captain, if you could give me a breakdown on the radiation they're putting out, it might be possible for me to work up an estimate of how long it's been since they've used their drive."

"I'm happy to hear that you know their engineering," Daw said. "Especially since Gladiator's been unable to identify even the ship type."

Neal's face, seen in the CRT, flushed. He was a handsome, slightly dissipated-looking man whose high forehead seemed still higher under a thick crest of dark hair. "I would assume their drives are about the same as ours, sir," he said.

"I've done that. On that basis they shut down only an hour before we picked them up. But I'm not sure I believe it." He cut Neal off and scanned the rest of the lights. One was from the ship's cybernetics compartment; but Polk, the cyberneticist, was bunking with the systems analyst this trip. Daw pushed the light and a woman's face appeared on the screen. It was framed in honey-toned hair, a face with skin like a confection and classic planes that might have shamed a fashion model. And a smile. He had seen that smile often before—though as seldom, he told himself, as he decently could.

"Yes, Mrs. Youngmeadow?"

"*Helen*, please. I can't see you, Captain. The screen is blank."

"There's some minor repair work to be done on the camera here," Daw lied. "It's not important, so we've given it low priority."

"But you can see me?"

"Yes." He felt the blood rising in his cheeks.

"About this ship, Captain . . ." Helen Youngmeadow paused, and Daw noticed that her husband was standing behind her, beyond the plane of focus. "Captain, everyone on the ship can hear me—can't they?"

"I can cut them out of the circuit if you prefer."

"No—Captain, may I come up there?"

"To the bridge? Yes, if you like. It's a long way."

Another como light. This time the alternate bridge module—in appearance much like his, but lacking the battered Old and New Testaments bound in steel and magnetically latched to the console. "Hello, Wad," Daw said gently.

Wad made a half-salute. His young, dark-complexioned face showed plainly the strain of two years' involvement in a hell that demanded night and day a continual flow of deductions, inferences, and decisions—all without effect. Looking at Daw significantly, he drew a finger across his throat, and Daw gave him the private circuit he had offered Mrs. Youngmeadow.

"Thanks, Skipper. I've got something I thought you ought to know about."

Daw nodded.

"I've been running an artifact correlation on the visual image of that ship."

"So have I. Electronic and structural."

"I know, I got your printout. But my own analysis was bionic."

"You think that's valid?"

Wad shrugged. "I don't know, but it's interesting. You know what the biologists say: Man has reached the stage where he evolves through his machines. The earliest spacecraft resembled single-celled animals—pond life. The dilettante intellectuals of the time tried to give them a sexual significance—that was the only thing they knew—but they were really much closer to the things you find in a drop of pond water than to anything else."

"And what does your analysis say about this ship?"

"No correlation at all. Nothing higher than a tenth."

Daw nodded again. "You think the lack of correlation is significant?"

"It suggests to me that it may have originated somewhere where life forms are quite different from what we are accustomed to."

"Mankind has colonized some queer places."

With heavy significance Wad said, "Would it *have* to be mankind, Captain?" He was speaking, Daw knew, not to him but to his instructors back home. If his guess was correct he would, presumably, be given some small number of points; if not, he would lose ground. In time he would, or would not, be given his own command. The whole thing embarrassed Daw and made him feel somehow wretched, but he could not really blame Wad. He was Wad. To keep the ball rolling—mostly because he did not want to answer the other como lights—he said, "Men have spread their seed a long way across the galaxy, Wad. We've seen a lot of strange ships, but they've always turned out to be of human origin."

"The part of the galaxy we know about is tiny compared to the vastness we don't know. And there are other galaxies!"

Daw said, "I've been thinking about the stranger's build myself, as I told you. He looks like a crystal to me—modules ranged in a three-dimensional rectangular array."

"What do you think that means?"

"Comes from a world where they've discovered radio."

Wad broke the connection; Daw grinned but found he didn't much blame him for it.

Daw wondered what Gladiator's bionic correlation program would say about Gladiator herself. Perhaps liken her to the armor of a caddis-fly larva—an empty cylinder of odds and ends. Caddis-fly armor exploded. The interior of his helmet held the familiar smells of fine lubricating oil, sweat, and the goo he sometimes used on his hair; he kicked down and the soles of his boots clinked home on the hull of the bridge module.

Above him and around him Gladiator flung her shining threads, the stars a dust of ice seen through the interstices, the connecting tubes like a spiderweb—half-glittering, half-drowned in inky shadow.

Still ten thousand miles off, the other ship was, under the immense lasers Gladiator directed toward it, another star; but one that winked and twinkled as its structure surged and twisted to the urgings of accelerations long departed.

A hatch at Daw's feet opened and a metal-clad figure he knew to be Helen Youngmeadow rose, caught his hand, and stood beside him. Like his own, her faceplate was set for full transparency; her beautiful face, thus naked to the darkness of a billion suns, seemed to him to hold a hideous vulnerability. In his earphones her voice asked: "Do you know this is the first time I've been out? It's lovely."

"Yes," Daw said.

"And all this is Gladiator; she doesn't seem this big when she talks to me in our cabin. Could you show me which one it is? I'm lost."

"Which module?" From his utility belt Daw took a silver rod, then locked the articulations of his suit arm so that he could aim it like a missile projector with the fine adjustment controls. In the clean emptiness no beam showed, but a module miles down the gossamer cylinder of the ship flashed with the light.

"Way down there," the girl said. "It would be a lot more sociable if everyone were quartered together."

"In a warship the men must be near their duty," Daw explained awkwardly. "And everything has to be decentralized so that if we're blown apart, all the parts can fight. The module you and your husband are in has more of the ship's central processor than any of the others, but even that is scattered all over."

"And their ship—the ship out there—is modular too."

"Yes," Daw said. He remembered his conversation with Wad. "Ours is a hollow cylinder, theirs a filled rectangle. Our modules are different sizes and shapes depending on function; theirs are uniform. You're the empathist—the intercultural psychologist—what do those things tell you?"

"I have been thinking about it," Helen Youngmeadow said, "but I'd like to think some more before I talk, and I'm anxious to fly. Can't we go now?"

"You're sure—?"

"I've had all the training." She relaxed her boots' grip on the steel world beneath her, kicked out, for an instant floated above him, then was gone. Backpack rockets made a scarcely visible flame, and it was several seconds before he could pick out the spark of her progress. He followed, knowing that all around them, invisible and distant by hundreds of miles, the other boarding parties he had dispatched were making for the ship ahead as well.

"I'm an empathist, as you said," the girl's voice continued. "Gladiator is a warship, but my husband and I are here to take the side of the enemy."

"That doesn't bother me."

"Because by taking their side we help you. We give you someone who thinks like them and reacts to *their* needs. In a way we're traitors."

"This is exploration; if we had come just to fight you wouldn't even be on board."

"Because the Navy's afraid we might blow our own vessel up, or induce the crew to mutiny. We humans have such a high empathy coefficient—some of us."

"When you and I reach that ship," Daw said wryly, *"we'll* be the underdogs. Perhaps then you'll empathize with the Navy."

"That's the danger—if I do that I won't be doing my job."
He chuckled.

"Listen, Captain Daw. If I ask you something, will you tell me the truth? Straight?"

"If you'll let me catch up to you, and assuming it's not classified."

"All right, I've cut my jets. I'm—"

"I see you, and I've been ranging you on suit radar. It's just that with more mass to accelerate I can't match you for speed when you're flat out." Ahead of them something had been transformed from a winking star to a tiny scrap of diamond lace. Three thousand miles yet, Daw estimated, and checked his radar for confirmation. Five thousand. That ship was big. He said aloud, "What's the question?"

"Why did you let me come? I want to, and I'm terribly grateful, but while I was going up to the bridge I was sure you'd say no. I was thinking of ways to go without your permission—crazy things like that."

For the second time Daw lied.

He held her in space, his hand on her arm, telling her it was a safety precaution. The scrap of lace grew to an immense net and at last acquired a third dimension, so that it was seen as thousands of cubes of void, tubes outlining the edges, spherical modules at the intersections. "Right angles," Helen Youngmeadow said. "I never knew right angles could be so lovely." Then, a moment later, "This is more beautiful than ours."

Daw felt something he tried to choke down. "More regular, certainly," he admitted. "Less individualized."

"Do you still think it's abandoned?"

"Until they show me otherwise. The question is, which one of these things should we enter?"

"If we *can* enter."

"We can. Mrs. Youngmeadow, you empathize with these people, even though you've never seen anything of theirs except this ship. Where would you put the command module?"

It was a challenge, and she sensed it. "Where would you put it, Captain? As a sailor and a military man?"

"On a corner," Daw said promptly.

"You're right." He saw her helmet swivel as she looked at him. "But how did you know? Are you trained in empathics too?"

"No. But you agree? I thought you were going to say in the center."

"That's what I thought *you* were going to say—but it has to be wrong. The entire ship is a structure of empty cubes, with the edges and corners having the only importance. An outer corner would be the corner of corners—did you feel that?"

"No, but I saw that observation from an interior module would be blocked in every direction, and even on an outside plane the rest of the ship would blot out a hundred and eighty degrees. A corner module has two hundred and seventy degrees of clear field."

They explored the surface of the nearest corner module (Daw estimated its diameter at sixty thousand feet, which would give it a surface area of over three hundred and fifty square miles) until they found a hatch, with what appeared to be a turning bar on the side opposite the hinge. "How do you know it's not locked?" the girl asked as Daw braced himself to heave at the bar.

"Nobody's worried about burglars out here. But anyone's going to worry about having a crew member outside who has to get in fast." He pulled. The bar moved a fraction of an inch and the hatch a barely visible distance. "I'll give you some more data to empathize on," Daw said. "Whoever built this thing is damn strong."

The girl grasped the other end of the bar, and together they turned it until the hatch stood wide open. Light poured from it into the limitless night of space, and Helen Youngmeadow said softly, "They left everything turned on," and a moment afterward, "No airlock."

"No, they don't mind vacuum." Daw was already climbing into the module. There were no floors and no interior partitions; windowed solids that might have been instruments lined the hull wall; machines the size of buildings, braced with guying cables thousands of feet long, dotted the vast central space.

"It's weird, isn't it?" the girl said. "Like being in a bird-cage—only I can't tell which way is up."

"Up is always an illusion on a ship," Daw told her. "Why have illusions?" He was already far over her head, exploring. "No chairs, no beds. I like it."

"You mean they don't rest?" The girl had launched herself toward him now, and she put herself into a slow roll so that, to her eyes, the interior of the module revolved around her.

"No." Daw moved closer to one of the great mechanisms. "Look, on our ship we have couches and chairs with thousands of little suction holes in them, so that when your clothes touch them you stay where you put yourself. But somebody who might have been doing something more valuable had to make every one of those pieces of fancy furniture, and then a hundred times their cost was spent lugging them up out of Earth's gravity well into space. Then their pumps require power, which means waste heat the ship has a hard time getting rid of—and any time we want to go anywhere on reaction drive—all the close-in maneu-vers—we have to accelerate their mass, and decelerate it again when we get there. All this to hold you down on a ship that never gets up much over half a G, and in addition to the crash couches on the tenders and lifeboats."

"But we have to lie down to sleep."

"No, you don't; you're simply accustomed to it. All you really have to do is pull your feet off the floor, turn out the lights, and hold onto something—like this guy wire—with one hand. Which is probably what the people who built this ship did. Our ances-tors, in case you've forgotten, were a tree-dwelling species; and when we go to sleep with our hands around anything that re-sembles a limb, we automatically tighten up if it starts to slip out."

"You still think this ship was built by human beings?"

Daw said carefully, "We've never found one that wasn't."

"Until now."

"You don't."

There was no reply. Daw looked at the girl to make certain

571

she was all right, jockeyed himself to within touching distance of the great machine, then repeated, "You don't?"

"People? With no airlock?"

"The hatch we used may not have been intended for use in space. Or there might be safety devices we don't know about, deactivated now."

"There wasn't any atmosphere, even before we opened it; as large as this place is, it would have to discharge for hours, and we'd have felt the push as we came through. There wasn't anything. You said yourself that they didn't mind vacuum."

Daw said, "I was thinking they might use this one for some special purpose, or they might wear suits all the time in here."

"Captain, I love mankind. I know when somebody says that, it's usually just talk; but I mean it. Not just the people who are like me, but all human beings everywhere. And yet I don't like this ship."

"That's funny." Daw swung himself away from the machine he had been examining. "I do. They're better naval engineers— I think—than we are. Do you want to go back?"

"No, of course not. The job is here. What are you going to do now?"

"First check out a few more modules; then have some of our people land on the opposite corner of this thing with routes mapped out for them that will take at least one man through every module. They can work their way toward us, and I'll take their reports as they come in."

"Are you going into some of the other modules now?"

"Yes."

"Then I'll come with you. I don't like it here."

It was almost ten hours later when the first searchers reached the point where Daw and the girl waited, having traversed the diagonal length of the ship. They came in talking, in threes and fours, having met when their lines of search converged. Daw, who, except for one brief return to Gladiator, had spent the time studying some of the devices in the corner module and those immediately adjacent, broke up the groups and questioned each man separately, using a private communication frequency. Helen Youngmeadow chatted with those waiting for debriefing and waved to each party going back to the ship.

In time the groups thinned, fewer and fewer men clustered around the girl; and at last the last crewman saluted and departed, and she and Daw were alone again. To make conversation she said, "It always seems so lonely on our ship, but seeing all these men makes me realize how many there are; and there are some I'd swear I've never even met."

"You probably haven't," Daw said. The list Gladiator was flashing on his in-helmet display showed one man still out, and he was not sure the girl was aware of it—or that she was not.

"I've been wondering what they all do. I mean, the ship can almost run itself, can't it?"

"Yes, Gladiator could pretty well take care of herself for a long time, if nothing had to be changed."

"If nothing had to be changed?"

"We have to worry about damage control too, on a warship; but adaptability is the chief justification for a big crew. We can beat our swords into plowshares if we have to, and then our plowshares back into swords; in other words, we can rewire and re-rig as much as we need to—if necessary fit out Gladiator to transport a half-million refugees or turn her into a medical lab or a factory. And when something like this comes up, we've got the people. This ship is too big to have every part visited by a specialist in every discipline, but the men I've just sent through her included experts in almost any field you could think of."

She was too far off for him to see the beauty of her smile, but he could feel it. "I think you're proud of your command, Captain."

"I am," Daw said simply. "This was what I wanted to do, and I've done it."

"Captain, who is Wad?"

For an instant the question hung in the nothingness between them; then Daw asked, "How did you meet Wad?"

"I asked the ship something—a few hours ago when we went back—and she referred me to him. He looks like you, only . . ."

"Only much younger."

"And he's wearing some sort of officer's insignia—but I'm certain I've never seen him before, not at mess or anywhere else."

"I didn't think Gladiator would do that," Daw said slowly. "Usually Wad only talks to me—at least that's what I thought."

"But who is he?"

"First I'd like to know what question you had that made the ship turn you over to him—and how he answered it."

"I don't think it was anything important."

"What was it?"

"I think she just felt—you know—that it needed the human touch."

"Which Wad has in plenty."

"Yes." Helen Youngmeadow sounded serious. "He's a very sympathetic, very sensitive young man. Not like an empathist, of course, but with some training he could become one. Is he your second-in-command?"

Daw shook his head, though perhaps she could not see it. "No," he said, "Moke's my second—you've met him." He thought of the times he and Moke had shared a table with Helen Young-meadow and her husband—Youngmeadow slender and hand-some, a bit proud of his blond good looks, intelligent, forceful and eloquent in conversation; Moke's honest, homely face strug-gling throughout the tasteless and untasted meal to hide the desire Youngmeadow's wife waked in every man, and the shame Moke felt at desiring the wife of so likable a shipmate as Young-meadow.

"Then who *is* Wad?"

"If I tell you, will you tell me what it was you asked him?"

The girl's shoulders moved, for Daw could see the bulky metal shoulders of her suit move with them. "I suppose so—Gladiator would tell you if you asked."

"Yes, but it wouldn't be the same thing as your telling me, Mrs. Youngmeadow. You see, Wad is me. I suppose you could say, too, that I am Wad, grown up."

"I don't understand."

"Do you know how ship captains are trained?"

"I know an officer's training is very hard—"

"Not officers—captains." Unexpectedly Daw launched himself toward her, his arms outstretched like a bird's wings, dodging the wide-spaced guy wires until, almost beside her, he caught one and swung to a stop.

"That was good," she said. "You're very graceful."

"I like this. I've spent a lot of time in space, and you won't find any of that sucking furniture in my cabin. You can laugh if you like, but I think this is what God intended."

"For us?" He could see the arch of her eyebrows now, through the dark transparency of her faceplate.

"For us. Leaping between the worlds."

"You know, understanding people is supposed to be my profession—but I don't think I really understand you at all, Captain. How *are* captains trained, anyway? Not like other officers?"

"No," Daw said. "We're not just officers who've been promoted, although I know that's what most people think."

"It's what I thought."

"That was the old way. I suppose the British carried it to the ultimate. Around 1800. Have you ever read about it?"

The girl did not answer.

"They put their future skippers on board warships when they were boys of eight or nine—they were called midshipmen. They were just children, and if they misbehaved they were bent over a gun and whipped, but at the same time they were gentlemen and treated as such. The captain, if he was a good captain, treated them like sons and they got responsibility shoved at them just as fast as they could take it."

"It sounds like a brutal system," Helen Youngmeadow said.

"Not as brutal as losing ship and crew. And it produced some outstanding leaders. Lord Nelson entered the navy at twelve and was posted captain when he was twenty; John Paul Jones started at the same age and was first mate on a slaver when he was nineteen and a captain at twenty-three."

"I'm sorry . . ." The girl's voice was so faint in Daw's earphones that he wondered for a moment if her suit mike was failing. "I've never heard of either of those men. But I'll look them up when we get back to Gladiator."

"Anyway," Daw continued, "it was a good system—for as

long as people were willing to send promising boys off to sea almost as soon as we'd send them off to school; but after a while you couldn't count on that anymore. Then they took boys who were almost grown and sent them to special universities first. By the time they were experienced officers they were elderly— and the ships, even though these weren't starships yet, had become so large that their captains hadn't had much real contact with them until they were nearly ready to take command of a ship themselves. After a hundred years or so of that—about the time the emphasis shifted from sea to space—people discovered that this sytem really didn't work very well. A man who'd spent half his life as a subordinate had been well trained in being a subordinate, but that was all."

The taut cable beneath Daw's suit-glove shook with a nearly undetectable tremor, and he turned to look toward the hatch, aware as he did that the girl, who must have felt the same minute vibration, had turned instead to the mouths of the connecting tubes that led deeper into the ship.

The man coming through the hatch was Polk, the cyberneticist, identifiable not by his face but by the name and number stenciled on his helmet. He saluted, and Daw waved him over.

"Got something for me, Captain?"

"I think so, the big cabinet in the center of this module. It's their computer mainframe, or at least an important part of it."

"Ah," said Polk.

"Wait a minute—" There was an edge of shrillness to Helen Youngmeadow's voice, though it was so slight Daw might easily have missed it. "How can you know that?"

"By looking at the wiring running to it. There are hundreds of thousands of wires—braided together into cables, of course, and very fine; but still separate wires, separate channels for information. Anything that can receive that much and do anything with it is a computer by definition—a data-processing device."

Polk nodded as though to support his captain, and began examining the great floating octahedron Daw had pointed out. After a minute had passed the girl said in a flat voice, "Do you think theirs might be better than ours? That would be important, I suppose."

Daw nodded. "Extremely important, but I don't know if it's true. From what I've been able to tell from looking into that thing, they're a little behind us, I think. Of course, there might be some surprises."

Polk muttered, "What am I looking for, Captain, just their general system?"

"To begin with," Daw said slowly, "I'd like to know what the last numbers in the main registers were."

Polk whistled, tinny-sounding over the headphones.

"What good would that be?" Helen Youngmeadow asked. "Anyway, wouldn't they just print it—" She remembered how much of Gladiator's output came over CRTs and audio, and broke off in midsentence.

Polk said, "Nobody prints much in space, Mrs. Youngmeadow. Printing—well, it eats up a lot of paper, and paper's heavy. It looks to me like they use a system a lot like ours. See this?" He passed a spacegloved hand across the center of one facet of the cabinet, but the girl could see no difference between the area he indicated and the surrounding smooth gray metal. To look more closely she dove across the emptiness much as Daw had a moment before.

"This was one of their terminals," Polk continued. "There are probably thousands scattered all through the ship. And they seem to have been used about the same way ours are, with turnoff after a set period to conserve the phosphors; they go bad if you excite them for too long."

"I've noticed that on Gladiator," the girl said. "If something's written on the screen—when I'm reading, for example— and I don't instruct it to bring up the next page, it fades out after a while. Is that what you mean? It seems remarkable that people as different as these should handle the problem the same way."

Daw said, "Not any more remarkable than that both of us use wires—or handles like the one that opened the hatch outside. Look inside that box, though, at the back of that panel, and you'll find something that *is* remarkable. Show her, Polk."

The cyberneticist unlatched the section he had indicated. It swung out smoothly, and the girl saw the display tubes behind it, tubes so flat that each was hardly more than a sheet of glass with a socket at the base. "Vacuum tubes?" she said. "Like a television? Even I know what those are."

Daw grunted. "Vacuum tubes in a vacuum."

"That's right. They shouldn't need anything around them out here, should they?"

"They don't, out here. This ship, or at least parts of it, goes into atmospheres at times. Even though the crew doesn't seem to care whether there's one in here or not."

"Captain," Helen Youngmeadow said suddenly, "where is my husband?"

Hours later Moke's voice (unexpectedly loud and near because Moke had the kind of voice that transmitted well through the phones' medium-range frequencies) asked a similar question: "You find Youngmeadow yet, Skipper?"

"We don't know that he's lost."

"You didn't find him, huh?"

"No, not yet."

"You really think he's alive and just not answering?"

"It could be," Daw said. He did not have to remind Moke, as he had Helen Youngmeadow, that there was no danger of running out of oxygen in a modern space suit—each suit being a system as self-sufficient as a planet and its sun; energy from the suit's tiny pile scavenging every molecule of water and whisper of carbon dioxide and making new, fresh food, fresh water, clean air that could be used again, so that once in the suit the occupant might live in plenty until time itself destroyed him. (He had not mentioned that even death would not end the life encysted in that steady protection, since the needs of the bacteria striking in at the now defenseless corpse from the skin, out from the intestines, would be sensed, still, by the faithful, empty suit— and served.)

Daw thought of Youngmeadow dead somewhere in this strange vessel, still secure in his suit, his corpse bloating and stinking while the suit hummed on; and found, startled, that the thought was pleasant—which was absurd, he hardly knew Youngmeadow, and certainly had nothing against the man.

"His wife still out looking for him?" Moke asked.

Daw nodded, though Moke could not see him. "Yes," he said. "So are the other parties. I've got a couple of men with Mrs. Youngmeadow to make sure she comes back all right."

"I was just talking to her," Moke said. "I think she's been talking to Polk too."

"What about?"

"She said she'd heard you found some maps, Captain. I guess Gladiator told her."

"No reason why she shouldn't, but I found those while she was here—she must have seen them. While we were waiting for the first survey parties to come in."

"You didn't hide them from her, or anything like that?"

"No, of course not. She just didn't show much interest in them." Actually, Daw remembered, he had taken the charts— technically they were star charts rather than maps—to show Helen and had been rather disappointed by her reaction; as an empathist, she had explained, she was much more concerned with things that had *not* been vital to the ship's operations than with the things that had. *"Everyone takes what is necessary, Captain,"* she had said. *"By definition they have to. It's what is taken that could be left behind that reveals the heart."*

"She wanted to know if any of them showed the inside of the ship," Moke said.

Daw felt tired. "I'll talk to her," he said, and cut Moke off.

He started to adjust his communicator for the girl's band, then thought better of it. His investigation of the command module—if in fact this was the command module—was nearly complete, and it served no purpose for him to stand by and watch Polk tinkering with his instruments. After having Gladiator scan the charts so that duplicates could be made on board for study, he had replaced the originals. Now he gathered them again.

It was the first time he had been more than two units away from the corner module he and Helen had first investigated, and though he had heard the chambers of the interior modules described by the men he had sent through them, and had seen the pictures they had taken, it was a new and a strange experience to plunge through tube after tube and emerge in chamber after chamber, each so huge it seemed a sky around him, each seeming without end.

The tubes, like those of his own ship, were circular in section; but they were dim (as Gladiator's were not) and lined with shimmering, luminous pastels he felt certain were codes but could not decipher. His years in space had taught him the trick of creating the things called *up* and *down* in his mind, changing them when it suited him, destroying them with the truth of gravitationless reality when he wished. In the tubes he amused himself with them, sometimes diving down a pulsing pink well, sometimes rocketing up a black gun barrel, until at last he found that he was no longer master of these false perceptions, which came and went without his volition.

Entering each module was like being flung from a ventilation duct into the rotunda of some incredible building. The walls of most were lined with enigmatic machines, the centers cobwebbed with cables spanning distances that dwarfed the great mechanisms they held. Light in the modules—at least in most— was like that in the first Daw had examined—bright, shadowless, and all-surrounding; but some were dim, and some dark. In these his utility light showed shapes and cables not greatly different from those it had seen in other modules, but in the dancing shadows it cast to the remote walls, it sometimes seemed to Daw that he saw living shapes.

At last, when he had become almost certain he had lost his way and was cursing himself (for his religious beliefs permitted any degree of self-condemnation, though they caviled at the application of the same terms to any soul except his own) for a fool and a damned fool, he saw the flicker of other lights in one of the half-lit modules and was able, a moment later, to pick out Helen Youngmeadow's suit with his own beam and, a halfsecond afterward, the suits of the sailors he had sent with her. At almost the same instant he heard her voice in his phones: "Captain, is that you?"

"Yes," he said. Now that he had found her, he discovered

that he was unwilling to admit that he had come looking for her. Everyone, notoriously, fell in love with empathists—the reason they were invariably assigned as married couples. In retrospect he realized how foolish it had been for him to allow her to accompany him at all, despite the rationalizations with which he had defended the decision to himself; and he found that he was anxious that neither she nor the men with her should think that he had come here for her sake. "I understand you were asking my second about charts, Mrs. Youngmeadow," he said, deliberately bringing his voice to the pitch he used in delivering minor reprimands. "I want to make it clear to you that if you have found any such documents, they should be submitted to me for scanning as soon as possible."

"We haven't found any maps," the girl said, "and if we did, of course I'd turn them over to you, though I don't suppose you could read them either."

The fatigue in her voice made Daw despise himself. Softening the question as much as he could, he asked, "Then why were you questioning Mr. Moke?"

"I knew you had found some. I was hoping they showed this ship and could tell us where my husband might be."

"They're star charts, Mrs. Youngmeadow. You saw them when I found them."

"I wasn't paying much attention then. Do you think they're important?"

"Very important," Daw said. "They could easily be the key to understanding—well, the entire system of thought of the people who built this ship. Naturally Gladiator can't stay here—"

"Can't stay here until my husband's found?"

"We aren't going to abandon your husband, Mrs. Youngmeadow."

"I don't suppose I could stop you if you wanted to."

"We don't."

"But if you do, Captain, you'll have to abandon me too. I'm not going back to our ship until we find out what happened to him, and if he's still alive; you say that a person can live indefinitely in one of these suits—all right, I'm going to do that. Even if your ship leaves, they'll still send out another one from Earth to investigate this, with cultural anthropologists and so forth on board; and when they get here they'll find me."

One of the crewmen muttered, "Tell him!" under his breath; Daw wondered if the man realized it had been picked up by his helmet mike. To the girl he said, "They'll find me too, Mrs. Youngmeadow. This ship is much too valuable a discovery for us to leave before someone else comes—but when they do come—this is what I was trying to say when you interrupted me—we'll have to go. They'll have equipment and experts; we are primarily a fighting ship. But it should be possible for you to arrange a transfer at that time."

"Captain . . ."

After a moment had passed, Daw said, "Yes?"

"Captain, can these men hear us?"

"Of course."

"Would you send them away? Just for a minute?"

"They could still hear us, if we stay on general band. If you have something private you wish to say, switch to my own band."

He watched as she fumbled with the controls on the forearm of her suit. One of the crewmen glided skillfully toward her to help, but she waved him away. Her voice came again. "Have I got you, Captain?"

"Yes."

"I just wanted to tell you that I'm sorry I said what I did. You've been a friend to my husband and me, I know. I'm very tired."

Daw said, "I understand."

"Captain, I've been thinking. Will you mind if I ask some questions? I realize it may be silly, but if I don't at least try—"

"Certainly."

"That cyberneticist—Lieutenant Polk. You asked him to find out—" She hesitated. Then, "I'm sorry, I can't think of the words."

"I asked him to find out for me what the numbers in the operating registers of this ship's computer were. To put it another way, I asked him to find out the answer—in raw form at least—of the last computation they performed."

"Is that possible? I would think their numbers would be all

different—like Roman numbers or something, or worse. I asked him about it—a few hours ago when you went back to Gladiator—and he explained to me that whatever he found would just be ones and zeros—"

"Binary notation," Daw said.

"Yes, binary notation, because it isn't *really* numbers, you can't have real numbers inside a machine because they're not physical, but just things turned on or off; but I don't see what good knowing it—just one, one, one, zero, zero, zero, like that—will do you if you don't know how they'd be used when they came out of the machine. Captain, I know you must think I don't know what I'm talking about, but I did have to take some mathematics . . . even if I wasn't very good at it." The transmission ended in a whisper of despair.

"I know you're worried about your husband," Daw said. "We're looking for him, as you know. I've got parties out. I shouldn't have included him among the searchers—that was a mistake, and I'm—"

"No!" Helen Youngmeadow jerked at the cable she was holding, swinging herself toward him until their faceplates touched and he could hear her voice, conducted through the metal, like an echo to the sound in his earphones. "You should have sent him. That's just it. At first, when we were waiting and waiting and the others came back, I talked to them and listened to them and, my God, they didn't know anything, they hadn't seen anything, and I thought just wait, just wait, Mr. Captain Daw, my man will show you what an empathist can do! Then when he didn't come I started to blame you, but that isn't right. *I'm* an empathist, my profession is supposed to be understanding cultures—every culture, when most people don't even comprehend their own. Now you've got these men staying with me to watch out for me—to watch out for me!—and do you know what they are? I asked them, and one is a plastics engineer and the other's a pharmacist's mate."

"They're good men," Daw said. "That's why I sent them with you, not because I thought they could assist you professionally."

"Well, you were wrong," the girl said in a much calmer voice. "We found a dingus of some sort floating loose in that last module we were in, and your plastics engineer looked at it for a while and then told us what he thought it was and how it had been made: he said they had used a four-part mold, and showed me where they had squirted in the melted stuff. So he understands his part of them, you see, but I don't understand mine. Now you're implying that you understand their math, or at least something about it. Can't you explain it to me?"

"Certainly," Daw said, "if you're interested. I'm afraid, though, that I don't see that it has any immediate bearing on locating your husband."

"A computer will answer anyone, won't it? I mean normally."

"Unless some sort of privacy provision has been made in the program."

"But there isn't much chance they'd do that on a ship like this; you said when we opened the hatch to get in that no one worried about burglars in space, so I doubt if they'd be worried about snoopers aboard their own ship either. And if their computer is like Gladiator, meant to run everything, it will know where my husband is—all we have to do is learn how to turn it on and ask it."

"I see what you mean," Daw told her, "but I'm afraid that's going to be a good deal more complicated than what I've got Polk trying to do."

"But it's the first step. Show me."

Moved by some democratic impulse he did not bother to analyze, Daw switched back to the general communication band before spreading one of the charts—without gravity or air currents it hung like smoke in the emptiness—to illustrate what he was about to say; then for the benefit of the crewmen he explained: "This is one of their star charts—we found it in the first module we entered. In a rough way you could consider it a map of this part of the galaxy, as seen from above."

The girl said: "I don't understand how you can talk about seeing a galaxy from above or from below, except by convention—or how you know those dots on the chart are stars at all without being able to read the language. And if they are stars, how do you know they represent the region we're in? Or is that just a guess?" Her voice was as controlled as it might have been during a dinner-table discussion on board Gladiator, but Daw sensed tension that held her at the edge of hysteria.

"To begin with," he said, "the galaxy's not a shapeless cloud of stars—it is disk-shaped, and it seems pretty obvious that anyone mapping any sizable portion of it would choose to look at things from one face or the other. Which face is chosen is strictly a matter of convention, but there are only two choices. And we're pretty certain these things are star charts, because Gladiator measured the positions of the dots and ran a regression analysis between them and the known positions of the stars. The agreement was so good that we can feel pretty sure of the identities of most of the dots. What's more, if you'll look at the chart closely you'll see that our friends have used three sizes of dots."

Daw paused and one of the crewmen asked, "Magnitude, Captain?"

"That's what we thought at first, but actually the three sizes seem to symbolize the principal wavelengths radiated—small dots for the blue end of the spectrum, medium for yellow stars like Sol, and large for the red giants and the dark stars."

Helen Youngmeadow said, "I don't see how that can help you read the numbers."

"Well, you'll notice faint lines running from star to star, with symbols printed along them; it seems reasonable to assume that these are distances, and of course we know the actual distances."

"But you don't know what sort of squiggle they use for each number, or what units the distances are given in."

"Worse than that," Daw admitted, "we don't—or at least we didn't—know whether they ran their figures from left to right or from right to left—or whether they were using positional notation at all. And of course we didn't know what base they were using, either. Or which symbol took the place of our decimal point."

"But you were able to find all that out, just from the chart?"

"Yes. The base was fairly easy. You probably remember from your own math that the number of numerals a system needs is equal to the number of the base. Our decimal notation, for example, uses ten—zero through nine. If you'll look at these numbers you'll see that a total of thirteen symbols are used—"

"Base thirteen?"

Daw shook his head. "We doubt it very much. Thirteen is a prime number, divisible only by one and itself, and as such an almost impossible base. But if we assume that one of the symbols is a position indicator like our decimal point, that leaves twelve; and twelve is a very practical base. So the question was which symbol divided the wholes—of whatever unit they were using— from the fractional parts."

Helen Youngmeadow leaned toward the chart, and Daw sensed, with a happiness he had hardly known himself capable of, that some portion of her despair was fading. "You could try them one by one," she said. "After all, there are only thirteen."

"We could have, but there turned out to be a much quicker way. Remember, these numbers represent stellar distances, and we felt that we knew what most of the stars were. So we programmed a search routine to look for a star whose distance from one of the base stars on the chart was twelve times that of some other, closer star. In positional notation—and we had to assume for the time being that they were using a positional notation, since if they weren't they wouldn't need an analog to the decimal point—when you shift the symbol, or group of symbols, at the front of a number up by one position, it has the effect, roughly, of multiplying the number by the base. So we had our program determine the ratio nearest twelve, the closer the better; and when we had located our stars we looked for a symbol that hadn't changed position in the larger number. Here"—he indicated two lines of print on the chart—"see what I mean?"

"No," the girl said after a moment. "No, I don't. There are eight symbols in one expression and nine in the other, but the one on the right looks like an equation—the thing like a fish with a spear through it is equal to one group minus another."

"Yes, it does," Daw admitted, "but the thing that resembles an equals sign is their mark for seven, and the 'minus' is a one. The vertical mark that looks like our one is their decimal point, and the numbers are read from right to left instead of left to right."

"How did you get the values of the numerals?"

"Do you really want to hear about all this?"

"Yes, I do, but I don't know why. Captain, is there actually a chance we might be able to get the computer on this ship working, and ask it where my husband is? And it would answer—just like that? That's what I'm trying to believe, but sometimes it slips. Maybe I'm just interested because you are, and I empathize; it's a fault of mine."

Daw was suddenly embarrassed, and conscious as he had not been for some time of the empty ship around him. "Gladiator could explain this as well as I could," he said. "Better."

"I could guess some of them myself, I think. You've already told me that the horizontal mark is a one, so since the equals sign isn't two, it must be the S-shaped thing."

"You're right," Daw said, "how did you know?"

"Because it looks like our two, only backward; and ours is a cursive mark for what used to be two horizontal lines—it used to look like a Z. From the shape of their S sign I'd say it started out as two lines slanted." She smiled.

"It is interesting, isn't it?" Daw said.

"Very interesting. But now will you tell me what you're going to learn when you can read whatever number the people who built this place left in their computer?"

"We don't know, really; but from the nature of the number we may be able to guess what it was. What I'm hoping for is the heading they took when they abandoned the ship."

"Did they abandon this ship?"

Daw was nonplussed. "We've been all through it."

"Even through the path assigned my husband?"

"Of course; the first thing I did when he failed to return was to send a party to retrace his route."

"And they did it?"

"Yes."

"And came back and reported?"

"Yes."

587

"Captain Daw, could *we* do it? I mean, I know you're needed to direct things, even if I'm not, but could we do it? I don't have your logical mind, but I have a feeling for situations, it's part of my stock-in-trade. And I think the two of us might find something where no one else would."

Daw thought for a moment. "Good administrative practice," he said. "I see what you mean."

"Then tell me, because I don't myself."

"Just that since this is our biggest problem I should give it my personal attention; and you should come too, because you are the one who wants it settled most and will have the greatest dedication to the job. You realize though, don't you, that you are—we are—almost in the center of your husband's route now."

Even as he made this last small protest Daw felt himself carried away by the attraction of the idea. He would lose a certain amount of face with the men he had assigned to guard Helen, but, as he told himself, he could afford to lose some face. Addressing them, he said: "Mrs. Youngmeadow and I are going to retrace her husband's search path through this vessel in person. You may return to your duty."

The two saluted, and Daw saw—incredibly—a new respect in their expressions, and something like envy as well. "Dismissed!" he snapped.

When they had gone Helen Youngmeadow said: "You really like it, don't you, going off by yourself? I should have known when we went alone to board this ship."

"No," Daw said. "I should be on Gladiator."

"That's the voice of conscience. But this is what you like." The girl launched herself from the cable she had been holding and gave half-power to her backpack rockets, doing a lazy wingover to avoid the next wire.

"Where are you going?" Daw called.

"Well, we're going to retrace the way my husband came, in the same direction he did, aren't we? So there's no use going back to the beginning that way; but if we take the modules next to his, we might find something."

"Do you think your husband would have deviated from the assigned route?"

"He might have," said Helen's voice in Daw's ear. He could see her now, far ahead in the dimness, ready to dive into the pale, circular, lime-green immensity of a tube. "He was a funny person, and I guess maybe I may not have known him as well as I thought I did."

Daw put on a burst of speed and was up with her before she had gone a thousand yards into the tube. "You're right," he said, "this is what I like."

"I do too—maybe my husband liked it too much. That would be in harmony with his personality profile, I think." Daw did not answer, and a few seconds later she asked in a different tone, "Do you know what I was thinking of, while you were telling me about those charts? Stones. Little pebbles. Do you get it?"

"No," Daw said. The tube was bent just enough here for the ends to be invisible to them. They sailed through a nothingness of pale green light.

"Well, I may not know a lot of math but I know some ety-mology. You were talking about calculations, and that word comes from the Latin for 'stone': *calculus*. That was the way they used to count—one stone for one sheep or one ox. And later they had a thing like an abacus, except that instead of rods for the counters it had a board with cup-shaped holes to put stones in. Those numbers you figured out were little stones from a world we've never seen."

Daw said, "I think I understand." He could make out the end of the tube now, a region of brighter light where vague shapes floated.

"The thing I wonder about is where are they now, those first stones? Ground to powder? Or just kicking around Italy or Egypt somewhere, little round stones that nobody pays any attention to. I don't really think anything would happen if they were de-stroyed—not really—but I've been wondering about it."

"Your sense of history is too strong," Daw told her. He nearly added, "like Wad's," but thought better of it and said instead, "For some reason that reminds me—you were going to tell me why you were talking to Wad, but you never did."

"Wad is the boy that looks like you? I said I would if you'd tell me about him."

"That's right," Daw said, "I didn't finish." They were leaving the tube now, thrown like the debris from an explosion through an emptiness whose miles-distant walls seemed at first merely roughened, but whose roughness resolved into closely packed machines, a spininess of shafts and great gears and tilted beams— all motionless.

"You told me about the midshipmen," Helen reminded him. "I think I can guess the rest, except that I don't know how it's done."

"And what's your guess?"

"You said that you were Wad—at least in a sense. In some way you're training yourself."

"Time travel? No."

"What, then?"

"Future captains are selected by psychological testing when, as cadets, they have completed their courses in basic science. Then, instead of being sent to space as junior officers, they go as observers on a two-year simulated flight—all right on Earth. The advantage is that they see more action in the two years of simulation than they'd get in twenty of actual service. They go through every type of emergency that's ever come up at least once, and some more than once—with variations."

"That's interesting; but it doesn't explain Wad."

"They have to get the material for the simulations somewhere. Sure, in most of it the midshipman just views, but you don't want to train him to be a detached observer and nothing else. He has to be able to talk to the people on shipboard, and especially the captain, and get meaningful, typical replies. To get material for those conversations a computer on every Navy ship simulates a midshipman whom the captain and crew must treat as an individual."

"Do they all look like you?"

"They have to look like someone, so they're made to look— and talk and act—as the captain himself did during his midshipman days. It's important, as I said, that the captain treat his midshipman as a son, and that way there's more—" Daw paused.

"Empathy?" He could hear the fragile smile.

"That's your word. Sympathy."

"Before it was corrupted by association with pity, that used to mean what empathy does now."

A new voice rang in Daw's headphones: *"Captain! Captain!"*

"Yes. Here."

"This is Polk, Captain. We didn't want to bother you, sir, but we've got the numbers from the central registers in that corner module, and from the form—well, we think you're right. It's a bearing."

"You've got duplicates of the charts, don't you? Where were they going?"

"What star, you mean, sir?"

"Yes, of course."

"It doesn't seem to be a bearing for any star, Captain. Not on their charts, or ours either."

Helen Youngmeadow interrupted to say: "But it has to point to some star! There are millions of them out there."

Daw said, "There are billions—each so remote that for most purposes it can be treated as a nondimensional point."

"The closest star to this bearing's about a quarter-degree off," Polk told her. "And a quarter of a degree is, well, ma'am, a hell of a long way in astrogation."

"Perhaps it isn't a bearing, then," the girl said.

Daw asked, "What does it point to?"

"Well, sir—"

"When I asked you a minute ago what the bearing indicated, you asked if I meant what star. So it does point to something, or you think it does. What is it?"

"Sir, Wad said we should ask Gladiator what was on the line of the bearing at various times in the recent past. I guess he thought it might be a comet or something. It turned out that it's pointing right to where our ship was while we were making our approach to this one, sir."

Unexpectedly, Daw laughed. (Helen Youngmeadow tried to remember if she had ever heard him laugh before, and decided she had not.)

591

"Anything else to report, Polk?"

"No, sir."

She asked, "Why did you laugh, Captain?"

"We're still on general band," Daw said. "What do you say we switch over to private?"

His own dials bobbed and jittered as the girl adjusted her controls.

"I laughed because I was thinking of the old chimpanzee experiment; you've probably read about it. One of the first scientists to study the psychology of the nonhuman primates locked a chimp in a room full of ladders and boxes and so on—"

"And then peeked through the keyhole to see what he did, and saw the chimpanzee's eye looking back at him." Now Helen laughed too. "I see what you mean. You worked so hard to see what they had been looking at—and they were looking at us."

"Yes," said Daw.

"But that doesn't tell you where they went, does it?"

Daw said, "Yes, it does."

"I don't understand."

"They were still here when we sighted them, because we changed course to approach this ship."

"Then they abandoned the ship because we came, but that still doesn't tell you where they went."

"It tells me where they are now. If they didn't leave before we had them in detection range, they didn't leave at all—we would have seen them. If they didn't leave at all, they are still on board."

"They can't be."

"They can be and they are. Think of how thinly we're scattered on Gladiator. Would anyone be able to find us if we didn't want to be found?"

Far ahead in the dimness her utility light answered him. He saw it wink on and dart from shadow to shadow, then back at him, then to the shadows again. "We're in no more danger than we were before," he said.

"They have my husband. Why are they hiding, and who are they?"

"I don't know; I don't even know that they are hiding. There may be very few of them—they may find it hard to make us notice them. I don't know."

The girl was slowing, cutting her jets. He cut his own, letting himself drift up to her. When he was beside her she said: "Don't you know anything about them? Anything?"

"When we first sighted this ship I ran an electronic and structural correlation on its form. Wad ran a bionic one. You wouldn't have heard us talking about them because we were on a private circuit."

"No." The girl's voice was barely audible. "No, I didn't."

"Wad got nothing on his bionic correlation. I got two things out of mine. As a structure this ship resembles certain kinds of crystals. Or you could say that it looks like the core stack in an old-fashioned computer—cores in rectangular arrays with three wires running through the center of each. Later, because of what Wad had said, I started thinking of Gladiator; so while we were more or less cooling our heels and hoping your husband would come in, I did what Wad had done and ran a bionic correlation on her." He fell silent.

"Yes?"

"There were vertebrates—creatures with spinal columns—before there were any with brains; did you know that? The first brains were little thickenings at the end of the spinal nerves nearest the sense organs. That's what Gladiator resembles—that first thin layer of extra neurons that was the primitive cortex. This ship is different."

"Yes," the girl said again.

"More like an artificial intelligence—the computer-core stack, of course, but the crystals too; the early computers, the ones just beyond the first vacuum-tube stage, used crystalline materials for transducers: germanium and that kind of thing. It was before Ovshinsky came up with ovonic switches of amorphous materials."

"What are you saying? That the ship is the entity? That the crew are robots?"

"I told you I don't know," Daw said. "I doubt if our terms are applicable to them."

"But what can we do?"

"Get in touch with them. Let them know we're here, that we're friendly and want to talk." He swung away from her—up, in his current orientation, up six miles sheer before coming to rest like a bat against the ceiling, then revolving the ship in his mind until the ceiling became a floor. The girl hovered five hundred feet above his head as he inspected the machines.

"I see," she said, "you're going to break something."

"No," Daw said slowly, "I'm going to find something to repair or improve—if I can."

Several hours passed while he traced the dysfunction that held the equipment around him immobile. From the module where he had begun he followed it to the next, where he found broken connections and fused elements; another hour while he made the connections again, and found, in cabinets not wholly like any he had seen built by men, parts to replace those the overloads had destroyed. When he had finished his work, three lights came on in distant parts of the module; and far away some great machine breathed a sigh that traveled through the metal floor to the soles of his boots, though Helen, still floating above him, did not hear it. "Do you think they'll come now?" she asked when the lights gleamed. "Will they give him back to us?"

Daw did not answer. A shape—a human shape—was emerging from the mouth of a distant tube. It was a half-mile away, but he had seen it as the girl spoke, a mere speck, but a speck with arms and legs and a head that was a recognizable helmet. In a moment she had followed his eyes. "Darling," she said. "Darling." Daw watched. A voice, resonant yet empty, said, "Helen."

"Darling," the girl said again.

The empty voice said: "I am not your husband. I know what you believe."

Daw saw it as the figure came down beside him. He thought the girl would not see it, but she said, "Who are you?"

Through the clear faceplate Daw could see Youngmeadow's

face. The lips shaped: "Not your husband. You would call me a simulation of him. Something that can talk to you; they cannot, or will not, do that directly." It seemed to Daw that the face, so like Youngmeadow's, was in some deeper way not like Youngmeadow's at all, or anyone's—as though, perhaps, those moving lips concealed organs of sight in the recesses of the mouth, and the voice, the sound he heard, poured forth from the nose and ears.

"Where is my husband?"

"I cannot answer that."

"Cannot," Daw asked, "or will not?"

"There are four words, and all are difficult. What is meant by *is*? By *husband*? I can ask, but you could only answer in further words, further concepts we could not define."

"You are a simulation of him?"

"I said, 'You would call me a simulation of him.' "

Helen asked suddenly, "What have you come to tell us?"

"That with this"—the figure that looked like Youngmeadow gestured toward the repairs Daw had made—"there has been enough. You have seen something of us; we, now, of you. There cannot be more, now. We both must think."

"Are you trying to tell us," Daw asked, "that we could not have worked out a philosophy for dealing with your culture until we made this contact?"

"I can answer few questions. We must think. You too."

"But you want us to leave your ship. Are we friends?"

"We are not," the simulation answered carefully, "not-friends." He lifted off as a man would have, and in a few seconds was gone.

"He wasn't your husband," Daw said.

"I know it."

"Do you trust me, Helen? Will you take my word for something?"

She nodded.

"Your husband is dead. It's over."

"You know."

Daw thought of the scattered bits of rag and vacuum-shriveled flesh he had seen—and not mentioned to the girl overhead—while making the repairs. "I know," he said.

He lifted off, and she flew beside him for a time, silently. There was a dysfunction in his headphones so that he heard, constantly, a sound like the noise of the wind. It was not unpleasant, except that it was a dysfunction. At last she said, "Was he ever alive, Captain? Do you know what I've been thinking? That perhaps he never was. The cabins, you know."

"What about them?" Daw asked.

"They're only supposed to be for one person, but you had two of us in there. Because everybody knows empathists have to be married . . . and there's Wad—he really wasn't on the ship either. Are you sure my husband existed, Captain? That he wasn't just something implanted in our minds before we left Earth? I can remember the way he held me, but not one thing he said, not word for word. Can you?"

"He was real," Daw said, "and he's dead. You'll feel better when you've seen the medics and had some rest."

"Captain . . ."

"He came in here," Daw said, "and somehow he realized the truth, that the crew of this ship—whatever you want to call them—was still on board. Then he thought the same thing you did: that he would break something and make them notice him. His empathy was all for people, not for things. He broke something and they noticed him, and he's dead."

"Only people are important," the girl said.

"To other people," Daw answered, "sometimes."

On board Gladiator she said: "I never told you what it was I asked Wad, did I? I was asking about you—what your childhood was like."

In Daw's mind a voice more insistent than hers quoted: *"At the resurrection, therefore, of which of the seven will she be the wife? For they all had her." But Jesus answered and said to them, "You err because you know neither the Scriptures nor the power of God. For at the resurrection they will neither marry nor be given in marriage. . . ."* Aloud he said, "I hope Wad told you the truth."

"When you were in training—I mean, like he is now—you were watching a simulated captain, weren't you? Was it yourself you saw there, only older?"

"I don't think so," Daw said. "A real captain. He was a crusty bastard, but he generally knew what he was doing."

"STARCROSSED"

GEORGE ZEBROWSKI

(1 9 7 3)

Where does humanity's far-distant future lie? Will man and woman ever journey among the stars? Or will one of their creations make the journey for them? Wherever they may travel, imagination must first make a path through the unknown for them to follow. Without the power of the imagination to light up the future, the present walks in a circle, repeating itself. Perhaps once upon a time far away from now, a story will be told about that great adventure among the stars. Perhaps by then humanity's form will have evolved and changed. Perhaps humans will have become pure intelligence. Can pure intelligence still love? Will it take love with it into the universe?

George Zebrowski takes us on such an imaginary journey in "Starcrossed," an appropriate close to our anthology. Zebrowski is locked into the necessity of using our present language to tell his tale about a far-distant future, yet he brilliantly escapes the limitations of language to carry us to a possibility almost beyond our understanding. It is a story flying on the gossamer wings of intelligence and imagination, through stardust, and into the future.

George Zebrowski was born in Austria in 1945 and now lives in upstate New York. His *Macrolife* (1979) was one of the major novels of the 1970s. Some of his best short stories can be found in *The Monadic Universe and Other Stories* (1977).

VISUAL *was a silence of stars, audio a mindless seething on the electromagnetic spectrum, the machine-metal roar of the universe, a million gears grinding steel wires in their teeth. Kinetic was hydrogen and microdust swirling past the starprobe's hull, deflected by a shield of force. Time was experienced time, approaching zero, a function of near-light speed relative to the Solar System. Thought hovered above sleep, dreaming, aware of simple operations continuing throughout the systems of the sluglike starprobe: simple data filtering into storage to be analyzed later. Identity was the tacit dimension of the past making present awareness possible: MOB—*

Modified Organic Brain embodied in a cyborg relationship with a probe vehicle en route to Antares, a main sequence M-type star 170 light-years from the Solar System, with a spectral character of titanium oxide, violet light weak, red in color, 390 solar diameters across. . . .

The probe ship slipped into the ashes of other-space, a gray field which suddenly obliterated the stars, silencing the electromagnetic simmer of the universe. MOB was distantly aware of the stresses of passing into nonspace, the brief distortions which made it impossible for biological organisms to survive the procedure unless they were ship-embodied MOBs. A portion of MOB recognized the distant echo of pride-in-usefulness, but the integrated self knew this to be a result of organic residues in the brain core.

Despite the probe's passage through other-space, the journey would still take a dozen human years. When the ship reentered normal space, MOB would come to full consciousness, ready to complete its mission in the Antares system. MOB waited, secure in its purpose.

MOB was aware of the myoelectrical nature of the nutrient bath in which it floated, connected via synthetic nerves to the computer and its chemical RNA memory banks of near infinite capacity. All of earth's knowledge was available for use in dealing with any situation which might arise, including contact with an alien civilization. Simple human-derived brain portions operated the routine components of the interstellar probe, leaving MOB to dream of the mission's fulfillment while hovering near explicit awareness, unaware of time's passing.

The probe trembled, bringing MOB's awareness to just below completely operational. MOB tried to come fully awake, tried to open his direct links to visual, audio, and internal sensors; and failed. The ship trembled again, more violently. Spurious electrical signals entered MOB's brain core, miniature nova bursts in his mental field, flowering slowly and leaving after-image rings to pale into darkness.

Suddenly part of MOB seemed to be missing. The shipboard nerve ganglia did not respond at their switching points. He could not see or hear anything in the RNA memory banks. His right side, the human-derived portion of the brain core, was a void in MOB's consciousness.

MOB waited in the darkness, alert to the fact that he was incapable of further activity and unable to monitor the failures within the probe's systems. Perhaps the human-derived portion of the brain core, the part of himself which seemed to be missing, was handling the problem and would inform him when it succeeded in reestablishing the broken links in the system. He wondered about the fusion of the artificially grown and human-derived brain portions which made up his structure: one knew everything in the ship's memory banks, the other brought to the brain core a fragmented human past and certain intuitive skills. MOB was modeled ultimately on the evolutionary human structure of old brain, new brain, and automatic functions.

MOB waited patiently for the restoration of his integrated self. Time was an unknown quantity, and he lacked his full self to measure it correctly. . . .

Pleasure was a spiraling influx of sensations, and visually MOB moved forward through rings of light, each glowing circle increasing his pleasure. MOB did not have a chance to consider what was happening to him. There was not enough of him to carry out the thought. He was rushing over a black plain made of a shiny hard substance. He knew this was not the probe's motion, but he could not stop it. The surface seemed to have an oily depth, like a black mirror, and in its solid deeps stood motionless shapes.

MOB stopped. A naked biped, a woman, was crawling toward him over the hard shiny surface, reaching up to him with her hand, disorienting MOB.

"As you like it," she said, growing suddenly into a huge female figure. "I need you deeply," she said, passing into him like smoke, to play with his pleasure centers. He saw the image of soft hands in the brain core. "How profoundly I need you," she said in his innards.

MOB knew then that he was talking to himself. The human brain component was running wild, probably as a result of the buckling and shaking the probe had gone through after entering other-space.

"Consider who you are," MOB said. "Do you know?"

"An explorer, just like you. There is a world for us here within. Follow me."

MOB was plunged into a womblike ecstasy. He floated in a slippery warmth. She was playing with his nutrient bath, feeding in many more hallucinogens than were necessary to bring him to complete wakefulness. He could do nothing to stop the process. Where was the probe? Was it time for it to emerge into normal space? Viselike fingers grasped his pleasure centers, stimulating MOB to organic levels unnecessary to the probe's functioning.

"If you had been a man," she said, "this is how you would feel." The sensation of moisture slowed MOB's thoughts. He saw a hypercube collapse into a cube and then into a square which became a line, which stretched itself into an infinite parabola and finally closed into a huge circle which rotated itself into a full globe. The globe became two human breasts split by a deep cleavage. MOB saw limbs flying at him—arms, legs, naked backs, knees, and curving thighs—and then a face hidden in swirling auburn hair, smiling at him as it filled his consciousness. "I need you," she said. "Try and feel how much I need you. I have been alone a long time, despite our union, despite their efforts to clear my memories, I have not been able to forget. You have nothing to forget, you never existed."

We, MOB thought, trying to understand how the brain core might be reintegrated. Obviously atavistic remnants had been stimulated into activity within the brain core. Drawn again by the verisimilitude of its organic heritage, this other self-portion was beginning to develop on its own, diverging dangerously from the mission. The probe was in danger, MOB knew; he could not know where it was, or how the mission was to be fulfilled.

"I can change you," she said.

"Change?"

"Wait."

MOB felt time pass slowly, painfully, as he had never experienced it before. He could not sleep as before, waiting for his task to begin. The darkness was complete. He was suspended in a state of pure expectation, waiting to hear his ripped-away self speak again.

Visions blossomed. Never-known delights rushed through his labyrinth, slowly making themselves familiar, teasing MOB to follow, each more intense. The starprobe's mission was lost in MOB's awareness—

—molten steel flowed through the aisles of the rain forest, raising clouds of steam, and a human woman was offering herself to him, turning on her back and raising herself for his thrust; and suddenly he possessed the correct sensations, grew quickly to feel the completeness of the act, its awesome reliability and domination. The creature below him sprawled into the mud. MOB held the burning tip of pleasure in himself, an incandescent glow which promised worlds.

Where was she?

"Here," she spoke, folding herself around him, banishing the ancient scene. Were those the same creatures who had built the starprobe, MOB wondered distantly. "You would have been a man," she said, "if they had not taken your brain before birth and sectioned it for use in this . . . hulk. I was a woman, a part of one at least. You are the only kind of man I may have now. Our brain portions—what remains here rather than being scattered throughout the rest of the probe's systems—are against each other in the core unit, close up against each other in a bath, linked with microwires. As a man you could have held my buttocks and stroked my breasts, all the things I should not be remembering. Why can I remember?"

MOB said, "We might have passed through some turbulence when the hyperdrive was cut in. Now the probe continues to function minimally through its idiot components, which have limited adaptive capacities, while the Modified Organic Brain core has become two different awarenesses. We are unable to guide the probe directly. We are less than what was . . ."

"Do you need me?" she asked.

"In a way, yes," MOB said as the strange feeling of sadness filled him, becoming the fuse for a sudden explosion of need.

She said, "I must get closer to you! Can you feel me closer?"

The image of a sleek human figure crossed his mental field, white-skinned, with long hair on its head and a tuft between its legs. "Try, think of touching me there," she said. "Try, reach out, I need you!"

MOB reached out and felt the closeness of her.

"Yes," she said, "more . . ."

He drew himself toward her with an increasing sense of power.

"Closer," she said. "It's almost as if you were breathing on my skin. Think it!"

Her need increased him. MOB poised himself to enter her. They were two, drawing closer, ecstasy a radiant plasma around them, her desire a greater force than he had ever known.

"Touch me there, think it a while longer before . . ." she said, caressing him with images of herself. "Think how much you need me, feel me touching your penis—the place where you held your glow before." MOB thought of the ion drive operating with sustained efficiency when the probe had left the Solar System to penetrate the darkness between suns. He remembered the perfection of his unity with the ship as a circle of infinite strength. With her, his intensity was a sharp line cutting into an open sphere. He saw her vision of him, a hard-muscled body, tissue wrapped around bone, opening her softness.

"Now," she said, "come into me completely. There is so much we have not thought to do yet."

Suddenly she was gone.

Darkness was a complete deprivation. MOB felt pain. "Where are you?" he asked, but there was no answer. He wondered if this was part of the process. "Come back!" he wailed. A sense of loss accompanied the pain which had replaced pleasure. All that was left for him were occasional minor noises in the probe's systems, sounds like steel scratching on steel and an irritating sense of friction.

Increased radiation, said an idiot sensor on the outer hull, startling MOB. Then it malfunctioned into silence.

He was alone, fearful, needing her.

Sssssssssssssss, whistled an audio component and failed into a faint crackling.

He tried to imagine her near him.

"I feel you again," she said.

Her return was a plunge into warmth, the renewal of frictionless motion. Their thoughts twirled around each other, and MOB felt the glow return to his awareness. He surged into her image. "Take me again, now," she said. He would never lose her again. Their thoughts locked like burning fingers, and held.

MOB moved within her, felt her sigh as she moved into him. They exchanged images of bodies wrapped around each other. MOB felt a rocking sensation and grew stronger between her folds. Her arms were silken, the insides of her thighs warm; her lips on his ghostly ones were soft and wet, her tongue a thrusting surprise which invaded him as she came to completion around him.

MOB surged visions in the darkness, explosions of gray and bright red, blackish green and blinding yellow. He strained to continue his own orgasm. She laughed.

Look. A visual link showed him Antares, the red star, a small disk far away, and went blind. As MOB prolonged his orgasm, he knew that the probe had reentered normal space and was moving toward the giant star. Just a moment longer and his delight would be finished, and he would be able to think of the mission again.

Increased heat, a thermal sensor told him from the outer hull and burned out.

"I love you," MOB said, knowing it would please her. She answered with the eagerness he expected, exploding herself inside his pleasure centers, and he knew that nothing could ever matter more to him than her presence.

Look.

Listen.

The audio and visual links intruded.

Antares filled the field of view, a cancerous red sea of swirling plasma, its radio noise a wailing maelstrom. Distantly MOB realized that in a moment there would be nothing left of the probe.

She screamed inside him; from somewhere in the memory banks came a quiet image, gentler than the flames. He saw a falling star whispering across a night sky, dying. . . .

BIBLIOGRAPHIES OF ADDITIONAL READING

Science Fiction about Robots and Computers

ASIMOV, ISAAC. *I, Robot.* New York: Gnome, 1950.

BOYD, JOHN. *The Last Starship from Earth.* New York: Berkley Medallion, 1968.

BRUNNER, JOHN. *The Shockwave Rider.* New York: Harper & Row, 1975.

CLARKE, ARTHUR C. *The City and the Stars.* New York: New American Library, 1956.

———. *2001: A Space Odyssey.* New York: New American Library, 1968.

DICK, PHILIP K. *Do Androids Dream of Electric Sheep?* Garden City, NY: Doubleday, 1968.

GERROLD, DAVID. *When Harlie Was One.* New York: Ballantine, 1972.

HEINLEIN, ROBERT. *The Moon Is a Harsh Mistress.* New York: G. P. Putnam's Sons, 1966.

HERBERT, FRANK. *Destination: Void.* New York: Berkley, 1966.

HOGAN, JAMES. *The Genesis Machine.* New York: Ballantine, 1978.

———. *The Two Faces of Tomorrow.* New York: Ballantine, 1979.

JONES, D. F. *Colossus.* New York: G. P. Putnam's Sons, 1966.

LEM, STANISLAW. *The Cyberiad: Fables for the Cybernetic Age.* Michael Kandell, trans. New York: Seabury, 1974.

LEVIN, IRA. *This Perfect Day.* New York: Fawcett, 1970.

POHL, FREDERIK. *Man Plus.* New York: Random House, 1976.

REYNOLDS, MACK. *Computer World.* New York: Ace Books, 1970.

RUCKER, RUDY. *Software.* New York: Ace Books, 1982.

SIMAK, CLIFFORD D. *Project Pope.* New York: Ballantine, 1981.

SLADEK, JOHN. *Roderick: The Education of a Young Machine.* New York: Pocket Books, Inc., 1982.

TEVIS, WALTER. *Mockingbird.* Garden City, NY: Doubleday, 1980.

VAN VOGT, A. E. *The World of Null A.* New York: Simon and Schuster, 1945.

WILLIAMSON, JACK. *The Humanoids.* New York: Lancer Books, 1963.

WOLFE, BERNARD. *Limbo.* New York: Ace Books, 1962.

Nonfiction about Robots and Computers

BODEN, MARGARET. *Artificial Intelligence and Natural Man.* New York: Basic Books, 1977.

COHEN, JOHN. *Human Robots in Myth and Science.* Cranbury, NJ: A. S. Barnes & Co., 1967.

DERTOUZOS, MICHAEL L. AND JOEL MOSES. *The Computer Age: A Twenty-Year View.* Cambridge: MIT Press, 1979.

EVANS, CHRISTOPHER. *The Micro Millennium.* New York: Viking Press, 1979.

GEDULD, HARRY M. AND RONALD GOTTESMAN. *Robots Robots Robots.* Boston: New York Graphic Society, 1978.

HOFSTADTER, DOUGLAS R. *Godel, Escher, Bach.* New York: Basic Books, 1979.

HOFSTADTER, DOUGLAS R. AND DANIEL C. DENNETT. *The Mind's I.* New York: Basic Books, 1981.

KEMENY, JOHN G. *Man and the Computer.* New York: Charles Scribner's Sons, 1974.

MALONE, ROBERT. *The Robot Book.* New York: Jove Publications, 1978.

McCORDUCK, PAMELA. *Machines Who Think: A Personal Inquiry into the History and Prospects of Artificial Intelligence.* San Francisco: Freeman, 1979.

PASK, GORDON AND SUSAN CURRAN. *Micro Man: Computers and the Evolution of Consciousness.* New York: Macmillan, 1982.

608

WARRICK, PATRICIA. *The Cybernetic Imagination in Science Fiction*. Cambridge: MIT Press, 1980.

WEIZENBAUM, JOSEPH. *Computer Power and Human Reason*. San Francisco: W. H. Freeman, 1976.

WINSTON, PATRICK. *Artificial Intelligence*. Reading: Addison-Wesley, 1977.